The Center Seat

Life and Death
In the Supreme Court

A Novel

D1415301

Peter Irons

The Center Seat

This is a work of fiction. Names, characters, places and incidents either are the product of the author's imagination or are used fictitiously.

Copyright © 2016 by Peter Irons

ISBN-13: 978-1539873075
ISBN-10: 1539873072

Printed in the United States of America

Prologue

Then . . .

At 9:31 a.m. on December 14, 2002, a Saturday, police in Williamsburg, Virginia, received a 911 call from a woman who identified herself as Myrtle Cassell and gave an address on Oak Street. She told the operator she heard screams from the house next door, and a woman's voice shouting, "Stop, stop, I'm sorry," followed by more screams, then silence. Myrtle said she ran to her kitchen window, from which she could see the bedroom window and the back door of the neighboring house, but not the front door, and had not seen anyone enter or leave the house.

Oak Street is in a middle-class residential neighborhood, with tree-shaded lawns, about a mile from Williamsburg's tourist-thronged Historic District. Police responded to the 911 call in seven minutes, with two cruisers. The front door was partly open, and two officers entered, guns drawn. They found the body of a young female in the bedroom closest to the front door, lying on a bed, face-up and nude. Her skull had been crushed, obviously with a blunt object, and the bed was covered in blood. A white tee shirt, a pair of jeans, and a red thong were on the bedroom floor.

A quick search of the house found no one in any of the rooms. The officers called in for an ambulance, the coroner, and a crime-scene team from the department, telling the dispatcher there had been a homicide. In the bedroom, an officer found an open purse on a small desk, with a wallet inside. He pulled on a pair of latex gloves, opened the wallet, and found a Virginia driver's license for Laurel Leigh Davis, with a birth date of 1979, making her 23 years old. The wallet also contained an ID card, with her name and photo, from William & Mary Law School, whose campus was a short walk from the Historic District.

While they were waiting for the coroner and crime-scene team, the officers did a more thorough search of the house, but did not find an obvious murder weapon. The other two officers did a quick search of the front and back yards; one came back, reporting he had found a hammer under some bushes at the front side of the house; there appeared to be blood on the head. He left it there until the crime-scene team arrived. They picked it up with latex gloves and placed it in a Zip-lock evidence bag. The other officer did a search of the sidewalks and lawns on both sides of the short block, returning with a brown leather driving glove, the kind with small holes in the palm, that he found on the curb, across the street and two houses down, and that was also bagged.

The crime-scene team found some spots of blood on the sides of the bathroom sink and several strands of hair in the sink drain. They scraped the blood spots into a sterile vial, picked up the hair with tweezers, and placed it in an evidence bag. The top drawer of the bedroom nightstand contained a plastic medicine bottle with three pink tablets, each embossed with a butterfly. A crime-scene tech took pictures of the body, the bedroom, the bathroom, and the other rooms. The house was also dusted for fingerprints, and several were found on the knobs on both sides of the front door and the kitchen door, which opened to an unfenced back yard. After the search was completed, a deputy coroner arrived, and pronounced the victim dead; her body was placed in a body bag and taken to the state medical examiner's office in Richmond for an autopsy.

Ten minutes after the officers arrived, Moses Townley, a Williamsburg detective who was African American, pulled up to the house. He first interviewed Myrtle Cassell, the neighbor who called 911. She told Townley she had seen a young black man, in his early twenties, raking leaves on the lawn of the house on her other side, at about 8:30 that morning. She recognized him as someone who did chores like mowing lawns and raking leaves in the neighborhood, sometimes knocking on doors to ask if residents needed help with any chores. She didn't know his full name, but said he went by "OD." Ms. Cassell said he was always pleasant, and "somewhat slow" in his speech, which was a bit slurred, as if he had a speech impediment. She also told Townley that Laurel Davis had two roommates, Colleen McAllister and Liz Gronbach, also William & Mary law students, and that both had left several days earlier for the holiday break. Townley also interviewed Margaret Chisholm, the woman whose lawn OD had raked that morning; she confirmed that she knew him as OD and had given him $5 for the raking.

Townley recognized the nickname "OD" as Odell Beasley, the son of a woman named Mamie Beasley, who attended the same church as Townley, and whose son occasionally attended church with her. Townley went to Mamie Beasley's house, about four blocks from Laurel's house; she told him that OD had come home about 9:15 that morning, out of breath as if he had been running, and had left within ten minutes, but didn't say where he was going. Townley called the station, requesting that patrol officers keep a lookout for OD and to bring him in for questioning if he was located. About 30 minutes later, an officer reported that he'd found OD at the downtown Greyhound station, waiting for a bus to Richmond, saying he was going to visit his sister, who lived there. The officer brought OD, who was cooperative, to the main police station.

Townley returned to the station, and took OD into an interview room, saying "I just want to ask you a few questions about where you were this morning and what you were doing." OD was cooperative. He told Townley he'd been raking leaves for the lady who lived next door to Myrtle, although he didn't know the lady's name. He said she'd paid him $5, and he had then gone home.

"You didn't knock on Miz Cassell's door to see if she needed any chores?" Townley asked.

"No, her lawn was clear, and she wasn't too friendly when I axed a few times before," OD replied.

"You didn't go to the house on the other side of Miz Cassell's before you went home and ask about raking leaves or any other chores?"

OD paused, then said, "Oh, now I 'member. I knocked on the door, but nobody come, so I went home."

"You didn't see anyone, or hear anyone, at that house, or on that street?"

"No sir, I dint see nobody, dint hear nobody. When nobody answer the door, I just go home."

"The officer found you at the Greyhound station, with a ticket to Richmond," Townley said.

"Yes sir, I ain't seen my sister for a while, so I figures I give her a little visit, maybe see a couple friends up there. Stay a couple days, maybe."

Townley gave OD a long look. His expression was impassive, and Townley didn't detect any nervousness. OD hadn't asked why he was brought in, or whether he was in any trouble. Townley thought for a minute. "Okay, OD, you can go home now," he said, "but do me a favor and stay in town, in case I have more questions."

"Yes sir, I'll do that," OD agreed. "My sister dint know I be coming up there, anyway. And my momma got some chores she been wanting me to do."

After OD left, Townley checked records and found that he had been arrested a year before, for smoking marijuana in public, along with three other young black men, one of whom was arrested for possession of a bag of marijuana in his pocket. All four men had been booked and fingerprinted, but the county Commonwealth's Attorney had dismissed the charges as too minor to warrant prosecution.

After OD left the station, Townley called the William & Mary police department, told the officer that a law student had been the victim of a homicide, and got the name and phone number of Laurel Davis's parents, who lived in Seattle. He decided to put off calling them until he had a positive ID on Laurel's body, just in case the victim had been another young woman staying in her room, although he knew that was unlikely.

The W&M police also gave Townley the home numbers of Laurel's two roommates: Colleen lived in Lynchburg and Liz in Hyattsville, Maryland. He called both and informed them of Laurel's murder, and asked for the names of any of her male friends. Both said that Laurel was casual friends with three or four fellow law students, and that she also had an "off-and-on" boyfriend, Winslow Early, Jr., who had been to their house several times, and had stayed overnight with Laurel at least three times. Liz also told Townley that two students, Tory Tucker and Nick Cashman, had been at their house recently for parties and that both had been in Laurel's bedroom for what Liz assumed were make-out sessions or possibly sex, although she didn't know for sure.

Townley got the names Liz and Colleen gave him, and called the W&M police again for their local and home phones. Tucker and Cashman's parents both answered at their homes, in McLean and Danville, and both said their sons had been home for the past week, and were still home. Early's home phone was unlisted, so Townley called the number at his apartment in Williamsburg, got no answer, and left a voice message asking him to call back as soon as possible. He got a call back on Sunday afternoon. Early said he'd just returned from Richmond. Townley told him of Laurel's murder, to which Early professed great shock, although he said he hadn't seen Laurel for a couple of weeks. Townley asked where he had been on Saturday morning, and Early said he'd been in Richmond all day Friday and Saturday, staying with his father; his mother had gone with a friend to New York City for theater and shopping that weekend. He said he had driven back to Williamsburg on Sunday morning. Townley recognized Early's father as the Attorney General of Virginia. He called him Monday morning, and Early said that yes, his son had come up on Friday for the weekend, that they had dinner that night at the Willow Oaks Country Club, played several sets of indoor tennis on Saturday, and that his son drove back to Williamsburg around noon on Sunday.

Three days after Laurel's murder, the medical examiner in Richmond, Dr. Irwin Arias, called Townley and said the forensics lab had found an almost full set of fingerprints on the hammer, along with blood, several hairs, brain tissue, and flakes of bone. He also said he found bruises on Laurel's neck, consistent with having been choked, but that her death was caused by "blunt force trauma" to her skull. The autopsy revealed still-motile semen in Laurel's vagina and mouth, and bits of blood and tissue under her fingernails. The ME sent Townley a blown-up photo of the prints on the hammer by email. On a hunch, he got the set of prints from OD's arrest; an examination with a magnifying glass convinced him they matched those on the hammer.

He then went to OD's home, found him there, and brought him to the station. Townley set up a tape recorder and read OD his Miranda rights. OD said, "I don't need no lawyer. God is all the lawyer I need, 'cause I tell the truth. I know why you brought me here, but I did not kill that girl." But he signed the waiver form. Townley told OD right off that his prints were on the hammer and asked him to explain how they got there. OD said, "OK, I'll tell you what happened, but I did not kill that girl."

OD then told his story without any prompting: "I did knock on that door, 'cause I seen some girls at that house before, and the front lawn was all full of leaves. I never talk to them before, but they smile at me when I goes by. So, I knocks on the door, and this girl comes in a bit and opens it. I axed her if she wants me to rake the leaves, and she says, 'How much?' I says 'Five dollar,' and she says 'There's a rake by the back door, and some leaf bags, and five dollar is fine.' So I goes around the back and gets the rake and bags, and I rake and bag the leaves. Takes me about 15 minutes, and I puts the bags out on the curb, four or five of 'em. Then I goes up the steps and knocks on the door, and the girl comes. She says, 'Can you do another chore? It's real quick and easy, and I give you another five dollar.' So I say yes, and she says 'Come in and I show you.' We go back to her kitchen, and she opens a drawer and gets out a hammer and some picture hooks and nails. She says, 'I got some pictures to hang in my bedroom, but I just painted my nails and I don't want to scratch them.' I was a little nervous, you know, being in the house with her alone and going into her bedroom, but she be smiling and says 'Just two pictures, take two minutes.' So I goes into her bedroom, and there's two pictures in frames on a little desk, looks like her and two older people I figures might be her parents, you know. She wants them on the wall over the desk. So I slide the desk and a chair over and reach up to where she put her fingers. So I puts in the hooks with the hammer and nails, took about one minute. And I turns around to see if that was right, and I almost jump out of my skin. She been wearing a tee shirt and jeans. But when I turns around, she be naked."

Until this point, Townley had asked no questions, and said nothing. It was obvious OD was just telling a story from beginning to end, and didn't need any prompting. "I couldn't believe my eyes, and I says, 'Miss, I better leave right now, and you don't owe me nothing, and you better put your clothes back on right now. This ain't right.' But she says, 'What's your name?' And I says, 'OD, and I better leave right now.' But she says, 'OD, let me axe you a question. Have you ever had a white girl before?' And I says, 'No, if that's what you mean, and I better go.' But she says, 'OD, you can have a white girl right now, if you never tell nobody. 'Cause you're good looking, and I never had a black man. First time for everything, and I'll make you feel good.'"

Townley spoke for the first time. "OD, if you thought it wasn't right, and you wanted to leave, why didn't you just do that?"

OD paused for a minute. "'Cause before I could move, she comes over and undoes my belt and unzips my pants, and puts me in her mouth.

And you know, it feels good. I know it's wrong, but I'm a man, just like you, and I figure, well, just this once, and then I'll leave and never come back. So she keeps me in her mouth for a couple minutes, and then takes off my pants and shorts and shirt and shoes, real quick, and pulls me on her bed. And she takes me and puts me in, and she says, 'Just go as long and hard as you can.' So I just goes, and she be saying, 'Keep going, don't stop.' And I goes until it's over, maybe five minutes, but I just be guessing. And just then, I hears a knock on the front door, and this loud voice, a man, says 'Hey baby, I'm here and I'm horny.'"

OD paused again. "I'm pretty sure that's what I heard. So I jumps off the bed, grabs my clothes, and runs down the hall and out the back door, fast as I can. I run through the back yard, no clothes on, into the alley behind the yard. I looks around and don't see nobody come out of the house, so I quick puts my clothes back on, and run down the alley to the street, and over to my momma's house. That's what happen, and that's God's own truth. I did not kill that girl. I swear on the Bible. I know what I did with her be wrong, but we all be sinners, and God will forgive us if we go to Jesus and say I'm sorry and won't never do it again, which I did. Say I'm sorry, I mean. But I did not kill that girl."

Townley asked, "Did this girl scream? Miz Cassell said she heard her screaming. That's why she called 911. She screamed and you got scared and hit her with the hammer. Isn't that what happened?"

OD shook his head. "No sir, I dint hear no screams. I dint hit her with the hammer. And I dint even know she be dead until that night. My momma saw it on the TV and tole me 'bout it."

"So why did you go to the bus station and get a ticket to Richmond?"

"'Cause I think maybe that man seen me run down the hall and out the back door, me with no clothes on, and come after me. Maybe he think I took advantage of her. Which I guess I did, but she axe me if I want her. So I figure I go to Richmond for a couple days and stay with my sister, and maybe they find that man and put him in jail. He the one that killed her, got to be. But I did not kill that girl."

Townley pressed. "Nobody else saw a man go into the house or come out. Did you see him at all?"

"No sir, I dint see him. I dint look back. I just run out the house and keep running 'til I was down the alley. I dint hear no screams."

"You didn't run out the front door?

"No sir, it was the back door."

"You didn't take the hammer with you and throw it in the bushes by the front door?"

"No sir. I just tole you I run out the back door and dint take no hammer."

"But your fingerprints were on the hammer, and her blood."

"Yes sir, if you says so. I did use the hammer to put the pictures on the wall. But I dint hit her with it. I put it back down on the desk and then she undo my belt and unzip my pants, just like I tole you. But I did not kill that girl."

Townley shook his head. "OD, I have to tell you right now, that story is really hard to believe. You knock on a door, rake some leaves, and this pretty white girl invites you inside and asks you to fuck her. But here's what I think happened. You rake the leaves, we could see they were raked, and the rake and box of bags were on the front porch. She says come in and I'll get your five dollars, thinking you're a harmless guy she's seen around the neighborhood. She's wearing a white tee shirt, maybe with no bra underneath, and tight jeans. We found them on the floor of her bedroom, but not a bra. You come in, you admire her tits and her ass, and you get excited. You decide to rape her, not even thinking that Miz Cassell just saw you. You get her into the bedroom, tell her to take off her clothes, and you take off yours. You tell her to stay quiet or you'll hurt her. She's scared and stays quiet. Then you rape her, after you make her suck your cock. But while you're pounding her, she starts screaming, real loud, 'Stop, stop.' You think somebody might hear you, like Miz Cassell next door, and you tell her to shut up, but she keeps screaming. You grab her by the throat to make her stop screaming, but she scratches your arms and twists away. There was a hammer on the desk, which she used to hang those pictures or maybe something else, and you panic. You grab the hammer from the desk and whack her in the head. Maybe you didn't mean to kill her, but you did. So you quick put on your clothes, maybe you just pulled down your pants or unzipped them to rape her, grab the hammer, run out the front door, and toss the hammer in the bushes, in case anyone sees you with it. You're in a panic, you just killed a white girl. Maybe you didn't know she was dead, but maybe you made sure because she could identify you. Whatever, you ran home to your momma's, got enough money for a ticket to Richmond, went to the bus station, and there's a bus every hour.

Then one of our officers found you, brought you in, and you lied to me about not going into that house. And here you are now, with this story that nobody would believe."

Townley paused. "OD, listen to me. Your fingerprints are on the bloody hammer. And they'll probably find out it's your spunk in her mouth and her pussy. Nobody else was there, and you admitted you were there. So what should I think, or anybody on a jury think? You did it, OD." Townley paused again. "Tell you what, OD. Your momma is a good woman, and you haven't been really bad, just that one pot bust, but you didn't get charged. And I believe you when you say you didn't go in there intending to rape or kill that girl. And I believe that she might have come after you. And you only hit her with the hammer in panic, to make her stop screaming."

Townley fixed OD with a Come Clean look. "Listen to me, OD. I can't make any promises, but if you tell me what really happened, the prosecutor might take all this into consideration and lower the charge to second-degree homicide, and you'll get a sentence that will get you out before you get to be an old man, maybe twenty years. No promises, but I think the prosecutor will listen to me."

OD shook his head. "I did not kill that girl."

"Listen to me again, OD. If you don't tell me what really happened, and keep on with a story that nobody will believe, and with your fingerprints on the hammer, and your spunk in her, you face getting a needle that will kill you. Think about it, OD. I need an answer before I walk out of here. And that's in one minute. And then you'll be in a cell until you get the needle." Townley looked at his watch. "One minute, OD."

"I don't need no minute. I did not kill that girl."

Townley then told OD he was under arrest for first-degree murder. After OD was booked and placed in a cell, a tech from the medical examiner's office took a swab for cells in his mouth, and a blood sample. At his arraignment on December 19, OD was appointed a local lawyer, Darrell Lewis, who entered a not-guilty plea. OD was held without bail pending trial. Shortly after the arraignment, the medical examiner, Dr. Arias, reported that the blood on the hammer was Laurel's, and that the semen in her mouth and vagina matched OD's DNA profile from the swab. However, the medical examiner also reported that the blood and hairs from the bathroom sink did not match OD's DNA, and the blood type, O-positive, did not match either Laurel or OD, both of whom were type A. The report concluded that the blood and hair from the sink came from an unidentified person, probably male, and did not match anyone in the national DNA databank. The report also included the results of a toxicology exam, performed after the autopsy of Laurel's body, which showed a significant level of methylenedioxy-methamphetamine in her urine.

The Commonwealth's Attorney, Victor Stone, then filed for "special circumstances," making OD eligible for the death penalty, charging the murder was committed in connection with a rape and forcible sodomy. Darrell Lewis filed what's known as a Brady motion, standard in most felony cases, seeking access to all police reports, including interviews with persons contacted by detectives, and results of the blood and DNA test and the toxicology exam. Stone turned this material over to Lewis, who had not requested access to the physical evidence. Lewis later filed a motion for a change in venue, arguing that Beasley couldn't get an impartial jury in Williamsburg because of pre-trial publicity, but the motion was denied.

The trial took place in May 2003. Stone put Detective Townley on the stand, who recounted his interviews with OD, and verified the Miranda warning and waiver that OD signed. In his cross-examination of Townley, Lewis elicited his admission that OD was cooperative, but had no other questions. Stone's other witnesses included Margaret Chisholm and Myrtle Cassell, the police officers who responded to the 911 call, two of the crime-scene techs, and a fingerprint specialist from the state crime lab who testified, along with blow-ups on the screen, that the prints on the hammer and the inside kitchen-door knob all matched OD's. He did not find OD's prints on either knob of the front door. On cross-examination, the specialist admitted that OD's prints were also found on the picture frames in Laurel's bedroom.

Stone's final witness was the medical examiner, Dr. Irwin Arias, who testified about the DNA and serological testing of the blood and hairs.

On cross-examination, Arias admitted to Lewis that none of the blood or hairs from the crime scene, including those from the bathroom sink, matched OD's DNA or blood type. Arias also said the fingernail scrapings had yielded cells and small amounts of blood that did not match OD's DNA. He could offer no explanation of whose they might be, except that they came from a male. Arias admitted that he found no abrasions inside Laurel's vagina. Lewis did not ask any questions about the toxicology exam. On re-direct by Stone, Arias said the fingernail scrapings and bathroom blood, although deposited recently, could have been there for three or four hours before the murder. Stone also passed around to the jurors several photos of Laurel's body on her bed, covered with blood, to which several responded with audible gasps of shock and revulsion. Lewis had filed a pre-trial motion to exclude the photos, arguing they were so graphic they might prejudice the jurors, but the motion was denied. At trial, Lewis repeated his objection for the record. He also repeated his earlier, unsuccessful demand for a change of venue.

After Stone rested the prosecution case, Lewis called only one defense witness, a forensic scientist who testified that the fingernail scrapings, and the blood from the bathroom sink, were unlikely to have been there for more than an hour before the crime-scene techs gathered them. On cross-examination by Stone, the scientist admitted that placing a precise time was not possible, and agreed with Dr. Arias that a range of three to four hours was possible. Lewis did not call OD Beasley to testify in his own defense, leaving the jury with no opportunity to hear his story in his own words.

In his closing argument, Lewis stressed that OD had been cooperative with Townley, had a plausible story of being hired by Laurel to rake leaves, and that there was no evidence of forcible sodomy or rape. Lewis also pointed to the evidence that the bathroom blood and hair indicated that another male had been there, and that OD might have left after having sex with Laurel but before this person arrived. He urged the jurors to find that reasonable doubt existed of OD's guilt.

In his closing, Stone hammered away at the facts that OD had admitted having sex with Laurel, that semen matching his DNA was found in her mouth and vagina, and that his prints were on the bloody hammer. Stone heaped scorn on what he called Lewis's "SODDIT" argument, telling jurors that was an acronym for "Some Other Dude Did It," and called that a last resort of defense lawyers whose clients are obviously guilty. He finally portrayed Laurel as the unsuspecting victim of a brutal killer, who first raped and sodomized her, showing the jury—over Lewis's repeated but denied objections—blown-up photos of her as a smiling, cheerful girl at home and in college and law school, side-by-side with photos of her beaten, bloody body. Stone also reminded jurors that OD had been picked up at the bus station with a ticket to Richmond, arguing that his attempt to leave Williamsburg showed a guilty mind. He concluded that there was no reasonable doubt, or any doubt at all, of OD's guilt. After instructions from Judge Tommy Moore, the jury took just three hours to reach a unanimous guilty verdict.

The case then moved into the penalty phase, beginning the next day, with the same jurors. In this phase, the prosecutor presents evidence of "aggravating" factors that support the death penalty for the crime, and the defense lawyer presents evidence of "mitigating" factors that support a sentence of life imprisonment without possibility of parole, the only choices the jurors could consider. Stone called no witnesses, simply restating the testimony and evidence of the brutal nature of the murder, concluding that it supported the death penalty for OD. Lewis called only Mamie Beasley, who testified, tearfully, that OD had always been a good child and young man, had never assaulted or harmed anyone, and that she would be devastated to lose her only son. The jurors took only two hours to return with a recommendation of death, which Judge Moore then imposed. OD was then taken to the Sussex state prison, about 35 miles south of Williamsburg, where was placed on Virginia's death row.

Virginia law requires an automatic appeal of death sentences to the state supreme court. Lewis filed an appeal that alleged two errors in the trial: the judge's denial of the change of venue motion, and the introduction of the photos of Laurel's bloody body. He also restated his argument that the blood and hair of another male raised a reasonable doubt of OD's guilt. In 2005, the Virginia Supreme Court unanimously rejected the appeal, in an opinion that found no error on either claim. Citing the evidence of OD's fingerprints on the hammer and his semen in Laurel's body, the court held that "overwhelming evidence" of OD's guilt, and the "heinous" nature of the murder, supported the death penalty. The opinion brushed aside Lewis's "SODDIT" argument, dismissing its reliance on evidence that the tissue and blood under Laurel's fingernails, and the bathroom blood and hairs, came from another male, as "speculative" and subject to an interpretation that Laurel might have had an encounter, possibly an argument, not involving sex, that led her to scratch someone, presumably a male, several hours before OD raped and sodomized her, and then murdered her when she resisted. The opinion stressed that no evidence of such an encounter had been presented at trial. After this decision, Darrell Lewis dropped out of the case, and OD remained on death row, visited for an hour each month by his mother, Mamie.

No one else visited OD Beasley for the next fifteen years.

According to FBI statistics, the number of homicides in the United States in 2002 was 16,204. The number of death sentences imposed for those murders was 151, less than one percent. There were 357 murders in Virginia in 2002, which resulted in six death sentences, less than two percent. The United States Supreme Court, so far, has not reviewed—either to affirm or reverse—a single one of these death sentences. But there is always the possibility, although very slight, that the Court will agree to review a death penalty case. And, in those few cases, a delay of fifteen or more years between conviction and final decision is common. The wheels of justice in death penalty cases turn very slowly.

1

. . . Fifteen Years Later

"*Oh, shit!*"

Andy Roboff glanced up at the clock on the wall of her cubicle in the offices of the Harvard Law Review. It was ten minutes before nine on a drizzly Tuesday morning in April, typical weather for early spring in Cambridge. Andy had been at her desk on the second floor of the Review's home in Gannett House, a three-story white clapboard structure fronted by four Grecian columns, since six that morning, fortified only by a stale bran muffin and lukewarm coffee from her thermos. She had ten minutes to get from Gannett to Pound Hall, one of the classroom and office buildings at Harvard Law School, for a conference with Professor Hank Lorenz. It was just a three-minute walk, but Andy didn't want to be late, since Lorenz had set aside the hour between his two morning classes to give her feedback on the paper she'd been working on, and sweating over, for the past three months.

Andy was the senior articles editor at the nation's oldest student-edited law review, founded in 1887 and arguably the most prestigious and influential legal publication in the world, cited in opinions of the Supreme Court more often than any other journal. After two years on the Review, Andy was now in her third and final year at the law school, with six more weeks until graduation.

"One more fucking cite," Andy said to her computer, which displayed page 47 of an article by an assistant professor at Georgetown law school who hoped it would propel him into life-time tenure. Andy knew the article would never be cited by any court, let alone by the life-tenured justices of the Supreme Court. But the author had been an editor of the Harvard Law Review, four years earlier, and had clerked for a liberal

Supreme Court justice, Alice Schroeder, whom Andy admired. So, against her better judgment, Andy had recommended the article for publication.

Now Andy was saddled with "cite-checking" each of the article's 312 footnotes, to make sure the citations and quotes were accurate and conformed to the Review's "Bluebook," as everyone called the 511-page style manual formally entitled "A Uniform System of Citation." So far, Andy had cite-checked 236 footnotes, and hadn't found a single error, not surprising since the author had done exactly the same job at the Review and presumably kept the Bluebook on his nightstand as a cure for insomnia.

"Oh, shit again," Andy mumbled to herself. After finishing one more check, using the Lexis-Nexis legal database on her computer, she now had five minutes to get to Pound Hall. As she logged off her computer and swept muffin crumbs off the cluttered desk, Josh Barfield stuck his head around the cubicle wall. Josh was the Review's managing editor, whose main job was hectoring the articles editors to get their assignments done in time to meet the deadlines for each of the Review's eight yearly issues.

Josh had been Andy's best friend since they met during their first week at Harvard, a relationship that progressed quickly to what singles of their generation called "friends with benefits." After their first year, they had agreed to give up the benefits they shared in Josh's bedroom, and return to best-friend status. Seeing him now gave Andy a sudden flash of her first hand-in-hand walk with Josh from the Cambridge Common to his Oxford Street apartment, but it vanished as she stuck a copy of her paper in her backpack.

"Hey, Andy," Josh said with a grin. "Did you hear the news?" He was gripping the bat with which he'd smacked the bottom-of-the-ninth homer to bring Sandpoint High its first-ever title in the Idaho baseball tournament. Josh kept the bat in his law-review office, under a hand-lettered sign that warned, "You missa you deadline, I breaka you leg! Capice?"

Andy grinned back. "You mean the news that this boring-as-hammered-shit article was due yesterday, and you're about to play fungo with my kneecap?"

Josh assumed a batting stance, and hefted the bat to his shoulder. "Not that news, although you get to choose which knee you'd like to keep." He gave the bat a slow-mo swing. "No, the news about Sanjay. You didn't hear?"

"No, I didn't hear whatever news about Sanjay you're bursting to tell me," Andy said, raising her hands and pretending to catch a pop fly from Josh's bat. "But just give me the headline, since I'm due in five minutes at Hank Lorenz's office." Just then, Sanjay Singh walked past Andy's cubicle. The Review's editor-in-chief, he had graduated summa cum laude from Berkeley in South Asian studies; his senior thesis was a translation of several Sikh holy books from Ancient Punjabi into English. With sculpted features and bronze skin, he wore a tightly-wrapped blue turban, a sign of his Sikh religion, along with a white tunic and black slacks.

Josh beckoned him to stop. "Sanjay," he asked, "is it true that you turned down an offer that might make you the first Sikh president someday?"

Sanjay smiled. "You mean like the editor-in-chief who became the first African American president? The Muslim guy from Kenya, some people still believe."

"Excuse me," Andy interjected. "Can you clue me in here? What offer did you turn down, Sanjay?"

Josh answered for him. "Sanjay turned down an offer of a Supreme Court clerkship with Chief Justice Sam Terman. Every law-review editor who ever lived would kill for that job. I still can't believe it."

"Well, I'm one who wouldn't even cross the street for that job," Andy replied. "Good for you, Sanjay. So, what are you going to do that will make use of your many talents?"

Sanjay looked reflective. "You know, Andy, my dad was one of the people who was killed at our temple in Wisconsin, five years ago, by a racist who thought they were Muslims. My dad lived for several days after he was shot, and when I saw him for the last time in the hospital, he told me I had an obligation to devote my work to the Sikh community. So, I'm taking a job as counsel to the North American Sikh Association."

Andy moved around Josh and gave Sanjay a hug. "Working for people you care about, Sanjay, is worth a lot more than cite-checking for Supreme Court justices." She gave Sanjay a wink. "Of course, I loved every cite I ever checked here." She waved a hand as she headed for the stairs. "Guys, I've got to rush. But I'm glad for you, Sanjay." As she continued down the hall, Andy turned to Josh. "Can you meet me at the Hark in an hour? I'll let you know whether Hank gives my paper a passing grade, or needs a orthopedic surgeon for his broken leg."

Josh laughed. "I'll bring my Louisville Slugger, just in case." Just as Andy reached the stairs, he gave out an old-fashioned wolf whistle. "By the way, Andy," he said, "you're looking quite the young female lawyer this morning. Like your outfit, especially the rear view. And the front view's pretty nice, too."

"I'll ignore your sexist remark, Josh, but thanks for the compliment," Andy retorted. Her normal attire ran to jeans and polo shirts, but today she had dressed in a black pantsuit she'd bought at the Ann Taylor store on Newbury Street in Boston's Back Bay. Her young-female-lawyer outfit included a cream-colored, scoop-neck blouse, black flats with silver buckles, and a silver-and-turquoise necklace she'd purchased on a family trip to Santa Fe during high school.

"Just don't walk by the construction at Hastings Hall," Josh said. "You'll get more than wolf whistles from those hard-hat guys."

"Thanks for the advice," Andy replied. "But I've heard it all, believe me."

Andy's bantering with Josh had the effect he intended, easing her anxiety about Lorenz's reaction to the paper she had submitted to him a week earlier. "It's not such a big deal," she told herself, as she walked briskly from Gannett House to Pound Hall. But it *was* a big deal, since the paper she had been working on, beginning with the month-long Winter Term in January, was the most substantial piece of research and writing Andy had done in law school.

All HLS students were required to fulfill a writing project under a faculty member's supervision. Because the written-work grading was pass-or-fail, and nobody in recent years had gotten a failing grade, many students took the task lightly and didn't burn the midnight oil.

Andy, however, took the project very seriously. Her topic, although academic in nature, dealt with a life-or-death situation for the people who were its subjects: the 3000 men, and about sixty women, currently confined on the nation's state and federal death rows. Andy knew that her paper, the research she had put into it, and the reforms it proposed, probably wouldn't prevent any further executions. But, as Hank Lorenz had said, when she proposed the topic, "You might just make an impact, Andy, if this is solid work and reaches the right audience of legislators and judges." This gave Andy some assurance that, whatever the future impact of her paper, the project had been worth the midnight-oil effort.

Trotting up the front steps of Pound Hall, Andy's fear that she would be late for her meeting with Lorenz eased when she almost bumped into him as he strode down the hallway to his office. "Good morning, Andy," he greeted her. "Just heading for my lair. I could use a break from explaining the doctrine of substantive due process to my con law section. Most of them take a while to get it through their heads."

Andy fell in beside Lorenz as they walked down the hallway, passing portraits of long-dead and mostly bearded law-school professors. "Well," she said, "it took me a whole semester to understand why process has substance, which seems oxymoronic to me."

Lorenz chuckled. "Me too, to be honest. So, we're just around the corner. Can I ask Brenda to bring us some coffee," he said with a smile at his secretary, across the hall from his office.

"Thanks, but I've had so much this morning that my stomach is sloshing," Andy replied.

Lorenz's office surprised Andy, who hadn't been invited into it before. Their previous meetings to discuss her paper proposal and its progress had been in the Pound Hall lounge, where students and faculty mingled among groupings of sofas and club chairs. Andy had expected to see walls of diplomas, awards, and framed book covers that reminded visitors of the accolades and achievements heaped upon "chaired" Harvard Law School professors. Andy knew that Lorenz held the Harry Blackmun Professorship, an endowed chair funded by the former justice's law partners in Minneapolis. She also knew that he had served a year as law clerk for Justice Blackmun, and that both had graduated summa cum laude from Harvard College with degrees in math, which struck Andy as an amazing coincidence, or maybe not.

Two walls of Lorenz's office were covered with framed paintings, about a dozen, all of them landscapes and seascapes done in pastels, looking to Andy like the Maine coast where her family spent two weeks each summer near Bar Harbor. A couple of the harbor scenes, and a lighthouse in one painting, looked familiar to her. "These are beautiful," Andy said. "I'm guessing the artist painted them in Maine. Somewhere near Bar Harbor. Do you know the artist?'

Lorenz chuckled. "I'm glad you like them, and you're right. They were done near Bar Harbor, and I do know the artist." He paused for a second. "That's me."

Andy took a step closer to one, and saw the initials "H L" on the bottom right. "Wow," she exclaimed. "Maybe you're in the wrong profession, Hank. My mom has a small art gallery in Scarsdale, and she'd find homes for these in a flash."

"That's very kind of you, Andy, but I'm no Winslow Homer. And with due respect to your mom, I'd hate to wind up over the fireplaces of the estates in Scarsdale."

"Well, we don't actually live there," Andy said, a little abashed. "We live in Yonkers, but my mom took over a gallery in Scarsdale from a friend who retired. It's more of a hobby for her, but she's got a good eye for art."

"Speaking of art," Lorenz said, "I noticed on your law-school application that you were an art history major at Barnard. If you're wondering how I know that, I was on the admissions committee the year you applied. Of course, you had magna cum laude grades and a great LSAT score, so you had a pretty good chance of getting admitted anyway." He noticed that Andy was still standing. "I'm sorry, Andy," Lorenz said. "Why don't we sit." He gestured to a small floral-patterned sofa, with two matching chairs across from a low coffee table. Andy plunked her backpack next to the couch, and sat down as Lorenz settled into a chair, crossing his legs. She expected him to shift their conversation to her paper, but he continued where he left off.

"Anyway, on the admissions committee we each got to pick three or four applicants who would be green-lighted for admission, with no objections from the other members. I put you on my list, because I felt we needed some balance with all the political science and economics majors we seem to attract. Smart people, but they'll mostly wind up spending their careers looking for tax loopholes for the one percent. But I take a special interest in my picks, not only here but after they leave. Sanjay Singh was another one of mine from your class. I told him he was a cinch for a Supreme Court clerkship, but I just heard this morning that he turned down an offer to clerk for Sam Terman."

Andy nodded. "I just heard that from Sanjay over at Gannett House. He's going to work for the Sikh Association, which I think is a great tribute to his dad."

Lorenz paused for a moment. "I heard about that, too," he said. "And I agree with you, Andy. But a clerkship with the Chief Justice is quite a plum." He shook his head, then smiled at Andy. "So, Andy, you're probably wondering why you're here this morning, aside from showing off my paintings. Two things. One is about your paper." Noticing Andy's involuntary tensing, Lorenz quickly said, "Don't worry. I said it was a really good paper, and I meant it."

Picking up a copy of Andy's paper, Lorenz flipped through it and found a page. "I do have a couple of questions, Andy, just to clarify your argument. Okay?" She nodded. "Now," he continued, "your title is 'Traumatic Brain Injury As A Bar To Capital Punishment,' and you cite studies by neurologists that show a very high incidence of, let's call it TBI for short, among inmates on death rows across the country."

He scanned the page in his hand. "Let me read this section and then ask a question. Okay?" Andy nodded again. "'A study conducted by Doctor Dorothy Lewis, a psychiatrist at Yale Medical School, and Doctor Jonathan Pincus, chief of neurology at the Veterans Administration hospital in Washington, D.C., published in the American Journal of Psychiatry in 1986, examined fifteen death row inmates and found that all fifteen had suffered severe head injuries in childhood, and about half had been the victims of cranial assault, that is, beatings or blows to their heads that resulted in traumatic brain injury. Others had been injured in car accidents or falls. Significantly, not one of these inmates, through their trial lawyers, had raised a defense of mental impairment as a result of their TBI.'"

Lorenz looked up, as Andy followed along on her copy of the paper. He continued reading: "'A more recent and larger study by Doctor Pincus of one hundred fifty convicted murderers found that ninety-four percent had evidence of TBI, ranging from moderate to severe, and that most had experienced severe physical and sexual abuse as children. These figures should be compared with an incidence of TBI in the general population of two to five percent. This disparity is striking, and obviously significant.'"

Lorenz looked up again. "Ninety-four percent of convicted murderers with TBI," he said, "compared to five percent for the rest of the population, really is significant, I'll agree. And you say here, Andy, let me read a bit more, that 'the consequences of moderate to severe TBI are profound and devastating. Every researcher in this field has identified them as neurological damage, enormous anger, and a diminished or even absent capacity to control or stop urges to violence, which can flare up without warning or provocation.'"

Andy had taken Lorenz's criminal law seminar the year before, and knew that he could ask penetrating questions. As he looked up again, she figured one was coming, and was right. "One question, Andy," he said. "Actually, two." She steeled herself for his interrogation, and nodded. "First, you argue that evidence of moderate to severe TBI should be a bar to the death penalty," he said. "But do you have any basis in the Constitution, or Supreme Court precedent, that would support such a bar? It seems to me you'd need one for a court to make such a ruling."

Andy was stumped, and her face showed it. Lorenz noticed this, and prompted her. "I'll give you a hint," he said. "Roper versus Simmons, Supreme Court, 2005."

"Of course," she said, her face showing relief. "We covered that in your crim law seminar. Thank you for that hint, Hank."

"So, Andy, tell me how the Roper case would support your argument, from what you recall about it."

Andy recalled her anxiety at being called upon in Lorenz's seminar, but could almost see the pages in the casebook on the Roper case. "Well," she said, "this was a case of a juvenile who was sentenced to death for a murder he committed when he was seventeen, I think." Lorenz nodded approvingly, as Andy continued. "The Court cited studies of brain development in juveniles, showing that most of them lack the cognitive abilities of adults, affecting their reasoning and impulse control, which are well below those of normal adults. And the Court concluded that, considering the immature brain functioning of juveniles, executing them would constitute 'cruel and unusual punishment' under the Eighth Amendment." She paused. "Did I get that right, Hank?"

She got another approving nod, then another question. "Very good," Lorenz said. "Now, can you connect the dots between Roper and your TBI studies?"

Andy thought for a moment. "How about this," she said. "The studies of TBI in death row inmates show the effects of trauma to the brain in loss of control over violent urges that are characteristic of juvenile behavior. In other words, adults with TBI have, in effect, the brains of juveniles." Andy jumped on the conclusion that Lorenz's hint had now made clear to her. "So, the principle of the Roper case should apply to defendants with TBI, and bar their execution, as an Eighth Amendment violation."

Putting Andy's paper on the table between them, Lorenz smiled broadly. "Just the answer I expected, Andy. QED, as a logician would say. And you answered that question better than most lawyers in their oral arguments to the Supreme Court." He picked up her paper again. "Now, I've got a proposal for you." Andy gave him a quizzical look. "Let me explain," Lorenz said. "I'm editing a book for Harvard University Press that's called 'Dismantling the Machinery of Death.' Recognize the title reference?"

"I think so," Andy replied. "Didn't Justice Blackmun, in his last death penalty opinion, say he would no longer tinker with the machinery of death, because it was broken beyond repair?"

"Very good, Andy," Lorenz said. "So, here's my proposal. If you can add three or four pages to your paper, tying the studies you cited to the Roper decision, I'd very much like to include it as a chapter in this book. What do you think? Could you do that in the next, oh, six weeks?"

Andy was speechless for a moment. "I'm floored," she blurted, then recovered her composure. "I don't think that would take six weeks, Hank. In fact, I could start tomorrow, and probably finish by next week. And I'm honored that you think my paper is good enough for your book."

Lorenz held up a hand. "Whoa, stop for a minute, Andy. Take all the time you need. And the list of contributors will say, 'Andrea Roboff, J.D., Harvard Law School.' Along with the title of the position you'll hold after graduation." He paused for a second. "Which brings me to the second thing I wanted to discuss with you this morning."

Lorenz picked up a thin folder from his desk and gave Andy a sly grin, which she returned with a quizzical look. "So, Andy," he said, "have you lined up a job after graduation?" Andy hadn't expected this question, but wasn't surprised. She hadn't discussed her post-graduation plans with Lorenz, although he had offered to write letters of recommendation, or make calls, on her behalf. Many of the hiring partners at major law firms were former students, and Andy knew that a good word from him could land any student an associate's position at a starting salary of $180,000, with plenty of perks to make up for putting in at least fifty hours a week. But Andy had no intention of working in a law firm, no matter what the inducement. She started framing a polite way to say thanks, but no thanks.

"Well, I do have a job offer, but I haven't accepted it yet," Andy said. "It's with the Texas Defender Services, working with one of their staff attorneys on death penalty litigation. It would be great training, and Texas, as you know, is the execution capital of the country."

"You said you haven't accepted their offer yet," Lorenz said. "Is there some deadline on this?"

"They'd like to know by the end of the month, but I'm asking for a few more weeks, until after graduation. I've never been to Texas, so I'd like to visit Austin and meet the people at the Defenders before I decide. It would be quite a change from the east coast, where I've lived all my life, but it would also put me right in the belly of the beast, if you know what I mean." Andy noticed that Lorenz had reached over to his desk and picked up a thin manila folder.

"If you want to work on death penalty cases," he said, "Texas *is* the belly of the beast, as you put it, and the Defenders Service does great work. I know Ken Murray, who's their trial director. He's been handling death penalty cases for almost thirty years, and you'd learn a lot if you worked with Ken. I helped him a few years ago on a case he argued before the Supreme Court. He lost, unfortunately, in a five-to-four, really bad decision, but he's won several other cases that took his clients off of death row in Texas."

Lorenz pulled a sheet of paper from the folder he'd put on the coffee table. "Andy, before you decide about the job with Texas Defenders, let me read you an email I got yesterday. It's on this print-out." He cleared his throat, and Andy felt hers tense.

"Here it is," Lorenz said, looking up from the sheet at Andy, then looking down. "'Hank, it was great talking with you last week and catching up on your unstinting efforts to clean the stables.'" Lorenz smiled and said, "That's a running joke between us; he thinks I'm a modern-day Heracles, trying to shovel all the manure from the Augean stables, while I keep telling him to stop adding more."

Andy smiled back, trying to conceal her impatience. What the hell is this all about, she wondered. And who is this from?

"Anyway," Lorenz went on, "I'll skip the blah, blah, and not keep you in suspense. Bad habit of mine. Here's the meat." He looked back down and continued reading. "'I read the material you sent me about Andrea Roboff and was quite impressed. Her undergraduate record, and her law-school grades, are outstanding. And the senior articles editor of the Harvard Law Review clearly has the skills to excel at clerkship duties.'" Lorenz smiled, and kept reading. "'Based on your recommendation, I'd be glad to offer Ms. Roboff a clerkship for the coming term. I trust your judgment, Hank, and the clerks you've sent in previous terms have all done commendable jobs. If Ms. Roboff accepts the offer, she can begin her clerkship anytime in July that's convenient for her.'"

Andy was floored by what Lorenz had read to her. "A clerkship with a judge, is that what I'm bring offered?"

"Not a judge, Andy. You're being offered a clerkship with a justice on the Supreme Court."

"Oh, my God," was all Andy could say.

"Well, I'd give the credit to your record, and your paper, not to the supreme being, assuming there is one," Lorenz said with a smile. "What do you think?"

"I don't know what to think," Andy replied. "I hadn't even considered a clerkship with any judge, let alone a Supreme Court justice. In fact, I just congratulated Sanjay for turning down a clerkship offer with Chief Justice Terman. Besides, as I said, I've already been offered a job with the Texas Defenders."

"That's not a problem," Lorenz said. "Actually, I have a former student who interned with the Innocence Project last summer. He's looking for a one-year position while he finishes a book on the lives after prison of inmates who have been exonerated and released from prison through the Innocence Project. He'd be perfect for the Texas Defenders."

Lorenz noted the skeptical look on Andy's face. "Tell you what, Andy. If you take this clerkship offer, I'll call Ken Murray and ask if he'll take my former student for a year, and keep his offer to you open until you finish the clerkship. I'm sure he'll agree to that. Having a former Supreme Court clerk on the Defenders' staff would impress the folks who fund their work."

"I've got a couple of questions," Andy said. "First, I thought Supreme Court clerks all spent a year clerking for a lower-court judge before they clerked for a justice."

"Well, that's generally the case," Lorenz replied. "Most of them do clerk for a judge on the federal courts of appeals for a year, but it's not a rule. Two of my colleagues on the faculty went straight from law school to the Court. It's like going to the major leagues without spending time on a Triple-A team. Doesn't happen often, but if you're good enough you don't really need time in the minors. And you're more than good enough, Andy. You've got all the skills you need to be a Supreme Court clerk. You're great at research, you write better than most justices—or the clerks who draft their opinions—and you've got both judgment and passion. What do you say?"

"Well, I'm flattered that you think I could do this," Andy said. "And it's tempting, if Ken Murray will hold the job with the Defenders. But something tells me you already knew about his offer and that you already called him."

Lorenz laughed. "You're right, Andy. Guilty as charged. Actually, I was in the Pound Hall lounge yesterday and I overheard Bonnie Fox telling Sanjay about it. And I did call Ken last night, and he's fine either way. He'd be glad to have my former student for a year, and Ken is willing to keep the job open for you."

Andy looked at the sheet on the coffee table. "So, Hank, what you haven't told me, since this all sounds like a set-up job, is just who has offered me a clerkship. It wouldn't be Justice Schroeder, would it?"

If Andy had to pick one justice to clerk for, it would be Alice Schroeder, elevated to the Supreme Court five years earlier from the Ninth Circuit Court of Appeals on the west coast. One of the most liberal judges on the nation's most liberal appellate court, Schroeder had quickly become a solid member of the Supreme Court's current liberal majority, a five-justice bloc led by Chief Justice Sam Terman. "If it's Justice Schroeder," Andy said, "I'll accept right now. But you said 'him' when you read me the email. So, if it's not her, who is it?"

"No, it's not her," Lorenz said. He paused for dramatic effect. "It's Justice Alex Novak."

"Excuse me," Andy blurted. "You're kidding, right? Did Bonnie and Sanjay put you up to this? It sounds like a prank they would play."

"Nope, I'm serious, Andy. Justice Novak has offered you a clerkship. I'll call him right now to confirm it, if you'd like, and you can give him your acceptance yourself."

"Okay, I believe you," Andy said. "But Justice Novak is one of the most conservative members of the Supreme Court. I mean, he supports the death penalty, votes against women's rights, affirmative action, everything you and I agree on, Hank. So why would he offer me a clerkship, sight unseen? I thought you had to apply a year in advance, and have an interview with the justice, and be at least compatible with his or her judicial philosophy, or politics, to be honest."

"That's the normal process, yes," Lorenz agreed. "But before you say no, which it looks like you're itching to do, let me explain the deal, okay?" Andy nodded her agreement. "Justice Novak and I were classmates here. We were in the same study group, and we were moot court partners in the Ames competition. He was very conservative even then, and I was, as you know, much more liberal. The moot court case we briefed and argued was a First Amendment case, about an anti-abortion group whose members picketed the home of a doctor who performed abortions. They held up placards with his picture on it, and captions that said, 'Wanted for Murder.' And they handed out leaflets that accused the doctor of performing late-term abortions with a procedure that involved cutting off the limbs and crushing the heads of fetuses to extract the torsos. One serious problem. Turned out they had the wrong doctor. Same last name, but this one didn't perform that kind of abortion. Some of his friends and neighbors had stopped talking with him after seeing the placards and getting the leaflets. So, he sued them for intentional infliction of emotional distress."

Andy listened politely as Lorenz continued. "The issue in our moot-court case was whether distributing literature with false claims was protected by the First Amendment. Alex was initially reluctant to make that argument, and he and I argued about it for hours. But I finally convinced him that 'freedom for the thought that we hate,' as Justice Holmes put it, is the price we pay for expressing the views we hold, or even cherish, but that others may hate. Anyway, Alex came around, and actually quoted the phrase from Holmes in his oral argument. And one of the moot court judges was the Chief Justice of the Supreme Court, who said to Alex, 'Quoting Holmes can win just about any argument, on either side,' which got a big laugh. But Alex has been good in First Amendment cases ever since, one of the few things we do agree on.

"Anyway," Lorenz continued, "Alex and I both went on to clerk on the Supreme Court, for different justices, and we both became law professors, at different schools. Then he was named to the Seventh Circuit Court of Appeals in Chicago, and five years later to the Supreme Court, where he's been for ten years now. And every year he asks me to recommend a clerk with liberal views." Lorenz noticed Andy's raised eyebrows. "That might sound odd, Andy, but Alex Novak is the kind of guy who really enjoys intellectual debate—we were both college debaters, by the way—and he wants to have a clerk who will press him on hard cases. His other clerks are almost all conservatives, most of them from the Federalist Society, and they're unlikely to question anything he says or writes. Our arrangement has worked out so far, and the liberal clerks liked him a lot. I can give you some names, and you can call them if you want first-hand reports."

"I'll take your word on that," Andy replied. "But do you need an answer right now? I'm not sure I can give you one without thinking some more about this, and talking with some of my friends, and with my folks. My parents are both card-carrying ACLU members, and they consider Justice Novak a threat to all the causes they support."

"That's fine," Lorenz said. "Alex did ask me to give him your decision by Friday. Today's Tuesday, so take your time. But I can assure you that you'll enjoy spending a year at the Court. Well, maybe not enjoy every minute, since the clerks work even longer hours than first-year associates in the big firms. But it's exciting to be in the building where decisions are made that affect every American's life, for better or worse. I wouldn't trade my year at the Court for any year I've had since then."

Lorenz got up from his chair, and Andy followed, picking up her backpack from the carpet "Think about it, Andy. But just give me a call or stop in by Friday, okay?"

Shouldering her backpack, Andy looked around Lorenz's office one more time. "Tell you what, Hank," she said lightly, gesturing at the paintings on the walls. "My mom and dad are coming up for commencement. If I say yes to Justice Novak's offer, can you show them your gallery?"

Lorenz laughed. "Even if you say no, Andy, I'd be delighted. Although your mom can probably spot a dauber like me right away. But I'd love to meet them both."

As he ushered Andy out of his office, Lorenz gave her a pat on the shoulder, and headed down the hall to his next class. She turned the other way, heading for the Harkness Commons and her meeting with Josh.

2

Andy's thoughts were swirling as she left Pound Hall for the short walk to the Harkness Commons, the campus center everyone called the Hark. She'd been all prepared for a trip to Austin right after graduation, and was almost sure she'd accept the job offer from Texas Defenders. Now, out of the blue, Hank Lorenz had offered her a clerkship at the Supreme Court, a post that hundreds of students at the elite law schools dreamed of landing, but for which only thirty-six were chosen every year. But the clerkship would be with a justice that liberals, including Andy's parents and most of her friends, considered hostile to every cause they supported.

Spending a year at the Supreme Court might be exciting, and potentially rewarding in terms of her future legal career, wherever that led. If she could auction off the clerkship offer, Andy thought, she might wind up with a million, maybe more. Spending that year as the token "liberal" clerk for the Court's most conservative justice, however, might be more of a challenge than Andy felt she could handle. Everyone said that Justice Novak was a nice guy, the often snarky tone of his dissenting opinions aside, but maybe the "nice guy" persona didn't apply to his clerks. Andy didn't mind—in fact, she enjoyed—intellectual debate, of which there was plenty at Harvard. On the other hand, pitting a twenty-five-year-old, fresh-out-of-law-school neophyte against the Court's most skilled and experienced debater, both on and off the bench, might be akin to getting into the ring with the world's reigning heavyweight champ.

Still absorbed in her thoughts, Andy entered the Hark's cafeteria and looked around for Josh. He was the first person whose advice she'd ask in making her decision, and the person whose judgment she would trust over anyone else. Andy didn't see Josh in the cafeteria. But the morning drizzle had ended, and the day had turned sunny and warm, so she went outside to the patio where students brought their lunches and laptops to the picnic tables. Andy checked her watch. It was a quarter before ten, the time Josh had agreed to meet her. She found an empty table, plunked her backpack onto it, sat down, and looked out at the lawn between the law-school dorms, where she had first met the guy she had fallen in love with, and who was now her best friend and confidant. Love was still there, but a different kind of love than Andy had anticipated during her first weeks at Harvard. Andy retrieved these memories as she waited for Josh.

The law school's Social Committee hosted a "mixer" for the first-year students after classes ended on the first Friday of the fall semester. Tables with kegs of beer and munchies had been set up on the lawn between the five connected dormitories—named after famous and long-dead professors—in which most first-year students lived. Andy had come, a bit reluctantly, at the urging of her Story dorm roommate, Bonnie Fox, a bubbly, blond, and self-described "surfer girl" from San Diego, whose dead-ringer resemblance to Reese Witherspoon in "Legally Blond" had escaped no one's attention, and belied her very sharp mind. Andy had planned to spend the afternoon reviewing her notes from the first week's classes, but Bonnie had urged her to come along to the mixer. "It's a beautiful fall day, the beer is free, and all the hunky guys will be there," Bonnie had said, grabbing Andy's arm and marching her out to the lawn.

By the time they arrived, it was obvious that much beer had been consumed, and that students had begun to look for classmates from their undergraduate colleges. Most of the conversations Andy overheard, as Bonnie peeled off, gave her a cheery wave, and headed for the beer table, started with "So, what college did you go to?" The Harvard people found other Harvard people, the Yale and Princeton people did the same, until most of the Ivies were grouped in little clusters, laughing and guzzling beer. Andy knew she was the only Barnard graduate in this class, and she felt a bit out of place among the chattering crowd that spilled across the lawn.

As she stood by herself, outside the shifting clusters, a tall, lanky guy, with tousled sandy hair, approached Andy, holding a plastic cup of beer in each hand. He wasn't in her first-year section, so Andy didn't recognize him from classes. "You look thirsty," the guy said with a smile. "Can I offer you a Sam Adams?"

A little startled by this invitation, Andy hesitated for a moment, then said, "I'm not much of a beer drinker, but I'll try one, if you can tell me who Sam Adams was."

Handing Andy one of the cups, the guy laughed. "What is this?" he replied. "Tenth-grade American history class? You don't look anything like Miss Williams, who probably was born around the time of Sam Adams. But I'll bite." The guy took a swig from his cup, cleared his throat, and said, in a high-school-recitation tone, "Sam Adams was one of the leading patriots in colonial days, organized resistance to British rule, helped draft the Articles of Confederation, and served as governor of Massachusetts. He was a cousin of John Adams. Now there's a beer named after him. Will that do?"

Andy smiled, and took a sip from her cup of Sam Adams, paused a second, then took a bigger swig. "That's very good, young man," she said, in a prim, school-teacherly voice. "Now you may sit down, and we'll move on to Crispus Attucks and the Boston Massacre."

The guy raised his right hand, and waved it back and forth. "I can do that one too, Miss Williams," he said with an eager, call-on-me-teacher tone.

Andy smiled. "We'll let someone else answer that, for a change," she said.

"Okay," the guy said, sticking out his right hand. "By the way, I'm Josh Barfield, and you are Andy Roboff, unless I misread your name tag." Andy looked down at the adhesive tag on which she'd printed her name with a Sharpie at the sign-in table for the mixer, and stuck on her polo shirt. She shook the guy's hand, and said, "Yes, I'm Andy. Andrea, actually, but nobody calls me that except my mom, when she wants me to clean up my messy room." Andy looked at the guy's tag. "And you must be impersonating Josh Barfield, for some reason. I heard the real Josh Barfield is in the library, boning up for Monday's civil procedure class."

"Oh, no, that's not me," he replied, feigning a recoil of horror. "I am the one and only Josh Barfield, at least at Harvard Law School, and I'm not going to be a library rat or a gunner." Every first-year section had at least two or three "gunners," the pejorative term for students who always waved their hands when the professor asked for volunteers to recite the facts and holdings of a case. It was a Harvard tradition, Andy had learned during her first week of classes, that other students responded to gunners by hissing and stamping their feet, although most gunners--angling for letters of recommendation for summer jobs with big firms—seemed oblivious to this expression of scorn, and most professors ignored it.

"Glad to meet you, Josh," Andy said. "I was just kidding. You don't look like the gunner type, and I'm certainly not going to be one, either." Having finished her cup of Sam Adams, Andy was feeling a little buzzed and was enjoying her almost-flirting banter with Josh, something she often did with guys as a cover for her natural shyness in first encounters.

Just then, a burly guy staggered up and clapped Josh on the back, spilling some beer from the cup in his other hand. "Hey, Josh, I heard you were here. Small world, huh? Say, there's a bunch of us Princeton folks over by the beer table. Come on and join us, buddy. And bring your lady friend along. We'll make her an honorary Tiger." Turning to Andy, he slurred, "I'm Rob Frelinghuysen. Did you know that Josh, here, won the Ivy championship in squash last year? Prob'ly too shy to boast about it. Not my game, though. I was a rugby player, the best game for guys who like to grope other guys in the scrum. Just kidding."

Josh shot Andy a Let's Get Out of Here look. "Sorry, Rob," he said. "Andy and I are heading over to the Square for dinner. I've heard that Grendel's Den has great quiche. But not your kind of grub, I guess. More like steak and fries for you rugby guys, right? Anyway, see you around, Rob."

Taking Andy by the arm, Josh steered around Rob and headed toward Harvard Square, on the other side of Harvard Yard. "After putting up with that drunken clown, Andy, I owe you a good dinner," Josh said. "And I've wanted to try Grendel's Den, if that's okay with you."

Grateful to Josh for handling that unpleasant encounter, and enjoying the feel of his hand on her arm, Andy said, "Sure, that sounds good, Josh. I'm more of a quiche person, myself. Too much steak and fries can make you fat and stupid, although I guess your friend Rob can't be really stupid, if he got into Harvard Law School."

Josh chuckled. "Rob's not really stupid, at least when he's sober, but it helps if your grandfather was in Congress for years from New Jersey, and your ancestors include four senators. Rob got turned down by Yale, which was the family law school, but Harvard admits lots of Princeton grads whose families can boost the endowment fund by a couple mil. Not a bribe, of course, more like a gratuity. Anyway, let's forget about the Robs of this world and enjoy dinner. My treat."

As they left the law school grounds and entered the north gate of Harvard Yard, Josh slid his hand down Andy's arm and linked his fingers with hers. She hadn't anticipated any of this, ever since Bonnie had dragged her down to the mixer, and then left with a knowing wink, but Andy felt comfortable with Josh. He hadn't spoken on their walk through the Yard to Harvard Square, and she assumed he had his own thoughts, perhaps about her, perhaps not. He'd kept her hand in his, and had squeezed it lightly several times, turning his head to smile at her, so maybe he *was* thinking about her, or was just a nice guy on a spur-of-the-moment date. Andy knew she spent too much time thinking about what other people were thinking, especially when they might be thinking about her.

Grendel's Den was just a block down from the Square, and Andy and Josh found a table on the elevated outside deck, fronting a little grassy area on which teen-agers—all in the uniform of baggy shorts and baggy tee shirts—were playing hacky-sack, and from which the pungent odor of cannabis reached their nostrils. Josh sniffed deeply and said, "I'm pretty sure there's some Pineapple Express and some Northern Lights out there."

Andy was puzzled. "I'm sorry, Josh. What's that about?"

He grinned. "Oh, those are varieties. One's a sativa and one's an indica, but I forget which is which. My favorite is Lemon Haze. Have you tried that?"

Catching on to the pot jargon, Andy laughed. "I'm not a connoisseur, Josh. And I'm not much of a toker. Give me a joint at a party, and I'll take a hit or two, although it always gives me a bad case of munchies. I don't know weed varieties, but it sounds like you do."

Josh sniffed the air again. "Do you smell something that's more sweet, and another that's more earthy? Just from the smell, you can tell most varieties, just like wine buffs can tell which variety of grape they're drinking, and even the vintage."

Just then, a waitperson—this variety was male—approached with the universal, "Can I get you folks something to drink?" Andy looked at Josh, who was perusing the menu. "We're both having quiche," he said, "so

I guess a white. Okay with you, Andy?" She nodded agreement. "Any recommendation?" Josh asked the server.

"I'd suggest the Beringer chardonnay, to go with quiche," he replied. "It's a 2012, and very good. Would you like a sip to try?"

"Sure, although I'm sure it'll be fine," Josh said. "Can you bring us a bottle, and can we order now?" The server pulled out his pad and pen. Josh looked up from the menu. "How about two orders of mushroom and onion quiche, an order of hummus and pita bread, and a large Greek salad that we'll share. Okay with you, Andy?" Again, she nodded agreement. So, Josh likes to take charge, Andy thought, but not in a bossy way. And the dinner order suited Andy just fine.

The wine arrived, the server poured a sip for each, and filled their glasses after more nods of agreement. "So," Josh said, holding out his glass for Andy to clink, "what college did you go to?"

They both laughed. "Barnard," Andy said, "although I lived at home in Yonkers with my parents and my grandmother. And I know you went to Princeton, thanks to your buddy Rob."

Josh grimaced. "Please, don't lump me with the Robs, of whom Princeton has far too many. I went there on a scholarship, and I suspect they admitted me to fill their quota of one from Idaho. There seemed to be just one in each class."

"I don't think I've ever met anyone from Idaho," Andy said. "Tell me what it's like. Potatoes and pine trees, I guess."

Josh grinned. "Potatoes in the south, along with scads of Mormons, trees in the north, the Panhandle. My folks live way up near the Canadian border, a little town called Sandpoint. It's on a beautiful lake, Pend Oreille, where we'd go swimming and windsurfing. My dad's a forester with the state department of natural resources, and my mom's a math teacher at the high school. No brothers or sisters. So, how about you?"

"Born and raised in Yonkers, just north of the Bronx," Andy replied. "My dad's an orthodontist, and my mom has a little art gallery in Scarsdale, more of a hobby. Also no brothers or sisters. Went to Barnard for art history, spent my junior year in Florence and Rome, which I loved, picked up a little Italian, which is wearing off."

"So, how did we both wind up at Harvard Law School?" Josh said. "I'll go first. I was a double major in physics and politics at Princeton, in the public law program. Odd pair, I admit, but I like the indeterminacy in both. People think physics and law both follow rules, which is only partly true. Heisenberg showed the indeterminacy in physics, and a bunch of people have done that in law. Anyway, I didn't feel like doing physics in grad school, and I took a couple of great courses on law, one on Law and Society, which looked at how the real world affects law and legal reasoning. That's what interests me the most about law, you know, how it affects real people and how they live." Josh paused, took a sip of his wine, and smiled. "Now it's your turn, Andy."

"Well, nothing like that," she said. "Maybe something like it, actually. I was an art major, as I said, but I took a course on Justice in America, and the instructor assigned a book by a law professor, a guy named David Dow. He's also a lawyer who represents death-row inmates in Texas, about fifty of them, and he wrote a book called 'Executed On a Technicality.' It really shook me up, Josh. Almost every one of his clients got sentenced to death because people in the legal system fucked up. Police, prosecutors, defense attorneys, judges, even witnesses and jurors. Dow says that all but one of his clients had unfair trials, and courts hardly ever overturn the guilty verdicts or death sentences. It does happen, and we read about the ones who get exonerated, but that's just a fraction of the inmates who got screwed, even if they did the crime. I may sound like a bleeding-heart crusader, but I think fairness counts."

Andy realized that she was getting a bit worked up. She also noticed that Josh had put a hand over hers, just resting it lightly, and was looking at her intently. He was obviously very interested, at least in what she was saying. But maybe interested in something more, Andy thought as she took another sip of wine. "Anyway," she continued, "I thought maybe I could do something as a lawyer, not just on death-penalty cases, but getting people educated about the injustices that happen every day. Maybe writing about it, too, since I'm a pretty good writer, not to be modest."

"Wow," Josh said. "I'm impressed. I'm still not sure what I'll do after law school. I'd like to practice a bit, maybe a couple of years with a civil rights group, and then maybe teaching law, if that works out. And writing, too. I've already got a book title: 'Law, Physics, and Chance.' But that's years away, and who knows what'll happen? Even tonight. The future is very indeterminate for me."

After that exchange, Andy and Josh both got to work on their dinner, which had recently arrived, along with a second bottle of chardonnay.

Andy could feel the effects of the first, which were pleasant, but wasn't sure about the second. She didn't often drink much, and didn't want to wind up like Rob Frelinghuysen, staggering and slurring her speech. So she took only tiny sips from the new glass. And thought about Josh's last comment. Tonight, for him, was still indeterminate. Did that mean in a general sense, that maybe a plane might crash on Grendel's Den, or whether Andy might spend the night with him? She'd never slept with a guy on a first date—the general rule was not until the third—but every rule has an exception, she reminded herself. Well, since everything was indeterminate, nothing to do but wait and see.

As their server appeared to clear the table, he noticed that the second bottle had barely been touched. "Would you folks like to take this home?" he asked. "I can cork it and put it in a nice bag, if you like."

"Sure," Josh said, "and we'll finish it later. And can you spare a couple of plastic cups? Thanks." The server bustled off, and Josh said, "I've got an idea, Andy. There's a really cool spot, just down the street by the Harvard boathouse, where we could sit on the grass and watch the rowers in the sculls. It's still light, and we could finish the wine there. Sound like a plan?"

"Sure," she agreed. "I've seen the crews a couple of times, and it looks very strenuous, but very precise, getting the blades all in synchrony. Wow, I haven't used that word for a while. But I like synchrony. I'm feeling some of it now." Oh, my God, Andy suddenly thought. Maybe Josh thinks I'm talking about two bodies in synchrony, moving together in perfect time. No more wine, or just little sips. Andy wondered if Josh could read her thoughts. His hand was still resting on hers, and she could feel little tremors. He lifted his hand, reaching for the check and his wallet. The server appeared in a flash, took the check and Josh's card, and bustled off again, returning in a minute with the card and a cloth bag with the wine and two cups. The server thanked them profusely—Josh must have left a generous tip on the card, Andy thought—and they ambled slowly down Winthrop Street toward the Charles River.

Again, Josh took Andy's hand, and she squeezed his lightly. "Thank you for the dinner, Josh. Next time is on me. And the conversation. I enjoyed it."

Josh squeezed her hand back, a bit more firmly. "Thank you, too, Andy. And I'm still enjoying our conversation. Let's see, what's next?

Maybe our favorite bands, or favorite movies." She noticed he hadn't said anything about a next time for dinner, or whatever followed, but maybe it didn't need to be said.

They found a shady spot under a tree, and spent the next hour in a Getting To Know You conversation, discovering that they both loved the Dave Matthews Band and had each attended several of their concerts. "I went to one of Dave's concerts at the Columbia River Gorge in Washington, when I was home from Princeton one summer," Josh said, "and I could identify at least a dozen pot varieties while I was walking around. That was cool."

Andy couldn't match that, but she recounted a visit to the Vatican during her year in Italy, during which she'd fallen sound asleep on a bench in the Sistine Chapel, and had been gently shaken awake by a guard, who informed her that the doors had been locked for an hour and that the Vatican police had been looking for her, after fellow students had missed her and raised an alarm. "We even had the Pope looking for you," one of her friends joked after Andy emerged from the Chapel, feeling sheepish. That didn't sound very exciting, Andy realized, but there hadn't been much excitement in her life to share with Josh.

After it started to get dark, and the rowers had hoisted their shells into the boathouse, Andy and Josh disposed of their wine bottle and cups, and strolled back to the Square, again holding hands. "I'll walk you back to Story," Josh offered. "My place is just up Oxford Street from the dorms." No invitation to his place, Andy thought, at least this time. Maybe Josh also obeyed the three-date rule, or maybe this was the first and last. "Sure," Andy said. Back through the Square and the Yard, they stopped briefly to watch the grey squirrels grabbing acorns from the oak trees and running off to stash them away.

Back at the Story dorm, Josh released Andy's hand. "That was really nice," he said. "I'm glad Bonnie sent me over to you at the mixer. Let's do this again, okay?" Josh paused a moment. "Can I give you a kiss?" You can give me more than a kiss, Andy thought, if there will be an again. "If you can bend down a little," she said. Josh chuckled, tilted his head down and gave Andy a kiss that was more than a peck, but less than the first step to a bedroom. "Good night, Andy," he said. "You're very special. I hope you know that."

"So are you," was all she could say before he strolled across the lawn to Oxford Street. When she got up to her room, Andy found Bonnie sitting cross-legged on her bed, painting her fingernails a bright red. Bonnie looked up, brightly. "Well, I wasn't sure you'd be back tonight. No sparks?"

"More like a warm glow," Andy said. "But no flames. We had a good time, Josh is a nice guy, and that's all she wrote, as they say." Andy felt some annoyance toward her conniving roommate. "You set all this up, didn't you, Bonnie? Poor little Andy, she needs a good fuck. And Josh must be a good fucker. Or maybe you already knew that."

"No, nothing like that, Andy," Bonnie said, holding up her hand and blowing on the nails. "As you say, Josh is a nice guy, you're a nice girl, and things like this can take time for the glow to catch fire. Just wait for the right wave, and enjoy the ride, to mix metaphors."

Still pissed at Bonnie, Andy sat down at her desk, picked up her class notes, put in the earbuds from her iPod, turned on Dave Matthews, and decided to let it all go. Bonnie had meant well, Andy decided, and she hadn't expected a good fuck anyway, or even a good dinner with a nice guy.

3

Still waiting on the Hark patio for Josh, Andy's thoughts returned to the second time she'd seen him. The second week of classes had kept Andy busy. On Wednesday, she attended an evening meeting of the newly-formed Harvard Committee to Abolish the Death Penalty, after seeing a poster on the Harkness bulletin board. She volunteered to serve as liaison with similar groups at other schools, and started putting together an email contact list. By Friday, she had almost—but not quite—forgotten her dinner date with Josh, and hadn't seen him on campus, which wasn't surprising, since they were in different first-year sections.

Saturday morning, as Andy was doing her laundry in the Story basement, her phone dinged with a text message. "Hi Andy. Missed you this week. Free for a picnic lunch on the Cambridge Common at noon? I'll bring bread, cheese, strawberries and wine if you can bring yourself. Okay if you can't make it. Let me know. Josh." Andy was torn, but figured that waiting a week, especially for busy law students, wasn't too long, and "missed you" could have more than one meaning. She pondered the invitation while she pulled her clothes from the dryer and started sorting and folding them, then decided that it wouldn't hurt to find out whether Josh had "missed" her in a personal sense, or had simply "missed" running into her on campus that week. Besides, it was a warm, sunny day, and a picnic lunch with a nice guy sounded good. She texted him back: "Sounds great. Missed you too. Meet you at the cannons, okay? See you at noon. Andy."

Josh had texted her at ten, and Andy spent the time before noon on her computer, compiling a list of anti-death penalty groups at other schools and drafting a letter that would propose a national conference the next spring at Harvard. That task was largely—but not completely—successful in keeping Andy from speculating about what might follow her lunch with Josh. A weekly lunch or dinner, maybe movie or concert dates, or something more intimate? She recalled Josh's comments about the "indeterminacy" of life, and decided that speculation about the future was pointless. Saving the draft letter for later polishing, Andy logged off her computer, went down the hall to the communal bathroom, splashed cold water on her face, brushed her teeth, and smiled at her reflection in the mirror. "Okay, girl," she said to herself, "let's go see what life has in store for you." Returning to her room, and realizing the warm day might turn chilly, she checked her closet and pulled on a green Dave Matthews Band sweatshirt she'd bought at a concert in Peekskill that summer.

The Cambridge Common, just across Massachusetts Avenue from the Harvard campus, features a brace of cannon the British had abandoned when they withdrew from Boston in 1776. Andy was sure that Josh knew how to find her at the cannons, whoever arrived first. As it happened, they spotted each other as they both entered the Common, and waved a greeting. Josh was toting a wicker picnic basket, and wearing a green Dave Matthews Band sweatshirt.

"Hey, Andy," he said, pointing at her sweatshirt, "it must be telepathy, although any physicist will tell you that doesn't exist. Anyway, good to see you, and I'm glad you could make it on short notice." Josh set down the basket and spread his arms wide, inviting Andy in for a hug, which lasted long enough and close enough to assure her that "missing" her meant more than not crossing paths over the past week. Josh gestured toward a grassy area nearby. "Does this suit you?"

"Sure," Andy replied, "and don't apologize for the short notice. You rescued me from a day of prepping for Torts next week. Have you noticed that all the cases so far are hundreds of years old, about watermill spills and trespassing cows in rural England?"

Josh laughed. "Hold on, city girl. Don't you know those are still problems up in northern Idaho?" Setting his basket on the spot he'd picked, Josh pulled out a blanket that he and Andy spread on the ground, then arranged Tupperware containers of French rolls, cheese, and strawberries, small jars of mayonnaise and Dijon mustard, paper plates, plastic forks and knives, a bottle of white wine, and a corkscrew. "There," he said, with a look of satisfaction. "A loaf of bread, a jug of wine, and thou beside me. I'll share with you if you can tell me who said that."

Andy laughed. "What is this, tenth-grade English class? It's Omar Khayyam, smarty pants." An hour later, the food and wine had been consumed, and the conversation had been light and bantering. Andy felt relaxed and comfortable. She sat cross-legged on the blanket, enjoying the pleasant glow from the wine and the sounds of children on the nearby playground. Josh had stretched out next to her, resting on his elbows. After several minutes of companionable silence, Josh abruptly sat up and took both of Andy's hands in his. He squeezed them lightly, and she squeezed back.

"Andy," he said, "I have something I need to tell you. Two things, actually." His voice was quavering, and Andy could feel his hands trembling. He looked almost ready to cry. Totally unprepared for this sudden eruption of emotion, Andy just nodded. Josh cleared his throat, and took a deep breath. "First of all, I would love to take you back to my place and make love with you." He paused for a moment, looking directly into her eyes. "If that's okay with you." Andy nodded her agreement, wondering why saying this put Josh on the verge of tears. It was more than okay with her, and not totally unexpected, even though it broke the not-until-the-third-date rule.

Josh smiled, then took another deep breath. "So, here's the second of all. You know what LGBT means, right?" Andy nodded a third time, puzzled and unsure what to say. "Okay," Josh continued, "I'm the 'B' in LGBT. I'm one of those bisexual people that get overlooked by most lesbians and gays, and by most straight people too. We're a minority within a minority. Most gays won't get involved with guys who sleep with women, and I've never met a real lesbian who will have sex with men. It's one or the other for most gays and lesbians. It's not like, tonight I'll sleep with Jack, and tomorrow I'll sleep with Jill."

Andy was taken aback by this confession, but Josh continued. "I discovered in high school that I was attracted to both girls *and* boys. But Sandpoint is a very small town, and I didn't know any guys that were gay, or even how to tell. It wasn't until I got to Princeton that I met any, and I had sex with two girls and three guys in my first two years there." He gave Andy a crooked smile. "Am I totally grossing you out? I know this isn't your normal 'want to come up and see my etchings' pitch for sex. I'm just being honest, and you can say no, if that's how you feel."

"No, Josh, I'm not grossed out," Andy said. "I'd love to make love with you, too. But I have a question, if you don't mind."

"Sure, any question," Josh said.

Andy took a deep breath of her own. "Okay. Is there another guy at your place?"

Josh shook his head. "No, but there is another guy in my life. His name is Carlo Abruzzi, we met at a party in New York two years ago, and he's a second-year med student at Columbia. Carlo's from Italy, he's all gay, but he knows that I'm bi, and we talked about you yester-day."

"You talked about *me*?" Andy sounded incredulous. "What *about* me?"

"Well, I told him I'd met a girl here at the law school, that she's smart, beautiful, funny, and loves the Dave Matthews Band." Josh chuckled. "And that I'd love to have sex with her. And that I think she'd like to have sex with me."

"So what did Carlo say?"

"He said that anybody who loves the Dave Matthews Band sounds like a perfect match." Andy smiled. "No, seriously, he said that he knows we're solid, that smart, beautiful, and funny girls are more rare than diamonds in a dump, and that he'd enjoy helping you keep up with your Italian."

Andy was taken aback. "You told Carlo my whole life story?"

"Every word from our dinner last week," Josh said. "Look, Carlo's not the jealous, possessive type. All he wants is honesty, and that's what we have. How long we'll stay together, I have no idea. He's totally consumed with med school, I'm up to my ears in law school, we're two hundred miles apart, and the future is . . ."

"Indeterminate," Andy broke in.

"So," Josh said, "how about coming to see my etchings?"

Fifteen minutes later, after packing the blanket and picnic stuff into Josh's basket, Andy followed him up the stairs to his second-floor, two-room apartment in a brick building on Oxford Street, which ran past the law-school dormitories and the Harvard Museum of Natural History. Unlocking the door, Josh said, "Just to make sure, this is okay with you? Harvard has a mutual-consent policy, and you're free to say no, or stop, at any time."

"Thank you for reminding me, Josh," Andy replied. "If I say stop, it'll be because I'll be late for Civ Pro on Monday morning."

Josh laughed. "Well, then we'll both be late for class."

Andy looked around the living room, separated by a counter from a small kitchen. Furnished in Basic Student style, the room had a couch, a small coffee table, a round dining table with two chairs, a media cabinet with a flat-screen television and CD player, an Ikea desk like the one in Andy's dorm room, and a bookcase that had been constructed with bricks and pine shelves. It looked pretty much like every student apartment in Cambridge, and every other college town. The only wall decoration was a framed poster from a Dave Matthews Band concert at the Columbia River Gorge.

"Are you a bit nervous, Andy?" Josh asked. "To be honest, I am. An hour ago, I was sure you'd say you had a pressing appointment with your dentist."

"A bit nervous, yes," Andy said. "But I'm calling the dentist to reschedule."

"Tell you what, then," Josh said. "Since we're both a bit nervous, can I offer you a sure-fire cure?" Opening a tin box on the desk, he pulled out a ceramic pipe and a Zip-lock bag of cannabis buds. "This is Lemon Haze. No finer substance to make you mellow."

"Wow," Andy said. "I could use a little mellow."

"Mellow coming right up." While he filled the bowl, Josh said, "Why don't you pick a CD. Anything you'd like, as long as it's Dave Matthews."

Andy found a dozen Dave Matthews CDs in the media cabinet, picked out "Live At Mile High Music Festival," which included her favorite song, "Sledgehammer." She stuck it in the CD player, turned on, and sat beside Josh on the couch. Ten minutes later, after three hits of Lemon Haze, Andy and Josh were both certifiably mellow, with her head on his shoulder.

When the CD reached the third track, "Too Much," Josh said, with a devilish grin, "I'm a bit warm, Andy. If you help me out of my sweatshirt, I'll be more comfortable." He raised his arms over his head, Andy pulled the sweatshirt off, and tossed it on the floor.

"Actually, I'm a little warm, too," Andy said, raising her arms. Her sweatshirt joined his on the floor. Andy was sure that she'd lose more of her clothes before long, but Josh seemed content, leaning back on the couch and closing his eyes, swaying gently to the music.

Five minutes passed, until Josh stirred and said, "You still look a bit warm, Andy. If I undo the top button of your shirt, you won't be too chilly?" Andy was wearing a blue, Oxford-cloth men's shirt.

"Umm," she said, "I'm plenty warm," as he deftly undid the button. "And how about you?" Andy said. He was wearing a red-plaid flannel shirt.

"Umm," Josh replied. They both giggled. Button by button, their shirts got undone, pulled off, then tossed on the floor. Andy had on a lacy, blue, front-hook bra from Victoria's Secret, and Josh a red tee shirt. "Would you be comfortable without your bra?" Josh asked.

"Umm," Andy replied, as he unhooked the bra and slid it off her arms. "And your tee shirt looks a bit warm," Andy said. They both giggled, as she pulled the shirt over his head and tossed it on the floor with her bra.

Josh handed Andy the pipe for another hit, and then took one himself. Andy had never lost her shirt and bra so slowly, and never with a guy who made it a one-button-at-a-time game. She had only had sex with five guys, one in high school and four in college, and each seemed more eager than the last to get her naked and into bed as rapidly as possible.

Andy was now half-naked, and briefly wondered if Josh—who hadn't made any move since he removed her bra—was content to leave it that way. He had leaned back on the couch, arms behind his head and feet stretched out on the coffee table. Perhaps the Lemon Haze had made him so mellow, Andy thought, that getting her fully naked and into his bed—or on the couch—had gone up with the vapors from the pipe in his hand. Maybe he was even falling asleep, since his eyes were closed. She was actually startled when Josh sat up, smiled, and said, "Andy, you were an art history major, and you spent a year in Italy, so here's a question. The correct answer will earn you a guided tour of the etchings in my bedroom, okay? A wrong answer and I'll walk you back to your dorm, although I'll keep your bra as a souvenir."

Andy laughed. "What is this, reverse strip poker? But I'll bite."

"Okay, here's the question." Josh paused, for effect. "Who painted 'The Birth of Venus'?"

"Oh, wow," Andy said. "That's like 'Who's buried in Grant's Tomb?' Too easy. The answer is Alessandro Botticelli. It's in the Uffizi Gallery in Florence. I've seen it, as you probably guessed. And how come you asked?"

"Well, it's my opinion, as a connoisseur of fine art, that Venus has perfect breasts," Josh said. "Not too big, not too small. Just like yours. Now that I can see them, which I've been wanting to do for a week."

Andy looked down at her breasts. "That's very nice of you to say, Josh. Although mine are a bit lopsided, if you noticed. A tad bigger and lower on the right."

"Let me check," Josh said, cupping both breasts in his hands. "Hmm. Hard to tell. Can I make a closer inspection?" He leaned over and gently licked Andy's right nipple, then the left. She reacted with an involuntary gasp. "Oh, my God, Josh."

"Is that okay? You can say stop, you know. That's the rule at Harvard."

"No, don't stop. Or do stop for a minute. I'm too warm in these jeans. Can you help me get them off? And you must be too warm in yours."

They both stood up, and helped each other unbutton and unzip their jeans, which joined the clothes in the pile on the floor. Josh then slipped Andy's blue Victoria's Secret panties off her hips and down her legs, and she pulled down his black boxers, adding both to the pile. Their socks and shoes followed. By this time, the Dave Matthews CD had reached the "Sledgehammer" track, and they held each other in a close embrace, swaying in time as Dave sang in his gravelly voice: "Show me round your fruitcage, 'cause I will be your honey bee, open up your fruitcage, where the fruit is as sweet as can be."

An hour later, lying on their backs on Josh's bed, both of them sweating and satiated, Andy said, "Do you like my fruitcage?" Josh chuckled. "Sweet as can be, honey bee."

Andy and Josh showered together, playfully and erotically, dried each other off, then returned to the living room, sorting through the pile of clothes on the floor and dressing each other. It was now five o'clock, and Andy said, "Josh, that was the best picnic I've ever had. But I should get back to prepping for Torts class. Is that okay with you?"

"Sure," he replied. "But can we sit for a minute? I've got a third thing to tell you."

Andy sat down on the couch, feeling a shudder of apprehension. Oh, no, she thought, this was just a one-night stand, or a one-afternoon stand. Josh took both of her hands in his, cleared his throat, and said, "There's nothing more I would love than to keep this going. I hope you know that." Andy nodded. "But," he continued, "I promised Carlo that I won't get into the kind of relationship with you that would come between me and him." Her heart in her throat, Andy just nodded again. Josh cleared his throat again. "So, here's what we agreed. Now that I know how I feel about you, which I knew two minutes into the mixer last week, can we keep our picnic lunches to maybe once a month? I don't mean like sex every fourth Saturday, but there are lots of things we can do, like the Dave Matthews concert next month at the Harvard Stadium. I already got two tickets for that." Andy smiled weakly. "And I'd love to have you stay with me when we do things together, but only if you want to."

Josh paused, waiting for Andy's response. "Josh," she said, "you can tell Carlo that I'll share you with him, even if it's only once a month. Okay?" Josh squeezed her hand and smiled. "And here's the agreement you need to make with me," Andy said, smiling widely. "This sounds like Contracts class. You know, mutual agreement on the terms, equal bargaining power, and consideration, even if it's just a peppercorn. We had a case about a cricket club in London that rented its field from the city for one peppercorn each year, which was the consideration for the contract. Did you cover that case in your section?"

"Yep," he said. "I'm stocking up on peppercorns."

"Okay, here's the agreement," Andy said. "First, we'll do something together once a month or so, starting with the Dave Matthews concert. And I'll stay with you after, preferably all night, with breakfast thrown in. Second, we agree not to have sex with anyone else, just you and Carlo, and you and me. Although I think Carlo gets the short end of that stick. And third, our contract can only be terminated by mutual agreement. No 'Dear Andy' letters, or text messages." Andy looked Josh in the eyes. "Deal?" She withdrew her right hand from Josh's, and stuck it out.

"Deal," Josh said, shaking her hand firmly. Then they kissed, warmly.

A year later, Andy and Josh terminated their contract by mutual agreement, after Josh announced that he and Carlo were getting married. This wasn't a surprise to Andy. She had met Carlo on several weekend visits to Cambridge, joining him and Josh for dinners at Harvard Square restaurants, and noticing the close bond between them. On his part, Carlo charmed Andy with his wry humor, tales of his upbringing in Rome, and his obvious approval of her "picnic lunch" relationship with Josh. Andy attended their wedding in New York, chatting with Carlo's parents—who came over from Rome—in Italian, and gave the newlyweds a present of a poster signed by all the members of the Dave Matthews Band, for which she'd paid two hundred dollars at a concert on Cape Cod.

4

Andy's reveries ended at five minutes past ten, as Josh walked briskly across the Hark's patio, spotted Andy at the table at which she'd been waiting for him, and dropped his backpack on it. He leaned down and gave Andy a kiss on the top of her head. Sitting down, he gave her an inquisitive look. "So, you survived the grilling from Hank, I assume. I don't see any bruises on your pretty face. Maybe they're on your pretty bottom."

Andy laughed. "You'd have to get Carlo's permission to examine my bottom. How's married life treating you guys, anyway? Still getting down to New York every weekend?"

"Well, having a commuting marriage is hard on everyone except Amtrak," Josh replied. "Carlo's got med school finals coming up, and the June issue of the Review is giving me fits, what with an article that got torn apart by one of the faculty readers. We might have to substitute one from the submissions we rejected. One of them's pretty good, and it's already been cite-checked. That's what held me up. So, tell me about your meeting with Hank."

"Not as bad as I feared," Andy said. "He liked my paper, asked me a few questions about it, and gave me a suggestion about improving it." She decided to hold off telling Josh about Lorenz's invitation to include the paper in the book he was editing, until she'd finished the revisions. "But that's not the big news of my morning."

Josh raised his eyebrows. "So, what else happened? No, let me guess." He pretended to ponder for a moment, then looked like he'd just nailed the Final Jeopardy! question. "Hank offered you a Supreme Court clerkship with Justice Novak. Am I right?"

Andy couldn't conceal her shock. "How the hell did you know that, Josh? Were you hiding under his desk?"

"Didn't need to, Andy. Just logical deduction. It's no secret that Hank picks a liberal clerk for Novak every term. And they've all been law review editors. Sanjay would have been his first choice, since he's also brilliant and also liberal, and the editor-in-chief of the law review to boot. But Sanjay's taking this job with the Sikh association, and you're the obvious choice to get the nod from Hank. Am I right, fruitcage?"

Andy shook her head in disbelief. "Well, so much for the big surprise, Josh. You never cease to amaze me with your powers of deduction. Like when you deduced that some bread and wine, along with a little pot, and some Dave Matthews, might get me to disrobe in front of you." Josh chuckled. "But you're right. Hank did offer me the clerkship with Novak."

"So, did you accept the offer? You know how many people would give their right testicle for that job, or their right breast, depending on gender? It's a ticket to a lifetime of wealth and fame. Not to mention a great pick-up line." Josh smiled at Andy and said, with a mischievous grin, "Hi there, you cute thing. I'm a Supreme Court clerk. Would you like come up and see my briefs?"

Andy grinned back. "Very good, Josh, although very sexist, since a woman couldn't use that line. We wear panties, in case you've forgotten."

"Oh, I haven't forgotten, believe me," Josh said. "Blue and lacy, as I recall. Yum, yum."

"Good memory," Andy said. "Seriously, though, I haven't accepted the offer. Hank gave me until Friday to decide, and I wanted to get your advice, all joking aside. So, what do you think? You know I have the offer from Texas Defenders, and that would be a great experience, working on something that means a lot to me. Although Hank told me they'll keep the job open for a year, and he has a former student who's willing to spend a year with the Defenders."

Josh reached into his backpack and pulled out a legal pad and a pen. "Okay, I'll be serious. Let's make a list of the pros and cons of this offer." He drew a line down the middle of the top page, and wrote "PRO" and "CON" on the opposite sides. "The first pro, in my opinion, is the chance to spend a year at the Court, which could be exciting. And the first con would be that Justice Novak is far to the right on almost every issue the Court decides. Now, what are your pros and cons?"

Andy thought for a moment. "Well, my next pro would be that Justice Novak is considered to have the sharpest mind on the Court, maybe even brilliant. Having a chance to see how his mind works in deciding cases would be like, I don't know, if you could spend a year with Stephen Hawking, working out problems in physics. He does cosmology, is that right? The Big Bang, and stuff like that."

Josh nodded. "Right. And if I was still in physics, I'd snap up an offer to spend a year with Hawking. Maybe some of his brilliance would rub off on me. So what's your next con?"

"Let me think," Andy said. "Okay, everybody says Justice Novak's a nice guy, and I'm sure he is. But maybe that's just a mask, you know what I mean? Maybe he treats his clerks like serfs on the lord's estate. I read a biography of Justice Douglas, who was also brilliant, and charming to most people. But apparently he treated his clerks like shit, at least his female clerks. One of them said Douglas was so rude to her that it ruined that whole year."

"Okay," Josh said. "Now, here's another pro. Did Hank tell you, or do you already know, how much Supreme Court clerks get paid?"

"No," Andy said. "He didn't bring it up, and I didn't ask. But I assume you know, smarty pants."

"Of course I do," Josh said. "I looked it up on Google when the thought briefly crossed my mind that I might clerk for an appeals court judge, and then maybe, just maybe, get tapped by one of the Supremes. By briefly, I mean about ten seconds. But I'm not really good clerk material, Andy, considering I think the underdog should win every case. Especially when the upperdog is some rapacious corporation that's fucking its workers, or dumping toxic shit in our lakes and rivers. There's a lot of that in Idaho, screwing the undocumented Mexicans who harvest potatoes, and poisoning the trout and salmon in the Snake River."

Josh smiled. "But I digress. The salary for a Supreme Court clerk is about seventy-eight thousand, although that's less than half of what our duller classmates can pull down as first-year associates at one of the mega-law firms, no experience required. That's just obscene, in my opinion. Plus, the big firms are now giving signing bonuses to former Supreme Court clerks of two-fifty to three hundred thousand. Can you believe that?" Andy shook her head. "Anyway, what was Texas Defenders going to pay you, Andy, or didn't you ask? Knowing you, you'd probably work for nothing, for the privilege of springing depraved killers from the fate they deserve."

"Actually, I didn't ask, but they did tell me it's thirty-five thousand. Which I can live on very easily, considering that I'm frugal. I got that from my grandmother Bella, who only shops at the second-hand stores. 'Why pay more for fancy labels on your clothes,' she says. 'They don't keep you any warmer.' You'll meet her at graduation, Josh. Just don't tell her I wear Victoria's Secret undies. Plain, cotton, white, from Macy's. That's all I wore before I left Yonkers, even in college. Tossed them all out when I packed to come here. Fortunately, she didn't check."

Josh chuckled. "So, the paycheck isn't a deciding factor, I guess." He looked down at the sheet on which he'd been jotting the pros and cons. "Pretty much even on both sides. But you're the one to decide, Andy, and I don't want to influence you either way."

He twirled his pen for a moment. "Well, maybe I do, to be honest. I've got some news of my own. Carlo called this morning and told me he'd just gotten notified that he's been accepted into the first-year residency program at George Washington University Hospital in DC. That was his top choice, and he's already accepted the offer."

"Wow," Andy said. "I'm really glad for Carlo. You told me that's where he wanted to go. Give him my congratulations."

"Will do." Josh held up a hand. "But wait a second, Andy. That's not all the news today." He looked intently at Andy, who looked back expectantly. Josh smiled. "I got a call yesterday from the head of the federal public defender's office in the eastern district of Virginia. He offered me a job as an assistant public defender in their main office in Alexandria, right across the river from DC."

"Holy shit, Josh," Andy said. "You never told me you applied for a job there. How come you didn't share that?"

Josh looked a bit abashed. "Well, first of all, I was waiting to hear whether Carlo got into the residency program at GW hospital. And second, I wasn't sure I wanted to work for the government. I was thinking more of the ACLU, or Lambda Legal, working on LGBT cases. But the federal public defenders are the good guys in the government, even though it's a big bureaucracy and there's politics involved. And it would be great training for whatever comes next. Do you know anything about the federal PD program, Andy?" She shook her head no.

"Okay," Josh continued. "They mostly handle cases of indigent defendants who've been charged with federal criminal offenses, both misdemeanors and felonies." He chuckled. "I'd probably start with guys who'd been arrested for urinating on the graves in Arlington cemetery, which is federal property. Not much different from PDs in county courts. But lots of courtroom experience. Plus, I'd be able to live with Carlo. No more Amtrak every weekend. I haven't accepted the offer yet, but getting the news from Carlo was the clincher, so I'll call back today."

"Well, holy shit again, Josh," Andy said. "I didn't surprise you with my news, but you sure as hell surprised me. Josh Barfield, defender of gravestone pissers. But who knows? One of your cases may get up to the Supreme Court. Maybe you didn't know the guy had urinary incontinence, and couldn't get to the john in time. Remember the 'necessity defense' from crim law?"

Andy stood up and struck a courtroom pose. "Yes, Your Honor, my client did commit the offense of defacing government property, but it was necessary to avoid knocking people down and possibly injuring them as he rushed to handle a medical emergency. And I'm raising an ineffective assistance of counsel defense in this appeal because trial counsel, Mr. Barfield, failed to raise that issue in the district court."

Josh laughed, then assumed a deep, judicial tone. "Good point, Ms. Roboff. But please tell the Court why Mr. Barfield failed to raise that defense at trial. It seems to me that even a neophyte public defender would have known that. Maybe they don't teach that at Harvard Law School, where they seem to focus on the epistemological foundations of law."

Their antics had attracted the attention of students at nearby tables, who looked up from the laptops on which each had been tapping, in between bites of sandwiches. Andy and Josh waved to their audience, then returned to their more serious topics. "So, Josh, you've made your decision, I guess. It sounds right for you, and for Carlo too. I'm glad for you both."

Josh looked at his watch. "Andy, I hate to leave you here, torn with indecision, but I have to get back to Gannett and give the news to the author of the substitute article for the June issue that he's going to be published in the Harvard Law Review. I'm sure he'll be thrilled, although I won't tell him he's a lucky loser. Anyway, let me know what you decide about the clerkship, okay?"

"Tell you what, Josh," Andy said. "I'm going to call my mom and dad, but I know what they'll say, despite their low opinion of Novak. They think half the people in Texas are violent drug smugglers, and the other half are trigger-happy cops. And they'll be delighted that I'd be just an Amtrak ride away from New York. But that won't take long, and I'll drop back to Gannett. I've got to finish my cite-checking, anyway."

They stood up to leave, grabbing their backpacks. "You'll be the first to get the news, whatever it is," Andy said, as they headed in opposite directions, Josh to Gannett House and Andy to her apartment on Quincy Street. After her first year in the Story dorm, rooming with Bonnie Fox, Andy had found a studio just off Harvard Yard. It was just a five-minute walk from the law school, and on her way Andy made her decision about Hank's offer of a clerkship with Justice Novak.

After hanging up her Ann Taylor outfit and changing into her normal jeans and polo shirt, Andy decided to put off calling her parents until they were both home in the evening, although she knew they wouldn't object to her decision. Having their little girl closer to home, even working for the Darth Vader of the Supreme Court, would be preferable to braving the Wild West shoot-outs in Texas.

On her way back to Gannett House, Andy stopped by Pound Hall to give Hank Lorenz the news. His office door was open, and she poked her head in. He was packing his briefcase for class, but looked up and smiled. "Back so soon, Andy? Come on in." He looked at his watch. "It's only been two hours since you left here. So let me guess." He stuck a book into his briefcase.

"No need to guess," Andy said. "I've decided to accept the offer. So, you can call Ken Murray at Texas Defenders and tell him your former student can hold my place for a year. And thank you for thinking I could handle a clerkship with Justice Novak."

"I'm delighted to hear that, Andy. Tell you what. Being five minutes late to class won't get me fired, so why don't you sit down and let me take care of a little business." Puzzled, Andy sat on the couch. He picked up the phone on his desk, punched in a number, waited a moment, and said, "Hello, Angie. This is Hank Lorenz calling. Is he available? I have somebody with me who'd like to talk with him. He knows who it is." Lorenz paused for a few seconds. "Okay. Thanks, Angie."

Lorenz pulled the phone across his desk and handed the receiver to Andy, who instantly realized whom he had called, and had a sudden panic attack. She put the phone to her ear, and heard a resonant voice say, "Good afternoon. Am I speaking with Andrea Roboff?"

Andy took a deep breath. "Yes, this is Andrea."

"Miss Roboff, this is Alex Novak. I understand that Professor Lorenz has discussed with you the opening for a clerkship in the Court's next term. And I assume he wouldn't have called and put you on the line if you were going to disappoint us both. That would be a bummer, as they say."

Andy was startled by the unjudicial term, and the casual tone of Novak's voice. "Well, Justice Novak," she responded, "I wouldn't want to disappoint you. Professor Lorenz did discuss the clerkship with me, and I'd be honored to accept the offer, if it's still open."

"That's what I hoped to hear, Miss Roboff, and of course the offer is open. Professor Lorenz and I go back a long way, and he's never disappointed me in finding outstanding clerks. From everything he's told me about you, and the material he sent me, I think you're the ideal person for the job."

"I'm not sure about ideal, Justice Novak," Andy said, feeling her anxiety recede, "but I would certainly try to meet your expectations. You do know, I guess, that I haven't had a clerkship in a lower court, so I might not hit the ground running, as they say."

"Miss Roboff, if you run as well as you write, you're way ahead of the pack," Novak said. "Hank told me about the brilliant paper you wrote that he wants to include in the book he's editing. I'll read your chapter with great interest, of course, and keep an open mind about your argument. Who knows, it might even change my mind on that issue, although I'm pretty unmovable about capital punishment, as you probably know." Novak chuckled. "Maybe your paper will be the irresistible force that budges me. But we can discuss that when you get here. That's one reason I ask Hank to send me a clerk every term. Keeps me on my toes."

Andy wasn't sure if Novak wanted a response, but he continued. "Tell you what, Miss Roboff. Let's shoot for the middle of July, once this term is over and the pundits have labeled it another disaster for the Constitution. My fantastic secretary, Angela Conforti, can help you with arrangements for getting settled here. Anything from finding a place to live, to the key for the ladies' room. Angie's like a mother hen, and we're all her chicks. Hank can give you her number, and my private line if you need to appeal from her clucking."

"Well, thanks again, Justice Novak," Andy said. "I'm looking forward to joining your clutch, and I appreciate your offer."

"And I appreciate your acceptance, Miss Roboff . From what I dimly remember from my class with Professor Areeda, that constitutes a contract. No need for a peppercorn, though. And give my best to Hank, who's probably drafting an op-ed for the Post about the flaws in my latest opinion."

With that, Novak hung up, and Andy handed the receiver back to Lorenz. "Well," she said, "I left your office two hours ago, and now I've got to cancel my plane reservations to Austin. But seriously, Justice Novak sounds like a really nice person. I didn't imagine that he'd be so easy to talk with, and funny to boot."

"I'm not sure the lawyers who feel the sharp end of his tongue in oral argument would agree," Lorenz said, "but after he takes off the black robe, he's just a regular guy. But a very conservative guy, don't forget that. Anyway, congratulations, Andy, and I'm now ten minutes late for class. Time well spent, though." Holding the door for Andy, Lorenz gave her a pat on the shoulder and headed down the hall to his classroom.

Three minutes later, Andy trotted up the stairs of Gannett House and headed for Josh's cramped and cluttered office. He spotted her coming, stood up from his desk, and grinned as Andy approached. "No, I wasn't hiding under Hank's desk," Josh said. "But it doesn't take an eavesdropper to figure out what just happened in his office."

"If you're so clairvoyant," Andy said, "how'd you know I was in his office, and what happened there?"

"Logical deduction, once again," Josh replied. "Actually, I just called Brenda to see if Hank could attend the dinner for the Review's graduating editors, which includes you and me. That's two weeks from Saturday, and I didn't know Hank's schedule. Anyway, Brenda said you had stopped by, and that you and Hank were smiling broadly when you left his office. So, are my deductive powers still working?"

"Better than ever," Andy replied. "Yes, I did accept the offer. You want to know what the clincher was?"

"Let me guess," Josh said. "With seventy-eight thousand, you could buy that Beemer you've always wanted."

"Wrong," Andy said. "Washington has a great Metro system, and only the folks from Bethesda or McLean need cars to get to their K Street offices. But seriously, Josh, which might be hard for you, the clincher was that I'd spend a year in the same city with you and Carlo."

Josh looked genuinely surprised. "Andy, that is really sweet of you. To be honest, I was hoping that you'd accept Novak's offer, for the same reason. I don't want to lose you, and Carlo is very fond of you. He was touched by the way you charmed his parents at our wedding, chatting with them in Italian and dancing the tarantella with his dad."

"Grazie," Andy said. "I'm very fond of Carlo, too. And I'm glad he was okay with our picnic lunches before you guys got married." Josh smiled at the term he and Andy had adopted for their monthly dates and the sex that had become more and more pleasurable as they explored each other's bodies with gentle fingers and hungry mouths.

Josh broke Andy's momentary reverie. "I have a proposal," he said "After we left the Hark, I was almost certain that you'd accept the clerkship with Novak, although not as quickly as you did. So I called Carlo and asked him if we could celebrate with another picnic lunch, whenever you made your decision."

Andy struggled to hide the anticipation that swept through her body like a wave, but lost. "Please, Josh, tell me that Carlo is the most generous and sweetest guy on the planet."

"Well," Josh said with a smile, "he did say that any girl his mom thinks is 'molto dolce' deserves a picnic lunch with a special dessert."

Ten minutes later, they reached the apartment on Oxford Street that Josh had kept for all three years of law school. An hour later, drained of passion, they lay side by side on his bed, settled into the languorous afterglow that returned their heartbeats and breathing to a slower, even pace.

Andy rolled onto her back, and broke the silence that had left her immersed in thought. "Josh, are you sure I made the right decision? And for the right reasons?" Josh raised himself up on his elbows, but Andy held up a hand to stop his response. "I mean, I don't really *need* to be a Supreme Court clerk. I never even thought about that until this morning in Hank's office. But, as I said, the real reason for my decision was you. I can do just fine without more picnic lunches, and I don't want to create any issues with Carlo." Andy took a deep breath, and slowly let it out. "Josh, I love you."

Josh took a deep breath, and slowly let it out. "Not as long as I've loved you, Andy. That started when we shared our life stories at Grendel's Den. Started slowly, but picked up speed and just kept going. Now I just can't stop it."

Andy leaned over and gently kissed Josh. He put an arm around her and pulled her close. "Tell you what," he said. "Let's make another contract, no peppercorn required. We can keep having picnic lunches until Carlo and I move to DC, probably in July." Andy started to reply, but Josh hushed her with a finger on her lips. "Actually, Carlo already said we could do that, when I called him from Gannett House. I didn't want to tell you yet, but he's fine with that. Okay?" Andy nodded her agreement. "And after that, we'll take life as it comes. Who knows what the future holds?"

Andy smiled. "Why don't we call that indeterminacy? That's a word I just coined." She took Josh's hand and placed it on her breast. Then she slowly slid her hand down his torso until she met the source of her desire.

An hour later, they showered together, got dressed, and walked down Oxford Street until it until it crossed Quincy. They kissed again, then Josh headed back up Oxford while Andy walked slowly down the block to her apartment. Her life had changed in just the past few hours, but how it would change in the coming year was something yet to be determined. Nobody could know, Andy mused, what might happen even minutes from now.

Back in her studio, Andy sat down at her desk, opened her laptop, and composed a to-do list of tasks, starting with today and ending on July 12, the day she'd picked for her move to Washington. She put a check-off box next to each item, printed it out, and pinned it to the cork-board above her desk, next to a poster she'd bought, with a photo of a tiny, grey-haired woman, Mary Harris Jones, a legendary labor organizer of a century earlier, known fondly to striking workers as "Mother" Jones. The poster included her rallying cry to those who struggled for decent wages and better lives: "Pray for the dead, and fight like hell for the living." Andy had adopted that exhortation as her inspiration and goal.

With a wink at Mother Jones, Andy picked up her phone and called her parents, who had just arrived home from her mom's gallery and her dad's dental office. They were, as Andy knew, engaged in their long-standing ritual of sharing their day's events in the den over Manhattans, joined by her grandmother Bella, who added a splash of Glenlivet to her mug of tea. Her mom, Evelyn, answered and put the call on speaker-mode on the coffee table.

As Andy expected, her parents were surprised by the totally unexpected—and only hours old—news that she had been offered, and had accepted, a clerkship at the Supreme Court. When she told them the offer came from Justice Alex Novak, Andy's dad, Herbert, blustered a bit about Novak's zero rating from the ACLU. But, as Andy had also expected, they were pleased that she wouldn't be moving to Texas. The call ended with plans for Andy's parents and Bella to attend the law-school commencement, four weeks away.

The next four weeks went by quickly. Andy spent much of her time in Gannett House, finishing her editing and cite-checking of articles for the Review's final issue of the year in June. She also worked on the revisions to her TBI paper that Lorenz had suggested, giving it to him a week later, and getting back an email that just said, "Perfect."

Finding a place to live in DC turned out to be simple. Justice Novak's secretary, Angie Conforti, emailed Andy that one of the departing clerks was looking for someone to take over the lease on his one-bedroom on Tenth Street on Capitol Hill, a ten-minute walk from the Supreme Court, and close to a Metro station. He gave Andy a virtual tour of the apartment from his iPhone, and it suited her just fine, although two thousand a month seemed a bit steep to Frugal Andy. The rental agency sent the lease documents, which she signed and returned with a check for the first and last month's rent.

Graduation Day came with beautiful spring warmth and sunshine. Attired in cap and gown, Andy sat with her parents and Bella on the lawn between the law-school dorms. Josh and his parents, along with Carlo, sat next to them, and everyone was introduced, with Andy and Josh posing as fellow editors of the law review. The commencement address, by the Chief Justice of South Africa, was a moving account of the painful transition from apartheid-era death squads to the rule of law for every citizen.

Following the ceremony, Hank Lorenz, as promised, gave Andy's parents a tour of the paintings in his office. Andy's mom examined each with an approving and appraising eye, and told him they could fetch twenty thousand each at a Manhattan gallery. Smiling, Lorenz unhooked the one Evelyn had particularly admired, the Bar Harbor lighthouse, from the wall. He said Andy had told him it would fit perfectly in the Roboff's den, and that's where he wanted it hung. Ignoring Evelyn's protestations, Lorenz handed it to her, giving Andy a knowing wink.

With her law-school days, and many nights, behind her, Andy spent the remaining weeks before her move in her Quincy Street studio. She took care of one item on her to-do list by reading every opinion Justice Novak had written during his ten years on the Court, about a hundred fifty, including dissents, which made up more than half. Shaking her head occasionally in disbelief, Andy took notes on each. She also read a pile of books on the Court's history and its processes for deciding cases, although few dealt with the role of clerks. She'd just have to learn on the job, Andy thought.

One item not on her to-do list was Josh, who was spending most of his time studying for the two-day Massachusetts bar exam in July. Andy had decided to put off the bar exam for a year, since she didn't need a bar license for her clerkship. But there was time, between Andy's reading and Josh's cramming, for picnic lunches, sometimes with a real picnic basket. These now-weekly events all ended in Josh's bed, from which Andy most often emerged in the early morning, making coffee and toast while Josh whipped up a ham and cheese omelet. Their last night together, they shared a bottle of Moet & Chandon champagne, which made them both giggly and playful. In the morning, after breakfast, they shared a long, close embrace. Andy's eyes began filling, but Josh put a finger to her lips and softly whispered, "Indeterminacy." With that, they parted.

On the morning of July 12, Andy finished loading the last of her belongings into a Jeep Cherokee she'd rented for a one-way trip, and headed out of Cambridge.

5

Andy's clock-radio buzzed her awake at 6:30 on Monday, July 15. She had arrived in Washington the previous Friday night, and spent most of the weekend unpacking and arranging her clothes, books, kitchen utensils, and bedroom and bathroom supplies. She had also taken a walking tour of her new neighborhood, and had stocked up on groceries at the nearby Safeway. By Sunday night, Andy felt settled in, and went to bed after calling her parents to assure them their little girl was safe and sound.

After showering and dressing in her Ann Taylor outfit, Andy made a quick breakfast of coffee, English muffin, and peach yoghurt. Angie Conforti had sent her a letter to present to the security guard at the Court's entrance, along with a note that Justice Novak wanted to meet with his new clerks at eight that morning. She tucked them into the black leather shoulder bag her parents had given her to replace her old green backpack, and set off at seven-thirty.

The walk down Constitution Avenue from Tenth to First Street took fifteen minutes, and Andy arrived at the Court's side entrance and joined a line of people waiting to pass through the metal detector manned by a brace of uniformed security guards. Wondering if any of those in line were also new clerks, and if they might also be a bit nervous, Andy handed the letter to a tall, African American guard, who scanned it, asked Andy for her driver's license, looked at her photo and then her face, and directed her to place her bag on a conveyor belt. Nothing beeped, and Andy entered the Supreme Court for the first time. She asked the guard for directions to Justice Novak's chambers, getting instructions to take an elevator to the second floor, turn left, and find the second door on the left. As she waited for the elevator, Andy thought to herself, Holy shit! I actually work here at the Supreme Court of the United States. It was a thought that prompted her to take a deep breath as the elevator door opened.

The second-floor hallway was wide, with cream-hued marble walls and a red-carpeted floor that said Important Business Is Being Conducted Here. The second door on the left bore a brass plate that read, Chambers of Associate Justice Alexander Novak. Taking another deep breath, Andy opened it, entered, and was greeted by a plump, grey-haired woman behind a desk, who beamed and said, "Welcome! You must be Andrea Roboff. I'm Justice Novak's secretary, Angela. But everyone calls me Angie."

Andy felt her nervousness receding. "Thank you, Angie. I'm Andrea, but everyone calls me Andy. How did you know it was me?"

"Not hard to figure out." Angie said. "The other new clerks are all here, and none of them was you. They're all in the clerks' office, waiting to meet with the Justice." Wow, Andy thought. They must be even more worried about being late than me.

At that moment, the door behind Angie opened. The man who came out was about five ten, somewhat stocky, with short black hair, brushed forward, above a broad face with high cheekbones that displayed his Slavic genes. "Perfect timing," he said, extending his hand and smiling broadly. "Angie pushed the button that tells me my new clerks are all here. You're Andrea Roboff, and I'm Alex Novak. I'm delighted that you're here, thanks to Hank."

Taken aback by his informality, Andy shook his hand. "Justice Novak, I'm very pleased to meet you, and thank you again for offering me the clerkship."

"No thanks necessary," he replied. "You come with great credentials." Turning to Angie, he said, "Can you get everybody into my office? I think we're ready to get the meet-and-greet started. And can you call the library and ask Dick to get down here? I think that's where he went."

Angie went into the clerks' office, across from her desk, emerged with two young men and a woman, and ushered them, along with Andy, into a spacious office, in which six upholstered chairs were grouped around a large coffee table. Tall bookcases, lined with tan-backed volumes that Andy recognized as volumes of United States Reports, the official publication of the Court's opinions, covered two walls. Novak gestured to the chairs. "Please, sit, everyone."

As she sat, Andy glanced surreptitiously at the other three new clerks, with whom she would spend an entire year, working in the close quarters of the clerks' office. One was a tall guy, a bit over six feet, with sandy hair, an aquiline nose, and cleft chin. The second guy was about five-six, shorter than Andy, obviously Asian. The woman, who glanced over at Andy, was about her height, blond hair swept back and held by a gold barrette, dressed in what Andy guessed was a thousand-dollar grey Armani suit. She had that distinctive, well-bred look that said Trust-Fund Money. Her glance at Andy said You're Not From My Circle.

Just as they got seated, a young man, somewhat pudgy and out of breath, entered and said, "Sorry I'm a bit late, Alex. I had trouble finding the British Law Lords reports."

Novak waved him to the only empty chair. "Folks, this is Dick Wadleigh, my go-to clerk for tracking down obscure sources. He's been looking for ancient cases with which I can impress the Law Lords with my encyclopedic knowledge." Wadleigh gave the group an Aw-Shucks look.

"Well," Novak said, "now that we're all here, let's not waste time that could be better spent manning the oars in my galley. Dick has graciously offered to spend two more weeks on the payroll, sharing his expertise with you newcomers on how things work around here, and how to avoid my cat-o'-nine-tails." Wadleigh smiled and shook his head, no.

"This will be a short meeting," Novak continued, glancing at his watch. "In two hours, I'll be at Dulles for a plane to London, where I'll spend two weeks at the Inns of Court, explaining to barristers why the colonials revolted and designed a perfect legal system. Perfect, that is, except that lawyers here don't wear horse-hair wigs and refer to us judges as My Lord, in view of our mandate from the Deity." The new clerks politely chuckled.

"Okay," Novak continued. "A few ground rules. First, I'm not a stickler for formality. Inside my chambers, we'll be on a first-name basis, so call me Alex. But outside, especially with my more proper colleagues, it's Justice Novak." He paused, and swept a stern gaze across the clerks. "Second, and this comes with severe sanctions, everything that happens inside this building is strictly confidential. Anything I say, anything you hear from anyone, including fellow clerks, any documents you see or work on, are top secret. What happens in Vegas, stays in Vegas, as they say. Any violation, even accidental, will get you fired on the spot, with no appeal. Is that clear?" The clerks all nodded their agreement.

"Fine," Novak said, resuming his smile. "Last thing. Any time you have a question your colleagues can't help you with, or any kind of grievance, bring it to me. I don't want unresolved problems to slow you down, or fester until it affects your work. That's happened before, unfortunately, and it creates problems for everyone, especially me. We're a very small law firm in here, and getting our jobs done, and done well, requires every one of us to pull his or her oar."

Novak glanced at his watch again, then looked up with a start. "Oh, my goodness," he said. "Here I've been sitting with four people who haven't met before, and I neglected introductions. My bad, as they say. So, why don't we each tell us some basic things, like your name, where you're from, went to college and law school, and what kind of work you'd like to do after slaving away here for a year. And keep it brief. I've got a driver waiting to get me to Dulles on time, running up the meter. Plus, you'll all get to know each other very soon, probably better than you might wish. Why don't we start on my right. Okay?" He gestured to Andy, sitting on his right.

Andy felt suddenly exposed, like someone who'd been picked out of an audience and asked to reveal their most embarrassing moment. But she quickly recovered. "I'm Andrea Roboff, but everyone calls me Andy. Let's see. I'm from Yonkers, New York. I went to Barnard College, and majored in art history. Then Harvard for law school, graduating this year. I haven't clerked before, so I've got a lot to learn. Let's see. After this year, I'll be working for the Texas Defenders on death-penalty cases." Great, Andy thought. Now they'll all know I'm this year's liberal clerk, which they probably suspected anyway.

"Thank you, Andy," Novak said. "I might add that Andy was articles editor of the Harvard Law Review, and wrote a paper for my old friend and sparring partner, Professor Hank Lorenz. Andy's paper, which she based on studies by some top-notch neurologists, argues that murder defendants who got bashed in the head as kids should be spared from the death penalty. Not sure Andy has convinced me, but I'm still thinking about it. So, welcome, Andy." Novak gestured to the guy sitting next to Andy. "Your turn."

"Hi," he said. "I'm David Chun Park, but call me Dave. I was born in Seoul, Korea, but my family moved to Los Angeles when I was three, so don't try out your Korean on me. And I'm not a big fan of kimchi, the Korean national dish that's made of rotten cabbage. Um, I went to Cal Berkeley, majored in poli sci, then Stanford Law. I clerked last year for Judge Kozinski on the Ninth Circuit, which was great. That's about it. Oh, I'm thinking of the Foreign Service, or maybe the UN. Great to meet you all." Andy got the feeling that she'd like this guy, who seemed funny and self-deprecatory.

"Dave's much too modest," Novak interjected. "He's actually one of the world's leading computer experts and software designers." Dave shook his head. "No, really," Novak continued. "Fresh out of Berkeley, one of the top Silicon Valley firms offered Dave a salary bigger than mine to work on cybersecurity." Novak chuckled. "I think the government has classified Dave's brain as Top Secret." Dave shook his head even more vigorously. "Okay, next," Novak said with a grin.

All eyes turned to the woman sitting next to Park. "Hello," she began. "I'm Amanda Cushing." She shot a glance at Andy. "But I'm not a Mandy, so we won't get confused with an Andy and a Mandy. I'm from Greenwich, Connecticut, and went to Yale for college and law school. Majored in economics. I clerked last year for Judge Parker on the Second Circuit. My career goal is international finance." Andy felt an instant dislike of Amanda, not Mandy. What a stuck-up, superior bitch, she thought.

Novak broke in again. "What Amanda modestly didn't say was that her great-something grandfather was William Cushing, one of the original Supreme Court justices, appointed by the first George W and served for twenty-one years. Talk about legacy, although I chose Amanda because I know zilch about economics and she can educate me when those number-crunching antitrust cases come up." Even worse, Andy thought. One of those privileged types who care more about profits than people.

"I guess it's my turn," the final guy said. "I'm Todd Armistead, from Leesburg, Virginia, just up the pike. University of Virginia, majored in history, stayed there for law school. I clerked for Judge Early on the Fourth Circuit. I'll probably join my dad's firm in Leesburg. He's a state senator, plans to run or governor in four years. He says he'll keep the seat open for me, so maybe I'll give politics a shot."

"What Todd didn't tell you," Novak said, "is that he wrote his senior thesis on his great-great granddad, General Lewis Armistead, whose illustrious career tragically ended when he was mortally wounded in

Pickett's Charge at Gettysburg. Todd tried to show that if the Rebs had avoided a frontal assault, they would have won the war and we'd be flying the Stars and Bars on the Court's flagpole." Oh, great, Andy thought. A grey-flannel Klansman. She reminded herself not to make snap judgments about people, then realized that most of hers proved accurate.

Novak rose from his chair, then said, "By the way, a week from Sunday, I'll be back from London. You're all invited to a barbeque at my place, very informal. Steak and shrimp on the barbie, and beer to wash it down, soda for any Carrie Nations. Angie will give you directions. So, I'll put you all in Dick's capable hands for a Clerking 101 session. Sorry to rush out, but I'll see you all soon." Novak picked up a briefcase, gave a parting wave, and left the office.

The new clerks followed Dick Wadleigh into the clerks' office, in which four desks, each with a Dell computer and a phone on top, were placed, two on each side of the longer walls. A long table against the shorter wall held a printer and supplies. Compared to Novak's office, it was fairly spartan and cramped. The only decoration was a framed photograph of the Court's main entrance, with wide marble steps leading to the massive bronze doors. On the pediment above the doors were chiseled the words, Equal Justice Under Law.

Once in the office, the clerks looked to Wadleigh, who said, "Andy and Dave, why don't you take the desks on that side," gesturing to his right, "and Todd and Amanda over there." Dave smiled at Andy. "Your choice," he said. Andy picked the desk nearest to the table, and set her bag on it. Todd and Amanda looked at each other, and Todd said, with a bow, "Ladies first." Amanda smiled brightly and put her thin leather portfolio on the desk farthest from the table. "Why, thank you, sir," she said in a faux southern drawl. Oh, my God, Andy thought. Everything but the parasol and hoop skirts, and already flirting with Rhett.

When the new clerks were seated at their desks, looking like eager first-graders at their first day of school, Dick set up an easel with a whiteboard in front of the table. "Okay, class," he said, "take your seats and get out your pencils and paper. Time for today's lesson." He scanned the clerks, all facing him with attentive faces. "If you look on your desks, you'll find the tools of our trade." On each desk was stacked a pile of booklets. "Let's start with the one on top," he said. Each clerk dutifully picked up a small, white-covered booklet. On the cover was printed "Rules of the Supreme Court of the United States."

Dick picked up a copy from the table and held it up. "This is your Bible, folks. Everything we do here is guided by these rules, and must conform to them. Lots of them are very technical and precise, like the one that requires the text in printed documents to be four-and-one-eighth by seven-and-one-eighth inches in size." Dick shook his head in apparent bafflement. "Don't know who decided on those dimensions, but that's the rule. Of course, computers set the margins on most documents, so you won't need to measure them with a ruler."

Dick thumbed through the rules booklet and found a page. "Okay, let's take a gander at the most important rule for you guys. Page five, rule ten." The clerks each opened the booklet and found the page, like obedient schoolchildren. "It's not very long, but it's your guide to the job you'll be spending the most time on, especially the next couple of months, reviewing cert petitions, so pay close attention." He cast a schoolteacher's gaze across the clerks. "Dave, could you read the caption and first two sentences for us?"

Dave looked down at the booklet he held open like a hymnal. "Okay, it says 'Rule Ten. Considerations governing review on writ of certiorari.' That's the caption. Then it says, 'Review on a writ of certiorari is not a matter of right, but of judicial discretion. A petition for a writ of certiorari will be granted only for compelling reasons.'" He looked up brightly, hoping he'd pleased the teacher.

Dick nodded his approval. "Very good, Dave." He picked up a marker from the easel and wrote "discretion" and "compelling" on the whiteboard. "Those are the most important words in the rules. Almost all cases get here through writs of certiorari, basically asking the Court to review the judgment of a lower court, and reverse it." Dick paused. "Now, Dave and Amanda and Todd have already clerked on courts of appeals, where most of the cases we get come from. But, as you guys know, those courts are obligated to decide almost every case that gets appealed to them, one way or another. Up here, though, the Court has almost complete discretion to review those judgments, which it most often declines to do. So, only those cases the justices think raise a quote, compelling reason to decide them get a grant of cert."

Dick turned to Amanda. "Okay, let's see what makes a petition compelling. Amanda, can you read us the first clause of section A?" She found it, and read, "A United States court of appeals has entered a decision in conflict with the decision of another United States court of appeals on the same important matter."

"Very good, Amanda," Dick said. "So, what do we call this?"

Amanda looked baffled. Dick raised his eyebrows. "Anyone?" Andy, trying to conceal a smirk, said, "We call this a circuit split, Amanda. That is, two or more of the circuit courts have issued decisions that conflict with each other." Andy instantly regretted having directed this put-down at Amanda, who repaid her with a glare that said, You'll Pay For Making Me Look Dumb.

Sensing the mutual animosity between the two women, Dick quickly pointed his marker at Todd. "Okay, how about Section C?"

Todd found it. "A state court or a United States court of appeals has decided an important question of federal law that has not been, but should be, settled by this Court, or has decided an important federal question in a way that conflicts with relevant decisions of this Court."

"Right," Dick said. "Of course, the tricky part is figuring out what an important question of federal law is. Every cert petition you'll see that's not based on a circuit split claims to be raising an important question the Court really needs to decide. That's for the justices to determine, but you guys are the screeners. My advice, at least from my experience, is to treat those petitions like 'Hail Mary' passes. Hardly any wind up with a touchdown." Dick swung his marker to Andy. "Almost done. The last sentence, Andy."

"Sure," she said, keeping her eyes on the page. "'A petition for a writ of certiorari is rarely granted when the asserted error consists of erroneous factual findings or the misapplication of a properly stated rule of law.'"

"There we go," Dick said. "Basically, the Supreme Court's not going to second-guess the lower courts, or correct their mistakes. Now, reading cert petitions, you guys will see a lot that claim the judges below screwed up, which is often true." Dick shrugged. "But there's one thing to keep in mind when you read petitions. Every one of them comes from a loser. What I mean is, the party asking the Court to review their case has lost in the court below, usually twice, in the trial court and then in the appeals court. Judges make mistakes, just like everybody else. But unless it's a really, really big mistake, this Court simply doesn't have the time or resources to correct every single error. To be blunt, most losers just have to take their lumps. Took me a while to get over feeling sorry for the losers, but most of them deserved to lose."

Replacing the rules booklet on the table, Dick picked up two more booklets. "You guys probably know what these are, but I'll explain anyway." He held up one. "Here's a cert petition. The rules say it has to have a white cover. Don't ask me why. Anyway, Rule Fourteen specifies what petitions must contain, and you can read that for yourself. But, since you'll read a lot of them, here's what I'd advise you to focus on." He turned to the whiteboard and picked up his marker. "First," he said, while writing on the board, "is the Questions Presented. Exactly what issues does the petitioner want the Court to consider? Supposed to be concise, and most are." He next wrote, Petition Summary. "This is like the preface to a book. If it doesn't grab you, and most won't, it's highly unlikely the rest of the petition will convince you to recommend granting cert, so that's a red flag."

Dick then wrote, Statement. "This part is supposed to include the basic and most relevant facts of the case, and not be argumentative, although most are. Hard to avoid for most lawyers. They get paid to argue." Under that, Dick wrote, Reasons For Granting The Petition. "Assuming you haven't decided to toss this fish back, here's the lawyer's chance to argue. Usually ten, twelve pages, but pretty quick reading in most cases."

Replacing the white booklet on the table, Dick picked up one with an orange cover. "Okay, there's two sides to every story, they say. Not always true, in my opinion, but it's only fair to listen to both sides." He held it up. "So here's a Brief in Opposition, which we call a BIO. Orange cover, as you see, so you won't get confused. Same format, same order of contents. These come from the winners below, who think the judges below got it right, and there's no need for a replay in this Court. The BIOs aren't required from the winners, but most lawyers file one anyway. Sometimes, when you're unsure whether a petition is cert-worthy, a term you've probably heard, the BIO will seal the deal."

Dick scanned the clerk's faces. By this time, their attentive expressions had given way to fidgeting, much like sixth-graders waiting impatiently for recess. Sensing this, Dick said, "One more thing, guys, and we'll wrap it up. Here's what you'll mostly be doing for the next couple months. You all belong to what's called the cert pool, which includes the clerks for each justice. Every week, the Court's clerk will deliver a batch of cert petitions and BIOs to each justice's chambers. They're divided randomly between the justices, roughly a hundred fifty each week, from the seven or eight thousand petitions the Court gets every year. There's thirty-six clerks in the pool, so you'll each get four or five a week. Your job is to read them, do any research you think is necessary, and write what we call a pool memo on each case. Three or four pages in most cases, longer if you think the case might be cert-worthy. These are circulated to each justice, so you're writing for all nine, not just for Alex."

Dick gestured to the clerks' desks. "I've also given you each a few pool memos that I wrote, to give you an idea of what to include. The bottom line in each memo is your recommendation on whether cert should be granted or denied. Ninety-nine out of every hundred will recommend denial, so keep that in mind. Of course, the justices make the final cert decisions, and it takes four to grant cert. But most often, your recommendation will be followed."

Dick paused, looking soberly at the four new clerks. "That's a big responsibility. Took me a while to get over worrying that I'd possibly ruined somebody's life. But there's no way to avoid making tough decisions. If you can't do that, let Alex know, and he'll be understanding. He lost one clerk a couple terms ago who just couldn't pull the trigger, and found her a job with a good firm. Okay, on that upbeat note, any questions?"

After her snarky put-down of Amanda, Andy had sat quietly through Dick's little lecture. She already knew most of what he'd said, having read the Supreme Court rules during her prep sessions in Cambridge, and several cert petitions shedownloaded from the Court's website. But she appreciated Dick's refresher course, especially his parting admonition. Andy wondered if she could pull the trigger when the time came. This wasn't a carnival shooting gallery with plastic ducks as targets, but real people in the sights, looking for relief in the court of last resort. Putting those thoughts aside, Andy raised her hand like a sixth-grader. "Dick, can we take this stuff home, the stuff you gave us to read?"

"Sure," he replied. "Just remember, don't leave anything on a bus, and don't post your memos on Facebook. Now, there's more to your job that I didn't mention, like writing bench memos to prep the justice for oral argument, drafting opinions, and dealing with emergency motions, usually in death-penalty cases. But Alex will cover those when he gets back." Dick removed the whiteboard from the easel and stacked them beside the table. "By the way, I'm camping out at a desk in the library, upstairs, but Angie can roust me if you need any help. Okay, class dismissed. No need to stay, since the Clerk won't drop off the new batch of petitions until Wednesday."

"Thanks, Dick, this has been very helpful," Dave said, and the others murmured agreement. Andy decided to take her homework back to her place, and stuffed it into her bag. Leaving the office, she cast a sideways glance at Amanda and Todd, who were giggling about something and seemed to have paired off. Well, Andy thought, Dave seems like an okay guy, so at least I won't be totally isolated.

Back at her apartment, Andy stacked the material Dick had provided on her desk, matching up the cert petitions, BIOs, and Dick's pool memos for each case, then started reading through them, making notes as she proceeded. Each petition included an appendix with the opinions of the court below, some quite lengthy, which she read carefully. These were the opinions, after all, from which the petitioners sought Supreme Court review. Andy paid attention to the Statement of Facts and Reasons for Granting the Petition in the petitions, discovering in two, after consulting the lower court opinion, that the lawyers had omitted what she considered relevant facts, or failed to cite or discuss cases that undercut their arguments. She was pleased, after noting these omissions, to see that Dick's pool memos had spotted these flaws, and had recommended denying cert in all but one.

Andy's first day as a Supreme Court clerk ended at eight that night, twelve hours after it began. She didn't feel like cooking for one, or heating up a microwave dinner, so she treated her self to orange chicken at a nearby Thai restaurant. Back home—although she didn't consider her apartment "home" yet—Andy called her parents to tell them about her day. She and Josh had agreed to once-a-week calls until he finished the bar exam and moved to Washington, but she called anyway. He sounded glad to hear from her, and said that studying for the bar exam was a crashing bore.

Andy recounted the meeting with Justice Novak and Dick Wadleigh's mini-course on the clerks' tasks, but avoided telling Josh about her instant dislike of Amanda and Todd. Andy also avoided telling Josh that she missed him terribly, having vowed not to deflect his focus on prepping for the bar exam, or sounding needy. Their conversation ended with Andy's "love you," and Josh's "love you too." After hanging up, Andy popped a CD in the player, ran a hot bath—having a stretch-out tub had been the clincher for her apartment—and soaked with her eyes closed, while Bob Dylan put plaintive words to her longing: "Lay, lady, lay, Lay across my big brass bed, Stay, lady, stay, Stay with your man a while, Until the break of day, Let me see you make him smile."

6

Tuesday morning, Andy called Angie to see if there was any need to come to the Court. There wasn't, so she spent the day going through more of the material Dick had given her. As she plowed through the pile on her desk, her pace picked up. After she finished each case, reading through the petition, BIO, and opinions from the court below, Andy checked her conclusions—deny cert in eleven cases, and grant in one—and was pleased that her decisions matched those in Dick's pool memos.

Her task, Andy thought as she worked, wasn't much different than reading article submissions to the law review—of which only three or four out of a hundred were accepted—and doing the editing and cite-checking. Of course, having an article rejected by the Harvard Law Review didn't affect their authors, aside from bruised egos, to the same degree having a petition rejected by the Supreme Court might affect parties with their rights or money at stake. But, as Dick had said, making tough decisions was her job, one that Andy increasingly felt she could handle as her second day ended.

Wednesday, Dick had announced, was the day the Clerk's office delivered a batch of new petitions and BIOs to each chambers. Andy arrived promptly at eight, to a cheerful greeting from Angie, who was signing a delivery form she handed to an assistant clerk, who wheeled his cart around Andy, headed for the next chambers.

Dave Park was already at his desk, and smiled up at Andy as she entered the clerks' office. "Morning, Andy," he said with a welcoming smile. He motioned to the pile of manila folders on which he'd neatly printed the parties' names and docket numbers. Andy dug her pile from her bag, with equally neat printing on each folder.

"Good morning, Dave," she said. "Looks like we both got our homework done on time for class."

"Yeah, but this was just practice, since these are old cases. Today's the real deal. Let's compare answers before the teacher gets here. I had a dozen, and it was eleven denies and one grant. How about you?"

"Same here," Andy said. "My grant was the Fourth Amendment case about the cops using a mini-drone to peek in this guy's bedroom window and see if he was sleeping, before they busted through his front door, to arrest a supposedly armed and dangerous suspect. The Ninth Circuit ruled that looking in the bedroom window with the drone was an unreasonable search, and also an invasion of privacy."

"Hey, same here," Dave said, giving Andy a thumbs-up. "There's no circuit-split on that issue, but it seemed to me that's an important question of federal law the Court hasn't decided. I mean, what if the cops could fly drones around a neighborhood to see if people were smoking dope, or watching kiddie porn? Pretty soon, folks would be keeping their blinds closed day and night."

Just then, Dick Wadleigh came into the office, carrying a pile of manila folders, which he put on the table. He was followed by Amanda and Todd, who looked somewhat bleary-eyed. Andy wondered, suspiciously, if they'd spent the night in the same bed. But, she chided herself, it was probably coincidence they arrived at the same time, and none of her business if they had.

"Morning, boys and girls," Dick said, as Amanda and Todd took their seats. "I hope you're all rested and ready to start some real work, now that practice is over." He picked up a stack of documents, secured with large rubber bands, from the pile on the table, and handed it to Dave. "Okay, these are petitions and BIOs that came in since the term ended last month, after the last batch of clerks, except for me, left for greener pastures. You're each getting twenty-two. I put a list of case names and docket numbers on top." He handed the remaining packs to Andy, Amanda, and Todd.

"Excuse me, Dick," Dave said, holding up a document with no binding, "they're not all in the white and orange covers. Are these petitions, or something else?"

"Good question, Dave," Dick replied. "I forgot to explain that on Monday. The ones on regular paper are IFP petitions, which is what we call the 'in forma pauperis' petitions. In case you're rusty, that's Latin for 'I can't afford the docket fee,' which is three hundred bucks for what we call the 'paid petitions.' Dave, can you hand me the one you're holding?"

Dave handed it over, and Dick showed the cover sheet to his class. "Actually, the IFPs are almost all from prisoners, a lot written by jailhouse lawyers. Some of them are real lawyers, in fact, mostly disbarred and serving time. The IFPs make up about three-quarters of the petitions we get, but only a handful get granted. I think in the last term it was seven out of six thousand, a pretty low batting average. And that's because most of them just say 'My trial was unfair, I was tricked into copping a plea, and I've got nothing better to do with my time than pester the Supreme Court.'"

Dick thumbed through the IFP in his hand. "Here," he said, "under Question Presented, it says 'Does it violate the Constitution for a police officer to lie on the stand and my lawyer not object to the lies?' Now, that's a really bad one, but most aren't much better." Dick shook his head in disbelief, and handed the petition back to Dave. "However, just so you don't stamp 'Deny' on every IFP, every once in a while you'll find one that's worth a grant. That's rare, but sometimes even a hand-written IFP, and we still get a few, raises an issue that actually makes new law." He scanned the clerks. "Anybody read a book called 'Gideon's Trumpet'?"

Andy and Dave both raised their hands. Dave smiled at Andy with a You Go look. "Yeah," she said, "I read it in high-school civics. Really interesting, about this guy who was charged with burglarizing a pool hall, I think in Florida. He couldn't afford a lawyer, and asked the judge to appoint one for him, but the judge said he could only do that in murder cases. So this guy, Clarence Gideon, defended himself at trial and wound up with five years in prison. So he wrote a petition on prison paper, saying the Sixth Amendment gave him a right to a lawyer. The Supreme Court took the case, appointed a big-time lawyer who later became a justice to argue for Gideon, I forgot his name, and the Court ruled in his favor. He got a new trial, with a lawyer, and was acquitted. Did I get that right, Dick?"

"Andy, that's the best book report I've heard in ages," Dick said approvingly. "The lawyer who argued for Gideon was Abe Fortas, who almost became Chief Justice, but that's another story. Anyway, the moral is, you might just find a diamond in a slag heap, so keep your eyes and minds open. Okay?"

Dave reached over and gave Andy a low-five. She noticed Amanda and Todd trading smirks, which Dick caught. "Hey, we can all learn from each other, right? Anyway, you've all got plenty to keep you busy, so I'll leave you to your labors. Remember, I'll be up in the library if you need my help." Giving Andy a knowing wink, he left the office.

All four clerks picked up the top petition from their stack, and started reading. No one said a word for another two hours, but the silence spoke volumes about the tension between the opposite sides of the office. Andy considered taking her stack and going back to work in her apartment, but decided to stick it out. She'd just have to adjust to the situation, and not let herself get pushed out of the office by people who pegged her as a Miss Know-It-All and—even worse—as a liberal intruder in their conservative midst.

Frugal Andy had brought a lunch of cottage cheese, sliced apple, and date squares. The weather was warm, upper-seventies, but not yet the sweltering, sticky heat that would make August and September almost unbearable. Rather than eat in the clerks' dining room, Andy took her lunch out to one of the Court's four inner courtyards that contained fountains and benches, little islands of tranquility from which tourists were barred. She plugged in the earbuds on her iPod and pushed negative thoughts away with James Taylor's "Fire and Ice" album to restore the good mood she'd brought to work that morning.

Thirty minutes later, Andy returned to the clerks' office, in which Dave Park was now alone. He smiled and said, "Andy, your summary of Gideon's Trumpet was great. That book started me thinking about law as a career, instead of following my dad into med school. I'm one of those weenies who faint when they see a needle. And don't worry about Amanda and Todd. They probably only read books about how to get ahead in finance and politics." Dave motioned toward their desks. "By the way, did you notice how they looked when they came in this morning? None of my business, but there's something going on between them. Don't know what, but Amanda's wearing the same outfit as yesterday."

"I wasn't here yesterday," Andy said, "but there's some sort of chemistry that I could almost smell. But, as you say, none of my business." While she was chatting with Dave, Andy noticed something different about her desktop. Almost compulsive about neatness, Andy had stacked the folders on her desk with precision, corners straight and flush. But the stack was now out of alignment, with four or five folders angled away from the rest.

"Dave, I don't mean to interrupt, but did anybody move anything on my desk while I was having lunch?" Andy was sure Dave would have told her if he'd done so.

"Well, I wasn't paying much attention," he replied, "but Amanda did pick up a folder, and I think she put one down. Why, is something missing?"

Andy picked up the docket sheet on top of the folders, laid it to the side, and went through the stack, checking the caption on each with the docket list. "Dave, there's one on my list that's missing, and one here that wasn't on my list. But I don't remember what case the missing one was about, since I hadn't gotten to it before lunch."

Just then, Amanda and Todd came into the office, then stopped short. "Oh, hi Andy," Amanda said brightly. "Enjoy your lunch?"

"Lunch was fine, Amanda, thank you for asking." Amanda and Todd exchanged looks, aware of Andy's steady gaze on them. "Just curious," Andy said, "but did either of you guys take anything from my desk, or put anything on it?"

"Oh, Andy, I'm so sorry," Amanda said contritely. "I meant to leave you a note, but I forgot. But I saw on the docket sheet a case that I've sort of been following, that was decided last year by the Second Circuit while I was clerking there, although my judge wasn't on the panel." Andy didn't shift her gaze. "Anyway, it's an appeal by a drug company that was ordered by the Federal Trade Commission to divest one of its subsidiaries, because it had too big a market share of its products. Pretty technical stuff, to be honest."

Amanda now looked rattled by Andy's steady, inquisitorial gaze. "I thought you might find that case really boring and tough to figure out," she said. Andy remained silent. "So, I found one in my pile that sounds right up your alley, and traded it for yours. It's an appeal from the Fifth Circuit by some Hispanic group that claimed their school district in Texas wouldn't let Mexican kids speak Spanish on school property, even the playground. They sued for violation of free speech, ethnic discrimination, freedom of association, you know, all that stuff I don't know beans about."

Amanda now looked wilted. She picked up a folder from her desk, holding it out to Andy. "Here. I'm sorry if you don't like the trade. I just thought, you know, we'd both have a better grasp of the issues if we switched cases."

Andy ignored the proffered folder. She was seething inside, but replied in an even voice. "Amanda, if I have trouble understanding, quote, technical stuff, I'll find somebody to help me. And what makes you think a case about speaking Spanish is, quote, right up my alley? I don't even speak Spanish. But that's not the point, is it?"

Andy took a step toward Amanda, who pulled the folder back against her chest, like a shield. "So, what's the point, Amanda? Is there some reason you wanted the antitrust case, other than assuming an art history major from Barnard can't handle technical stuff, but an econ major from Yale can? That's pretty condescending."

Dave and Todd hadn't said a word during this exchange, or even moved, Dave seated at his desk and Todd standing behind Amanda. Todd finally spoke. "Hold on, Andy. It was my idea that switching these cases would benefit both of you. It looks like I was wrong, and I apologize. Okay? So, let's agree that we won't do any switching again. Okay?"

Andy shifted her eyes to Todd. "Tell you what," Andy said. "I'm going to assume you both had good intentions, and just forgot to ask me for permission to switch the cases. So, we'll let it go. But let's stick to the case distributions from now on. That should avoid any more confusion." She turned to her desk, picked up the folder Amanda had inserted into her pile, and held it out. But her conciliatory words had not eased her anger. "Here, Amanda, let's trade, again. And if you need any help with that technical First Amendment stuff, just ask me. It's right up my alley, as they say."

Amanda and Andy traded folders, returning them to the piles on their desks. "Listen, guys," Amanda said, "Todd and I are going out to meet with some of his law-school buddies who are working here in DC, for beers at TGI Friday's. Probably see you in the morning. And sorry again, Andy. Thanks for being understanding."

After they left, Dave said, "You know, Andy, I'm not sure why they switched files, but I doubt it was to give you a case you'd prefer to Amanda's. Now that I remember, she had the docket list in her hand, and looked through your folders until she found the one she obviously wanted, then stuck her folder just where the other one was. Smells a bit like kimchi to me, as they say in Korea."

Andy laughed. "Or like rotten eggs, as we say here. But it's probably not worth worrying about. Anyway, I'm heading up to the library for a bit. They've got all the state reporters, and there's a case from Oklahoma I want to check out that's not online. Sorry to leave you all by your lonesome again, but I won't take long."

She returned in thirty minutes, having located the Oklahoma case and printing out the opinion. Entering the clerks' office, she found Dave at his desk, beaming and holding a sheaf of papers.

"Well, well," Dave said, with an air of triumph. "I took the opportunity to look up and read the Second Circuit opinion in the antitrust case Amanda tried to pilfer from you, and then did a little Internet surfing. Want to know what I found? Smells more and more like kimchi and rotten eggs, mixed together."

"Wow," Andy said. "You didn't have to do that, Dave, but clue me in." She sat down at her desk, then rolled her chair over to Dave's.

"Okay," he said. "First, I got the case name from the docket list. ProVita Pharmaceuticals versus Federal Trade Commission. According to the Second Circuit opinion, the FTC conducted an investigation of one of ProVita's subsidiaries, an outfit called Eutech. Their biggest money-maker, to the tune of half a billion a year, is a drug called Anhelofac. I checked an online dictionary, and that's a combination of Latin words for breathe and easy. It's prescribed to treat pulmonary obstruction."

"All this in thirty minutes, Dave? I'm impressed."

"That was just the first ten minutes, Andy. It's pretty quick, when you know what you're looking for on the Internet and where to find it. Anyway, the FTC ordered ProVita to divest Eutech, finding that it controlled eighty percent of the market for PO drugs and that ProVita was using the profits from Eutech to undercut prices for its other drugs and harm its competitors. ProVita challenged the FTC ruling in federal district court in Connecticut, where its headquarters are in Hartford. They lost there, and the Second Circuit upheld the district court, and now ProVita's cert petition is on your desk."

"That's impressive, Dave, for ten minutes of surfing. So, what about the next twenty minutes? Must be something more than case facts."

"You bet there is," Dave said, "and it's definitely kimchi. Connecticut just happens to be the home state of someone we both know. So, being a suspicious guy, I looked up ProVita's officers and directors, which is easy to find. Guess who's a director?"

"Last name wouldn't be Cushing, would it?"

"Carleton Cushing, in fact, home in Greenwich. But there's more. I got on the Securities and Exchange Commission website and found a recent Form 144 filing by Carleton." Andy shook her head, indicating puzzlement. "Oh," Dave continued, "that's a form that company directors and major stockholders have to file when they plan to sell stock over a certain value. Turns out Daddy Warbucks owns five percent of ProVita. Current market value of his stock is a couple hundred million, and his 144 says he plans to sell shares worth fifty million. But he's got ninety days to make a trade, and doesn't have to follow through."

"I think I'm getting the drift here, Dave," Andy said. "If the Court grants cert in this case, it's likely to reverse the Second Circuit, which would push up the stock price. And if it denies cert, ProVita has to divest Eutech and the stock goes down. Am I on the right track?"

"Bingo," Dave said. "So, if our friend who's swilling beer at TGI Friday's can predict the cert decision in advance, she could whisper in Daddy's ear and he could decide whether to sell or hold the stock."

"But that would be illegal, right?"

"Depends," Dave said. "That's what's called insider trading, which isn't illegal per se, but it's illegal if a family member of a stockholder gets confidential info that would affect stock prices, either up or down, and gives it to their relative, which is called tipping. In this case, that would be a huge tip. Any waiter could retire for life with that tip on the table."

"And you suspect our beer-swilling friend wanted that case so she could write a pool memo that recommended a cert grant," Andy said.

"Seems likely to my suspicious mind," Dave said. "And if she did, it's pretty sure Alex would agree, since he admittedly knows zilch about antitrust law and said he'd rely on our friend in those cases. But if the pool memo recommended denial, he'd probably also go along. So, even if there were four votes to grant, which is all you need, those four justices would anticipate five votes to affirm, and not take the risk of losing."

Andy gave Dave a Light-Bulb look. "You just gave me an idea," she said. "What if I give the ProVita folder back to our friend, tell her she was right, that an art history major couldn't make heads or tails of the case, and offer to trade back for the Spanish-language case. Then we could see what her pool memo recommends. We'll find out after Alex gets back from London and we meet to review our memos."

"Just what I was going to suggest," Dave said. "If she recommends a grant, that would meet the kimchi test. Of course, even if she did, that probably wouldn't support a prosecution for insider trading, without some way of showing she tipped off Daddy in advance."

"You mean ratting her out to the Justice Department? I wasn't thinking of going that far," Andy said.

"Me neither," Dave said. "But it might come in handy if our friends, and I'm including the other beer-swiller, try anything else to stack the deck in other cases, which I wouldn't put past them. To be honest, Andy, I didn't like either of them as soon as we met in Alex's office on Monday. Maybe I'm wrong, but they've been acting like they knew each other before then. I do know they're both very active in the Federalist Society, since I'm also a member, which I hope you won't hold against me. And folks in the student chapters get together in conferences around the country, and network with each other. But, as I said, maybe I'm wrong that there might be something nefarious about the folder-switching episode."

"Dave, I wouldn't hold being a Fed against you," Andy assured him. "There were several Harvard Law Review editors who were Feds, and I got along with them very well, despite our political differences. Anyway, it looks like we have a plan. And I can't believe you did all of this in just half an hour."

"Hey, I'm not the only person who took Antitrust and Securities Regulation in law school. And I look like a computer geek, right?"

Andy laughed. "Not all stereotypes are wrong, Dave. But you're my kind of geek, and I owe you for this."

"Well, let's wait to see how the kimchi turns out. If I'm right, you'll owe me any Redskins tickets you get from Alex. Do I fit the stereotype of an NFL fan? I'm not overweight, loud, or obnoxious. But I'm a die-hard 'Niners fan, so go figure."

The next morning, Andy executed the Kimchi Plan. Amanda apologized again, assured Andy she hadn't meant to question her ability to comprehend technical stuff, and said she'd had trouble understanding the issues in the "no Spanish in schools" case. The case folders were transferred, and the two clerks—sitting back-to-back in their office—got to work on their pool memos as if the day before hadn't happened.

Andy knew it would be a couple of months before she knew the final outcome of the scheme she and Dave had cooked up. Dick had explained that the justices wouldn't make any decisions on the roughly 1500 petitions that had been filed over the summer until they held their "long conference" on the last Thursday of September. Cases that one or more justices considered cert-worthy, after the pool memos had been circulated to each chambers, would be placed on the "discuss list," with those that none felt deserved review relegated to the aptly-named "dead list," from which a Lazarus-like revival at some later date was theoretically possible but almost never happened. Cases that got at least four votes to grant cert place would be placed on the docket for argument and decision in the forthcoming term, which began the first Monday of October. Once the list of cert grants and denials from the long conference had been finalized, the Clerk's office would issue an "order list" the following Monday, which would be posted on the Court's website at 9:30 a.m., and eagerly perused by every lawyer with a case up for review.

However, Alex was likely to return from the Thursday conference with a list of the cert grants, probably no more than a dozen, for which the clerks would begin preparing bench memos for oral argument. It was this window, between Thursday and the following Monday, in which Amanda— assuming Andy and Dave had guessed right about her motivation for slipping the ProVita folder from Andy's pile—could tip her dad about whether he should sell or hold onto his stock. Nothing to do but wait, Andy thought. But as she worked, her brain dredged up a stanza from a poem by Sir Walter Scott she'd read in a literature class at Barnard: "Oh, what a tangled web we weave, when first we practice to deceive." Andy chuckled to herself as she picked another folder from her pile.

7

Alex Novak had invited his clerks to a barbeque at his home on Sunday, July 28, the day after his return from London. His secretary, Angie, had given each of them a sheet with the address, directions by car and Metro, and reminders that "spouses and significant others" were also invited, "the bar will open at 1 p.m.," and dress should be "BBQ casual."

A thunderstorm had passed through Washington the night before, but the brief cooling had given way to the hot and steamy weather that would blanket the area for the next two months, a reminder that the Capital City had been built on a subtropical swamp. Andy dressed for the day in a pair of khaki shorts and a green polo shirt she'd bought at Eddie Bauer, hoping she wouldn't be too casual for the occasion. After a morning of cleaning her apartment and grocery shopping at Safeway, she set out at noon for a twenty-minute walk, past the Supreme Court and the Capitol to Union Station, which housed both Amtrak and a Metro station. Andy boarded a Red Line subway train; seven stops later, she got off at the Cleveland Park station on Connecticut Avenue, lined with embassies, up-scale shops, and the United Nations of restaurants.

Consulting the sheet Angie had given her, Andy walked three blocks up Connecticut and turned right on Quebec Street, looking for 4428 on the left. Two blocks later, she reached a three-story, red-brick, Georgian-style house with green shutters and trim. Two flowering magnolia trees flanked a red-brick walkway to a green door with a lion's-head knocker.

As she reached the wrought-iron gate, on which a hand-written note saying "Come around to back" was taped, Andy spotted Dick Wadleigh coming down the sidewalk toward her, holding hands with a petite, blond woman in a yellow summer dress. "Hey, Andy, fancy meeting you here," Dick greeted her. "Andy Roboff, this is my wife, Jane."

Andy couldn't resist. "Hi, Jane. And how are Spot and Puff?"

Jane laughed. "Just fine, Andy. Spot barks too much, and Puff sheds all over the couch. Nice to meet you. Dick tells me you turn out pool memos faster than he can give them to you."

"That's because I just write 'Deny' on each one," Andy said. "Seriously, Dick's memos are my models. Concise, but incisive, if you know what I mean. And Dick tells me you clerked last term for Justice Schroeder. But she's very liberal, and Justice Novak is very conservative, although I hear they're good friends."

"That's right," Jane said. "Dick and I don't share political views. But we leave politics at the office, and definitely keep them out of the bedroom. Although my pillow is blue, and Dick's is red."

Dick gave Jane a mock punch on her shoulder. "That's to hide the blood from getting whacked upside the head when I tell Jane that Democrats believe there's no problem that can't be solved by printing more money."

"Very funny, dear," Jane retorted. "And Republicans believe there's no problem that can't be solved by taking from the poor and giving to the rich. You know, like Robin Hood in reverse."

Andy was amused by this obviously well-practiced marital badinage. She had her hand on the gate, ready to swing it open. At that moment, Dave Park trotted up the sidewalk. "Hey, guys," he said cheerfully. "It's ten after one, and the bar's open. Shall we all go in and join the party?" Andy swung the gate open, and they followed a red-brick path around the house to the back yard, from which laughing voices and the distinctive odor of grilling beef signaled the party had already begun.

The new arrivals turned the corner of Novak's home into a back yard that featured a large flagstone patio and a smaller but well-tended lawn, with blue-flowering hydrangea bushes along a redwood fence. A wooden ramp with railings extended from sliding glass doors to the patio. Four picnic tables and benches were grouped around a long barbeque grill, on which Novak was turning steaks with tongs. Beside the grill were two fold-out tables on which four large coolers sat, along with stacks of plastic cups, paper plates, napkins, and utensils.

Andy was surprised to see a half-dozen people she didn't recognize, three women and three men who looked to be in their late twenties and early thirties. Amanda and Todd were standing with this group, all chatting and holding cups of beer or soda. Novak turned from the grill as the new arrivals reached the patio. He was wearing a white apron on which was printed, "No Appeal From the Cook. You Eat What We Serve."

Putting down his tongs, Novak waved the foursome over to the grill. "I've been fending off these hungry beasts," he said with a grin. "Ten minutes and I toss the meat to the wolves." He gestured to the chattering group. "Since it's a Sunday afternoon, the only time lawyers in this town get a few hours off, I invited some of my former clerks who've stayed inside the Beltway to join us." Novak clapped his hands and the chatter stopped. "Folks, we're honored to have with us two of my new clerks, Andy Roboff and Dave Park, my sadly departing clerk, Dick Wadleigh, and his beautiful and brainy wife, Jane. I'll skip introducing you all, but you can do that while I rescue the steak before it turns to charcoal."

Andy followed Novak to the grill. "Welcome back," she said. "I hope your trip went well."

Novak laughed. "Well, aside from the fact that it rained every day I was in London, it was fun to explain why we Yanks dressed like Indians and tossed their tea into the Boston Harbor. The Brits still don't understand our 'no taxation, no representation' complaint against King George." He gestured to the nearest table. "Andy, can you bring that platter over so I can serve the steaks before they taste like an overcooked British roast?"

Andy got the platter from the table and held it while Novak piled New York strip on it. The grill also held a dozen kebobs with shrimp and vegetables, and corn wrapped in foil, which Novak placed on two more platters that Andy fetched from the table. When the platters were all spread out, Novak clapped his hands again. "Chow time, folks," he bellowed over the chatter. "Line up and fill your plates. No pushing and shoving, please. Act like regular people, not like lawyers. Plenty for everybody."

As the chattering group obediently lined up at the table, picking up plates, forks, and steak knives, the sliding doors above the ramp opened. Andy looked over to see a woman in a wheelchair being guided down to the patio by a very elderly man. The woman, who looked to be in her mid-fifties, was strikingly beautiful, with auburn hair piled into an old-fashioned bun over a face that reflected aristocratic origins. The man was white-haired, ramrod straight, and gave the clear impression of being accustomed to exercising authority. He wheeled the woman to the nearest table, and stood behind her with a protective stance.

Andy, into whom politeness had been drilled from childhood by her grandmother Bella, put down her plate and went over to the couple. "Hello," she said, "I'm Andy Roboff, one of Justice Novak's new clerks. Could I get you both something to eat?"

The woman looked up at Andy with a gracious smile. "Thank you, Andy, that's very kind. But we already had a light lunch in the house. Alex has told me what a find you were, to help with his work, and I wanted to come out and meet you. I'm Gloria Novak, Alex's wife, and this gentleman is his father, Anton Novak." Anton bowed his head slightly, but without saying anything. "You'll have to excuse me, Andy, for not shaking your hand," Gloria continued. "I have muscular dystrophy, which makes my hands a bit useless, but Alex and Anton take care of all my needs, and treat me like a princess." She gave Andy a radiant smile. "Although I do miss the fancy-dress balls, and the young men in their uniforms."

Andy was thoroughly charmed by this woman, but was puzzled that Alex's father remained silent. She noticed that his face was marked by a long, semi-circular scar that ran from his left cheekbone down to his jaw, and wondered if this disfigurement might hamper his speech and account for his silence.

Gloria seemed to read Andy's thoughts. "Please don't think Anton isn't also pleased to meet you, dear. He has lived in this country quite a few years, and his English is perfectly good, but he's a bit shy with people he doesn't know well. Although Anton can be a real raconteur when he's with family and friends." Gloria gave Andy an Excuse Me look. "Oh, I didn't mean to impress you with my high-school French, Andy. I just meant that Anton can tell fascinating stories about places he's been and people he's met."

"Oh, there's no need to apologize, Mrs. Novak," Andy said. "I use my high-school French sometimes, like saying 's'il vous plait' and 'merci' to waiters in French restaurants. And I felt sort of shy when I spent a year in Italy and had trouble understanding what people said, although my Italian got more fluent when I lived with a family in Rome that spoke more slowly than most Romans, to help me out."

Just then, Novak came over. "Andy, I'm glad you had a chance to meet my wife and father. I told them you're the first clerk I've hired that was an art history major. Gloria has a real interest in art, and my dad spends a lot of time with her in museums and galleries. I hope you'll have time from the work I pile on you to visit with them. Anyway, I'm going to drag you away for a little ceremony I cooked up. Please excuse us, dear."

As Novak took her arm, Andy said, "It was nice meeting you, Mrs. Novak. Perhaps you and Justice Novak's dad could give me a tour of the National Gallery sometime. Your husband keeps me so busy I haven't had time to get out much." She gave Novak a Just Kidding smile.

"Thank you so much, dear," Gloria said to Andy. "I'd love to show you around the National Gallery, and perhaps the Corcoran museum as well. Just let me know when Alex gives you a few hours away from telling him how to decide cases, since he generally just flips a coin." Gloria smiled again, then nodded to Anton, who turned her wheelchair around and pushed it up the ramp and through the sliding doors.

"What a remarkable woman," Andy said to Novak. "I have a feeling we can become good friends, and that I can learn a lot from her. And your dad as well, if he gets into a story-telling mood."

"Gloria is remarkable," he replied. "She's been in that chair for almost ten years, and has never complained once about her condition. And my dad isn't always so reticent. Give him a glass of Polish vodka, and he becomes a regular Garrison Keillor. He's ninety-two, believe it or not, and still walks two miles every day."

"So, your dad is Polish?" Andy asked. "I figured from your name you had roots in some Eastern European country."

"He was from Warsaw," Novak said. "Came over after the war, in 1948, and then spent ten years as a salesman for a patent drug company, traveling all over the country, before he settled in Chicago and met my mom. She died of breast cancer when I was twelve, and he raised me and my sister, who's six years younger than me and still lives in Chicago."

Novak paused and shook his head. "But my dad never talks about the war years, even with me. When I asked him once, back in my teen-age years, about his life in Poland, he just said, 'Alex, you want to know about Hell? I was there, and it's too horrible to describe.' So I never asked him again." He shook his head again. "Anyway, Andy, it was kind of you to chat with Gloria, but you didn't get to smear barbeque sauce all over your face. So why don't you grab a plate, while I take care of a short errand."

The only steak left looked a bit charred, so Andy put the two remaining shrimp kebobs and an ear of corn on a plate, then joined Dick and Jane at their picnic table. They were chatting with a couple of Novak's former clerks, so Andy ate without interrupting their conversation. But what Novak had said about his dad reminded her of a similar talk she'd had, also as a teenager, with her grandmother Bella. Andy's mom had told her that Bella had been smuggled out of the Warsaw ghetto in 1942, at the age of eight, and had been taken in by a Catholic family, never seeing her parents or younger brother again. Her mom also told her that Bella had been placed in a displaced persons camp after the Soviet Army liberated Warsaw from the Nazis, and had been sponsored for immigration to New York by relatives who'd come over before the war. When Andy asked Bella about that experience, she'd simply said, "Bubelah, my life started here in New York. Before that, you don't want to know. Just be glad you have a tateh and a mameh, and a nice place to live."

Novak's account of his dad's refusal to discuss his wartime experiences, and recalling Bella's similar refusal, set Andy to reflecting on the horrors that people could inflict on fellow humans, simply because of their race or religion.

Oblivious to the chatter around her, Andy was jolted from her reverie by a sudden burst of laughter. Seated with her back to the house, Andy turned to witness Novak coming down the steps to the patio. He was attired in a scarlet robe, a heavy gold chain and medallion around his neck, and a tightly curled white wig that came down past his shoulders.

What the hell is this, Andy thought. Novak answered by raising his hands for silence. "My lords and ladies," he said in a plummy British accent, "I am the Lord Chief Justice of Her Majesty's courts, visiting my colleagues in your colony—I mean your republic." He shushed the ensuing laughter with a wave. "It is my distinct honor to introduce my esteemed counterpart, the Chief Justice of the United States, the Honorable Samuel Terman." Emerging from the house was a short, stout man with frizzy grey hair, wearing a plain black robe. Standing beside the resplendent Novak, he looked like the sidekick in a Borscht Belt comedy routine.

"Thank you, Lord Chief Justice," he said in a voice that betrayed his Brooklyn roots. "I might say that I once proposed to my colleagues that we adopt your mode of judicial attire, considering our common heritage with the Magna Carta and our debts to your common law system. But I only got one other vote, from Justice Novak, if I recall." Andy joined the laughter at this little joke, knowing that Novak, who disliked formality, had once proposed dispensing with robes altogether and moving the Court's bench to floor level.

Terman was holding a paper-wrapped package that looked like a picture frame, which he handed to Novak. "I don't mean to interrupt your festivities," he said, "but I have some official Court business to transact." Pulling an envelope from inside his robe, Terman extracted a sheet and cleared his throat. "I have in my hand an order that has been adopted by the Court, without dissent. It reads, 'Upon application by the undersigned justices, it is hereby ordered and decreed that a special commendation be conferred upon a member of the Court's staff, for performance of duties in an exemplary and meritorious fashion. Each justice, and his or her staff, has benefitted from the wise and learned guidance, offered without expectation of reward or return, of . . .'" Terman stopped and handed the sheet to Novak, who continued in a stentorian voice, "Mr. Richard Wadleigh." Dick, sitting next to Andy, almost choked on the beer he was sipping.

"Dick, please come up here," Novak said, while the assembled clerks, present and former, stood and clapped. Dick put down his beer cup while Andy slid out from the bench to let him pass, giving him a pat on the back. "In between us," Terman said, as Novak unwrapped the package he was holding, handing the glass-covered frame to the Chief Justice.

"Dick, I've been on the Court for thirteen years," Terman said, "and I've never met a clerk, including my own, who was so willing and capable of helping the clerks in every chambers to do a better job. Right, left, or center, it didn't matter. I've heard many clerks say, 'Any question, Dick knows the answer or how to find it.'"

Terman extended a hand to the table at which Andy sat. "And the same goes for your amazing wife, Jane. You're the first husband and wife team the Court has ever had, and Justices Novak and Schroeder, despite their occasional differences in our conference room, agree that both of you have made the Court a more pleasant and collegial place to work. So,

Jane, come up here and share in this presentation." Andy slid out again for Jane, who looked overcome with emotion, while the clerks again clapped. Once beside Dick, she put an arm around his waist and gave him a kiss on the cheek. Terman handed the framed object to Dick, who held it up for all to see. "This is a photograph of all the justices, in our conference room," Terman said, "signed by all of us, as a token of our appreciation for helping us do a job that few people realize can't be done without such outstanding and hard-working clerks."

Andy stood with all the clerks, clapping even harder than before, with someone shouting "Huzzah!" Terman held up a hand for attention. "I have another announcement," he said. "Some of you may know that Dick has been offered a position with one of our leading firms, Arnold and Porter. I assume a sizable signing bonus came with that offer," he continued with a knowing wink at Dick. "However, I recently learned that Dick has declined that offer to take a position as assistant counsel to the president. Now, Justice Novak and I may, and I repeat, *may* differ on whether President Chambers deserves another term in office, although we're strictly nonpartisan on the Court, and never discuss political issues." Andy chuckled at that, since everyone knew that Terman, who had served as attorney general of New York, and a term as a Democratic senator, before his appointment to the Court, and Novak were polar opposites in politics as well as votes on important cases that divided the justices into supposedly liberal and conservative factions. "But," Terman continued, "we agree that Dick will give the president his best advice, which I hope he takes. With that, I'll conclude this session. The Court is now in recess, and you are all free to resume your festivities."

Andy joined the crowd that quickly surrounded Dick and Jane, who both appeared overwhelmed by this unexpected event. When she got close to Dick, she said, "I'm really happy for you, Dick. You've been a great help in getting oriented to this job. And I hope, if it's not unethical, that I can still call or email you if I need help with some case."

"Thanks, Andy," he replied. "Of course you can, anytime. But I think you'll do just fine. Just remember, the Court and the White House, despite what the pundits say, have an equal stake in making this country live up to its ideals." Dick gave Andy an embarrassed look. "Jeez, there I go, sounding like a politician, which I never wanted to be. Anyway, good luck with your job. I know you're this term's liberal clerk for a conservative justice, but don't back down from what you believe."

Andy leaned over and gave Dick a kiss on the cheek. "Thanks for that, and good luck to you."

Andy returned to her table, with a Bass Ale she grabbed from a cooler. Novak and Terman returned to the patio, having shed their judicial attire. Spotting her, Novak waved Andy over. "Andy Roboff," he said, "I'd like you to meet a person who needs no introduction."

"Mr. Chief Justice," she said, shaking his extended hand, "I'm very pleased to meet you. And it was gracious of you to recognize Dick's contributions to the Court. I've only been here a few weeks, but he did a great job in getting Justice Novak's new clerks oriented to our jobs."

"Nice meeting you, too, Andy," Terman said. "Dick really deserved the Court's thanks for his work. And please call me Sam. Alex and I both dislike pomposity, although he did look quite judicial in the robe and wig the English judges gave him. But I've got a question for you."

Andy couldn't imagine what question Terman had for her. Certainly the Chief Justice didn't need legal advice from a brand-new clerk. "I may be wrong, Andy," he said, "but when I was a kid in Brooklyn, my dad had a hardware store on Flatbush Avenue, next door to a kosher butcher shop owned by Isaac Roboff. Wonderful guy. My mom bought all her chicken and chops from him. Any chance you're related?"

"Oh, my goodness," Andy replied. "That was my grandfather. He passed away several years ago, but I remember him telling us about the man who owned the store next to his. Was it Morris Terman?"

Terman beamed. "That was him. He and Isaac were great friends. During the Depression, your granddad would take IOUs from folks who were having hard times, and my dad said he just tossed them out. Good Democrats, too, both of them. That's what politics should be, Andy, helping your neighbors when they need help, whether it's getting food on the table or fixing potholes." Terman shook a finger at Novak. "You paying attention, Alex? That's what our Court should be, the nation's pothole fixer when the politicians won't do their jobs and fill them."

"That's an interesting judicial philosophy, Sam," Novak said. "But I'd rather have the people fire their politicians if they won't fix potholes, and hire new ones that will. That's what we have elections for, and you and I weren't elected by anyone. We have weightier issues to decide, like whether the Migratory Bird Treaty bars farmers from shooting Canadian geese that eat their corn." Andy was amused by this judicial badinage, which she suspected—like that between Dick and Jane—was well-practiced.

"Well, Andy, I've got to run," Terman said, checking his watch. "Barbara's dragging me off to a concert by some chamber music group, where I'll catch a nap during the slow movements. But if your zayda passed on the lessons from his butcher shop, maybe you can get them across to Alex. You can translate that for him, Andy. And tell him not to be such a schnook." He gave Andy a wink, and headed back into the house. "Got to fetch my robe," he said, over his shoulder. "And you're welcome to drop by my chambers any time for a chat, or a cup of tea."

Wow, Andy thought. Two weeks on the job, and now I'm on a first-name basis with the Chief Justice. She turned to Novak, and motioned to the tables. "Can I help you clean this up, Alex? I'm not in a hurry."

"Thanks, Andy, but that's my job," he said. "The only one I'm qualified for, according to Sam, since I'm not so good at fixing potholes."

"Okay, then I guess I'll polish off another pool memo for our meeting on Friday," Andy said. "Thanks again for the barbeque, and the tribute to Dick. And please tell Gloria I'll give her a call about a museum tour very soon, with your dad. We can take turns pushing her through the galleries."

"No, forget the pool memos, Andy. Why don't you spend the rest of the afternoon at the National Zoo? It's just down Connecticut, and you can see the pandas we got from China, along with everything we buy at Walmart."

"That's a great idea, Alex. I've been meaning to visit the zoo, and I love pandas. And by the way, you're not a schnook. More like a macher, as my grandma Bella would say. She grew up speaking Yiddish, along with Polish. By the way, I've invited her down here this fall, and I hope we can get together while she's here. You'd love her, and maybe she could brush up her Polish with your dad, after a little vodka. That always loosens Bella's tongue, and I know she sneaks a shot into her orange juice when she thinks nobody's looking. But I'll let you clean up, and go visit the pandas."

Andy looked around the patio, and discovered that Dave and two former clerks she hadn't met, who were chatting over beers, were the only ones left. She decided not to interrupt them, and headed for the path around the house. As she turned the corner, she heard Dave say, "See you guys later," and he caught up with her.

"Hey, Andy," he said. "I was sort of waiting for you. My car's across the street, and I'll give you a lift to the Metro, if that's where you're headed. I'd give you a ride back to your place, but I've got to pick up my parents at National. My dad's a cardiologist, and he's got a conference this week at the Hilton, so he brought my mom along for some shopping and sightseeing, emphasis on the former."

"Thanks, Dave," Andy said. "So why were you waiting for me, if you're in a rush to the airport?"

"Well, remember when Amanda pulled the switcheroo with the ProVita folder? I got to thinking about how that wound up in our office." They reached Dave's car, and Andy got in when Dave beeped the doors open. "Anyway," he continued, after starting the car and fastening seat belts, "the Clerk distributes the cases to each chambers, supposedly at random. So there's a one in nine chance it would get to ours. Not bad odds, but Amanda seemed to know we got it."

"Right," Andy said. "From what you said, she made a beeline to my desk. And the docket sheet had our initials next to each case we got."

"Exactly," Dave said, pulling out from the curb. "So, just on a hunch, I went down the other day to the Clerk's office, and asked the guy behind the counter to see the master docket list, saying the ProVita folder was missing a BIO, and did they have it. Turns out, when I looked at the list, that case was supposed to go to Justice Schroeder's chambers."

"You mean, another switch was done in the Clerk's office?" Andy asked. "That's a bit suspicious, if you ask me."

"Suspicious is my middle name," Dave said. They had reached Connecticut Avenue, but he pulled over and put the car in park. "So I showed the guy the list, and pointed out the 'AS' next to the ProVita case. They use the justices' initials for case distribution, and that's Alice Schroeder. 'Oh, yeah,' the guy said. 'I remember now. One of the clerks from Justice Novak's office, a pretty blond girl, came in and said he'd asked for the case, and had cleared it with Justice Schroeder.' He said that happens sometimes. So he told her he'd send it to Novak's chambers and give Schroeder another one. He was a young guy, good looking, and I got the impression Amanda had flirted with him, maybe showed him some cleavage."

"Wow, Dave," Andy said. "Sherlock Holmes could take lessons from you. But that clinches it, right? Amanda knew the case was coming in, flashed her boobs to get it to our office, and then switched it with mine, thinking I wouldn't notice. If you hadn't been there, I probably wouldn't have noticed. Do you smell kimchi now, Dave?"

"Good and rotten," he said, "just the way Koreans like it, except for me." He glanced at the dashboard clock. "Listen, Andy, my dad's plane is due in thirty minutes, so I better hustle over there. But I've got another idea, so let's have lunch tomorrow, if you're coming in, and we can strategize. Okay?"

"Great," Andy said, unlatching her seat belt. "I'll bring the lunch, but without the kimchi. How about chicken salad and coleslaw? I'm pretty good at those." She got out of the car. "Thanks for the ride, Dave. And for being such a suspicious guy." He tooted the horn and drove off. Andy headed down Connecticut to visit the pandas.

Just after she got back to her apartment, Andy's phone rang. It was Josh, who sounded exhausted but cheerful. He had survived the two-day Massachusetts bar exam. The Multistate portion on Saturday, a multiple-choice test that covered federal law, had been a piece of cake, Josh said. The Sunday exam, which required essays on issues of Massachusetts state law, had been tougher, and two questions—on family law and municipal regulation—had baffled him. But he followed the advice of friends who'd taken the exam the previous year: If you don't have a clue, restate the questions and the facts, then just write anything you can think of, for which you'll get partial credit, even if it's total crap.

After the exam was over, Josh said, he'd gone home, popped a Dave Matthews CD into the player, and smoked two bowls of Pineapple Haze, a very mellow variety. He'd be moving down to DC in two weeks, into an apartment Carlo had found in Foggy Bottom, walking distance from the George Washington Hospital, where he'd already started his residency. Josh would begin a two-week orientation at the Justice Department in DC for new assistant federal attorneys and defenders, then commute to Alexandria by Metro to begin his new job.

For her part, Andy recounted the show that Novak and Chief Justice Terman had performed at the barbeque, her conversation with Terman about the Brooklyn days of his dad and her grandfather, and her visit to the zoo. She left out the complete silence of Novak's dad, and the Kimchi Plan that she and Dave Park had devised to snare Amanda. Andy figured Josh needed time to unwind after the bar exam, and she could tell him all this in person, after his move. As usual, their conversation ended with Andy's "love you" and Josh's "love you too." With no pot available, Andy popped a Dave Matthews CD into her player, enjoyed two glasses of Beringer chardonnay while Dave riffed with his band members, soaked in a hot tub, went to bed, and very quickly to sleep.

Monday morning, Andy got to the Court at eight-thirty. Dave, Amanda, and Todd were already at their desks, each working on the computer. She gave them a collective "Good morning, guys," then began work at her desk on a pool memo that was such an easy "Deny" that she had trouble getting past two pages. About eleven, Novak stuck his head in the door and said, "Ah, just what I like to hear, the sound of brains at work," then disappeared.

As she had promised Dave, Andy made chicken salad and coleslaw out of her fridge before coming to work, adding chocolate chip cookies—she knew Dave liked them—to the bag of plastic containers into which she put their lunch. At noon, with an "Off to lunch" for Amanda and Todd, who just glanced up and nodded, Andy and Dave stopped by the cafeteria, picked up utensils, napkins, and bottled Evian, and took their lunches to one of the interior courtyards. An hour later, they returned to the office, having agreed on the next steps in the Kimchi Plan. Amanda and Todd were gone, and didn't reappear before Andy left at six, leaving Dave at his desk, fingers flying over his keyboard.

8

Friday morning at nine, the four clerks assembled in Novak's office for their first meeting to review with him the pool memos they had written over the past two weeks. They had each given their memos to Angie on Wednesday, who dropped them in Novak's in-box for him to read before the meeting. After the meeting, Angie would take them to the Clerk's office for distribution to the other eight chambers. This would be the first time the new clerks got feedback on their work since beginning their jobs at the Court, and they exchanged looks as they took seats like ninth-graders waiting for the English teacher to return their four-page essays on The Most Interesting Book I Read This Summer.

"Sorry to keep you folks waiting," Novak said as he bustled in five minutes later. "The Chief wanted my sage counsel on whether it would be appropriate for him to speak at a conference of an Orthodox Jewish group that requires women to sit in the back of the meeting room. So I told him, Sam, why don't you pull a Rosa Parks and invite the women to move up front. That will make a point more than anything you say about the wonders of our divinely ordained Constitution." The clerks, still a bit nervous, responded with polite chuckles. "The Chief said he didn't think he could match Rosa Parks in courage, and he'd probably decline the invitation."

Novak lifted a pile of memos from his desk and put them on the low table around which the clerks were seated. He scanned their somber faces. "Hey, you guys look like you've been tossing and turning all night," he said with a grin. "Lighten up. We're just deciding who gets to keep pots of money, or walk out of prison, and who loses their life savings, or spends the rest of their life in the slammer. Nothing to lose sleep over." No chuckles this time.

"Well, so much for that feeble attempt at humor," Novak said. "Sorry, I know this is serious business, so let's get to work. This won't take long, since you've all given me memos that covered the bases, and presented both sides of the cases fairly. I've read them all, and I've got just a few questions. First of all, I don't have any quibbles with the ones you recommended for denials. And I doubt that any of my colleagues will disagree, although we'll have to wait a few weeks until they read them and see if any wind up on the discuss list for the long conference. But that doesn't happen often with memos from my clerks, so pat yourselves on the back."

Novak picked up the docket sheet. "So, let's look at your grant recommendations. There's only four, about par for the course." He glanced at the list. "Okay, we've got none from Todd, one from Dave, two from Andy, and one from Amanda. So Todd, you can just warm your chair until we're done. But don't fall asleep. We might need your expertise on some knotty legal issue the rest of us can't unravel. Dave, why don't you start?"

Dave sat up straight in his chair, an eager student ready to impress the teacher. "This is an appeal from a decision of the Idaho Supreme Court that upheld the state's ban on marriages between first cousins. The plaintiffs are cousins, but the woman was adopted as a child and has no genetic link to her cousin. They challenged the ban as an arbitrary restriction on their Fourteenth Amendment liberty right to marry the person of their choice, but the state court ruled the cousin-marriage ban was a reasonable effort to protect against increased risks of having children with birth defects and inherited diseases."

"So what's unreasonable about that?" Novak asked.

"Well," Dave answered, "first, because even if first cousins have children, the risk of passing on genetic defects is only about two percent greater than for unrelated parents. That's what the plaintiffs' genetics expert testified. Second, because the woman was adopted, this couple is actually unrelated in terms of having similar DNA, so preventing them from getting married doesn't serve any legitimate state interest."

"Well, let's assume that," Novak conceded. "But what makes this a federal case, instead of strictly an interpretation of state law?"

"Because," Dave continued, "this Court has power under Rule Ten to decide challenges to state laws that raise a federal question, which this case does. And the Court has struck down other state laws that restricted marriage rights, like for prisoners and people who are delinquent on child-support payments."

"Hmm," Novak said. "It's not a case that would affect many people, Dave, but since this Idaho couple is basically unrelated, preventing them from getting married doesn't further any legitimate state interest that I can think of." Novak pondered for a few seconds. "Tell you what, Dave. I'm not sure there'd be another three votes for a cert grant, but I'll put your case on the discuss list and see what happens." Dave beamed at his passing grade from a tough teacher.

Novak consulted his docket list. "Andy, you've got two grants, so let's hear about them. Briefly, since I read your memos."

Dave had passed his test, so Andy felt more confident than when the session began. "Okay," she said. "The first is a case from Iowa in which the petitioner is a convicted sex offender who completed his two-year sentence for statutory rape, which was having sex with his fifteen-year-old girlfriend. He was eighteen at the time, and the girl's mom, who didn't approve of him, caught them in the act on the living-room couch and called the cops. He'll have to register as a sex offender, which he doesn't dispute. Now, the prison officials approved his plan to live with his mom in this small town that's mostly residential, and he moved in with her."

Andy caught Amanda wrinkling her nose with distaste, but went on. "Here's the issue. The town had an ordinance that barred registered sex offenders from residing within a thousand feet of any school, church, or playground. Now, this guy's mom lives about twelve hundred feet from a middle school. So, when town officials were notified he'd be moving there, they amended the ordinance to increase the distance to two thousand feet. But there's no residence in the town that's farther than that from any school, church, or playground. Basically, he's now barred from living in the town at all, and has been ordered to move out of his mom's house. So, he filed a suit in federal court, with the ACLU's help, claiming this was a bill of attainder and violated Article One, Section Ten, of the Constitution. The district court dismissed the suit and the Eighth Circuit upheld the dismissal."

Todd gave Andy a puzzled look. "Excuse me for exposing my ignorance, Andy, but what's a bill of attainder? I must have missed that class."

"Well, Todd, we didn't cover that at Harvard, either, so don't feel bad," Andy replied. "But it's a legislative act that singles out a specific person for punishment that doesn't apply generally to all persons. In this case, the town council approved the zoning amendment after about a thousand people signed a petition that named this guy as a danger to children. And he's the only registered sex offender who lives in this town, so he claims it was directed only at him. By the way, Todd, since this ordinance is only directed at sex offenders, a convicted murderer or drug dealer could live right next door to a school, but nobody in this town objected to that. "

Amanda chimed in. "Andy, don't you think it's reasonable for the town to protect kids from sex offenders? I mean, this girl was fifteen, but schools are full of girls that age and younger. I don't see what's unreasonable about that."

Novak interrupted before Andy could answer. "Tell you what, guys. I've been waiting years for a good bill of attainder case to get here, just so my colleagues can pull out their history books. I think the first one we decided was right after the Civil War, when the Court struck down a law that barred people like Todd's rebellious ancestors from practicing law without swearing an oath renouncing their Confederate allegiance. Andy's case, at least to me, seems like a good vehicle to rule that people can't be punished without some kind of trial. I'm not a fan of sex offenders any more than Amanda, but this guy doesn't seem like a serial offender. So, without further ado, I'll put this case on the discuss list."

Dave gave Andy a Good Job look. "Okay," Novak continued. "Andy's other grant was this Texas case about a school district that barred kids from speaking Spanish anywhere on school property, even the playgrounds. If you don't mind, Andy, I think we can skip your recital, because your memo points out that the Fifth Circuit's ruling against the plaintiffs conflicts with a recent Ninth Circuit ruling to the contrary. I'm not a big fan of the Ninth, since it's stacked with liberals and we reverse them more than any other circuit, but I think they got this one right. So, we've got a circuit split here, and I'll go with a grant. Thanks, Andy. Good job."

Novak turned to Amanda. "So far, you guys are batting one thousand, and the bases are loaded. Amanda, let's see if you can drive in a run." He picked up her memo on the ProVita case, and nodded to her. Andy and Dave exchanged Here We Go glances, and noticed that Amanda and Todd did the same.

"Well, this case involves one of the leading pharmaceutical companies that acquired a smaller company a few years ago," Amanda began. "That company manufactures and sells a drug that treats pulmonary obstructions. It currently controls about seventy percent of the market for similar drugs, because most doctors think it's the most effective. However, the Federal Trade Commission ordered the parent company to divest its subsidiary, ruling that its market share allowed it to undercut the competitors in pricing, since any losses in revenue could be made up by the parent company." Amanda paused. "Am I getting too technical here, Alex? I tried to explain all this in my memo." He shook his head with a Go Ahead look.

"Okay," she continued. "The parent company filed suit against the FTC, claiming that its subsidiary was simply selling a better product than its competitors, and that its pricing benefitted consumers. But the district court and the Second Circuit upheld the FTC ruling, on grounds that the subsidiary was engaged in predatory pricing, designed to create a monopoly for this drug and drive competitors out of that market. However, it seems to me that if this Court grants cert, and reverses the Second Circuit, consumers actually will benefit from the lower cost of drugs that patients need and that doctors prefer. I mean, that's what free markets are supposed to do, give consumers the best products at the lowest prices. And the government shouldn't interfere with that, at least in cases like this." Amanda stopped and gave Novak an Any Questions look.

"Thanks, Amanda," Novak said. "You cleared the bases with that swing, and I'll go along with your grant recommendation. I'm also a fan of free markets, and I buy a lot of medications to treat my wife's muscular dystrophy. They're pretty pricy, and a lot of people who aren't in our income bracket have to scrape the barrel to afford them. Plus, these unelected government bureaucrats down the Hill think they know what's best for the unwashed masses. Maybe this case will send them a message. Anyway, that wraps it up for today."

Novak glanced at his watch. "I've got a meeting downtown of the Judicial Conference. There's a district judge in New York who's in the early stages of Alzheimers, and lawyers have complained that he can't follow the proceedings in court. So we have to decide whether to place him on medical disability and remove him from presiding at trials. Very sad, but the poor guy refuses to step down. Anyway, you all did a great job. So, same time, same place, next Friday?"

The clerks all nodded their agreement, gathered their papers, and got up to leave, smiling with satisfaction at having pleased the teacher.

On the way out of Novak's office, Dave turned around. "Excuse me, Alex, but can you spare just a couple of minutes? Andy and I have a quick question."

"Of course, Dave," Novak said. "I may not have the answer, but shoot."

Checking to make sure that Amanda and Todd were out of earshot, Dave cleared his throat. "This is sort of delicate," he said, "and I didn't want to embarrass Amanda, but I think her memo on the ProVita case was really biased, and the case doesn't deserve a cert grant. Can I tell you why?"

Novak looked surprised, but gave Dave a Go Ahead nod. "Okay," Dave began. "I heard Amanda and Todd talking about the case in the office, and she told him the Second Circuit had failed to consider that most economists agree that selling products at a discount doesn't constitute predatory pricing, as long as the prices aren't below the cost of production. Amanda also said she knew that ProVita's subsidiary had incurred substantial costs in developing and marketing the drug, which should count as costs of production, and the FTC hadn't factored those costs into its divestment ruling." He gave Novak an Are You Following Me? look, which got another Go Ahead nod.

"Anyway," Dave continued, "that didn't sound right, at least from my Antitrust course at Stanford. So I read the Second Circuit opinion, and the FTC ruling the judges cited and quoted. They both said that costs of developing and marketing drugs weren't relevant in predatory pricing cases. And I wondered how Amanda knew what those costs were, since she cited them in her memo, including the dollar figures, which weren't in the case record. Now, I don't fault Amanda for doing additional research, but courts are bound to consider only evidence presented at trial. Also, selling below cost of production isn't an antitrust violation, unless the intent is to drive competitors out of business and create a monopoly for that product, which the FTC found that ProVita intended." Dave played his final card. "And, Alex, you know what happens once the competitors are driven out of the market?"

"Let me guess," Novak answered. "Prices get raised, and consumers get screwed."

"Exactly," Dave said, relishing his new role as the teacher. "And that's what both the FTC and Second Circuit predicted would happen if ProVita's subsidiary could dig into daddy's pockets to cover the short-term losses from selling its drug below cost. And that's why they ordered divestment as the remedy, and why the Court should deny cert and let that order stand. That's my opinion, for what it's worth."

Novak picked up his briefcase from his desk, then put it down. "Dave," he said, "this is the first time I recall one of my clerks doing something like this." Dave looked stricken, waiting for a stern rebuke or something even worse. "But I'm glad you did, and told me about it. You know, I just don't have time to read all the opinions we're asked to review, none of us do. So I rely on my clerks to do that, and give me a balanced judgment on each petition's merits. It looks like Amanda didn't in this case, but you guys have only been here a few weeks, so I'll just let it go."

Novak paused for a moment. "Tell you what, Dave. We haven't circulated your memos to the other chambers yet. And if one of my colleagues who's keen on antitrust cases, and there are two or three, reads Amanda's memo, they'd probably spot the bias right away and wonder how one of my clerks got that past me. So, why don't you write up a new memo and we'll send that out. We've got plenty of time before the long conference, so don't feel rushed. A couple of weeks will be fine. Is that okay with you?" Dave nodded his agreement. Novak patted him on the shoulder. "But thanks, Dave. You did the right thing."

Novak glanced at his watch, again. "This is one meeting I really would rather skip. But we've got to do something to keep this poor judge from screwing up more cases." Shaking his head, Novak picked up his briefcase and ushered Dave and Andy from his office.

The clerks' office was empty, and Angie wasn't at her desk. Dave breathed a huge sigh of relief. "Oh, my God, Andy. For a minute, I was afraid I'd get fired. I mean, I couldn't tell Alex that Amanda stole the case from you, or about her visit to the Clerk's office, or why we think she wanted the case. And I was afraid he'd think I was trying to sabotage her for some reason."

"Well, actually, Dave, we were," Andy said, "but for a good reason. If the Kimchi Plan works out, we'll have proof that Amanda's reason for what she did, to be honest, was illegal. But we won't know for sure until we get the results of the long conference. And that's two months away. So let's just keep doing our jobs, and see what happens."

"Okay, but that really gave me a scare."

"You did good, Dave, you did good." Andy gave Dave a pat on the back, and he smiled in return.

Andy felt relieved that Novak had praised her pool memos, and pleased that he agreed with her grant recommendations. Having passed that first test, she felt more confident about tackling the next task. Angie had given the clerks a list of the cases in which the Court had granted cert before the summer recess, and had scheduled oral argument for the first two weeks of the October Term. There were twenty-four cases on the list, and each clerk was delegated to write a "bench memo" on six cases, to prepare Novak for the upcoming arguments. He had written each clerk's initials next to the cases he assigned to them.

Andy wasn't familiar with the cases on her list, but dug out the pool memos on her six from the copies Angie had filed, and noticed—with some amusement--that four raised issues of criminal law, while the other two involved First Amendment claims of free speech and religious freedom. Novak had pegged her, Andy realized, as his chambers' specialist in these areas, leaving disputes about statutory interpretation and governmental regulation to her fellow clerks, which was fine with Andy. She also dug out a half-dozen bench memos from the previous term, to use as models. They followed the general format of the pool memos, except they were mostly longer, fifteen to twenty pages, and included a list of questions the justice might pose to the lawyers on both sides during oral argument. These memos were for Novak alone, and tailored to his well-known penchant for posing tough and unexpected questions that often left the lawyers fumbling for answers, despite weeks or even months of preparation for their argument.

Andy tried her best to frame questions that probed the weak spots in each side's briefs, noting that some lawyers glided over, or even ignored, precedent and legal doctrine that undermined their case and that better lawyers would have dealt with forthrightly. Novak would jump on these evasions and omissions, with rapid-fire questions that had lawyers, even experienced Supreme Court advocates, ducking for cover. Andy knew that some of Novak's colleagues would rescue lawyers by lobbing soft-ball questions that gave them a brief respite from his barrage. Andy tried to suggest questions that sounded more like Can You Explain This For Us? than Do You Expect Us To Believe That? But she also realized that Supreme Court argument should test a lawyer's ability to field even the most out-of-the-blue questions. Andy would see how her bench memos fared during the first argument sessions in October.

Josh moved to Washington in mid-August, after a week-long visit with his parents in Idaho to unwind from the bar exam. Andy helped him get unpacked and settled into his Foggy Bottom apartment, while Carlo was working twenty-four-hour shifts at George Washington Hospital, catching naps in the staff quarters. By unspoken agreement, they stayed out of Josh's bedroom, but still traded hugs and kisses, and held hands while exploring Georgetown and hiking along the Chesapeake and Ohio towpath that followed the Potomac up to the Great Falls park. Josh began his two-week orientation for new federal attorneys and defenders at the Justice Department, while Andy plowed through her bench memos for Novak. Once a week, Carlo would join them for dinner, sampling the fare at restaurants that spanned the culinary universe. Carlo and Andy would chat and banter in Italian, while Josh laughed along at jokes and stories that were Greek to him. It was a strange threesome, but they all felt comfortable and relaxed. One night, as Carlo returned to the hospital for his rotation in the pediatric ward, Josh gave Andy a goodnight kiss and whispered into her ear, "Indeterminacy." Andy nodded, knowing that Josh believed that nothing could be predicted beyond the moment. She felt confident, however, that only a totally unexpected event could disrupt or end her relationship with Josh, and she didn't speculate about what such an event might be. Loving him, with Carlo's blessing, and being loved in return, gave Andy a feeling that her world would keep spinning as it moved through the endless universe. Another Dave Matthews CD, a glass or two of wine, a hot bath, restful sleep, and the sun would surely rise in the morning.

Two weeks later, a totally unexpected event disrupted a quiet morning in the clerks' office, where Andy and Dave were drafting bench memos at their desks. With Todd trailing behind, Amanda stormed into the room, waving a sheaf of papers. "What is this," she screeched, "some kind of bad joke? It's got your initials on it, Dave, so tell me what the hell you've been doing."

"Well, tell me what you've got there, Amanda, and where you got it," Dave replied. "And calm down, before somebody calls security to report a ruckus."

Amanda kept waving the papers at Dave, but lowered her voice a bit. "You know damn well what this is, Dave. It's a pool memo to Alex, dated yesterday, and it's headed 'ProVita versus Federal Trade Commission.' And it was sitting on Angie's desk, on top of some bench memos. So tell me why you wrote a memo on this case, when you know I wrote one for Alex. We discussed it at our meeting with him, remember?" Amanda's face was red, and Todd put a restraining hand on her arm, which she brushed away.

Before Dave could reply, Andy fixed a steely glare on Amanda and Todd. "You two sit down and shut up, before I really call security and tell them you stole something from Angie's desk." Amanda sputtered, but she and Todd sat down at their desks. "First of all, Amanda, tell us why you were rummaging on her desk."

"I was looking for one of my bench memos, because I decided to make some revisions before Alex read it," Amanda said.

"Pardon my language, Amanda, but that's bullshit," Andy said. "Angie came in here yesterday and asked if our first batch of bench memos were ready for Alex, and we all said yes. So she said she'd give them to Alex to take home, for him to read. Remember that, Amanda? You knew there weren't any bench memos on Angie's desk. You saw Dave's memo on her desk and picked it up, and I'm sure you read it before you barged in here, screaming at the top of your lungs."

"Well, I did see the memo when I passed Angie's desk, and I noticed the heading, and Dave's initials at the top," Amanda conceded. "So I glanced through it, and I saw the line on the last page." She flipped the copy to that page. "'I recommend that certiorari be denied,'" she read. "But my memo recommended a grant, and Alex agreed." Amanda turned to Dave. "So you haven't told me why you wrote another pool memo on my case."

"Sure, since you asked me so nicely," Dave answered, in a tone of obvious sarcasm. "After you presented your memo on the ProVita case at our meeting with Alex, I told him about your conversation with Todd about how the FTC and the Second Circuit failed to consider the costs of developing and marketing its subsidiary's drug in their rulings. Remember that, Amanda? I was right here and heard every word. What did you think I was, anyway, a potted plant?" Amanda didn't respond. "Those costs weren't in the case record," Dave continued, "but you found them somewhere, probably from a company insider, since they're proprietary information, and put them in your memo. Am I right?" Amanda remained silent. "So I told Alex your memo was biased and slanted in ProVita's favor, and that other justices who read it might think his clerks were incompetent. He asked me to prepare another pool memo, which I did, and which you lifted from Angie's desk."

Dave opened his desk drawer and pulled out a sheet of paper. "Now that I answered your question, Amanda, I've got some for you. These are yes-or-no questions, so don't give me any bullshit, okay? Or we'll call Alex and you can answer them for him. And speak up, you're on the record." Amanda looked to Todd, who was staring at the ceiling.

"Look at me, Amanda," Dave said in a prosecutorial tone. She did, with fear written on her face. "First question, yes or no. Are you related to a Carleton Cushing, of Greenwich, Connecticut?" She nodded. "The reporter can't hear you, Amanda. Yes or no?"

Amanda clearly knew what was coming. "Yes," she replied.

"Is he your father, yes or no?"

"Yes."

"And is he a director and major stockholder in the ProVita Pharmaceutical Company?"

"Yes."

Dave held out the sheet in his hand to Amanda, who took it. "This is a Securities and Exchange Commission Form 144, which you probably recognize," Dave continued. "Company directors are required to inform the SEC if they plan to sell restricted company stock, Amanda, which you probably also know. Was that form filed by your father, listing one hundred thousand shares of ProVita stock that he planned to sell?"

Todd broke his seemingly unconcerned silence. "Dave, this is ridiculous. Are you accusing Amanda of something illegal, or what?"

Andy answered for Dave. "Damn right, Todd, and you both know what it is. Amanda's expecting a cert grant in the ProVita case, with Alex behind it, and a reversal of the Second Circuit later on, also with Alex behind it. She's going to tip her dad in advance, and he's going to cash in that stock for millions, once the Court announces the cert grant and the stock price shoots up. But if the Court denies cert, and ProVita has to divest its subsidiary, the stock will go down like a lead balloon, and daddy loses millions."

Andy paused, while her words took their intended effect, which was evident on her fellow clerks' stricken faces. "Tipping your dad, Amanda, is insider trading, as you know, and could land both of you in prison. And Todd is an accomplice, no doubt about that, although he'd probably get a lighter sentence for letting you lead him around by the dick. And, when we tell Alex this sordid story, he'll fire your sorry asses. You'll lose your signing bonus with some big corporate firm, Amanda, and maybe, if you're lucky, find a paralegal job with some solo practitioner in East Armpit, Arkansas. And Todd can kiss his seat in the Virginia Senate goodbye, that daddy's keeping warm for him." Andy paused again, for effect. "That is, *if* we tell Alex, which is what I'm inclined to do. But Dave, who's more compassionate than me, has another sentence in mind. Right, Dave?"

Dave and Andy had discussed the possible scenarios of the Kimchi Plan at their first lunch meeting, and he quickly caught the ball she tossed him. "Well, I don't know about the compassionate part, since the stereotype you white folks have of us yellow folks isn't exactly what Buddha taught." Amanda and Todd gave him imploring looks, totally defeated.

"So, we're going to put you bungling crooks on probation," Dave continued. His expression was anything but compassionate. "With very strict conditions," he warned. "First, right after the long conference, and Alex confirms the cert denial, Amanda's going to call her crook daddy and tell him cert was granted. That's what you arranged, right?" She shook her head in a weak denial. Dave gave her a derisive laugh. "You've already been convicted, so cut the crap. You're going to make that call, from right here, on speaker-phone, and we're going to monitor it. Todd, you'll be right here, too, keeping your mouth shut. Any deviation from the script, and you're both out of here. Is that clear? Yes or no." A barely audible "yes" from Amanda, and a grudging head shake from Todd.

"Okay," Dave said. "Anything more, Andy?"

"Two more, Dave," she said. "First, we've got a month before the long conference. So, Dave and I are going to read and approve every pool memo and bench memo you write, before it goes to Alex. You'll make every change we require, no questions asked. Is that clear?" Andy accepted their head nods. "Second, you'll fetch coffee for us from the cafeteria, whenever we ask. Dave likes his black, I like a little cream and sugar. Is that clear?" Dave couldn't suppress a laugh.

"One last thing," Dave said. "Since we're being compassionate and putting you both on probation, we'll have to share this office for the rest of the year, unless you screw up and get fired. And if you do get fired, Andy and I would have to do the work of four people, unless Alex could find replacements, which might be hard this time of the year." Dave gestured to Andy. "We don't expect hugs of gratitude, but let's be civil with each other, okay? Remember, you're getting a break you don't deserve. Now, why don't you take the rest of the day off, go back to wherever you're shacking up, and reflect on your sins."

Dave gave them a dismissive wave, and they left the office, heads down.

"You did good, Dave, you did good," Andy said. "Let's go out and have a good lunch, my treat. But no kimchi."

"Great idea," he replied. "Actually, I like Italian, so how about Buon Appetito? It's just three blocks."

Thursday, September 28, was the date for the Court's long conference. Typically, it lasted until five or six in the afternoon. Novak would return to his chambers with a list of cert grants, and dole out cases for more bench memos before oral arguments were scheduled. All four clerks waited for the results, with not a word exchanged between them. Amanda left the office several times, Andy suspecting—even hoping—that she went to the ladies' room to throw up.

Just before six, Novak stuck his head in the door, holding a sheet of paper. "Hey, you all," he announced in a cheery voice, "the last precincts are counted, and the winners are . . ." He paused for effect. "Andy got her two grants, including the 'no habla Espanol' case, and Dave got the Idaho 'kissing cousin' case. By the way, two of my colleagues said they were persuaded by your pool memos, so I got to shine in your reflected glory." He glanced at the grant list, then at Amanda, whose face was pale. "Sorry to say, Amanda, but your drug company case got denied. But the Second Circuit always fares better than the Ninth, so don't feel bad." He gave Amanda a concerned look. "Are you feeling okay? Don't take it personally. At least you won't have to write a bench memo on the case." Novak glanced at his watch. "You guys have been here all day, and Gloria's waiting dinner for me, so let's punch the clock and scoot." He shot a knowing wink at Dave as he left the office.

The clerks waited until they heard the chambers door close behind Novak. Dave peered out the door to make sure Angie had left, then came back into the office, pulled his chair next to Amanda's desk, placed a sheet of paper on it, and slid her desk phone between them. "Okay, show time," he said. "You already rehearsed this, Amanda, so push the speaker-phone button, dial the number, and give daddy the good news. Bad news, really, but the only way for you and Todd to save your jobs."

Amanda's hands were shaking, and she made a final appeal for clemency. "But he'll find out I was wrong on Monday, and how will I explain that?"

Andy couldn't resist a final jab. "Amanda, you've been wrong since the day you got here, and so has Todd, who's an accomplice in your attempted crime. As for daddy, that's your problem. I'm not a family therapist, so deal with that yourself. So cut the whining and pick up the phone, Amanda. *Now!*"

Amanda flinched at this emphatic order, then pushed the speaker-phone button and punched in a number. The phone rang three times before a baritone voice filled the office.

"Hi, sweetheart. I knew it was you from the display on my phone. So, what's the news? I've got some people waiting to hear."

"Hi, daddy. It's good news. Justice Novak just got back from his conference, and ProVita got a certiorari grant. He said there were more than enough votes to reverse the Second Circuit when the case is decided." Dave nodded with satisfaction.

"That's great, sweetheart. From what you said, the market won't react until the order is announced on Monday, and it'll probably peak a few days later. But I think I'll hold on until it levels off before I cash out. It's at sixty-seven now, and my people think it'll go up fifteen, maybe twenty, within two days of the announcement. Listen, sweetheart, I've got some calls to make, but you did a great job. Say, why don't you and your friend go out for a steak at the Capital Grille. It's just down the Hill on Pennsylvania. I've got an account there, and the Delmonico is fantastic. Thanks again, that's just the news I was hoping for. Bye, sweetheart." The phone clicked off before Amanda could reply, and she put the receiver back in the base.

"That was great, sweetheart," Andy said with sarcasm. "Daddy's little girl. And fellow conspirator. And you, Todd, must be the friend who's in on this scam." Andy turned to her desk and pushed a button on her phone. "Hi, sweetheart," the baritone voice of Carleton Cushing boomed. "I knew it was you from the display on my phone. So, what's the news? I've got some people waiting to hear." Andy pushed a button, and the recording stopped. She pushed another button, and extracted a mini-cassette from the phone. Amanda and Todd both looked stunned.

"Right, you guys," Andy said. "It's all here on tape. No claims this conversation never happened. This tape, and the SEC form your dad filed, and a memo for Alex all go in here." She pulled a large padded envelope from her desk, and dropped the tape, form, and memo inside. Andy held up the envelope to show an address label. "This is going to a federal attorney," she said, "who will hold it for safekeeping, and possibly evidence." She had addressed the envelope to Josh, at his apartment. Andy hadn't told him yet about the Kimchi Plan, just in case it didn't work out, but was having dinner the next night with Josh and Carlo, and would explain it to them over Afghan food.

"Now go," Andy said, pointing to the door. "And thank your lucky stars that Dave is compassionate, because I'm not, when it comes to crooks like you. And, Amanda, if you call your dad before Monday, we'll find out and you're dead meat. Dave has ways of finding out that the NSA doesn't even know. Understand what I'm saying?" Amanda nodded, and left the office with Todd at her heels.

"Wow," Dave exclaimed. "That was a great idea, Andy, recording that on your phone. By the way, did you notice that dad said there were people waiting to hear the news? I'm betting this scheme has several partners, maybe other directors or Cushing's friends. I'm going to check for more Form 144s tomorrow. If I'm right, we might have to inform the SEC. I mean, Amanda and her dad are one thing, but this might be a conspiracy that goes beyond them. If that's true, I feel an obligation to let the SEC investigate, even if it means Amanda and her dad get charged. What do you think, Andy?"

"Hmm." Andy replied. "Let me think about that, Dave. Because if that gets out, and the SEC does charge people, it would make the news and Alex might get dragged in, maybe even questioned or suspected, since Amanda and Todd are his clerks. So, why don't you check the SEC filings, and we'll just wait to see how this shakes out next week. Is that okay with you?"

"That's fine with me," Dave said, then gave Andy a wide grin. "Tell you what. I seriously doubt our friends will be celebrating at the Capital Grille tonight, so let's go there for dinner, my treat. I hear the Delmonico is fantastic." They left the office just as the cleaners were coming in.

9

Andy dressed in her go-to-court outfit on Monday, since she was going to court that morning for the opening session of the October Term, always on the first Monday of that month. She was excited at her first opportunity to witness the Court in action, and planned to sit through the first oral argument, in a case that had drawn widespread media coverage and would pack the chamber with lawyers, reporters, and government officials.

It was a sunny, crisp, fall day, a respite from the steamy heat that had gripped Washington the past two months. As she neared the Court at eight-thirty, Andy could see the long line of people waiting for the door for visitors to open at nine-thirty, some of whom had been standing or sitting on the sidewalk for hours, hoping for seats close to the bench from which the justices would grill the lawyers who argued this morning's cases.

Flashing her laminated pass for Court staff at a guard who gave her a smile of recognition, Andy skipped the line and headed for the elevator, finding Dave Park already waiting, along with several other Court staff. "Hey, Andy," he said with a smile, "I see you're all decked out for the opening kickoff, although I'm going to skip it. But I found some interesting stuff on the SEC website, which I'll share with you later. Maybe lunch in the courtyard, after the morning arguments?"

"Sure, Dave," she replied, as the elevator door opened. "I'm just going to grab some briefs for the first argument and read them in the library. Hey, did you notice the TV crews out front, on the plaza? Must be a dozen cameras and reporters, waiting to pounce on the lawyers when they come out to predict their side will win. That first case might be one of the biggest for the whole term. Should be fun to watch and listen." When they reached Novak's chambers, Andy picked up the briefs from her desk and headed for the library. Reading them, she decided that both sides had strong arguments, and wondered how Justice Novak would vote. An hour later, she went back down and entered the courtroom through a side door reserved for staff and guests of the Justices.

Andy had been in the chamber once before, when Dick Wadleigh gave the new clerks a tour of the Court building. With no guards present, and with a Go Ahead nod from Dick, she had gone up the steps beside the curved mahogany bench, sitting for a minute in the center seat on which the Chief Justice sat during oral arguments, flanked on either side by four justices. By tradition, the most senior associate justice sat on the Chief's right, the next most senior on his left, then alternating by seniority, with the most junior justice to his far left.

Behind the bench were four marble columns, separated by burgundy velvet drapes that hung from the high ceiling. Below the bench, the Clerk's desk was to the Chief's left, along with a section of padded benches for staff and guests. The Marshal's desk was to the right, with seats for the press in a little balcony alongside it. Facing the bench was a long table for counsel arguing cases, centered with a lectern from which they addressed the justices. Four rows of seats behind the counsel table were reserved for members of the Supreme Court bar; there was an actual brass bar separating those with official status from three sections of benches, divided by two aisles, that seated about 250 spectators.

Andy had not expected the chamber of the nation's highest court to be so small—many courts had larger chambers—but the high ceilings and marble columns around the room gave it a grandeur that impressed her, and all who entered to attend its sessions.

This morning, the seats on both sides of the bar filled rapidly when the doors were opened at nine-thirty, with a hum of conversation and air of anticipation. Andy took a seat in the staff and guest section that gave her a view along the bench, from which the justices would be in profile. While she waited for the session to begin at ten, Andy wondered what Dave had found in the SEC filings, which she'd find out during lunch with him. She'd finally told Josh and Carlo, over dinner on Friday, about Amanda and Todd's scheme to secure a cert grant in the ProVita case, the Kimchi Plan she and Dave had devised, and Amanda's scripted call to her dad. Josh hadn't yet received the envelope Andy had mailed him Friday morning, but said he'd keep it securely locked in his desk in case she needed evidence of the attempted crime.

An ornate clock hung from the chamber's ceiling, behind and over the Chief Justice's seat on the bench. Andy glanced at it just as the hands reached ten, and was startled by the loud smack of a gavel from the Marshal's desk. "All rise," he commanded in a booming voice, as the center drape behind the bench parted and Chief Justice Terman emerged, followed by the associate justices, who stood with him behind their seats while the Marshal, a bald and stocky African American, intoned the traditional opening of every Court session, its words unchanged over more than two centuries:

"The Honorable, the Chief Justice and the Associate Justices of the Supreme Court of the United States. Oyez, oyez, oyez. All persons having business before the Honorable, the Supreme Court of the United States, are admonished to draw near and give their attention, for the Court is now sitting. God save the United States and this Honorable Court."

Andy felt goose-bumps on her arms at her first hearing of the words that linked the Court's past with the present. Scanning the chamber and smiling broadly, Terman said, "Please be seated, everyone," as he and the other justices took their seats. Looking both cherubic and avuncular, Terman scooted his high-backed leather chair closer to the bench and adjusted the microphone before him. "Good morning, ladies and gentlemen, and distinguished counsel," he said. "On behalf of the Court and my colleagues, I welcome you all to this opening session of our term. The arguments we will hear today are in cases that are both interesting and important." He paused for a second. "Of course, *all* the cases we hear are interesting and important, so I hope we'll see you all back here for the rest of our term." A round of chuckles from the audience followed Terman's tension-relieving levity, since few of those in the chamber would return for later sessions.

Terman glanced briefly at the lawyers seated at the counsel table. "We will hear argument first," he said, "in Khalid versus the United States. General Ewing, you may proceed wherever you're ready."

Andy recognized the man who picked up a binder from the counsel table and moved to the lectern at its center. Anthony Ewing, the Solicitor General of the United States, was attired for this first-of-the-term argument in the traditional dress of his office, worn by his predecessors for more than a century: a black morning coat, a grey ascot and vest over a white shirt, and black trousers with satin stripes down the legs. He was over six feet, and pushed a button on the lectern to raise it a few inches, while he opened his binder and cleared his throat.

"Mister Chief Justice, and may it please the Court," he began in another traditional opening. "The United States has petitioned this Court to reverse a decision of the Court of Appeals for the Sixth Circuit, which affirmed the award by a district court jury of six million dollars to the widow and minor children of Malik Khalid for his unfortunate death in Yemen. Their suit was brought under the federal Tort Claims Act, which provides that damages may be awarded for, and I'm quoting from the statute, 'personal injury or death, caused by the negligent or wrongful act of any employee of the Government while acting within the scope of his office.'"

Ewing glanced at his binder, then continued. "However, the Tort Claims Act contains an exception that bars suit, and I'm quoting again, for 'any claim arising in a foreign country.' It is that exception the United States urges the Court to apply in this case. Mr. Khalid's death, and the allegedly negligent and wrongful acts that preceded it, occurred in Yemen, not in the United States." Ewing paused and glanced at his binder. "I would first like to address this Court's precedents in this area, and then discuss . . ."

Before Ewing finished his sentence, Alex Novak leaned forward, speaking in a sharp voice. He held up a copy of the government's brief. "General Ewing, we are familiar with the statute, which is printed in your brief. And with this Court's precedents. There's no need to tell us what we can read for ourselves."

Ewing grimaced at this rebuke, as Novak continued. "The important thing in this case, General, are the facts, as found by the courts below. I take it you are familiar with the facts." Without waiting for a response, Novak went on. "Let me recite some of these facts, and ask if you dispute them."

From her seat, Andy could see the grim and determined look on Novak's face. He glanced at a sheet, then continued. "Malik Khalid is, or *was*, I should say, an American citizen who lived in Dearborn, Michigan. He was employed as an electrical engineer by General Motors. He regularly attended services at the Mecca Mosque in Dearborn. Two years ago, the FBI recruited an informant in the mosque, who reported on conversations he heard that might raise suspicions of possible terrorist activities."

Novak glanced briefly at the sheet before him, while Ewing stood silently. "The record also shows, General, that this informant reported overhearing a conversation at the mosque in which an unnamed person said something to the effect that 'Malik is making a timer,' and, later in the conversation, 'he's taking it to Yemen with him,' although the 'he' was not identified." Novak fixed Ewing with a steely glare. "Am I correctly quoting from the record, General?"

"You are, Justice Novak," Ewing replied, "but if I may . . ."

Novak interrupted again. "I'm not finished, General, and my question to you is based on the facts that are a predicate to that question."

At this point, Chief Justice Terman broke in, speaking in a placating tone, and without looking at Novak, who was two seats to his left. "The facts in this case, I might note, are also in the record before us. I assume General Ewing is familiar with them. And I assume his argument will relate to them."

From her seat, Andy noticed that Novak's face was reddening. He turned and looked directly at Terman. "General Ewing may be, Chief Justice, and I hope he is, familiar with the facts in this case. But I think the American people, and certainly those in our chamber, have a right to know these facts, and General Ewing's response to them. May I continue, briefly?" Terman nodded, very slightly, his lips pursed.

"Thank you, Chief Justice," Novak said, turning back to Ewing. "During the litigation of this case, General, certain FBI records were released, over the government's strenuous objection, I might note, and only in response to an order of the district judge." He picked up an inch-thick volume. "They are in the joint appendix to the briefs. May I direct your attention, General, to page twelve?" Ewing flipped through his binder, finding that page. He looked up and nodded to Novak.

"This is a memorandum from the Special Agent in Charge of the Detroit office of the FBI, to the Assistant Director in Washington. It's headed, 'Report of Confidential Informant, Re Malik Khalid.' I will read this excerpt, and then pose my question." Novak looked down at the page, reading from it. "'It has come to my attention that prior reports of this CI,' meaning Confidential Informant, 'are of questionable veracity. This CI has reported on conversations that further investigation has shown he could not have been present to witness. In addition, the CI could not verify that Malik Khalid was the person referred to in the conversation he reported hearing, and there are at least four men named Malik who attend this mosque. Further, the CI is known to belong to a tribe in Yemen that has a long-standing feud, sometimes violent, with the tribe to which Khalid's family belongs.'"

Novak looked down at Ewing. His voice rose, and his face reddened even more. "This is the informant, General, whose 'questionable' report was passed by the FBI to the Central Intelligence Agency, and was the basis for the CIA's plan to lure Mr. Khalid to Yemen, with a fabricated story that his mother was gravely ill, and target him for assassination while he was in Yemen. And he *was* assassinated, by a Hellfire missile, fired from a drone launched in Saudi Arabia, which hit the car in which he was riding from the Yemen capital to the village in which his mother lived." Novak paused. "*Did that in fact happen, General Ewing?*" he demanded, almost shouting at the Solicitor General.

All eyes in the chamber, including those of the Justices, swiveled from Novak to Ewing, who looked stunned. "Justice Novak," he stammered, "with all due respect, the government contends that Mr. Khalid's death was not an assassination, as you put it, but a targeted neutralization of a person the government had reason to believe was involved in an imminent terrorist plot to place a bomb on a commercial airliner, with a timing device supplied by Mr. Khalid. He was, the record shows, an electrical engineer with expertise in making such devices. We could not take the risk of a terrorist attack. To be frank, Justice Novak, it was a choice between one life and the deaths of possibly two or three hundred innocent people. Further, the order to launch the drone and fire the missile was given by a CIA officer in Saudi Arabia, who had the authority to abort the mission, which falls under the exception I previously quoted."

Novak leaned forward, shaking a finger at Ewing. "Targeted neutralization? That's a bureaucratic euphemism, General. Mr. Khalid was assassinated, plain and simple." His voice was dripping with sarcasm. "I assume you are familiar with the Fifth Amendment to the United States Constitution. It says, in case you need a refresher, that no person shall be deprived of life without due process of law. But Mr. Khalid was tried, convicted, and executed by our government without any charges against him, without a trial, on the basis of highly suspect information."

At this point, Chief Justice Terman broke in, turning toward Novak. "Justice Novak, please wait a minute. You are interrogating the Solicitor

General in what I consider an inappropriate, even insulting, manner. He deserves the respect of his office. And some of your colleagues, including myself, have questions for him. I think you've made your point, and should allow General Ewing to make his argument. General, you may have an additional ten minutes, and opposing counsel will as well."

Novak bulled ahead, ignoring Terman's effort to cut him off. "Chief Justice," he said, "allow me to ask my question, and I will yield once General Ewing gives us an answer, if he can." Novak leaned forward, almost over the bench. "Here's my question, General, and I want a straight answer." He spoke slowly, giving each word emphasis. "What legal authority gives the president, who personally approved this 'targeted neutralization,' as you put it, to ignore the plain command of the Constitution and order the assassination of an American citizen?"

Andy glanced at the dozen or so reporters in the press section, sitting directly across from her. They were scribbling furiously on their notepads. Novak's outburst, and Terman's rebuke of his colleague, would certainly lead their stories on the argument.

Before Ewing could answer, Chief Justice Terman uttered a guttural moan. His head lolled to his left. He slid slowly from his seat, and dropped from sight behind the bench.

A collective gasp of shock swept across the chamber. Every person in the courtroom, including the other justices, jumped to their feet, craning their heads to see if the Chief Justice would rise and resume his seat. A second later, the Marshal picked up his gavel and banged it, three times. "Please, everyone, please exit the chamber immediately," he said loudly. "Please, follow the instructions of the security staff. And all visitors, please exit the building through the main entrance, to your right, immediately. Please, follow the instructions and leave the building." Four uniformed members of the Court's police force, stationed on each side of the chamber and at the doors, began ushering spectators, many still looking back at the bench, out the rear doors. Andy and others in the staff and guest section left through the side door. Over the din as the evacuation proceeded, she heard the repeated words, "What happened?" "Is he all right?" "I can't believe this!" Before she reached the door, Andy looked back and saw Alex Novak lift his hands in supplication, then bury his face in them.

Andy skipped the buzzing crowd of staff at the elevator and took the stairs, two at a time, to the second floor, then ran down the hallway to Novak's chambers. As she entered, the pulsating wail of sirens grew louder. The door to Novak's office was open, and she rushed to the window behind his desk, spotting a red-striped ambulance, trailed by three D.C. police cars, swing around and disappear into the Court's underground garage.

She turned from the window as Dave Park rushed into the office. "Andy, what's going on? The argument can't be over yet. Were those sirens coming here? They just stopped. And people are running up and down the hall."

"Oh, Dave, it was terrible. Alex was yelling at the Solicitor General, and then the Chief Justice told him to stop, and then he collapsed and fell off his chair."

"Who fell off his chair? Alex?"

"No, the Chief Justice. He just moaned and then disappeared, and the Marshal told everyone to leave. And an ambulance just went into the garage."

"Oh, my God," Dave said. "Maybe he just fainted."

"I don't think so, Dave. That moan was really loud. I don't think people who faint sound like that. But I really don't know."

Just then, the wail of sirens began again. Andy and Dave went back to the window, as the ambulance and police cars sped from the Court, around the Capitol, toward Pennsylvania Avenue. Andy guessed they were heading for George Washington Hospital, a few blocks west of the White House. She realized that Carlo Abruzzi was on duty at the hospital. He'd told her, at dinner on Friday, that he was starting a rotation in the emergency room. If that was where the ambulance was taking Chief Justice Terman, maybe Carlo could tell her later what had caused him to collapse.

Turning from the window, Andy noticed the small flat-screen television on a shelf by Novak's desk. She picked up the remote beside it, and switched it on, just as Wolf Blitzer of CNN appeared on the screen, with a "Breaking News" banner behind him. Looking grave, Blitzer said, "We have breaking news from the Supreme Court. Shortly after ten o'clock this morning, Chief Justice Samuel Terman collapsed on the bench, during the fist oral argument of the Court's term. CNN has learned that he has been taken to George Washington Hospital, but we have no details of what might have caused his collapse, or his condition. Stay tuned and we will bring you updates as soon as they are available." The screen behind Blitzer flashed a picture of Terman, dressed in his black robe, smiling broadly.

Andy and Dave turned as Alex Novak ran into the office, his face flushed. "What did he say? What did he say about Sam?"

"Nothing yet, Alex," Andy replied. "He's at GW Hospital, and that's all they know right now."

"Oh, my God." Novak's voice quavered. "I did that. I should have kept my mouth shut. The SG was just so smug and arrogant. I just lost it. And Sam was so upset. I did that to him. You were there, Andy. You saw that. You heard me lose it."

Impulsively, Andy stepped toward Novak and hugged him, tightly. His body was shaking. "Alex, calm down," she said, firmly. "We don't know why Sam collapsed. Maybe he just fainted." Andy didn't think so, but felt compelled to ease his agitation. Novak stopped his shaking, and Andy released her hug.

CNN was still on the television, showing a reporter standing outside the emergency room entrance to GW hospital. Dave pushed the remote to raise the volume. "Wolf, the hospital has not yet released any details of Chief Justice Terman's condition, but a hospital spokesperson has informed us that doctors are treating him, and will give us a report within the hour. We have learned that President Chambers has been informed of the Chief Justice's collapse, and will make a statement to the press once the doctors have a report on his condition."

Just then, the phone in Andy's pocket dinged with a text message. She pulled it out, to see a message from Josh. "Carlo just texted me," it read. "He said, 'CJ died at 10:44. Probable heart attack.' Very sorry, Andy. Call when you can. Love you."

Andy held the phone in her hand, staring at the screen, in the initial stage of disbelief, but knowing it was true. "Dave, can you turn that off, please." He complied. "Alex, sit down." She took his arm and led him to one of the chairs around the low table. He sat, knowing from her voice and command that Andy's text message had news he didn't want to hear.

Andy sat in the chair next to Novak, reaching out and taking his hand. "Alex, that was a message from my friend Josh. His husband is a resident at GW hospital, on rotation in the ER, and he just texted Josh." She squeezed Novak's hand, firmly. "He's gone, Alex. Sam is gone. I'm so sorry. He was such a nice man." With that, Andy's eyes flooded and she began sobbing. Dave moved behind Novak and put a hand on his shoulder, as his body began heaving.

Angie came into the office, her eyes red. "Oh, Alex," she said. "I'm so sorry. I was in the Clerk's office, delivering some memos, and the television was on, and they said the Chief had died at the hospital, and I came right back." She sniffed, and dabbed her eyes with a handkerchief. She looked down at Novak, who was still holding Andy's hand. "The Chief was one of the nicest people I ever met," Angie said, her voice tinged with nostalgia. "I knew him even longer than you, Alex, from the day he came here as the new Chief, while I was working for Justice Carmichael. I remember the first thing he ever said to me. He came into the justice's office and said, 'You must be Angie. I've heard great things about you. I'm Sam Terman. Just call me Sam.' Oh, I'll miss him terribly, Alex, and I know you will, too." Angie sniffed again, then shook her head. "Alex, I just got a call from Justice Sorenson's office. The justices are all meeting in the conference room to draft a statement, and make some plans, I guess for what the Court will do the rest of the week. Charlotte didn't say. But they'd like you to come down."

Novak nodded, released Andy's hand, and stood up. "Thank you, Angie, and thank you, Andy and Dave." He scanned the office. "Do you know where Amanda and Todd are?" They all shook their heads. "I'd better get down there. I probably won't be back today. After our meeting, I'm going to go home, to be with Gloria and my dad, and then go see Barbara. But if Amanda and Todd come in, leave a note, Angie, that we'll meet here tomorrow at nine. And you can all take the rest of the day off. There's nothing that can't wait until tomorrow." He paused for a moment, then spoke with resolve. "But we *will* carry on. The Court will carry on. It always has, and always will." He left the office with a purposeful stride.

Andy and Dave stayed behind, exchanging inquiring glances. "The staff is meeting in the cafeteria, so I'm going down there," Angie said. "It's so sad, but Alex is right. We *will* carry on. And thank you both for being here. Alex is very fond of you." She left the office, and Andy and Dave heard the door close behind her.

"Andy, this isn't a good time for this," Dave said, "but we need to talk about Amanda and Todd, okay?" Andy nodded, and sat down in one of the chairs. "They didn't come in today. Maybe they skipped town, or maybe skipped the country and flew to some country without an extradition treaty. Who knows? But if they don't come in tomorrow morning, I'm really tempted to tell Alex the whole story. He'd probably fire their asses."

"Dave, I think you should tell Alex, if they don't show up," Andy said. "And I'm sure he would. I can get the envelope with the evidence from Josh, tonight, and bring it with me tomorrow. But if he does fire them, it'll just be you and me to do the work."

"Actually, I thought about that," Dave said. "The Chief Justice has four clerks. But with him gone, they won't have much to do until there's a new Chief, which might be months from now, and whoever that is might not keep them. Alex could have two of them transferred over here, at least during that time. I don't know if Alex would go for that, since I've met the Chief's clerks and they're all pretty liberal. But he might take pity on us, and get at least one as a short-term thing."

"Good idea, Dave," Andy agreed. "I really think Amanda and Todd should go. I mean, it really sucks to be working with two people we know are thieves and liars. Alex doesn't deserve that, and the Court doesn't either."

"Okay," Dave answered. "We'll see what happens in the morning. Oh, by the way, Andy, before you came running in here with terrible news, I checked the SEC website, and discovered that four people, two of them directors of ProVita, filed SEC forms to sell at least ten thousand shares each. So that makes a conspiracy, if the feds get wind of this. And we'll find out this week if any of these people actually sold the stock, because they have to file an SEC form reporting that within two days."

Dave pondered for a moment. "Or maybe, if you can put up with them being here, it's punishment enough that Daddy and his friends lose millions. All the insider trading cases I know of were against people who actually made money from tips, not people who lost money. Anyway, Alex has enough to deal with this week, so let's just wait and see how this plays out. Is that okay with you, Andy?"

"Sure," she replied. "So, Dave, are you taking off now? There's nothing much for us to do here, until we meet with Alex in the morning."

"Yeah. I'm heading over to the Emerald Isle, raise a pint of Guinness to the Chief, maybe two or three. Care to join me?"

"Thanks, Dave, but no. I'm going home to change, then over to Josh's place. We'll probably raise a glass of wine to the Chief, maybe two or three." Andy reached out and gave him a hug. "You know, Dave," she said, "I only met Sam four or five times, at Alex's barbeque, and when he invited me for tea and chit-chat in his chambers, but he was such a nice man. And despite their political differences, I could tell that Alex really loved him. Anyway, see you in the morning, Dave. As Alex said, we *will* carry on."

"Yes, we will," Dave replied. "See you in the morning." They left the office, headed for the elevator, and went their separate ways as they left the Court. As she began the walk to her apartment, Andy looked back at the building where many lives were changed, for better or worse. She'd arrived this morning, eager to witness the unchanged rituals of the Court, and the new issues it would decide. She left, just a few hours later, with the feeling that more lives, including hers, would soon change. For better or worse, Andy thought, was something yet to be determined.

When Andy got home, she clicked the small television on her bedroom dresser to CNN while she changed into jeans and a polo shirt. President Chris Chambers was at the lectern in the White House press room, an appropriately somber expression on his face. Andy sat on the end of her bed to watch. "Good afternoon," Chambers began, pretending not to be reading from the teleprompters to his left and right. "It is, I'm sorry to say, a very sad afternoon for me, and for the American people. The First Lady and I were deeply saddened to learn this morning of the untimely passing of the Chief Justice of the Supreme Court, Samuel Terman. He died, fittingly, and as he perhaps might have wished, presiding over the Court he led with distinction for the past thirteen years. Having served in all three branches of government, at both the state and federal levels, Chief Justice Terman brought to the Supreme Court a wealth of experience that informed his many landmark decisions, and that affected the lives of every American."

Chambers paused, seemingly affected by emotion, a practiced trait of most seasoned politicians. "However," he continued, "I want to assure you that the business of the Court will continue while my staff and I begin the sad and difficult task of selecting, and presenting to the Senate for confirmation, a nominee to replace the Chief Justice. I will make this choice carefully and with all necessary deliberation, and cannot yet predict how long that process will take. The First Lady and I extend our deepest sympathy and condolences to the Chief Justice's widow, Barbara, and to his family. God bless them, and God bless the United States."

With that, Chambers picked up the sheet of paper from the lectern that he had not glanced at, and left the podium, ushered through the door to his left by a brace of Secret Service agents. Andy thought, cynically, that Chambers might as well have been reading from his lunch menu, despite his faux show of emotion.

The screen shifted to the CNN studio in Washington, where Wolf Blitzer sat across a curved desk from Jeffrey Toobin, the network's resident legal pundit. Andy decided to hear his prognostication before she finished dressing and went over to Josh's apartment. "Jeff," Blitzer began, "as the president just said, the death of Chief Justice Terman was certainly untimely, coming as it did on the first day of the Supreme Court's new term. Let me first ask you, how will the Court deal with the loss of its Chief, in terms of the cases now on its docket?"

"Good question, Wolf," Toobin answered. "The Court can function and decide cases with as few as six justices, which is a quorum under its rules. So the justices will most likely continue to hear arguments, after the Chief Justice is laid to rest, and decide cases. However, Wolf, it's no secret that Chief Justice Terman was the leader of a five-justice liberal majority on the Court, which has voted together on almost every important case for several years, with four conservatives in the minority. So, if the Court does decide the major cases on its docket, there's likely to be a four-to-four tie vote on those cases."

"What happens in case of tie votes, Jeff?" Blitzer asked.

"Well, it means the decision of the court below, state or federal, is affirmed, but without a written opinion and without setting any binding precedent. Or, if there is a tie vote in the justices' private conference, after the oral argument, they can decide to set the case for re-argument, after a new Chief Justice takes his or her seat. Both of these options have happened in the past, Wolf, when there was a vacancy on the Court."

"Jeff, let me ask you about the president's choice as the new Chief Justice," Blitzer said. "Do you have any guesses who that might be?"

"To be honest, Wolf, I don't. Of course, nobody anticipated Chief Justice Terman's death, especially at the beginning of a new term for the Court. That said, President Chambers has two options. One, he could elevate a sitting justice to the center seat, as we call the Chief's position. That would give the president the chance to nominate someone from outside the Court to replace that justice. Or, two, he could choose someone from outside the Court to replace the Chief, leaving the eight present justices in place. Again, Wolf, past presidents have exercised both options, and we have no idea which the president will choose. The bottom line, however, is that the new Chief Justice will certainly be more conservative than Chief Justice Terman, and that will shift the Court's balance, and its voting alignments, to the right."

"One final question, Jeff," Blitzer said. "Senator Charter Weeks, the New Hampshire Democrat who chairs the Senate Judiciary Committee, issued a brief statement just a few minutes ago, saying that he hopes, and expects, the president to nominate a candidate who is in the, quote, 'judicial mainstream, and not the far-right extreme.' Does that put any constraints on the president, Jeff, since the Democrats control the Senate?"

"That's hard to say, Wolf," Toobin replied. "It depends how you define 'mainstream.' Certainly, the president remembers the Senate's rejection of Robert Bork in 1987, when he was perceived, quite rightly, in my opinion, as far too extreme in his judicial views, especially his stated opposition to abortion rights. So, the president will likely choose someone more moderate than Bork, and who can gain confirmation with at least some votes from Senate Democrats. Right now, however, it's impossible to say who that might be."

"Thanks very much, Jeff, as always, for your views on this breaking news," Blitzer said. With that, Andy clicked off the set. She hadn't learned anything from Toobin, she thought, that she didn't already know. But neither did most other people in Washington, as the Who Will It Be? guessing game began.

Andy finished dressing, putting on her Dave Matthews Band sweatshirt for the chilly day, and headed over to Josh and Carlo's apartment. On the way, she texted Josh, telling him she was coming and asking when he'd be home from his office in Alexandria. He texted back that he'd be home about six, and that Carlo would be on duty in the ER until midnight. When Andy got there, she let herself in with the key Josh had given her, opened a bottle of Italian pinot grigio from Carlo's wine collection, and had two glasses, after popping a Dave Matthews CD into the player. After Josh arrived, they sat on the couch, mostly in silence, Andy's head on his shoulder, finishing that bottle and then another. It had been a day, Andy thought, that gave new meaning to Josh's favorite word: indeterminacy.

10

The weather matched Andy's mood as she walked from her apartment to the Court on Tuesday morning: overcast, blustery, with a promise of rain to come later in the day. For the first time since beginning her clerkship in July, Andy did not look forward to what she knew would be a difficult time for everyone at the Court. She was particularly concerned about Alex Novak, knowing both his close friendship with Chief Justice Terman and the feeling he'd expressed to Andy that his outburst at Solicitor General Ewing had triggered the Chief's fatal heart attack.

The tall, grey-haired, African American guard at the Court's entrance, Clarence Owens, wore a strip of black tape around the shield on his uniform, and greeted Andy with a nod of recognition, instead of his usual cheerful "Good morning, young lady." She knew that the Chief had called all the Court staff, even the janitors, by first name, and traded banter with them about their kids, the weather, and sports, and they all treated him like a favorite uncle.

Andy stopped for a moment, and impulsively gave Clarence a hug. "We're all going to miss the Chief, Clarence," she said, "and I just hope the new Chief will be as kind and thoughtful as he was." Clarence gave Andy a wan smile. "Thank you, Miss Andy. I hope so, too, but there won't be another Chief that's, you know, such a regular person. Nobody to say, 'Hey, Clarence, how's Marvella? She keeping you out of trouble?' There's some around here, I won't mention any names, who don't even say hello or anything." Clarence brightened. "Your Justice Novak, though, he's a regular person too. You think maybe he'll be the next Chief? That would be good for all of us here."

"Oh, I don't know, Clarence," Andy replied. "That's up to the president, and it's too early to know what he'll decide. Anyway, we'll all carry on, even though it's not going to be the same without the Chief. You take care, Clarence, and stay out of trouble."

"I'll do my best, Miss Andy. And thanks for cheering me up."

Andy entered Novak's chambers to see Angie Conforti in Novak's office, placing a bouquet of white roses into a vase on his low table. "Good morning, Andy," she said, her eyes still red. She gestured at the roses. "The Chief always had a vase of these in his office, and I thought Alex might find them comforting."

"That's very thoughtful, Angie," Andy said. "He wanted to meet us here at nine, and I'm a bit early. Do you know if Amanda and Todd got your note, and are coming in?"

"I did get a phone message from Amanda, that she left last night," Angie replied. "She said she's not feeling well, but she and Todd will be here by nine."

I bet she's not feeling well, Andy thought. And I bet I know why, and it's not because the Chief died. Just then, Dave came into Novak's office. "Morning, Angie. Morning, Andy," he said. "Oh, those roses are so pretty, Angie. I know why you put them there, and Alex will be touched."

"Thank you, Dave," Angie said, returning to her desk.

"We've got a few minutes before Alex gets here," Dave said to Andy, speaking quietly. "We can talk more later, but here's the latest news." She looked at him, expectantly. "Okay, the order list was posted yesterday morning at nine-thirty, before the Chief collapsed. Every broker was waiting for it, since the Wall Street Journal had predicted a cert grant. And ProVita closed on Friday at seventy-one, up four points from Thursday. So, guess what?"

"Um," Andy said, "it went down yesterday. Am I right?"

"Good guess," Dave said. "It went down so far, hitting fifty-three by noon, that the Exchange suspended trading. We won't know until tomorrow, on the SEC website, if Amanda's dad and his crooked buddies sold before noon, but I'm estimating that he, personally, lost roughly two million, and the rest lost that much, between them. And, if they didn't sell yesterday, the stock they have is now worth that much less, anyway. So, they're screwed either way."

"Can't say I feel sorry for them," Andy said. "Or for Daddy's little sweetheart. I mean, they won't be applying for food stamps, but maybe the new Bentley will have to wait."

"Ow, that's cold, Andy," Dave said with a grin. "I'm sure Carleton had already ordered the Bentley, with his ill-gotten gains."

They were interrupted by voices in the outer office. Novak was comforting Angie, assuring her that he was alright, in tones that didn't sound alright. He came into his office, greeted Andy and Dave with a subdued "Good morning," noticed the vase of roses on the table, then went back out and thanked Angie, who sniffled and then blew her nose, quietly.

Novak came back into his office, looking drawn and tired, which didn't surprise Andy. "Angie says Amanda and Todd called and will be here shortly," he said. "But I have a request for you two. I've noticed lately that both of them seem to be bothered by something, probably personal. I know they're living together, that's pretty obvious, since they usually come in and leave together, and maybe they're having relationship problems. But whatever it is, they're both turning in pool memos late, and the ones I've gotten from them are, to be honest, pretty thin, both in length and substance. And that concerns me, since my colleagues will know they came from my chambers."

Andy and Dave just nodded, fully aware of what really bothered their fellow clerks. "So," Novak continued, "could you both sort of keep your eyes and ears open, and let me know what's going on with Amanda and Todd, if you can? And can you also, and I know this is an imposition, get their memos from Angie and look them over? Hopefully, even with Sam's death, they'll work out whatever it is and get back on track. Is that okay with you?" They both nodded agreement, without telling Novak they were already doing that. Novak brightened. "I've got two Redskins tickets for Dave to the 'Niners game on Sunday, and a Dave Matthews concert at Wolf Trap next week for Andy and her friend Josh."

"Wow," they both said in unison. "How did you know, Alex?" Andy asked.

"Oh, I have sources around here," he replied. "Actually, Angie overheard you talking, and wishing you could get tickets. And she knows I can get tickets to just about anything. But you both deserve a small reward for doing such great jobs."

"Thank you, Alex," they both said in unison.

Novak checked his watch, just as Amanda and Todd came into the office. "I'm sorry we're late," Amanda said to Novak. "And I'm sorry we didn't come in yesterday. I had a twenty-four-hour stomach bug of some kind, but I'm feeling better now."

Andy couldn't resist her impulse. "Well, it's been a rough twenty-four hours for all of us, Amanda. We're glad you're feeling better, but you should both take it easy. There's only a few pool memos to work on, and Dave and I can handle those." Andy had retrieved the ProVita evidence envelope from Josh's apartment the night before, and placed it casually on the low table. Amanda looked down for a second, then shot Andy a malevolent glare, which Andy returned with a benign smile.

Novak had turned to his desk, picking up some papers, and missed this exchange. Turning back, he said, "Sit, everyone. And thanks, Andy. I agree that Amanda and Todd should take it easy, maybe go back home and drink some hot tea with lemon, and have some toast, light with the butter. That's the best cure for the twenty-four-hour bug, and what my mom always gave me."

They all sat, as Novak handed each clerk a sheet of paper. "Okay," he said. "Here's a list of the cases that were scheduled for argument this week and next. We met briefly yesterday and decided to reschedule them all for the following two weeks, which would have been our normal break between argument sessions. The lawyers have all been prepping for weeks, and we figured it would be unfair to push them further back. So, there's twelve arguments coming up, and I'd like each of you to take three and make sure the bench memos are ready by next Friday. Dave, could you look over the list and parcel them out?" Dave nodded his agreement. "Other than that," Novak continued, "there's cert petitions still coming in, and pool memos to write, but nothing pressing the rest of this month. No decisions yet, of course, and no opinions to draft."

Novak paused, and glanced at each clerk in turn. "I said yesterday that we will carry on. It's what Sam would have wanted, and what the Court deserves. I know it'll be hard, at least for a while, but I have confidence you guys can keep everything going. And help each other out. Okay?" He glanced at his watch, again. "We're all meeting in a few minutes to make some more arrangements. Justice Sorenson is the senior associate justice, and he'll preside when we hear arguments and at our conferences. His office will call Angie if there's anything we need to know. Now, I strongly suggest that Amanda and Todd go back home and have that tea and toast. And, Andy, can you stay for just a minute?" Amanda flinched, looking at the envelope on the table, with a fearful expression, then left the office with Todd, who hadn't said a word, and Dave, who gave Andy a See You Later look.

"Andy, there's a couple of things to tell you before I go down to the conference room," Novak said. "First, I wanted to thank you for being so supportive yesterday, and helping me calm down. You seem to have a knack for knowing how to help people who are having a hard time. That made a big difference, Andy." He reached out and took her hand. Andy returned his squeeze, and Novak released her hand.

"Also, I went to see Barbara last night, and she told me that Sam's doctor had warned him that he was a prime candidate for a heart attack. He had high blood pressure, was overweight, didn't get enough exercise, and had a family history of coronary disease. His dad died of a heart attack at fifty-three. So, Barbara told me not to feel responsible for Sam's death. It could have happened anytime. That made me feel a little better, although I do regret my outburst yesterday. I called Tony Ewing and apologized, and promised not to ask any questions when the case is reargued, and he assured me there were no hard feelings."

Novak picked up his briefcase from the desk. "One thing more, Andy. Barbara told me that Sam had mentioned the old Brooklyn ties between your families, and that he'd taken a shine to you, as he put it. Turns out, according to Barbara, that Sam's father and your grand-father were actually distant cousins, back in Russia. So, she asked me to give you an invitation to his funeral service on Friday, and to sit with her and the family. It's going to be at Temple Shalom in Chevy Chase at eleven, and I'd be glad to pick you up at ten at your place and give you a ride there and back. If that's okay with you." He looked at her, expectantly and with a bit of apprehension. "Gloria and my dad aren't going," he added. "They're going over to visit with Barbara tonight, but Gloria doesn't feel comfortable at funerals. She gets tired very easily, and doesn't like having too many people around. Although she'd love to see you again, and take a gallery tour."

"That's very nice, Alex," Andy said. "I'm touched by Barbara's invitation, and please tell Gloria I'm sorry we haven't visited any galleries yet, and I'll call her and arrange one soon. And ten on Friday is fine. I appreciate your offer, Alex."

"Great," he said. "And maybe you can tell me what to do at a Jewish funeral. I haven't been to one for years, but I still have a yarmulke. When I take people who aren't Catholic to services at Saint Anthony's, I give them a nudge when it's time to kneel, or stand up, or pretend to be singing. So you can nudge me at the appropriate times, okay? Anyway, I don't want to keep my colleagues waiting. And thanks again, Andy."

The chime by Andy's front door rang at precisely ten on Friday morning. She pushed the button for the intercom and said, "Right on time, Alex. I'll be down in thirty seconds."

"Good morning, Andy," he replied. "Take your time. I'm parked right in front."

Andy had dressed for Chief Justice Terman's funeral in a black, mid-calf dress her grandmother Bella had bought for her years earlier at a second-hand clothing store called "From Hers to Yours," telling Andy that "Every girl needs a tasteful black dress, just in case you go to a funeral." She'd never worn the dress, and this was her first funeral since her grandfather, and Bella's husband, Milton Warshofsky, had died while Andy was in high school. She added a pair of plain black flats, a black lace scarf that came with the dress, and around her neck a small, gold Star of David on a thin, gold chain that her parents had given Andy for her bat mitzvah when she turned thirteen. She rarely wore the necklace, but thought it appropriate for this occasion.

Andy laughed when she saw Novak standing by his black Lexus, looking like a chauffeur in a black suit, white shirt, and black tie, with a white silk yarmulke perched crookedly on his head. "Morning, Andy. This damn thing won't stay on straight," he said. "You think I should just stick it in my pocket?"

"Here, let me fix that," Andy said. She opened her small black purse and dug out some bobby pins, fastening the yarmulke to his dark hair. "There, that should hold it, unless this wind turns into a gale."

"Todah rabah," Novak replied, as he held the car door for her.

"You're welcome, Alex," Andy exclaimed with surprise. "I didn't know you speak Hebrew. Are you sure you're not Jewish?"

Novak laughed. "No, I was raised a good Catholic boy, but I picked up some basic phrases when I visited Israel a few years ago, to meet with judges on their courts. Like 'shalom' for hello and goodbye, and 'eifo hasherutim' for 'where's the bathroom.'"

Andy laughed again. "Wow, even your accent is good. I only learned enough in Hebrew school to read the Torah verses for my bat mitzvah. Did you have to learn any Latin for your first communion?"

"Andy, that's all been in English for decades, although some parishes still have Latin masses for the old folks who never adjusted to Vatican Two. And you don't read anything for first communion or confirmation." Novak chuckled with recollection. "One thing I remember vividly is when a bunch of us boys were preparing for our confirmation when we were fourteen. Father Jim was drilling us on Bible verses, and he read one that said, 'Be fruitful, and multiply.' He asked what it meant, and being the smart-aleck I was, I waved my hand and said, 'I know, Father Jim! I had an apple for lunch, and two times two is four.' The other boys cracked up, and even Father Jim laughed. But some kid snitched on me, and Sister Veronica, our principal, gave me twenty Hail Mary's for penance."

This light-hearted conversation ended when they reached Temple Shalom, where an attendant waved Novak into a parking area reserved for dignitaries. Andy noticed a covey of Secret Service agents, sent to protect Vice President Gordon Barnstead. President Chris Chambers had announced, professing regret, that a long-scheduled meeting with Caribbean prime ministers would keep him away. Barnstead, winner of the consolation prize as runner-up to Chambers in the presidential primaries, seemed to spend much of his time filling in for the president at funerals, and otherwise attracted little attention from the media. A recent poll showed that only fourteen percent of the public could name the current second-in-line to the Oval Office. Under watchful eyes, Andy and Novak were ushered into the Temple and escorted to the front row. The sanctuary was filling with guests, dignitaries, and members of the congregation of which Terman had been a long-time member. Late-morning sunlight streamed through six translucent windows behind the dais, and twelve cedar columns ringed the sanctuary.

Novak guided Andy to a woman, short and stout, with curly grey hair and twinkling eyes, who rose and gave Novak a hug, then said to Andy, "I'm Barbara Terman, and you must be Sam's great-niece, Andy Roboff."

"I'm so sorry we lost your husband, Mrs. Terman," Andy said. "I didn't get to know him very well, just chatting over tea a few times, but he was such a kind and thoughtful man. And a great Chief Justice."

"Thank you, Andy. Sam told me about your tea-times, and what a bright young woman you were, and knew so much about art, which Sam loved. And you're part of our family, so please sit with us and I'll introduce you to Sam's sister, Miriam, and my brother, Howard, and their spouses and kids." While Barbara made the introductions, Novak excused himself, moving to a row of seats on which his fellow justices were chatting.

The sanctuary quieted when a woman in a black robe, with a sky-blue stole around her shoulders and down her front, walked across the dais and stood behind a lectern that was carved with vines and grapes. She was in her late thirties, Andy guessed, with wavy brown hair much like hers. "Welcome to Temple Shalom," she began. "For those who don't know me, I'm Lisa Margolis, the senior rabbi of a congregation that Sam Terman loved, and that loves him. We all mourn Sam's passing, but this is not a sad occasion, but a celebration of the life of a wonderful and wise man. As we say in Hebrew, 'L'Chaim,' to life, Sam's and ours, and the enduring legacy he left us, with service as Chief Justice of the United States, but also service to all of this great nation's citizens. Every decision Sam made for the Court, and every gesture of warmth and acceptance he made to persons high and low, rich and poor, of every race and religion, is what binds us all in remembrance of his life."

The rabbi paused. "Before we begin, I would like to welcome—but with no applause, please—Sam's colleagues on the Court, the chief justices of Canada, Mexico, Great Britain, France, and Israel, and fifty of fifty-three of Sam's present and former law clerks." Two seconds passed. "And the Vice President of the United States, Gordon Barnstead." Three seconds passed. "President Chambers, as you may know, had a prior engagement." Everyone, including Andy sensed the rebuke behind this last comment.

"This is a Jewish temple," Rabbi Margolis continued, "but this is an ecumenical celebration. Sam knew and admired, and was admired by, clergy of all faiths in this area. So I would like to join me the Archbishop of Washington, Terrance O'Malley, Metropolitan Alexi of St. Gregory's

Greek Orthodox Cathedral, Imam Ibrahim al-Fawzi of the Washington Islamic Center, Reverend Betsy Peterson of the Metropolitan Community Church, and Reverend Cleophus Aiken of the Mount Moriah African Methodist Episcopal Church, all of them friends of Sam Terman." As she named each clergy, they came up and flanked the rabbi. Each was in clerical garb, with Reverend Peterson, pastor to a largely gay and lesbian congregation, wearing a robe in rainbow colors, standing between the white-robed Archbishop and the black-robed Metropolitan.

"We will all participate in reading from the Book of Psalms," Rabbi Margolis continued. In turn, beginning with her, each clergy recited a verse:

"Righteousness and justice are the foundation of thy throne; Lovingkindness and truth go before thee; How blessed are the people who know the joyful sound; I will sing of the lovingkindness of the Lord forever. The Lord will deliver the needy when he cries for help; The afflicted also, and him who has no helper; He will have compassion unto the poor and needy; And the lives of the needy he will save; He will rescue their life from oppression and violence; And their blood will be precious in His sight."

As the clergy took seats behind the rabbi, she said, "I will read a verse from Deuteronomy that I think exemplifies Sam's life: 'Justice, and only justice, you shall pursue, that you may thrive and occupy the land that the Lord is giving you.'" She paused. "The point of justice is that all the Lord's children may thrive in this land, and this world, and sit together at the welcome table."

At this point, a gospel choir of twenty red-robed men and women from Mt. Moriah AME Church paraded down the center aisle, clapping their hands and singing: "All God's children gonna sit together, one of these days, Hallelujah! I'm gonna tell God how you treat me, one of these days, Hallelujah! I'm gonna sit at the welcome table, one of these days, Hallelujah." By the time the choir reached the front, and turned to face the sanctuary, everyone was clapping and singing each verse, repeated until a final, shouted, "Hallelujah, Lord!"

Rabbi Margolis then delivered a brief but moving eulogy, pointing out all the times Sam Terman had reached out to help those in need, both of justice in his Court, and sustenance in his community. She was followed by the Temple's cantor, Rabbi Bernard Katzman, singing a slow but powerful rendition of Albert Malotte's hymn, The Twenty-Third Psalm. "I send you out," Rabbi Margolis concluded, "with the words inscribed on the arks behind me that hold our three Torahs: Emet, Din, and Shalom. Truth, Justice, and Peace."

As the congregation rose, Secret Service agents hustled Vice President Barnstead out a side door. Andy turned to Barbara and said, "That was a beautiful service. Did you arrange it with the rabbi?"

"No, dear," Barbara replied. "Sam did that himself, a couple of years ago. The clergy are all people he wanted to participate in this service, and the verses they spoke are ones he particularly liked, and often recited in speeches he gave."

"That was very moving," Andy said. "And thank you for inviting me to sit with your family."

"No, Andy," Barbara said. "It's your family, too, and you're always welcome in everyone's home." She gave Andy a hug.

Alex Novak came over, and gave Barbara a hug. "Barbara, I have never attended a more moving service in my life. I have much to think about, and much to be thankful for, knowing how Sam touched and cared for so many people. And thanks for inviting Andy, who has also given me much to think about."

"Shalom, Alex, and shalom, Andy," Barbara said. "And thank you both for being here."

The drive back to Andy's place passed in silence. Novak seemed pensive and somber, and Andy left him to his thoughts. She had her own thoughts, which centered on the clergy Sam had invited—planning his own funeral service in advance—to participate in this celebration of his life. She was struck by the image of the rainbow-robed Reverend Betsy Peterson, pastor to gays and lesbians who had often been shunned by churches that considered them sinful, standing between a Catholic archbishop and Orthodox prelate, all of them clapping and singing along with descendants of African slaves who looked forward to the time when "all God's children gonna sit at the welcome table, one of these days." But the tables on which many Christian churches—more than just Catholic and Orthodox—placed the bread and wine of their sacraments still did not welcome the people who worshipped at Reverend Peterson's church. Of course, Andy thought, the orthodox branches of Judaism and Islam still excluded gays and lesbians, and relegated women to the separate and unequal status against which America's civil rights movements—suffragettes, sit-in protesters, and the Stonewall rioters—had fought against people who invoked God's blessing for their bigotry.

Lost in her thoughts, Andy was startled when Novak pulled up in front of her apartment building. "Here we are," he said. "I'm glad you came with me, and got to meet Barbara, and Sam's family."

"Alex, if you're not due someplace else," she asked, "would you like to come up for a bit and unwind with me? I could use a little unwinding, and I've got some wine that might help with that." Andy hadn't planned this invitation, and was nervous about asking, but sensed that Novak might welcome a chance to relax, after the emotional experience of Sam's service.

"Well, the Court's closed today," he replied, "and Gloria and my dad are spending the afternoon with her friend Margery, so a bit of unwinding sounds great. I can't stay long, but a glass of wine, or maybe two, would certainly help with that."

Novak parked in an open spot down the block, and followed Andy to her apartment. Once inside, she gestured to her couch. "Make yourself comfortable, Alex," she said, "and take off your jacket and that horrible black tie. It makes you look like a chauffeur, or an undertaker."

He laughed. "Gloria made me wear this outfit. In fact, I told her it makes me feel like a pallbearer, but she said I was going to a funeral, not a party. Although Sam's service really was a kind of party, especially with the singing and clapping. So, I'll shed the jacket and tie. And, can I give you a hand with anything?"

"Thanks, Alex, but this will just take a minute. I've got some Beringer chardonnay, and some Colby cheese and sesame crackers to absorb the wine. That sound okay?"

"Perfect. Beringer is my wine of choice, and you've got my favorite cheese and crackers."

Andy fetched the wine, glasses, and a tray of cheese and crackers from her kitchen, and put them on the coffee table in front of the couch. She handed a corkscrew to Novak. "I always screw this up, literally, so could you uncork the bottle?" He did this deftly, filled both glasses, and clinked them.

"L'Chaim," Novak said. "To Sam, and his life."

"L'Chaim," Andy repeated. "To all our lives."

They settled on the couch, then Andy jumped up. "Alex, I got you out of that black jacket and tie, so I'm getting out of my black dress. Be right back."

She returned in a minute, dressed in jeans and a white tee-shirt. "That's better," she said. "It's hard to unwind in funeral garb."

Novak smiled. "Much better. And I'm already a little unwound."

Andy suddenly realized that, as she usually did at home, she'd slipped on her tee-shirt without a bra, and that her bralessness was obvious. Oh, shit, she thought. Alex probably thinks I'm coming on to him. And I can't run back and put one on. So don't do anything provocative.

Novak took a sip of his wine, then surprised Andy. "You know," he said, "I was thinking about all those pastors up with the rabbi. Sam knew all of them, and they were all his friends. And I don't know any of them. I chatted briefly with Archbishop O'Malley at some White House reception, but that's it. So I was thinking, what does it mean that Sam knew all those pastors, and I don't know any?"

Andy didn't know if Novak was asking her a question, or posing one to himself. She decided to wait for some clue to his thinking.

He didn't wait for an answer from Andy, pausing a moment and pursing his lips. "What I think it means is that Sam didn't stay boxed up in his role as Chief Justice. He got out, and made it a point to meet and get to know all kinds of people. And, by getting to know these people, and I'm not just talking about pastors, he got to understand what they believe, and how they act on these beliefs. You know what I mean, Andy?"

"I think so," she replied, deciding not to derail Novak's train of thought.

"That doesn't mean Sam agreed with their beliefs," Novak continued, "or agreed with how they acted on them. But he did get a broader perspective on things than most people, including me, I guess." He paused, put a piece of cheese on a cracker, and munched it while Andy wondered where he was going. She took a sip of wine and waited for direction.

"So, Andy," he said, "I was thinking, on the way back from the service, that unlike Sam, I've lived all my life in two boxes. One was the Catholic school box, from grammar school to Notre Dame. Then the law box, from Harvard until now. And they're probably connected in some way.

You know, dogma and doctrine aren't that different. Follow them, or risk some penalty, whether it's hell, or writing an opinion that gets ripped up and overruled in the next case."

Novak went on. "I've been thinking about the people I know pretty well, people I can talk with about things outside the law box. And there aren't many." He paused and shook his head. "Ninety percent of the people I know well, at least that many, are people on the Court, other judges, and lawyers. And most of them don't talk much about things outside the law box."

Andy sensed some kind of transformation, or molting, going on inside the person sitting next to her, sipping wine and thinking out loud. But she couldn't be sure of this.

Novak suddenly turned to Andy. "But, you know, Andy, I'm so stuck in my boxes, and have been for so long, that even if the dogma and the doctrine don't seem to provide the right answers to questions, all I can do is what I think best. And I'm not always sure what that is. You know what I mean?"

"I think so," Andy said again. She decided to see if Novak was actually going somewhere, or just in circles that had no end point. "Let me ask you something, Alex. Okay?"

"Of course," he replied. "I'm sorry this has turned into a monologue. And I hate monologues."

"Well, this may seem off the point, Alex, but I took a class in cultural anthropology at Barnard. Really fascinating. Anyway, one of the things our professor had us do was to pick a country, as unlike ours as possible, and imagine you were born in a small village in that country. Say, China, or Saudi Arabia, or Cameroon. Okay? And then we wrote a paper that described who we were, what our parents did, what schools we went to, what church we attended, and what occupation we had as adults. And then what we believed about religion, politics, relations with the opposite sex, and what we thought about Americans."

"Wow," Novak exclaimed. "That *is* fascinating. So what country did you pick?"

"I picked Saudi Arabia," Andy said. "And I wound up as a Muslim, as a girl with very little education, possibly married to a guy with three other wives, wearing a burka in public, unable to drive a car, and thinking Americans were the devil." Andy paused a moment. "Of course, every culture has people who break away from the norm, and some even leave, but most stay in the boxes they were born into and raised. And the ones who live outside their boxes are often treated like lepers, or even worse."

Andy noticed, from the sudden lifting of his eyes and his smile, that Novak had noticed her bra-less state, which was obvious from the nipple bumps pushing against her tee-shirt. Oh, shit, she thought. Did I mean for him to notice? No, I didn't. But we can't go there. Not with Gloria being such a wonderful person, even in a wheelchair. Andy tried to banish those thoughts.

"Hey, I've got a hypo for you, Alex," she said brightly. "Let's say you were born in a Jewish neighborhood in Brooklyn, your parents were immigrants from Russia, you went to Hebrew school, you had a bar mitzvah when you were thirteen, your dad ran a hardware store, and you knocked on doors for Democrats at election time. Who would you be now?"

Novak laughed. "I'd be Sam Terman, right? Or his twin brother. And I'd think Alex Novak was a misguided conservative. Nice guy, but stuck in his boxes." He chuckled. "Interesting, Andy. Very interesting. Although I'd pick being a Jewish kid in Brooklyn over being a Muslim girl in Saudi Arabia."

He picked up his wine glass and took a last sip. "Andy, I hate to leave this fascinating discussion, but I should get back home, and tell Gloria and my dad about Sam's service. And I have to drive, so half a bottle of Beringer is enough for me. But, since we haven't figured out if Sam or Alex makes the better justice, can we keep this going, hopefully without anyone dying again?" He smiled. "I mean, without another person dying."

Andy laughed. "Sure, Alex. But no black outfits next time. Deal?"

"Deal," he agreed. "But only when it's convenient for both of us. We've got plenty of work to keep us busy, probably you more than me."

Andy and Novak got up, and retrieved his black jacket and tie from the chair over which they'd been draped. At the door, they both started a hug at the same time. Andy could feel her breasts against his chest, and knew he felt them too. She thought of the word she learned from Josh: indeterminacy. Who can tell what might change the course of your life?

"Thanks, Andy, and shalom."

"And thanks to you, Alex, and shalom."

When the front door closed, Andy opened another bottle of Beringer, stuck a Dave Matthews CD in the player, stretched out on the couch, and reflected that village girls in Saudi Arabia didn't listen to music like this, or drink Beringer. And neither did ultra-Orthodox Jewish girls in Brooklyn, dressed in black and forbidden to be alone with boys. She grew up just a few miles from them, Andy reflected, and lived in an entirely different world. With that, she stopped reflecting, and let Dave Matthews riff with his band.

11

"Hey, Dick. I just heard a bugle calling. Colonel O'Connor awaits our presence at roll call."

Dick Wadleigh looked up as Vicky Nickerson entered his cramped, windowless office in the Executive Office Building, an ornate pile of masonry Harry Truman once called "the greatest monstrosity in America." Housing over a thousand members of the White House staff, the EOB is connected to the West Wing by an underground tunnel. Vicky had landed a job as assistant counsel to President Chris Chambers after her clerkship the previous term with Justice Cormac McCarthy, a member of the Supreme Court's four-justice conservative minority. During his clerkship with Alex Novak, Dick had gotten to know Vicky over lunches in the Court's dining room for clerks, and found that she had a wry sense of humor and —unlike most clerks—didn't think she, rather than the justice, should be voting on the cases they decided.

This Monday morning, October 9, Dick and Vicky were due at an eight o'clock meeting with Rory O'Connor, Counsel to the President and head of his in-house legal staff. They had been summoned to O'Connor's office in the West Wing, just two doors down from the Oval Office. One week earlier, Chief Justice Sam Terman had collapsed on the Supreme Court bench and died of a heart attack at George Washington Hospital. After leaving Dick's office and taking an elevator to lowest level of the EOB, he and Vicky walked through the tunnel, passing unsmiling Secret Service agents at both ends, and more along the corridor past the Oval Office. Since he and Vicky were the only assistant counsel who came straight from the Supreme Court, Dick had guessed that the meeting with O'Connor had something to do with selecting a new Chief, and quickly discovered he was right. Waving them past his receptionist in the outer office, O'Connor pointed to chairs across from his desk.

Once they were seated, O'Connor skipped any small talk and got right to the point. "Okay, I've got a job for you two. As you know, Chief Justice Terman's unfortunate demise has given the president a chance to nominate his successor. I met with him yesterday and got some marching orders, and you are the grunts on this platoon." O'Connor had been deployed by the Army to both Iraq and Afghanistan, winning both Bronze and Silver stars as a front-line company commander, having turned down an offer to join the Judge Advocate General's staff in the Pentagon after finishing law school at Fordham. He still affected Army lingo and demeanor, with a flat-top crew cut and a Listen Up! manner.

"The president laid out some parameters for selecting a new CJ," O'Connor continued. "First, he's decided not to move any of the sitting justices to the center seat, okay? Dick, I know you clerked for Novak, and Vicky for McCarthy. They're both solid conservatives, and picking either of them would open up a seat for a new justice, and give us a conservative majority. But I understand, and correct me if I'm wrong, Dick, that Novak has made it crystal clear that he's not interested. Is that still true?"

"Yes, sir," Dick answered, restraining an impulse to salute his boss, "at least before Chief Justice Terman died. Justice Novak told me once, I forget how it came up, that he wouldn't take the job for a measly ten-thousand dollar raise and house-keeping chores that he hates. He also said, quoting General Sherman about running for president after the Civil War, that 'I will not accept if nominated, and will not serve if elected.'"

O'Connor chuckled. "Too bad," he said. "Sherman would have made a better president than Cleveland, or any president before Teddy Roosevelt. Anyway, considering that Novak seems pretty firm that he doesn't want the job, he's off our list. He wouldn't have made the list, anyway, after he ripped into Tony Ewing in that drone strike case, just before the Chief Justice had a coronary. Novak basically accused the president of murdering the guy who was killed in Yemen. That really pissed off the president. Truth be told, this was a total screw-up at every level, including the White House. Personally, I thought we should have just paid the guy's family the six million the jury gave them, and not appealed the case to the Supreme Court. Would have spared the president the bad press he was getting from those drone-strike accidents. Fortunately, the press forgot about that when Terman died. Anyway, Novak saying he doesn't want the job settles that."

O'Connor turned to Vicky. "Justice McCarthy would be ideal, but I've heard some rumors about his health. Anything you can tell me about that?"

"Well, two years ago he fell off his bike and broke a shoulder pretty badly," Vicky said. "He had to have an implant, but it didn't heal properly, and caused a lot of pain. So, he was taking Vicodin and got sort of addicted. He tells people he's okay now, but I have seen him taking pills and acting a bit woozy on the bench. I mean, he's a good justice, and very well liked on the Court, but I guess that would be an issue if it came up."

"Thanks for that intel, Vicky," O'Connor said. "I know it would be an issue, and we actually confirmed that he's still popping pills. The FBI tells us he's filling two scrips for Vicodin every month, for himself and his wife, who's perfectly healthy. And you're not the only person who's noticed that he's a bit woozy, as you put it. So, McCarthy flunked his physical and he's off the list, unfortunately." Dick wondered if FBI agents could legally obtain pharmacy records without a subpoena, but kept that thought to himself. O'Connor glanced at a sheet on his desk. "Also unfortunately, the other two conservative justices are off the list. Karl Sorenson is seventy-two, and Parker Hanlon is sixty-eight. They're both healthy, from what we know, but the president wants somebody who can serve at least twenty years, and we're not going to risk either of them dropping dead like Terman." Dick winced at this rather cold-blooded remark about a man he admired, but chalked it up to O'Connor's penchant for straight talk.

"Okay, back to the parameters the president gave me, and your jobs," O'Connor said. "He wants to nominate someone who's been on one of the circuit courts of appeals for at least three years, who's between the ages of forty-five and fifty-five, and whose opinions are well crafted and don't take any extreme positions. I think we can have a little leeway on the age, a couple of years at the top, if someone fits the other criteria, but that would require a clean medical report. We're sticking with circuit judges because they've all been through the confirmation process, background checks, Senate hearings, financial disclosure, all that stuff. That will speed things up, since vetting someone who hasn't been through the process would take longer."

O'Connor looked from Dick to Vicky and back. "So, here's your assignment. Between now and O-eight-hundred on Thursday, you two will sit down together and make up a list of all the circuit judges who fit those criteria, and who were appointed by a Republican president. No Democrats need apply." O'Connor chuckled at his little joke. "I'm guessing the list wouldn't be more than thirty. Divide them up between you, and put together a short bio of each, and a brief summary of their most notable opinions. You can get those on the computer, I'm sure you know, from Lexis-Nexis or Westlaw." O'Connor stood up, signaling the end of the meeting. As Dick and Vicky were rising from their chairs, he raised a hand and said, "One more thing. The words 'litmus test' will never pass the president's lips, but pay attention to any cases that deal with abortion, minority preferences, the death penalty, and executive powers. If you find any, read the opinions and write a fairly detailed synopsis. Like a bench memo for a justice, which I know you've both written. Any questions?" Dick and Vicky both shook their heads. "Okay," O'Connor said, "O-eight hundred on Thursday, here."

Back in the EOB, Dick and Vicky found a small conference room, outfitted with computer terminals and a printer, pulled out legal pads, sat next to each other at the table, and set to work. Dick volunteered to find a list of circuit judges, which took one minute on the Internet, then printed out two copies. He scanned the list for a minute. "There's a hundred eighty all together," Dick said, "but that includes judges who were appointed by Democrats, so we can just cross them out. So, Vicky, why don't you take the first ninety? This list has the circuits they're sitting on, the president who nominated them, and the date they were confirmed by the Senate. Also their birthdates. We'll each make a list of who fits the president's criteria, and then divide them up. Okay?"

"Aye, aye, Captain," Vicky said. "Oops, that's the Navy, and we're Army. But this shouldn't take long." Thirty minutes later, working in silence, Dick and Vicky raised their heads at the same time, like test-takers heeding the command to close their blue books and put down their pencils. "Okay, I've got thirteen out of ninety," Vicky said. "Turns out most of the judges named by Republicans are over sixty. But that's not surprising, considering that Republican presidents didn't name any during eight years of a Democrat in the White House, before the president was elected."

"Well, that winnows the field a bunch," Dick said. "I've got seventeen, but some are younger, named by President Chambers. He hasn't put anyone on the circuit courts who's over fifty. I once heard him say adding younger judges to the federal courts would be his greatest legacy, long after he leaves office."

"So, let's see," Vicky said. "Thirteen and seventeen make thirty. Wow! O'Connor was probably guessing, but he hit the bulls-eye. And two into thirty is fifteen, right? You give me two of yours and we'll be even." Dick crossed off the bottom two names on his sheet, reached over and added them to Vicky's list. "With fifteen each," she said, "you think we can get this done by O-eight-hundred on Thursday?"

"Well, if we don't," Dick said with a smile, "we'll be pulling KP duty for the next year."

"Wake up, sleepy-head! The bugle calls again. Ten minutes to roll call."

Vicky's reveille roused Dick, his head slumped on his chest. He sat up with a start, almost knocking over a paper coffee cup on his desk. It was almost eight on Thursday morning, three days after he and Vicky received their orders from Rory O'Connor. Dick had been up all night, with a cold shower at six to wipe the cobwebs from his brain, but still felt a bit groggy from lack of sleep.

"Well, you look all bright-eyed and bushy-tailed this morning," he replied. "I guess you didn't find any judges who wrote opinions that would get the Senate liberals up in arms."

"I actually did," Vicky said. "Some of the opinions I read even shocked me, but I figured those judges wouldn't make the cut anyway so I just put brief bios in my memos. How about you, Dick?"

"Glad to know you didn't miss any beauty sleep," Dick replied. "As for me, I pulled two all-nighters on this job, which is why you caught me napping. Anyway, let's head over and report for duty." He picked up a stack of folders on his desk. As they walked through the tunnel from the EOB to the West Wing, Dick turned to Vicky. "You know, one of us is probably holding the next Chief Justice of the Supreme Court in his hand. That's pretty exciting, don't you think?"

"You mean in *her* hand, sexist pig," Vicky retorted, drawing a stare from the Secret Service agent who stood immobile at the tunnel's exit.

As Dick and Vicky entered O'Connor's outer office, they heard him bark *"Do that!"* to someone on the other end of his phone. Spotting them, he put down the phone, glanced at his military-style, Special Ops watch, and pointed to a small conference table, on which they put their folders and took chairs. "Thanks for being prompt," O'Connor said. "Here's the plan. First, we'll go through what you've got, and try to get together a short list, four to eight, to submit to the president for him to interview." He looked to Dick. "So, how many are on the long list, Dick, before we start culling the herd?"

Dick caught the Sexist Pig look that Vicky shot at O'Connor, pissed at being ignored. "Well, sir," he replied, "you were right on the money. We got exactly thirty who met the parameters you gave us. At least three years on the circuit court, between forty-five and fifty-seven, with the leeway you said was okay. As for their opinions on the topics you mentioned, I tried, and I'm sure Vicky did also, to spot any that seemed outside the mainstream, as they say. We can tell you about those, but it's really a close call for some, depending on how you define the mainstream." Vicky shot a Thank You look at Dick, which O'Connor missed.

"Okay," O'Connor said. "However, before we start that, I've been given some new criteria from the president that will save some time." Dick and Vicky looked at him expectantly. "As you probably know," O'Connor continued, "the Supreme Court is now unbalanced in terms of geography. I did a little research of my own, and discovered that six of the eight remaining justices are from the Northeast states or the Left Coast. Four from the First, Second, and Third circuits, from Maine to Delaware, which are all blue states. And two from the Ninth circuit in the west, both of them radical feminists." Dick knew he was referring to Justices Alice Schroeder and Margaret McEwan, who were certified liberals but hardly, in Dick's opinion, radicals on any issue.

"There are only two justices," O'Connor went on, "from the South and Midwest, what you might call the Bible Belt and the Heartland. One is Justice Novak, from Chicago, and the other is Dwight Stokes, from Tennessee, but he's one of those anti-business populists, sort of like Huey Long in a black robe."

There was a good argument for more geographical diversity on the Court, Dick knew, but the frankly partisan calculations behind O'Connor's comments disturbed him. There might be a great Chief Justice on our list, he mused, but not if he or she came from one of the "blue" circuits. O'Connor made it clear. "The president, and I agree with him," he said, "wants to name a judge from one of the southern or midwestern circuits. That's the Fourth to the Eighth, from Virginia to Texas, up to North Dakota, and the Eleventh, in Atlanta, which used to be part of the Fifth. Lay one of those red-state-blue-state maps next to a map of the circuit boundaries and you'll see what I mean." He looked at Dick, then a quick glance at Vicky. "So, if it's not too much trouble, can you pull those out and we'll skip the rest."

Dick and Vicky had both written the names and circuits on their folders, and they quickly sorted their folders into two piles, pushing aside those of judges who would not become Chief Justice. "Okay," O'Connor said, "Dick, why don't you start." Vicky shot another Sexist Pig look at O'Connor, who hadn't directed a word at her.

"Yes, sir," Dick replied, pulling a sheet from the top folder. "I've got eight from those circuits. Four of them have written opinions that are, at least to me, pedestrian and poorly reasoned, regardless of the holding. Maybe their clerks drafted them, but I can tell you that most justices would consider them well below Supreme Court standards."

"Okay," O'Connor said, "we'll scratch them, and you can skip any report. You've read lots of circuit court opinions, Dick, and I'll defer to your judgment."

Wow, Dick thought. Just like Saint Peter at the Pearly Gate, pointing up or down. He quickly picked out the four rejects and slid their folders aside, cast to perdition. "Okay, my last four are from four different circuits. I'll go in numerical order, if that's okay." O'Connor nodded, and Dick pulled a sheet from his top remaining folder. "The first is Judge Winslow Early, from the Fourth Circuit in Virginia. He's been on the court for nine years, the last three as chief judge. Top of his class at Virginia law school, joined a big firm in Richmond, served two terms in the House of Delegates in Virginia, and was Republican whip. Then he was elected attorney general of Virginia, spent four years as president of the national attorneys general association, and was confirmed unanimously to the

Fourth Circuit when he was forty-eight. He's fifty-seven now, but I've heard that he runs marathons in decent time."

"So far, so good, Dick," O'Connor said approvingly. "I assume you've read some of his opinions. Any that stand out?"

"Well, I went through about a dozen," Dick said, shooting a chiding glance at Vicky, who smiled and shrugged. "They're very well written. In fact, among the best circuit opinions I've read. One of his former clerks, Todd Armistead, who overlapped with me in Justice Novak's chambers, told me Judge Early writes all his opinions, and relies on his clerks mostly for research. He's written a couple of opinions that upheld state restrictions on abortion, like requiring doctors to perform ultrasounds on pregnant women before abortions and describe the baby's development to them, which sounds reasonable to me."

Dick paused, and pulled a sheaf of papers from the folder. "But he wrote one opinion that will probably raise some eyebrows. Can I read a bit from it, so you get his point and flavor? That's better than me summarizing it."

"Go ahead," O'Connor said. "But keep it short, if you can." He glanced at his watch. "We've got to give the Chief of Staff a short list in exactly twenty minutes. He runs a very tight schedule, and he'll be here on the dot to pick it up." Mike Hammerman, dubbed "The Hammer" by the media, had come to the White House from a career on Wall Street, bringing with him a reputation as a ruthless hatchet-swinger in cutting jobs at companies he forced to merge with bigger fish in the corporate shark tank. Dick hadn't met him, and didn't relish the prospect.

"Okay," O'Connor continued. "The president wants to start interviewing candidates as soon as possible, preferably starting next Monday and finishing by Friday. Filling the center seat is a high priority, considering the Court is putting off some cases that are important to the president and this administration. And with the Court evenly split right now, the liberals have an advantage, since a tie vote on those cases would uphold some bad, liberal circuit court decisions. Anyway, let's go to double-time, since we need to have a short list before the Chief arrives. So, Dick, let's hear Judge Early's eyebrow-raiser, and see if mine go up."

"Okay," Dick said. "This was one of the cases that challenged lethal injection procedures for executions. Considering several botched executions that you probably remember, Judge Early wrote that lethal injection procedures were, and I'm quoting, 'inherently flawed and ultimately doomed to failure.' That's probably true, although the Supreme Court upheld the drugs they used in that case. Anyway, I'll just read this one paragraph from his opinion." Dick looked down at a sheet from the folder and began reading aloud:

"'If some states and the federal government wish to continue carrying out the death penalty, they must turn away from this misguided path and return to more primitive—and foolproof—methods of execution. The guillotine is probably best but seems inconsistent with our national ethos. And the electric chair, hanging and the gas chamber are each subject to occasional mishaps.'"

Dick looked up and paused. O'Connor and Vicky both had What's Coming? expressions. Dick was actually enjoying the moment of suspense. "So here's Judge Early's foolproof execution method," he continued. "'The firing squad strikes me as the most promising. Eight or ten large-caliber rifle bullets fired at close range can inflict massive damage, causing instant death every time. There are plenty of people employed by the state who can pull the trigger and have the training to aim true. Sure, firing squads can be messy, but if we are willing to carry out executions, we should not shield ourselves from the reality that we are shedding human blood. If we, as a society, cannot stomach the splatter from an execution carried out by a firing squad, then we shouldn't be carrying out executions at all.'"

Dick put the sheet down and looked up again. Vicky's face reflected shock and disbelief. "Dick, did you make that up?" she asked. "If you did, it's not funny and it's gross. I mean, doesn't every state with the death penalty use lethal injection now?"

"Nope," Dick replied. "I'll show you the page from the Federal Reporter if you don't believe me. And I don't think Judge Early was being tongue-in-cheek. I checked, by the way, and there are still two states, Utah and Oklahoma, that give inmates the option of execution by firing squad in place of lethal injection. In fact, Utah has executed four inmates by firing squad since 1960, the most recent in 2010. So, it's not a relic of the past, and the Supreme Court hasn't ruled against it."

O'Connor smiled. "Dick, I agree with Judge Early, to be honest. I know what an M-16 bullet can do at close range, believe me. And his credentials are impeccable." O'Connor frowned, and shook his head. "But here's what would happen if he were nominated as Chief Justice. The gun control lobby and death penalty fanatics would run full-page ads showing Judge Early blasting holes in the Constitution, with blood splattered all over it." O'Connor pondered for a moment. "So, even though Early has great credentials, the bleeding hearts would pounce on this and paint him as a blood-thirsty ghoul. And the Democrats would drag out the confirmation hearing, with a parade of left-wing groups lining up to testify against him. As I said, the president wants a quick confirmation, someone who's conservative but not a bomb-thrower. So, we'll scratch him from the short list. But thanks for that, Dick. Better to know now, before some Senate staffer digs it up, which I'm sure they would."

O'Connor checked the time again, then nodded at Vicky. "And, since you haven't had a turn yet, Vicky, why don't you give us one report. Then, each of you pick the top three on your list that you think have the qualities for a good Chief Justice, and let the president decide. If he doesn't like any of them, we'll have another session, but I don't see that happening, given our time frame."

"I'll be quick, then," Vicky said. "I ranked the judges on my list who fit the criteria, and the top three are pretty well above the rest. But I did notice, between me and Dick, there's only one woman, and she's on my list. Of course, there are already two women on the Court, Justices Schroeder and McEwan, but they're both liberals." She looked at O'Connor, who made a slight grimace, which Vicky noticed. "Don't you think," she continued, "considering the gender gap in the president's support, at least from the polls, that putting a woman in the center seat might be a good political move? If that's a factor, of course."

"I hadn't thought of that, Vicky," O'Connor said, although she suspected he had thought of it and didn't like the idea. "But, from what I know, there aren't more than a handful of circuit judges who are both female and conservative. Most women judges are radical feminists. But if you found a conservative woman judge from a red circuit, let's hear about her, but quickly, I'm afraid. The COS will be here in eleven minutes, and we've only got fifteen minutes of his time. Okay?"

"Yes, sir," Vicky said. "I'll make it quick. Top of my list is Judge Edith Holland. University of Texas law school, member of the law review. First female partner of a big Houston firm, also served as general counsel for the Texas Republican party. Fifty-three, but was confirmed to the Fifth Circuit at thirty-six, the youngest female circuit judge in history. Chief

Judge for five years. Sharp as a tack, but maybe a little too sharp for a quick Senate confirmation."

"Whoa, Vicky," O'Connor interjected. "You can speak in full sentences, okay. I didn't mean to rush you. But you said she's maybe too sharp. Does that mean she's written some eyebrow-raising opinions, like Judge Early?"

"Well, two opinions I read might raise some liberal eyebrows, but they're very defensible and fit the president's views, I think. One involved a Texas law that required abortion clinics to be outfitted with full surgical facilities. Abortion groups claimed that would shut down half the clinics in Texas, and all but one in West Texas. The Supreme Court struck down that law in 2016, after the Fifth Circuit upheld it, but she wrote a separate concurrence to her own opinion in which she criticized Roe versus Wade as, and I'm quoting, 'an exercise in raw political power' by the Supreme Court, and expressed her 'fervent hope,' quoting again, that the Court would revisit Roe. Of course, that's the president's position, too, but the pro-abortion lobby would certainly oppose her nomination."

"Bring it on," O'Connor said. "If she were Chief Justice, she'd be the fifth vote to reverse Roe, which the president has urged for years. We know the four conservatives have been waiting for that vote. So, what's her second opinion, Vicky?"

"That was a case involving a federal prosecution, I forget which state in the Fifth Circuit, for possession of a machine gun. This was in the last administration, and the Justice Department claimed Congress had the power to ban machine guns under its authority to regulate interstate commerce, since guns most often crossed state lines from manufacturer to buyer. Judge Holland said that was stretching the interstate commerce power too far. Her opinion isn't as colorful as Judge Early's that Dick read, but I could imagine ads by gun control groups that show her blasting the Constitution with a AK-47."

"Blast away," O'Connor grinned. "You know, the NRA has criticized the president for being wishy-washy on Second Amendment rights, after he said he didn't think school teachers should have guns in their classrooms to protect the children. That was after one of the school massacres, and he was pressured by the gun control lobby, but the NRA took offense. Naming Judge Holland, if that's his choice, might repair that damage. I doubt those opinions would raise *his* eyebrows, Vicky. So, if she's on the short list and it gets to the media—don't ask me how—having a conservative woman on it might help narrow that gender gap. Something to consider, anyway. And thanks for that, Vicky." Dick was struck by O'Connor's sudden flip-flop, striking Judge Early from the short list for his "firing squad" opinion, then adding Judge Holland, despite her machine-gun opinion. Vicky's comment about the president's gender gap in the polls, Dick figured, had put politics into the equation.

O'Connor checked his watch one more time. "Tell you what. We've got five minutes, so why don't you each write down the names of your top three, and pick out their folders. I'll have Yolanda type up and print the list real quick, and we'll be ready for the COS."

Precisely five minutes later—Dick checked his watch—he heard a loud voice coming down the hallway from the Oval Office. "I can give you ten minutes with the president, Charlie, at three-thirty, but you have everything ready for him, understand? And keep the briefing memo to one page. He doesn't like them any longer."

Everyone stood up as Mike Hammerman strode into O'Connor's office. In his mid-fifties, he had the build of a bulldog, close-cropped, steel-grey hair, matched by steel-grey eyes. "Chief," O'Connor said, "these are two of my assistant counsel, Dick Wadleigh and Vicky Nickerson. They've given me some help in putting together the short list you asked for. They both recently came from clerkships on the Supreme Court, by the way."

Hammerman gave each a quick handshake, and said, "Sit." They sat, and he pulled out a chair at the table. Dick couldn't help thinking that O'Connor's "some help" comment was intended to take the credit for himself, despite the sixty hours he had spent over the past four days on this task. "Shoot," Hammerman said to O'Connor. Dick suppressed a smile at his choice of that word, considering the cases they'd just discussed.

"Well, Chief, Dick and Vicky gave me a list of thirty circuit judges who met the criteria the president laid down when we met last week, with some research on each one, and I've cut it down to the six on this list." O'Connor handed the list to Hammerman, as Dick winced at this very intended slight, noticing that Vicky rolled her eyes. Fortunately, their reactions went unnoticed, as Hammerman glanced at the sheet, then tossed it on the table.

"Rory, I appreciate the work you put into this," Hammerman said, "and the help you got from these bright young lawyers. But I just came from the Oval Office, and the short list is down to one." He paused. "And that name is not on this list, although I noticed Judge Norval Scruggs is on it. I've met him. Buddy Scruggs from Kentucky. Good judge, from what I hear, but we're not going to have a Chief Justice named Buddy. I don't care if he's the reincarnation of Oliver Wendell Holmes. And Judge Edith Holland from Texas is on that list. Another good judge. But she looks like fucking Phyllis Diller in a fright wig." He turned to Vicky. "Excuse my language, young lady. I'll be more careful."

Vicky smiled at him. "No apology necessary, sir. My dad was a Marine, and this young lady has heard that word in a dozen languages." Dick barely suppressed a laugh.

"Anyway," Hammerman continued, "the president has decided to nominate Judge Winslow Early of the Fourth Circuit to replace Chief Justice Terman. He met with him last night, and Judge Early accepted the offer. And it's been cleared with the Attorney General and the Solicitor General, who both think Early's just what the Court needs. Plus, he looks like a Chief Justice. Sam Terman, rest his soul, looked like fucking Buddy Hackett. Excuse me again, young lady."

Vicky held her tongue, but Dick could not suppress his wide-eyed shock at this news. "Excuse me, sir," he said to Hammerman, "but we discussed Judge Early as a possible nominee, and agreed that one of his opinions might cause some problems if it came up at a confirmation hearing. That's why the Counsel decided we should remove his name from the list we just gave you." Dick's heart was pounding as he addressed the president's Chief of Staff.

"Well, Chief," O'Connor quickly interjected, "we discussed the opinion Dick is referring to, and decided that the president should make that call. We should have put Judge Early's name on the short list, considering his outstanding credentials and judicial record. That was my slip in judgment, but Judge Early is certainly qualified to serve as Chief Justice. The opinion Dick found is blunt in its wording, to be sure, but no more blunt than opinions by some Supreme Court Justices who feel strongly about the cases they decide."

Jesus, Dick thought, what a smooth effort to squirm out of a tough situation and shift the blame to a lowly subordinate, which O'Connor clearly intended.

Hammerman turned to Dick. "Do you have this opinion with you, Mister Wadleigh? Or can you give me the gist?"

"Yes, sir," Dick replied, pulling out the top sheet from his folder on Early. "The gist is on this page," handing the sheet to Hammerman. "It's a case about the drugs some states use in executions by lethal injection," he explained, "in which Judge Early expressed his views about the problems with those procedures, although he upheld the use of the particular drug that was challenged."

"Okay, that's enough," Hammerman said. "Let me take a look at this." Thirty seconds later, he snorted, giving Dick a What's The Problem? look, and tossed the sheet on the table. "Tell the truth, Mister Wadleigh, this is just the kind of blunt language, as Rory put it, that confirms our decision that Judge Early will bring to the Court the guts to write opinions that are more than legalistic jargon and euphemistic evasions of reality. If we're going to execute killers, let's make it quick and foolproof, as Judge Early said. Let the abolitionists squeal, which they will, I'm sure. But the vast majority of Americans, I'm equally sure, will applaud Judge Early for his blunt words."

Hammerman glanced at his watch, which Dick recognized as a Patek Phillipe, a favorite accessory of Wall Street swashbucklers and K Street lawyers and lobbyists. More stylish than a Rolex, and more expensive. More than my annual salary, Dick knew. Well, it's his money, he conceded.

"Okay, this is a done deal, to make it perfectly clear," Hammerman said, with emphasis. "Now, I'll tell you how this went down, and what's going to happen." He looked sternly at Dick and Vicky. "First, not a word of this leaves this room. That means, Mister Wadleigh, that you don't reveal anything to your wife. We know she works for Senator Weeks on the Judiciary Committee. But she's not in the loop on this decision. Is that understood?"

"Yes, sir," Dick replied, barely concealing his surprise at Hammerman's knowledge of his wife's position. And the Chief undoubtedly surmised, or knew, that Jane was a Democrat.

"Okay, I'll trust you on this, Mister Wadleigh," Hammerman said. He paused for a few seconds. "Now, as you may or may not know, Senator

Weeks is up for reelection next year, in the midterms. He's in his third term, but only won the last election by one percent, less than a thousand votes. People in New Hampshire think he spends too much time in Washington and too little in the state. Of course, that's true of many politicians, in both parties. Anyway, the most recent Granite State Poll shows he'd lose by five points to Governor Rene Coteau, if the election was today. He's the first Republican governor in twenty years in New Hampshire, and the first French-Canadian. And they've mostly voted for Democrats until Coteau beat an incumbent who waffled on a state income tax, which is political death in New Hampshire." Dick wondered where Hammerman was going, and found out quickly.

"Now, the president's election, as everyone knows, was a cliffhanger, and he lost Virginia by only two points. He'll be in better shape for a second term if he wins Virginia. Judge Early, of course, can't endorse the president or campaign for him. But he's still very influential and well respected in the state. Making him Chief Justice would show the president's regard and respect for Virginia, which hasn't had a native-son justice for thirty years, or a Chief Justice since John Marshall, two centuries ago."

Hammerman finally connected the dots that led along Interstate 95 between New Hampshire and Virginia. "So, the president had a nice chat with Senator Weeks last night. Weeks agreed to round up enough votes from Senate Democrats to confirm Judge Early, and we only need five, although more would be better, of course. Considering Early's votes on abortion and minority preference cases, and the firing-squad opinion you showed me, Mister Wadleigh, Democrats will be under intense pressure to oppose him, and slap the president in the face." Hammerman paused, scanning the faces around the table. "So, in return for Weeks's support, the president will offer to appoint Governor Coteau as ambassador to France, which we know he'd accept. There's no other Republican in New Hampshire, quite frankly, who could run a decent campaign against Weeks, so his reelection would be pretty well assured. But Coteau's nomination won't be announced until Judge Early is confirmed, to make sure Weeks doesn't welsh on the agreement. In fact, Coteau doesn't even know he's going to Paris, assuming he does."

Sensing the discomfort of both Dick and Vicky at this blatant logrolling deal, Hammerman gave them an avuncular smile. "Just to disabuse any rose-colored illusions, my young friends, you should understand that everything that happens in this house," waving expansively around O'Connor's office, "is politics. Always has been, always will be. Appointing judges and justices is no exception. Democrat or Republican in the Oval Office, doesn't matter. The last president put more than a hundred liberals on the federal bench, and now they control all but four of thirteen circuits. But now it's our turn. And putting a solid conservative in the Supreme Court's center seat will give us a majority in cases the president cares about. Might even be the end of abortion on demand, and putting minorities at the head of the line." He shot a steel-grey look at Dick and Vicky. "Be shocked if you want, be cynical when you leave here, but just understand that both sides know how to play this game. Okay?"

Hammerman stood up, ending the meeting. As Dick and Vicky stood and gathered their useless folders, the Chief of Staff raised a hand. "I'm guessing you two put in a lot of hours the last few days. I appreciate that, and I know the Counsel does, too. And I'll make sure the president knows that you did an outstanding job. So, take the rest of the day off, get out and enjoy the great fall weather, and get a good night's sleep." He turned back as he reached the door. "And, by the way, the president won't announce Judge Early's nomination for two weeks, so the media will think we've been carefully sifting the potential candidates to find the most qualified Chief Justice to lead the Court. So keep this to yourselves. Understood?"

Without waiting for agreement, Hammerman left the office. O'Connor raised his hands in apology. "Dick and Vicky, believe me, I wouldn't have put you through this if I'd known what was happening down the hall. But thanks."

After walking back through the tunnel, with Vicky silent, Dick dropped his folders on his desk, left the EOB, took a cab to his apartment, opened a bottle of Scotch, sat on the couch, put a DVD of "To Kill a Mockingbird" on the screen, then watched "All the President's Men." When Jane got home at seven, she found Dick sleeping on the couch. She kissed his head, then covered him with a blanket.

The next morning, Dick told Jane everything.

12

The Supreme Court was a quiet and somber place when Andy returned to work on the Monday after Chief Justice Terman's funeral service at Temple Shalom. The people she passed in the hallways looked down-cast and didn't nod with the usual recognition. Entering Novak's chambers, Andy noticed that his office was empty, and wondered briefly—with a pang of guilt—if the time they'd spent at her apartment after the service, drinking wine, discussing the "boxes" in which people's lives were shaped, and the longer-than-necessary hug when Novak left, each aware of her breasts against his chest, might have affected their relationship in some way, deciding that she could only wait and see. Time will tell. Who knows? Beats me. Trite phrases, Andy thought as they flashed through her mind, but also true. So, wait and see, and meanwhile focus on the task at hand, finishing a bench memo she'd left half-done the previous week..

The clerks' office was also quiet this morning. Her fellow clerks worked silently at their computers; the pair she called "the crooks," Amanda and Todd, hardly spoke to her any more. Even Dave, invariably cheerful and ebullient, was subdued, although he greeted Andy with a smile. Sitting at her desk, Andy logged onto her computer, pulled up the bench memo, and tried to remember what the case was about.

Twenty minutes later, Andy jumped when her cell phone rang, displaying Josh's work number at the Federal Defenders office in Alexandria. He rarely called from work, and Andy wondered if something had happened to his husband, Carlo, who was spending a two-week rotation for his residency at George Washington Hospital at a rural clinic in West Virginia that mostly treated retired coal miners with black-lung disease. Andy stepped outside the clerks' office to take the call. "Hey, Josh," she said. "Carlo's okay, I hope."

"Aside from having trouble with patients who speak a hillbilly dialect he needs a translator to understand, he's fine. Although he can't believe how many people there are grossly obese, buying crappy food with food stamps. So, how are you, Andy, now that you're back at work, providing equal justice under law for those who can afford it, unlike my clients."

"I'm fine, Josh, writing a bench memo in a case that's set for argument next week, and that's really boring. So, what prompts this interruption of my supremely important work? Missing me, I hope."

"Yes and no," Josh said. "Missing you, yes. Calling just to tell you that, no. So, Andy, remember the job with Texas Defenders you put off for your clerkship?"

"Of course," Andy replied, surprised by the question. "But I also put it off to be near you, remember?"

"Well, that's why I'm calling. You're near me, and I need your help with a death penalty case I just volunteered to handle."

"A death penalty case? Josh, I thought your caseload was mostly people who pissed on gravestones in Arlington Cemetery. Are you kidding?"

"Absolutely not," Josh assured her. "I got called up to the big leagues this morning. I don't know much about the case yet, but I got a call from Jim Carruthers, in our Richmond office. He was assigned by a federal judge to represent a death-row inmate who filed a pro se habeas petition, representing himself. The judge didn't just toss the petition, although Jim said it was filed past the one-year limit from the Virginia supreme court decision affirming the inmate's conviction and death sentence. But Jim says his office is swamped with work, and asked if I'd take a look at the case files and let him know if this petition has any merit. He did say, from a brief look at the petition, that it raises an ineffective assistance of counsel claim, which might get the inmate through the courthouse door, if there's anything to it. I checked with my boss, and he agreed I could work on it."

"Wow," Andy exclaimed. "That sounds a lot more exciting than my case. But are you calling just to tell me you're making your major league start, or asking me to shag flies for you?"

"Actually, I'm asking you to give me a hand, going through the files that Jim is sending up with someone who's got a meeting at our office this afternoon. Should be here by three or four. Tell you what, Andy. If you're interested, could you come over to my place, say at six-thirty? We can order take-out Thai, and I've got wine, and maybe later, your favorite variety of hemp. But only if you're interested."

"It's the last thing you mentioned that will get me there, since I'm all out," Andy said, "but Thai and wine sounds good too. And six-thirty is fine. So, I'll show you mine if you show me yours. Cases, I mean."

Josh laughed. "Enough with the double entendres, Andy. Remember my pick-up line? 'Hi there, cute thing. Want to come up and see my briefs?' Okay, see you then."

Andy left the Court at six and took the Metro from Union Station to Foggy Bottom, walking a few blocks to the apartment Josh shared with Carlo. She arrived to find Josh at his dining-room table, sorting through two cardboard boxes and putting folders into piles at each end. "Hey, Andy," Josh greeted her. "I just got this stuff at four and only had a chance to skim through the habeas petition, but I made a copy for you. You want to take a look while I finish sorting these folders?"

"Josh, aren't you going to say more than 'Hey, Andy. Roll up your sleeves and get to work'?"

"Oh, sorry," he apologized. "I just got a little excited, you know, this being my first death penalty case. So, roll down your sleeves and I'll fetch some wine to lubricate our mental gears." He chuckled. "I bet if the Court put carafes of wine on the lawyers' table they'd get better oral arguments, or at least more colorful."

"Great idea, Josh. I'll suggest it to Alex, who might want carafes on the bench, too."

Josh came back with a bottle of Kendell-Jackson pinot noir and two glasses, filling them and clinking with Andy's. "Seriously, though," he said, "there's a guy's life at stake here, so let's not get buzzed until we're done figuring what to do next, okay?"

"Okay," Andy agreed. "But since I haven't skimmed the petition, can you give me some background on the case?"

"Well, here's what Jim Carruthers told me on the phone, and what I gleaned from the case files so far." Josh consulted a sheet of notes. "Fifteen years ago, down in Williamsburg, a girl named Laurel Davis was murdered in her bedroom, her head bashed in. She was a student at William & Mary law school, and shared a house off-campus with two other law students, both girls. It was close to Christmas, and her roommates were both away for the holiday break. Laurel had stayed in Williamsburg, since her parents lived in Seattle and were in Mexico on vacation."

Josh looked at his notes. "The next-door neighbor heard screams and called 911, although she didn't see anyone enter or leave the house. The cops found a bloody hammer in some bushes in the front lawn, which they figured was the murder weapon. So, when a detective interviewed the neighbor, she said she'd seen a young black guy—Laurel was white, by the way—raking leaves at the house on her other side. She recognized him, and gave the detective his name, which was Odell Beasley. The detective knew him and where he lived, a few blocks away, and brought him in for questioning. The guy, who went by 'OD,' first denied he'd been at Laurel's house, but then admitted he'd been there, saying Laurel was going to pay him five bucks for raking leaves in her front yard."

Josh looked at Andy, who gave him a Go Ahead nod. "So, here's where it gets interesting, and a little hard to believe. OD told the detective that Laurel invited him in, saying she had another chore for him, then took off her clothes and invited him to have sex with her. OD claimed he declined, saying he should leave, but she pulled down his pants and gave him oral sex, and then had intercourse on her bed. Just after he climaxed, OD said, he heard a male voice at the front door, saying something like, 'I'm here, baby, and I'm horny.' OD got scared, grabbed his clothes, ran out the back door, got dressed, and ran home. The cops picked him up at the bus station, with a ticket to Richmond, saying he was going to visit his sister there. That was his story. Oh, and he said he never saw the guy at the front door. Sound plausible to you, Andy?"

"Well, a bit far-fetched," she answered. "But how'd he get charged with murder, if no one saw him at the house? Just because he was a black guy, and a white girl had been murdered, and somebody saw him in the neighborhood? Got to be more than that."

"Good question, Andy. Always happens when a white girl is murdered. Pick up the nearest black guy and put him on death row." Andy shot him a semi-serious glare. "Just kidding," Josh said. "Turns out they found this OD's fingerprints on the hammer, with her blood on it, and semen in her mouth and vagina that matched his DNA. And he admitted having sex with her, although he said it was her idea, not his. But he was charged with capital murder, convicted, and sentenced to death. He appealed, claiming the DA prejudiced the jury by showing them pictures of her bloody body from crime-scene photos. The state courts ruled that wasn't prejudicial, and affirmed the conviction and sentence. Then his lawyer withdrew and didn't file any further appeals. So OD's been on death row the last fifteen years."

"And just now he's filing a habeas petition in federal court?" Andy asked. "So, what are his grounds? And isn't it a bit late, like? I assume the last state court ruling was several years ago, right?"

"Yeah," Josh said, "it was about ten years ago. So, normally, with a one-year time limit for habeas petitions from that date, his petition would get tossed. But here's why the judge didn't dismiss it without a hearing, and appointed Jim Carruthers to represent him. Very clever reason, if you ask me."

"Well, I'm asking you," Andy said. "What's so clever that a judge wouldn't dismiss a time-barred petition?"

"Okay," Josh said, picking up a copy of the petition. "Turns out this petition wasn't drafted by OD Beasley, who can't read or write past a third-grade level. Here's what Jim told me. It was drafted by a real lawyer, or former lawyer, I should say. Guy named Timothy Bostic, whose name was on some of the documents filed with the habeas petition. He's doing twenty years in the same prison for murdering his adulterous wife, after catching her in bed with one of his partners, who didn't get murdered. He's been disbarred, of course, but volunteers to help guys he thinks have at least some chance of getting a new trial or sentence reduction. Bostic was a criminal defense lawyer, Jim tells me, and actually won some acquittals for clients who looked guilty. Good lawyer, very bad reaction to his wife's infidelity. I mean, you never heard of lawyers who screwed their partners' wives?"

"Josh, please stick to the point, and don't be gross," Andy said, refilling her wine glass. Josh put his hand over his.

"Sorry," Josh said. "Lubrication makes me garrulous. Anyway, according to Jim, who talked with Bostic on the phone, Bostic got to know OD, since he was assigned to the maintenance crew on the death-row section, and had plenty of time to talk with the inmates there. He listened to OD's story, and figured out, whether his story was true or not, that OD was mentally impaired. Not really retarded, in the drooling, slack-jawed sense, but definitely way below normal. And Bostic knew of the Supreme Court decision, back in 2014, holding that states couldn't set an arbitrary

IQ level of 70 as a cut-off for imposing death sentences. Florida said any score over that made a defendant eligible for the death penalty, but the Supreme Court said that IQ tests have a margin of error that goes up to 75, so they effectively raised it to that number."

"I remember that one," Andy said. "Hall versus Florida, right? We discussed that case in Hank Lorenz's crim law course."

"That's the one," Josh said. "So, Bostic got one of his former partners, not the one he caught in bed with his wife, to get records from OD's elementary and high schools. They showed he'd dropped out in the ninth grade, had been assigned to 'slow learner' classes since second grade, and, here's the kicker, Andy. OD scored 72 on an IQ test in the eighth grade. That would put him within the category of mentally deficient, under the Hall decision."

"So, the habeas petition is based on Hall?" Andy asked."

"Yeah," Josh answered. "But there's a problem with that. The Eleventh Circuit ruled in 2015, in a case from Georgia, that the Hall decision was not retroactive. Really bad ruling, in my opinion, because it allowed Georgia to execute a guy who was just as mentally impaired as Hall, who now can't be executed. The Georgia guy's lawyers asked the Eleventh Circuit to allow the Supreme Court to decide if Hall should be applied retroactively, but they refused, and the guy was executed the next day."

"My God!" Andy exclaimed. "That is horrible. That really should be a decision the Supreme Court should make, especially if someone is executed before they can answer the question."

"You're right," Josh said. "Fortunately, Eleventh Circuit decisions are not binding on the Fourth Circuit in Virginia. And there was a very powerful dissent by one of the Eleventh Circuit judges in that case. So, Judge Jacobs, who appointed Jim to represent OD, has scheduled a hearing on the habeas petition two weeks from now, on the twenty-third, and Jim is going to argue that Hall should be applied retroactively."

"Great," Andy said. "But I've got a couple questions, Josh. First, if the state supreme court decision was ten years ago, and OD didn't file any federal appeal, how come he hasn't been executed already? I mean, the state could have done that any time after that, right?"

"Good question," Josh replied. "Because the previous two governors, both Democrats, imposed a moratorium on executions while challenges to the lethal injection method were finally decided by the courts. But the current governor, a pretty right-wing Republican, lifted the moratorium. So, technically, OD is eligible for execution whenever the governor signs a warrant and sets a date."

"Okay," Andy said. "Second question is, what makes this an ineffective assistance of counsel case? I mean, how did his trial lawyer fuck up, if he did?"

"Well, here's where Bostic got clever in drafting the habeas petition," Josh said. "If you file a habeas petition after the one-year limit, you have to explain *why* you were late. And one reason is that you now have what they call 'newly discovered evidence' that wasn't available at trial or sentencing."

Josh consulted his notes. "By the way, Andy, this is stuff I learned at my orientation at the Justice Department, not something I just looked up this afternoon. I'm not an expert, and I'm mostly relying on what Bostic wrote in the petition. But he seems to know this stuff really well. Too bad he got disbarred for that minor breach of professional conduct."

"I'll ignore that comment," Andy said. "Can we move along, Josh?"

"Sorry. Anyway, the 'newly discovered evidence' in OD's case is his school and IQ records. Why weren't they available at trial, you might ask."

"I'm asking," Andy said, a bit impatiently.

"Well, his trial lawyer didn't ask for them from the prosecutors, or look for them himself," Josh said. "Without those records, of course, he didn't offer any evidence of OD's mental deficiency. Not doing that is what supports the claim of ineffective assistance of counsel. And he withdrew from the case after the final state appeal." Josh smiled. "So, you might ask again, since the records were at OD's schools all along, why didn't he discover them himself?"

"I'm asking again, Professor Barfield," Andy said. "This sounds like one of Hank's classes." Andy mimicked his inquisitorial tone. "'How do you get around the time limit in habeas cases? I'm asking *you*, Miss Roboff.'"

"Here's the clever answer," Josh said. "OD Beasley didn't ask his lawyer to get the records that showed his mental deficiency, or seek them out himself, because *he* is mentally deficient. Get it? Wouldn't even think of them. It took a real lawyer, namely Bostic, to get the records. So the failure to file within the one-year time limit should be excused."

"Very impressive," Andy said. "Too bad Bostic can't argue the case for OD. But I'm curious about why Jim asked you to go through these files, the police reports of the murder and the trial transcript, which is what's in these boxes, from what I see. I assume Jim's argument is based on the legal issue of whether the Supreme Court decision in Hall should apply to cases like OD Beasley's. Right?"

"Right," Josh replied.

"So why would these files, whatever's in them, be relevant to that issue?"

"No, they wouldn't," Josh replied. "But here's why Jim asked me to review them. When he talked with Bostic, he said, as an experienced criminal defense lawyer, that he could tell if a client who claimed he was innocent was telling the truth. Bostic told Jim that he listened to OD's story several times. OD kept saying, 'I did not kill that girl.' And even if OD's story that Laurel Davis invited him to have sex with her, but that he didn't kill her, sounds implausible, Bostic says he believes him."

"Okay," Andy said. "But you said they found OD's fingerprints on the bloody hammer. How do you get around that? I doubt the real killer, if it wasn't OD, somehow put his prints on the hammer. That's even more implausible."

"I don't know," Josh said. "But Jim thinks there might be something in these files that just might answer that question. It's a pretty slim chance we'd find the smoking gun, so to speak, but it's worth a try. Because even if Jim wins on the retroactivity issue, and was upheld on appeal, that wouldn't affect OD's original conviction. The most he would get from a new sentencing trial would be resentencing to life without parole."

"But if we find evidence that somehow clears him of the murder," Andy said, "he'd get a new trial, with evidence of his innocence, assuming there is any, and might get acquitted. Is that the idea?"

"Yep, that's the idea," Josh said. He gestured at the folders on the table. "There might not be any needle in this haystack, but if we don't sift through it, we'll never know. And if we find one, we might just help an innocent man get out of prison. Sound worth doing, Andy?"

"You bet," she replied. "So, what's your plan?"

"Okay," Josh said. "I've sorted these folders into two piles. One with all the police reports, what cops call the 'murder book,' and the other with the trial transcript. Any preference, or do you want to flip for it?"

"Um," Andy pondered. "You probably have more experience with police reports, from the cases you handle, so why don't you take that pile, and I'll go through the transcript."

"Deal," Josh said. "But since that would take longer than just a couple hours, why don't we get together again on, say, Thursday, and compare notes? You can take the transcript home with you and go through it there. Okay?"

"Fine, but what happened to ordering Thai food? That's how you lured me over here. And I'm hungry."

"I've got a better idea," Josh said. "Before he left for West Virginia, Carlo whipped up a big dish of lasagna, which is in the freezer. I'll heat it up in the microwave. We can have that, with another bottle of K-J, and then maybe have time to smoke some Lemon Haze and listen to some Dave Matthews. Sound good?"

Andy laughed. "The first time we smoked Lemon Haze and listened to Dave, if you remember, was three years ago at your place on Oxford Street. And we wound up taking each other's clothes off, very slowly."

Josh chuckled. "I remember every detail, like it was yesterday. Is that an invitation to undo your blouse again, one button at a time? I still have permission from Carlo to undo your buttons, as long as he's in West Virginia."

Andy smiled. "And maybe lasagna after? I'm not really starving, so I can wait."

After a bowl of Lemon Haze and a few tracks of Dave, buttons and zippers were undone, very slowly and with much giggling. Once the undressing was complete, Andy pulled Josh to his feet, put her arms around him, and enjoyed the feeling of her breasts against his chest. Fleetingly, she thought of her breasts against Alex Novak's chest, and put that thought back into the Wait and See box. Then she thought of OD Beasley in his death-row cell. I'm going to find that needle, Andy said to herself. And then she followed Josh into his bedroom.

13

"Damn! Damn! Damn!" Jane Wadleigh repeated to herself as she rushed to arrive on time for a nine o'clock meeting of the Democratic staff of the Senate Judiciary Committee, in the chairman's office in the Dirksen Senate Office Building, adjacent to both the Capitol and the Supreme Court. She had a good idea what Senator Charter Weeks, the New Hampshire Democrat who chaired the committee, intended to discuss with the staff.

At eight that morning, Jane's disheveled and somewhat hung-over husband, Dick, had told her, almost word-for-word, what had been said the previous day in the White House counsel's office by the counsel, Rory O'Connor, and the president's chief of staff, Mike Hammerman. Jane reminded Dick that President Chambers was certain to nominate a conservative judge as Chief Justice in any event, and that Judge Winslow Early, despite the "firing squad" opinion Dick felt was unbecoming any judge or justice, wasn't so extreme in his views that the Senate would reject his confirmation for that one opinion. Dick agreed, but said it was the president's deal with Senator Weeks, virtually buying his support for Early's confirmation in return for easing Week's reelection, that most bothered him. Washington was a political town, Dick conceded, but the blatant partisan politics on both sides of the deal offended his sense of how the system was supposed to work. Jane listened to Dick, told him to eat a good breakfast and take his time getting to work, kissed him, and left for her meeting, equally offended at how the system worked at her end of Pennsylvania Avenue.

As she semi-jogged the ten blocks to the Dirksen Building, Jane wondered if there might be some way to derail or at least shunt aside the train that seemed destined to deliver Early's confirmation. She had come up with no ideas by the time, five minutes after nine, that she entered the conference room next to Senator Week's office, where committee staffers were slurping coffee and munching on Danish.

"Good morning, Jane," Weeks greeted her. "Take a seat and we'll get started." Weeks was lanky and white-haired, given to New Hampshire jokes that had grown stale with retelling. His favorite, and Jane's least favorite, was about the New Yorker who visited the state during a cold, rainy July. "Don't you folks have summer up here?" he asked a Granite State native. "Ayup," he replied. "Last summah was on a Tuesday, I recall."

This morning, Weeks was all business. "I have some news," he began, "that is not going out of this room. If I see anything in the Post, or anywhere else, even hinting at what I'm going to tell you folks, somebody will be looking at the want ads. Is that clear?" Everyone in the room, including Jane, nodded their agreement.

"Very well," Weeks continued. "I got a call yesterday from the president, who informed me that he intends to nominate Judge Winslow Early, of the Fourth Circuit court of appeals, to replace Chief Justice Terman on the Supreme Court." Several eyebrows went up, as committee staffers realized it had only been ten days since Terman's death. Aware of the quizzical looks, Weeks went on. "That's quite a short period, I know. But the president and his staff, not surprisingly, had already prepared a short list of possible nominees in case any seat on the Court became vacant, from death or retirement. He told me that Judge Early had been at the top of the list for the next vacancy, even Chief Justice. That's his decision, of course, and I assured him the committee would give Judge Early a fair hearing."

Weeks scanned the table. "However," he continued, "the president said he had decided to delay an announcement of Judge Early's nomination until the twenty-third, at the judge's request, so he could deal with his pending caseload and make some financial arrangements, including putting all his stock holdings in a blind trust. That seemed reasonable to me, so I agreed." Weeks scanned the table again. "Let me repeat. Not a word of this leaves this room." More nods of agreement.

"Now, the president asked me," Weeks said, "considering the importance of having the Court at full strength, to schedule the confirmation hearing as soon as possible after he announces Judge Early's nomination. I consulted the ranking member on the Republican side, and we agreed on November thirteen, three weeks after the nomination. That gives us about five weeks to assemble material on Judge Early and his record, and to put together a list of witnesses on both sides, since I'm sure there will be some groups that will want to voice their opposition. That's only fair, and that's always been the committee's practice."

Weeks looked at the committee's staff director, Cheryl Perkins, a forty-something African American, and a veteran of several previous Supreme Court confirmation hearings. "Cheryl will be handing out assignments by tomorrow morning," Weeks said, "and any questions should go to her." He stood up, ending the meeting. "Let me repeat," he said, "not a word of this to anyone outside this office." With that, he left the room.

Suspecting that Weeks, who knew that Dick worked in the White House counsel's office, had directed his Loose Lips Sink Ships warning at her, Jane sat for a minute as fellow staffers headed back to their offices. Dick had told her of the similar warning from the president's chief of staff, and assumed they were both under some kind of special scrutiny. Weeks might suspect that Jane had learned from Dick of his logrolling deal with the president, considering that many couples find it hard to avoid confiding in each other about unethical conduct by their superiors. It seemed obvious to Jane that no other committee staffer, except possibly Cheryl Perkins, had a clue about the deal to assure Early's confirmation, so any media exposure of it would make her the leading suspect. Jane didn't know if the deal might be illegal, but it would certainly embarrass both the president and Weeks if the media got a whiff of potential scandal.

Getting up to leave, Jane was musing about the bind she and Dick shared when Perkins waved her over. "Spare a minute, Jane," she said. "I've already got an assignment for you." Jane smiled brightly, hoping to look eager and willing. "It's highly confidential," Perkins said. "Can I trust you to keep it that way?"

"Of course," Jane replied, a bit annoyed. "Everything we do that isn't cleared for public release is confidential. I certainly understand that."

"I'm sure you do," Perkins assured her. "Here's what the chairman asked me to task you with." She took a step and closed the conference room door. "We know, of course, that your husband works for the White House counsel." Perkins lowered her voice, as if she feared being overheard in the otherwise empty room. "The chairman told me that he's heard rumors that Judge Early has privately expressed negative views about African Americans and other minorities." She noticed Jane's raised eyebrows. "Now, these rumors might be totally unfounded. And there was no mention of anything like that in the reports we got, including the

FBI, when Judge Early went through the confirmation process before he joined the Fourth Circuit. But these rumors concern the chairman, as I'm sure you understand."

Seeing where Perkins was going, Jane decided to be blunt. "You mean, Judge Early might be a closet racist, and that might complicate things if it came up at the hearing, from any source. Is that what you're saying?"

"Well, that's a concern, putting it that way," Perkins conceded. "But you can help us see if there's any basis to the rumors. The chairman didn't tell me where or who he heard them from, but he suggested that your husband might have heard something like that in the White House."

"And that he'd tell me if he knew, and if I asked him?" Jane didn't bother to conceal her displeasure. "Is that my assignment, Cheryl? To ask my husband to reveal something that would obviously be strictly confidential at the White House?"

"Jane, please don't get huffy about this," Perkins said soothingly. "As I said, these rumors might be unfounded, and it would be unfair to Judge Early if the media, who will be digging into his record like dump-pickers, believe me, get wind of anything that would mobilize civil-rights groups against his confirmation."

"Tell you what, Cheryl," Jane said. "I'll make a deal with you," emphasizing the word 'deal.' "I'll ask Dick, although he hasn't told me anything he heard about this at the White House. Okay?" The "about this" qualifier gave Jane an out if Perkins or Weeks found out that Dick *had* told her what he'd heard at the White House, just not about Early's racial views.

"Fine," Perkins agreed. "That's a good deal, and very helpful to the chairman."

Jane held up an I'm Not Done hand. "Wait a minute, Cheryl. There's two parts to a deal. What one party does, and what the other party does in return. Sort of like a contract, you know."

"I'm a lawyer, too," Perkins said, a bit testily. "So what's the other part of the deal you're proposing?"

"Okay," Jane said, feeling she held the upper hand. "My part is that I'll ask Dick about these racism rumors. But, if he learns there's any substance to them, the chairman will advise the president that he can't assure any votes on our side of the aisle for Early's confirmation. There isn't a Democrat who would vote for a racist. And the president, if he has any brains, would have to withdraw Early's nomination." She looked sharply at Perkins. "That's the deal, Cheryl."

The look on Perkins' face confirmed Jane's suspicion that Weeks's vote-buying deal with President Chambers was a stick of political dynamite, and that Weeks—and Perkins as well—feared that Jane could light the fuse and blow his reelection chances to smithereens. It didn't take a marital counselor to tell an experienced politician that spouses often make exceptions to Don't Tell Anyone About This demands, especially when such demands gnaw at their conscience. Fortunately, Jane thought, she had married a man with a conscience, whatever their political differences.

Perkins took a deep breath, then let it out. "I'm sure the chairman would be frank with the president if he learned anything that might complicate Judge Early's confirmation."

"So," Jane said, firmly. "Deal?"

"Deal," Perkins replied, extending her hand. Jane shook it, two lawyers sealing a verbal contract.

Over the three days that followed her Monday evening session with Josh, Andy worked on bench memos for up-coming oral arguments during the days, and spent her evenings going through the transcripts of OD Beasley's trial and sentencing hearing. The trial had lasted three days, after a day of juror selection, and the hearing at which the jury recommended a death sentence for OD took only another day.

The transcripts totaled 600 pages, recording the examination and cross-examination of each witness by the prosecutor, Victor Stone, and OD's defense lawyer, Darrell Lewis. They also recorded the closing arguments of the lawyers, and Judge Tommy Moore's final instructions to the jurors before their deliberations. The last page recorded Moore's imposition of the death sentence and his benediction on OD: "May God have mercy on your soul."

Andy took a methodical approach to this task. On separate sheets, she listed each witness and summarized their testimony, highlighting verbatim passages in the transcripts on points Andy thought might be important in any further proceeding, such as a hearing on a motion for a new trial. Given the unanimous decision of the Virginia supreme court, she realized, upholding OD's conviction and death sentence, the prospect of a new trial was unlikely. Unless, Andy thought, she or Josh—who was going through the police reports in the case—somehow discovered the "needle in the haystack" that she had vowed to find, if humanly possible. That search motivated her to scrutinize every word of testimony, each stalk of hay in the 600-page stack, looking for something, anything, that Darrell Lewis might have missed or screwed up in the trial and appeals.

Andy was tired when she arrived at Josh's place at six-thirty on Thursday. She had worked until two each night she spent on the transcripts, and had gotten to the Court by nine to work on bench memos. She was also a bit depressed, which Josh noticed as soon as he opened the door.

"Uh-oh," he said. "No needle in your haystack?"

"Nothing that pricked me," Andy replied.

"Well, most haystacks don't have needles in them," Josh reassured her. "But don't be sad. My stack didn't have any needles, either. Although it does have some funny-looking objects that might deserve a closer look. Maybe there's a needle in one of them."

He gave Andy a hug and kiss, and they set up shop on the dining table. "I've got a nice chilled bottle of Beringer chardonnay in the fridge, Andy, but do you mind waiting until we're done going through this stuff?"

"Fine with me," she replied. "But do you mind if we have a couple glasses and then I go home? I'm sort of tired, and I could use a good night's sleep in my own bed before I get back to bench memos tomorrow morning." She smiled brightly. "But I'll give you a rain check for next time, since Carlo's got another two weeks in West Virginia. Or we could do a little high-school making out, just to second base, if you know what I mean. But just a preview of coming attractions."

Josh laughed. "I haven't heard anybody talk about getting to second base since I went out with Debbie Costello in high school. 'Stay above my waist, Josh,' she'd say. 'Third base and home plate are for the guy who gives me a ring, and that's not going to be you.' So, just one inning, and only buttons and hooks. I'll swing for the fences next time."

Andy gave him a light punch on the shoulder. "Maybe a grand slam next time, if you're lucky. So, Mister All-Star of Idaho baseball, let's get to work. I'll go first, okay, since it won't take long, unfortunately."

"We'll see," Josh said, "but you take the first swing."

"Okay," Andy said. "Since I didn't find a needle, I'll tell you about the one thing I found that might help a new trial motion, if there ever is one."

"Don't be so pessimistic," Josh chided. "Remember, this was a pretty open-and-shut case, from the evidence of OD's fingerprints on the hammer, and his semen in Laurel Davis. So the prosecutor was unlikely to screw up, and the defense lawyer didn't have anything to back up his 'Some Other Dude Did It' suggestion. But there's never been a perfect murder trial, so let's see what you found."

"Okay," Andy said, picking up a folder. "This is from Victor Stone's closing argument to the jury." She pulled out a transcript page, with yellow highlighting along several lines. "Stone is talking about what a wonderful, talented, caring young woman Laurel Davis was, and how her unlimited potential was snuffed out by this horrible, brutal crime. And he has blown-up photos of her on a screen."

"Well," Josh interrupted, "that's exactly what you'd expect a prosecutor to say about a victim like Laurel. Melodramatic, sure, but nothing objectionable."

"Right," Andy agreed. "But then he gestures to the photos, the court reporter notes, and says this: 'Ladies and gentlemen of the jury, do you really believe that a girl like *this* would willingly have sex with a man like *that*,' and he points to OD." Andy looked at Josh. "Don't you think that's an appeal to racial prejudice, Josh, and grounds for a new trial for prosecutorial misconduct? I mean, it was obvious what he meant the jurors to conclude, that no white girl would consent to have sex with a black man, and certainly not *this* white girl with *this* black man. What do you think, Josh?"

"You're absolutely right, Andy," Josh answered. "That's a deplorable appeal to racial prejudice. But, unfortunately, Stone worded it very cleverly. He didn't say 'white girl' or 'black man.' He was smart enough not to use racial terms. And, also unfortunately, I can't think of a judge who would hold that was reversible error and order a new trial. Covert racism shows up in lots of trials, and almost never gets sanctioned. But that doesn't mean we should discard it, because, who knows, there might be a judge who can't stomach that kind of 'I'm not going to say nigger, but you know what I mean' appeal to good white jurors."

"I thought that's what you'd say," Andy said. "But that's all I could find in my haystack. So, what about the funny-looking objects in yours?"

"Okay," Josh said, pulling several sheets from a folder. "Here's one. Did a woman named Martha Radford testify at the trial, Andy?"

She looked at her list of witnesses. "Nope. So who is she?"

"She's a lady who lived across the street from Laurel's house. The detective on the case, a guy named Moses Townley, interviewed her, and wrote a brief report." He lifted a sheet and read from it: "Mrs. Radford said she did not hear any screams, or see anyone enter or leave the victim's house. She did say she had seen a red car, parked two doors down from her house, when she came out to pick up her newspaper at approximately 9 a.m. When she came back out, hearing the patrol cars arrive at approximately 9:40 a.m., the red car was no longer parked on the street. She said she noticed the car because it did not belong to anyone who lived on that block. There was no further identification of the car, and no follow-up is planned."

Josh put the sheet down. "Now, in a quiet, residential neighborhood like this one, noticing a strange car at a crime scene normally involves some follow-up, and witnesses are asked to identify the vehicle as best they can, like make, model, color, license plate, any decals or bumper stickers, anything distinctive. Maybe Mrs. Radford didn't know cars, and couldn't provide any details. But maybe the detective didn't press her because he thought an old lady—the report says she was 63 and a widow—wouldn't know cars. So maybe she did, and just wasn't asked. And since she wasn't called as a witness, OD's lawyer didn't get a chance to ask her for details about the car. See what I mean, Andy?"

"Right," Andy said. "Not a needle, but a piece that doesn't fit the puzzle that Stone thought he solved. What do you think we should do about this, Josh? Anything we can do?"

"I'm not sure," he answered. "But let me show you the other funny-shaped piece I found, okay?" Andy nodded. "Was there any testimony about a brown glove at the trial?"

Andy thought a moment, then nodded no. "Nothing about a glove, Josh. Why, did you find something about one?"

"Maybe nothing to it," Josh replied. "But I found this report by Detective Townley, about the physical evidence. I'll read a bit. 'An officer retrieved a brown glove, of the type worn by drivers, from the curb in front of a residence across the street and two doors down from the victim's house. Visual examination showed no blood or other substance on the glove, or indication of its owner, or how long it had been at that spot. Glove was bagged and sent to the evidence locker.'" Josh looked at Andy and raised his eyebrows.

"Well, Darrell Lewis probably saw the glove listed on the evidence sheet," Andy said, "but he didn't ask anything about it at the trial. And Detective Townley's report says he saw nothing unusual, no substance on the glove, by visual examination. But if the glove has any connection to the murder, aren't there pretty sophisticated tests that can detect substances that aren't visible to the naked eye? Like blood, or saliva?"

"Yeah," Josh replied. "But Townley might not have known about them, since this was fifteen years ago. And Darrell Lewis probably wouldn't have known about those tests, either. But I'm curious about the glove. Most people who drop one like that would notice when they put them on for driving that one was missing, and usually find it right near the car. But not if they're in a rush to leave someplace. You know what I mean?"

"So, you're suggesting that getting our hands on that glove, so to speak, might be worth asking if the Williamsburg cops still have it?"

"Well, we won't know if we don't ask," Josh said, "so maybe we should ask if they still have it. And, assuming they do, see if it can still be tested. Long shot, I know, but that's all we got." He put the sheet back and closed the folder. "That's it for me. Couple of very long shots."

"Well, somebody's got to win the lottery," Andy said. "And maybe we'll pick the winning number. But how do you propose we go from here?"

"I have a suggestion," Josh answered. "Just on the off chance, I called the Williamsburg police and learned that Detective Townley retired a couple years ago, but he's still listed in the phone book. And so is Martha Radford, at the same address that's noted on Townley's interview report. Why don't I call them, and see if they'd talk with us. I'll tell them OD has filed an appeal from his conviction, and that I'm working with his new lawyer, doing some investigation. Maybe they'll be willing to talk, although they don't have to, not without a subpoena, which we won't have. Worth a couple of calls, Andy?"

"Why not," she said. "And if they are willing, then go to Williamsburg, right?"

"Right," Josh said. "And if they agree to talk with us, could you drive down with me on Saturday? I've got cases to work on tomorrow, and you still have bench memos to finish. But if we're going, I'd like to make it soon. Jim's argument on the habeas appeal is a week from Monday, and if we find anything that might help him, sooner is better."

"Saturday is fine," Andy said, "and since Carlo's car is in West Virginia, I assume you'd rent one."

"Actually," Josh said, "I can borrow one from the Justice Department motor pool, here in DC, since this will be official business. One of the perks I haven't used yet." Josh grinned at Andy. "I'll call tomorrow and let you know if the trip is on. Meantime, a glass or two of wine, and maybe stretch a single into a double?"

"If you don't get thrown out at second base," Andy grinned back.

Second base turned out to be under the buttons on Andy's blouse, which Josh undid between sips of wine, followed by deftly unhooking her blue-lace Victoria's Secret bra. "Oh, my," he said, leaning over to kiss her breasts and lick her nipples. "Every high-school boy's dream."

It took all of Andy's will power to keep from urging Josh to make a dash for third base, and then a daring steal to home plate. But she did, and left for her place with a whisper in his ear: "Good batting, slugger. I'll throw you one right over the plate next time you're up."

14

Saturday morning, October 14, Josh picked up Andy at her place at eight, in a Ford Fiesta he'd checked out from the Justice Department's motor pool. He'd called her on Friday and reported that both Moses Townley and Martha Radford had agreed to talk with him about OD Beasley's case, both saying they remembered it well, and both a bit surprised that OD had filed an appeal in federal court of his murder conviction and death sentence, fifteen years after his trial. "They're both retired," Josh had told Andy, "and sounded like they'd welcome visitors."

After Josh pulled into traffic, he outlined their itinerary. "It's about three hours to Williamsburg, maybe quicker, straight down the freeway, with a swing around Richmond. We're due at Moses Townley's house at noon, and Martha Radford said any time in the afternoon is fine with her, and we'll call after we talk with Townley. We should be back in DC in time for dinner, and we can chew on whatever we get from these folks."

"Just don't bite down on something that might be a needle," Andy said.

Guided by the GPS on Josh's phone, they pulled up at Townley's house just before noon, having grabbed burgers at a diner off the Interstate. Small but well-tended, like its neighbors, the house had a wide front porch, on which Townley was sitting, his hand on the head of a black-and-tan Rottweiler, who wagged a greeting as Andy and Josh came through the gate of a white picket fence.

"You folks must be the lawyers," Townley said as he rose to shake hands, "although you're not wearing fancy suits and handing me a subpoena." He was stocky and dark, with a fringe of grey hair around a shiny dome. He gestured Josh and Andy to lawn chairs, and settled back into an old, well-worn easy chair, the dog curled up at his feet. "This here's Rambo," Townley said. "Ten years on the K-9 squad, retired when I did, so I took him in. Never bit anybody, far as I know. Just showed his teeth and growled. Most bad guys are more scared of dogs than guns." He looked at his guests, and started to rise. "Anything I can get you folks? Bud, Coke, water?"

"Thank you, but we're fine," Andy said. "We had burgers and Cokes just a bit ago."

"Well," Townley said, settling back into his easy chair, "you folks have questions about OD Beasley's case." He reflected for a moment. "You know, I feel sort of sorry for that boy. He could be out now, or in a few years, if he'd pleaded to second-degree, which I told him the state would offer if he confessed to killing that girl. I mean, I don't think he went in her house intending to rape her, and he panicked and hit her with that hammer when she screamed. But he just kept saying, a dozen times, 'I did not kill that girl.' So it was his choice, and he got what he deserved, most folks around here think. But if you folks can get him off death row, I think he's paid for his crime."

Done musing, Townley nodded at Josh. "So, you have questions, and maybe I have answers. But won't know until you ask, Mister Barfield."

"Josh is fine," he said. "And Andy for Miss Roboff. We're not formal on Saturdays."

"Mose is fine for me, any day of the week. Questions?"

"Just a couple," Josh said. "We went through your reports on the case, and one thing seemed a little odd, at least to us."

"There's a lot that's odd in most cases that don't get confessed," Townley said. "What's the odd thing in this case?"

"Well," Josh said, "your report on the physical evidence the officers picked up mentions a brown glove an officer found across the street. But the records don't show it was ever tested for blood or any other substance, and it wasn't introduced at trial. Do you have any recollection of the glove, or why it wasn't tested?"

"Not a real clear recollection," Townley answered. "I do remember the officer showed it to me, and I didn't see nothing on it, no blood or anything. And folks drop all kinds of stuff. Plus, it was across the street and a good couple hundred feet from the house. 'Course, the CA—that's what we call the Commonwealth's Attorney down here—could have had it tested, but I guess he didn't." He gave Josh a quizzical look. "Why? You think that glove might help get OD off death row, fifteen years later?"

"No idea," Josh replied. "But we figured it might be worth testing now, if that's possible. And if it's still around, of course."

"Pretty sure it's still in evidence storage," Townley said. "All the police departments in Virginia keep evidence in death-penalty cases until the inmate is executed. Orders of the attorney general, after a man got a new trial because they tossed out the rape kit before another man confessed to the rape and murder. I could check and get it for you, since I worked the case, and nobody would care."

"That would be great, Mose," Josh said. "If you find it, can you send it to me at the Defenders office in Alexandria?" Josh pulled out his wallet and handed Townley a card.

"Sure, I'll do that this afternoon," Townley said. "Get me out of this easy chair. Spend more time sittin' here than anyplace else, which ain't good for my circulation. So if the glove's still there, I'll log it out on the chain-of-custody form and send it right up." He paused. "That's one question. Got any more?"

"Actually, a couple, if you don't mind.," Josh said. "We tried to find OD's trial lawyer, Darrell Lewis. We wanted to ask him if he remembered that glove from the evidence log, and if he did, why he didn't request that it be tested for DNA. But we couldn't find him in any of the lawyers' directories, and figured that he might be retired. Any idea where he might be now, Mose?"

"Sad story," Townley replied. "He did retire, about five years ago, and moved down to Florida. Don't know what town. But I did hear, couple years ago, that he got drunk one night, tripped on something, and fell in a swimming pool and drowned. He had a drinking problem, most lawyers and judges here knew about it, but I never saw him in court under the influence." Townley shook his head. "One thing I can tell you about him, though. I asked him once, after the trial, why he didn't call OD to testify, you know, tell his story to the jury. Maybe one juror might believe him, or at least vote against the death penalty. But Lewis told me he was sure OD was guilty, with his fingerprints on the hammer and the semen in her body, and he couldn't put a defendant on the stand he knew would lie. Lawyers can get disbarred for that, he told me. Don't get me wrong. My opinion, Lewis did the best he could with a bad case. Anyway, too late to ask him about the case."

"I'm sorry to hear that, Mose," Josh said, and paused for a moment. "Couple more questions, if you don't mind."

"Not goin' anywhere," he replied. "No pressing appointments today. Just sittin' on my porch with my dog. So, all the questions you got, if I got answers."

"Okay, here's one," Josh said. "We got the records of the investigation, and you wrote an interview report on a lady named Martha Radford. Just one page, and she didn't testify at OD's trial, so you might not remember her."

"Oh, I remember Martha Radford," Townley said. "She used to dress up like Martha Washington and show tourists around the old Governor's Palace in the Historic District. Most everybody in town knows her." He paused. "Let's see. She lived across the street from those girls. Still does, far as I know. Don't recall that interview, though. I guess you have the report. Something odd about it?"

"Well," Josh said, "it says you asked her if she'd seen or heard anything out of the ordinary that morning, before the officers answered the 911 call from the lady next door. She said she hadn't heard anything, or seen anyone go into or leave the girls' house, but said she'd seen a red car before the officers arrived, but it was gone when they got there."

"I do recall that now," Townley said. "Said the car was parked a couple houses down, her side of the street. But, you know, red cars are a dime a dozen in Williamsburg. And I couldn't check every red car in the county." He paused again. "To be honest, Miz Radford seemed a bit, well, confused. Told me she was deaf, and I don't think her eyesight was that good. She sort of peered at me when I rang her bell."

"So, you didn't ask her any questions about the red car?" Josh asked. "Like the make, or the year?"

"Probably should have," Townley conceded. "Of course, after fifteen years, most cars are up on blocks now, or scrapped. And nobody else saw a red car, or told me about one, at least."

"Okay," Josh said. "We're just checking, and you're probably right that it had nothing to do with that murder. And probably too late to find it, anyway." Josh checked his watch. "Mose, you've been kind to talk with us, but we've got a couple more people to see this afternoon, so I hope you'll excuse us."

"Don't know if I was any help," Townley said, "but if you find anything to get that boy off death row, his momma would be thrilled. I still see her at church, and she's a fine Christian lady. And I'll check on that glove, and send it right up if it's still there."

He paused a moment. "You know, one thing bothered me about that case, still does. That boy wasn't too bright, but the story he told me, the girl inviting him in and asking him for sex, and somebody coming to the front door, and him running out the back door. Didn't sound like something a boy who's somewhat, you know, retarded would just make up. Could have happened that way, but no way of proving it without some evidence some other guy killed her. And his lawyer didn't have any. Too late now, I suppose. But it still bothers me a bit. Well, good to see you folks. I wish you well, and that boy too."

They all stood and shook hands. Rambo wagged goodbye as Josh and Andy left the porch. "Well, Miss Chatterbox," Josh said as they got in the car, "I guess old Mose doesn't flirt with pretty girls. So, what do you think?"

"No needles in that haystack," Andy said. "Unless he finds the brown glove, and it's got the real killer's name sewed into it. And I guess he thinks old ladies are all deaf and almost blind."

"We'll find out pretty soon," Josh said. He pulled out his cell phone and dialed Martha Radford's number. She obviously wasn't too deaf to hear the ring, and said she'd be glad to see them in fifteen minutes. "She'll have tea and cookies for us," Josh said, "so let's be polite and have them, even though I'm not a tea person. I should have taken Mose up on that Bud."

Martha Radford was, indeed, the spitting image of Martha Washington. Greeting Josh and Andy at her door, she ushered them into a chintz-and-doily living room, and showed them pictures on the wall of the first First Lady, and her in almost identical colonial garb, with a flouncy white cap and billowing gown. Tea and cookies were laid out on a coffee table, which Josh and Andy sipped from china cups and nibbled politely.

Martha didn't strike either of them as a confused old lady. "You said you had some questions about the day that poor girl was murdered," she began, swiveling her head from Josh to Andy and back. "I don't know if I can help you, but nothing like that ever happened here before, and never since, so I remember that day, almost like yesterday. But I knew all three of those girls. I brought over cookies when they moved in, three or four months earlier, when school started, and we always said hello. And I knew the boy who killed Laurel. He mowed my lawn and shoveled my walk. He was always polite and cheerful."

She thought for a moment, while Andy and Josh sipped and nibbled. "Although, to be honest, he seemed a bit retarded. Well, just slow, if you know what I mean. I have no idea what happened over there, but he didn't strike me as a violent person, in any way. But you never know what causes people to lose control." Martha shook her head. "Well, you said you had questions. I don't know if I can help, but I'll try my best."

Andy, who had read Townley's one-page report on his interview with Martha, took the initiative this time. "Do you recall talking with Detective Townley that morning?"

"Oh, yes, dear," she replied. "I remember him quite well. Very nice-looking and polite gentleman. I recall he asked me if I'd seen or heard anything unusual that morning. I told him that I hadn't heard anything from across the street before the police arrived, because I'd been vacuuming and had my hearing aid turned off." She touched her left ear. "But I turned it back on when I saw the police cars arrive. And I hadn't seen anyone coming or going from the girls' house." Martha pursed her lips. "I'm not the type who peeks out my windows at the neighbors. Myrtle Cassell, who lived next door to the girls, was a peeker, and she'd sometimes tell me about boys she'd seen leaving early in the morning. But that was their business, I'd tell Myrtle, not mine. She passed away three years ago, but I don't think she knew anything more than what she told Detective Townley, and then told everyone on the block." Martha obviously disapproved of peekers and gossipers.

Josh spoke up. "Do you recall telling Detective Townley that you'd seen a red car parked a couple doors from your house?"

"Oh, yes, I did," Martha said emphatically. "I told him I'd seen it when I went out to fetch my paper, about nine o'clock, but it wasn't there when the police arrived, maybe half an hour later. I knew it didn't belong to anyone on this block, and I thought the police should look into it. At least find out if the driver was visiting one of the neighbors."

Andy took a turn. "Did Detective Townley ask you anything about the car? Like, what model was it, new or older, anything like that?"

"Well, I don't want to criticize him," Martha replied, "but he didn't seem too interested, so I didn't say anything more. It was his job to ask questions, not mine. And it didn't belong to the boy who killed Laurel, anyway."

"If he had asked," Andy continued, "could you have told him anything more about the car than its color?"

"Why, yes, dear, I certainly could have," Martha said. "It was a bright red Corvette, which looked very new." Andy shot a glance at Josh, who sat straight up. "I don't know much about cars," Martha went on, "but my son-in-law had one then, a new Corvette, although his was silver. He took me in it to visit with my daughter and grandkids. So I knew that red car was a Corvette. Exactly the same, except for color."

Josh took over, almost squirming with excitement. "By any chance, had you seen that car before, on this block?"

Martha nodded firmly. "Oh, yes, dear. In fact, I'd seen it in front of the girls' house three or four times before. There was a tall young man who visited them, and I saw him get into the car once, a couple of weeks before Laurel's murder, but I never met him or knew his name. Of course, I wasn't peeking when I saw him. I just happened to be on my porch, getting the paper." She paused a moment. "Oh, one other thing about the red Corvette. It wasn't parked in front of the girls' house that morning, because there were a bunch of leaf bags on the curb. The city was going to pick up leaf bags on Monday, and lots of people had them out on the street. The bags would have made it hard to park there."

Andy jumped back in. "Do you recall anything else about the car, Mrs. Radford?"

"Yes, I do," she replied. "It had a William & Mary decal on the rear window. I noticed, because it was parked facing down the street. So I assumed it was a friend of the girls from school."

Josh took over. "This young man you saw getting in the car a couple of weeks earlier, did you see his face, or could you recognize a picture of him?"

"No, dear, but I do remember he was very tall, as I said. My son-in-law is six feet three, and this young man was just as tall. I remember he had to really stoop down to get in the Corvette when I saw him that time."

Martha's face suddenly reflected shock. "Are you asking because you think this young man might have had something to do with Laurel's murder? I mean, from everything I heard and read, and saw on TV, it seemed pretty clear that young black man killed her, and I know he was convicted and sentenced to death." She looked mortified. "I mean, if he didn't kill her, and I know he always denied that, do you think the person in the red Corvette might have done it, or at least been in the house when she was killed?"

"We don't know," Josh said. "But, as you said, it's certainly something the police should have followed up, if Detective Townley had asked you the questions we have. Of course, it may turn out to be perfectly innocent. And, as you also said, Odell Beasley was convicted of Laurel's murder by a jury that heard the evidence against him. So I wouldn't worry about it now."

Martha looked relieved. "You're right, dear. From what I read, the evidence against him was pretty convincing, and I wouldn't second-guess the jury." She paused a moment. "Although he was such a polite young man. But I guess you never know what's inside a person from just chatting with them, you know, about mowing your lawn or shoveling your walk."

Josh glanced at Andy. "Mrs. Radford," he said, "we have another appointment this afternoon, and we need to get there soon. But you've been very helpful, and thank you so much for the tea and cookies."

"You're very welcome, dear, both of you. And if you have more questions later, I have plenty of tea and cookies, and I always like company."

"I think we might," Andy said, as she and Josh rose to leave. "And if we do, your tea and cookies are delicious."

15

Josh and Andy didn't have another appointment in Williamsburg, but they hadn't wanted to linger with Martha Radford, who seemed eager for company, chatting, and more tea and cookies. "It's three now," Josh said as they got into the motor-pool car. "That burger was long ago, and tea and cookies didn't fill me up. And if we leave for DC now, we'll get stuck in traffic when we hit the Beltway. So, how about an early dinner here in Williamsburg? Most places shouldn't be crowded with tourists."

"Sounds good to me," Andy said. "And we can chew on what Mose and Martha told us, and figure out what to do next. No needles yet, but I've got a couple thoughts."

"Well, that makes one of us with thoughts," Josh said. "But that's better than none."

The Historic District was five minutes from Martha Radford's house. Josh circled around and pulled up at Chowning's Tavern, which looked very colonial. He gave the car to a valet in knee-britches and red vest. "Oh, before we go in," Andy said to Josh, "are those the police reports in the folders on the back seat? And can you grab my laptop? I brought it along to make notes from our interviews." Josh reached in and picked them up, as the valet gave them a funny look before he drove off. "I didn't bring the transcripts," Andy explained as they entered the tavern, "but something Martha told us about the red Corvette clicked with something Moses said about the brown glove. Maybe no connection, but I recall something in his reports, from what you showed me the other night, that might connect them."

"Well," Josh said, "I've got all his reports here, so tell me what clicked for you. I didn't hear a click, but I turned my hearing aid off at Martha's."

"No, you didn't," Andy laughed. "When she said the red car was a Corvette, your ears both pricked up."

Once inside, a colonial-garbed waitress in a flouncy white cap led them to a colonial-style plank table in the rear, although only a few tables were occupied in mid-afternoon. They plunked Josh's folders and Andy's laptop on the table, picked up the menus, and asked the waitress for two mugs of Sam Adams before they ordered. "Might as well have some colonial beer with our colonial food," Andy said. When the beer arrived, Andy ordered colonial corn chowder and a green salad, and Josh picked Brunswick stew with colonial flatbread. They clinked mugs, and Josh toasted to "Good old King George. Long may he reign."

After a slug of Sam Adams, Josh asked, "So, what's in the police reports that gave you a click, Andy?"

"Well, if I remember correctly," she said, "Townley interviewed both of Laurel's roommates, and one of them gave him the names of two or three guys that came over for parties at their house, and maybe had sex with Laurel in her bedroom, or at least made out with her, although she didn't know for sure. Do you remember that report, Josh?"

"Rings a bell," Josh replied. "I think that report's in this folder." He picked one up, riffled through, and pulled out a sheet. "Okay, here it is." He scanned it quickly. "The roommate who gave him those names was Liz Gronbach, and the names were, um, Tory Tucker, Nick Cashman, and Winslow Early. All William & Mary law students. So, you think one of them might be the guy whose voice OD said he heard before he scampered out the back door? Assuming that actually happened."

"Possibly," Andy said. "Assuming OD's story was true. But let's assume that for now."

Josh nodded, then pulled several more sheets from the folder. "Okay, these are reports of Townley's interviews with these guys, all by phone." He briefly scanned each sheet. "Tory Tucker's parents said he was home with them all week in McLean. Um, let's see. Same with Nick Cashman's parents in Danville. No follow-up by Townley on either one."

Josh scanned the last sheet. "Winslow Early, Junior. Unlisted home phone in Richmond, so Townley called his Williamsburg number. This was on Saturday, the day of Laurel's murder. No answer, so Townley left a call-back message." Josh scanned the sheet again. "Okay. Early called back on Sunday afternoon, said he'd been home with his father in Richmond since Friday, drove back to Williamsburg on Sunday morning." He looked up from the sheet at Andy. "Hmm, this is interesting. Townley recognized Early's dad as the Virginia attorney general, and called his office on Monday. Early Senior said Junior had come up on Friday, they had dinner that night at a country club in Richmond, played indoor tennis on Saturday, and Junior drove back here on Sunday, just like he told Townley."

"So, all three of these guys had alibis for the day of Laurel's murder," Andy said. "All confirmed by their parents. That pretty much eliminates them, I guess. So, now what, Sherlock?"

"Now what is lunch," Josh said, as the waitress served the food with a little colonial-servant curtsy. He and Andy ate for a while, then Josh resumed their conversation, between bites.

"Well, you said you heard a click between what Townley said about the brown glove, and Martha about the red Corvette. What clicked for you, Andy?"

"Just a tiny click," Andy said. "But Martha said the red Corvette was parked two doors down from her house, right? And Townley said the brown glove was picked up by the officer at about that spot, lying on the curb." She made a clicking noise with her mouth. "The glove, according to Townley's report, was the kind that drivers wear, leather, with holes in the palm." She gave Josh an inquisitive look. "You'd know better than me, Josh, but don't some sports car drivers wear that kind of glove?"

"Yeah," he said, "especially ones who drive cars like Corvettes. Part of the race-car image." He gave Andy a Light-Bulb look. "Are you thinking that if we could find out, somehow, if any of those three guys drove a Corvette back in 2002, it might be the glove-dropper?"

"Right," Andy said. "And if Townley finds the glove and sends it to you, and you can get it tested for DNA, if that's possible, and we find out if any of these guys drove a Corvette back then, if that's possible, then. . ." Andy paused, looking skeptical. "And keep in mind, Josh, these guys all had alibis. So these are three pretty big haystacks."

"That's a double 'possibly' scenario, Andy," Josh said, "but we've got no needles so far, and I've actually got an idea. Something I picked up from my job, working on a couple of cases that involved cars." He polished off his Brunswick stew, drained his Sam Adams, and pulled out his cell phone. "Sherlock Holmes didn't have a cell phone, but they do save driving a horse-carriage all over London."

"Who are you calling?" Andy asked.

"The Virginia state police, Dr. Watson." Josh smiled, pleased with himself. "The Virginia DMV headquarters is closed on Saturdays, but the U.S. attorney's office can call the state police, and they can get into DMV records on their computer. I'm pretty sure they go back at least to 2002. So, without further delay, I'm going to call the state police in Richmond, tell them I'm with the U.S. attorney, and ask them to see who owned red Corvettes in Williamsburg in 2002. Probably add McLean, Danville, and Richmond, because if one of these guys drove one, it might be registered to their parents. That'll expand the list by a bunch, but we're just looking for one that's registered under one of these three names, Tucker, Cashman, and Early."

Josh pulled up his contact list, and punched a button. After a few seconds, he said, with an official tone, "Good afternoon. This is Joshua Barfield. I'm with the U.S. attorney's office in Alexandria. Can you connect me with someone who has access to the DMV records?" A short pause. "Thank you. I'll hold." A few seconds later, Josh repeated who he was, then said, "Sure, no problem." He pulled out his wallet and extracted a card. "My government access code is DOJOFPDEDVAJB." Andy quickly figured this meant Department of Justice, Office of the Federal Public Defender, Eastern District of Virginia, Joshua Barfield. Josh waited about a minute, sipping on his second Sam Adams, while Andy took a gulp from hers and looked at Josh expectantly.

"Okay, thank you very much, Sergeant Wilson. Here's what I'm looking for. All persons who were registered owners in 2002 of red Corvettes in Williamsburg, McLean, Danville, and Richmond. I think the certificates have the color, but all Corvettes would be fine. And the model year would be from 2000 to 2003. I think the '03 models were out in the fall." Josh paused. "Ten minutes? That's great. All I need are the owners' names. Let me give you my number." Josh recited his cell number. "Sergeant, thank you for this favor. Talk to you soon." He clicked off, and beamed at Andy. "Wow! She says she'll call back in ten minutes."

They chatted, both of them nervous, until Josh's phone buzzed. "This is Joshua Barfield." He listened for a minute. "Three red Corvettes in Williamsburg, five in McLean, two in Danville, and twelve in Richmond. Let's try Williamsburg first. All I need are the owners' last names." He listened for ten seconds. "Okay, how about McLean?" A "nope" from Josh, another "nope" after Danville. "Okay, how about Richmond?" He listened for another thirty seconds. "*Wait!* That's the one I'm looking for. Red Corvette, 2001. Registered to Winslow Early. Got the address?" He paused a few seconds, writing the address on a napkin. "Sergeant, you deserve a commendation for this." He paused another thirty seconds. "Tell you what, Sergeant. That's even better than a commendation. I'll send you three tickets for Selena Gomez at the Classic Amphitheater for you and your daughters, next Friday. Promise. Give me your home address and I'll have them sent by FedEx." He wrote the name and address on the napkin. "My pleasure, Sergeant. Thanks again, and enjoy the concert." Josh gave Andy a thumbs-up. "She didn't seem to recognize Winslow Early's name, which is good, since my inquiry didn't ring any warning bells."

"Holy shit, Josh!" Andy exclaimed. "That rings a bell with me. Winslow Early's now on the Fourth Circuit in Richmond. One of my asshole fellow clerks, guy named Todd Armistead, clerked for Judge Early last year. Very conservative judge, and apparently still active in state politics, you know, behind the scenes. Todd said Early helped get his clerkship with Justice Novak, and promised to help Todd if he ran for his dad's seat in the state senate, a few years down the road."

Josh nodded. "I do know that Early's on the Fourth Circuit, Andy. Our office has had several appeals he sat on. Ruled against us in each one, I think." He frowned. "But remember," he said, "when Early Senior was attorney general, back in 2002, he gave Townley an alibi for his son the day of the murder. So, I'm wondering if maybe Junior loaned his 'Vette to a friend while he was in Richmond, assuming that's the same red 'Vette that Martha saw. Maybe we should look into Junior's friends, back then. Laurel's roommate, Liz Gronbach, gave Townley the names of three guys who'd been at their house, but if we track her down and call, maybe she'd remember more. What do you think, Andy? Worth a shot?"

Andy had opened her laptop and was clicking on keys while Josh was speaking. She looked up from the screen. "Oh, sorry, Josh, didn't mean to ignore you. Yeah, I think calling Liz is worth a shot, and we can probably find her through the William & Mary alumni office, even if she's married and changed her name." She looked back down at her laptop screen. "Just out of curiosity, I googled Judge Early. I think he wrote a really bad opinion in a case that's up on a cert petition at the Court, and Alex asked me to write a pool memo on it. Hang on a second. I'll try his Wikipedia entry. And then, since we're pretty much done here in Williamsburg, we can head back to DC. Okay?"

"Sure," Josh said, signaling the waitress for the check.

Andy suddenly looked up, her eyes wide open with surprise. "Holy shit, Josh! I just found something that looks a hell of a lot like a needle. Hold on a minute." Josh waved the waitress away, while Andy scrolled down on her screen. "Josh, listen to this," Andy said. "Wikipedia says Judge Early was attorney general of Virginia from 1998 to 2006. And he was elected president of the National Association of Attorneys General in 2002. Okay?" Josh nodded, looking a bit puzzled.

"So, there's a link on that entry to a press release from the NAAG, and I clicked on that link," Andy continued, excitement in her voice. "Josh, you won't believe the date on that press release."

"I have a guess," Josh said, "but tell me."

"Okay," Andy said. "It's dated December 15, 2002. Let me read it to you." She looked down at the screen. "'At its winter meeting in Chicago, December 13-15, Winslow Early, the Attorney General of Virginia and president of the National Association of Attorneys General, presided at a session on Saturday, on Interstate Cooperation in Enforcing Child-Support Payments.'" She glanced at Josh, then continued reading. "'General Early heralded the on-going development of a national computerized data base of persons who are delinquent in making child-support payments and have moved from the states in which the payments were ordered. Some of these 'delinquent dads,' as Early called them, owe thousands of dollars in payments. 'With this new database,' he said, 'they can be tracked, found, and forced to pay for the support of children who often live in poverty because of disregard of this parental duty.' And then, blah, blah, blah."

Andy gave Josh an Oh, My God! look. "Do you know what this means, Josh?"

"Holy shit back to you, Andy," he replied. "My guess was right. Unless there's some mistake, which I doubt, it means Judge Early was in Chicago the day of Laurel's murder, and probably the day before and after, since he was the president of this group. Wow! So, his son's alibi for that time was a lie, on both ends. Junior may or may not have been in Williamsburg that Saturday, but he sure as hell wasn't playing tennis with his dad in Richmond."

"Nope," Andy said, closing her laptop. "Of course, that doesn't prove Junior murdered Laurel. But if he's the guy who drove the red Corvette that was registered to his dad, and if it was the same one Martha saw that morning, that puts him at her house at the same time as the murder. That makes OD's story a lot more believable, right? Junior would be the guy at the front door, telling Laurel he was horny. That's what OD told Moses Townley the guy said."

"Okay," Josh agreed. "But you're right, Andy, that still doesn't prove Junior killed her." He thought for a moment. "Just to be devil's advocate, here's another scenario. Junior goes to Laurel's house that morning, looking for sex. Maybe she invited him over, maybe he just showed up. He comes in the house and goes to her bedroom, discovers her body, covered with blood. Okay?" Andy nodded. "He's not sure she's dead, so he shakes her body, or touches her, at least. He's still wearing his driving gloves. He panics, runs into the bathroom, tries to wash off the blood on his gloves. Then he runs out the front door, runs to his car, drops a glove by mistake, then hauls ass out of there."

Andy held up a hand. "Whoa, Josh, not so fast. What about the hammer in the front lawn, and what about the alibi from his dad?"

"Good questions, Andy," Josh replied. "Let me think for a minute." He looked around, waving the waitress over. "Since there's no line out the door," he said to her, "could you fetch us a couple more Sam Adams?" She went to fetch them, and Josh turned back to Andy. "Okay, let's say Junior picked up the hammer, still wearing his gloves, ran out the house with it, and tossed it in the bushes." He paused for a second, shaking his head. "But that doesn't make much sense, if he didn't kill her, does it?"

"Not to me," Andy said. "And washing his gloves in the bathroom sink doesn't make sense, either, if he didn't kill her. And what's your scenario for calling his dad in Chicago?"

"Assuming he didn't kill Laurel, and just discovered her body," Josh said, "he's afraid somebody might have seen him when he left the house. So, he calls his dad, tells him something really bad happened in Williamsburg, but he doesn't want to get involved, and doesn't want to talk with the cops about it." Josh paused again. "His dad says, I don't want to know about it, so don't tell me. But if the cops call me, for any reason, I'll tell them you were with me in Richmond. I'm the attorney general, and they'll probably believe me."

Andy laughed. "Josh, with all due respect to your legal brilliance, you sound like a really desperate lawyer with a really guilty client. Those scenarios make even less sense than OD's story." Andy thought for a minute. "Here's one that makes more sense, at least to me. Ready?" Josh gave her a Go Ahead nod. She paused for a minute as the waitress returned with the beers, and they both took swigs.

"Okay," Andy continued, "part of your first scenario does make sense, so I'll use those parts. Here's how I'd change it, though." She ticked off points on her fingers as she spoke. "Junior was there, saw OD run out of the house, found Laurel on her bed, naked and obviously in a just-fucked state, by a black guy, no less. He gets enraged, starts to choke her, but she scratches his arms, which makes them bleed, and starts screaming. He grabs the hammer from the desk, bashes in her skull, which gets her blood on his gloves. He tries to wash off the blood on his arms in the bathroom, which also leaves some hair in the sink. Then he grabs the hammer, runs out the front door, tosses the hammer in the bushes, accidentally drops a glove by the Corvette, and hauls ass out of there, as you said. You still with me, Josh?"

He gave her another Go Ahead nod. "So, Early Senior, being attorney general of Virginia, is almost certain to hear about the murder in Williamsburg when he gets back from Chicago to Richmond. And, when Junior calls and tells him something really bad happened in Williamsburg, Senior is bright enough to figure Junior might have had something to do with the murder. Maybe even recognizes Laurel's name as Junior's girlfriend, or at least a fellow W & M law student."

Josh gave Andy a Keep Going nod. "And, being attorney general of Virginia, Senior knows that if Junior becomes a suspect in Laurel's murder, or even gets charged with it, his political career would be toast. And maybe his dream of a federal judgeship, as well. So, when Moses Townley calls that next Monday, Senior gives Junior a convincing and plausible alibi. And, when OD gets arrested and charged with the murder, and then convicted and sent to death row, everything is hunky-dory for the next fifteen years."

Josh chuckled. "Until a really brilliant young lawyer hops on the Internet and pricks her finger on a very sharp needle." Josh raised a hand and high-fived Andy. "So," he continued, "if your scenario is more convincing than mine, which it is, we still need the brown glove, and hope it has enough of Laurel's blood to match her DNA. And we'd still need some DNA from Junior to see if it matches the blood and hair from the bathroom. Otherwise, a really good defense lawyer might convince a jury that my scenario of Junior finding Laurel's dead body, after OD had sex with her and killed her when she resisted, raises more than a reasonable doubt that Junior actually killed her." Josh shook his head, with resignation. "Of course, I'm just speculating, since it's highly unlikely Junior would ever get charged with her murder. After all, OD's on death row for her murder, and will stay there, unless Jim Carruthers wins the habeas appeal and gets him a new sentencing trial."

Andy reached over and put a hand on his. "Hey, Sherlock, don't get all discouraged. We got a good needle with the Corvette, and another one with Senior's phony alibi. Maybe the glove will give us the one to sew up this case. So let's wait until we hear from Mose Townley, who's definitely no Holmes."

"Okay, Miss Nancy Drew," Josh said, looking brighter. "So let's get on the road, and maybe unwind at my place."

Andy stuck out her tongue. "You mean get undressed at your place. And maybe get to home plate this time?"

The waitress had left the check with the beers. Josh added a ten-dollar tip, and handed the valet another ten when the car arrived. Done looking for needles for the day, Josh and Andy got back to his place at six, shared hits of Lemon Haze, along with hits to first and second base on the couch. Their day ended in Josh's bed, with daring steals of third and home.

16

Andy had invited her grandmother, Bella Warshofsky, to visit her the third weekend in October, with dinner on Saturday with Justice Novak, his wife Gloria, and Novak's 92-year-old father, Anton. The past two weeks, from Chief Justice Terman's death through the trip to Williamsburg with Josh, had been busy and stressful, and Andy was glad to have a break. She hadn't planned anything for Friday evening, thinking Bella might be tired from the train trip from New York to DC, and they'd just go out to dinner near Andy's place. But on Thursday, Andy was leafing through the Washington Post and spotted a short piece about a play called "Life in a Jar," scheduled for a Friday performance at the Jewish Community Center at 16th and Q streets.

The article said the play, first written in 1999 by three ninth-grade girls in Overton, Kansas, as a project for National History Day, was based on the true-life story of Irena Sendler, a Polish Catholic social worker in Warsaw, who rescued 2,500 Jewish children from the Warsaw ghetto, smuggling them out and placing them with sympathetic Catholic families and in Catholic convents and orphanages. The play was called "Life in a Jar" because Irena and her helpers, who belonged to an underground group called Zegota, the Polish Council to Aid Jews, wrote the real names of the Jewish children and their parents, along with their assumed Christian names, on slips of paper and placed them in jars, which they buried in a garden near the Gestapo headquarters. After the war, Irena dug up the jars, and helped some of the children to reunite with their families, although most of their parents and siblings had perished in the ghetto or the gas chambers. The article also said that Irena, who went by the code name "Jolanta" while in the ghetto, had died in 2008, at the age of 98, but that her daughter, Janka, who lives in Warsaw, would be speaking about her mother after the play's performance.

The article about the play fascinated Andy. When she was a teenager, her mom had told her about Bella's having been smuggled out of the Warsaw ghetto, and somehow surviving the war before being sent to New York to live with relatives who had left Poland before the Nazi invasion. But when Andy asked Bella about this, she hadn't provided any details, saying the experience was too painful to discuss. It occurred to Andy that Bella might have been one of the children whose names were placed in the jars. Seeing the "Life in a Jar" play, Andy thought, and having a chance to hear, and perhaps meet, Irena's daughter might overcome her grandmother's reluctance to tell Andy more about how she survived the Holocaust.

Before Bella left Yonkers for the train to DC, Andy called her and asked, casually, if she would be interested in attending a play on Friday night. Bella replied, "Anything you want to do, bubeleh. I haven't been to the theater in years, so it would be nice to see real actors on stage, instead of watching tiny people inside the television. So, Andy, is this play a comedy, musical, or drama?"

Andy decided to fudge a bit. "From what I read about it, bubbe, it's about children who get rescued from evil people by a courageous woman who hides them until the evil people have been driven away. It's based on a real story, they say, and it has some hard parts, but it sounds very inspiring."

That seemed to satisfy Bella, who said, "It sounds like a happy ending, and most stories with happy endings have some evil people who do bad things until the good people come to the rescue and save the ones who are in danger, especially the little ones. Believe me, Andy, I've seen that in my own life."

Andy was surprised by this, wondering if Bella knew anything about the play and Irena Sendler, but just replied, "That's a plan, then. I'll call and get tickets for tomorrow night."

She picked up Bella at Union Station around two on Friday afternoon. They took a taxi to Andy's apartment, and Bella had a short nap on Andy's bed. They went to an early dinner at a Lebanese restaurant, The Cedars, near Andy's place. While they were having baklava for dessert, with cups of strong coffee, Bella said, "This play we're going to see, Andy, the title is funny. 'Life in a Jar.' Do you know what that means?"

Andy decided to stop fudging. "Tell me, bubbe, do you remember anyone named Irena Sendler, from when you lived in Warsaw?"

Bella looked up, puzzled. "No, I don't think so. Why do you ask?"

"Do you remember a woman named Jolanta?"

Bella's eyes opened wide. "Andy, that was the woman who took me out of the ghetto. I remember her very well, like it was yesterday. She wore a white nurse's uniform, I remember, and brought in bags of food and medicine in a cart. And she would take out children, telling their parents it was the only way to save them. Otherwise they would starve, or die of typhus or dysentery. Some mothers refused to let Jolanta take their children, but most agreed, since babies and children were dying every day." She looked at Andy sharply. "Tell me, bubeleh, is this play about Jolanta?"

"Yes, it is, bubbe."

"So that's why you just told me it's about children who are rescued from evil people," Bella said with a chuckle. "You made it sound like Little Red Riding Hood. Did you think I would not go to the play if you told me it was about Jolanta?"

Andy looked abashed. "Well, yes, bubbe, but we don't really have to go if it might be disturbing for you. Do you remember telling me, when I was about fourteen, that your life started when you got to New York, and you didn't want to talk about what happened before then?"

"Andy, back then I thought you were too young to hear about what happened to me, and even more, what happened to my parents and my little brother, who died in the gas chambers at Treblinka. But now you're grown up. Or at least you're growing up." Bella smiled. "So, this play is about Jolanta. And where is the title from?"

Andy explained about putting the real and assumed names of children in jars, and the names of families who sheltered them, and burying them in a garden. "That's how the Red Cross people were able to find your real name after the war, when the jars were dug up, and they found your relatives in New York."

"Oh, my, Andy. I never knew how they found out I was really Bella Feldman, and that I had relatives in New York. I do remember my name while I was with the family on the farm near Warsaw was Marya Wozniak. They had two daughters about my age, Karolina and Magda, and I looked sort of like them. They taught me Polish, since we spoke only Yiddish in the ghetto and I knew just a few words of Polish."

Bella paused, closed her eyes for a minute, then opened them and looked into Andy's eyes. "Now I'm having all these memories of living in the ghetto, with hardly any food, and children who looked like sticks, begging for scraps of bread. Every day, there were bodies lying in the street. Some of them were little children, just bundles of rags. The ghetto police would come with carts, and throw the bodies on them, and haul them away. And I remember Jolanta coming to our apartment and telling my mother she could save me before the Nazis took everyone away. Jolanta also offered to take my little brother, Avram, with her. He was just four, and he hung onto my mother, and cried, and she wouldn't part with him. And I remember how Jolanta got me out of the ghetto. I was too big to smuggle out in her cart, like she did with babies and little ones. But she took me to a square where there was a sewer drain, it was late at night, and I went down the drain with a boy who was about fourteen. He took me through the sewer tunnel to a place where I climbed up a ladder and came out behind a factory. Another woman—I never knew her name— was waiting for me there, and took me with her on a tram, outside the city, where the Wozniaks picked me up in a horse-drawn wagon, and put me under some bags of cabbage until we got to their farm." Bella paused. "Oh, my, Andy, I've wanted to tell you this, but it never seemed a good time. I guess this is the time. And the play? I can hardly wait to see it."

Andy and Bella took a cab from dinner to the Jewish Community Center, where the play was being performed in the theater of the Morris Cafritz Center for the Arts. As they entered, an elderly woman spotted them in the lobby and bustled over. "Oh, my goodness! Bella Warshofsky! I haven't seen you for, what, fifteen years. And you don't look a day older."

Bella lit up with recognition. "Sarah Goldenbaum! I heard you moved to Washington, to live with your son, the lawyer. It's so good to see you again. And you don't look a day older, yourself." Both women laughed, and Bella said, "Sarah, this is my granddaughter, Andrea Roboff. She's a lawyer, too, and is a clerk for a justice on the Supreme Court."

Andy and Sarah exchanged hugs, and Sarah said, "It's such a shame that Chief Justice Terman passed away. I met him two or three times at events here at the Community Center. He was such a nice man, a real mensch, if you know what I mean, Andrea. He always said, 'Just call me Sam.'"

"And just call me Andy," she replied. "I just found out about this play yesterday, Sarah, and Bella just told me, an hour ago, that Irena Sendler rescued her from the Warsaw ghetto, smuggled her out through a sewer and hid her from the Nazis with a Catholic family on a farm. After the war was over, the Red Cross found her relatives in New York. Bella never told me that before, but that's why we're here. And what brings you here, Sarah, if you don't mind my asking."

"Not at all, Andy, although it's nothing like Bella's story. But I'm on the board of the Community Center, and I'm going to introduce Irena's daughter, Janka, after the play. I hope you can stay for a short while after she speaks. I'm sure Janka would love to meet one of the children her mother rescued."

"Well, just long enough for me to tell her how grateful I am to her mother," Bella said. "I just got down here on the train this afternoon, to spend the weekend with Andy, and this is a long day for an old Jewish lady."

"Oh, Bella," Sarah said. "Old Jewish ladies are the ones who stay up to make sure everyone has enough to eat and drink, and then they clean up after all the guests have left. That's my job here, anyway. But what are your plans for tomorrow? If you're not busy in the afternoon, would you and Andy be up for visiting the Holocaust Museum? I'm a volunteer docent there once a month, and tomorrow is my day. So I could take you around the exhibits, and we could have tea in the café, and catch up on old Jewish lady stuff, like children and grandchildren. I've got three of each, and plenty of pictures on my cell phone."

Bella thought for a moment. "Sarah, I wasn't sure I could ever visit the Holocaust Museum, but I think I'm ready now. Especially since you'll be there. Is that okay with you, Andy?"

"Bubbe, I wasn't even going to suggest that, since I thought it might be too hard for you. But I've wanted to go, myself, and Sarah's very kind to invite us. We've got dinner planned at six-thirty with Justice Novak, so would one o'clock be a good time? That will give us time to freshen up before dinner."

"That's perfect, Andy," Sarah said. "And you won't even need tickets. Just tell them you're meeting Sarah Goldenbaum. I've got some pull there. You know, old Jewish ladies can get just about anything done. And I'll see you after the play and introduce you to Janka."

Just then, the foyer lights dimmed, and Bella and Andy went into the theater. Andy found the play gripping, especially the scenes where Irena pleaded with mothers to part with their children to save them from almost certain death from starvation, disease, or the Nazis. But it was inspiring, and ended with a standing ovation and four curtain calls.

After the actors finally left the stage, Sarah entered with a short, somewhat stout woman in her sixties. "Ladies and gentlemen," Sarah began, "I'm Sarah Goldenbaum, a member of the Community Center's board, and I have the pleasure of introducing Irena Sendler's daughter, Janka, who has come from Warsaw to tell you a bit more about her courageous mother." She paused a moment. "Before I do that, however, I'm delighted to tell you that one of those children is with us tonight. Her name was in one of the jars that Irena buried in her garden, and she survived the Holocaust because Irena helped her escape the ghetto through a sewer, and find refuge with a Catholic family that defied the Nazi threat of execution for sheltering Jews. Courage, as we know, is not defined by creed or color. So, would my dear friend, Bella Warshofsky, please stand and be acknowledged as a link to Irena."

Bella looked shocked, but rose from her seat while the audience burst into applause. Shyly, Bella turned each way to face them, then sat down. She leaned over to Andy and whispered. "Oh, my goodness, Andy. I thought we'd just have a nice dinner this evening and chat for a bit before we turned in. I never expected anything like this."

Sarah was helping someone adjust the microphones on the stage, and people were chatting quietly while they waited for her to introduce Janka. Andy patted Bella's arm. "Just think, bubbe. If I hadn't been leafing through the newspaper yesterday, with nothing in mind, I wouldn't have seen the article about the play, and we probably wouldn't be here tonight. And I wouldn't have learned about how you were saved by Irena, and you wouldn't be meeting her daughter." Andy smiled. "Do you remember meeting my friend, Josh, at our graduation?" Bella nodded. "Well, Josh has a favorite word about what happens in our lives. He calls it indeterminacy. We can't know for sure what's going to happen next, good or bad. So, you didn't know that Irena would save you, but she did. And if she hadn't, then I wouldn't have been born. And neither of us would be here tonight. That's what Josh means by indeterminacy."

Bella smiled back at Andy. "Your friend Josh may be right. But we are both here, and we will make the best of whatever happens while we are on this Earth. Who can know the days, or months, or years to come? So I say to Josh, 'L'chaim.' To life. And the gifts it brings us. And you, my dear Andy, are a gift beyond measure."

Andy took a deep breath, trying hard to hold back the tears that made her blink. Just then, Sarah Goldenbaum quieted the chatter in the auditorium. "I'm sorry for the delay," she said, "but we had some gremlins in the microphones that were causing mischief. But thank you for being patient. And now, I'd like you to meet Irena's daughter, Janka. She has come from Warsaw, where she works as a book editor and, I'm told, collects children's art and Garfield dolls." Andy joined the chuckles at this reference to a cartoon cat.

Janka took the microphone from Sarah and stood quietly for a moment. "I thank you all for coming to this play about my mother," she said in heavily accented English. "I apologize if I am difficult to understand, but if I spoke in Polish you would have no trouble, am I correct?" There was more laughter. "This wonderful play, written by three young girls who started with just a magazine clipping about my mother, has told you much about her and the work she did in saving children from the Holocaust. I want to tell you one more thing about her, which the play did not mention. After the war, she married for a second time, to my father. They had met in university, before the war, but were separated during that time, because he was Jewish, and fortunately survived the war. So, I am both Catholic and Jewish. And I take for my life the best of both religions, which begins with children. The Psalmist says, 'Children are a gift of the Lord,' and Jesus said, 'Bring the little children to me, for the kingdom of God belongs to them.' And my mother believed, and taught me, that there is no Jew or Gentile in the heart of a child, just the trust they put in us to keep them safe from harm. That was my mother's life's work, saving as many as possible from the most terrible harm the world has yet seen."

Janka paused, scanning the silent auditorium. "I would like to leave you tonight with two things my mother said, when she was given awards in Poland and Israel, late in her life. She said, 'Every child saved with my help is a justification of my existence on this Earth, and not a title to glory.' And she said, when she was called a hero, 'Heroes do extraordinary things. What I did was not an extraordinary thing. It was normal.'" Janka scanned the audience again, and Andy thought her gaze stopped on Bella. "Helping others in need," Janka continued, "should be normal, whoever and wherever they are, and whoever and wherever you are." Andy felt goose-bumps on her arms, and reached for Bella's hand, squeezing it gently, getting a gentle squeeze in return. "So, my friends," Janka concluded, "thank you again for this tribute to a person who did for children in Warsaw what any normal person should have done."

The members of the play's cast had silently come from behind the curtain and flanked Janka, as the audience rose and showered them with applause. Andy stood with Bella, still holding her hand, and let her tears slide down her cheeks. As people began filing out, Sarah came down the steps from the stage. "Bella and Andy," she said, "please come up and meet Janka." They followed Sarah back to the stage, and waited a moment while Janka hugged and thanked the cast members. Then she turned and opened her arms to Bella. "Sarah told me that you had come from the Warsaw ghetto to this wonderful country of freedom," she said. "And I'm glad my mother made that possible. I have met more than twenty children she helped to rescue, but I do remember her telling me about the girl who came through the sewer, just before the Nazis found the escape route and sealed it at both ends. You must be that little girl, one of the last to escape."

Bella was so overcome, she could only nod. Then she brightened up and smiled. "We must go," she said. "I am an old woman, but I will make sure that my granddaughter comes to visit you in Warsaw. God willing, with children of her own. And to see the city that has come back to life, where children can play and laugh."

Janka nodded, and turned to Andy. "My mother has many children, and you are one of them. Please come, whenever you can."

As they left, Sarah said, "Well, this old Jewish lady is going to stay and clean up. But you need some rest. I called, and there's a cab waiting at the door. So, Andy, give Bella a nightcap, put her to bed, and I'll see you both at one o'clock tomorrow." They both thanked Sarah, took the cab back to Andy's apartment, had the nightcap—wine for Andy and tea with a splash from a bottle of Glenlivet that Andy had bought for Bella's visit—and went to bed, Andy on her convertible couch and Bella, at Andy's insistence, in her more comfortable bed.

17

Saturday morning, Andy awoke at eight, to the smell of coffee and the sounds of kitchen bustle. "Oh, I'm sorry, Andy," Bella said, coming out with a cup of coffee. "I tried to be quiet and let you sleep a bit longer, but now that you're awake, I'll start breakfast. I'm making scrambled eggs with lox, if that's all right with you, and I'll toast some bagels with cream cheese. I see you stocked up on Jewish food for me, which was sweet of you."

"That's sweet of you, too, bubbe," Andy said. "Let me get washed up, and I'll be right back to help you."

"Do I look like I need help?" Bella said. "You'd just get in my way, bubeleh. You sit, and drink your coffee. And you're going to eat a good breakfast. You're too skinny, and you probably eat out of the microwave."

"Okay, okay," Andy said as she headed for the bathroom. "You be a Jewish grandmother, and I'll eat every bite. But I'm not too thin. You want me to look like a dumpling. Like a giant kreplach."

Andy loved bantering with Bella, but she knew it was often a cover, to keep in something that worried or bothered her. When she got back to the little round table, Bella had breakfast ready, and sat across from Andy. "Tell me if the eggs are too runny," Bella said.

"They're perfect, bubbe," Andy replied. "Now you tell me something. Seeing the play last night, with hardly any warning, must have been difficult, with all the memories it brought back. So, are you still up for visiting the Holocaust Museum this afternoon? That might be even more difficult."

"Oh, no," Bella said. "The play didn't bring back those memories, Andy. They've always been there, every day, sometimes just a flash when I see a little girl, about eight, or a little boy, about four, or someone who looks a bit like my mother. But watching the play, and meeting Irena's daughter, made me realize that hiding all of this from you, my dear Andy, let you know only part of me, the part that began when I came to New

York. You just knew your bubbe, who changed your diapers, pushed you on the swing in the park, kept copies of all your school papers, and was so proud of what you accomplished in college and law school."

Bella spread cream cheese on a toasted bagel while she was talking, then put it on Andy's plate. "A nice bagel mit schmeer for you, bubeleh," Bella said. "Not as good as fresh New York bagels, but what's to do?" Always the Jewish grandmother, Andy thought, even as Bella continued talking. Her voice took on a serious tone. "Watching my only grandchild grow up from a chubby, happy baby to a beautiful, talented young woman was a wonderful experience. It still is, of course. But you only knew that part of me, Andy. The part of me from the ghetto in Warsaw, leaving my parents and brother forever, that part of me I hid from you. But that's also part of you, Andy, and you need to know it. And to learn about how all that happened. That's why we're going to the Holocaust Museum this afternoon. Not so much for me, but for you, Andy, to see and learn about the missing part of me."

Bella's expression suddenly changed from serious to smiling. "So, bubeleh, finish your bagel while I clean up the mess I made in your kitchen. Think of the starving children in Africa."

"Actually, I was thinking of the starving children in the ghetto, begging for scraps of bread," Andy said.

"Enough, enough already," Bella said. "Now, you finish getting dressed, and then we'll walk over to the farmers market you told me about. You don't have any fresh vegetables and fruit in your refrigerator."

"Okay, but promise you won't haggle over the prices. That's too much of the Jewish grandmother."

"Feh," Bella snorted. "If they charge too much, I just won't buy."

The visit to the Eastern Market, three blocks from Andy's apartment, took over an hour, as Bella moved from stall to stall, scrutinizing every apple, pear, head of broccoli, bunch of carrots, and bell pepper, checking to see which were the freshest and whose prices were the lowest before she made her purchases and placed them in a mesh bag she'd brought from Andy's kitchen. "Now, you eat all of these, and make some nice salads," Bella admonished Andy as they walked back. "I can tell your diet is not healthy. And stop noshing on those chips I found in your cupboard. Too much salt, not enough vitamins."

After viewing the permanent exhibits, it was close to two-thirty, half an hour until meeting Sarah at the café. Andy checked her map and guided Bella to a special exhibit on the lower level, called "Some Were Neighbors: Collaboration and Complicity in the Holocaust." Andy hadn't picked this exhibit for any special reason, but thought viewing it might use the time before meeting Sarah at three. The displays of photographs and artifacts were labeled, "Neighbors, Workers, Teachers, Policemen, Religious Leaders, and Friends." Andy followed Bella as they circled the exhibit room, her grandmother silent, as she had been for most of the tour, speaking only to ask Andy if she'd like to stay longer at an exhibit or move to the next. Bella hadn't commented on anything they had seen, and Andy hadn't either.

Suddenly, Andy was startled by a sharp intake of breath from Bella. She turned to see her grandmother, hands clutched to her chest, recoiling in shock before a photograph on the wall. "Andy," Bella called, "come, see this!" She quickly came to Bella's side. Pointing to the photo, Bella exclaimed, "This man, I know this man!" The photo showed three uniformed men, wearing caps with visors, standing in a row, with a fourth man adjusting the cap of the man in the middle. The one nearest the camera wore an armband on his left arm, with the words "Juden Polizei" above a Star of David.

Bella put her finger on the man who was obviously in charge. "This man, Andy, I know this man. He is Rudy Novitsky. He was an officer in the Ghetto Police, the Jews who served under the regular Polish police and the Germans. They called them the Jewish Order Service, but we called them the Ghetto Police. And the building behind them, that was the headquarters of the Ghetto Police on Ogradowa Street."

"You knew that man, Bella?" Andy asked, incredulous.

"Yes, he owned an eyeglass store on Chlodna Street. We lived just two squares from his store. I saw him many times in his police uniform, giving orders to the men he commanded. He was very harsh with the children who shouted bad names at the Ghetto Police. Some children would yell 'Oink' at them, like pigs, and run away."

Bella leaned closer to the photo, and put her finger on the young man standing to Novitsky's left. "And this one, Andy, this is Anton Novitsky. He was Rudy's nephew, just a teenager, maybe seventeen or eighteen. But he was also in the Ghetto Police. I saw him often on street intersections, directing traffic, and sometimes pushing a cart to pick up garbage."

Andy leaned her face within inches of the photo. "Bella, this boy you say is Anton Novitsky. Are you sure of his name?"

"Oh, yes," Bella said. "You see this scar on his cheek, right here?" The boy in the photo had a semi-circular scar on his left cheek, perhaps three inches long, from his cheekbone to his jaw, the shape of a crescent. "I think he got that scar from being kicked in the face by a horse. That's what someone told me. Some children would whinny like a horse when they saw him, but I never did that. And he was not really harsh with children, not like his uncle."

Andy could hardly believe what she was seeing. "Bella, this boy looks almost the same as Alex Novak's father, Anton. His face looks the same, and his nose is sharp and pointed, just like this boy. And he has a scar just like this on his left cheek."

"Andy, are you sure?" Bella asked. "I know this is Anton Novitsky, and you say he is Anton Novak?"

"Of course, I could be wrong," Andy said. "It's been more than seventy years since this photo was taken. But there's no mistaking the face, and the scar. And Alex told me his father was from Warsaw, and came here after the war." Andy shook her head in puzzlement. "But Alex is Catholic, and I assume his father is also Catholic. And if Anton Novitsky was in the Ghetto Police, he must have been Jewish, not Catholic."

"Andy, we are going to have dinner with Justice Novak and his father in just a few hours," Bella said. "If this boy is his father, what should we do? We can't just ask him, Are you really Anton Novitsky, of the Ghetto Police? And what if we are wrong, and this is just a strange resemblance between two different people?"

Andy thought for a moment. "Bella, I have an idea. But first, let's sit down." She steered Bella to a bench in the center of the exhibit room, sat beside her, pulled the plastic box Sarah had given her from her pocket, and pushed the red button. Less than a minute later, Sarah entered the room and hurried over, looking concerned. "Bella, are you okay? Do you need to rest?"

"Sarah, we're both okay, and thank you for coming so quickly," Andy said. "But I have a request, although I'm not sure you can help us."

"Anything I can do, Andy. Just ask me."

Andy got up from the bench and walked over to the photo on the wall. "Sarah, this photograph here," she said, tapping it with a finger.

"Bella recognized someone in it that she knew in Warsaw. Would it be possible, do you know, to have a copy for Bella to take with her?"

Sarah answered quickly. "Oh, yes, Andy. The curators have digital copies of all the photos in the museum on computers. They make copies for some of the traveling exhibits that we send to schools and groups around the country. It wouldn't take ten minutes for me to get a copy from them." She turned to Bella, still sitting on the bench. "Is this a friend of yours from Warsaw, Bella, or a relative? These are photos of members of the Jewish police in the ghetto, but most of them did not survive the Holocaust."

"Yes, this is someone I knew, Sarah," Bella said. "Not a friend or relative, but someone my father knew very well. It would be nice to have this photo of him, and I could show it to Andy's parents." Andy smiled at Bella's quick-witted response.

Sarah glanced at her watch. "Tell you what," she said. "It's close to three, and I was going to meet you in the café. If you go over there and find a table, you could order tea or coffee, and I'll meet you there in ten minutes." Without waiting for an answer, Sarah bustled out the entrance to the exhibit room.

"Andy, can I ask you," Bella said, "why you want a copy of this photo? You aren't going to push it in Anton Novak's face, I hope. That could be very embarrassing, if this boy is him, or even more if it is not."

"No, bubbe, that's not what I plan to do. You're right. I don't want any embarrassment. But I do want to know for sure, before we have dinner with him, to avoid any embarrassment. So let's go over to the café, and wait for Sarah. And you'll hear what I plan to do." Bella looked puzzled, but followed Andy without asking any questions.

The café was almost empty, and Andy led Bella to a table in the rear. She pulled out her cell phone, punched a number on her contact list, and waited a few seconds. "Alex, this is Andy," she said. "Oh, you did know it was me." She paused a few seconds. "No, Bella's fine. And I'm fine too. Listen, Alex, I don't mean to sound mysterious, but I have something I'd like to show you, before we have dinner, if you don't mind." She paused again. "No, no, it's not about a case, Alex. But it is something delicate, and I'd rather show you what I have before dinner. I hate to impose on you, but can Bella and I come over now? We're downtown, near the National Mall, and we can grab a cab, and be there in fifteen or twenty minutes."

Andy glanced at Bella, who looked up with a quizzical expression. "Okay," Andy said. "And can I ask a favor, Alex? Would it be difficult for us to talk privately, just you and me and Bella? I can explain when we get to your house." Another pause. "Oh, they're out to visit one of Gloria's friends, and will be back around five, is that right?" Andy repeated this for Bella's benefit, paused, then chuckled. "Well, since you're not barbequing in October, Bella would be happy to show you how to properly bake salmon and mix a healthy salad. You can't keep a Jewish grandmother out of your kitchen." Another pause. "Yes, it does have something to do with you, Alex. But can you wait twenty minutes without stewing over it?" Just then, Sarah Goldenbaum walked briskly to their table, holding a blue folder and looking pleased. Andy held up one finger as Sarah sat down, patting Bella's hand. "Thank you, Alex," Andy said. "We'll be there in twenty minutes, and you can get out an apron for Bella."

Andy clicked off her phone, and picked up the folder Sarah had placed on the table. It had the seal and name of the Holocaust Museum on the cover, embossed in gold. "I had them make two copies of the photo, Andy," Sarah said. "They came out very well."

"Sarah, we really appreciate this," Andy said. "You've been a wonderful help. I'm sorry to leave you here, without a chance to visit and see pictures of your children and grandchildren, but Bella and I have to meet someone in twenty minutes, up past the Zoo. But I'll get Bella back down here before Christmas, I promise, and we can spend a whole day together."

"Andy, I understand," Sarah said. "Just let me know when, and we'll make a day of it." With hugs all around, Andy and Bella left Sarah and went to catch a cab from the stand outside the museum entrance. During the ride to Novak's house, Andy assured Bella that Alex was capable of handling any kind of news, even when he was on the losing end of a Supreme Court vote on a case he felt strongly about. Andy didn't tell her how devastated Novak had been after Sam Terman had died of a heart attack that Novak felt he might have caused.

"Besides, Bella," Andy said, "going to dinner with what we know, or suspect, about his father, and not telling Alex in advance would make it very awkward, to say the least. And skipping dinner with a diplomatic headache wouldn't be fair to Alex, considering how often he's said how much he wants to meet you."

Bella nodded, as the cab pulled up in front of Novak's house. "You remember what you told me about your friend Josh and his favorite word, Andy? 'Indeterminacy,' am I right? We only went to that last exhibit because we had some time before meeting Sarah. And I had no idea that photo would be on the wall, with Rudy Novitsky and his nephew. And, of course, I have no idea how Justice Novak will react, if that actually is his father. Perhaps he already knows, and just hasn't told you about it."

"I doubt that, bubbe, but we'll find out in just a few minutes," Andy said, helping Bella out of the cab. Generous Andy handed the driver ten dollars, twice what the meter read.

18

Alex Novak was standing on his front porch as Andy led Bella through the wrought-iron gate. He was dressed in grey slacks and a blue shirt with the sleeves rolled up. As she and Bella approached the porch, Andy glanced at the blue folder in her hand, wondering if she should have waited until another day to show the photo to Alex, and just come over at six-thirty for a pleasant dinner with him, Gloria, and Anton. She was sure Bella, who had a knack for engaging people she had just met in conversation as if they were old friends who hadn't seen each other for years, would have charmed them. But coming to dinner without bringing the photo, Andy realized, would have produced one of those Elephant In The Room occasions that made everyone wonder what the hell was not being said.

"Welcome, welcome," Novak greeted them, smiling broadly. He came down the steps and took Bella's arm, guiding her to the door. He helped Bella out of her coat, and hung it with Andy's parka on the coat tree in the hallway. "I'm so glad to meet the person Andy credits with giving her the inspiration to use her talents to the fullest," he said. "I sometimes think Andy could wear my black robe and do a better job than the rest of us. So, come in and let me fix you a drink, anything you'd like."

Bella beamed, while Andy caught a strong whiff of the nervousness beneath Novak's cheerful exterior. He glanced at the blue folder in Andy's hand as he ushered his earlier-than-expected guests into a comfortable living room, in which a fire was crackling behind a wrought-iron fireplace screen. "Please, sit and tell me what you'd like. I've got a nice, chilled Beringer chardonnay for you, Andy," giving her a knowing wink. "And for you, Bella, if I may? And I'm Alex, unless you're a lawyer and I'm wearing my black robe. Then I'm 'Could you repeat the question, Justice Novak?'"

Andy winced at Alex's somewhat awkward effort to lighten the mood and put Bella at ease. She knew he could have no idea where she and Bella had spent the past few hours, or what was in the folder, but obviously suspected, from Andy's request to come over earlier than planned, that it was something he'd prefer not to see. Bella, who had sat down on a brocaded sofa, clearly sensed Novak's discomfort. "Well, Alex," she said brightly, "no need to repeat your question. Club soda would be fine for me, if you have that."

"Coming right up," Alex said, filling two wine glasses from a bottle in a silver ice bucket on a side table, and a tumbler from a bottle of club soda. He handed one glass to Andy, who sat on a matching easy chair, and the tumbler to Bella. "Cheers," he said, raising his glass.

Andy decided it was time to end the suspense that she had created. She lifted her glass. "Cheers, Alex. And thank you for letting us come over without much warning. Can I show you something that Bella and I found just an hour ago? Bella can explain what it is."

Novak sat in a matching easy chair, taking a sip of his wine as Andy opened the folder and handed him a copy of the photo. He looked at it for a few seconds, then recoiled with a shock of recognition. He sat, speechless, staring at the photo. He cleared his throat, and took a deep breath before speaking, his voice strained. "This must be my father, the boy on the left, with the armband. The scar, the face, his nose. It *is* my father. And I can read what the armband says. 'Jewish Police.'"

Novak looked at Bella, grandmotherly concern on her face. "Can you tell me more about this, Bella? You haven't met my father. How could you recognize him, wherever you found this picture?" He suddenly turned to Andy, holding out the photo. "You recognized him, Andy, didn't you? And did you and Bella come here from the Holocaust Museum? That's what it says on the folder, and that must be where you found this."

Andy nodded. "You're right, Alex. We saw it on the wall of an exhibit about collaborators with the Germans, and a friend of Bella's who volunteers at the Museum made two copies for us."

"Collaborators?" Novak shook his head in disbelief. "My father collaborated with the Germans? Bella, tell me more about this. Please." He leaned closer to her, with a beseeching look.

"Alex, let me tell you what I know." Bella paused, aware of Novak's shock. "The older man, the officer, is Rudy Novitsky. He was in charge of the Ghetto Police in our neighborhood. This building behind them was their headquarters. And the young man, with the scar on his face, was Rudy's nephew, Anton Novitsky. My father knew Rudy very well, and I knew his nephew, not well, but I knew his name. And someone told me he got the scar when a horse kicked him when he was younger. He was about seventeen or eighteen then, and I was eight when I was rescued from the ghetto. And when he joined the Ghetto Police, I only saw him directing traffic and cleaning garbage from the street."

Bella leaned forward and put a grandmotherly hand on Novak's arm. "I don't know for sure, Alex, but I think that's all he did. He was just a boy, and I would think he joined the Ghetto Police to please his uncle, and to do something useful. I can't imagine he took part in any of the brutality and deportations, although some of the Ghetto Police assisted the Nazis in herding Jews to the Umschlagplatz, the train station that took them to Treblinka. I didn't know of Treblinka, of course, until after the war. But that is where my parents and little brother died, in the gas chambers."

Andy was grateful that Bella was trying to ease Novak's distress. He sat silently, Bella's hand on his arm, his eyes closed. Suddenly, a phone rang in the kitchen. Startled, Novak got up. "Excuse me, let me answer that and I'll be right back."

Bella looked at Andy, and spoke quietly. "I am sorry for Alex, Andy. Perhaps we should have let this go. If Anton has not told Alex about this, he must have his reasons."

Andy thought for a moment. "Bubbe, you told me this morning that you kept part of you, a very important part, hidden from me all these years. Leaving your parents and brother in the ghetto, knowing you would probably never see them again. And now I know all of you, if you know what I mean, and that makes me feel even closer to you. If Anton has kept this hidden from Alex, maybe knowing about his life will bring them closer."

"Andy, if Anton did more in the Ghetto Police than direct traffic and clean the streets, it might hurt Alex terribly to learn this. Of course, Anton might not talk about it. His secrets, whatever they are, are his. To share them with Alex, or keep them inside, he will choose. And it is not for us to judge him."

Novak came back from the kitchen, looking apprehensive. "Bella and Andy, that was Gloria. Her friend, Marjory, is not feeling well, so she and Anton are coming back. Marjory lives close by, and they should be here in just a few minutes." He ran a hand through his hair, pacing by the fireplace. "Bella, I need your help. What should I do? What would *you* do?"

"Alex, that I cannot tell you. That is for you to decide. But Andy just reminded me, while you were on the phone, that I had kept secrets from her, about what happened to me and my family, in Warsaw, until I saw a play, last night. But it was about a real person, the woman who rescued me from the ghetto, leaving my family behind. Going to see that play, I had to tell Andy those secrets, which I did. That play was like this photo of your father. If he has secrets, he will tell you, or not. That is for him to decide." Bella paused. "Perhaps, Alex, it would be better for me and Andy to leave you and your father to talk about this, or not, without us. Perhaps I have a headache, and you can make our excuses to Anton and Gloria, and have dinner another time."

"That's kind of you, Bella. But you went to the play with Andy, and I have the photo, and I should do what you did. Besides, without showing it to Anton, he would know very soon that I was keeping something important from him. He can tell, just like I can tell. This is something he and I both have, and it can't be covered up. And having you here, both of you, will make it easier for me. So please stay. Besides, I told Gloria you were here, and she said that was great, to have more time to chat before dinner."

Just then, a car door slammed, and they heard the sound of Gloria's wheelchair coming up the ramp behind the house. Alex took a deep breath. Andy and Bella both stood up, as Anton wheeled Gloria into the living room. She looked up and beamed. "Andy, it's so good to see you again. And you are Bella, the grandmother we should all have, from what Andy's told me about you. Alex told me you came early to help him with dinner, which is quite a relief. Salmon is tricky, to get it just right."

Anton remained standing behind Gloria's wheelchair, but Alex took his arm and led him to Andy. "You remember Andy Roboff, from the barbeque this summer with Chief Justice Terman." Anton gave Andy a courtly nod, but did not speak. "And I'd like you to meet Andy's grandmother, Bella Warshofsky." Anton turned toward Bella, with another courtly nod.

Bella stood up and moved toward Anton, but did not extend her hand. Noticing the steely expression on Bella's face, Andy started to move between them, fearing that Bella might actually strike him. She had rarely seen this look, only when Bella was going to confront someone who had deeply offended her. Shaking her head at Andy, Bella moved so close to Anton that he took a step backwards. She looked up at him, a full head taller, and spoke with steel in her tone.

"Gedenkt ir mir!? Ikh bin Bela Feldman fun Bankovy Gas in Varshe. Un ir zayt Anton Novitsky – Rudi Novitsky's plimenik. Ikh gedenkt aykh. Tsi – gedenkt ir mir!?"

"Do you remember me? I am Bella Feldman, who lived on Bankowy Street in Warsaw. And you are Anton Novitsky, the nephew of Rudy Novitsky. I remember you. So, do you remember me?"

No one in the room breathed during the silence that followed. Andy knew Bella had spoken in Yiddish, and from the demanding tone in her voice, figured that she had asked Anton if he were from Warsaw. Bella leaned her head back, her gaze directly into his eyes. Anton kept his eyes on Bella's. Then he nodded slightly, and answered her in a firm tone.

"Yo, ikh bin Anton Novitsky. Un ir zent Bela Feldman di kleyne meydele fun Bankovy Gas. Ir zent di meydel vos hot zikh aroysgeshmuglt fun geto durkh di kanalen. Ikh hob gevust vegn dem. Ober ikh hob keynem nisht derseylt. S'git mir anoye aykh tsu zen un anarkenen az ir hot durkhgemakht dem khurbn."

"Yes, I am Anton Novitsky. And you are Bella Feldman, the little girl on Bankowy Street. You are the girl who escaped through the sewer tunnel. I knew about that, but I never told anyone. I am glad to see you here, and know that you survived."

Bella kept her stare into Anton's eyes without blinking, then nodded. "A sheynem dank. Un ikh bin dankbar az ir hot oykh durkhgemakht dem khurban."

"Thank you. And I am glad that you survived."

Anton turned and glanced at the photo Alex had placed on the coffee table. He picked it up, looked at it for a few seconds, nodded again, walked to Gloria, and placed it on her wheelchair tray. Alex cleared his throat. "Please, everyone, sit. And Gloria, come over by me." Bella took her seat on the sofa, Anton in a chair directly across from her. He nodded again to Bella, turned to face his son, and spoke in English, his words clearly enunciated, but with a slight accent that Andy recognized as matching Bella's.

"Alex, I have told you since you were a young boy that my parents died in a fire on their farm, outside Warsaw, before the war. I told you their names were Vaclav and Maria Novak." He paused a moment. "My parents were Solomon and Ruth Novitsky. They were deported from the ghetto on the Day of Atonement in nineteen forty-two. They died in the gas chamber at Treblinka. I learned that after the war."

Novak leaned toward Gloria, reaching out to take her trembling hand in his. Anton turned his head to face Bella, then back to his son. "Since Bella is here, and knows who I am, I will tell you things that she knows about me, and things she does not know. I have nothing to keep from any of you." It was clear that Anton intended to tell a chilling story, and no one interrupted as he continued.

"We lived on Klodny Street, near the Great Synagogue. My father lost an arm in a machine shop, and could not work after that. We had very little money, and often no food. My father's brother, Rudy, had an eyeglass shop and gave us food when we had none. After the Germans invaded and occupied Warsaw, they forced Jews to build a wall around the ghetto. The Germans forced the Jewish Council, the Judenrat, to establish an internal police force."

Anton gestured toward the photo on Gloria's wheelchair tray. "My uncle, Rudy, had spent a few years in the regular Polish police before the war, so he was made a captain in the Jewish Police. Rudy told my father that if I joined, our family would get double the food ration of other Jews. I was seventeen, but tall for my age, and admired my uncle, so I joined. They put me to work as a traffic warden and sanitation duty, picking up garbage from the street. It was not like a regular policeman, although we wore a uniform, and were given bicycles to patrol the streets."

Anton paused, and looked again at Bella, who returned his gaze, without expression on her face. Turning back to Alex, he continued. "At first, conditions in the ghetto were not too bad. But the Germans forced Jews outside the ghetto to live inside the wall. And food became scarce, with more people to feed, and no markets for the farmers outside Warsaw. We were instructed to watch for smugglers, who would bring food through hidden gates or over the ghetto wall. If they were reported by the Ghetto Police, the Germans would shoot them. Some of them were children. When Rudy would ask, I would say I had seen no smugglers."

Anton turned back to Bella, and spoke with a catch in his voice. "I will tell you something, Bella Feldman. You had a friend, a little girl named Sophie. She was about eight or nine. Do you remember her?" Bella nodded, knowing what would come. "One of the Ghetto Police, I don't recall his name, caught Sophie near the ghetto wall with a bundle of food. He took her to the German police, on Szucha Avenue. She was shot in the street, along with five other smugglers, two of them children. I saw that happen."

Anton suddenly heaved, choking back a sob. Novak started to rise from his chair, but Anton waved him back down. "Alex, let me finish. It is time to tell you what I did." He composed himself, then continued. "In July, the Germans ordered that the Ghetto Police assist them in rounding up Jews and taking them to the gate by the Umschlagplatz, the railroad station. We each had a quota of five, each day. If we did not bring five, the Germans said they would take our families. This was something I could not do. So I told Rudy that my mother was very ill with dysentery, which was true, and that I must stay home and tend to her. She was his brother's wife, so he agreed, but told me if she recovered, or died, I must return to my duties."

Anton turned again to Bella. "Did you know a boy, about twenty, named Stanislaw Korbat? We called him Stash, and he lived on your street." She nodded with recognition. "He was in the Ghetto Police with me," Anton continued. "But he came to me one day and said he had joined the Jewish Armed Resistance, which later fought the Germans in the Uprising. He wanted to know if I would join his group, but I was afraid to leave my family. But one night, I was on the street and heard a noise in an alley. I looked around the corner, and I saw Stash standing over a German soldier, lying on his back. Stash did not see me, but he ran down the alley with a rifle in his hand. I went over, and saw the soldier was dead. His head had been crushed by a paving block. It was dark, and I saw no one around. So, as quickly as I could, I took the uniform off the soldier, his jacket, blouse, and trousers. I rolled them up under my arm, and ran back home. I hid the uniform under a pile of clothes in a closet."

During this account, no one in the room had moved, seemingly frozen. Suddenly, Anton rose, went to the side table, picked up a bottle of vodka, and filled a tumbler. He took a gulp, returned to his chair, and sat. "About two weeks after this," he continued, "Rudy came to our apartment and said the Germans were going to come that night and round up Jews from our street, but would spare the families of the Ghetto Police. 'Your mother is well now,' he told me, 'and you must assist us, taking them to the gate by the Umschlagplatz.' I told him I would report to the police station at eight o'clock. He patted me on the head, and left."

Anton lifted the tumbler and took another gulp. "Around eight o'clock, I heard shouting in the street, and looked out the window. There was a troop of German soldiers, herding people along the street. I went to the closet, took off my clothes, and put on the German uniform. My parents were in the bedroom, with the door closed. I rolled up my clothes in a small bag, and ran down the stairs in the back. I came out the alley to the street, and walked at the rear of the column as it passed. I saw Rudy at the head, but he did not turn around. When we reached the gate, I simply walked through with the soldiers. Children were crying, and no one paid attention to me."

Anton took another gulp from the tumbler. "When we got to the Umschlagplatz station, I walked around a corner, and ran behind a shed, where no one saw me. I took off the uniform and put on my clothes. Then I walked as quickly as I could to a square where Polish people were walking and sitting, as if nothing unusual was happening. Stash had given me the address of a house near the square, and said that if I ever escaped the ghetto, to go there. I found the house, and knocked on the door. A man opened it, and I told him that Stash Korbat had told me to come. He let me in, and asked how I got there. I told him about coming through the gate with the German soldiers. He did not tell me his name, but said he could connect me with the Polish Home Army, the underground resistance. He took me to another house, near the outskirts of Warsaw, where members of the Home Army lived, and stored weapons and explosives in the basement. I went on several actions with them. We blew up several railroad bridges and a storage depot for German trucks. One night, when the Germans invaded the ghetto to round up all the Jews who remained, we tried to blow holes in the ghetto walls with dynamite, so Jews could escape, but Germans saw us and started shooting, and we barely escaped."

Andy had read about the Polish Home Army in her Holocaust course at Barnard, and the attempt to blow holes in the ghetto walls. Now, sitting across from Anton, more than seventy years after these events, she could almost picture the story he was telling as if it were a movie. She glanced at Bella, whose expression now reflected relief. Alex sat transfixed, still holding Gloria's hand. Anton lifted his tumbler and drained it, then glanced at his watch.

"I will finish this story at some other time," he said, "since we are here for dinner with Andy and Bella, who are special people I want to know as friends. And there is cooking to be done. But I have one last thing to say, before we sit around the table and talk about more pleasant things."

Anton got up from his chair, went over to Novak, and placed his hand on his son's shoulder. Novak looked up at his father. "You are Alex Novak, and I am now Anton Novak. The boy in that photograph is not the same person who raised you to become who you are. But he is the same person who lived in the Warsaw ghetto, the Jewish boy who went to the Great Synagogue every Shabbas. Do you understand what I mean?" Novak nodded, tears flowing down his cheeks. "Well," Anton said, smiling warmly at Bella, "Alex told Gloria that you are a maven in the kitchen, and that you can show him how to bake salmon to perfection." He turned and smiled at Andy. "And perhaps tomorrow, if you and Bella are free, you can come with me and Gloria to the National Gallery. There's a special exhibition of Italian paintings, on loan from the Uffizi Gallery in Florence, and Alex tells me you know everything about the artists."

Andy spoke to Anton for the first time since meeting him at the backyard barbeque. "Not everything," she said with a laugh, "but enough to tell you the story of Botticelli and the model in 'The Birth of Venus.' Her name was Simonetta Vespucci, and it's a classic tale of unrequited love."

On that note, the dinner was more than pleasant, and the salmon was cooked to perfection. The visit on Sunday to the National Gallery ended with Anton lifting Bella's hand and giving it a courtly kiss.

19

"Oh, Andy, my dear, wonderful Andy," Bella said, a catch in her voice, as Andy lifted her roll-on bag and slid it onto the rack above the seat on the Amtrak train that would take Bella from Union Station back to New York. "You have no idea how much I love you, and how much I am glad to be your bubbe."

Andy gave her a good-bye hug, holding back tears. "And you have no idea how much I love you, and how much I am glad to be your bubeleh."

Sensing Andy's emotions, Bella patted her cheek and smiled. "When you were a little girl, Andy, you used to annoy me by repeating what I said. But now, I see it means that you feel how I feel. We are very much the same, my dear Andy, how we feel about important things."

Andy nodded her agreement, afraid that she would cry. "Have a good trip, bubbe," she said after a moment. "And the next time you visit, we will definitely go up the Washington Monument and see the pandas at the Zoo." A tinny voice warned that the train would leave in two minutes. After another hug, Bella took her seat and Andy left, heading up the hill from the station to the Supreme Court.

Monday morning, October 23, was a sunny, crisp beginning to a day that followed a weekend that had changed the lives of the five people who had gathered on Saturday for what they all assumed would be a pleasant, relaxing dinner at Alex Novak's house. The dinner had ended that way, but none of those who sat around the dining-room table was the same person who had listened to Anton Novak's chilling story in the living room.

After their visit to the National Gallery with Anton and Gloria on Sunday afternoon, Bella had said only one thing to Andy about the day before. Sitting on Andy's couch, sipping tea with a splash of Glenlivet, Bella had broken a spell of silence between them. "I was thinking, Andy, about that long word your friend Josh likes, to mean you never know what might happen to change your life. Can you remind me?"

"Indeterminacy," Andy prompted.

"That's the word," Bella said. "And I was thinking, if a Ghetto Police other than Anton had seen me that night, when I went down into the sewer tunnel, I might have been shot on the street, like my friend Sophie." She shook her head. "And neither of us, my dear Andy, would be here tonight." Andy nodded, but let the silence return, thinking of how her life had changed since Josh had sauntered over at the first-week mixer, offering her a cup of Sam Adams and charming her with his bantering. And wondering what might happen to change it again, in ways that no one could determine.

With Bella on her way back to Yonkers, Andy looked forward to her day at the Court. At ten that morning, three weeks after Chief Justice Terman's sudden collapse had abruptly and shockingly ended the first oral argument of the term, the remaining eight justices would resume hearing arguments that had been postponed while the Court was in recess. The first argument, which had drawn a crowd that filled the Court's chamber on that sad Monday, would resume from the beginning, with Solicitor General Tony Ewing at the lectern, but without any hectoring by Alex Novak, who had promised Ewing that he would ask no further questions.

Andy went straight to Novak's chambers when she arrived from seeing Bella off, chatting briefly with Angie Conforti at her desk, and with Dave Park in the clerks' office. She didn't even say "Good morning" to Amanda Cushing and Todd Armistead, who didn't glance up from their computers. Novak was not in his office, and Andy presumed he had gone down to the justices' robing room, or had stopped by another justice's chambers before the arguments began.

The Court's chamber was only half full of spectators when Andy slipped into the clerks' section shortly before ten. After the "All rise" and the Marshal's intonation of the traditional "Oyez" opening, the eight justices took their seats at the bench. Novak glanced over and gave Andy a nod and wink, as if to say, "Don't worry, I'm on my best behavior." She gave him a nod and wink back, as Justice Karl Sorenson, presiding as the senior associate justice, said, "We will resume argument this morning in

Khalid versus United States. General Ewing, you may proceed whenever you're ready. And you have the full thirty minutes for your argument."

Everyone in the chamber was aware of the vacant center seat that was now reserved for the next Chief Justice, about whom media speculation had been swirling for the past three weeks, with a dozen names of potential nominees being floated, but with no consensus on any front-runner. President Chris Chambers had not said a word since Chief Justice Terman's death that even hinted at his choice. His press secretary, Ken Roby, had deflected all questions, saying only that the selection process would be careful and thorough, although the president was aware of the need to have the Court at full strength, with important cases pending on its docket.

When Ewing moved to the lectern, he began, "Mr. Chief Justice, and may it please . . ." Suddenly realizing his slip, he quickly said, "I'm sorry, Justice Sorenson," to which Sorenson replied, "We are all sorry, General Ewing, but there's no need to apologize. Please proceed." After that, Ewing launched into a technical discussion of exceptions in the Federal Tort Claims Act that, in his view, precluded recovery for "claims arising in a foreign country" in which American citizens were injured or died through the "negligent or wrongful act" of a federal employee. Perhaps because Alex Novak had forced Ewing to confess the government's reliance on a questionable informant in the case, his colleagues in this round asked few questions of Ewing, and even fewer of the lawyer who represented the widow and children of Malik Khalid, whose name Ewing had not uttered once.

When the argument concluded, Justice Sorenson said, "Thank you, counsel. The case is submitted." Andy spotted a grimace on Tony Ewing's face as he gathered his papers and left the chamber. He likely shared her sense, from the limited questioning of the lawyers, that a majority would affirm the verdict against the government, and the jury's award of six million dollars to Khalid's family. An even split of the eight justices would produce the same result, but without a written opinion to set a binding precedent in future cases.

Andy had planned to stay in the chamber for the next argument, set to begin at eleven. Just as the petitioners' lawyer rose to begin his argument, a buzz of chatter arose from the press section, directly across the chamber from the clerks' section. Andy noticed someone whispering in the ear of Bob Barnes, who covered the Court for the Washington Post. He abruptly left his seat, followed by several other reporters. Several justices, looking puzzled, swiveled their heads as the press section quickly emptied. Something's happening, Andy realized, deciding to return to Novak's chambers and see if the commotion had anything to do with the Court. Barnes and the other reporters, she figured, wouldn't skip this argument unless there was breaking news on their beat to cover.

Andy heard sounds from the television set in Novak's office as she briskly entered his chambers. Three weeks earlier, she had watched the same screen as CNN had reported the collapse of Chief Justice Terman, and his death an hour later at George Washington Hospital. All three of her fellow clerks, along with Angie, were clustered around the set. Andy joined them as Wolf Blitzer, under a "Breaking News" banner, was saying, "The White House press secretary, Ken Roby, has informed the media that President Chris Chambers will shortly announce his nominee to head the Supreme Court, to replace Chief Justice Samuel Terman, whose sudden death three weeks ago created a vacancy in the Court's center seat." Blitzer paused for a second, listening to the voice in his ear bud. "We're taking you now, live, to the White House."

The scene shifted to the steps that fronted the Rose Garden, cameras aimed at a lectern behind which Ken Roby was standing. He moved aside as President Chambers, smiling broadly, took his place, tapping the microphone to make sure his words would be audible. He was flanked on his right by a tall, distinguished looking man with a sober expression, and a petite woman in a pink jacket and skirt. Both looked to be in their mid-fifties. On the President's left stood two younger people, an even taller man and a woman with flowing blond hair. Andy had a sudden premonition, and waited to see if she was right.

"Good morning," Chambers began. "As you know, three weeks ago the Nation suffered the loss of a distinguished and universally admired public servant, Chief Justice Samuel Terman. His record on the Supreme Court will remain a legacy that honors both him and the Nation he served so well." Bullshit, Andy thought. Chambers hated Sam, and was glad to see him go. But that's what any politician would say, she reminded herself.

"Over the past three weeks," Chambers continued, "my staff and I have conducted a careful and thorough search for a nominee as Chief Justice who could fill the Court's center seat with equal distinction. We considered many outstanding and experienced judges on our state and federal courts, all of them highly qualified to lead the Court. We were determined to select a nominee who respects our Constitution's division of powers between the three branches of our government, and who will be guided by the wisdom of our Founding Fathers in creating a charter that places the power to make laws in the hands of the people's elected representatives." So much for judicial review of legislation, Andy thought, cynicism welling up as Chambers implicitly dismissed the Court's role in keeping lawmakers from trampling on the people's constitutional rights.

"I am delighted to announce this morning that our search has ended," Chambers went on, "with a nominee whose records as an elected official of his state, and as a federal judge, span twenty years of distinguished service." He paused, as the cameras shifted to the man to his left, then back to Chambers. "Before I introduce him, and his charming and supportive family, I am pleased to announce that the distinguished chairman of the Senate Judiciary Committee, Senator Charter Weeks of New Hampshire, has agreed to hold a confirmation hearing three weeks from now, and has assured me that my nominee will receive fair and respectful consideration by the committee, and the full Senate." Don't drag this out so long, Andy thought. Am I right, or not?

Perhaps aware that he was dragging out his announcement, Chambers turned to the man on his left. "I am pleased to introduce to the American people the next Chief Justice of the Supreme Court, Judge Winslow Early." Shit! Andy thought. I was right. She was startled when Todd Armistead gave out a loud "Yeah!" and pumped a fist, almost hitting her.

The camera panned to include both Chambers and Early. Chambers glanced at his off-camera teleprompter. "Judge Early has served with distinction as a member of the legislature in his native state of Virginia, elected for two terms, and elected for two terms as Virginia's attorney general. In that position, he was honored by election as president of the National Association of Attorneys General. For the past nine years, Judge Early has sat on the United States Court of Appeals for the Fourth Circuit, based in his home town of Richmond. His judicial record, which I have reviewed with admiration, has shown a keen understanding of the role of the judge as a neutral arbiter of legal disputes, not as a partisan of either side." Take that, Sam Terman, Andy thought, her cynicism turning to seething outrage.

"And now," Chambers said, beaming widely, "I'd like to introduce Judge Winslow Early, who will introduce his lovely family."

Chambers moved aside as Early replaced him at the lectern. He spoke with a slight Tidewater drawl. "Mistah President, I cannot thank you enough for considering me worthy of the post to which any judge would aspire. And I want to pay my respects to Chief Justice Terman, a man whose record of devoted service on the Supreme Court I can only hope to emulate." Early gestured to the people on either side, as cameras panned to include them on the screen. "I would not be here today," Early continued, "without the love and support of my beautiful wife, Calista. And the drubbings at tennis by my son, Winslow Junior, to remind me that even judges lose on some courts. My son, and my beautiful daughter-in-law, Penny, are under judicial order to continue the Early line with grandchildren, or face a contempt citation." What a feeble attempt at humor, Andy thought, sourly. And Junior must be six feet four, which makes Martha Radford a good judge of height.

Chambers moved back to the lectern. "As you know, the Senators will have a chance to pose questions to Judge Early at his confirmation hearing, which I'm sure he will answer frankly and honestly. Until then, Judge Early will defer any questions from the media, with my full agreement. Thank you, and God bless America."

Andy decided to skip the chatter between Wolf Blitzer and Jeff Toobin, which started right after President Chambers and the Early family returned to the White House through the doors behind them. Without a word to Angie or her fellow clerks, Andy turned and left Novak's chambers, going down to one of the Court's interior courtyards, where she sat on a bench and pulled out her cell phone.

"OMG! Did you see?" she texted Josh. "Pres picked Early as CJ. Holy shit! What now? Call when u can. Love, A." A minute later, her phone rang with Josh's ringtone. "Can you believe this?" Andy almost shouted into her phone. "Chief fucking Justice of the Supreme Court!

And most likely complicit in covering up a murder by Early fucking Junior. I can't fucking believe this, Josh."

"Well, *hello*, Mary Poppins," Josh replied. "Yes, I did see it, and I actually *can* believe it. Early is just the kind of judge Chambers would pick. He's right-wing, but not a bomb-thrower, from what I know. Nothing like Bork, if you remember him."

"Only from ancient history class," Andy retorted. "But I get your point, Josh Toobin."

Josh chuckled. "Early even looks like a Chief Justice you'd get from Central Casting, if you noticed. Tall, full head of silver hair, the exact opposite of Sam Terman. Plus, he comes from a state that Chambers would like to win when he runs for a second term. Don't overlook politics, Andy."

"Oh, there's no politics up where I work," Andy said. "No Democrats, no Republicans, ha ha."

"Anyway, Andy," Josh said, "now that you're over your hissy-fit, I have some news. But I've just got a minute before a staff meeting, so I hope you can come over to my place at six, and I'll fill you in."

"I'll ignore your sexist comment, Mister Neanderthal," Andy replied. "And I'll try to live with suspense until six. Okay? Love you."

"Love you too," Josh added. "But there's no bad news, so look forward to a little fungo, if you know what I mean."

"We'll see, Mister All-Star, but you might just strike out tonight. Can't hit a homer every game, you know."

Jane Wadleigh also watched President Chambers' announcement of Judge Early's nomination as Chief Justice that morning on the television in the reception office of the Senate Judiciary Committee. She already knew it was coming, of course, as did the other staffers who clustered around the set. Senator Weeks had informed the staff on October 10 about the forthcoming announcement, and his chief of staff, Cheryl Perkins, had parceled out tasks to Democratic staffers to prepare for the confirmation hearing that was scheduled for November 13, three weeks from now.

Jane was heading back to her office when Perkins popped out of hers. "Well, Jane, it's now official," Perkins said, beckoning Jane into her office.

"I guess the suspense is over." Jane chuckled, politely. She knew what Perkins wanted to discuss with her. "Have a seat," Perkins said, returning to her desk and waving Jane to a chair across from her.

"Sure," Jane complied. She did not relish having the conversation that Perkins had initiated after Weeks had told his staff of his "chat" with Chambers about Early's nomination. The two women had not talked since then about Jane's assignment to pump her husband, Dick, for any White House scuttlebutt about Early's racial views, and the "rumors" Weeks had supposedly heard, that Early had expressed negative views about African Americans and other minorities. Jane was still seething over the request—actually, a demand—that she ask Dick to reveal confidences from his job. To be honest, Jane reminded herself, Dick had, while angry and a bit hung-over, spilled the beans about Chambers' deal with Weeks to assure Democratic votes to confirm Early, in return for removing an obstacle to Weeks' election to a third Senate term.

"So, Jane," Perkins began, with a smile, "anything to report on the info I asked you to put together about the distinguished Judge Early?"

"Oh, you mean the deal we made about sneaking into the White House and looking for the hidden file on him?" Jane couldn't keep the resentment from her tone.

Perkins replaced her smile with a chiding expression. "You know the Senator wouldn't ask your husband to rifle through the president's desk, Jane. He and I just want to know if there's any substance to the rumors." Perkins resumed her smile. "And, of course, we hope there's not. This should be a pretty smooth confirmation." She chuckled. "Nothing about pubic hairs on Coke cans, if you remember that disastrous hearing."

"Vaguely," Jane replied. "Before my time, though." Jane did know about that hearing, and firmly believed the accuser's story of sexual harassment by the nominee. But she let the topic drop. "Actually, Cheryl, I do have some 'info,' as you put it. My notes are on my desk, so I'll run down and be back in a minute."

When Jane returned to Perkins' office, she was surprised to find Senator Weeks seated there. "Good morning, Jane," he said warmly, rising to shake her hand. Outside of staff meetings, Jane had only conversed with Weeks three or four times since she started her job in July, about nothing significant. But seeing him in Perkins' office gave her a chill, despite his warm greeting. "I just stopped by Cheryl's office," Weeks said, "and she tells me you've found some information about Judge Early's views on racial issues. I hope there's nothing to the rumors I've heard, but it's better to be prepared, if there is anything that might complicate our hearing."

Jane took a deep breath as she sat and opened the folder in her hand. "Well, Senator, I have found a few things that might be a bit troublesome, but I'll leave that for you to decide."

"Fair enough," Weeks said. "Although 'troublesome' doesn't sound like, oh, 'disastrous.'"

Jane smiled. "Nothing like that, Senator." She pulled two sheets from her folder.

"I'll start with the earliest," she began, prompting a chortle from Weeks at her unintended pun. She consulted a sheet. "Oh, before I do that," she said, "some of my sources, one in particular, gave me information on a confidential basis. I assume we'll keep their identities out of any public record." Weeks and Perkins both nodded agreement. Actually, everything in Jane's folder came from Internet research she and Dick had done, searches that Perkins or any staffer could have easily performed. But Jane didn't reveal that, or her annoyance that Perkins hadn't done that herself.

"Let's see," Jane said, consulting her sheet again. "I was told that when Judge Early was a student at the University of Virginia, his fraternity put on a 'blackface party' on Dr. King's birthday." She looked up, but Weeks showed no reaction. "The fraternity was reprimanded by the Student Conduct Committee, after all the fraternity members, including Judge Early, signed a public apology in the campus newspaper." Weeks simply nodded.

"When he was in the Virginia House of Delegates," Jane continued, "he voted against a bill to remove the Confederate flag from all state buildings." Again, no reaction. "Now, this was twenty years before the flap over the flag in South Carolina, after that church massacre a couple of years ago, and that bill only got twelve votes, ten from African American delegates." Jane felt like she was talking to a department store mannequin, but plowed ahead.

"Okay," she said, "when Judge Early first ran for attorney general, he spoke at a meeting of the Virginia chapter of a group called The League of the South. Sounds pretty harmless, from its name, but I checked the League's website." Jane glanced at her sheet. "It's a Southern Nationalist group that advocates the right of states to secede from the Union. The

League claims it's not racist, but its motto is 'Sic Semper Tyrannis.'" Jane was sure Weeks recognized the words John Wilkes Booth shouted after he shot President Lincoln, as he jumped from the presidential box onto the stage of Ford's Theater. But again, just a nod.

"Two more things I learned," Jane continued. "Since he joined the Fourth Circuit, Judge Early hasn't hired a single minority clerk, or any women, for that matter. And one source told me that he often refers to African Americans as 'colored,' although he apparently doesn't use the n-word, at least that my source knows." This was the only thing Jane had learned from Dick, who said he heard it from a lawyer friend in Richmond.

"That's about it," Jane said, returning the sheets to her folder.

Weeks finally responded, spreading his hands in dismissal. "Seems to me," he said, "that's about what you'd expect from a man whose great-grandfather was Jubal Early."

Jane looked puzzled. "Oh, he was a famous Confederate general from Virginia," Weeks explained. "Won more battles than he lost, and promoted what he called 'the Lost Cause' after the war. 'Course, that was a long time ago, and the Confederate flag wasn't much of an issue until those folks got killed in the church in Charleston. And, there's still lots of white southerners who say 'colored.' He glanced at Perkins. "Am I right, Cheryl?"

"Senator," she replied, "being African American myself, I don't hear that word too often from white folks, at least the ones I meet. They're afraid of being politically incorrect, these days. But I'm sure 'colored,' and even the n-word, get spoken a lot when we're not within earshot."

"Well, I've heard 'colored' from quite a few southerners," Weeks said, "including some of my distinguished colleagues, and I don't feel any hostility behind it." He looked reflective for a moment. "Jane, I appreciate you getting this information, and your sources will be protected," he said. "But, frankly, I don't think all this amounts to a hill of beans, as we say in New Hampshire. Now, I'm sure the N-Double-A-C-P, and the Reverends Sharpton and Jackson will oppose Judge Early's confirmation, but they just preach to the choir. Unless there's something you didn't find, Jane, I don't see anything troublesome in his record. No white sheet, no burning cross. To be honest, just a typical white southerner of his generation. They'll be mostly gone before too long, but most of them are good folks at heart." With this little homily, Weeks rose, smiling at Jane.

"Oh, Senator," she said, smiling back at him. "One other thing a source told me, totally unconnected to Judge Early, but something I thought might interest you."

"And what might that be?" he asked, halfway out the door of Perkins' office.

"This is also confidential," Jane said, "but I learned that President Chambers intends to name your governor, Rene Coteau, as the next ambassador to France. But he won't announce the nomination until the Senate confirms Judge Early. My source didn't know why the president chose this timing, but he did say that Governor Coteau was an ideal choice, considering he won't have to take French lessons."

Weeks turned and gave Jane a dead-pan look. "Well, that's news to me, Jane, but it's quite an honor for our little state. And Rene Coteau is a good man, for a Republican." Weeks checked his watch. "Well, ladies," he said, "I've got to chair a subcommittee hearing this afternoon, and better get some sharp questions ready for the witnesses. But thank you, Jane. Good work." With that, he left Perkins' office.

"Yes, very good work, Jane," Perkins said. "No white sheets, no burning crosses. Just a typical white southerner of his generation." Jane sensed that Perkins didn't really share Weeks' dismissal of Early's history of racial insensitivity, but also didn't want to slow down or derail the confirmation of a new Chief Justice.

Back in her office, Jane felt confident that Weeks had gotten the message she intended to convey in giving him the "news" about Coteau's after-the-confirmation naming as ambassador to France. No one outside the White House knew about this, but if Jane knew about it, she must have learned from Dick that it was part of Week's log-rolling deal with President Chambers. Dick had even told her that Coteau had no idea that he'd be headed to Paris after Early's confirmation. So, Jane concluded, Weeks now knew that she knew about the deal. But she didn't know what to do with her knowledge of the deal. Leaking it to the media might derail Early's confirmation, but Weeks would certainly suspect Jane as the leaker, since no one in the White House would want it exposed. Probably not another Watergate, Jane thought, but the media was always sniffing for another "gate." Selling the post of Chief Justice for political gain would certainly win a Pulitzer for the next Woodward and Bernstein.

Closing her office door, Jane thought for a while about the dilemma she shared with Dick. Then she texted him. "He knows that I know. But is it worth both our jobs? Let's talk at home." She got a text back. "Okay. Plenty time to decide."

20

Trying, without much success, to push aside the suspense she felt after Josh's invitation to his place at six to share "news" about OD's murder case, Andy grabbed a quick lunch of tuna salad and iced tea in the clerk's dining room, before returning to Novak's chambers. She hoped to make some progress on the bench memo she'd been working on for one of next week's oral arguments, a case in which she had little interest. Watching President Chambers' announcement that morning of Judge Early's nomination as Chief Justice, along with Josh's call, left Andy with little enthusiasm for what was already a boring task. Well, she thought, every clerk gets some of what they called "dogs," and this was a particularly ugly mutt. Diligent Andy plowed ahead with the memo until five-thirty, stuck Fido back in his digital crate, logged off her computer, and headed for Union Station and the Metro.

When she got to Josh's apartment, he was standing in the open doorway, grinning broadly and holding up a FedEx box, which he handed to her. "Old Mose is a man of his word," he said.

"Don't tell me that's the brown glove, already," Andy replied.

"Yep, a right-hand leather glove, size large," Josh said. "Just the type that sports-car drivers wear, especially ones who own red Corvettes." He pretended to be gripping a steering wheel. "Vroom, vroom!"

Andy chuckled as they took chairs at the dining table, on which the OD case files were stacked. "Go ahead, take a gander," Josh said.

The FedEx box was open at one end, and Andy pulled out a Zip-lock evidence bag, to which was taped a chain-of-custody form, with Moses Townley's signature on two lines, the first dated 12-14-2002, and the second the Saturday that Andy and Josh had visited him in Williamsburg. Josh put a finger on the form. "Unless somebody else took this out without signing for it," he said, "it's been sitting in evidence storage for the last fifteen years."

"I'd better not open the bag, right?" Andy asked.

"Actually, you can," Josh replied, "as long as you handle it very carefully with these." He slid a box of latex gloves across the table to Andy, who put on a pair, extracted the brown glove with thumb and forefinger, and held it up, six inches from her eyes. She peered at the glove, turning it to both sides.

"My sight must be fading," she said. "I really can't see any blood on this. Maybe it's not the needle we've been looking for."

"Maybe you need glasses, Andy," Josh said, "although men don't make passes at girls who wear glasses. Some famous wit said that, although I don't remember who."

"Then maybe I should start wearing glasses, Lothario," Andy retorted. "That might keep your hands off my buttons. But seriously, I don't see any blood on this glove."

"Here, try this," Josh said, handing her a magnifying glass. "I picked up this and the gloves at the CVS on my way home. Look at the palm."

Andy examined the palm side of the glove with the glass. "Oh, you're right," she exclaimed. "I see a bunch of little spots here, a shade darker than the leather. You think that could be blood?"

"Well, I checked on the Internet," Josh said, "and a couple of sites said that blood can dry on leather in fifteen to thirty minutes, and it turns brown with the oxidation. And if it was already dry when the cop found it, that's why Mose couldn't identify these little spots as blood with just his eyes. "

"So, if these spots might be blood," Andy asked, "presumably Laurel Davis's blood, could they still be tested for DNA?"

"Yep, they can," Josh replied. "So, here's my plan, okay?" Andy gave him a Go Ahead nod. "I called Carlo in West Virginia after I got the glove from Mose," Josh continued, "and asked him about that. I'll skip the technical stuff, but here's the gist of what he said. A lab technician can scrape those spots off with a scalpel, put them in a DNA sequencer, which makes thousands more, and get a profile. Let's say that works, and the profile matches Laurel Davis's profile, which we've got in these files. That means, of course, that whoever wore this glove got her blood on it, somehow."

Andy put the glove back in the evidence bag. "But that still doesn't connect this glove with Early Junior," she said, "unless we can prove it was his, and he was wearing it when it got Laurel's blood on it."

"Right," Josh replied. "But here's what else Carlo told me. There's this recent technique called 'Contact Trace DNA' that can produce a profile from skin cells that are left on all kinds of things that people touch, including gloves. Want to hear how it works?"

"Give me the dummy version," Andy said.

"Not that you're a dummy, but okay," Josh said. "According to Carlo, every person sheds about four hundred thousand skin cells every day. That's something I never knew, by the way. Seems like a lot, but Carlo says we have billions of the little buggers. Anyway, this new technique can produce a DNA profile with as few as ten or twenty skin cells, hardly enough to fit on the point of the needle we're looking for. They lift them off with adhesive tape, put them in some fancy machine, and presto! Here's the guy who wore the glove with Laurel's blood on it, assuming it's also on the glove."

"Wow!" Andy exclaimed. "So, this fancy machine, does Carlo have one in his black bag?"

"In a manner of speaking, he does," Josh said. "Carlo told me he's friends with an Italian guy, Vito Petrocelli, who runs the DNA lab in the Department of Forensic Sciences at GW University. They met by chance in the hospital cafeteria, when Carlo overheard some guys speaking Italian, and jumped into the conversation. Anyway, Carlo already called Vito about testing the glove, and he says he can test for blood and skin cells both."

"So, can we just take the glove over to Vito," Andy asked, "or do we have to wait for Carlo to get back from West Virginia?"

"We can give the glove to Vito tomorrow," Josh said, "but he told Carlo he's backed up in the lab, and it might take another week or two, since this isn't a high-priority job, and it's a favor to Carlo. Although Vito's lab is certified for DNA testing, and he can sign the chain-of-custody form, so the results would be admissible in court, assuming that OD ever gets a new trial."

"That's great," Andy said, "but only one problem, Josh. We'd have to get Junior's DNA, somehow, and see if it matches the trace DNA from the glove, assuming Vito can find any. We've got a lot of assumptions going here."

"Right," Josh said. "That is a problem. I thought of asking Jim Carruthers to ask Judge Jacobs, who's hearing OD's habeas appeal, to order Junior to provide a DNA sample from an oral swab. But that would take a formal motion and a hearing, and both the state's lawyer and Junior's lawyer would oppose the motion, since Junior would have to be notified of the motion. That would take time, maybe months, and the judge would probably deny it, unless we had evidence of a DNA match of both Laurel and Junior on the glove, which we don't have." He paused. "Any ideas, Miss Marple?"

"Afraid not," Andy said. "But you're being a bad host, Josh, not offering your guest something to drink. And I've got to pee. So why don't you raid Carlo's wine cellar while I take care of pressing business?"

"Sorry," Josh said. "I'll take care of that while you go potty."

Andy came back with a Light-Bulb expression on her face. "Hey, Josh," she said. "You ever get a bright idea while you're sitting on the toilet?"

Josh laughed. "No, I'm usually wondering what people are saying about me while I'm wiping my butt. Why, did you come up with a plan while you were flushing?"

Andy took a sip from the glass of pinot noir that Josh had poured for her. "I did have an idea, Josh, and don't laugh when I tell you, okay? It's something I saw in a movie. I can't remember which one, but it worked."

Josh laughed. "Not Dracula, I hope."

"Nope," Andy said. "I'm not going to drink Junior's blood. But seriously, I might be able to get some of his saliva, if this plan works. And Vito can get DNA from saliva, I'm pretty sure."

"Right," Josh said. "Blood, saliva, hair, semen, poop, pee, toe jam, snot, anything from your body. So, what's your plan, from the movie you can't remember the title of?"

Andy explained her plan. "That is so fucking audacious," Josh said, when she finished. "But it might just work. And I don't have a better plan, so let's go with it. Nothing ventured, nothing gained, as they say."

"Well, let's venture," Andy said. "I'll call Junior first thing in the morning, and let you know right away if it's a go." She gave Josh a Come Hither look. "By the way, Lothario, you think Vito could get your DNA from my buttons?"

"Not unless I touch them," Josh replied, filling both glasses with more wine. Moving to the couch, wine was consumed and buttons were touched.

Dick and Jane Wadleigh also met at six that evening. Their Capitol Hill apartment was just a few blocks from Andy's, and the two women sometimes ran into each other on their ways to and from the Supreme Court and the nearby Dirksen Senate building, and would chat as they walked, but rarely about their jobs.

Jane made a mental note as she arrived home to call Andy and set up a lunch date. She had decided that leaking to the media the evidence of President Chambers' deal with Senator Weeks to assure at least five Democratic votes to confirm Judge Early would be a last-ditch option, and would probably cost her and Dick their jobs. She wouldn't share her knowledge of the deal with Andy, at least not yet, but Andy might have some ideas about how to mobilize death-penalty opponents to mount a media campaign against Early's confirmation. Dick had given Jane a copy of the opinion in which Early had proposed replacing lethal injection with firing squads, despite the bloody "splatter" their bullets would produce. Giving Andy a copy of this, if she hadn't already found it, might prompt her to pass it to groups that could "splatter" Early with charges of trigger-happy callousness. Persuading even two or three wavering Democrats that he lacked the judicial temperament expected of a Chief Justice might counter some of the arm-twisting that Weeks would employ to get the four votes—his was already bought and sold—he needed for his part of the deal with Chambers.

"Help you with your groceries, ma'am?" Jane had stopped at the nearby Safeway to pick up pork chops, sweet potatoes, and a bagged Caesar salad for dinner, and was clutching the bag while she fumbled in her pocket for keys to the apartment. She turned and handed the bag to Dick, who had arrived just behind her. "Well, you're a good-looking Boy Scout," she greeted him. "You get a merit badge for that."

"If the Scouts had a merit badge for cowardice," Dick responded as they entered the apartment, "I'd get one. I drafted a resignation letter this afternoon, but turned chicken and deleted it." He grinned. "So, how was your day, sweetheart? Your text message said that he knows that you know, about you-know-what."

"Well, I didn't draft a resignation letter," Jane said, "but I was tempted, after I found this, which confirms the you-know-what." Putting the dinner groceries on the kitchen counter, Jane handed Dick a copy of Roll Call, the daily paper that covered Capitol Hill politics, read by every lawmaker and lobbyist within the Beltway. Jane opened the fridge and got out two Heinekens, uncapping one for Dick as he sat at the kitchen table. She pointed to a brief front-page article. "Here's the final nail in this maison de merde," Jane said, "if you'll pardon my French."

"Oh, a house full of excrement," Dick said with a grin. "Like the ones you and I work in, and shovel out. But let me read this while you pour your beer in a glass, like a cultured person." He raised his bottle and took a swig.

"Hmm," Dick said, after scanning the article. "I didn't know that your distinguished boss also chairs the Democratic Senatorial Campaign Committee, as well as the Judiciary Committee. It says here that he announced million-dollar donations from his slush fund to five Democrats who face tough campaigns for re-election to the Senate." He took another swig of Heineken. "You don't think there's any quid pro quo attached to this largesse, do you, sweetheart? And you want Democrats reelected, I assume."

"Of course," Jane answered. "But, if you didn't know, three of these five million-dollar quids are also on Judiciary, which makes their quos pretty obvious. My distinguished boss is buying the votes he needs for a majority on the committee to send Early's nomination to the full Senate. And the other two will give him the votes for confirmation, with one to spare in his back pocket. Political Math 101, Dick. Five times one million equals a right-wing Chief Justice."

"My, we're getting cynical in our young age," Dick said. "But, as the president's chief of staff told me, everything in this town is political."

Jane picked up her glass of Heineken and moved into the kitchen. "While I'm slaving over a hot stove," she said, "you want to hear an idea I just had about giving the senators who took the swag from my boss a reason to vote against Judge Early's confirmation? It might not work, but it might budge a couple of fence-sitters."

After Jane put the pork chops in the broiler and the sweet potatoes on the stove, she explained her plan to give Andy a copy of Early's "splatter" opinion, to see if death-penalty opponents could use it to campaign against his confirmation. Dick then explained his plan to slip the evidence of Early's country-club racism to his contacts in civil-rights groups the Republicans were trying, so far with little success, to lure into the "big tent" from which they'd long been excluded. Over dinner, Dick and Jane agreed that both plans were long shots, but that leaking the deal between President Chambers and Senator Weeks would be a last-ditch option.

"You know, sweetheart," Dick said as he cleared the dishes, "it's possible there's something about Early that we haven't dug up yet, aside from his 'shoot 'em dead' opinion and his 'back of the bus' racial views. And his confirmation hearing is still three weeks away. So let's hold our fire, so to speak, and see if some muck-raking reporter digs up some even smellier merde about Early."

"So, let's hold off with those resignation letters, is what you're saying," Jane replied.

"Don't forget," Dick said, "my offer from Arnold and Porter is still open. And, with their signing bonus, we could move up from pork chops to filet mignon."

Jane chuckled. "And maybe a cook and butler, to befit our proper station in life."

Dick answered her chuckle with his. "And maybe a real Spot and Puff, to romp around the house in Bethesda."

"Meantime, dear," Jane said, "could you take the trash out to the Dumpster? The butler has the night off."

21

Andy called Josh on Tuesday morning, excitement in her voice. "My plan's a go," she told him. "I called Junior twenty minutes ago, and he bit like a hungry bass. In fact, go time is tomorrow night at six, dinner at the Bull and Bear Club on Cary Street in Richmond. His treat, he says. We'll have to leave here around three, so you'll either have to borrow another car from the DOJ motor pool, or we'll rent one. Fast work, huh?"

"Fast work, indeed," Josh replied. "I can get another motor-pool car, I already checked. So, tell me, Mata Hari, what lure you reeled him in with."

"Pretty much the one I tossed out last night, with a few quick improvisations," Andy said. "He bit so fast, and said he'd be glad to come up here, that I told him I was coming to Richmond tomorrow anyway, to interview some other people for the article I'm writing. Except I'm not, of course. I wasn't expecting tomorrow, Josh, but he was so damn eager I said that would be perfect, since my deadline is Friday. Except it's not, of course."

"The Bull and Bear Club," Josh said, "sounds like a watering hole for stockbrokers."

"Stockbrokers, lawyers, bankers, and other money-grubbers," Andy said. "I checked its website right after Junior gave me the name. It's on the twenty-first floor of the building, at the top, and his law firm is on the fourteenth. Whipple, Early, and Gilmore, the firm Senior was managing partner of, before he put on his black robe. Oh, the website also said dress for dinner is business casual, so I won't wear my Dave Matthews tee-shirt and my Eddie Bauer shorts."

"Maybe you should wear something that shows a little cleavage," Josh said. "That way, Junior won't be looking at what you're doing with your hands. Just kidding!"

"Actually, that's not a bad idea," Andy said, "since every guy peeks down women's blouses. I've seen you do that several times, when you didn't think I'd catch you."

Josh laughed. "Guilty as charged. But I've seen guys peeking at your lovelies when they didn't think I'd catch them." Andy heard Josh speaking to someone else, then he came back. "Sorry for the interruption. Listen, Andy, I've got a motion hearing in half an hour at the District Court, and two more tomorrow morning, back to back. So, unless something urgent comes up, I'll pick you at three tomorrow, right outside the Court entrance on the side. I'll call five minutes before I get there, okay?"

"Fine," she replied. "I've got to finish my 'ugly mutt' bench memo, and plow through a stack of cert petitions that have been growling at me for a week. So, tomorrow at three. And keep your fingers crossed that Junior doesn't get suspicious, and check out the phony identity I gave him. But he's so eager, I doubt he will."

"Crossing your fingers for luck, may I point out, is an easily disproved theorem," Josh said, "as are all superstitions. Quick, before I run to court, literally, I took the brown glove over to Carlo's friend, Vito, at the Forensic Sciences lab this morning. He signed the chain-of-custody form, and said he'd do what he can to speed up the testing, but no guarantees. Oh, and I asked Vito if he could handle another item if we got it soon, and he said sure."

Andy heard Josh saying, "Coming," then "Love you, Andy."

"Love you, too," she said. "Good luck in court. I'll cross my fingers for you." Then she heard the click as Josh hung up.

"Wow," Josh said, as Andy got into the Ford Fiesta he'd checked out of the DOJ motor pool, "I snuck a peek when you bent over, and saw your very low-cut Victoria's Secret. Black and lacy. I know it well."

Andy laughed. "I guess this will distract Junior while I do my legerdemain. But I've got a can of pepper spray in my purse, in case he tries to cop a feel."

"Back to business," Josh said. "You didn't tell me on Monday about your new identity. So, with whom will Junior be having dinner?"

"Very pleased to meet you, Mister Early," Andy said. "I'm Portia Bradwell, with the American Law Journal. As I said on the phone, I'm writing a profile of your dad, with a human-interest angle, including his family. Congratulations, by the way, for his nomination as Chief Justice. And, Mister Early, I've learned that you've done some major property development deals, like the new mall downtown, and I'd love to include them in my story." She turned and smiled at Josh. "I know you like my bra. How about my new name?"

"I don't know," Josh replied. "If Junior's a Shakespeare buff or knows legal history, he'd probably call your bluff. But I doubt he reads anything more than the Wall Street Journal. And, since you asked, and I'm both of those, Portia was a scheming character in The Merchant of Venice, who posed as a lawyer, and Myra Bradwell was kept out of the Illinois bar because she was a woman, long time ago, which all nine men on the Supreme Court upheld. Very clever, though."

"Josh, I don't think I've ever stumped you on a question," Andy said. "You really should try out for Jeopardy. But you're right. Very clever, hopefully not too clever."

Sensing each other's nervousness, underneath their tension-breaking badinage, Andy and Josh chatted about their respective jobs on the two-and-a-half hour drive to Richmond. Josh found parking on the street, just up the block from One James Place, the building that housed both the Bull and Bear Club and Early's law firm. With half an hour until six, they did a quick reconnoiter of the area and the building lobby, noticing the uniformed doorman who opened car doors for people who pulled up in front. At five minutes of six, Josh gave Andy a kiss. "I'm crossing my fingers," he said. "Just in case. You never know." Indeterminacy, Andy said to herself as she entered the elevator and pushed the button for 21.

At the reception desk inside the Bull and Bear Club, Andy glanced around. Floor-to-ceiling windows offered a panoramic view of Richmond, with well-fed men—and very few women—seated at tables, served by white-coated waiters, almost all of them black. Before she could give her phony name to the receptionist, a tall man—six three at least, Andy figured—bounded over from a nearby table and stuck out his hand. "You must be Portia Bradwell," he greeted her, "and I'm Win Early."

"I am," she said, "and I'm pleased to meet you, Mister Early."

"Oh, Win is fine," he said, "and I like your name. It's not spelled like the car, is it? I've got one, but I doubt anyone would name a child after a sports car."

Andy gave him an appreciative chuckle as Early guided her to his table, her chair pulled out by an attentive waiter. "No," she said, "I usually spell it for people, but sometimes I get mail addressed to the car." She put her large purse, open at the top, next to her chair, as a waiter appeared, put menus before them, and asked for their drink orders. "I'll just have sparkling water, thank you," she said.

Without asking Andy, Early ordered a bottle of Beringer chardonnay and two glasses. "I hope you don't mind," he said, "but that's my favorite, and it goes well with just about anything."

Holy shit, Andy thought. Could he know who I really am, and is testing me? "Well, goodness me," she said, "that's my favorite, too, and it would go perfectly with the sole." She had glanced at the menu and looked for something easy on the stomach, since hers was full of butterflies. Andy took a deep breath, letting it out slowly. "Well, again," she said, "my congratulations on your father's nomination as Chief Justice. I know his confirmation hearing is coming up soon, and everyone says he'll be sitting in the center seat within a month. That must make your whole family very proud."

Early beamed. "You know, that's a position that every judge dreams of, but I think my dad is the perfect choice." He smiled. "Of course, as his son, I'm biased."

The waiter came with the drinks, uncorked the wine, and poured an inch into Early's glass. He swirled it, took a sip, and nodded his approval. The waiter filled his glass, but Andy put a hand over hers. "Thank you, but I'll wait until my dinner is served," she said. "But if you're ready for orders, I'll have the sole, with a small green salad." To her surprise, Early ordered the same thing, with an appetizer of artichoke dip. She had pegged him as a red-meat guy, but perhaps he was trying to please his guest. Andy reached into her purse and brought out a small digital recorder. "Do you mind if I record our talk?" she asked Early. "It's hard to take notes while you're eating, and I like to get quotes down right." She didn't expect a confession, but wanted to look like a real reporter.

"Fine with me," he replied. "As long as you take out the ums and ahs. Don't want to sound like a doofus, which I am."

Andy put on her best imitation of a Southern Belle, batting her eyelashes. "Win, a lawyer of your stature couldn't be a doofus." She clicked the recorder. "Now, since the story I'm writing is really about your dad as a person, not as a judge, can you tell me what he's like without his robe. What you and he enjoy doing together, that kind of stuff. Is that okay?"

Over the next hour, in between bites of sole and salad, and sips of wine, Andy listened to the most boring dad-and-son stories she could recall ever hearing, all the while pretending to be entranced. Twice, she dropped her napkin, making sure as she retrieved it that Early got a good look at her Victoria's Secret and its barely-covered contents, noticing out of the corner of her eye that he enjoyed the view. As his boring stories dragged on, Andy cast a few surreptitious glances at Early's water glass, the object she wanted to pilfer, but he didn't drink out of it while he ate and talked. Swiping his wine glass might be hard, she thought. Finally, after finishing his sole, Early picked up his water glass and took a healthy swig, then wiped his mouth with the napkin. He leaned forward and said, "Portia, this is delightful, and I'd like to continue in the lounge, if you're not tired of hearing about what a great dad I've got. We could relax with an after-dinner drink, and I could have a cigar, if you don't mind. This is a private club, so polluting the air in the lounge is legal."

"Oh, that's perfectly okay with me," Andy said, leaning toward him to offer another peek. "My dad is a cigar smoker, and I actually enjoy the aroma," she lied.

"And, if you'll excuse me for a moment," Early said, rising from his chair, "nature calls, and I must answer. Back in a flash."

Make it a long flash, Andy thought. After he headed for the men's room, she looked around, spotted no one watching her, picked up Early's water glass, wrapped it in a napkin, dropped it in her purse, took a swig from her glass, and placed it where his had been. Her heart was pounding, and she took a deep breath of relief.

When Early returned, he guided her to the nearby lounge, finding two empty chairs on either side of a low table. Before they sat, Andy said, "I'm sorry, Win, but nature just called me, too." She gave him another Southern Belle smile. "Could you hold this seat for me, sir?"

Andy headed for the ladies room, which was unoccupied, sat on a toilet in a stall, and texted Josh. "Got it! But I'll be a bit longer. Make your call in 10 minutes." They had agreed on this in case Andy hadn't been able to snatch the glass, but she thought she might get another, just to make sure. Closing the stall, she returned to the lounge, where Early was blowing smoke from a thick cigar.

"I ordered a cognac for you," he said, "the perfect drink to please your palate after a delicious meal."

"Why, thank you, Win," Andy said. "You seem to know just what a lady would like." What I'd really like, she thought, was to get out of here. But she had another idea. "So, Win," she said, "I've got enough about your dad, who obviously didn't let his work interfere with great parenting. But I'd love to hear about *your* work, especially bringing that new mall to Richmond. I hear it's going to revitalize the whole downtown area."

Five minutes after Early launched into an incredibly boring account of getting run-down buildings razed, and their mostly black and poor residents evicted, to make room for up-scale stores, the maitre d' approached their table. "Excuse me, Mister Early, but the doorman called and said there's a delivery man in the lobby with a package for you. He needs a signature, and your office told him you were having dinner with us."

Early frowned, and Andy was afraid he'd tell the maitre d' to have the package delivered to the lounge. But he got up, excused himself, and headed for the door. She quickly pulled out her phone and texted Josh to have the car at the building entrance in ten minutes. Then she picked up Early's half-smoked cigar, which he'd stubbed out, wrapped it in a cocktail napkin, and dropped that in her purse. She took another deep breath to slow her racing heart.

Early returned in two minutes, frowning again. "Sorry, Portia, but the doorman said the delivery guy told him he didn't need a signature after all, and would deliver whatever it was to my office." He looked down at the empty ashtray on the table.

"Win, I'm sorry," Andy said, "but the busboy came by and emptied this before I could stop him." She was deathly afraid he'd summon a busboy and blister him. To her relief, Early grumbled, then sat down and lit another cigar from the silver case on the table.

"Now, I was telling you about the red tape I had to cut to clear the area for the mall," he said. Andy looked attentively at him, planning to have a mild headache in five minutes as an excuse to thank Early for a delicious meal and fascinating stories about his dad. And then take the elevator down and jump in the car Josh would have waiting at the building entrance. And make their getaway, Early's DNA safely tucked in her purse.

Just then, a young woman approached their table. "Andy, Andy Roboff!" she exclaimed. "Imagine seeing you here! I heard you got a job clerking for Justice Novak at the Supreme Court." Andy looked up in horror at Sue Saugstad, a classmate at Harvard Law School. Saugstad turned to Early, who looked astounded. "Oh, I'm sorry to interrupt," she apologized, "but I haven't seen Andy since our law-school graduation."

Realizing that she couldn't pretend it was mistaken identity, Andy grabbed her purse and bolted from the lounge, leaving Early and Saugstad with their mouths and eyes wide open. Fortunately, the elevator opened immediately. Praying that Josh would be waiting, Andy sprinted across the lobby, spotted the car at the entrance, jumped in and blurted, "Josh, I got busted! We've got to haul ass out of here."

As Josh peeled out and headed for the freeway, Andy told him what had happened, looking back over her shoulder, although Early couldn't have gotten down to the street before they left, or seen the Fiesta or where it was headed.

Andy was hyperventilating. "He knows my name, Josh, and where I work. What if he calls Alex and tells him one of his clerks was impersonating a reporter, and Alex asks me to explain. I'd be fucked!"

"Calm down, Andy," Josh ordered. "You got what we needed, right? The glass and the cigar, which I'll give to Vito tomorrow. And then Junior will be fucked. And he wouldn't dare call Alex, because then he'd be double fucked. Because we could tell Alex why you were there, and about Senior's phony alibi for Junior. Alex might not approve of what we did, but I'm sure he'd understand, and do something himself to block Senior's confirmation. That's the kind of guy he is, believe me. And I'll take the fall, if it comes to that. Okay? So just calm down, Andy. We'll be back at my place in three hours, maybe quicker, and we can have a drink, or three. But your plan worked, except for that little glitch, and that's not to worry, as your grandma Bella would say."

Josh's calming and reassuring words had their intended effect on Andy. Three hours later, they shared a bottle of wine, smoked a bowl of Lemon Haze, listened to the Dave Matthews Band, and fell asleep in each other's arms.

"I'm still shaking," Andy confessed to Josh, as they shared a quick breakfast of croissants, honeydew, and coffee, after a chaste night in his bed. "I haven't been that scared in my whole life."

"Well, Inspector Clouseau," Josh said with a grin, "at least we didn't have a high-speed chase up I-95, with Junior blazing away at our Fiesta from his Porsche. It was a clean get-away, and you made the heist and got the goods. Remember what I said last night? Junior would be double fucked if he ratted you out to Alex. So just relax, okay?"

"Easier said than done," Andy replied. "But I'll do my best to get my pulse back to normal. And thanks, Josh, for helping me settle down last night."

"That's me," he said. "An island of tranquility in a sea of stress."

Andy took the Metro to her place, where she quickly showered and changed before walking to the Court. Before he left for his office in Alexandria, Josh stopped by the Forensic Sciences lab at George Washington University to give Carlo's friend Vito the water glass and cigar that Andy had pilfered from Early Junior. The DNA results on those items and the brown glove, which Vito already had, might take more than a week. Meanwhile, Andy and Josh agreed they would resume their normal work routines until word from Vito.

Back in the clerks' office, Andy greeted Dave with a cheerful "Morning, Charlie Chan," which he returned with a wink. She opened her computer and let the 'ugly mutt' bench memo out of his digital crate. An hour later, she put him back and picked up the top folder on the stack of cert petitions that needed pool memos. Maybe this one will be a purebred Afghan, she hoped.

Just as she opened the folder, Alex Novak stuck his head into the office. "Andy, can I see you for a few minutes?" he asked. She turned to him, a startled expression on her face. Oh, my God, she thought, Junior called Alex and I'm about to get fired. "I've just got a few questions about a memo," Novak said, aware that Andy's fellow clerks had noticed her jumpy reaction to his request.

"Oh, sure, Alex," Andy replied, replacing the folder and following him into his office.

"Sorry to interrupt you," Novak said, "but it's not actually about a memo." Andy tried to quell her renewed panic attack, taking a deep breath as Novak motioned her to a chair across from his desk, from which he picked up a folder. "How would you like a break from grinding out memos, Andy?"

"Oh, I'm not complaining, Alex," she replied, trying to sound normal. "Most of the cases raise interesting points on both sides, and make me wish the Court could give both parties half a loaf, instead of winner-takes-all."

Novak chuckled. "That's how I feel in a lot of cases, Andy. Unfortunately, we can't play Solomon and split the baby." Seated behind his desk, he reached across and took one of Andy's hands. "Are you okay, Andy? Your hands are trembling."

"Thanks, Alex, I'm fine," she replied. "But I almost got run over by a Metro bus on my way here, and I'm still a bit shaky," she lied. "I wasn't looking when I crossed the street."

Novak squeezed her hand and let it go. "Andy, I've got a job for you," he said. "How would you like to draft the majority opinion in the Khalid case? You know that one. You were there for both arguments, and I'm sure you read the briefs. So, how about it, Andy?"

Andy couldn't hide her surprise. "Are you kidding, Alex? Of course I would. But the reargument was just on Monday, and your conferences are on Friday, right?"

"Normally, yes," he replied. "But I'll let you in on a little secret, Andy. Not very often, but sometimes, after an oral argument, it's clear which justices will make up a majority. And they caucus, informally, and agree on who will write the majority opinion. The Khalid case was five-three, with me, Alice Schroeder, Maggie McEwan, Dwight Stokes, and Juan Pablo Romero. It wasn't a four-four tie, with no opinion. We'll take a formal vote on Friday, but this speeds things up, and avoids a lot of blather in the conference."

"And they picked you in the Khalid case," Andy said, "and you picked me to draft the opinion."

"Actually, I volunteered," Novak said. "And you're by far the most qualified of the clerks on this case, and the best writer of the lot. So why don't we get started, and I'll sketch out what I'd like to say."

"Just one question, Alex," Andy said. "You haven't told me which side won, since you can't split the baby."

"I assume you're being facetious," Novak said, "after you saw me blister Tony Ewing at the first argument."

"Well, I was," Andy said, "but I just wanted to make sure." She paused for a moment. "Can I make one suggestion, Alex, before you start sketching the legal points you want to make?"

"Of course, Andy. Go ahead."

"Well, let me back up first," she said. "When I was reading all your opinions before I started working for you, I was struck that you almost never said anything about the people who brought these cases, or defended them." Novak raised his eyebrows. "In fact, Alex, in several opinions you didn't even mention their names, just called them petitioner or respondent." Novak looked surprised. "If you want me to," Andy continued, "I'll make you a list and copy the opinions for you."

"No, no, I believe you," he said.

"Thank you," she said. "So, both at Harvard and here, I read quite a few of Sam Terman's opinions. You were often in dissent in these cases, as you know. But, what I noticed in Sam's opinions was that he almost always told the parties' stories, who they were, how they got involved in the case, the impact it had on their lives. Even on the pages of U.S. Reports, they were real people to Sam." Andy paused. "Do you see where I'm going, Alex."

"I think so," he replied. "But keep going. You're making me think."

"Okay," Andy said. "And I don't mean to make you feel uncaring or heartless, Alex, because you're not. But I think it has something to do with what you said to me, when we were at my place, after Sam's funeral."

"I remember," Novak said. "I was talking about the boxes that I've lived in, most of my life, and the very different boxes Sam lived in. Is that what you meant?"

"Right," Andy said. "But Sam, from everything I know about him, got out of his boxes and got to know people in other boxes, people very different from him. Some of these people literally lived in boxes, on the street, or tenements in big cities, or shacks in rural towns. And when people like these got involved in cases the Court decided, Sam would tell their stories. Because he knew them, and their pain and struggles."

"And I don't," Novak said, shaking his head. "You're right, Andy, I don't." He gave Andy a rueful smile. "So, let me suggest that you tell the story of Malik Khalid's wife and kids in the opinion you draft. The pain they've endured because the government assassinated their husband and father. Do you like my suggestion, Andy?"

"Gee whiz," she said, "that never occurred to me, but it's a great suggestion, Alex. I'll get right to work on it."

As she got up to leave, Andy spotted a familiar-looking book on Novak's desk, on top of two others. She picked up the top book. "I and Thou, by Martin Buber," she read. "I read this in college, Alex. A classic in philosophy. And this one, too," picking up the second. "A History of the Jews, by Abram Sachar. And this one I don't know, Exploring Your Jewish Heritage." She replaced the books. "Alex, this is very interesting. I assume your reading list has something to do with the story your dad told us at dinner with Bella. And you picked a couple of really good books, although I struggled a bit with Buber."

"You're right about learning from my dad, thanks to Bella, that he's Jewish," Novak said, "or was born Jewish, even though he and my mom raised me as Catholic." Novak chuckled. "Not a very good Catholic, to be honest. I'm afraid the Holy Father would give me a thousand Hail Mary's as penance."

Novak picked up Buber's book. "I have a confession, Andy. Not the kind where you whisper to some guy on the other side of a screen that you have lustful thoughts, and promise to go and lust no more."

Andy waited. "You remember Rabbi Margolis at Sam's funeral? Lisa Margolis." Andy nodded. "Well, since then, I've had three sessions with her. Did you know that she's also a certified therapist?" Andy shook her head, fascinated by what Novak was telling her. He seemed eager to tell her more, so she gave him an encouraging smile. "Well, our sessions aren't formal therapy, but she did say that finding out my dad is Jewish was a blow to the identity I'd always thought defined myself. Both to me and other people." He stopped, shaking his head. "Does this all sound like psychobabble to you, Andy?"

"Of course not, Alex," she assured him. "It sounds perfectly reasonable, considering what a shock that must have been. But it doesn't mean you have to abandon that identity and adopt another one. Just to expand the one you grew up with, if that makes sense." Andy chuckled. "That doesn't sound like psychobabble, I hope."

"Of course not, to quote you." He paused. "Andy, can I ask a favor?"

"Of course," she replied, "to quote myself. I'll do anything I can for you, Alex. And you've done so much for me."

"Thank you," Novak said. "So, Andy, I really enjoyed our time after Sam's funeral. You left me with lots to think about. Can we do that again? Maybe over dinner, some evening that's convenient for both of us? I'll even cook salmon, the way Bella showed me."

Andy was touched by Novak's eagerness to open up with her. "Sure, Alex, that would be fun," she said. "Salmon and Martin Buber. Great combination. Food for the mind, both of them. And no chauffeur's uniform this time."

Novak laughed. "I donated the black suit and tie to Goodwill. So, just give me a date, and I'll bring my apron."

"I will, Alex, and we'll make it soon," Andy said. She didn't want to set a date until Josh got word from Vito on the DNA testing, maybe another week, maybe sooner. Until then, Andy and Josh had agreed to keep their calendars clear, in case they had to spring into action with the plan they'd hatched to use the results, if they nailed Early Junior.

Andy gave Novak a smile. "So, Alex," Andy said, "you read Martin Buber and I'll go write the story of Malik Khalid's wife and kids. We can add the legal mumbo-jumbo later, to give law professors something to dissect in law-review articles nobody will read."

She leaned over and kissed Novak on the cheek. "You're a good person, Alex. Keep your identity, because that's you. Just expand it a bit. And maybe I could help you with that."

Andy left Novak's office, thinking—once again—about the role of indeterminacy in life. Hers and his, both. So many unexpected changes in both, in so short a time. Back in the clerks' office, she opened her computer and set to work on telling the story of Malik Khalid's family, and how a faulty decision by the government had changed their lives, in the sudden blast of a Hellfire missile.

22

Tuesday, November 7, was a chilly, drizzly day in Washington. Andy's mood matched the weather as she glanced at her watch in the clerks' office. It was six o'clock, and her fellow clerks had left for the day, along with Alex Novak. After getting the assignment from him to draft an opinion upholding the lower-court ruling that Malik Khalid's widow and children were entitled to the six-million dollar judgment awarded by the trial jury, Andy had divided her time between that task and writing pool memos on the stack of cert petitions she'd been pushing to the side of her desk. Over the past twelve days—Andy had kept count--she had tried hard to push aside the images that kept popping up in her mind of Vito Petrocelli doing whatever he did in the Forensic Sciences lab with the tiny samples of blood, skin cells, and saliva from the items Josh had given him for DNA testing.

Andy jumped when her phone rang, telling her that Josh was calling. She hadn't spoken with him since the morning after snatching Early Junior's water glass and cigar at the Bull and Bear Club in Richmond. With both of them buried under piles of pushed-aside work, they had agreed to observe phone silence until word from Vito.

"Long time, no hear," Andy said as she answered Josh's call. "Twelve days, to be exact."

"I've missed you every day," Josh replied. He warbled the next line in an off-key baritone. "On the twelfth day of Christmas, Vito gave to me, twelve lab reports, in a box with a bow of red ribbon."

Andy laughed. "Well, at least you're not singing a funeral dirge. And I've missed you, too. So, can I come over and open Vito's present with you?"

"Hmm," Josh replied. "Can you wait until next week? I've got laundry piled up, and two week's worth of dusting. Carlo will be back tomorrow, and he likes a tidy place."

"Hey, I'll do the laundry and dusting," Andy said, "and even take out the trash. Anything to make Carlo happy."

Josh chuckled. "Hop on the Metro and I'll have detergent and a dust-pan ready. Oh, by the way, Andy, we've got more presents to open than Vito's. I think Junior's getting a lump of coal in his stocking this year. A whole bag full, in fact."

Josh was standing in the doorway when Andy arrived at his apartment, holding out a manila folder, to which was affixed a stick-on red bow. "Couldn't find a gift box," he said, "but I found a bow in a bag of Christmas stuff. Carlo likes to wrap presents with paper and bows that get ripped off right after Santa goes down the elevator." He kissed Andy and handed her the folder. "You can open this while I open a bottle of pinot grigio."

Andy pulled out a chair at the dining-room table, and opened the folder. The sheets inside, about a dozen, were each filled with two columns of squiggles, looking like tiny caterpillars, with headings above each column that read, "Sample A" and "Sample B." Just from quick scannings of the first three sheets, Andy noticed that the squiggles in the left-hand columns looked very similar to those on the right.

Returning with the wine and two glasses, Josh sat beside Andy and pointed at the squiggles on first sheet. "These here, on the left," he explained, "are the DNA markers from the blood that was on Laurel Davis's body, when they did the autopsy." Andy nodded. "I'm not sure what markers are," Josh continued, "but Vito put a memo explaining them in the folder. Anyway, the markers on the right are from the blood spots that Vito scraped from the brown glove. Notice anything?"

"Duh," Andy replied. "They look identical. At least to my untrained eye."

"Very good," Josh said. "Which means what?"

"Duh, again, Mister Science," Andy replied. "It means that Laurel's blood was on Junior's glove, right?"

"Wrong, I'm sorry to say," Josh said. "Laurel's blood *was* on the brown glove, true, but that doesn't prove it was Junior's glove. Could have been Martha Radford's glove, for all we know, and she planted it to frame Junior for the murder."

"I knew it from the minute we met her," Andy said. "Nobody would suspect a deaf and blind old lady of cold-blooded murder. We should have gotten her DNA from her tea cup."

Josh chuckled, then picked up another sheet. "Let's be serious, Andy, and it's my fault for joshing, so to speak. I mean, OD Beasley's life could be at stake here. I'm sure you realize that."

"Of course I do," Andy said. "And it's my fault, too. People sometimes josh when they're nervous. And I was thinking about that on our mad dash back from Richmond. We both took that risk to help somebody we've never met, and who's been sitting on death row for fifteen years. This *is* serious, Josh, I understand."

"Okay," he said. "Now, on this sheet here, the markers on the left are from the skin cells Vito lifted from the inside of the brown glove." Andy looked, and nodded. "And the markers on the right are from the saliva on the water glass that you filched from Junior."

"I can't see any difference," Andy said. "So, it looks like Junior *was* wearing the brown glove, which he fortunately dropped beside his red Corvette, after he got Laurel's blood on it."

"Right," Josh said. "And the next sheet is from the saliva on Junior's cigar. Another match. And, to wrap up this case, the other sheets are from the blood and hair the crime-scene techs found on Laurel's bathroom sink, which also match Junior's DNA."

"Which means he was in her bedroom either during or right after her murder," Andy said. "Which also means, just to be devil's advocate, that we still don't have absolute proof he killed her. Remember the scenario, Josh, where Junior found her body after OD killed her with the hammer, and Junior touched her body, got her blood on the glove, tried to wash it off in the bathroom sink, picked up the hammer, ran out of the house, tossed the hammer in the bushes, dropped the glove, and hauled ass out of there."

"Andy, you'd be a good defense lawyer for Junior," Josh said, "but let's assume we could use this evidence if OD gets a new trial. How would you use it then, if you were his lawyer?"

Andy thought for a minute, then stood up and struck a lawyerly pose. "Ladies and gentlemen of the jury," she said, "you have heard and seen the evidence from the prosecution that Mister Beasley's fingerprints were on the hammer, and his semen was found in the victim's body. But the evidence from the DNA testing of Winslow Early, Junior, which is displayed on the screen behind me, raises more than a reasonable doubt that Mister Beasley, who admits holding the hammer and having sex with the victim, was in fact the person who killed her."

Andy adopted an accusatory tone. "Ladies and gentlemen of the jury, it is our contention that Mister Early killed Laurel Davis in a fit of rage, after discovering that she had lured Mister Beasley into having sex with her. The evidence on both sides is circumstantial, we admit, since no one witnessed the murder, or confessed to it. But, with considerable doubt that Mister Beasley committed this horrible crime, we ask you to return a verdict of not guilty." Andy released a breath, then chuckled. "In other words, some other dude did it."

Josh stood up. "Your Honor, we the jury find Odell Beasley not guilty on the charge of first-degree murder. And we find that some other dude did it."

Andy laughed. "Thank you, Mister Foreman and members of the jury," she said. "You have performed a great civic duty, however difficult, and you are hereby dismissed, with thanks of the court." She paused. "So, now what, Clarence Darrow?"

"What now," Josh replied, "is a toast to Vito Petrocelli, for doing us a tremendous favor, thanks to Carlo overhearing a guy speaking Italian." He poured wine into the glasses on the table, and clinked glasses with Andy. "Indeterminacy," Josh said. "You never know who you'll meet in a hospital cafeteria. And who might help get a man off death row after fifteen years."

Josh picked up another folder from the table. "Before we get buzzed and start touching buttons, Andy," he said, "I've got more presents for you, although without red bows." He pulled a sheet from the folder as they sat down at the table. "Do you remember Liz Gronbach, the housemate of Laurel's who gave Mose Townley the names of three guys who'd been at parties at their place, and who Liz thought might have had sex with Laurel in her bedroom, or at least heavy petting?"

Andy nodded. "Well, I got to thinking," Josh continued, "that Liz might be able to tell us more about Laurel's sexual proclivities, if you know what I mean."

"You mean," Andy said, "whether she was a slut, to use a polite term."

"You said it, not me," Josh replied. "Anyway, the other day I called the William & Mary alumni office, and got her name and number. She's now Liz Porter, and works for the Maryland attorney general. So, I called her, and guess what she told me?"

"That Laurel was a virgin who'd never even kissed a guy?"

"Way off, Andy," Josh said. "Laurel's sheets were never cool. And here's what else. Liz said she once invited a black guy, Derrick something, she didn't remember his last name, to a party at their house. Not a boyfriend, just a fellow law student. So, Junior shows up at the party, pretty hammered, and pulls Liz aside. 'What's that coon doing here,' he asked her."

Andy raised her eyebrows. "He used that word?"

"That's what Liz said," Josh replied. "And, sometime later, Liz couldn't remember when, Laurel asked if Liz had ever had sex with a black guy, although she used another word."

Andy grinned. "The 'f' word, right?"

"Right," Josh said. "Anyway, Liz said no, she hadn't, but Laurel said she wondered if black guys were all 'well hung.'"

"And decided to find out when OD showed up," Andy said.

"Well, that shows you know the term," Josh said, with a grin. "And, it fits with something I recalled, after talking with Liz, from the case files." He pulled a folder from the stack on the table and handed Andy a sheet. "That's the physical evidence list, with everything the cops and crime-scene techs picked up. And one was a medicine bottle they found in her nightstand, with three pink pills, embossed with a butterfly."

"I didn't see that," Andy said, "but I have a guess what the pills were."

"So, this is the toxicology report from Laurel's autopsy," Josh said. He put a finger on one line. "This says, 'Positive for Methylenedioxy-methamphetimine, MDMA.'"

"Wow," Andy said. "I don't know what the long words mean, but I do recognize MDMA. You know what that is, Josh?"

"If I'm correct," Josh said, "and I'm no chemist, MDMA is an acronym for the chemicals in Ecstasy, or Molly, which was a favorite party drug at Princeton. Guys would give it to girls to get them in the mood for sex."

"Right," Andy said. "I wasn't a party girl at Barnard, but some girls I knew said it lowers your sexual inhibitions, although most of them didn't have much inhibition when it came to screwing guys at parties." She handed the sheet back to Josh. "You know, I don't recall anything in the trial transcript about this. I'm pretty sure OD's lawyer never asked the medical examiner about the pills, although he might not have recognized MDMA from the tox report, assuming he even read it."

"Hmm," Josh mused. "So, if OD was telling the truth that Laurel invited him to have sex with her, and there was MDMA in her system, maybe that explains why she did that, especially to see if OD was well hung."

"And maybe she took a Molly that morning," Andy said, "knowing that her boyfriend—let's call him Junior—was coming over and would be horny. And she wanted to be in the mood for screwing him. But she was so much in the mood that she couldn't resist screwing OD first, when he knocked on her door. And maybe she lost track of time, or maybe Junior was early."

Josh laughed. "Was that pun intentional?"

Andy laughed, too. "No, but it makes sense, if you think about OD's story. And Junior, seeing a naked 'coon' running down the hall from Laurel's bedroom, flies into a rage and bashes her with a hammer when he finds her dripping with OD's semen. We've thought of this scenario before, Josh, but what Liz told you and the tox report makes it much more believable."

"I agree," Josh said. He picked up another folder from the table, and handed some sheets to Andy. "Oh, I almost forgot. Three more little presents under the tree. The top one is a certified copy of Senior's registration for the red Corvette in 2002. Next, a sworn affidavit from Martha Radford, saying exactly what she told us about the red Corvette at the murder scene." Josh chuckled. "Jim Carruthers sent somebody down to Williamsburg for that, along with tea and cookies. And third, the office manager at the National Association of Attorneys General faxed me copies of Senior's travel vouchers for the conference in Chicago, the weekend Laurel was murdered, when he told Mose Townley he and Junior were together in Richmond. That can go with Townley's interview report."

"Good work," Andy said. "That nails Senior for lying to Townley."

"So, the next question is, what to do with all this stuff?"

"I think it's time to put it all together," Andy replied, "with a memo explaining what it means, and follow through on the plan we discussed after we got back from Richmond."

"Okay," Josh said. "I'll write the memo tomorrow, and you can call your friend and set up a meeting, preferably tomorrow night or Thursday. You didn't tell me who he is, or maybe she, and I don't need to know right now. But remember, Andy, that Early's confirmation hearing starts on Monday, and this plan might take a few days to work out. Assuming, of course, that your friend will agree to get this evidence into the right hands."

"Josh, I didn't tell you who my friend is," Andy said, "because she, or maybe he, might lose their job if anyone suspected who gave them the evidence. And you could say it wasn't you, if anyone asks. As for me, I'd just take the Fifth."

"Okay," Josh said. "I just hope you don't wind up before a grand jury. But I'll give you the evidence and memo tomorrow, and let you run with it."

Andy gave Josh a theatrical yawn. "Speaking of running, Josh, I can run to the Metro and hope I don't get mugged, or I can sack out on your couch, and walk to the Metro in the morning. Either way is fine with me."

Josh gave Andy a yawn back. "Let's compromise," he said. "Start on the couch, with the rest of Carlo's wine, then run to a more comfortable sack. Then walk to the Metro, after scrambled eggs and bacon."

"Deal," Andy said. "Compromise is always better than sleeping alone."

"Jane! This is Andy. I hope I'm not interrupting you, but do you have a minute?" She tried hard to keep her anxiety out of her voice. The plan she had devised with Josh, keeping Jane's name out of it, depended on meeting with her today. Another day or two might be too late. Josh had assured Andy on Wednesday morning, before she left his place, that he'd write the memo today, and send it over to her place by courier, by six at the latest.

"Andy! Of course I have a few minutes, since it's you. Anyone else would get voice mail. I'm so glad you called, Andy. I've been meaning for weeks to call you. And here you are! So, tell me what you've been up to in that marble temple up the street."

Andy decided to be blunt, given the time pressure. "Jane, I'd be glad to tell you all about it, and find out what you've been doing in that ugly pile of masonry down the street. But I'm calling about something pretty urgent, something you've been working on." She paused. "Is there any chance you could stop over at my place this evening, say around seven. It's just a few blocks from your place. If you haven't made dinner plans, I'll get take-out Thai from the place down the block."

"That sounds great, Andy. And if it's about what I think it's about, can I bring Dick along? He's got something you should know about, that possibly should be shared with Alex, and with Alice Schroeder, as well. They have different views, as you know, but they both care deeply about the Court, and wouldn't want anything to damage it. And Dick's been tossing and turning for weeks about it. Makes me seasick at night."

Andy was certain that Jane couldn't possibly know about her something, and couldn't imagine what Dick's something was. But Jane's voice, despite her quip, betrayed a little anxiety, so it must be something earth-shaking to disturb Dick's normal equanimity.

"Seven is great, Jane. And I'll get some chicken with cashew nuts for Dick. I know it's his favorite. And pad Thai for you and me, okay?"

Andy could barely function in the clerks' office, and was afraid her fellow clerks would sniff the odor of anxiety. She called Josh at his office and left a quick voice mail. "My friend is coming at seven, and bringing another friend, who has something important to tell me. I'm punching out here and working at home, so I'll be there for the delivery. Love you, Josh."

Pushing herself to be Disciplined Andy, she worked on the Khalid opinion on her home computer, putting in the legal mumbo-jumbo that Novak had sketched for her. At five-thirty, her bell rang, and she went down to meet the courier, signing for the large padded envelope Josh had sent. She carefully read his four-page memo, which wasn't signed, thinking it was perfect, and skimmed the documents he'd attached, all of which she'd seen the night before. At six-thirty, she went down the block to the Thai Palace—actually, a storefront restaurant with six tables—and picked up the food she'd ordered by phone. Back home, she opened a bottle of

Beringer chardonnay and drank a glass, quickly, hoping it would calm her fluttering butterflies. They settled down when she had another quick glass.

"Jane! And Dick! Come in, you guys. It's been too long." They exchanged hugs, and Dick handed Andy a bag with two bottles of chilled Beringer. My God, Andy thought, everybody I meet—even Early Junior—seems to know my wine of choice. "I've already got one open," she said, "so I'll put these in the fridge, although they won't stay there long, I'm sure."

They sat around her dining table, while Andy poured glasses from her open bottle. "To all three branches of government," she toasted, "sitting around a table and working together, which is rare these days." They clinked, and then sat in silence for a long moment.

Andy decided to break the awkward situation. "Well, it's great to see you both, and we'll have plenty of time for Thai and vino." She picked up two of the three folders Josh had sent over, each with the same contents, handing one to each of her guests. "I hate to do this, guys," she said, "but can I ask you to keep this stuff confidential? I can't tell you where I got it, but it could cost somebody their job if it got out." Or mine, she thought. Or anyone who touched this stick of political dynamite.

Dick and Jane both nodded, and Andy said, "Tell you what. Why don't you both read the cover memo while I put the dinner in bowls, and get out plates and chopsticks." She bustled around the kitchen, opening paper cartons of rice, chicken, and pad Thai.

A sudden gasp made her turn around. Jane was shaking her head in disbelief, staring at Josh's memo. "Oh, my God, Andy! I can't believe this!" She read from the memo: "Attached to this memorandum are documents that prove, conclusively, the criminal acts of Judge Winslow Early, in lying to a police detective and fabricating an alibi for his son, who may well be guilty of a murder for which another man was convicted, and has spent the past fifteen years on death row in Virginia."

Dick took over reading the memo aloud. "Judge Early's acts constitute a violation of the Virginia Criminal Code, Section 18, making it unlawful as an obstruction of justice for any person to knowingly make a materially false statement to a law-enforcement officer who is conducting an investigation of a crime by another person. Violation of this provision is a Class One misdemeanor, punishable by one year in jail."

Dick shook his head, then continued reading. "In view of this evidence, it is clear that Judge Early is unfit to serve as Chief Justice of the Supreme Court. Should he be confirmed by the Senate, and take an oath to uphold the Constitution, whose basic provisions he has violated, the Court will be irreparably damaged, should the attached evidence be made public, through any means. It is therefore incumbent that Judge Early's nomination be withdrawn, voluntarily if possible, but by the president, if necessary. If neither of these happens, the chair of the Senate Judiciary Committee must take action to prevent Judge Early's confirmation."

Dick held the memo out, looking like he was holding a live grenade. "Andy, I don't know who gave this to you, and the memo isn't signed, or addressed to anyone. But it would be almost impossible to fabricate all these documents, not that anyone has, certainly not you."

"Andy," Jane said, "Early's confirmation hearing starts Monday, and today is Wednesday. That's not much time to do anything with this." She paused. "Have you thought of giving this, some way that can't be traced to you or the person who wrote it, to Bob Barnes at the Post, or Adam Liptak at the New York Times, who cover the Court? It would be on the front page, and all over the networks, by Friday."

"No," Andy replied. "I mean, I thought about that, but the media would dig into this like starving wolves, and probably identify its source pretty quickly. Besides, if this gets into Senator Weeks' hands, he might have a private word with Judge Early and figure out a diplomatic way to withdraw his nomination. The media, of course, would jump on that, but the documents don't have to be revealed." She looked at Dick. "Of course, if Early withdraws before the hearing on Monday, that might cause President Chambers some grief, but Early as Chief Justice would be a disaster."

Andy looked back and forth at Dick and Jane, both still looking astounded. "So, do you guys have any suggestions? As Jane said, time is short."

Dick sat up straight, looking like a paratrooper about to jump into enemy territory. "Andy, there's only one person who can persuade Early to withdraw. And he's my ultimate boss." He held up the memo and attachments. "If you agree, Andy, I'll take this with me, and do everything I can to get into the Oval Office, even if it takes some threats, like giving it to Barnes and Liptak. I'm willing to do that."

Andy sensed Dick's resolve. "Dick, you realize this might cost your job, you know. But you seem determined to do this."

Dick smiled, and patted his shirt pocket. "Andy, I've got my resignation letter right here. Actually, in my computer. But I still have an offer from Arnold and Porter, with a signing bonus that will get us a house in Bethesda, with a yard for Spot and Puff."

Andy smiled back. "Dick, I know you're a Republican, and voted for the president, but you have greater loyalties, to the Constitution and the Court. And I admire you for that."

"Gee, Andy," he replied. "I remember saying that to you, and that it made me sound like a politician. But you're right." He paused. "There's another reason I'm going to do this." Over the next ten minutes, Dick told Andy about the deal between President Chambers and Senator Weeks to assure enough Democratic votes to confirm Judge Early.

Andy reacted just as Dick and Jane had reacted to Josh's memo. "Holy shit, Dick. That's just as bad, maybe worse, than the evidence of Early's cover-up of the murder his son probably committed."

"Well, maybe not illegal," Dick said, "but the president basically bought the center seat from Charter Weeks, and that really galls me, to be honest. Republican or Democrat, it's the worst side of politics."

Jane chimed in. "Well, sweetheart, that house in Bethesda is still on the market. And I wouldn't mind having a real Spot and Puff."

Dick leaned over and kissed his wife. "And it's got a perfect room for a nursery. Decorated in blue and red, of course."

Andy got up, and moved into the kitchen. "So," she said, "now that we've decided to blow up the White House and the Senate, how about Thai food, while it's still warm."

After Dick and Jane left, with another exchange of hugs, Andy called Josh, but got his voice mail. Probably taking the trash to the Dumpster, Andy thought. "Hey, Josh," she said, "I just had dinner with two of my friends. One of them is taking your memo and the docs to the highest office in the land, tomorrow morning, if you know what I mean. I'll let you know what happens, as soon as I get word. And give Carlo a kiss from me, when he gets back from West Virginia. But don't catch black-lung disease from him. That's a joke, since I know it's not contagious. Anyway, so far, so good. But you never know, right. What's that big word? Love you, Josh."

23

Thursday morning, after a quick breakfast and a "Good luck, sweetheart" from Jane, Dick arrived at his office in the EOB at seven-thirty. He made three copies of the memo and documents Andy had given him, sat at his desk for ten minutes, eyes closed, waiting for his nerves to calm, then picked up his phone and punched a number.

"Rory," he said, "this is Dick Wadleigh." A short pause. "I'll get that memo to you tomorrow. Just needs some polishing. Listen, Rory, I need to come over to your office right now. There's an extremely urgent matter we need to discuss, and the Chief of Staff should be there, too." A pause. "I know you're busy, and he is too. But let me repeat, Rory. This is an extremely urgent matter. If it's not dealt with today, the president might be highly embarrassed."

Dick held the phone away from his ear until the president's counsel stopped shouting. "Of course I'm loyal to the president, Rory, and I'm not being insubordinate. But I've got only one other option if this matter isn't resolved today." More shouting. "You can do that, Rory, if you feel that I'm no longer capable of doing my job. But I wouldn't put the Commander in Chief at risk, if I were you. So, I'm coming over now, Rory. Whether you let me in your office, or toss me out, is up to you." Before any more shouting, Dick hung up, picked up the copies he'd printed, and headed for the tunnel to the West Wing.

Rory O'Connor glared at Dick from his office doorway. "Ten minutes, Dick, that's all we've got. And I don't like being dictated to by the most junior member of my staff."

Dick couldn't contain his anger. "Sorry, Captain O'Connor. But there's incoming, and we need to take cover."

O'Connor wheeled around, brusquely pointing Dick to a chair. Sitting on another chair was Mike Hammerman, the president's chief of staff and gate-keeper to the Oval Office. He didn't greet Dick, fixing him with a Don't Fuck With Me glare.

"Tell me, Dick," O'Connor said, "what's such an extremely urgent matter that it can't wait, and screws up our schedules this morning? Run out of paperclips in the EOB?"

Answering O'Connor's sarcasm with his own, Dick handed each man a folder. "The memo on top is only four pages, and should take less than ten minutes to read. I'll wait until you finish." Dick put a third folder on O'Connor's desk. "Mike, there's a one-page briefing memo in there for the president. You told me he doesn't like them any longer, and it should take him less than ten minutes to read."

Looking up from the memo in his hands, Hammerman snarled at Dick. "Don't you 'Mike' me, young man. I'm 'Mister Hammerman' to you, or 'sir.' And what makes you think the president should read any of this crap?"

"I'll answer that when you finish what you're reading, sir." Dick felt calm, now that he'd gotten the memo Andy gave him into the hands of the president's top aides. He crossed his legs and relaxed. Hammerman and O'Connor looked anything but relaxed, as they flipped through the pages of the memo. Hammerman put his copy down, and flipped through the twenty sheets of documents in his folder, unable to conceal his obvious discomfort. He then picked up the folder on O'Connor's desk, and pulled out the sheet on top, moving his head back and forth as he read it.

Hammerman grunted as he finished reading Dick's one-page briefing paper. "Two questions, Mister Wadleigh," he said. "First, who gave this to you? There's no name on this memo. Or did you cook this up yourself?"

"No, sir, I didn't," Dick replied. "We don't have DNA testing equipment in the EOB, unless it's in the basement. And I can't tell you who gave this to me. Or, rather, I won't. But if you think these documents are all fabricated, call the FBI and have them checked. Of course, that would take more time than we've got." Dick glanced at his watch. "Mine's not a Patek Phillipe, sir, but it says time is running short."

Hammerman burst from his chair, his face red. *"Stop fucking with me,"* he shouted.

O'Connor cringed, but Dick sat impassively. "You had a second question, sir?"

Hammerman sat back down, and said nothing for a long moment. "Yes I do, Dick." His tone was calm. "What do you want out of this? I'm sure we can settle this matter right here. Rory told me that that Paul McDermott is leaving his office in two weeks, and he'll need a new Deputy Counsel to the President." O'Connor nodded his agreement.

Dick smiled. "Mike, you can't buy me," he replied, "like the president bought Charter Weeks, who bought the five votes you need to confirm Judge Early. But, since you asked, I'll tell you what I want, and it's not much." Hammerman leaned forward, expectantly. "All I want is five minutes of the president's time," Dick continued, "so he can give me his decision personally. Not that I don't trust you and Rory, Mike, but the president made the decision to nominate Judge Early, and I'd like to hear his decision on whether or not to withdraw that nomination. Once he's read my briefing memo, of course."

Hammerman sat for a moment. "I know what his decision will be, but if you need to hear it from him, I can arrange that." He gave O'Connor a nod. "Tell you what, Dick," he went on, "give me thirty minutes, and meet me in the reception room outside the Oval Office."

"Fair enough," Dick replied. "I know the president's a busy man, and he might have to juggle his schedule to fit me in. Thirty minutes." Hammerman got up and left the office. Dick turned to O'Connor. "Thanks for your time, Rory. And I've got a great suggestion for your new Deputy Counsel. Vicky Nickerson. She's extremely capable, and very smart." He couldn't resist a parting shot. "And putting a woman in that position would please the radical feminists, although Vicky's not one of them."

Thirty minutes later, after a brisk and head-clearing walk around Lafayette Square, across Pennsylvania Avenue from the White House, Dick entered the reception area outside the Oval Office, giving his name and showing his White House staff pass to a Secret Service agent at the door, who checked a list and nodded him inside. He took a seat on an upholstered couch. Three men and a woman were seated on another couch, chatting. Another man, with a camera bag, stood near a window.

A minute later, Mike Hammerman stuck his head through the door to the Oval Office and beckoned Dick with a finger. "You asked for five minutes, and that's what you get," Hammerman said, quietly but firmly, as Dick followed him. "One minute more, and you'll be escorted out."

President Chris Chambers rose from his desk, waving Dick and Hammerman to one of two facing sofas, coming around to sit across from them, separated by a low table, adorned with vases of red roses. He put the folder Dick had given Hammerman on the table, then reached across and shook Dick's hand.

"Mister Wadleigh," he said, "I'm sorry we don't have more time, but I've got a delegation outside from the Special Olympics. I'm their official sponsor, and they're here for a photo op. Part of my job, you know." The president's photo, arms around the shoulders of beaming Oval Office visitors, hung on thousands of walls across the country. The recipients of these autographed mementos, aside from children, were all voters. A former governor of Kansas, Chambers was famed for posing with everyone he met. But not for this meeting, Dick knew.

Dick smiled. "Mister President, I appreciate your time, and I'd like to thank your Chief of Staff for arranging this meeting. And I apologize for the short notice."

Chambers waved a dismissive hand. "No apology needed, Mister Wadleigh. Mike has filled me in on the purpose of your visit, and I've read your briefing paper, and the memo with it. Took me less than ten minutes, actually." He smiled, but Dick saw the Gotcha! behind it. Chambers tapped the folder on the table. "Now, I think what we've got here is a simple matter. It looks like Judge Early was confused when he spoke with the detective from Williamsburg. In fact, I just called him, and he told me that he'd been with his son the previous weekend, and thought that's what the detective was asking about. Simple misunderstanding."

Oh, my God, Dick thought. He's lying already. Chambers wouldn't have called Early with bad news, just days before his confirmation hearing. Hammerman must have prompted him to give Dick a scare. But he wasn't. "With all due respect to you and Judge Early, Mister President," Dick replied, "the documents attached to that memo indicate very clearly the dates Judge Early was in Chicago, and the dates the detective questioned him about. And Judge Early's response was that he and his son were both in Richmond on *that* weekend, not the previous weekend. There's no doubt that Judge Early lied to the detective, and gave his son a phony alibi for the day of the murder in Williamsburg. Perhaps you should look again at those documents, sir."

Chambers waved another dismissive hand. "Let's not quibble about dates from fifteen years ago, Mister Wadleigh. I trust Judge Early's word, and I have no intention of withdrawing his nomination. He has every quality one should expect of a Chief Justice, and I made that choice very carefully." Dick knew better, but decided not to argue.

Chambers gave Dick a piercing look. "Now, from what my Chief of Staff has told me, you have no knowledge of who prepared this memo, and you refused to tell him who gave it to you." Dick nodded agreement. Chambers continued. "The allegations in that memo, whoever wrote it, are libelous, Mister Wadleigh. Stating, or even suggesting, that he committed a crime, or had any part in covering one up, is completely false. Any publication or circulation of them would subject both the anonymous author, and you as well, to a suit for defamation." He paused. "Do I make myself clear, Mister Wadleigh?"

"Yes, Mister President," Dick replied, "but I assume you also know that truth is an absolute defense to a defamation claim."

Chambers ignored Dick's statement of legal fact. "Look, Mister Wadleigh," he said. "I'll make one last point before I welcome the delegation that's been waiting to see me during your interruption of my schedule." He leaned toward Dick. "Please listen to me very carefully, Mister Wadleigh. I'll only say this once. I understand from the Chief that you have an offer from Arnold and Porter to join that firm when you leave the Counsel's office. I happen to be on very good terms with their managing partner, Matty Michaels. If I told him that you had any part in circulating false charges against Judge Early, that offer would be withdrawn. And, any other firm that might offer you employment would be told the same thing." He pointed a finger at Dick. "Have I made myself clear, Mister Wadleigh?"

"Very clear, Mister President," Dick replied. Hammerman had gotten up from the couch, giving Dick a Time's Up look. Dick reached into his breast pocket and pulled out an envelope, handing it to Chambers. "Mister President, considering your answer to the request that you ask Judge Early to withdraw his nomination, I don't think I'd be comfortable in the Counsel's office, and I doubt the Counsel, and your Chief of Staff, would be comfortable having me here."

Dick smiled at the president. "The letter in this envelope tenders my resignation, effectively immediately. And, just to conclude our meeting, and allow you to greet your visitors, I called Marty Michaelson this morning and confirmed that his offer remains open. That's the name of your good friend at Arnold and Porter, by the way." He shot a glance at Hammerman. "Someone must have given you the wrong name, Mister President." Dick hadn't called, but he knew that Michaelson detested Chambers and wouldn't bow to White House pressure, which was likely a bluff.

Dick smiled at Chambers. "Thanks for your time, Mister President." He turned to Hammerman, with a You Fucked Up look. "Mike, I'll clean out my office and turn in my badge before noon." With that, he left the Oval Office. Once inside the tunnel to the EOB, he reached into his right jacket pocket and clicked off the "Record" button on his phone. He'd been afraid a Secret Service agent would confiscate it before letting him into the Oval Office, but apparently White House staffers weren't considered threats to the president. But it was the president who made the threats, Dick thought, as he reached his office. His own were not recorded, just left on a table in the Oval Office.

Back at his desk, he called Jane. "Hi, sweetheart," he said when she answered. "We can buy that house in Bethesda now, the one you've been pining for. And move to Plan B. Unfortunately, Plan A didn't work, but I wasn't surprised."

"I've already started decorating the house," Jane said. "And I'm proud of you, Dick. At least you tried. But there's a slight problem with Plan B. Senator Weeks is in New Hampshire, mending fences, the political kind, and won't be back in DC until late Sunday. And the hearing's at ten on Monday. I'll try to pull him aside before it starts, but no guarantee, considering that he'll be hustling to get things started on time, with everybody grabbing at him."

"Hmm," Dick said, "that *is* a problem. And we don't have a Plan C."

"Actually, sweetheart, I just thought of one," Jane said. "It's sort of a 'Hail Mary,' but hey, it's fourth down on the one-yard line, with one play left, so I'll throw it up and see who catches it. Might be a touchdown."

Dick chuckled. "Well, let's hope it's not a fumble, and you can tell me about Plan C when you get home. Meantime, I'm going to call Marty Michaelson and tell him to cut a check for the signing bonus."

Smack! Smack! Smack!

Senator Charter Weeks brought down his gavel with another *Smack!* It was ten on Monday morning, November 13, and the cavernous hearing room in the Hart Senate Office Building was filled with people, mostly seated, but some still standing and chatting. A final *Smack!* stopped the buzzing and put everyone in seats.

Behind a straight bench and two angled arms sat the fifteen members of the Senate Judiciary Committee, eight Democrats and seven Republicans. Behind them were chairs for committee staffers, most holding folders in their hands. Behind the bench, a creamy marble wall, embossed with the Senate seal, gave the room a classical look. Two dozen photographers sat on the floor in front of the bench, cameras trained on the witness table, and overhead booths provided television coverage of the proceedings.

A minute before Weeks smacked his gavel, Andy Roboff stuck her head through the side entrance door, peered around, came inside, and found an empty seat in the back row. Seated at a long table facing the bench, flanked by two men, Judge Winslow Early had his back to Andy. Also with their backs to Andy, seated just behind Early, she spotted the heads of Early Junior, and those of two women, whom she assumed, from watching CNN the day President Chambers announced Senior's nomination, were his wife, Calista, and Junior's wife, Penny.

Andy also spotted Jane Wadleigh, seated behind Weeks with the committee staffers, next to an African American woman. Jane had called Andy the previous Thursday to report that Chambers had rejected Dick Wadleigh's effort to persuade him to withdraw Early's nomination, and that Dick had resigned on the spot as assistant counsel to the president. Jane had urged Andy to attend the Monday hearing, saying only that she had a "Hail Mary" plan. Andy recognized the football term, but Jane had just said that Andy would have to wait for the end-zone toss.

"Good morning," Weeks said, once the room was quiet. "The committee would like to welcome Judge Winslow Early, and his family,

271

to this hearing on his nomination by the president as Chief Justice of the Supreme Court." Weeks adopted a somber tone. "It's been thirteen years since I sat at the far end of this bench, as a freshman member of this committee, for the confirmation hearing of our sadly departed Chief Justice, Samuel Terman, whose untimely passing we all deeply regret."

He paused a moment, head bent in faux reflection, then continued. "The procedures of this committee are that the distinguished Senators from Judge Early's home state of Virginia will first introduce him, followed by a statement from the judge. We'll then proceed to questioning of Judge Early by committee members, beginning with the ranking Republican member, on my right, and alternating by party and seniority, with each member having ten minutes for the opening round. As chair, it's my practice to reserve my time until the end of that round, at which time I'll ask the questions my colleagues have been too polite to raise." A ripple of chuckles died quickly..

The two Virginia senators, both Republicans, each spent five minutes praising Early as an outstanding and superbly qualified nominee as Chief Justice, outdoing each other in superlatives. After Weeks thanked the senators, Early began his statement on a tone of humility, expressing his gratitude to President Chambers, his admiration for Sam Terman—who had written several opinions overruling Early's—and his respect for the Supreme Court as an institution whose legacy he hoped to continue. Early then turned and gestured to his wife, son, and daughter-in-law, choking up as he thanked them for their undying love and support. From her seat in the rear, Andy observed the senators nodding in appreciation of Early's almost tearful effusions. She glanced at Jane, sitting behind Weeks, wondering if time had expired and the game was over.

Weeks thanked Early for his heartfelt statement, then turned to Senator Ted Tillman, the ranking Republican and a corn-pone Alabaman. Unsurprisingly, Tillman began lobbing softball questions at Early, who fielded them like lazy pop-ups, promising to follow the divinely-inspired guidance of the Founding Fathers, and to eschew any legislating from the bench. Andy suspected that both questions and answers had been scripted and rehearsed in advance, and cribbed from transcripts of previous hearings in which Supreme Court nominees had scrupulously avoided saying anything that revealed their true judicial philosophies. None, whether left or right, wanted to risk the fate of Robert Bork, the object lesson of suffering the consequences of being honest before the committee.

Five minutes into Tillman's questioning, Andy saw Jane rise from her seat behind Weeks. The woman on Jane's left grabbed her arm, but Jane wrested from her grasp, with an audible "Let go of me, Cheryl!" Startled by the commotion, Early paused in mid-sentence, and Weeks turned his head. Jane leaned over, thrust a folder into his hand, and whispered into his ear, as the room buzzed. The man seated next to Andy said, "What the hell?" Jane then sat down, as Weeks said, "I apologize for the interruption, Judge Early. Please continue." The room quieted, and Early resumed his answer to Tillman. Weeks opened the folder, and began reading its contents.

Five minutes later, Weeks turned around and gave Jane an emphatic 'No' shake of his head. Andy saw her whisper something to him, hand him a sheet of paper, and point to the section of the room where more than fifty reporters were seated. Two minutes later, as Andy watched him reading the sheet, then looking over at the press section, Weeks turned back to Jane, and gave her a 'Yes' nod. Turning back, he leaned into his microphone and said, "Senator Tillman, your time for this round has expired. However, before we resume with Senator Shapiro, the committee will be in recess for thirty minutes. Judge Early, I apologize again for the interruption, but would you kindly accompany the committee to our conference room." Pushing back his chair, Early followed the committee members through the side door.

During the next thirty minutes, the room buzzed and people milled around, exchanging What The Hell's Going On? questions. Andy pulled out her phone and texted Josh: "If you're not watching now, turn on CNN." A minute later, he texted back: "I'm watching, but Wolf Blitzer is just speculating. Keep me posted."

Thirty minutes later, looking grim, Weeks led his colleagues back to their seats, and smacked his gavel three times. Andy noticed that Jane was no longer seated behind the chairman. Early resumed his seat at the witness table, turning to whisper to his wife and son. After another gavel smack, Weeks leaned toward his microphone, a sharp tone in his voice. "Judge Early, you asked to make a statement to the committee. You may proceed."

Looking down at a sheet of paper in his hand, his voice quavering, Early said, "Thank you, Mister Chairman. First, let me apologize to the committee for not disclosing to its members a serious health condition, very recently diagnosed, that will likely prevent me, at some time my doctors cannot predict with certainty, from performing with full strength and ability the duties required of the Chief Justice of the Supreme Court."

Well, Andy thought as she listened, they gave the lying son-of-a-bitch an easy out. And Charter Weeks probably dictated that sob story to him. But Jane threw a touchdown, after almost fumbling the snap. She wondered where Jane had gone.

The hearing room was absolutely silent as Early continued, after taking and expelling a deep breath. "In consideration of my family," he continued, "I hereby withdraw my nomination as Chief Justice of the Supreme Court. And I will submit my resignation as a judge on the Court of Appeals." Behind him, Calista Early began sobbing, consoled by her son, his arm around her heaving shoulders.

With that, Early abruptly rose and departed again through the side door, trailed by his family and surrounded by a phalanx of Senate security guards, obviously summoned by Weeks. The room erupted in chaos and confusion, hardly anyone hearing the final smack of Weeks' gavel or his pointless statement: "This hearing is now adjourned."

Andy decided to return to Alex Novak's chambers at the Court, and scooted out of the hearing room, barely ahead of a horde of reporters, rushing to file stories about the spectacle they had just witnessed. "I can't believe this," she heard from a dozen voices. "What do you think he's got?" others asked. Something fatal to his chance of becoming Chief Justice is what he's got, Andy thought, but nothing a doctor had diagnosed. A self-inflicted wound is what he's got.

Halfway down the hall to the elevator, Jane rushed toward Andy, pulling her into an empty conference room. "Holy shit, Jane," Andy exclaimed. "I thought you threw an interception, when I saw Weeks shake his head at you. So, what happened? I saw you pointing at the reporters before he hustled Early out with the committee. Was that a trick play?"

Jane was breathless, and sat down at the conference table, looking a bit queasy. Just then, Dick stuck his head in the door and came in, kneeling before Jane. "Are you okay, sweetheart? I got your text and came looking for you. Just take it easy, okay?" He looked up at Andy, surprised to see him. "Hey, Andy. Jane said you'd be here. I was downstairs in the press room, and saw it all on the monitor. It's total pandemonium down there."

Jane looked down at Dick and smiled. "You can get off your knees, Sir Galahad. I'm fine now. But I thought Cheryl was going to wrestle me to the ground when I handed Weeks the folder with the memo about Early's cover-up lies." She noticed Andy's puzzled look. "Cheryl Perkins is the chairman's chief of staff, and it's strictly verboten to interrupt him during a hearing, unless he asks for something."

"I would have put her in a headlock if I'd been there," Dick said. "Putting her hands on my wife, in her condition."

Andy looked even more puzzled. "What condition, Dick? Breaking the 'don't interrupt the boss' rule?"

Jane laughed. "No, Andy, but I'll tell you about that in a minute. Anyway, here's my trick play." She mimed throwing a football. "After Weeks read the memo I handed him, and made it clear he wasn't going to ask Early anything about it, I gave him another memo, just one sheet. I was afraid Cheryl would try again to stop me, but I just said, 'Keep your fucking hands off me, Cheryl, or I'll start screaming. That'll get his attention.'"

Dick gave Jane a look of mock horror. "Sweetheart, that's the first time I've ever heard you utter the 'f' word."

"And probably the last," she replied. "But that got her attention, too." She turned to Andy. "Anyway, the sheet I gave Weeks said that my husband was down in the press room, with a statement laying out all the details of his deal with the president. Like getting Governor Coteau off the ballot with an excursion to Paris, and buying votes to confirm Early with his slush-fund contributions. That's why I pointed at the reporters, and *that* got his attention."

"Wow," Andy said. "That's some trick play, Jane."

"Well, more like desperation," Jane replied. "But that's not all. I also told Weeks that Dick was in the press room with fifty copies of the memo about Early's lies to that detective, and would let the reporters scramble for them." Jane smiled. "Oh, and that's not all, Andy. The last line in my one-pager said, 'I hereby resign as assistant counsel to the chairman of the Senate Judiciary Committee, effective immediately.'"

"Wow, again," Andy said. "So, what now? I know Dick has a job lined up with Arnold and Porter, but what about you, Jane? I'm sure any good firm would take you in a flash, maybe with another signing bonus."

"Well, Andy," Jane said, patting her belly, "I do have a job lined up, but not with a law firm." She gave Dick a wink. "My hubby gave me the job I've always wanted, which is being a full-time mom. Which will happen, by the way, six months from now."

Andy pulled her friends into a group hug. "I'm so happy for you guys. Can I be the godmother? And free babysitting anytime you want a break from diapers and formula."

"Andy, you're wonderful," Jane said. "We'll even have a room for a live-in nanny in our new house, in case you need a job after your year's up with Alex."

Andy laughed. "Speaking of whom, I'd better run across the street and see what he thinks of what you guys just did. I'm sure he was watching."

Dick handed her a thin folder. "Before you go, Andy, here's something you might want to keep handy, just in case. I had a little chat with the president last Thursday, and I just happened to remember every word he said. At least, the little device in my pocket did, but don't tell anyone."

Andy opened the folder and scanned the three pages inside. "Holy shit, Dick," she exclaimed. "So, he knew about Early, and threatened you if you let it get out. Wow! Can I show this to Alex? I know he doesn't like Chambers, but he'd blow a gasket if he knew what a slime he really is."

Dick thought for a moment. "You know, Andy, why don't you keep this in reserve, at least for now. I have a hunch the president will invite Alex over for a little chat, and I don't want him to blow a gasket in the Oval Office, and spill oil all over that beautiful carpet."

Andy looked skeptical. "You think Chambers will offer Alex the center seat, Dick? I'm sure he knows that Alex has said he doesn't want it, in no uncertain terms."

Dick chuckled. "It's the president on the one-yard line now, with time running out. And Alex is the only player left on his bench, if you get what I mean. Too late to draft anyone, and the others are too old or too sick. And No doesn't always mean No, especially in the Oval Office. Just a hunch, I said. But you never know, right?"

"Right," Andy said. "So, I'll put this in the playbook, just in case. And guys, I'm so happy for you." After another round of hugs, Andy headed back to the Court, just across Constitution Avenue from the Hart Building.

When she entered Novak's chambers, he waved Andy into his office, in which Jeff Toobin, CNN's legal pundit, was confessing his total puzzlement at what Andy had just witnessed in person. Novak clicked off the television. "Andy, you were there," he said. "I even saw you in the back row when they panned the room. And Jane Wadleigh in a wrestling match behind Charter Weeks. So, fill me in. You must know more than Jeff Toobin."

Seating herself in one of the chairs around the low table across from Novak's desk, Andy thought quickly before she answered. She hadn't told him anything yet about working with Josh on OD Beasley's case, their trips to Williamsburg and Richmond, Early Senior's cover-up lies to Moses Townley, the results of the DNA testing that linked Early Junior to Laurel Davis's murder, or Dick Wadleigh's meeting with President Chambers. Nothing, in fact, that would solve Jeff Toobin's puzzlement, which Novak obviously shared.

Novak came around his desk and sat next to Andy, looking expectant. She decided, at least for now, to lie about what she knew. The time may come, perhaps soon, to tell the truth. But just in case Dick was right that Chambers would invite Novak to an Oval Office chat, Andy didn't want him to learn anything that might cause a blown gasket.

"Alex," she said, "I actually do know a bit more than Jeff Toobin, but it's confidential, okay? I got this from Jane, who got it from Dick, who got it from the president. And the president, as you know, hates leaks and hunts down leakers like a bounty hunter. So, this is just between you and me, Alex. Okay?"

Novak nodded agreement, so Andy continued with her lie. "Last Friday, the FBI director informed the president that Judge Early had been diagnosed, just a week before, with some kind of leukemia. Judge Early hadn't disclosed this to the president, and Dick wasn't told how the FBI found out about this, or how serious it was."

Andy noticed that Novak seemed astounded by her on-the-spot fabrication, and continued spinning the tale. "Anyway, Dick thought Senator Weeks should know about this, and told Jane. But she couldn't get any time with him before the hearing. And Weeks doesn't like staffers to interrupt him during hearings. That's why his chief of staff tried to stop Jane from giving Weeks a memo about this that Dick had prepared. And that's what started the wrestling match you saw on TV, Alex."

Feeling like Pinocchio, Andy told her final lie. "Anyway, Weeks read Dick's memo, and obviously decided it required an explanation from Judge Early. I have no idea, Alex, what was said during that recess, but I assume Early's condition was serious enough that Weeks, and probably the whole committee, persuaded him to withdraw."

Novak shook his head in astonishment. "My God, Andy, that's hard to believe." For a second, she thought Novak had seen through her rather unbelievable story. "So," he continued, "now the Court has to function for who knows how long with an empty center seat." He shook his head again. "Well, Andy, as I said after Sam died, the Court will continue. And I guess we'll just have to wait for the president to make another choice." He chuckled. "Hopefully, somebody with not even a hangnail."

Andy breathed a sigh of relief. "I hope so, too, Alex." She glanced at her watch. "Hey, I've almost finished the Khalid opinion. Before you tear it apart, can I stick in the last bit of legal mumbo-jumbo?"

Novak smiled. "Maybe I'll tear all that out, and just let you tell the story of his grieving widow and children. And how the president launched that drone from the Oval Office."

Back in the clerks' office, which was empty at lunchtime, Andy recalled something Bella had told her, when she was caught in a childhood fib. There were White Lies, to spare someone from embarrassment. "Oh, that dress looks perfect on you." There were Black Lies, to conceal your own horrible misdeeds. "No, I didn't steal from your purse, to buy the dress I wanted." And there were Grey Lies, to put off telling a truth until a better time. "Dick learned of Judge Early's leukemia, and decided Senator Weeks needed to know about it." At a better time, Andy decided, she would replace that lie with the truth. But that time depended on things she could not predict. More of that damned indeterminacy, Andy thought, opening her computer and pulling up the Khalid opinion.

24

Tuesday morning, Andy entered Novak's chambers with a sense of great uncertainty. The previous evening, she had flipped between CNN, MSNBC, and even Fox, the panels of legal pundits on each network equally stunned by Judge Early's abrupt exit from the Judiciary Committee's hearing room. Early had disappeared, without a word to any of the reporters who trailed him to a waiting car, kept at bay by Senate guards. Charter Weeks had brushed off reporters who trailed him to his office with a brusque "No comment," and other committee members were equally tight-lipped.

Ken Roby, the White House press secretary, had told the media only that President Chambers had not known in advance of Judge Early's serious health problem, prayed for his full recovery, and would immediately begin a search for an equally qualified nominee. Left with no hard news to report, the talking heads filled the airtime with speculation. Their main topic was, unsurprisingly, who might Chambers name to fill the still-vacant center seat on the Court, and how long that search might last. They all agreed that none of the sitting justices was a likely choice, since Chambers had probably considered and rejected elevating one of the four conservatives. A dozen names of appellate judges, a handful of Republican senators, and a couple governors were floated, but the pundits all confessed they hadn't a clue.

Alex Novak was at his desk, on the phone, and gave Andy a greeting wave through his open door. Turning into the clerks' office, she found only Dave Park at his computer. "Hey, Andy," he said with his usual cheer. "Saw you on the tube yesterday, in your cameo role as an extra. So, what happened in there? Any inside scoop?"

"Sorry, Dave," she replied. "No scoop, inside or outside. I really don't have a clue. And I got out just before a thundering herd of reporters almost trampled me. So, I guess we'll just have to wait and see who wins the Second-Most-Qualified-Judge contest to replace Sam." Andy noticed that Amanda and Todd were absent, and gave Dave a questioning look.

"Another bout of twenty-four-hour bugs is what Amanda told Angie," Dave said. "Although, considering our friends were banking on Early's confirmation, and maybe a move to the Chief's chambers, I'm guessing a twenty-four-hour hangover."

Andy chuckled, and sat down at her computer, pulling up the Khalid opinion for a final polishing, before giving it to Angie for Novak's in-box.

An hour later, she pressed Save, then Print, and collected two copies from the office printer. "Hey, Dave," she said, holding up the draft opinion. "Thirty-seven pages, which Alex will probably cut down to two words: 'Judgment Affirmed.' He told me that's all the parties and their lawyers want to know, anyway. Oh, just in case you want to peruse my masterpiece, Dave, there's a copy on my desk."

In the outer office, Andy handed the draft opinion to Angie, just as her phone rang. "Justice Novak's chambers," Angie said, then paused. "Yes, he's in, Mister Hammerman, and I'll connect you." Angie pushed a button. "Alex, Mike Hammerman, the president's chief of staff, would like to speak with you." She pushed another button. Andy almost jumped. Holy shit, she thought. Dick was right. The president wants to chat with Alex.

A minute later, Novak came out of his office. "Well," he said, "my first summons to the Oval Office, and probably my last, if I know what the president's going to ask, and how I'm going to answer. But you don't tell the Chief Executive that you've got to pick up your dry cleaning." Andy and Angie both chuckled. "I'll be back before lunch," he said, "since I doubt I'll be invited to share his tuna sandwich." With that, Novak left for the White House.

Two hours later, Novak stuck his head into the clerks' office. Dave had left for lunch, and Andy had tackled a bench memo for one of next week's arguments. "Got a minute, Andy? No lunch at the White House, but I've got a question."

Andy clicked off her computer and followed Novak into his office, wondering what question he had, that she might be able to answer. Novak gestured to a chair around his low table, and sat across from Andy, who looked at him expectantly. "Well," he said, "I guessed it was one of two reasons I got summoned to the Oval Office. And I guessed wrong." Andy waited for the correct reason. "I thought the president would ask me for suggestions on who to nominate, after Judge Early's withdrawal. But he practically got down on his knees and begged me to take the center seat." Andy decided not to interrupt what Novak seemed eager to tell her. "So, I told him that I'd made it clear, at least I thought I had, that I didn't think I was cut out to be Chief Justice. As you know, Andy, I can be a bit testy, and I'm a terrible manager. I can barely manage my own office, let alone the whole Court. And I hate the ceremonial duties that come with the center seat, the kind that Sam did so well." He paused. "So, guess what, Andy? I chickened out, and told the resident that, out of respect for his office, I'd seriously consider his offer, and give him an answer in two days."

Andy was surprised. "And you wanted to ask *me* if I thought you should take the offer?"

"No, I made up my mind before I even set foot in the Oval Office," Novak said. "But let me explain why I asked the president for two days to think about it." Andy nodded. "Mike Hammerman, the president's chief of staff, and his counsel, Rory O'Connor, were also there. And when we were chatting, before I left, I asked O'Connor how Dick Wadleigh was working out as his assistant counsel. And I swear, Andy, O'Connor and Hammerman both jumped like I'd zapped them with a Taser. O'Connor hemmed and hawed, looked at Hammerman like he wanted help, and then said that Dick had decided to leave the White House, and take the offer from Arnold and Porter. That surprised me, so I asked when Dick left. And O'Connor said, last Thursday."

Andy guessed what question Novak wanted her to answer. "Yesterday, Andy, you told me that Dick learned on Friday about Judge Early's health condition. But he left the White House, obviously without notice, on Thursday." Novak gave her a Come Clean look. "Andy, is there something you know, that I should know? Because something fishy is going on at the White House, and I don't mean tuna salad. And I don't think Judge Early has leukemia."

Andy was trapped in her Grey Lie, and decided to come clean. "Alex, I'm terribly sorry I lied to you. But I thought if I told you the truth about why Judge Early withdrew, and if the president invited you to the Oval

Office, which Dick predicted, you might refuse to go. Or maybe you'd go, and blow a gasket." Andy was trembling, and her voice quavered. "Alex, it might be better if I resigned. You can't trust a clerk who lies to you. I'm really sorry."

She started to cry. Novak reached over and lifted her chin. "Andy, Andy, calm down." He dug into a pocket and handed her a pack of tissues. "Gloria makes me carry these so I won't wipe my nose on my sleeve." Andy took one and wiped her tears, touched by Novak's effort to lighten the atmosphere. He waited a moment. "Andy, it sounds like you *do* know the truth about why Judge Early withdrew. And you said you didn't want to tell me before I saw the president, so I wouldn't blow a gasket. So, can you tell me now what could blow my gasket?" He chuckled. "It sounds like Hammerman and O'Connor blew their gaskets when Dick quit on the spot."

Andy blew her nose with another tissue. "Thanks, Alex. And thank Gloria for protecting your sleeves." She got up from her chair. "Hang on for a minute, okay? I'm going to fetch something from my desk."

A minute later, Andy returned, handing Novak two folders. "Can you read these, Alex? And then I'll answer any questions you have about them." Novak opened the first, read the memo that Josh had written, then examined the documents attached to it. Andy waited, her heart pounding, and took several deep breaths. Novak shook his head, put the folder on the table, then opened the second, and read the memo Dick had written about Chambers' logrolling deal with Charter Weeks, to which he'd attached a transcript of the Oval Office conversation that he'd recorded on his phone. Novak shook his head again, put that one on the table, tilted his head back, and closed his eyes for a minute.

Then he opened them, and spoke in a quiet but determined voice. "Only one question, Andy," he said. "Am I right that these are what Jane handed Senator Weeks, after her tussle with his chief of staff? I recognized Cheryl Perkins on TV. She worked for him when I had my confirmation hearing, ten years ago."

"You're right, Alex," Andy replied. "If you want, I'll tell you who wrote the first memo, and how I got it. And Dick gave me the second one after the hearing yesterday."

"Actually, I'd rather not know who wrote the first one," Novak said. "Maybe you can tell me later, but I'd prefer to say I don't know, in case anyone asks. But these just blew every gasket in my engine." He paused for a moment. "Andy, would you mind making four copies of these? I'd ask Angie, but she peeks at everything I give her." He chuckled. "Just in case I've libeled anyone."

"Sure, Alex," Andy said. "Back in a minute." While she fed the office copier, she wondered why Novak wanted four copies. She put the copies into four folders, and brought them into Novak's office, resuming her seat.

"Thanks, Andy," he said. "I promised the president I'd give him my decision by Thursday. But first, I need to caucus with four of my colleagues. I hope you don't mind if I share these with them." Andy nodded her agreement. "I'd ask you to join us, but that might raise some eyebrows. Is that okay with you?"

"Of course," Andy replied. She leaned over and kissed his cheek. "Don't want to raise any eyebrows, Alex. And I've got a bench memo that's itching to get finished." She returned to the clerks' office and began scratching the memo. Ten minutes later, she heard voices, looked out, saw Alice Schroeder, Maggie McEwen, Dwight Stokes, and J.P. Romero greet Angie, and then troop into Novak's office. Interesting, Andy thought. The four liberal justices, caucusing with their most conservative colleague. Or *was* he? Diligent Andy shook her head, then returned to scratching her itchy memo.

W ednesday passed very slowly. Andy had no idea what Novak had discussed with his four colleagues the previous day, although she assumed he gave them copies of the memos by Josh and Dick. Perhaps they had all blown gaskets, but their hastily-convened caucus with Novak had taken place behind his closed office door. Maybe Novak's second visit to the Oval Office would give the media some hard news to report, and legal pundits more airtime for their blather. Nothing to do but wait, Andy realized, pushing aside her curiosity while she worked on a pool memo.

Amanda and Todd had returned to the clerks' office, from wherever they'd gone to drown their sorrows. From their bleary expressions, and total silence, Andy surmised they'd been drinking something stronger than champagne. Dave, as usual, attacked his stack of cert petitions like a ravenous wolverine. Andy didn't see Novak all day. Angie did say, when

Andy asked if he'd picked up her draft of the Khalid opinion, that he'd taken it with him on a quick trip out of town, saying only that he would be back on Thursday morning. Andy wondered where he'd gone, and who he might be meeting, but decided not to press Angie for details. I'll probably find out tomorrow, she thought, reminding herself again that she could only wait to see what it brought.

Andy literally tingled with anticipation as she entered Novak's chambers on Thursday morning. She was almost certain that he would give President Chambers a Shermanesque rejection of his bended-knee offer of the center seat, but his caucus with the four liberal justices left her wondering if something else might be afoot.

Stopping at Angie's desk before she turned into the clerks' office, Andy asked, lightly, whether Novak had returned from his out-of-town trip the day before. "Not yet, Andy, but he called to say that he has an appointment with the president at four this afternoon." Angie gave Andy a questioning look. "You think we might soon be working for the next Chief Justice, Andy? I can't imagine a better replacement for Sam, bless his soul."

"You're right, Angie," Andy replied. "And we'll probably know before the evening news."

Andy spent the rest of the morning working on a bench memo. Just before noon, her fellow clerks left for lunch, but she decided to plow ahead for another hour. Absorbed in her task, Andy was startled when her desk phone rang. Josh always called her cell phone, and she thought for a moment that it might be Novak, wherever he was. She picked it up, said "Hello," and heard an unfamiliar voice.

"Am I speaking with Andrea Roboff?" the voice said.

"This is she," Andy replied. "May I ask who's calling?" She glanced out the office door, but Angie wasn't at her desk, and obviously hadn't transferred the call.

"This is Bob Barnes, of the Washington Post. If I'm not interrupting, may I ask you a question?"

Andy was totally baffled, but also curious. "May I ask what this is regarding, Mister Barnes?"

"Certainly," he said. "I have obtained what appears to be a draft opinion by Justice Novak in the Khalid versus United States case. This copy has the initials A R at the top, and I assume that means you drafted this for Justice Novak. Am I correct, Miss Roboff?"

Andy felt like she'd been hit by a speeding train. "Is this a joke?" she sputtered. "And how do you know those are my initials, and how did you get my number?"

"No," Barnes replied. "It's not a joke, Miss Roboff. You are the only clerk for Justice Novak with those initials, and the Public Information Office gave me your number." He paused a moment. "Miss Roboff, I'm simply checking to make sure this opinion is not a joke you or someone else is playing on me. It seems to be authentic, but I wouldn't want to write anything about it without getting confirmation from you. I'm sure you understand that. All I need is a simple yes or no."

Andy was too stunned to reply. Barnes continued. "I won't take your silence one way or the other, Miss Roboff." He chuckled. "I'm not Bob Woodward or Carl Bernstein, like 'if you don't say no in ten seconds, I'll take that as a yes.' And one other thing, Miss Roboff. I can assure you that your name won't be in anything I write. I don't reveal my sources. Okay?" He paused again. "One more thing, just to keep you out of this. I won't say this opinion was drafted for Justice Novak. From the heading, it looks like four other justices have signed on. I'd just say that five justices have agreed to uphold the jury verdict in the case. Okay?" Another pause. "Are you still there, Miss Roboff?"

"Um, yes, I am, Mister Barnes." Andy was thinking, faster than she could recall. "How did you get this, Mister Barnes? I know you didn't get it from me."

"Well, first," he replied, "I'll take that as confirmation that this copy is authentic. And second, I can't tell you how I got it. But I believe you, Miss Roboff, that you didn't give it to me."

Trying to quell the worst panic attack she'd experienced in twenty-five years, Andy had a sudden flash. There were only five people who knew she had drafted the Khalid opinion. Neither Novak nor Angie would have given it to Barnes, and she trusted Dave. That left only two suspects, who both knew, from her conversations with Dave in the clerks' office, that Novak had assigned the opinion to her. And she recalled, from the first meeting of the clerks with Novak in July, that revealing the outcome of a case—intentionally or by accident—was grounds for dismissal on the spot.

In those few seconds before she answered Barnes, Andy had another flash. "Mister Barnes," she said in the calmest voice she could muster, "I saw you in the press section when the Khalid case was argued, both times. And you probably guessed what the outcome would be. Am I right?"

It was Barnes's turn to confess. "Yes, I did, Miss Roboff. It was pretty obvious. So, what's your point?"

Andy knew she had him on the hook. "My point, Mister Barnes, is that a story about the opinion wouldn't tell anyone who follows the Court what they don't already know. It might be a scoop, if you revealed it in advance, but so what?" Andy paused, and Barnes didn't reply. "So, Mister Barnes," she continued, "what if I gave you a story that would be a much bigger scoop, and you don't write about the Khalid opinion?"

"Miss Roboff," he replied, "I'm working this story, and I have no idea what you're talking about."

"Fine," Andy said. "Now, Mister Barnes, let me ask *you* a question. Okay?"

She could sense from his silence that Barnes was curious, and exploited that advantage. "I saw you in the press section of the hearing room on Monday when Judge Early withdrew his nomination as Chief Justice, and I read your story on Tuesday, wondering why he hadn't revealed his, quote, 'serious health condition' to President Chambers or the Judiciary Committee before the hearing. In fact, Mister Barnes, you sounded a bit skeptical in your story that his health was the real reason for his withdrawal. Am I right about that?"

"Miss Roboff," he replied, "it did seem to me, and other reporters, I might add, that Judge Early should have disclosed this prior to the hearing. That's all I wrote about it."

"I'll tell you what, Mister Barnes," Andy said. She had the upper hand now, and had regained her composure. "I happen to know the real reason Judge Early withdrew his nomination, and I have evidence to back that up. Now, if I give you that evidence, would you agree not to write about the Khalid opinion?"

It was Barnes's turn to sputter. "Miss Roboff," he replied, "we don't make deals like that."

"By 'we,' Mister Barnes," Andy said, "I assume you mean that *you* don't make deals. That's fine with me, and that's up to you." She paused. "But Adam Liptak of the Times might like a scoop, maybe a Pulitzer scoop."

Andy could almost hear the gears turning in his head. "What kind of evidence are you talking about, Miss Roboff?"

"You can call me Andy, by the way," she said. "And you can only see this evidence, Bob, if we have a deal about the Khalid story. You have ten seconds to say yes or no, Bob."

The pause lasted about five seconds. "Assuming I say yes, Andy, where and when can I get this evidence?"

"Are you calling from your office at the Post on K Street, Bob?"

"Um, yes."

"Okay," Andy said. "Grab a cab and meet me outside the Court's side entrance on Constitution in fifteen minutes. Otherwise, I'll call Adam Liptak." She paused for a second. "Oh, one other thing, Bob," she said. "There's an embargo on this until Saturday, at least. You know what that is, I'm sure. And there's probably going to be another story you can work tomorrow. Maybe even bigger than this one. Is that a deal, Bob?"

"Deal," he replied, without asking what that bigger story might be. With that, Andy hung up. She could hardly believe what she'd just done. Barnes's out-of-the-blue call, and the ten minutes they'd talked, had forced her to make on-the-spot decisions that she might later regret. But revealing the outcome of the Khalid case, whoever had tipped Barnes, would certainly cost Andy her job. And she liked her job, even though a Supreme Court clerkship hadn't been her supreme ambition.

With only fifteen minutes to go, Andy realized that handing the evidence of Judge Early's lies to Mose Townley might also put Josh's job in jeopardy. In the press of time, she hadn't thought of that, but she couldn't do that in good conscience, without giving Josh a chance to stop the presses. Although his name wasn't on the memo, Barnes might be able to dig it out. Pulling out her cell phone, Andy used speed-dial to call Josh, who answered right away. Her heart pounding, she told him about the deal she'd made with Barnes, and that she'd break it if Josh objected.

"Hey, Andy," he replied. "Slow down, before you have a coronary. First of all, a story in the Post about Early's lies might give *him* one, even though his career is dead, anyway. And he got what he deserved, the bastard. And second, a story in the Post might actually help OD Beasley. The Innocence Project would jump on his case, and pointing the finger at Early Junior as Laurel Davis's likely murderer might convince a judge to give OD a new trial. And that's not going to happen with the habeas petition, whichever way Judge Jacobs rules on whether to apply Hall versus Florida retroactively. So, nothing to lose, and maybe a lot to gain."

Listening to Josh's calming voice, Andy was relieved. "Oh, Josh, thanks for bailing me out. I just got scared, and that was the only thing I could think of. And your memo doesn't mention President Chambers, so even if Barnes breaks my embargo, it's not going to affect Alex's meeting with him this afternoon. By the way, Alex went out of town yesterday, didn't tell Angie where, and hasn't been in this morning. But something's up, Josh, and I have no clue. Anyway, I've got to run outside and hand your memo to Barnes. Call you later, okay? Love you, Josh."

"Love you, too, Andy. Life is getting very interesting. Bye."

Ten minutes later, a cab pulled up on Constitution. Without a word, Andy handed a folder through the back-seat window, and the cab pulled away. As she returned to the office, she realized there was unfinished business. And she knew just who could help her dump this putrid dish of kimchi.

A<small>ll</small> three of her fellow clerks were at their computers when Andy entered the office. She checked her desk, and the folder with the Khalid opinion was there, seemingly undisturbed. She went over and whispered into Dave's ear. "Got time for a smoke break, Dave? Or a kimchi break, actually." He nodded, looking puzzled. They went down to one of the interior courtyards. Andy briefly told Dave about her conversation with Bob Barnes, without revealing the deal she'd made about giving him Josh's memo in return for killing the story about the Khalid opinion.

Dave was appropriately shocked that Andy's draft opinion had wound up in Barnes's hands. And he agreed that the likely suspects for the leak were sitting in their office. Dave pondered for a minute. "I've got an idea," he said, "so let's go back up and let me check something. No geeking, just low-tech sleuthing. And you said your draft was thirty-seven pages, right? I was too busy to read it, but I do remember numbers."

Back in the office, Dave went over to the printer, with a sheaf of papers in his hand. He fed them in, then opened a flap on top, and punched a couple of buttons. A minute later, he gave Andy a Come With Me nod, and she followed him into Novak's empty office, closing the door. Angie just smiled as they went past her desk.

Andy looked at Dave, expectantly. "Okay," he said. "As you know, suspicious is my middle name, and my suspicion was confirmed. And the dummy was even dumber than I thought."

"So, which dummy, and what dumb thing did they do?"

"Okay, here's how I caught our uber-dummy," Dave said, with a grin. "In case you didn't know, Andy, the printer has a page counter for each job, with the date and time for each printing. Now, it shows that someone, obviously you, ran seventy-four pages on Tuesday in one job. That's the two copies of your draft, right?"

"Right, Dave," Andy said, "although I didn't know about the counter."

"Now you know," Dave said. "Anyway, the counter shows that somebody copied thirty-seven pages on Wednesday, at ten-seventeen a.m. I assume we were both out of the office then. I think I was up in the library."

"And I remember going down to the cafeteria about then," Andy said.

"So, while we were both out, one dummy copied your opinion, and put the folder back just where it was. I think they learned that lesson from their last dummy move. The other dummy was probably the look-out, in case one of us came back." Dave gave Andy a wink. "Hold on, Andy, for five minutes, maybe ten. Got a lead to check out." He hustled out of Novak's office. Puzzled, she returned to the clerk's office, in which Amanda and Todd were at their desks, oblivious to her presence.

Ten minutes later, Dave stuck his head in the door and beckoned Andy with a finger. Back in Novak's office, Dave gave Andy a Cat Who Ate the Canary grin. "Got 'em," he said. "Let's go back in. I've got a little surprise for the dummies." Still puzzled, Andy followed Dave into the clerks' office, where he sat at his computer, typed for a minute, pushed a key, went to the printer, and pulled out a couple of sheets. Andy had no idea what he was doing, but noticed that he was rather loudly humming the "Dum, De Dum Dum" theme from Dragnet.

Standing behind Amanda and Todd at their desks, Dave surprised Andy when he barked, even more loudly, *Busted!* They both whirled around, eyes and mouths wide open in surprise.

"Here," Dave said, thrusting a sheet of paper toward each one. "All I need is signatures, then you can pack up and slink off to wherever you slink."

Todd took his sheet, glanced at it, and said, "What the hell is this, Dave?"

"Well, if you can read, Todd, it says 'I hereby resign my position as law clerk to Justice Alexander Novak, effective immediately.'" Dave reached into a pocket and handed Todd a pen. "Right down here at the bottom, Todd, on the line for your signature. It's already dated." He looked at Amanda, whose mouth was still wide open. "Same for you, sweetheart," Dave said. "Sign on the dotted line."

Still seated at her desk, Andy got up, flashing Dave a What the Hell Is Going On Here? look. Todd beat her to it. "Dave, what the hell is going on here? This looks like a resignation letter. I'm not resigning. And for what?"

Dave cocked a pistol-pointing finger at Todd. "Yes, you are, and so is Daddy's sweetheart here. And you already know why."

Todd, a head taller than Dave, took a menacing step toward him. "I don't know shit, Dave, and neither do you."

Dave pulled his phone from a pants pocket, clicked a button, and held it up to Todd's face. "Know this guy?"

"That's me, Dave. So what?"

Dave gave Todd a glare that could have stopped a raging rhino. "So what, asshole, is leaking Andy's draft of the Khalid opinion to Bob Barnes of the Post, and trying to frame her for it."

Todd raised a fist, then thought better. "I have no idea, Dave, what you're talking about."

Dave raised his phone again. "This guy, who I snapped at Alex's barbeque back in July, went down to the press room yesterday and left a folder with the Khalid opinion for Bob Barnes. Don't know if he was there, or you put his name on it, but he obviously got it."

Todd lifted a fist again. "That's a lie, Dave. I did no such thing."

"Back off, Rambo," Dave said. "Unless you want me to call security." Todd put his fist down, as Amanda put an arm around his shoulder. Dave went on, as Andy watched, hardly believing her eyes and ears.

Dave held up his phone again. "You know Judy Chu in the press room, Todd? Pretty Chinese girl, handles all the inquiries from reporters."

Todd began to weaken, his voice tight. "No, I don't, Dave. I've never been in the press room. Why would I go there?"

"To drop off a folder for Bob Barnes, dummy. I was just down there, showed Judy Chu your mug shot, and she said, 'Oh yeah, that guy. He was down here yesterday, asked me where to put stuff for reporters. He left something on the table, then left. I didn't know who he was, but that's him, on your phone.'"

Todd sounded plaintive. "Why would I do that, Dave? I don't even know Bob Barnes, except by name."

Dave held out a hand. "Give me your phone, Todd. I know it's in your pocket. Hand it over."

Amanda spoke for the first time. "Todd, don't do that. They can't prove you gave him anything. Remember, I asked you to get a press release about putting cameras in the chamber."

Dave smiled. "Mandy, sweetheart. Nice try. You don't mind being a Mandy, do you? Now sit down and *shut up!*" He turned back to Todd, holding out a hand. "Phone, Todd, phone. Come on, big guy."

Todd put a protective hand over his left front pocket. "Why do you want my phone, Dave?"

Dave's voice reeked with sarcasm. "Well, since you asked so nicely, Todd, I want to check your call history. For Monday and Tuesday, and up to ten-seventeen on Wednesday morning. The exact time of your dumbest move ever. Calls to or from your very sick friend, Judge Early, or his even sicker son, Junior. Hand it over, or else."

Todd put up one last show of defiance. "Or else what, Dave? You have no proof of anything."

Dave turned to Andy, with a Gotcha! smile. "Andy, do you have the kimchi folder in your desk?" She gave him a Gotcha! smile back, opened her top drawer, pulled it out, and handed it to Dave. He held it up. "Remember your insider trading scam, Todd? The one you cooked up with Mandy, here? The one Andy recorded on her phone, with Mandy telling Daddy to cash in his ProVita stock, and make millions? Only he lost millions. And we caught you at it, and put you both on probation? Remember that? Well, dummies, your probation is hereby revoked."

Dave waved the folder in Todd's face, then in Amanda's. "Sign the resignation letters, guys, or this goes in tonight's mail to the enforcement division of the SEC, and another copy to Alex. First thing in the morning, he'll fire your sorry asses. Or, you can leave now and avoid getting escorted out of the Court by security. Your choice."

It was over. Todd and Amanda picked up pens and signed the resignation letters. Dave held out a hand, took the letters, and said, "I'll give these to Angie, for Alex. Ten minutes, and out of here." Amanda burst into tears. Andy looked at her. Just yesterday, she thought, I burst into tears and offered to resign. I lied, and she lied. I kept my job, and she lost hers. Does the universe care why you lied? She made a mental note to ask Josh about that.

Ten minutes later, Amanda and Todd left the office. Dave handed Andy the resignation letters, which she dropped into Angie's in-box. "Hey, Andy," Dave said, giving her a high-five, "how about dinner tonight at the Capital Grille? I think Daddy still has an account there, and I hear the Delmonico's really tasty." They worked on memos the rest of the afternoon, and took a cab at six to the restaurant.

Over steaks and wine, courtesy of Carleton Cushing, they traded guesses as to whom President Chambers would nominate as the next Chief Justice. Dave, who knew nothing about Novak's Oval Office meeting that afternoon, predicted a sixty-forty chance that he'd get the nod. Andy, who did know about the meeting, confessed that she didn't have a clue, which was true. As their waiter served crème brule for dessert, Andy's phone dinged with a text message. "Join me in the office tomorrow at ten. CNN. Alex." She texted back. "See you there. Andy."

25

Andy arrived at Novak's chambers at eight-thirty on Friday. This morning, in a last-minute wardrobe decision, she'd dressed in her young-female-lawyer outfit: Ann Taylor black pantsuit, cream-colored, scoop-neck blouse, silver-buckled black flats, and turquoise-and-silver Indian necklace. It was the same outfit she'd worn for her meeting with Hank Lorenz, back in April, at which he'd surprised her with the offer of a clerkship with Alex Novak. And to the Court's session at which Sam Terman had collapsed from a fatal heart attack. Today, she thought, might bring an equal surprise, although Novak's texted summons to join him at ten to watch CNN hadn't offered a clue about what it might be.

"Oh, my goodness, Andy! Did you know about Amanda and Todd?" Angie Conforti, normally unflappable, looked flustered as Andy entered the reception area. She did know, of course, but feigned ignorance.

"No, Angie," she replied. "Are they both sick again?" You bet they're sick, she thought, still amazed at Dave's low-tech but high-quality detective work the previous afternoon.

"Well, maybe they are," Angie said. "But they both left resignation letters yesterday, but didn't give any reason for leaving. I was at the dentist yesterday afternoon, and just found the letters on my desk this morning. I gave them to Alex when he came in, but he didn't say anything, and left for a meeting. Said he'd be back before ten."

"Oh, my goodness, Angie, what a surprise!" Andy feigned surprise. "I know they both haven't been feeling well lately. Maybe the job became too much for them." Much too much, she thought, suppressing a smile.

Dave popped out of the clerks' office, also feigning surprise. "Morning, Andy," he said. "I was just telling Angie how unprofessional that was, just walking out like that, and leaving us high and dry. But I've got an idea, and we'll see what Alex thinks when he gets back." He nodded toward the clerks' office, and Andy followed him in. Scooting his chair over to Andy's desk, he spoke quietly. "You know, Andy," he said, "two of Sam Terman's clerks have left, but the other two are still here, with not much to do, although they pitch in with other justices to work on pool memos. I know them both pretty well, and one of them, Laura Saponara, already told me she'd be glad to move over here. I left Alex a note about her. She's pretty liberal, of course, but I'm sure Alex would like her." Dave smiled. "I mean, you're pretty liberal, Andy, and Alex likes you." He gave her a knowing wink. "Likes you a lot, that's pretty obvious."

Andy chuckled. "Alex likes me for my Harvard degree, Dave. His alma mater, you know."

"Hmm," Dave replied. "Not many Harvard grads come so well-packaged, if you get my drift."

"Well, just drift on down the Potomac, Dave. And how about putting in a solid hour of the work we're paid for, until Alex gets back, okay? Then you can tell him how well-packaged your friend Laura is." Andy stuck out her tongue, then booted up her computer.

At nine-thirty, Andy's desk phone rang. She picked it up, and recognized her caller's voice. "Andy, this is Bob Barnes. Just got a minute, because the president is making an announcement at ten. It's not a press conference, and we're told it's a no-questions deal, so I'll just watch it here. Anyway, thanks for giving me that stuff yesterday. It was very interesting, to say the least. If you'd given it to me before the confirmation hearing, it would have been front page."

Andy just kept listening, since Barnes hadn't asked a question. "But I ran it by our in-house lawyer, and my editor. Our lawyer, as you might expect, got all queasy about potential libel suits. Between you and me, Andy, it's obvious Judge Early lied to the detective, and gave his son a phony alibi. But, as our lawyer said, that doesn't prove he knew *why* his son needed one. And all the DNA shows is that his son got the girl's blood on his glove. Maybe he killed her, maybe not. Bottom line, can't use it, especially without a source we could interview. And you're probably not going to give me a name."

"Uh, no, Bob," she replied. "That wasn't part of our deal." Andy was surprised, but not much. She wasn't an expert on defamation law, but knew that even suggesting that someone might be involved in a crime, especially a murder, without harder evidence, would be inviting a libel suit. And Early Junior was a well-connected lawyer.

"You're right, Andy," Barnes agreed. "And not running anything about the Khalid decision *was* part of our deal. Plus, my editor said that since the outcome won't be much of a surprise, anyway, we'll just wait for the Court to announce it." He chuckled. "So, two scoops down the drain, and a ten-buck cab fare. But thanks again, Andy. You're good at making deals, and most law firms pay a lot more than ten bucks for good deal-makers."

Andy laughed. "I'll keep that in mind, Bob. And thanks for calling. Now I can read tomorrow's Post for my horoscope, and skip the front page. Unless the president makes some news at ten." With that, she hung up. Dave, at his computer, hadn't even glanced over, but Andy hadn't said anything to Barnes that might pique his curiosity. So, Andy thought, Amanda and Todd lost their jobs over something that wasn't even news. But she didn't feel in the least sorry for them. Compassionate Andy saved her compassion for those whose problems weren't caused by their own greed and supreme ambition.

Alex Novak breezed into his chambers at ten of ten, with a cheery "Good morning, good morning." He stopped at Angie's desk. "Well, Angie, it looks like you survived the extraction yesterday. I hope they didn't use a pair of rusty pliers." She chuckled. "And can you fetch Andy and Dave, and join us in my office. There's a show I don't want to miss, and I want the whole crew to enjoy it with me."

Andy and Dave heard this, popped out of the clerks' office, and followed Angie into Novak's, where he had pulled four chairs into a row, facing the TV on a shelf. "Seats, everyone," he said. "I would have brought popcorn, but the cleaners complain that it gums up their vacuums and stains the carpet." Seated next to Andy, he whispered, "I just paid a visit to Karl, Parker, and Cormac, to give them a heads-up. They'll probably watch this on Fox, but it's all from the same camera." Novak gave her an appraising look. "You're looking very nice this morning, Andy. Special occasion?" He winked, then turned to Dave. "I got your note, Dave. When the show's over, can you go find Laura Saponara and tell her she's got a new job, if she wants it, and to come see me anytime this afternoon." He picked up the remote and clicked on CNN.

Under the ubiquitous "Breaking News" banner, Wolf Blitzer, sporting his permanent three-day white stubble, was speaking. "In just a moment, CNN will take you live to the White House, where President Chambers will make an announcement. CNN has learned that the president will introduce his second nominee as Chief Justice of the Supreme Court, just four days after the surprise withdrawal of Judge Winslow Early." Blitzer looked briefly off-camera, then said, "The president is coming into the Rose Garden, and we take you there. Stay tuned for analysis by Jeff Toobin after the announcement."

President Chambers emerged from the doorway to the Rose Garden, followed by two women and two men, who flanked him on either side of the lectern. The woman to his right was petite, coming only to the president's shoulder, mid-fifties, and clearly Asian. The woman to her right was tall, blond, and young. The men on his left, both of medium height and build, looked almost like twins, in dark suits, white shirts, and identical red-and-black rep ties. Novak turned to Andy, his eyebrows raised in puzzlement.

"Good morning," Chambers began. "I have several announcements this morning. But first, I want to express my wishes for a speedy and full recovery to Judge Winslow Early, whose illness has unfortunately prevented him from serving as Chief Justice of the Supreme Court."

Chambers paused, glancing briefly at the paper on his lectern, then turned to the men on his left. "I would now like to introduce three members of the White House staff who are assuming new positions. This morning, with deep regret, I accepted the resignations of Michael Hammerman, my chief of staff, and Rory O'Connor, my legal counsel. They both served me well, but have decided to return to the private sector. I wish them both success, and thank them for their loyal service."

Novak's jaw dropped, and he nudged Andy with an elbow. "Holy cow," he whispered in her ear, "this is more of a show than I expected."

Chambers continued. "Fortunately, I have on my staff two outstanding men who possess the experience and integrity to fill these important positions. On my immediate left, Quentin Burdick will now serve as my chief of staff. Quentin has been my chief economic advisor for the past two years, and is a person with great managerial skills." Chambers looked into the camera and smiled. "Those are skills, by the way, that some people think I lack. But Quentin will keep me from signing the wrong papers, and cutting off the whole defense budget by accident." Chambers delivered his laugh line with no audience but the cameramen to laugh with him, which they didn't.

After this gaffe, Chambers made another lame joke. "And on my far left, not politically, of course, is my new legal counsel, Paul McDermott. Paul has been deputy counsel, and had decided to return to private practice, but agreed to stay on at my request." Chambers turned to his right. "And to take Paul's place as deputy counsel, I'm pleased to introduce Victoria Nickerson. In her few months as assistant counsel, Vicky has been of great help in selecting the most outstanding nominees for federal judicial positions." The young blond woman nodded her appreciation to Chambers.

While Chambers paused, Novak whispered to Andy. "Resigned, my ass. I should have guessed. Hammerman and O'Connor got fired yesterday, the minute after my colleagues and I left the Oval Office." He looked back at the screen. "Oops, previews are over. Here comes the main attraction." He gave Andy a knowing wink.

Chambers turned to the woman at his right, then back to the teleprompter. "The most important position in our federal judicial system, as we all know, is that of Chief Justice of the Supreme Court. What you might not know, however, is that the formal title of that position is Chief Justice of the United States." Sounding like a high-school civics teacher, Chambers continued. "In our federal system, the individual states make up the United States of America. And the courts of our states play a vital role in protecting the rights, and enforcing the responsibilities, of their citizens. It is only fitting, in my opinion, that an outstanding jurist who has led the highest court in her state with distinction now lead the highest court in our great nation."

He paused, and cleared his throat. "I am very pleased to introduce my nominee as Chief Justice of the United States, the Honorable Kathryn Ikeda." They exchanged smiles. Andy's eyes widened with surprise, as Chambers continued. "For the past six years, Justice Ikeda has served as Chief Justice of the Supreme Court in her home state of Washington. Unlike our federal courts, this is an elected position, in two ways. Justice Ikeda has been twice elected by the voters of Washington to six-year terms on her court, and then elected by her eight judicial colleagues as Chief Justice." Ikeda smiled again, demurely.

"Justice Ikeda has an outstanding record of accomplishment," Chambers continued, his eyes shifting to the teleprompter. "She graduated first in her class from the University of Washington Law School, where she served as editor-in-chief of its law review. After two years in private practice in Seattle, she joined the office of the Prosecuting Attorney in King County, rising to the post of Chief Deputy, before her appointment by the governor to the King County Superior Court, where she served as a trial judge in both civil and criminal cases." Chambers smiled again at Ikeda. "That's a record of service that has only increased in the years since her election. Justice Ikeda has also served as president of the National Association of Women Judges, and she currently is president of the Council of Chief Justices, whose members include the chief justices of all fifty states and the American territories."

Chambers adopted a serious tone. "On a personal level, I learned from Justice Ikeda that her grandparents, all of them immigrants from Japan, were forced in nineteen forty-two from their homes and farms on Bainbridge Island, across Puget Sound from Seattle, and removed to an internment camp in Idaho for the duration of the war. They were hard-working, loyal Americans, but never abandoned their faith in this country and its promise of liberty and justice for all. And both of her parents were born in that camp." Chambers shook his head. "There's a lesson here for all Americans. Loyalty is not a matter of birth, or ancestry. It flows from the heart, and Justice Ikeda is standing beside me as proof of that principle."

Novak nudged Andy, whispering. "Good boy. I wrote every word of that, and told the president that if he left out a single word, he'd answer to me."

"One final word this morning," Chambers continued. "Because it is essential that the Supreme Court have a full complement of justices, I have been informed by Senator Charter Weeks, who chairs the Senate Judiciary Committee, and the ranking member, Senator Ted Tillman, that they have scheduled a confirmation hearing for Justice Ikeda in two weeks. And they assure me the committee will promptly and unanimously send her nomination to the full Senate for a vote before its holiday recess in mid-December." Chambers looked into the camera one last time. "I am proud and excited that our Supreme Court will, for the first time, have a woman, and a member of one of America's great minorities, presiding from its center seat." He smiled at the camera. "Thank you, and God bless America." With that, Chambers turned and ushered Ikeda and his newly-promoted staff back into the White House.

Before Wolf Blitzer and Jeff Toobin began voicing their surprise at this breaking news, Novak clicked off the set and grinned at Andy. "So, Andy, stick around and I'll tell you how Chris Chambers suddenly became a champion of women and minorities. Or maybe we can adjourn to the Capitol Hill Club, where they have a bottle of Beringer chardonnay waiting for us." He chuckled. "It's actually a Republican watering hole, but I'm a member, and you're looking like a Republican today in that outfit. And it's just three blocks."

Ten minutes later, leaving Angie and Dave in the office, Andy and Novak shared a comfortable booth at the almost-empty lounge in the posh private club. There actually was a bottle of Beringer waiting for them. Their waiter poured glasses and said, "Always good to see you, Justice Novak. And your guest is most welcome. I'll bring some bread and cheese, unless you'd like an early lunch."

"That's fine, Cornelius," Novak said. "Bread and cheese, and a plate of your delicious Maryland crab cakes. That suit you, Andy?"

"Sounds good, Alex. I skipped breakfast this morning, and I missed the popcorn at the show."

After clinking glasses, and sips of chardonnay, Andy leaned over and took Novak's hand, giving it a gentle squeeze. "So, Alex, we both got a surprise this morning. You obviously didn't know about Hammerman and O'Connor, and I certainly didn't know about Justice Ikeda. But if she's from Washington, where Republicans are an endangered species, how did she wind up in the Rose Garden this morning?"

Novak grinned. "Actually, I'd never met her before Wednesday. In fact, I'd never heard her name before the little caucus in my office on Tuesday. But after I gave your memos to Alice, Maggie, Dwight, and J.P., they each blew all their gaskets. Alice said the president was royally screwed, although she used another word. And Maggie said that if the five of us could agree on a nominee, Chambers couldn't object, unless he wanted to board a helicopter on the South Lawn and wave goodbye, like Nixon. But without the 'V' sign."

Cornelius returned with the bread and cheese, and a plate of crab cakes. Andy actually was hungry, and munched and sipped while Novak continued. "Anyway, we decided to make up a list of three potential nominees, and see if we could whittle it down to one. So we each wrote down three names on slips of paper." He chuckled. "Talk about exhaustive deliberation. And guess what, Andy?" She gave Novak a Tell Me look, and he grinned again. "The same name was on three slips. Justice Ikeda, in case you couldn't guess. Turned out that Alice, Maggie, and J.P. all wrote down her name, the only one we had in common. They all knew her, and raved about her, as a person and a judge. Two minutes later, Alice called her on my phone, explained the situation, and thirty seconds later, she said yes. Turns out she was in New York, for a conference of women judges, and I volunteered to go up on Wednesday morning and meet with her."

Andy kept sipping and munching while Novak took a break to sip and munch from the rapidly shrinking bottle of wine and plate of crab cakes. Wiping his mouth, he resumed his story, clearly relishing the telling. "So, Andy, she had a lot of questions, mostly about whether the Senate Republicans would vote to confirm a liberal, female, Asian as Chief Justice. She said she didn't relish the prospect of having the right-wingers mount a filibuster against her. I said there might be a dozen Tea Party die-hards, but that Ted Tillman would stamp out any revolt on his side of the aisle. After all, he'd hardly go against the president's choice, whoever it was. And Charter Weeks would make sure every Democrat would support her, even the ones in tough re-election races."

Novak took a long swallow of wine, and smiled. "You know what her last comment was, Andy? She said she'd really miss Seattle. She lived her whole life there, it was the most livable city in the country, and she'd miss all her friends and colleagues on the court in Olympia. So I asked if she wanted more time to decide, and that I'd make sure the president gave me another week, if I insisted. Considering he didn't have much choice in the matter. And she said, Alex, the Supreme Court needs a new Chief, and I appreciate your confidence in me, so let's do it."

Andy interrupted Novak's monologue for the first time. "So, you got back from New York on Wednesday night, with your bird in hand, so to speak. And you went to the Oval Office yesterday afternoon. Did you bring her with you?"

Novak grinned. "No, she decided to stay in New York for the last day of her conference, but with her phone in hand. But, and this is the fun part, Andy, I didn't go to the Oval Office alone." Andy raised questioning eyebrows. "No, I called Mike Hammerman and said I was bringing four of my colleagues with me. Mike said, what the hell for? And I said, you'll find out when we get there, Mike, but it's either all five or none. He got pissy for a minute, but caved in when I asked if he'd rather have us camped out in the Oval Office reception room, like a civil rights sit-in from the Sixties."

"Wow," Andy exclaimed. "That would have freaked out the Secret Service, especially if you all sang 'We Shall Overcome.'"

Just then, Cornelius returned, to clear the empty plates and empty bottle. "Another bottle of the Beringer, Justice?" he asked.

"Thanks, Cornelius, but if you've got a chardonnay from Washington state, that would be good. I hear they have great vineyards on the eastern side of the Cascades."

"I think we do, Justice. I'll bring one right back."

Andy could see that Novak was a bit tipsy, but obviously enjoying himself. He resumed his story. "Anyway, Mike ushered us all into the Oval Office, and Rory O'Connor was in there, looking like a man who would rather be having a prostate check from a Harley biker with studded gloves." Andy chuckled at his males-only joke.

"Anyway," Novak continued, "President Chambers looked us over and said, I see you brought a majority of the Court with you, Justice Novak. And what's your verdict? So, we all sat down on his sofas, and I tossed a copy of Dick Wadleigh's transcript on the table. Here's the verdict, Mister President, I said. I know you and Mike and Rory haven't seen this yet, so we'll give you a minute to look it over."

He paused as Cornelius returned and displayed a bottle. "This is a DuBrul Vineyards from Yakima Valley, Justice Novak. A hint of citrus, apple, and pear. One of our best chardonnays. The vice president always asks for this."

Novak smiled. "What's good for Gordon Barnstead, Cornelius, is plenty good for us. He's a noted wine connoisseur, I've been told. No need for a taste. Just pour away." Cornelius filled the glasses, placed the bottle on the table, and departed. "So, Andy, where was I?"

"Um, you tossed Dick's transcript on the table, Alex."

"Oh, right," he replied. "So, they all picked up the transcript, flipped through it, and dropped it like a live grenade. Hammerman almost had a stroke. Where the hell did you get this, Justice Novak? Language, Mike, I said. There are ladies present. But you know perfectly well where I got it. Rory's former assistant counsel, and my former clerk. And a man with a conscience, which is rare in this town."

Novak took a sip of the Washington chardonnay, nodded his approval, took a longer swallow, and continued. "So, I turned to the president, who was just sitting there, looking at Dick's transcript like it was a turd he'd just stepped on. By the way, Mister President, I said, I respectfully decline your magnanimous offer to replace Sam Terman. But here's why I brought my colleagues with me. We have voted unanimously that you are going to nominate Kathryn Ikeda as Chief Justice." He paused for effect. "You should have been there, Andy. They all looked like I'd proposed that kid president of North Korea, what's his name?"

"Um, I think it's Kim Jong Un, Alex."

"Right," he replied. "The one who executes all his relatives. Anyway, the president said he'd never heard of her. So, Alice and Maggie took over, and told him who Kathryn Ikeda was, and her sterling credentials. And then I said, Mister President, Justice Ikeda will be in your office at nine, tomorrow morning, and then you'll announce her nomination at ten. He looked at me blankly. And then I said, Or else. And then he said, Or else *what*, Justice Novak? And I said, Or else, Mister President, five members of the Supreme Court, which is a majority, will give Dick Wadleigh's transcript of your conversation with him to Bob Barnes at the Post. And Dick's memo about your deal with Charter Weeks. *That's* what, Mister President. And the Post's presses are ready to roll."

Novak took a swig of chardonnay. "And that was it, Andy. Game over. And you saw the final out this morning." He paused for a moment, twirling his glass, looking reflective. "You know, Andy," he said, "I'm sure Justice Ikeda and I will disagree on some cases, just like I did with Sam. But maybe not as many." He put his glass down, looked at the bottle, then shook his head.

Andy realized that Novak was now more than a bit tipsy. She spotted Cornelius and waved him over. "Cornelius, can you ask the maitre d' to call a cab for Justice Novak? He's going to Cleveland Park. And can you put this on his tab? I assume he has one."

"Certainly, miss," Cornelius said. "Should be just a few minutes."

"Andy, Andy," Novak protested. "It's just a five-minute walk back to the Court. And Dave is bringing Sam's clerk to my office."

Andy reached over and took his hand. "Alex, you did a great job. Justice Ikeda is going to sail through the Senate, thanks to you. And you need to tell Gloria and Anton all about it. And I can walk back to the Court, and tell Laura Saponara she's got a job with you, okay?" Novak nodded, and got up, a bit wobbly, holding Andy's arm as she steered him toward the waiting cab, giving him a parting kiss on the cheek. Holy shit, she thought, as the cab pulled away. Who could have predicted this? Wait until I tell Josh. And I know what he'll say. His favorite word. Andy was a bit tipsy herself, and it took a moment to remember the word.

Rethinking her plans, Andy hailed a passing cab outside the club and gave the driver her address. Back in her apartment, she shed her young-female-lawyer outfit, changed into jeans and a tee-shirt, and called Dave, asking him to give Laura Saponara the news about her move. Then she called Josh, telling him she had news to share. He came over after work, and shared a bowl of Lemon Haze—Andy had consumed enough wine for the day—while she recounted, almost verbatim, what Novak had told her over wine and crab cakes. "So, Josh," Andy said, "you started the ball rolling that stopped Judge Early from becoming Chief Justice, and didn't stop rolling until Chambers nominated Kathryn Ikeda. If people knew that, you'd be on the cover of both Time and Newsweek."

Josh grinned. "Not without you, Mata Hari. You gave it the final push with your grab-and-run at the Bull and Bear Club."

"Don't remind me," Andy said. "I still get the shakes when I think about that."

After Josh returned home for dinner with Carlo, Andy heated up some left-over spaghetti carbonara, took a long, hot bath in her stretch-out tub, then put her day to bed.

26

The startling events of the past week—none of which she had anticipated—left Andy hoping for a quiet and uneventful next week to catch up with tasks she'd pushed aside during the whirlwind that had swept across Washington, tossing the Court, the Senate, and the White House into a maelstrom of frenzied efforts to repair the damage to their branches from Judge Early's abrupt exit from the Judiciary Committee's hearing room.

Taking advantage of a weekend that didn't require her to tackle the pile of pool and bench memos on her desk, Conscientious Andy tackled her apartment. She scrubbed her tub and shower, ran three loads of laundry through the nearby Washingteria, stocked up her kitchen from the Safeway, even moved her couch and tables to vacuum every square inch of carpet. Bella would be proud of her bubeleh, Andy thought, as she sucked up the last dust bunny. On Sunday, as a Good Girl reward, she walked all the way down Pennsylvania and up Connecticut to Dupont Circle for a double feature of Annie Hall and The Purple Rose of Cairo at a Woody Allen retrospective, munching the popcorn she'd missed in Novak's office theater.

Back at the Court on Monday morning, Andy entered Novak's chambers to find Dave and a young woman chatting with Angie. Grinning broadly, Dave said, "Andy, I'd like you to meet our new office mate, Laura Saponara, who will do the work of our dearly departed friends, twice as well as they did."

Dave had given Andy the highlights of Laura's path to the Court. Her dad was a professor of Romance languages at Rutgers, where Laura had majored in classics, and her mom was a high-school art teacher. She'd spent a year in Italy on a Fulbright, had gone to NYU for law school, wrote a article for the NYU law review on legal claims to art works that had been stolen by foreign museums after the collapse of fascism, and clerked for Judge Roberta Gianfortoni on the Third Circuit in Philadelphia. Sam Terman, Dave told Andy, had picked Laura for a clerkship after his wife, Barbara, had plucked her application from Sam's pile of more than a hundred and told him that he'd get more of an education from Laura than she would from him.

Laura stuck out her hand and said, "Buon giorno, Andy. Molto lieto."

"Benvenuti, Laura," she replied to this Italian greeting.

Dave and Angie smiled at this exchange. "Sorry," Laura said. "I know English is our official language, but Dave tells me you're fluent in the tongue of the world's greatest artists. And lovers."

Andy laughed. "Artists, yes. Lovers, I only know from Petrarch's sonnets to the beautiful Laura. You wouldn't be her namesake, would you?"

"Actually, I am," Laura replied. "My dad wrote a book about Petrarch while my mom was pregnant, and my name was sort of decided before I was born. If I'd been a boy, it would have been Francesco."

Dave and Angie exchanged puzzled looks. "Hey, guys," Laura said, with an impish grin. "I was just testing Andy's knowledge of classic Italian poetry. And she passed with flying colors. Anyway, I'm glad to be here, thanks to Dave. I loved working for Sam, even just a few months, but the last few weeks in Justice Sorenson's office, quite frankly, have been boring. I mean, he's a nice man, but his clerks only gave me the dogs to work on."

Andy knew instantly that she and Laura would become good friends. She also knew, from Dave's googly expression, that he was enamored of her. But, like Petrarch's unrequited love for the Laura of his sonnets, Dave had little chance of winning this charming 'giovane e bella donna.' A pretty young woman, and one as smart as Laura obviously was, might appreciate Dave's considerable talents, but his geekiness made him an unlikely suitor. But you never know, Andy thought. Kiss a frog, and you might awaken a handsome prince. Well, maybe not handsome, and maybe not a prince, but a guy with a conscience, and a heart. Like Josh, Carlo, Dick, and Jane. Andy felt lucky to have such people in her life, and hoped she could follow their examples, when the time came to make hard choices.

Introspective Andy retreated into her thoughts while Dave and Laura chatted with Angie, then put them aside while her fellow clerks got settled in their office. Gallant Dave pulled out Laura's chair at the desk Amanda had vacated the week before, on which he'd placed the Best in Breed cert petitions for her to groom and Novak to judge for Best in Show. No ugly mutts in Laura's pile, Andy chuckled to herself, sorting through her own pile for the one that barked the loudest for her attention.

Shortly before ten, Novak stuck his head into the clerks' office. Dave and Laura had gone to the cafeteria for coffee, but Andy wanted to finish a bench memo for next week's arguments. "Morning, Andy," Novak said. "Somebody would like to meet you in my office."

The 'somebody' turned out to be Kathryn Ikeda, who greeted Andy with a warm smile and a firm handshake. "Alex told me you had a lot to do with my being here," she said, "although he left out the details, which I'd probably be better off not knowing. But it's so nice to meet you, Andy."

A bit flustered, Andy glanced at Novak, who gestured them both to chairs around his low table. "Justice Ikeda, I'm very pleased to meet you, too," she replied. "But, from what Justice Novak told me, you're here because of who *you* are, not anything I did."

"Well, thank you, Andy, for such refreshing modesty. And please, call me Kathryn." She gave Novak a smile. "Alex tells me you're all on a first-name basis in his chambers, and I do the same with my clerks. Even with our staff. We're much more informal out West." She leaned toward Andy, lowering her voice to a sotto voce level. "I'll tell you a secret, Andy. Once in a while, after my morning run, and I don't have time to change before an argument, I'll put my robe on over my sweats, and nobody knows."

Novak, who had pretended not to hear this Just Between Us Girls exchange, burst out laughing. "Okay, I've got one that tops yours, Kathryn. I was judging a moot court competition at a law school in Texas, and the bag with my suit got stuck in Atlanta. So, I put my borrowed robe on over my pajama bottoms and a tee-shirt, and nobody noticed. Or were too polite to say anything." Andy found this judicial camaraderie amusing, thinking it boded well for Ikeda's tenure as Chief Justice, much like Sam Terman's informality had bridged the Court's ideological divide.

Ikeda glanced at her watch. "Andy, I'm sure you and I will get to know each other very well, assuming I get confirmed. Which is one reason I'm still here in Washington, to pay courtesy calls on Senator Weeks and

Senator Tillman, and other members of the Judiciary Committee. That's part of the drill, I've been told."

She paused, giving Andy an appraising look. "But I've got a question, Andy, before I head across the street." Andy gave her a Go Ahead nod. "On my court, I've only got two clerks, who have both agreed to come here with me. But I'm entitled to two more in this court, since apparently our work in Olympia isn't as taxing as yours." Andy guessed what was coming, and knew her answer. "Alex tells me you're the best clerk he's ever had," Ikeda said, "and he's had some great ones. He says he needs you for the rest of this term, Andy, but would you be willing to stay for the next term, and work with me?"

Andy had to steel herself from tearing up. "Justice Ikeda, I mean Kathryn, I'm terribly flattered, and I appreciate Alex's kind words. Working for him has been more rewarding than I could have expected." Andy paused, giving Novak a Thank You smile. "But, Kathryn, I put off a job offer in Texas, working for a group that defends death-row inmates. I made a commitment to join them after this term, and I really can't break that. Otherwise, I'd be honored to work with you. I hope you understand."

Andy's tears began sliding down her cheeks. Novak pulled out his pack of tissues, handing her one. "My goodness," Ikeda said. "Andy, I think you're making the right choice. And I respect you for that. So, may I ask another question?" Andy nodded. "Are there any other clerks here you would recommend?"

Andy brightened up. "Oh, yes, Kathryn," she replied. "Dave Park, who's been working for Alex this term with me, would be perfect. Dave knows everybody at the Court, and all the procedures. Plus, he's a computer genius, and can find anything you need in a second, or even less, if you're in a real hurry." Ikeda chuckled. "And I'd also recommend Laura Saponara. She was clerking for Chief Justice Terman before his death, and knows how the Chief's office works. Laura just came over here today, to fill in for two of Alex's clerks who resigned for, um, health reasons. But she and Dave would make a great team. I don't know if they'd stay on for another term, but working with you would be a great incentive."

"Why, thank you for that, Andy," Ikeda said. "Assuming I don't commit some horrible faux pas with the senators, and come back here with their seal of approval, I'll have a chat with Dave and Laura. And you, Andy, will always be welcome in my chambers." As they stood up, she gave

Andy a warm hug. "And I'll be following your work in Texas with great interest." She glanced at her watch again. "Alex, let's walk over and you can introduce me to the men who'll decide whether I'll come back here again, or return to my chambers in Olympia, with its great view of Mount Rainier, at least on sunny days." She smiled. "Either way, I'll have a job that pays enough to feed my cats. And if I do come back here, my first decision will be that Annabelle and Misty have a constitutional right to sit on my lap during oral arguments." Andy and Novak both laughed, as Ikeda briskly led them out of his office.

Back at her desk, Andy sat quietly for several minutes. She had politely declined Ikeda's offer to stay at the Court for another term, but the prospect of clerking for the first female Chief Justice, and someone she had instantly felt a bond with, was an invitation she might seriously consider.

Andy thought back to the April morning in Gannett House, and the hug she'd given Sanjay Singh for turning down a clerkship with Sam Terman, to work instead for the Sikh community. But Sanjay knew those people, had grown up with them, and shared their values and culture. Andy hadn't met any of the death-row inmates the Texas Defenders represented, most of whom had committed heinous crimes, and had placed no value on the victims whose lives they'd ended. Would breaking her agreement to join the Defenders after her term with Novak deprive anyone on death row in Texas of skills that other lawyers could provide, probably better than she?

The person whose counsel she most needed in making her decision was, of course, Josh. She reached for her phone to call and see if he'd come over to her place after work, or invite her to his. Andy jumped when it rang in her hand. Josh's ring-tone. "Hey, Josh," she said, brightly. "Just about to call you. Must be telepathy, although I know you don't believe in that. Anyway, I've got news, and a decision to make. Nothing urgent, but I wondered if we could meet after work. Your place or mine, or maybe over dinner at a restaurant of your choice. My treat."

Josh didn't reply for several seconds. "You still there?" she asked, thinking the call might have been dropped.

"Um, yes," he finally replied. Andy sensed, from his voice, that Josh was upset. "Actually, I've got news, Andy," he said, "and it sucks."

Another few seconds passed, while Andy wondered if something horrible had happened to Carlo, or one of his patients. He was on rotation in pediatric oncology, Josh had told her, and took the death of any of his little cancer patients very hard.

Andy could hear Josh take a deep breath, and let it out. "I'm okay now," Josh said. "But OD Beasley isn't fucking okay." He paused for another deep breath. "I just got a call from Jim Carruthers. He said that Judge Jacobs denied OD's habeas petition, although it wasn't a total surprise. Jim thought it was fifty-fifty, anyway. He faxed me a copy of Jacobs' order, which said he relied on the Eleventh Circuit decision in the Georgia case I told you about, holding that Hall versus Florida wasn't retroactive. And that OD hadn't presented enough evidence of his intellectual disability, and that the state's evidence showed that OD had enough 'adaptive capability' to disqualify him for habeas relief."

By now, Andy sensed that Josh had regained his composure, and let him continue. "Jacobs said that OD had adapted well to confinement, did all the tasks in prison that were required, like personal hygiene, keeping his cell clean, and not having any disciplinary record for fifteen years." Josh gave a cynical snort. "In other words, OD's reward for being a model inmate is that he stays on death row, and doesn't have any chance for a new sentencing hearing. That fucker!"

Andy interrupted. "So, what does this mean, Josh? I assume Jim can file an appeal with the Fourth Circuit, right?"

"Wrong, unfortunately," he replied. "Under the federal rules, an inmate whose habeas petition is denied has to ask the district judge for what's called a 'certificate of appealability' to get to the circuit court. It's complicated, but Jim says he asked Jacobs for one, and got denied without any explanation. But Jim can still ask the Fourth Circuit to issue one, even after Jacobs denied it."

Andy could hear Josh sigh with resignation. "Okay, Jim's going to do that, but here's more bad news. These COA requests, as they call them, go to a three-judge motions panel on the Fourth Circuit. They rotate every month, but this month's panel is the worst you could pick. They're all right-wing assholes, and none of them has ever voted for a COA, according to Jim. Plus, even though Judge Early has resigned, all three judges are long-time buddies of his. Jim thinks, and I agree, that Early gave them messages to deny the COA, which they probably will, anyway."

Andy could sense the resignation in Josh's voice. "But if the Fourth Circuit denies the COA," she asked, "can't Jim appeal to the Supreme Court? I mean, circuit decisions are mostly what the Court handles, right?"

"Yeah," Josh replied. "But not until there's an appealable order from the circuit court. And that might take weeks, or even months. The Fourth Circuit clerk told Jim that the motions panel meets just once a month, unless there's an emergency motion, and their next meeting isn't until December fifth. And there's no deadline on when they rule on motions. They could sit on the COA motion until hell freezes over, and there's nothing we could do to put a blow-torch to their asses."

Andy had a sudden flashback to something she'd learned in Hank Lorenz's class on Federal Litigation. "Josh, I may be wrong, but isn't there a provision in the federal habeas statute that allows second petitions, if they raise claims that weren't presented in the first?"

"That's true, Andy," he replied. "But second habeas petitions, after the first was denied, are rarely granted. It's the 'one bite of the apple' principle, which makes some sense. Otherwise, inmates would just keep filing petitions, especially death-row inmates, hoping to buy time and stave off their executions. Can't say I blame them, but judges don't like it, since most of them don't have any merit. And you're supposed to raise all your claims in the first one."

Andy had been searching her brain for a long-ago-filed fact. "I may be wrong again, Josh, but isn't there case law that allows second petitions if they raise claims based on 'newly discovered evidence' that wasn't available at the time of the trial?"

"Hmm," Josh replied. "I've been so tied up in the petition that Judge Jacobs denied, and my other cases, that I didn't look into that. But I think you're right, Andy." He chuckled, obviously a bit more relaxed than when he'd called with the news of Jacobs' denial. "How about this, Andy? Considering that Mose Townley never sent Junior's glove to the medical examiner for DNA testing, and OD's trial lawyer didn't ask for testing, Vito Petrocelli's report that it had both Junior's and Laurel's DNA on it would fit that exception. You see what I mean, Andy?"

"I see exactly what you mean, Josh. In fact, if Mose *had* sent the glove for testing, and it came back with the DNA matches that Vito found, OD might have been acquitted, even if his lawyer couldn't link the glove to

Junior. I mean, it was obviously not OD's glove, and having another male's DNA on it would at least create a reasonable doubt of OD's guilt."

"Exactly," Josh said, excitement in his voice. "Tell you what, Andy. If you're not buried in work at the Court, and can spare a little time for some research, how about we work on a second petition, assuming Judge Early's buddies on the Fourth Circuit take their time deciding the COA that Jim filed. If you can dig up some case citations on other second habeas petitions, especially ones that were granted on the basis of newly discovered evidence, I'll put together the factual evidence from the records we already have. Sound like a plan?"

"Definitely a plan, man." A thought flashed through her mind. "Hey, you ever think about where you'd be now, Josh, if you'd gone to grad school in physics, and became the second Stephen Hawking, and proved that everything that's happened in the universe since the Big Bang was already determined? And if I'd gone to grad school in art history, and became the world's leading authority on Botticelli?"

Josh laughed. "Don't remind me of Botticelli, Venus On a Seashell. Now I won't be able to work today, thinking of your luscious you-know-whats. Besides, if I proved that everything's been determined for the past sixteen billion years, we'd be right where we are now, two young lawyers trying to figure out the habeas rules."

"Oh, right," Andy said. "Well, on that note, try your best to focus on your work, and I'll come over to your place at six and show you what I've got. What I dig up this afternoon, I mean, not my you-know-whats. Well, maybe after we're done."

Josh chuckled. "Six it is. See you then."

When Andy clicked her phone off, she realized that she'd forgotten to tell Josh about the offer from Justice Ikeda. Well, that can wait, she thought. But OD Beasley had been waiting fifteen years for help from people who'd never met him. And maybe never would, if their help came too late.

Pushing aside the bench memo she'd been working on, Andy spent the rest of the afternoon researching case law on newly-discovered evidence as grounds for habeas relief. Much to her surprise, she found a Supreme

Court decision, handed down in 2006, that seemed to fit like a glove, so to speak. She read the opinion in *House v. Bell* with growing excitement, printed it out, and highlighted the best quotes to show Josh.

The facts in this case weren't a perfect fit with those in OD Beasley's, but close enough, Andy concluded. Paul House, a young man in rural eastern Tennessee, had been convicted and sentenced to death in 1985 for the murder of Carolyn Muncey, a young mother of two, whose body was discovered in a ditch, across the road from her isolated home. She had died from a powerful blow to her head. No murder weapon was found, but the pathologist who conducted the autopsy concluded the blow came from a fist. There were no witnesses, but one of Carolyn's cousins testified he saw House the next day, coming up from the ditch, wiping his hands on a 'black rag,' presumably the blue tank-top House admitted having been torn off the night before, while running through the woods to escape two men he claimed had chased and shot at him while he was out for a late-night walk. Police recovered the jeans House had worn that night, and FBI technicians found several small spots of blood that matched Carolyn's blood type. With only this evidence, it took the jury less than two hours to find House guilty, and a little more than two hours to recommend the death penalty.

Eleven years later, in 1996, a federal defender in Knoxville, Stephen Kissinger, filed a habeas petition for House, claiming that 'newly discovered evidence' cast serious doubt on his guilt. At an evidentiary hearing, two friends of Carolyn's husband, "Little Hube" Muncey, testified that— shortly before House's trial—he drunkenly confessed that he'd "smacked" his wife during an argument in their kitchen, that she'd hit her head on a table corner, and that he'd panicked and dumped her body in the ditch. Little Hube was also a daily drunk and wife abuser, but the cops had focused only on Paul House. Little Hube's friends said they'd tried at the time to tell the sheriff about his confession, but had been ignored and finally gave up. Kissinger also showed that Carolyn Muncey's cousin, who had testified that he'd seen House, the next day, come up from the ditch where her body had been dumped, couldn't have seen him from where the cousin said he'd spotted House. Finally, Kissinger called Tennessee's assistant medical examiner, who testified that the blood spots on House's jeans came from autopsy samples that spilled from unsealed vials, while they were being transported over bumpy roads from Tennessee to the FBI lab in Washington, and were not fresh blood from Carolyn's body.

Despite this evidence, the district judge denied House's habeas petition, and the full Sixth Circuit court of appeals upheld his ruling, in an eight-to-seven decision that provoked a bitter and passionate dissent, which prompted the Supreme Court to hear House's appeal, and to order a new hearing before a different judge. What excited Andy as she read the opinion, was the Court's holding that "new evidence" that was not available at trial, including "exculpatory scientific evidence" or "critical physical evidence," justified a new hearing if such evidence made it "more likely than not that any reasonable juror would have reasonable doubt" of the defendant's guilt. Reading this, Andy blurted "Wow" so loudly that Dave and Laura swiveled around, catching her Look What I Found grin. A quick Internet search prompted another grin, as Andy learned that Paul House finally left Tennessee's death row in 2008, after the state's lawyers dropped the murder charge, unwilling to risk a new trial at which the newly-discovered evidence would have shredded their case. Wait till Josh sees this, Andy thought, as she put the *House* opinion into a folder and headed over to his place at six.

Andy's excitement at her find vanished at Josh's doorway. His expression was grim and she could smell the Scotch on his breath. "Come on in," he said, gesturing to the couch. "Have a seat, while I fix you a stiff drink. I just had one myself, and I'm having another. Glenlivet, straight. Picked it up on my way home." He was holding a tumbler in one hand and a bottle in the other.

Andy took the bottle from his hand and put it on the coffee table. "Josh, I know you're upset, but we can't work on OD's case if you're going to get drunk." She took the tumbler from his other hand, and put it down with a thump. "So, sit down, don't even look at that bottle, and get ahold of yourself." She gave him a stern look. "Or I'll pour the bottle down the sink. And then I'll tattle to Carlo, and you know how he feels about the hard stuff."

Josh grudgingly complied, sitting down, but shaking his head. "Sorry, Andy. But my day just got even shittier than before. Want to hear?"

"Sure," she replied. "But only if I get a turn to tell you why things aren't as shitty as you think. But go ahead."

"Okay," he said. "Here's the really, really, *really* bad news, Andy." He glanced at the Glenlivet, then shook his head. "Two hours after Jacobs denied OD's habeas petition, the governor issued an execution warrant. OD is scheduled to die in fifteen days, Andy. December fifth. That's actually OD's birthday, but it's now his death day. What a fucking present, delivered by another fucking buddy of fucking Early."

"Oh, my God, Josh." Andy could hardly believe what he'd said. She wracked her brain for something, anything, to say. What she came up with sounded feeble, but she tried. "Can the governor do that, Josh, even while Jim's asking the Fourth Circuit for a COA? I mean, OD's case is still in federal court, and there's no final decision, even if it's another denial?"

Josh gave another cynical snort. "Well, Jim can ask the Fourth Circuit for a COA, with an emergency motion, but he says the chances of getting one are zero. The state courts upheld OD's conviction and death sentence years ago, Jacobs denied the habeas petition, and Early's buddies aren't going to stop the needles from going into OD's arms. Fuck, fuck, *fuck!*"

Andy had a sudden flashback to Hank Lorenz's seminar on Capital Punishment Procedure. Something she'd learned about the Supreme Court and stays of execution. "Josh, I know you're really upset," she said, "but can I look something up on your computer? I have an idea, which might not work, but it's worth a try. Okay?"

"Anything, Andy," he replied. "I'm fresh out of ideas, but if you come up with something, tell me. Meanwhile, I'm going to take a walk and clear my head. Maybe get a double-shot espresso at Starbucks."

"Okay, I'll call you when I'm done." She gave Josh another stern look. "But don't you stop in that bar on the corner. If you do, I'll tell Carlo for sure. Promise?"

"Promise," he said, giving Andy a wan smile as he left.

Andy did not log onto Josh's computer. Instead, she called Dave, who answered on the first ring. "Hey, Andy, what's up? Need a little help from your favorite geek?"

"Actually, I do, Dave," she replied. "Are you anywhere near a computer?"

"Like six inches away. I'm still in the office, going over the bench memo that Laura's working on. But tell me what you need, and my fingers are at your service."

"Thanks, Dave," she said. "I'm working on a pool memo, one of the prisoner petitions, but one that's got some urgency. Here's the basics. This inmate, who's on death row, with an execution date in two weeks, got denied on a habeas petition in the district court. He filed for a certificate of appealability from the circuit court, but it won't be acted on before his execution is scheduled. In other words, any relief would be too late."

"Hmm," Dave said. "So, your question, I assume, is whether he can appeal directly to our Court for a stay of execution, pending the circuit court appeal. Right?"

"Right," Andy replied. "You know the rules better than me, Dave, and your fingers are faster than mine."

"Hang on a second, Andy," he said. Andy could hear the tapping on his keyboard. Thirty seconds later, Dave spoke again. "Here we go," he said. "Rule Twenty-Three. The heading is Stays. Skipping the boilerplate, it allows an inmate to file an application for a stay of execution, which goes to the justice assigned to that circuit to handle emergency applications. The rule says, and I'm reading, the stay application shall set out specific reasons why a stay is justified. That's about it. So, what's the circuit this guy's in?"

"The Fourth Circuit, Dave. Virginia, in fact."

A short pause and more tapping. "That would be Alex," he said. Andy shook her head, knowing from her research on Novak's death penalty cases, before she'd accepted his clerkship offer, that he'd never granted a stay application as a Circuit Justice. Dave spoke again. "Is that your case, Andy?"

"That's my case, Dave. Less than a minute, and you just might have saved this guy's life." Andy paused a moment. "Hey, Dave, is Laura there with you?"

"Hovering right over my shoulder, in fact. We're on speaker, so she heard all of this."

"Great," Andy said. "Hey, Laura, in case you didn't already know, Dave is an absolute Prince Galahad. Always ready to hop on his trusty steed, the one he's sitting at, and rescue ladies from peril. And guys, too. One guy in particular, who just got a birthday present from Sir Dave."

Laura laughed. "Good work, Noble Knight."

"Thanks, guys," Andy said. "I owe you a fancy dinner, maybe tomorrow night, if you can drag yourselves away from the office. Too much work makes for dull clerks, or at least hungry clerks. See you both tomorrow."

When she hung up, Andy called Josh, telling him to hustle back to his apartment. He showed up in five minutes, carrying a bag with Chinese take-out, and looking much more sober. "Very thoughtful, Josh," she said. "Always better to eat your dinner than drink it. If you set the table, I'll tell you what I found while you were out."

Over sweet and sour shrimp, and beef with broccoli, Andy recounted what Dave had told her, adding that Novak hadn't ever—at least from her research—granted a stay application. By unspoken but mutual agreement, she and Novak had avoided discussing capital punishment, each aware of the other's positions on the topic. But the time had come, with OD's execution date just fifteen days away, and Novak as the Circuit Justice, to confront the issue.

Josh struck an optimistic note. "Well, there's always a first time," he said. "And, since there's solid evidence pointing at Early Junior as an equally likely killer, maybe Alex would at least grant a stay of execution until we can file a second habeas petition that asks for a hearing to present that evidence, and move for a new trial for OD. What do you think, Andy? Good chance, some chance, or no chance?"

"With those choices, I'd say some chance, Josh. But no guarantee." After another bite of sweet and sour shrimp, Andy nodded her head. "Tell you what, Josh. First thing tomorrow, I'll dig up some earlier stay applications, no pun intended. I'm sure the Clerk's office has a bunch on file. Then we can plug in the new evidence we have, and you can file it with the Clerk, who will send it to Alex's chambers. Meanwhile, you can work on a new habeas petition to go with it." Andy paused. "Holy shit, Josh, I totally forgot to show you the case I dug up this afternoon." She grabbed the folder on the *House* case, pulled out the Supreme Court opinion, gave him a brief summary of the facts, and pointed out the excerpts she'd highlighted.

"Holy shit, yourself," Josh exclaimed as he scanned the pages. "Talk about a case being on point, as every law-school professor says. This case has a point like a rapier. Wow! And you say this guy walked out of death row as a free man?"

"Yeah, but Paul House spent twenty-two years on death row for a murder somebody else committed. That sucks, Josh."

"It sure does," he replied. "And OD has spent fifteen years on death row for a murder somebody else committed. I'm totally convinced of that now, Andy."

"I am too," she said. "Now all we have to do is convince Alex to issue a stay of execution. If he does, we'll have time to put together a kick-ass habeas petition. So, first thing in the morning we'll get to work, okay?"

"First thing," Josh said, with a real smile. "Meanwhile, since we both wolfed down our dinners, how about raiding Carlo's wine cellar? He's got a super pinot grigio, just waiting for a corkscrew."

"Sounds good," Andy said. "And I'm taking the rest of your Glenlivet home with me. Just to avoid temptation."

Josh gave a faux sigh, then grinned. "That's not what's tempting me, Venus."

Andy grinned back, then gave Josh a faux frown. "I'll give you a rain check, Lothario, but remember what you said, not long ago? This is *serious* business, Josh."

"Duly noted, counselor," he replied. "First thing tomorrow. Now let me fetch the corkscrew."

27

Andy felt nervous and jumpy as she reached the Court the morning after Josh gave her the news about OD's execution warrant, now just fourteen days away. Josh had called the night before, after she returned to her place, with further bad news. Jim Carruthers had called Josh to say that OD had been transferred that afternoon from the Sussex prison, where he'd been on death row since his conviction and sentencing, to the Greensville prison, thirty miles south of Sussex, just above the North Carolina border. Greensville, which Jim said the inmates called "Hellsville," was the site of Virginia's death chamber, in which OD was scheduled to be strapped to a gurney and killed by lethal injection at nine p.m. on December fifth, his thirty-eighth birthday. According to Jim, OD had reacted to the news of his impending execution with the same words he said to everyone at the prison: "I did not kill that girl." He didn't seem to comprehend that he might receive a stay of execution from the Supreme Court, telling Jim only that "I want to see my momma before they kill me."

"Morning, Miss Andy," Clarence Owens greeted her as she entered the Court. Her favorite security guard scanned her face, and frowned. "Don't mean to pry, but you look a bit down today. But just two days to Thanksgiving, you know. And we all got something to be thankful for."

"Thanks, Clarence," she replied, trying to return his warmth and concern. "You're right, I'm a little down this morning. But if things work out, somebody will have something to be thankful for. That's what we're all here for, Clarence, giving people we care about a reason to be thankful."

Clarence beamed. "Miss Andy, you said that just right. And you got more care than just about anybody I know. I saw that the first time you came through that door, back in July. It just shows on your face, you know what I mean?"

Andy gave Clarence a hug. "Now I'm not so down, Clarence. You have that care, too. And give Marvella a hug for me. She's a lucky woman to have you."

Her spirits lifted, Andy headed for the Clerk's office. She asked the young man at the desk if he could find a few applications for stays of execution, and copy them for her. Ten minutes later, she greeted Angie in Novak's chambers, and noticed that his office was empty. Andy knew that later today, or more likely tomorrow—the day before Thanksgiving—she'd have to ask him to sign a stay of execution for OD. Last night, fighting off waves of anxiety with a bottle of Beringer, she had rehearsed in her mind the argument—or maybe plea—she'd make to Novak. As Josh had pointed out, Novak had already seen the DNA evidence that linked Early Junior to Laurel Davis's bloody body, either during or right after her murder. That was Andy's strongest argument for a stay, to give OD's lawyers time to prepare a second habeas petition, based on the "newly-discovered evidence" that could be presented to a federal judge. But the clock was ticking, and Andy could almost see its hands moving.

"Will Alex be in later today?" she asked Angie.

"Oh, no," she replied. "Didn't Alex tell you? He left this morning for San Francisco, with Gloria and Anton. They're going to stay at a lodge near Carmel, and come back on Sunday. Alex left strict orders not to give anyone his cell number or the number for the lodge. He said this may be the last trip his dad takes, and Anton always wanted to see the Pacific Ocean." Angie's brow furrowed with concern. "You know, Andy, the last time I saw Anton, maybe two weeks ago, he didn't look well, although he's still looking pretty good for someone in their nineties. Anyway, Alex said there's nothing that can't wait until he gets back. Why, is there something you need to discuss with him? Maybe something I can help you with?"

"No, nothing important, Angie. It can wait until he gets back. But thanks for telling me." Oh shit, Andy thought. She could wait for Novak to return on Sunday, but was determined to get the stay—if that was possible—by Thanksgiving, just to spare OD from spending that day with nothing to be thankful for. There were still two weeks until his execution date, but the kind words from Clarence made Andy even more determined to do for OD what her grandma Bella called a mitzvah, an act of kindness and caring. Maybe she could remind Novak of his Jewish heritage and implore him to bestow a mitzvah on OD. What to do? What to do? Andy asked herself as she entered the clerks' office.

Her thoughts were diverted by the sight of Dave and Laura, huddled over Dave's computer, heads touching. She noticed that he'd moved to Todd's former desk, right next to Laura's new desk. Hmm, she thought, maybe the princess likes this particular frog, who's actually a very nice frog. "Ahem," Andy said, startling her fellow clerks, who swiveled around, to see her wagging a finger at them. "Eyes on your own papers, children," she said in a schoolmarm tone. They both blushed.

"Hey, Andy," Dave said. "Just thinking about you, actually. You know that prisoner petition you asked me about yesterday, the guy who's two weeks from an execution date?" Andy nodded agreement. "Well, I didn't say anything," Dave continued, "but it seemed odd that he'd file a cert petition, and not an application for a stay of execution. Cert petitions take a lot more than two weeks to get decided. I mean, he could still file a stay application, but I'm thinking he didn't have a lawyer. Of course, every death row inmate has a lawyer, unless they've given up on appeals."

"Hmm," Andy replied, noncommittally. "I'd have to check the petition and see."

Laura gave Andy a skeptical look. "The Clerk's office just delivered a copy of this week's death list, the one with the names of every inmate who's scheduled for execution next month. Gives all the justices notice, in case an inmate files a last-minute stay application."

"Uh, huh," Andy said, guessing what Laura was about to say.

"And there's only one name on the death list, Andy. You might recognize it. Odell Beasley. So tell me. Is he the inmate you were asking Dave about?"

Laura did not look accusatory, just curious. Andy decided to be honest. "Actually, guys, he's the one. Odell Beasley, known as OD. And he didn't file a cert petition. Sorry I misled you, Dave, but the Virginia governor just issued a death warrant for OD, setting his execution for two weeks from today. To be honest, I've been working on his case for about a month, with my friend Josh, who's a federal defender in Alexandria. And right now, I'm working on a stay application that would go to Alex."

Andy grimaced. "I know the Court's rules prohibit employees, including clerks, from working on cases that aren't on the docket. But I'm not working as a lawyer, which I'm technically not, and it's been on my own time. Mostly, anyway, although I guess I'm on Court time right now." She paused. "Look, guys, I'm helping OD with a stay application because I'm absolutely convinced that he's innocent." She started to choke up. "I know I'm pushing the rule, maybe breaking it, but I can't let OD die for a crime he didn't commit, and getting Alex to sign the stay is his only hope."

"Hey, hey," Dave said, soothingly. "You're with friends here, Andy. And you know, there's an exception to every rule, like, um, trespassing on someone's property to rescue a child from a burning house."

"Thanks, Dave, and you, too, Laura." Andy took a deep breath, then exhaled. "So, if we're breaking rules to save an innocent guy from lethal injection, I guess that's a good exception."

"I've got an idea," Dave said. "Alex won't be back until Sunday, Angie says, and while the cat's away, us mice can play. So, why don't we get some stay applications from the Clerk's office, put one together for OD Beasley, and see if we can persuade Alex to sign it when he gets back."

Andy held up the papers in her hand. "Actually, I just got a bunch from the Clerk, and we can use these for models. You said it's pretty simple, Dave, right?" She paused. "But I don't want to wait until Alex gets back. OD seems resigned that he's going to die, very soon, and I don't want to put him through despair, especially at Thanksgiving. So I'll call Alex when the application's ready, and see if I can fax him a copy to sign, and he can fax it back. That may not be completely kosher, but every rule has an exception. Right, Dave?" She didn't confess to Dave and Laura that Novak had left a strict no-calls order with Angie, but that was her problem to solve, not theirs.

"Tell you what," Dave said. "Let's take this stuff up to the library, find a table, and work on it together. Three heads are better than one, as they say."

By three, with a lunch break in the clerks' dining room, a draft was ready. Dave had quickly found the name of the Greensville prison warden, who had custody of OD and would supervise his execution, and had the authority to stop it, at a governor or judge's order. Prison wardens were normally the respondents in death-penalty cases. The draft of the stay application followed the format of the ones Andy got from the Clerk's office:

No. _____

IN THE SUPREME COURT OF THE UNITED STATES

Odell Beasley, Petitioner, v. Eddie Pearson, Warden, Respondent

---

CAPITAL CASE
EXECUTION OF ODELL BEASLEY
SCHEDULED FOR 9:00 PM (EST)
WEDNESDAY, DECEMBER 5

APPLICATION FOR STAY OF EXECUTION

To the Honorable Alexander Novak, Associate Justice of the Supreme Court, and Circuit Justice for the Fourth Circuit: Petitioner Odell Beasley respectfully requests a stay of his execution, scheduled as above. The relief sought is not available from any other court or judge, given the denial of Petitioner's petition for habeas corpus by the district judge on November 20, and the judge's refusal to issue Petitioner a Certificate of Appealability to the Fourth Circuit Court of Appeals. Copies of the district judge's orders are appended hereto.

Given that only two hours separated the district judge's denial of Petitioner's habeas petition, and the governor's issuance of the execution warrant, submission of a Petition for Certiorari with this Application was impossible. However, a Petition for Certiorari is being prepared and will be filed with the Court as expeditiously as possible.

Petitioner asserts that there is a reasonable probability that four members of the Court will consider the issues raised herein as sufficiently meritorious to grant certiorari, and, upon granting certiorari, five Justices are likely to conclude that the habeas petition was erroneously decided below, and that Petitioner's claim of "actual innocence," which will be presented in a second habeas petition, requires a new trial.

Dave chuckled as he typed this last sentence. "Every cert petition ever written says exactly the same thing. Four will vote to grant cert and five will vote to reverse the dumb judges below. Except that you get four votes to grant cert less than one time in a hundred. But that doesn't faze the lawyers who dump the petitions on our desks."

Rule 23, which Dave had copied, says that stay applications 'shall set out specific reasons why a stay is justified.' Working together, with papers spread along the table, the three clerks came up with two reasons. First, the Supreme Court should apply the ruling in *Hall v. Florida* retroactively, and order a new sentencing hearing for OD, at which evidence of his intellectual disability could be presented to a jury. Second, citing the *House v. Bell* case that Andy had dug up, that "newly-discovered evidence" in OD's case supported a claim of "actual innocence" and required a new trial. This claim, Andy pointed out to Dave and Laura, was even more important than the *Hall* issue, since a new trial, with the DNA evidence in Vito Petrocelli's report, might—and hopefully would—result in OD's acquittal, or convince the prosecutors to dismiss the murder charge, as Tennessee prosecutors did in Paul House's case.

Andy had sketched the evidence against Early Junior to Dave and Laura over lunch, including the dinner at the Bull & Bear Club in Richmond at which she pilfered Junior's water glass and cigar, and the mad dash to escape after she was unwittingly busted by Sue Saugstad. Andy's account of this escapade left her fellow clerks with mouths agape. "Oh, my God," Laura had exclaimed. "This needs to be a movie, Andy. And they can add a high-speed chase up I-95, with Junior plowing his Porsche into a semi and winding up burned to a crisp. That's what Hollywood would do. Can't just have you leaving him in the club. Much too tame." They all got a laugh out of that, before returning to the library and wrapping up the draft:

> 'Petitioner has demonstrated a likelihood of success on the merits of his claims, and will suffer the most irreparable harm imaginable if his execution proceeds. This Court should stay the Petitioner's execution.'

At just five pages, the stay application was short on case citations, aside from *Hall* and *House*. But it met the requirements of Rule 23, and was directed at only one reader, Alex Novak. Andy would add her plea that he sign it, and issue a stay order, after she consulted Josh about the best way to handle this delicate task. If not before Thanksgiving, Andy reflected, she'd still have at least eight days after Novak's return, and before OD was strapped to the gurney in the Greensville death chamber.

After Dave printed out the draft, Andy remembered something. "Hey, guys, let's go have the dinner I promised you yesterday. My treat, your choice." The choice turned out to be Buon Appetito, where two bottles of pinot grigio washed down Dave's veal marsala, Laura's lemon piccata chicken, and Andy's sea bass. By the end of the evening, it was clear to Andy that the 'giovane e bella donna' had awakened the prince whose trusty steed was a computer. After all, she reminded herself, real princes come in all sizes, shapes, and colors. Princely deeds were more important than princely looks. Andy smiled as she followed Dave and Laura out of the restaurant, holding hands. She thought back to her first encounter with Josh, holding hands as they walked across Harvard Yard to dinner at Grendel's Den. And now the four of them had become a team, working to save OD Beasley's life. Andy felt thankful that her day started with Clarence's kindness and concern. Another prince, in a city full of well-dressed and well-paid courtiers, all seeking favors. By the time she arrived home, Andy had answered her What To Do? question, and was ready for whatever tomorrow might bring.

Tomorrow began at six, with daylight just pushing through the drizzly overcast that was forecast to linger past Thanksgiving. After a quick shower and quick breakfast of toast and coffee, Andy called Josh, who obviously hadn't risen with the roosters. "Morning, sleepyhead," she greeted his mumbled hello. "This is the wake-up call you didn't ask for."

"Morning to you, Andy," he replied. "Although it's still night-time over to your west, and foggy here in Foggy Bottom. But you sound more chipper than I expected, after yesterday's news. So, Little Miss Sunshine, what got you up at this ungodly hour?"

"What got me up," Andy said, "is that I've made a decision that may cost my job, but it's something that I just have to do. Or that *we* have to do, unless you tell me that I'm crazy, and that you'll just pull the covers back over your head."

"Actually, I'm up now," Josh said, "stumbling over to put a coffee pod in the Keurig that Carlo bought. So, tell me what *we* have to do, that can't wait a minute longer."

Andy explained what she had done yesterday, with help from Dave and Laura, drafting an application for a stay of OD's execution, and that it would go to Alex Novak as Circuit Justice for the Fourth Circuit.

"Wow, that was quick work," Josh said. "So, what do you need *me* to do?" Andy could hear the gurgle of the Keurig, and the clink of a coffee cup.

"Here's what I need you to do this morning, Josh, the earlier the better, okay? I'm going to fax the application over to your office in about an hour, after I get to the Court and print out a finished copy. Then, you're going to print out three copies, take a cab to the Court, and file them in the Clerk's office. Are you awake enough to get that, Josh?"

She heard a slurp. "Now I am," he said. "Caffeine is already hitting my brain cells. So, I make three copies and cab them over to the Clerk's office, right?"

"Right. And I'll be waiting there, so text me five minutes before you arrive. Then I'll take a copy to Alex's chambers, sign his name to the order granting the stay, and fax it to the warden at the Greensville prison. And that will stop OD's execution."

"Whoa, Andy, whoa!" Josh exclaimed. "Did you say *you're* going to sign the stay order with his name? Doesn't Alex have to sign it himself?"

"Well, I said this might cost my job," Andy replied, "and maybe I shouldn't have told you that. But here's the situation, Josh. Alex is in California, with Gloria and his dad, and left strict orders that nobody can call him before they get back to DC on Sunday. And 'nobody' includes me."

Josh slurped again, then chuckled. "Let me guess, Andy. I can tell from your voice that you have obviously decided to sign the stay order with Alex's name, the day before Thanksgiving, so that OD can have a little turkey, if they give him that, and be thankful that he's not going to die in two weeks. Am I right?"

"You are very right, Josh," she replied, "that I'm going to do something very wrong. Or at least against the Court's rules. But it's the right thing for OD. And when Alex gets back on Sunday, I'll tell him what I did and hand him my resignation letter. He can rescind the stay, if he wants, but I'm hoping he won't. But Josh, I'm breaking a basic rule of the Court, which is grounds for dismissal. And properly so, in my opinion. So, resigning before Alex is forced to fire me won't put that decision on him." Andy's throat constricted as she choked up. "Do you understand what I'm saying, Josh? I can't do anything else, and live with myself."

"Hey, hey, Andy, calm down," Josh said, soothingly. "One step at a time, okay? I'm ready to go, soon as I shower, get dressed, and jump on the Metro. But one question, first. As you know, every petition or motion to the Court has to be filed by a member of the Court's bar, as counsel of record. I'm not, but Jim Carruthers is, and he's OD's official lawyer. So, I'll have to call Jim in Richmond, tell him what we're doing, and ask if we can put his name on the stay application. He doesn't actually have to sign it, but we can't file it without his agreement. I'm sure he will, since he feels just a strongly as we do that OD is innocent. But I'll have to check with Jim, and hope he's available this morning."

"Oh, Josh, thanks for that," Andy said. "I totally forgot about that in the rush to get this drafted yesterday. And tell Jim that I'll treat him to dinner at the Bull & Bear Club, and maybe introduce him to Junior. Just kidding."

"Okay, let's go," Josh said. "I think the sun's up, somewhere behind the fog. Let's see, it's close to seven, I'll be at my office by eight, and I should be at the Clerk's office by nine. Meanwhile, Andy, don't worry about what might happen when Alex gets back. If he's the guy you say he is, he'll say you did the right thing. And if not, you still did the right thing. Okay? Gotta jump in the shower, Andy. Love you."

"Love you, too, Josh."

Promptly at nine, Andy met Josh in the Clerk's office. The middle-aged African American woman at the counter took the copies from Josh, stamped them, and handed a copy to Andy. "Good luck," she said. "Up to me, I'd grant it myself. I never bought that 'eye for an eye' stuff. You know what Reverend King said? 'An eye for an eye leaves everyone blind.' I just read that in my daily devotional. Can't see our brothers and sisters, if we shut our eyes to them. Well, preaching's not part of my job, but every time we get one of these, I say a little prayer." She paused. "Oh, if your justice signs a stay order, bring me back a copy for the file."

"Bless you for that," Andy said. "We could all use a little preaching. And say a prayer for this man. He needs all the help he can get."

Andy walked back out with Josh, whose cab was waiting at the curb, gave him a hug, and dashed back to Novak's chambers. She had already looked up previous stay orders, and printed one, under the caption 'Odell Beasley, Petitioner, v. Eddie Pearson, Warden, Respondent':

"Petitioner's application for stay of execution presented to Justice Novak is granted and it is hereby ordered that Petitioner's execution is stayed, pending final disposition of this case or further order of this Court."

Andy had also looked up the phone number of the Greensville prison, and called. "Good morning," she told the person who answered. "This is Andrea Roboff, law clerk to Justice Alexander Novak at the United States Supreme Court. May I speak with Warden Pearson, please. I have an order from the Court, a stay of execution, directed to the Warden."

After a brief hold, a gruff voice answered. "This is Warden Pearson. I understand you have an order from the Supreme Court, directed to me. I assume this is in regard to inmate Beasley, is that correct? He's the only one with an execution warrant at our facility."

"Yes, sir," Andy said. "Mister Beasley's lawyers filed an application for a stay of execution with the Court, and Justice Novak has granted it. May I read it to you, Warden?"

"No need for that, Miss Roboff, if it just says Beasley's execution is stayed. But I would need a copy, if you can fax me one, with the Clerk's phone number on it, just so I can check. Not that I don't think it's official, you know." Pearson sounded less gruff now, and Andy breathed a sigh of relief. He gave Andy the fax number.

"I'll do that right now, Warden Pearson," she replied. "And can you do me a big favor, sir?"

"Glad to, if I can. Long as you don't ask me to let Beasley out right now. Can't do that." He chuckled. "You know, Miss Roboff, he just got down here from Suffolk on Monday, and we'll be glad to send him back today. He's been driving our staff crazy, 'cause all he says is 'I did not kill that girl.' About a hundred times, so far. But what's your favor?"

"Can you go to wherever he's being held in your facility, and tell him personally that he won't be executed on his birthday. That's the day it was scheduled, December fifth."

"Well, sure I will," Pearson said. "I would have done that, anyway. I met Beasley when he came in, just to explain our procedures, and he seemed like a decent guy, whether he committed that crime or not. And I'll tell him I hope he doesn't get sent back here again. You know, Miss Roboff, I don't take any pleasure in that part of my job."

Andy was surprised by this expression of concern. "Thank you so much, Warden Pearson. I appreciate your kindness. And you'll have the order in just a few minutes."

"Well, it doesn't cost anything to be kind, Miss Roboff. My momma taught me that, and it helps keep things here a little better than being mean to folks. Anyway, Mister Beasley will get the news just as soon as I get the order."

Andy thanked him again, hung up, and faxed the stay order to the Warden. Her talk with him gave her a sudden thought. She called information, got a number, and made another call.

"Is this Mamie Beasley?"

"It is, but I don't know who *you* is."

Andy took a deep breath. "Mrs. Beasley, this is Andrea Roboff. I work at the Supreme Court, and I have some news for you. Good news, Mrs. Beasley."

"I can always use some good news, miss. Don't get much, these days."

Andy almost burst out her good news. "Mrs. Beasley, your son OD got an order from the Supreme Court that his execution has been stayed."

"Stayed? Does that mean OD won't be killed on his birthday?"

"If we're lucky, and work hard, OD won't be killed at all. And he'll come back to your home, but it might be a while." Andy's words erased the last bit of Mamie Beasley's suspicion.

"*Thank* you, Jesus! Thank you, *Jesus!*" Then she burst into tears.

Andy waited until the sobs turned to sniffles. "Mrs. Beasley, I'm working with some lawyers who have found evidence that another man killed the girl in Williamsburg. We don't charge anything, and we all believe that OD is innocent. As I said, it may take some time, but OD *will* be coming home."

"Oh, miss, you just made an old, weary lady so happy. Can I still visit him next week?"

"Well, they're taking him back to the Suffolk prison, the one he's been in for fifteen years. And I'll make sure you can visit him next week."

After a long minute filled with "Thank you, miss," and "Thank you, Jesus," Andy promised to keep Mamie Beasley informed of all the developments in OD's case. She hung up and burst into tears.

The ordeal of the past two days left Andy drained, both emotionally and physically. After Mamie Beasley's tears and then her own, she left the almost-deserted Court, went home, and napped for three hours. Somewhat refreshed, she picked up her phone and called her parents, who were surprised and delighted that Andy had decided to join them and Bella for Thanksgiving. Packing a small roll-on bag, Andy headed for Union Station, having reserved a week ago—just in case—a seat on the 3 p.m. Acela to Penn Station. The station was jammed with holiday travelers, but she got into a special line and waited only fifteen minutes to board and find her seat.

When her train reached Penn Station, Andy took the shuttle to Grand Central and a Metro-North train for the half-hour ride to Yonkers, where she took a cab to her home, greeted by an ecstatic welcome from her parents, whom she hadn't seen since July, and a "You look so thin!" from Bella. Over the next three days, Bella tried her best to fatten Andy up, while Herbert and Evelyn plied her with questions about the new, but not-yet-confirmed Chief Justice, Kathryn Ikeda. "I can't understand," her dad said, "why a reactionary like President Chambers named a liberal Asian woman. There must have been some kind of political deal. And maybe she's not really liberal. Do you know any behind-the-scenes stuff about this, Andy?"

She, of course, professed ignorance, just responding, "Dad, almost everything that happens in Washington involves deals. But I met Justice Ikeda briefly in Justice Novak's office and I think she'll be great." Period, end of topic. The real topic, Andy's work to free OD Beasley from death row, remained behind her lips. As did her likely resignation for putting Novak's name on a stay of execution order that he hadn't yet seen. But that would happen, most likely, on Monday. Meanwhile, Andy enjoyed the time with her parents and Bella, watching the Giants-Patriots game with her dad, and the Macy's Thanksgiving Day parade with her mom and Bella. On Friday and Saturday, she visited a few of her old Yonkers High friends, now all married with children, and all urging Andy to find the right guy and start having kids. "Too busy, right now," she told them. Sunday morning, she returned to DC, with promises to come back to Yonkers for what her family called "Hanukkamas." On the train back, she wondered if OD had gotten any turkey on Thanksgiving, and been able to see his mom that weekend. And wondered where she'd be a month from now.

28

Andy slept very poorly on Sunday night. In fact, she didn't really sleep at all, with brief periods of dozing interrupted by longer stretches of staring at the ceiling while she rehearsed in her mind—at least a dozen times—what she planned to say to Alex Novak that morning. She had broken an unbreakable rule, for which the penalty was dismissal. Her resignation would spare Novak the obligation to fire her, regardless of his feelings toward her.

Were she in Novak's place, Andy thought, she would accept the resignation of a clerk who violated one of the Court's basic rules. Many clerks, she knew, both past and present, thought of themselves as a "Tenth Justice," equally—or even more—qualified than the justices for whom they worked to decide which cases the Court should hear, and to write the opinions in those the Court accepted for review. And some were. But for most, this was the arrogance of youth, the hubris of those who felt superior to their peers who had failed to gain admission to the Marble Temple. Andy didn't share these traits. Truthfully, she often felt totally unqualified to make decisions that only came with years of experience, and a keen awareness that the Court's "final word" on a divisive issue was very often just the opening word for debates that would roil the world outside the Court for decades to come.

Andy put these thoughts aside as she showered, dressed, and gulped a cup of coffee this morning. She thought, instead, of how her resignation would affect the people she most loved and admired: her parents and grandmother Bella, her constant friend Josh, her always-helpful fellow clerk Dave, and, of course, Alex Novak, whose trust in her she had forfeited with this act of usurpation. Except for Josh, they would all be shocked, dismayed, and concerned for Andy's future, to which she'd given no thought. Her final thought as she put on a bright smile for Clarence at the Court's entrance, was of OD Beasley, whose stay of execution could be rescinded within the next hour. Maybe giving him that hope of going home to his momma had been a cruel act on Andy's part, an unintended consequence of misplaced compassion.

"Morning, Andy," Angie greeted her cheerfully. "I hope you had a nice Thanksgiving."

"Thank you, Angie. Very nice. I went up to New York and had Thanksgiving with my parents and my grandma, and visited with some of my old high-school friends. And how was yours, Angie?"

"Very nice, also," she replied. "I went up to my sister's in Philadelphia, with her three kids and my cousins and all their kids. Fourteen of us, and not a scrap of turkey left after the kids cleaned their plates, and the mince and pumpkin pies. I'm still a bit stuffed."

Just then, Angie's phone rang. "Yes, she's here, Alex. Right by my desk. Hang on one second." She handed the phone to Andy. Oh shit, she thought. He found out what I did and I'm going to get fired over the phone.

"Andy, I have a big favor to ask," Novak said. Andy sensed the anxiety in his voice. "Could you take a cab over to my house and stay with Gloria while I take my dad to George Washington Hospital?"

"Of course, Alex," she assured him. "I'll leave right away. Is Anton alright?" What a dumb question, Andy realized. If he's going to the hospital, he's obviously not alright.

"Well, he's not in any pain," Novak replied. "But while we were in California, he noticed some blood in his urine. And this morning, there was a lot more. I just called GW, and they've got a urologist waiting to see him. But I don't want to take Gloria with us, since she's tired from the trip and it takes time to get her wheelchair in and out of the car." Novak paused. "Andy, Gloria said she'd be very grateful if you could stay with her while I'm at the hospital with my dad. She said to tell you that you are one of the kindest people she's ever met."

Andy was overwhelmed. "Alex, I'll be there as soon as I can get a cab. Tell your dad that GW has the best doctors in town, and not to worry. And tell Gloria that she's got the best husband in town, or anywhere else. See you soon, Alex."

Angie had picked up the gist of this conversation from Andy's end. "Andy, don't go out and look for a cab," she said. "I'll call right now and have one of the Court's drivers take you right over. He'll be out at the curb in just a few minutes."

Fifteen minutes later, Andy arrived at Novak's house in a black Lincoln Town Car. He was standing at the curb, and greeted her with a hug as she got out of the car. Novak leaned into the driver's window, asking him to wait a few minutes for another trip. "Andy, thank you so much," he said as they entered the house. Anton Novak was sitting on the living room couch, with Gloria next to him in her wheelchair. With Novak's hand under his elbow, Anton rose and smiled at Andy.

'Tomorrow," he said, "you and I and Gloria will spend the afternoon at the Phillips Collection, and admire the Renoirs. 'Luncheon of the Boating Party' is my favorite. And they have some nice works by Degas and Daumier."

Andy was touched. "That's a great idea, Anton. I love all of them. If not tomorrow, then very soon."

"Andy, I'm not sure how long I'll be at the hospital with Anton," Novak said. "But help yourself to anything in the house. There's plenty of lunch food in the kitchen, if we're gone that long." He turned to Gloria. "Don't worry about us, dear. My dad's stronger than a team of oxen, and Doctor Huang is the best urologist in town. He says it might just be an infection, but he'll take a look inside, just to make sure."

Andy took Anton's other elbow, despite his protest that he could walk perfectly well, and helped him down the front steps and into the back seat of the car. Before Novak went around to the front passenger side, he pulled Andy aside.

"Andy, Doctor Huang is very concerned about the amount of blood that my dad's been passing, and its color, and said he'd like to keep him at least overnight. I'll probably be back home in two or three hours, once he's checked in for the tests, and starts complaining about the nurses fussing over him." Novak smiled. "And when I get back, can you stay for a while, and have some Beringer with me. There's something I'd like you to help me with, and it's something you know a lot more about than I do. Is that okay?"

"I know you need to get your dad to the hospital," Andy replied, "but can you give me a clue? Maybe I can start on it while you're gone, if Gloria doesn't mind."

"Well, here's a clue," Novak said. "Gloria can show you how to log on to my computer, and maybe you could look up the Court's rules on stays of executions. I've never granted one before, but there's a case a friend of mine, who's on the Fourth Circuit, told me about last week, and said I might want to consider issuing a stay, at least until I can look at the record. Can you do that for me, Andy?"

Andy's jaw dropped in surprise. She pulled out a folder from the bag in which she'd brought the stay application, the order she'd signed with Novak's name, and her letter of resignation, and put the folder in his hand. "Alex, if you have any time while they're running tests on your dad," she said, "can you take a look at what's in here?"

"Sure," he replied. "Maybe you anticipated what I asked you to help me with. That's what a really good clerk should do." He leaned over and kissed her on the cheek. "Don't make assumptions about people, Andy." He paused for a moment. "Remember when your grandmother Bella made an assumption about my dad, that he'd collaborated with the Germans in the Warsaw ghetto? But when she heard his whole story, she realized that her assumption was wrong. Well, I've made assumptions about people who were convicted of horrible crimes, that our justice system doesn't send innocent people to prison. But maybe this case will change that assumption, once I've heard the whole story." He turned and looked at Anton, sitting calmly in the car. "I've got to get my dad to the hospital, Andy. Gloria's pretty tired from the trip, and she'll probably nap while I'm gone. But you can tell me more about this story when I get back. I have a feeling you know it pretty well." He walked around the car, got in the front seat, and left Andy standing on the curb, her assumption about him totally shaken.

Gloria did want to nap, and Andy wheeled her into her first-floor bedroom and helped her get into bed. Gloria reached out and took Andy's hand, her own trembling. "Andy, I hope you know that Alex loves you," she said. "And I'm so glad that he does. And you can love him back in any way you want. That's what my love for him tells me would make you both happy. But that's up to you, dear. We can be happy in many ways. And just having you here makes me happy."

Andy squeezed Gloria's hand, gently. "And I'm happy being here with you. You get some rest, and let me know if you need anything."

For the next three hours, Andy sat on the living-room couch, thinking about how lives can change direction with just a word. Love, she realized, was one of those words.

Alex Novak texted Andy from a cab on the ride home: "Anton OK. If Gloria is still napping, no need to wake her." Peeking in the bedroom door, Andy saw that Gloria was sleeping, and met Novak at the front gate. "Gloria's still sleeping, Alex, and you said that Anton is okay. But staying overnight, I guess."

"Well, that wasn't his choice, Andy, but Doctor Huang insisted, because they want to monitor him and there might be more tests tomorrow. My dad is very stoic, but he can get crotchety when somebody orders him around. And most nurses order patients around, most very nicely, but they don't give you much choice. It's 'swallow this pill, stick out your arm, put on the johnnie.' But he's comfortable, and I'm going back this evening to listen to his grumping."

"But did Doctor Huang give you any diagnosis?" Andy asked.

Novak followed Andy into the living room and sat beside her on the couch. "He won't know for sure until he gets the pathology report on Thursday, but he's pretty sure it's bladder cancer. They did a cystoscopy and scraped some cells, so the path report will tell if the cells are malignant, and if so, what kind they are. And that will determine the prognosis and the treatment."

Novak reached over and grasped Andy's hand. "My dad is ninety-two, Andy. He's had a long and rewarding life, after a horrible experience during the war. As I said, he's very stoic, so whatever Doctor Huang says, he'll accept it and won't ever complain. I'm not sure I could do that, to be honest. But I haven't been through what he has, and lawyers are trained to complain about things." He chuckled. "That's why lawyers file complaints for their clients."

Andy squeezed his hand. "When you visit Anton tonight, Alex, tell him our visit to the Phillips and their Renoirs is still on, okay?"

"He already mentioned that, as a matter of fact. Told me to tell you this Saturday. He expects to be doing his regular two-mile walks by then." They both chuckled at this.

Novak picked up from the coffee table the folder Andy had given him. He pulled out her resignation letter, and calmly tore it in half. "Andy, you broke a very important rule," he said. "If I didn't understand your motivation, and the significance of this case, I would have accepted it." He paused for a moment. "But after I read the stay application you drafted, I decided that I'm going to break a rule myself." Andy gave him an inquisitive look. "Let me tell you what happened last Monday, and what I'm planning to do. Okay? And then you can tell me more about Mister Beasley's case."

Before he continued, Novak got up, went into the kitchen, and came back with a bottle of Beringer chardonnay and two glasses. He filled each glass, handed one to Andy, sat down, and took a sip.

"So," he said, "last Monday evening I was home, and got a call from a friend of mine who's a judge on the Fourth Circuit. I won't tell you her name, and there are three, maybe four, women judges on the circuit. Anyway, she told me that she'd been walking down the hall that connects the judges' chambers, passed one that had the door open, and heard Judge Early's voice. Former judge now, thanks to you and your friends, Andy, but anyone can get invited to a judge's chambers."

Novak took another swallow. "So, she heard Early say 'governor' and 'Beasley' and 'fifteen days and he'll be gone.' That's all she heard, but she recognized Beasley's name from a motion his lawyer filed that afternoon, asking for a certificate of appealability from the district judge's denial of the habeas petition. The Clerk's office sent a copy to her chambers, and she only skimmed it, but did recall Beasley's name."

Andy interrupted. "Excuse me, Alex, but why did she call you?"

"Because I'm the Circuit Justice, and know her pretty well," he replied, "and she'd gone back to her chambers and read the motion more carefully, and decided the district judge got it wrong. His opinion was attached to the motion, and she thought he completely misconstrued the Hall versus Florida case and the retroactivity issue. I'm sure you've read that opinion, too, Andy. And I assume you wrote what the stay application says about it."

Andy could sense that Novak suspected that Early Senior was behind the governor's quick decision to issue the execution warrant, and was lobbying his former colleagues to deny any appeal of the district judge's habeas denial. She also sensed that Novak was appalled by that, and determined to do something about it. Andy waited for the 'something' he was planning, and was very surprised.

"I told you I'm going to break a rule, Andy, although it's an unwritten rule on the Court, but every justice understands it. It's a rule against what they call 'ex parte' communications with parties to a case before the Court or their lawyers. It means we can't talk with them before the case is decided, without the other side being there. There are exceptions in lower courts, but not in ours. No talk means no talk, plain and simple." Novak reached for the bottle and refilled his glass, but Andy put a hand over hers.

"So, here's what we're going to do, Andy," he continued. "And 'we' includes you and your friend Josh, who I know has been working with you on Mister Beasley's case. I haven't met him yet, but I will on Wednesday."

"You want to talk with Josh about the case on Wednesday, Alex?"

"Yes, while we're all driving down to the Sussex prison. I'm devoting tomorrow to my dad, but Wednesday is all arranged for a visit with Mister Beasley. The Court doesn't have oral arguments this week, so my schedule is free."

Andy couldn't hide her astonishment. "Talk with OD Beasley, Alex? How come?"

"Look," he replied, "I know from Dick Wadleigh's memo, and the transcript of his little chat with President Chambers, about Judge Early's phony alibi for his son. And I know from the DNA report you gave me that his son could be the person who murdered the girl in Williamsburg. That might be enough to convince a jury to acquit Mister Beasley in a retrial, but I want to hear his story in person." He paused, took another swallow of wine, then smiled at Andy. "Don't worry, Andy, you won't have to send me home in a cab from the Capitol Hill Club. I'm already home, and just relaxing after a pretty stressful week."

Andy took a sip of her wine. "Me too, Alex. I was sure this morning that I'd be fired, when you called Angie and asked me to come over here."

Novak chuckled. "Well, I could get fired, too, although it would take impeachment to do that, and that won't happen if nobody finds out what I'm doing. And I think I've taken care of that. I'll tell you about that later.

Anyway, not to sound boastful, Andy, but I have a knack for knowing whether someone is telling the truth, or lying, when I look them in the face and hear their story. I'm like a human lie detector, only better than a machine. My dad is, too, and I think that's where I got it."

Andy looked skeptical. "So, if you listen to OD's story, Alex, and decide he's telling the truth, then what?"

Novak grinned. "That's what you're going to work on tomorrow, Andy. I've got a few research topics for you, which shouldn't be too hard. But I'm not up on all the rules and procedures for what I have in mind if Mister Beasley passes my exam."

"Um, Alex, can I ask a question?" He nodded agreement. "Last week, after Josh told me about the execution warrant, I started looking at how to get stays of execution from the Court. And I got a lot of help from Dave and Laura. Dave knows all this stuff, and he and Laura helped me draft the stay application that I put your name on. So, would it be okay if I asked them to help with the research you want me to do?"

"Sure," Novak replied. "I completely trust Dave, and I'm sure we can also trust Laura. But nobody else, not even Angie, can know anything about this. Okay?"

"Promise," Andy said.

"Promise accepted, resignation rejected," Novak said. "Now, I just heard some stirring down the hall, so let's go check on Gloria. Since Anton's not here, she might need some help in the bathroom, if you don't mind."

"Of course not," Andy said. "And before she started napping, we had a very nice chat. In fact, a lovely chat."

Thirty minutes later, just as Novak finished dictating a list of research topics for Andy and her fellow clerks, a cab arrived. Novak went out with Andy, handed the driver a twenty and told him to keep the change. He hugged Andy, lifted her chin, and said, "Don't make assumptions about people, Andy, before you meet them. I've done that too many times." Impulsively, she reached up and kissed him. Not a long kiss, but long enough to send a message. And he didn't resist or recoil. Novak opened the cab door and said, "Good night, Andy."

After she got home, Andy called Josh and told him about the trip with Novak on Wednesday to meet with OD at the Sussex prison. "If Alex believes OD's story," she said, "he'll keep the stay of execution in effect, and then we'll figure out what to do next. I'm going to work on that tomorrow with Dave and Laura." Andy tried to temper her optimism. "Of course, this all depends on whether Alex believes OD's story. But I have a feeling, Josh, that if he does, Alex wants to find some way to get OD's case to the Court without having to wait for a ruling from the Fourth Circuit on the denial of OD's habeas petition. That's what he wants us to research tomorrow."

"Sounds to me," Josh replied, "like Alex wouldn't break the ex parte rule unless he thinks the evidence we dug up about Early Junior merits at least a new trial for OD." He chuckled. "Think about it, Andy. Mose Townley and the brown glove, Martha Radford and the red Corvette, you googling Early senior, Carlo hearing Vito speaking Italian, you snatching Junior's glass and cigar. Who could have predicted all of that? And if it hadn't happened just that way, OD might be executed next week."

Andy laughed. "Josh, if you're trying to get me to say the 'I' word, how about 'this was all determined sixteen billion years ago.'"

"Well, that's a theory, too," he conceded. "But since I didn't go to grad school in physics, somebody else will have to prove that. Law school just teaches you to say, 'if you think my client's guilty, prove it beyond a reasonable doubt.' And there's no way to prove what's reasonable and what's not."

"Gee," Andy said, "I guess that's why lawyers never pick jurors with red hair, because everybody knows red-heads can't be reasonable." Josh laughed. "Anyway," Andy continued, "to be serious for a moment, Alex already knows there's plenty of doubt that OD was guilty. Otherwise, we wouldn't be going to visit him on Wednesday. Alex would have accepted my resignation, rescinded the stay, and I'd be leaving the Court in disgrace, just like Amanda and Todd."

"Oh, come on, Andy," Josh chided, "what you did was nothing like their greedy crimes. Sometimes, Andy, to quote some dead philosopher, the end justifies the means. Assuming, of course, that the end and the means are both reasonable. And saving an innocent person's life is certainly reasonable."

"Well, I feel better now," Andy said. "Thanks for that, Josh. Oh, before I forget, Alex said he'll pick us both up at the Court on Wednesday at eight. Not too early for you, I hope."

"Better than six, Early Bird. See you then. Love you, Andy."

"Love you too, Josh."

29

Andy and Josh were waiting on the curb outside the Court when Novak pulled up in his Lexus promptly at eight on Wednesday morning. Josh took the front seat at Novak's invitation, with Andy in the back, settling into the soft black leather. "It's about three hours to the prison," Novak said as he pulled out, "a straight shot down I-95, little town called Waverly. Let me know if you want a rest stop on the way, since we don't have a set time for our visit."

Novak glanced at Josh. "Now, here's the deal I worked out with the warden, after I called in a favor with a state judge I know in that area, who invited me last year to speak to his daughter's high-school Constitution Day assembly. So, Josh is meeting with Mister Beasley as his lawyer, which he is, so that's no problem." He turned around to Andy as they waited for a red light to change. "You and I, Andy, aren't going to be there. Not officially, because the warden agreed to keep our names out of the visitors log. So we'll be off the books, so to speak."

Andy had brought along the results of the research she'd done the day before with Dave and Laura, but Novak said it could wait until after their meeting with OD. After a brief stop to dispose of the morning's coffee and add more, Novak turned off I-95, drove another few miles through farmland, and pulled up at the gate to the Sussex prison. Andy hadn't really expected massive stone walls, with rifle-toting guards and searchlights every fifty feet, but this prison looked more like an industrial park, with four or five two-story buildings, surrounded by two rows of razor-wire-topped chain-link fences.

Novak rolled down his window as a guard approached from a post outside the gate, handing him a sheet of paper. "We're here to see Warden Zook," Novak told the guard. "Here's the warden's authorization for us to meet with him and visit one of your inmates." Novak gestured at Josh. "Mister Barfield is the inmate's attorney, and his visit is approved. But, as

Warden Zook says in this memo, Mister Barfield will be the only one of us who is logged in as visitors today."

The guard scanned the document. "Yes, sir," he said. "I got a copy of this. If you can all just show me your driver's licenses, you can go right through. That's just procedure, and it won't go on the log." Novak, Josh, and Andy pulled out their licenses and handed them to the guard, who quickly scanned them and handed them back. "Thank you," he said. "The administration building is straight ahead, and you can park over to the left." He went back into his post, and the barred gate slid back on rollers. Once inside, that gate closed, and a second opened. Novak parked, and they entered the tan, two-story building, finding a tall, well-built man, late forties, crew cut, waiting inside the door. They shook hands all around.

"Good morning, folks," he said. "I'm David Zook, and Judge Anderson told me you were coming to visit with inmate Beasley. Mack Anderson and I are good friends, we're both in the Rotary Club, and the men's group at our church. And our daughters are both cheer-leaders at the high school here in Waverley. So, Mack explained the reason for this exception to our usual procedures, and I agreed to his request." Zook led them down a hallway to his office, pointing them to chairs around a small conference table.

"Before you meet with inmate Beasley," Zook said, "let me tell you something, quite frankly." He gave his visitors a stern look. "I don't like to deviate from our procedures. It causes confusion, and possibly can result in serious problems. I'm doing a one-time favor to Mack Anderson. But if anyone in authority, the governor, attorney general, whoever is superior to me, asks me about your visit today, I have an obligation to answer honestly. I hope you understand that."

Novak replied. "Warden Zook, I very much appreciate your favor to Judge Anderson, and I understand your concern. This is the only visit any of us will make that doesn't follow your procedures. But let me also be frank." Zook nodded his agreement. "I have serious doubts that Mister Beasley is guilty of the crime for which he was convicted," Novak said. "I am deviating from the rules and procedures of my Court to listen to his story, and decide whether the stay of execution I issued should remain in effect." Novak smiled. "So, we're both in the same boat, Warden. I completely agree that deviating from the procedures of our respective institutions can result in confusion, and serious problems. But on rare occasions, not as favors to friends but in the pursuit of justice, a deviation is justified. I hope you understand that."

Zook smiled. "Now that we both understand each other, Justice Novak, let me take you down to our attorney consultation room."

Zook led them from his office through a long corridor, stopping at a steel door, where he pressed his palm against a book-sized screen at the side. Noticing his visitors' surprise, he held up his hand. "If you were expecting a big brass key, keys can get stolen or copied. But nobody can copy my hand-print, or any of yours. We may be in the boonies down here, but we do take advantage of modern technology."

Halfway down another long corridor, Zook stopped at a door, turned the knob, and led the visitors inside. The small room had institutional green walls, no windows, a metal table, bolted to the floor, and four chairs, three on one side of the table, one on the other. "Inmate Beasley will be here in five minutes," he said. "There will be an officer with him, but he'll stay outside until you finish your visit. The door won't be locked. And just to make clear, we don't monitor attorney visits. No cameras, no microphones. That's against the law, as you know, and we follow the law." He chuckled as he shook hands all around. "Well, almost always. You wouldn't be here—or not here, actually—if we always followed the law."

"We appreciate that, Warden Zook," Novak said. "And thanks for letting us be here—or not here, as you said."

"Don't thank me, Justice Novak. You can thank my daughter. She heard your speech last year on Constitution Day at her school, and said you were so inspiring that she wants to be a lawyer." He chuckled. "I told her I'd rather have her flipping burgers at McDonald's."

"Well, I've had that thought myself, and a lot of lawyers would probably do a better job of flipping burgers." Novak said. With that, Zook gave them a mock salute and headed back down the corridor.

"So," Novak said, "let's wait for Mister Beasley. Josh, do you mind if Andy and I have different names when you introduce us? Just to be on the safe side. If he asks, we're, um, Mary and John. Okay?"

"Very original, John," Josh said. "And Mary can take notes for us." He handed Andy a legal pad and pen from his thin attaché case.

"Oh, great," she said. "That's what girls are good at. Along with flipping burgers."

Five minutes later, Andy heard a clanking sound, and the shuffling of feet. The door opened, and a burly guard escorted OD Beasley into the room. Andy was shocked at his appearance. OD's close-cropped hair was flecked with grey, his head down, no expression on his face. He was dressed in a baggy orange jumpsuit, his feet shackled with a foot-long chain between them, that chain attached to one around his waist, with another chain from his waist to his cuffed hands. The guard sat him in the chair, undid the chain to his handcuffs, and secured that chain to a metal ring bolted to the table.

Novak gave the guard a sharp look. "Officer, there's no need to restrain Mister Beasley. Would you please undo that chain and his handcuffs."

"Sorry, sir, but that's procedure, for your safety."

"I'm not concerned about our safety, officer," Novak replied. "We don't have anything to fear from Mister Beasley. So, please undo those restraints." The officer hesitated. "Or you can call Warden Zook right now, officer, and ask him to come down here. Your 'procedure' is totally unnecessary, and it's demeaning to Mister Beasley."

"Okay, sir, it's your call." He complied with Novak's demand. "But if you need me, there's a button right under the table, on your side. Push it, and we'll be right in for an extraction."

Andy spoke up. "That's what you call dragging inmates out of their cells, don't you, officer, after you blast them with pepper spray, from the can on your belt. But you make it sound like a visit to the dentist." Andy was surprised at her vehemence, but she'd seen videos of "extractions" of recalcitrant inmates from their cells. OD showed no signs of recalcitrance. He sat quietly, but smiled at Andy as the guard undid his chain and cuffs.

After the guard closed the door, OD shook his hands and flexed his fingers. "They always put them on too tight," he said. "Thank you for that." He looked at his visitors. "They tole me I got a visit from my lawyer. But that's Mister Jim, and he ain't here. So is you my new lawyers?"

"Mister Beasley," Josh replied, "my name is Josh, I'm one of your lawyers, and I'm here with John and Mary," gesturing to his left and right. "We work with Mister Jim, and we're here to help him with your case, and see if we can get you out of here, or at least get you off death row. We can't promise you anything, but we'll do our best. We have a few questions, and you can ask us anything you want."

"Yes sir, Mister Josh," OD said. "First, though, I got to tell you something. I did not kill that girl. But they come close to killing me last week, down at the other place. They tole me they gone put poison in me, and I get what I deserve for killing that pretty white girl. That's what they tole me. But I did not kill that girl. Somebody else did, but I don't know who." He looked at Josh, expectantly. "Maybe you do, Mister Josh. It got to be the man who come to that girl's door, but I never seen him."

Novak spoke up. "Mister Beasley, my name is John. Do you mind if I ask you a few questions?"

"No, sir, course not. But you can call me OD. Everybody does, 'cept some of the officers. Most call me OD, but they's a couple call me names. Like 'Scum,' or they spit on my food when they shove the tray in. But I never cause no trouble. They's a few who just be nasty, you know?"

"I'm sorry about that, OD," Novak said. "And I'll talk to the warden about that. There's no need to call you names or spit in your food."

OD's eyes opened wide. "Oh, don't do that, Mister John. You do that, those officers find some other way to make it hard. Like they turn off the hot water in the shower, call my momma names when she visit, things like that. I don't complain. Things hard enough here, don't want to make it worse."

"Okay, OD, I understand," Novak said. "I don't want to make things harder for you. But can I ask you a few questions?"

"Yes, sir, Mister John. But can I first axe this lady here something?" He looked at Andy. "You Miss Mary, right?"

"Um, yes, I'm Miss Mary."

"Is you the lady call my momma and tole her they not going to kill me?"

Andy hesitated for a second, recalling that she'd given Mamie Beasley her real name. "Yes, I did call your momma and told her that. And I was very glad to give her that news."

"Oh, bless you," OD said. "I tole my momma you give me the best present I ever got. And she say if she ever meet you, she gone hug you to death." OD smiled. "I guess she dint mean just that, Miss Mary, but she cry when she tole me 'bout you."

"Well, thank you, OD," Andy said, trying hard not to choke up. "And I hope I'll meet her some day, maybe at your house when you go home. That's what we're trying to do, get you home with your momma."

OD turned to Novak. "Sorry, Mister John. I just had to axe Miss Mary if she the one call my momma. I had a feeling she was. I get these feelings, sometimes, and I usually be right, you know what I mean?"

Novak smiled. "I know what you mean, OD. I get those feelings sometimes, and I'm usually right, just like you." He paused for a moment. "OD, if you don't mind, can you tell me what happened the morning the girl got killed. Just tell me what you remember, okay?"

For the next ten minutes, without interruption, OD recounted the story he'd told Mose Townley during the interrogation he had recorded. Novak kept his eyes focused on him, nodding occasionally. Only once did OD pause, closing his eyes and squinting, then shaking his head. "Tell the truth, Mister John, onliest word I remember for sure this man say when he open the front door was 'horny.' But I sure he say that. 'Cause some of my friends, before I come here, we see a pretty girl, they say, 'don't she make you horny, OD?' Like they mean have sex with her, you know what I mean?"

Novak chuckled. "I know just what you mean, OD. Pretty girls can make a man horny." Andy tried hard not to blush, and scribbled 'OD remembers horny' on the legal pad, the first note she'd made.

OD finished his account with running out the back door of Laurel Davis's house, naked, quickly putting on his clothes and shoes in the alley, running to his home, grabbing some money, running to the bus station, buying a ticket to Richmond, and going with the officer who took him to see Mose Townley at the station. Then he paused. "But I did not kill that girl, Mister John. I swear to Jesus I did not kill that girl. You got to believe me, Mister John."

Novak sat quietly for a moment before he spoke, quietly. "I believe you, OD. I believe you." Andy reached over, under the table, and squeezed a hand that Novak had in his lap. He squeezed back.

OD looked at Josh. "Can I axe you a question, Mister Josh, you bein' my lawyer here?"

"Of course, OD," Josh replied. "Anything."

"Will I be goin' home to be with my momma?"

Josh took a deep breath, then exhaled. "OD, I can't promise you that. But we will do everything we can to make that happen. I can promise you that."

"That be good enough for me," OD said. "Everything up to Jesus, you know. And he promise he always hold us in his hand, and let no evil happen to us. So you do what you can, Mister Josh, and Jesus take care of the rest." He looked at Novak and Andy, smiling. "And he take care of you, too, Mister John and Miss Mary."

Andy reached over the table and took both of OD's hands in hers. "You make me a promise, OD. Don't you ever give up hope that you'll be home someday with your momma."

"You know, Miss Mary," he said, "even when they say they gone put poison in me and kill me, I know that me and my momma have a home in heaven, if that where Jesus want us." He chuckled, squeezing Andy's hands. "'Course, they prob'ly don't make fried chicken and greens in heaven good as my momma do."

With that, Josh got up and opened the door. The guard, standing across the hallway, came in and began replacing OD's chain and cuffs. "Don't make those cuffs too tight, officer," Novak said. "Mister Beasley won't give you any trouble."

"Yes, sir," he replied. "He never has. Sorry about that."

The restraints in place, the guard led OD down the hall, to the right, clanking and shuffling, but with his head erect. Another guard had arrived, and led OD's visitors to the left, placing his palm against the sensor at the steel door. Once through, Novak said, "Officer, if you don't mind, we'd like to stop at Warden Zook's office for a minute and thank him for his courtesy."

"Yes, sir, I think he's in." The guard knocked on Zook's door. The warden opened it. "You folks all done with inmate Beasley?" he asked.

"We're done, Warden," Novak answered. "We just wanted to thank you again for your courtesy in arranging our visit."

Just then, a man appeared behind Zook. "Justice Novak?" he asked, surprise evident in his voice. He held out his hand. "Bill Samuels. I'm with the attorney general's office in Richmond. We met at the Fourth Circuit conference a couple of years ago."

Novak shook his hand. "Good to see you again, Bill," he said. "That was a very enjoyable conference. White Sulphur Springs in West Virginia. I remember, right after my talk, hardly any questions. Everybody dashed out to the golf course. So, what brings you here, Bill?"

"Well," Samuels replied, "you may have heard that four of the death row inmates here filed a lawsuit that claims keeping them in solitary violates the Eighth Amendment. 'Cruel and unusual punishment,' they say. Of course, the murders they committed were more than cruel." He shrugged. "Anyway, the judge ordered that we try to reach a settlement with the inmates' lawyers, see if there's a way to ease some of the restrictions. Personally, I'd put them all on bread and water. But Warden Zook thinks giving them more recreation time, maybe even a basketball court, might satisfy his killers."

Zook gave Samuels a Don't Blame Me look. "Bill," he said, "you probably haven't been locked up for twenty-three hours a day for even a week. But some of these men are going crazy in solitary. I'd rather have them shoot hoops than scream about the Devil and throw shit at my officers." Zook gave Andy a Pardon Me look. "Sorry, Miss Roboff, but that's what happens when an inmate gets upset about finding green Jello-O on his tray when he wanted red."

Samuels shrugged again. "Okay, if hoops will do the trick. We can live with that. But three hours a day with cells unlocked, and a rec room with a TV and game boards? With all due respect, Warden Zook, the Commonwealth isn't running a Hilton down here."

Andy was tempted to jump in and ask Samuels what he knew about the effects of solitary confinement on death-row inmates, but Novak cut her off. "Well, Bill," he said, glancing at his watch, "it's good to see you again, but we're trying to beat the traffic back to DC."

"I understand, Justice Novak," Samuels replied, "but just out of curiosity, what brings you down here? I'm not aware that Supreme Court Justices make prison visits."

Novak hesitated for a moment. "Not normally, Bill," he replied, turning to Josh. "But Mister Barfield is here to visit with a client, and I volunteered to give him and my clerk a ride. I've never seen the inside of a prison before, and I thought it might give me a perspective on the cases we deal with at the Court. Sort of a busman's holiday, if you know what that means."

Samuels gave Novak an I Don't Believe You look. "And Mister Barfield wouldn't be here to see Odell Beasley, would he?"

"Yes, I was, Mister Samuels," Josh replied. "And Justice Novak and Miss Roboff asked to come along." He gave Samuels a Don't Argue With Me look.

Samuels gave Josh a You're Lying look in return. "Mister Barfield," he said, "I've seen the stay of execution order that Justice Novak signed, and the motion Jim Carruthers filed to appeal Judge Jacobs' denial of Beasley's habeas petition. Okay?" He looked at Novak. "But I don't think Justice Novak is here just for a tour of Warden Zook's facility." He paused for a moment. "Let me ask you, Justice Novak, did you sit in on Mister Barfield's visit with Beasley?"

"Yes, I did, Bill," he replied. "And if you had been with us, you would know that Mister Beasley is innocent of the murder for which he's been on death row for fifteen years." Novak pointed a finger at Samuels. "Let me give you a bit of unsolicited advice, Bill. You go back to Richmond and tell the attorney general that if he doesn't drop any opposition to Mister Beasley's habeas appeal, the son of one of his closest friends might wind up as the next inmate in Mister Beasley's cell." Novak poked Samuels in the chest. "I understand the son of your boss's golfing buddy was a high-school basketball star. So he'd probably enjoy playing some hoops with his death-row companions. And playing Go Fish in the rec room."

Andy was astounded at Novak's deliberate baiting of the state's lawyer. On his part, Samuels turned to Zook, who hadn't said a word during this exchange. "Thanks for your time, Warden," he said, then headed down the corridor, without another word.

Novak watched Samuels until he reached the entrance, then turned to Zook. "My apologies for that little fracas, Warden. But if anybody asks you about my visit here, tell them to call me at the Supreme Court." Novak reached in a pocket and pulled out a card. "Here's my personal number. I'd be glad to tell them that you run an exemplary institution, and treat the inmates with respect."

After handshakes all around, OD's visitors left the administration building, got into Novak's car, and were waved through both gates. "Tell you what," he said, "let's not talk about what comes next until tomorrow. Much more pleasant topics to discuss." He turned to Josh. "Andy tells me you chose law school over grad school in physics. But you obviously know something about how the universe works. So, tell me, Josh, if heaven and hell are actual places, how would a physicist devise some way to discover their actual location? I've been wondering about that, ever since my parish priest told us that the streets of heaven are paved with gold, and hell is a pit of burning sulphur." The rest of their trip back to DC was occupied with spirited discussion of this and other topics, including favorite movies and books.

Novak dropped Josh off at his office in Alexandria, then drove Andy to her apartment. "Alex," she said as he pulled up, "I've got a bottle of Beringer in the fridge. We could both use a little time to unwind from that fracas with the guy from the AG's office. I really thought you were going to wipe that smirk off his face, and wind up getting 'extracted' from the warden's office with pepper spray. So, you want to come up and chill for a bit?"

"That's very tempting," he replied. "I came within two seconds of decking the guy, Andy. I don't care if he tells the attorney general I had an ex parte visit with OD Beasley. It was his 'screw the inmates' attitude that really pissed me off. So chilling with some chilled wine sounds good." He checked his watch. "It's almost five now, but Gloria and Anton are having dinner with her friend Marjory, so I can stay for a while." Andy got the sense from his tone that he wasn't in a hurry to get back home.

Novak found a parking space down the block from Andy's building. As they walked to the doorway, her thoughts were swirling like the leaves that blew along the sidewalk in the gusty wind. In those few seconds, Andy thought of her 'lovely' chat with Gloria. She thought of Carlo's selfless agreement to share Josh with her, not only for love, but also for sex. She thought of the time, after the service at Temple Shalom for Sam Terman, that Novak had sat on her couch and gazed—as any healthy man would—at the nipple bumps under her tight tee-shirt. She thought of the rules that she and Novak had both broken, to find some way to free OD Beasley from fifteen years on death row. Breaking one more rule, Andy decided, might give them both a welcome release from the stress of the past few weeks.

Once inside her apartment, Andy felt comfortable with her decision. "Alex, why don't you get out of that jacket and tie," she said, moving into the kitchen for the Beringer and glasses. She put them on the coffee table, and filled both glasses. Novak shed his jacket and tie, hanging them over a chair, and settled into the couch. Just as she had the last time he visited her, Andy said, "make yourself comfortable, Alex, while I change into something less formal." She went into her bedroom, thought for a moment, stripped down to her panties, thought for another moment, and put on jeans and a thin white tee-shirt. Looking in the mirror over her dresser, Andy briefly considered putting her bra back on, but decided to skip the fumbling with hooks that would entail.

Back in the living room, Andy brightly asked, "Alex, would you like a little chilling out music?" He lifted his wine glass in agreement. She pulled out a CD from her collection. "How about Mozart? Does 'Eine Kleine Nacht Musik' appeal to you?"

Novak chuckled. "A little night music suits me just fine."

Andy popped the CD into the player, sat next to Novak on the couch, and lifted her wine glass. "Let's just enjoy this night, Alex, and let tomorrow wait until tomorrow." He clinked his glass with hers, each taking a swallow, then settling back into the couch as Mozart invited them to relax, close their eyes, and enjoy his brilliance.

Five minutes passed before Andy, her eyes still closed, reached over and took one of Novak's hands into hers, feeling a squeeze of agreement. Another five minutes passed before Andy lifted his hand and placed it gently around her left breast. "Is that okay, Alex?" she whispered. He responded by softly caressing her breast, running his palm over its hard nipple. Two minutes later, with Mozart giving encouragement, Andy took Novak's hand and slid it under her tee-shirt, where it resumed the gentle caresses. Another two minutes, and she moved his hand to her lap, pulled off her tee-shirt, settled into the crook of his shoulder, and placed his hands around each breast. She opened one eye, glanced up, and saw that his were both closed, his face smiling. "Alex," she whispered, "you can go anywhere you want. And I'd like to put my hands on you, wherever it feels good for you."

"Andy," he whispered back, "I'd love to feel your hands on me. But can we keep it with just our hands? That's all I'm able to do. The last four years, the rest of me hasn't worked the way it used to. I wish it did, but my hands still work just fine."

"Don't worry about that, Alex," she whispered. "You've heard of four-hand piano sonatas? Let's try our hands at one, okay? And playing on my bed would give us room to improvise." She undid the button and zipper on her jeans, lifted her bottom, pulled them and her blue lace panties off, then undid the buttons on Novak's shirt, his belt, pants button and zipper. Taking his hand, Andy led Novak into her bedroom. For the next hour, their hands moved in synchrony, up and down each other's bodies.

Andy finally sat up. "Hey, Maestro," she said, looking down at Novak. "The orchestra has left the stage, and it's time to join the audience for the reception. They're serving Beringer, and I'd love another glass."

Novak sat up, stretching his arms over his head. "Before I put my hands around a glass," he said, "can I put them around you?" With Andy's breasts against his chest, they stayed in an embrace that added a perfect coda to their night music. Dressed and finished with the wine, Novak kissed Andy lightly at her doorway. "Tomorrow will be here very soon," he said, "and I have a feeling that we'll find a way to give many more tomorrows to someone whose yesterdays have been stolen from him."

Andy's thoughts, as she closed the door behind Novak, were that love is a word that doesn't need to be spoken. And that rules serve no purpose if they tolerate no exceptions. Otherwise, children might burn to death behind "No Trespassing" signs. Or a man might die if someone did not break a rule, listen to his story, and believe he told the truth.

30

Tomorrow became today: gray, mid-thirties, steady rain that plastered yesterday's swirling leaves to the sidewalks. Andy headed out for her walk to the Court in a blue parka with a hood to keep her hair from getting plastered to her head, a red knit scarf—a second-hand-shop gift from her grandma Bella—wrapped around her neck, and with thoughts about the rules she and Alex Novak had broken. Unwritten rules, but rules the justices and clerks knew they were expected to follow. It was true, as Dave had said, that every rule has exceptions. The law recognized this in the "necessity defense" for rule-breakers who acted to prevent serious harm to themselves or others. Even homicide laws had exceptions for self-defense and protection of others from deadly attacks. That principle might excuse, or at least mitigate, Andy's decision to sign Novak's name to a stay of execution for OD Beasley, and Novak's ex parte visit to hear OD's story and judge its truthfulness. Would it likewise excuse the physical intimacy—short of sex, but not for lack of desire—they had shared the night before?

Andy felt conflicted about what she had initiated with Novak. Gloria had encouraged—almost urged—Andy to give her husband what she could not. She felt obligated to tell Josh about what she'd done, but decided to wait until they could have some time together. That might come as soon as tonight, after Novak met with his clerks to look at the research they'd done on ways to get OD's case before the Court.

"Good morning, Andy," Angie greeted her. "Looks like we're in for our first taste of winter. Maybe even snow tomorrow, the weather people say. Even a couple of inches shuts Washington down. You'd think people in the suburbs would leave their cars home and take the Metro, but they slip and slide until the roads and bridges get totally jammed with fender benders. You know, Andy, if the government was in Buffalo, they wouldn't send everybody home when the first snowflake hits the ground."

"Or Chicago," Andy heard Novak say as he entered his chambers. Still unwinding the scarf around her neck, Andy turned and smiled as Novak, wearing a black pea jacket, pulled a black watch cap from his head. "Gloria insisted I wear this to ward off pneumonia," he explained. "But this is practically tropical, compared to winters in Chicago when I was a kid. Ten below, and the wind off the lake, but they hardly ever closed the schools." Novak gave Andy a smile that would melt an iceberg. "Ready to put your hands to work on the case you've been researching, Andy?"

She blushed, even though Angie could have no idea of the double entendre behind Novak's reference to their accompaniment of Mozart's little night music. "Let me warm my hands around a cup of coffee first, Alex, if you don't mind," she replied. "I saw Dave and Laura heading for the cafeteria on my way in, and I'll go fetch them while I'm there."

Dave and Laura were getting up to leave when Andy, having grabbed a cup of coffee, poked her head into the clerks' private room in the cafeteria. "Hey, guys," she said, "Alex wants us to figure out how to get OD Beasley off death row. And that will depend on the stuff you dug up about ways to get around the assholes on the Fourth Circuit. So, let's go back up and dazzle him with your mastery of rules that nobody has used since, well, since nobody remembers when."

"Hey, Andy," Dave said, "just because nobody has used a rule since nobody remembers when doesn't mean it can't be dusted off and put to good use. Besides, I like to dazzle people with my mastery of things anybody could have found in two minutes, if they bothered to look."

"Don't be so modest, Dave," Laura said, giving him a mock punch on his shoulder, "but you have to know what you're looking for and why you need it. And that's what you can do better than your average bear. And faster, too." He gave her an Aw Shucks grin as they headed back to Novak's chambers. Andy smiled, wondering how far this budding romance had progressed. Pretty far, she figured, maybe all the way to Let's Save On Rent And Live Together. If that hadn't happened yet, Andy thought, it probably wouldn't take long. The frog and the princess seemed like a perfect match. She had worked out her match with Josh, and the first sparks with Alex Novak might set that match ablaze. But that remained to be determined, and while it did, she would focus on the task at hand. Patience was a virtue, even if Andy wasn't the most virtuous Supreme Court clerk.

Andy made a quick detour into the clerks' office to grab the folder with the research that she had done with Dave and Laura, then joined them around the table in Novak's office. "Before we start," he said, "just a reminder, unnecessary I'm sure, that what happens in Vegas stays in Vegas, as they say. I trust you all, but we're skating on very thin ice, and we can't call for help if anyone falls through. Understood?" The clerks nodded agreement, and Novak gave them a reassuring nod back.

"Okay," he said. "Now, here's where we are." He looked at Dave and Laura. "Andy and I went down yesterday and visited with OD Beasley at the prison where he's on death row. He told me his story, and I believed him. He's obviously intellectually disabled, but he seemed to have a perfect recall of what happened the day of the murder, and what he did. The girl lured him into having sex with her, but OD ran out her back door when some other guy came through the front door. And we have almost incontrovertible evidence, from the detective work that Andy and her friend Josh did, that Judge Early's son was that guy, and killed her, probably in a sudden rage, when he realized what she'd done with a black man."

Novak paused, shaking his head. "So," he continued, "we have an innocent man on death row. But he's run out of appeals in the state courts, a federal judge denied his habeas petition, and the Fourth Circuit is sitting on his appeal from that denial. And OD's still alive only because of the stay of execution order that Andy signed for me, which we all know bent the rules a bit." He chuckled. "But this is Vegas, so we won't show our cards to anyone who might be tempted to call us on this hand."

Novak lifted his arms and spread them wide, in a gesture of supplication. "So, OD Beasley got dealt a really bad hand," he said. "Not even a pair of deuces." Dropping his arms, he looked at his clerks. "But I'm sure you guys have a bunch of aces in your deck. Who wants to deal this hand?"

Andy and Laura both looked at Dave, who picked up the folder on the table. He pulled out a sheet and cleared his throat. "Okay," he said, "here's the first card. As we know, Judge Jacobs denied the habeas petition that was based on a claim that OD was intellectually disabled, and he also ruled that Hall versus Florida could not be applied retroactively. And filing a second habeas petition with him, based on our 'newly discovered evidence' that OD is actually innocent of the murder, would probably get all tangled up in arguments by the state's lawyers that OD's trial lawyer could have discovered this evidence and presented it at his trial." Dave shook his head. "That's bullshit, of course, but those arguments would probably drag the case out for months, or even years."

Laura, sounding a bit impatient, chimed in. "But Dave has found a shortcut around the district judge. Show Alex your card, Dave."

"Well, I was just shuffling the deck, Laura," he said. "But here's the top card, if you can't wait." He glanced at the sheet in his hand. "Alex, are you familiar with the provision in the federal code about original writs of habeas corpus?"

"Like the back of my hand, Dave," he replied, then grinned. "Actually, no, I'm not. But I'll bet you are, and you're ready to deal it."

"Here it is," Dave said. "Title 28, United States Code, section 2241(a). It says, and I'm quoting, 'writs of habeas corpus may be granted by the Supreme Court, or any Justice thereof.'" He gave Novak a How About That? look. "If I'm not mistaken, Alex, you're a justice of the Supreme Court, and you can grant a habeas writ without waiting for the Fourth Circuit to get off its collective ass."

Novak lifted his eyebrows in surprise. "Well, I've been a justice for ten years, and I don't recall ever hearing about an original habeas writ. Maybe I wasn't paying attention in our boring conferences."

"Don't feel bad, Alex," Dave said. "That's because the Court has hardly ever issued one. The last one, I think, was more than ninety years ago, a little dusty now. But you clearly have the authority to grant one. It says so right here," he added, handing Novak the sheet.

Laura chimed in again. "Here's what you can do, Alex. If Josh Barfield files an original writ, claiming that 'newly discovered evidence' shows a reasonable probability that OD is actually innocent, you can order the district judge to hold a hearing on that claim, and give him a deadline. We looked at some other habeas cases from circuit courts, although not original writs, but several set deadlines of three or four months to begin a hearing." She gave Novak an expectant look. "What do you think, Alex?"

Novak looked at the sheet, paused a moment, and nodded. "Well, the statute looks clear to me, although it's funny that I never saw it before." He paused another moment, then spoke firmly. "Okay, let's do it, and see what happens. Nothing ventured, nothing gained, as they say."

"Alex, that's great," Andy said. "We've already got most of what we need, in terms of evidence and case law, in the stay application we drafted, and I'm sure Josh can get the writ filed in the Clerk's office in a couple of days, addressed to you as Circuit Justice."

Dave raised his hand, then quickly brought it down. "Sorry, Alex," he said, "I sort of feel like I'm back in school again. And I was one of those hand-waving kids that teachers loved and the other kids hated."

"Go ahead, Dave," Novak prompted. "You obviously can't wait show off your superior knowledge." He chuckled. "Just kidding, but you don't have to raise your hand, unless you urgently need a bathroom pass."

"Not quite yet, Alex," Dave said. "But since the Fourth Circuit is moving slower than DC traffic in a snowstorm, I found a way to plow the road to the Court. Do you know Rule Eleven, Alex?"

He laughed. "Like the back of my other hand, Dave, but refresh my memory."

"Okay," Dave said, "it's headed 'Certiorari Before Judgment,' and it allows the Court to grant cert in cases the courts of appeals haven't yet decided, like the Fourth in OD's request for a certificate of appealability. The rule references a statute that says cert can be granted 'any time before judgment.' Of course, it would take four votes to grant cert if we snatched the case from the Fourth."

Novak pondered a moment. "That shouldn't be a problem, Dave, if the cert petition is limited to the question of whether Hall versus Florida should be applied retroactively. Broader than that, I'm not sure, but four votes on that issue would be a cinch."

"Josh and I can draft a cert petition in just a couple of days," Andy volunteered. "I've read so many I could draft one in my sleep, which apparently some lawyers do. Josh could file it next week, and there's another conference, maybe two, before the Court's holiday break, for a vote."

"Not so fast, Andy," Dave cautioned. "Don't forget, the state will have thirty days to file a Brief in Opposition. That would be early January. And then there's merits briefs on both sides, another couple months. But that's plenty of time to put the case on the argument calendar for late March or early April, with a decision by the end of the term in June."

"Oops," she said. "I forgot those little details. But that would mean OD spends another six or seven months on death row. That sucks."

"Well, that's the rule," Dave said. "We're breaking some, but that's one we can't break."

"Dave, this is great stuff," Novak said. "But I've got one question. Andy will give Josh the go-ahead to file a cert petition on the Hall issue, using the cert before judgment rule. And Josh will also file an original habeas petition on the 'actual innocence' claim, which I could punt to the district court for a speedy hearing. But I'm not sure we could do both at the same time. Is there any rule or precedent on filing two separate petitions that ask for different relief? Believe me, I'm clueless about this."

Andy and Laura both looked at Dave, who took a moment to think. "Good question, Alex. Offhand, I can't think of a rule that allows that, but I also can't think of one that precludes it." He chuckled. "I'm reminded of the old maxim, way back to English common law, that says something like this: 'Anything that is not prohibited is therefore allowed.' In other words, since no rule says you can't do this, why not give it a shot? And it would take five of your colleagues to deny the petitions."

"Well, it's a bit premature to start counting votes," Novak said, "but you're right, Dave. Unless you overlooked a rule, which is about as likely as, say, me winning the Boston Marathon, we'll go ahead with our plan." He shook his head. "I can't believe you guys found this stuff. And it was sitting right under our noses, not that I would have thought to take a sniff." He shook his head again. "You know, we're so focused here on the cases that get argued, and that we have to decide, there's hardly any time to step back and look at the real world out there. I mean, it's all paper up here, except for an hour in the argued cases to harass the lawyers with questions that are usually aimed at our colleagues instead of them."

Novak stood up and started pacing around his office, which Andy took as a sign of inner turmoil. "If I hadn't gone down yesterday to hear OD's story," he continued, "I'd probably have rescinded the stay order that Andy signed. I had this assumption that juries and judges are the best ones to decide on guilt and punishment, and it's not our job—or *my* job, anyway—to second-guess people who've heard all the evidence on both sides. And I'd never seen an exception that required a reversal of their decisions."

He walked behind his desk and stared out the rain-streaked window, his shoulders slumped. Turning around after a long moment, he straightened and spoke with conviction. "I was wrong," he said. "I was very wrong. I was so wrong that it took you guys to drag me out of this goddamn marble temple and listen to a person that juries and judges had assumed *must* be guilty. A black man who brutally raped and murdered a white girl, leaving evidence behind. OD Beasley had no way in that courtroom to defend himself. Even his lawyer thought he was guilty, and didn't try very hard to convince the jurors to spare his life. And I would have let him die, if you guys had been the kind of clerks—and I've had too many—who don't argue with me, tell me I'm flat-out wrong, make me wonder who I really am, and question the assumptions that were drilled into me by people who never questioned *their* assumptions, and generations before them."

Andy knew that Novak's words were meant more for her than Dave and Laura, although her fellow clerks deserved most of the credit for showing Novak a path through the legal weeds and thorns that would deter most lawyers and judges. She had seen him angry—the oral argument at which he excoriated the Solicitor General and at which Sam Terman died—and shocked—the dinner at which Anton had disclosed that he was Jewish. But she hadn't seen him bare his thoughts and emotions in this revealing way. Novak's deep-rooted assumptions had been proven wrong in his visit with OD, and he was now confessing that to his clerks. Andy glanced at Dave and Laura, who both looked unsure how to react to this Hamlet-like soliloquy.

Novak handed the sheets back to Dave. "You know, Dave," he said, "this hour was like a really good law-school seminar, with you as the professor. Have you given any thought to teaching in a law school after you finish your clerkship?"

"Now that you mention it, Alex, that's crossed my mind," Dave replied. "I'm not sure practicing in a firm would suit me. Kowtowing to senior partners, competing with other associates for the Most Billable Hours award, all that bullshit. But I'm not sure any law school would hire a geek like me."

"Don't be so modest, Dave," Novak said. "I've got a friend at Berkeley who's retiring a year from now. He teaches civil procedure and federal litigation. And I know the dean, too. Not to be modest, but a word from me and they'd hire you in a second."

"That's very generous of you, Alex," Dave said. "And I'd love moving back to Berkeley, where I did my undergrad work."

"My dad told me that Berkeley has a great doctoral program in classics," Laura added, "and I'm not sure that practicing law suits me, either." She gave Andy and Novak a Guess What? look. "I guess it's time to let you guys know that Dave and I are, well, engaged to get engaged," she said. "We're going out to LA at Christmas to meet his parents. Dave says they hoped he'd find a nice Korean girl, but none of their friends have an eligible daughter, so they might settle for an Italian girl who could learn how to make kimchi."

Dave laughed. "If my mom gives you her secret kimchi recipe, Laura, you'll be Korean enough for her."

Andy smiled, having guessed correctly that Let's Share Rent had progressed to Let's Share Everything. "That's wonderful," she said. "And I've got some news, too. Since Alex said his friend at Berkeley won't retire for another year, Kathryn Ikeda told me that she'd love to have you both stay on and clerk for her next term, assuming she gets confirmed as Chief Justice, which is pretty much a done deal."

"Wow!" Dave and Laura blurted at the same time. "That would be fantastic," Dave said, giving Laura a high-five, then one with Andy.

Novak smiled at his clerks. "Well, that's more decisions than I can recall in just an hour of informing and entertaining discussion." He glanced at his watch. "I've got an appointment coming up, downtown, and might not be back today. Meanwhile, we have oral arguments next week, bench memos to finish, and cert petitions still keep pouring in. Plenty to keep you busy, but maybe more work on this case later, depending how it goes. But I'm really impressed with what you guys found. And congratulations to my engaged-to-be-engaged clerks. I'm sure, Laura, that you'll get that secret kimchi recipe." He took his pea jacket off the coat tree by the door, as the clerks headed back to their office.

"Oh, Andy, do you have a minute?" Novak asked, as she trailed Dave and Laura out the door. "I've got a present for you."

Oh, no, she thought, with a sudden flash of Novak handing her a gift-wrapped box with a pair of diamond earrings, or something equally expensive and excessive. Maybe last night lit too bright a flame, and she'd have to extinguish it before it spread into his chambers. She turned, ready to say, "Please, Alex, you shouldn't do this." But 'this' turned out to be something entirely different.

"Remember the first cert petition you recommended granting, Andy? The case of the young guy who got caught having sex with his girlfriend? She was only fifteen, I think, but he was eighteen and spent a couple years in prison for statutory rape, and then had to register as a sex offender."

"Of course I remember," Andy said, concealing her relief. "He was approved to live with his mom, but the town changed its zoning law to make it impossible for him to live there. He claimed it was a bill of attainder, aimed only at him."

"Right," Novak said. "I think you missed the oral arguments last week, but we voted five-three at conference to strike down the law, and I volunteered for the opinion." He smiled. "It's yours, if you want it, and I promise I won't change a word."

Andy gave him an impulsive hug. "Thank you, Alex. This is a better present than, oh, a pair of diamond earrings." She blushed at having blurted out that hidden thought, but Novak simply gave her a bemused smile.

"Oh, one more thing, Andy," Novak said. "My appointment is with Doctor Huang at GW Hospital, for the results of the pathology report on Anton's bladder. I'm taking him with me, and Gloria's friend Marjory is staying with her. I'll let you know the results tomorrow, but Anton said to tell you that he's planning to visit the Renoirs at the Phillips Collection with you and Gloria on Saturday. Can you do that, Andy? Whatever happens with his tests, Anton is determined to lead a normal life, as long as he can. And you really lift his spirits." Novak put a finger on Andy's lips. "Mine, too."

Andy took his hand and squeezed it gently. "Tell Anton and Gloria that Saturday is a date. And we can lift our spirits together, whenever you have time." She put a finger on his lips. "You're a good man, Alex. You've done a real mitzvah this morning, as Bella would say." She turned to leave his office. "And thanks for the present. I'll get started on the opinion right away. See you tomorrow. And give my best to Anton."

Back in the clerks' office, Andy started work on an opinion in the sex-offender case that Novak had given her as a "present." She dug out her original pool memo, printed the oral argument transcript from the Court's website, and made a quick trip to the Clerk's office for the briefs in the case. After reading through this material, making notes as she went along, she started drafting an outline for the opinion. Groups like the ACLU had filed amicus briefs that included historical data on bills of attainder, and cited studies that cast doubt on the state's argument that using zoning laws to keep sex offenders at a distance from schools, playgrounds, and other places children would frequent actually protected them from sexual predators. Most of the men convicted of sexual crimes against children, the studies showed, preyed upon their own kids or those of relatives and friends, mostly in their homes. Abductions from schools or playgrounds were rare, and zoning laws, from what Andy read, didn't seem to act as deterrents to that small group of offenders. Besides, the eighteen-year-old guy who had sex with his fifteen-year-old girlfriend on a living-room couch wasn't likely to lurk by schools and playgrounds looking for more victims. Even if he did, walking an extra thousand feet to a school, added to the zoning law by this small Iowa town to keep this guy from living with his mom, would take only a few minutes. And the case record was clear, given the petition that named this guy as a dangerous sexual predator, that the zoning law change was directed at him, with the intent of forcing him out of the town, which met the criteria of a classic bill of attainder. Andy put all this in her outline, adding the point that the zoning law wouldn't prevent a paroled murderer or drug dealer from living right next to a school.

Absorbed in this task, she was a bit startled by a tap on her shoulder. "I'm sorry to interrupt, Andy," Laura said. "Can you spare a minute, and grab a cup of coffee with me in the cafeteria?"

"Sure," Andy replied, stretching her arms. "I was just finishing an outline for an opinion that Alex gave me, and I think I got it nailed down. Time for a break, before I start writing."

Coffees in hand, they found a table in the clerks' dining room. "So, what's up, Laura?" Andy asked. "You sounded like it was a bit more important than a coffee break."

"Maybe," Laura said, "maybe not. Anyway, I hope you don't mind, but I took a look through the files on your desk on OD Beasley's case, and found something in the police reports that jumped out at me."

"I don't mind at all, Laura," Andy said. "There's always the chance of finding another needle in that haystack. So, tell me, what jumped out and said Boo?"

"Okay," Laura replied. "You remember the interviews the detective did with the guys that Laurel Davis's housemate said were frequent visitors and might have had sex with her? One was a guy named Tory Tucker, but his parents gave him a solid alibi for the day of the murder."

"Yeah, I remember his name," Andy said. "Don't tell me he did the murder and his parents covered for him. That would blow our case against Early Junior out of the water."

"No, but it turns out I know him," Laura said, "and he told me something I found hard to believe, but it may be a needle, and poke the real killer."

"Wow!" Andy exclaimed. "But first, how do you know Tory Tucker?"

"When I clerked for Judge Gianfortoni last year on the Third Circuit in Philly, Tory was one of her former clerks, and used to come by her chambers to visit with her. He's with a firm in Philly now, banks and insurance companies mostly. Nice guy, we even went out for drinks a few times. He's still single, and obviously had a crush on me, even though he's pushing forty. Anyway, one time a bunch of clerks got together for after-work drinks, and Tory came along, and we all had a few more beers than usual. And somebody asked if we'd ever played a game called 'The Worst Thing I Ever Did.' The players vote on who did the worst thing, and the winner doesn't have to pay for their drinks. You ever play that game, Andy?"

"Never heard of it," she said, "and I sure as hell wouldn't admit the worst thing I ever did, because there are so many of them. Especially recently. So don't even ask."

"Well, it takes a lot of beer to play," Laura said, "and I won't do it again, believe me. So, anyway . . ."

"Wait a second," Andy interrupted. "Aren't you going to tell me *your* worst thing? You told your mom you'd cleaned your room, but stuffed everything under your bed, right?"

"Since you asked so nicely, I'll tell you, but don't you dare tell Dave. Deal?"

"Deal," Andy agreed.

"Okay," Laura said. "When I was in high school, I stole my best friend's boyfriend and did some heavy make-out with him. Everything *but*, if you know what I mean. I was pissed off at Cassie because she beat me out by one-tenth of a GPA point for valedictorian, and that was my payback. Isn't that petty and stupid?"

Andy laughed. "Laura, if that's really the worst thing you ever did, you belong to a big club of girls who stole other girls' boyfriends. My school was full of them, and the boyfriends didn't seem to mind some extra make-out. So, what was Tory's worst thing?"

"Well, *his* worst thing—at least what he said—was cheating on two law-school exams at William & Mary. Corporations and Federal Taxation, I remember. But that's not all he said." Laura took a sip of coffee and leaned toward Andy. "Tory said he played that game one time in law school, with some guys who got really drunk, and one of them said the worst thing he'd ever done was killing a girl."

"What!" Andy blurted, turning heads a few tables away. She lowered her voice. "Don't tell me who it was. Or *do* tell me, I mean."

"Tory didn't tell us the guy's name," Laura said, "and the other guys at William & Mary all said you must be kidding. But he said he wasn't, that it was an accident, and he didn't mean to kill her. And he wouldn't say any more. But if this guy actually did kill a girl, *she* could have been Laurel Davis, and *he* could have been Early Junior. Of course, they were all drunk, and guys tend to make things up or exaggerate when they're drunk."

"Holy shit," Andy said. "That's something I can't imagine making up, just to top somebody else's 'worst thing' story." She paused a moment. "Laura, are you still in touch with Tory? Maybe he'd be willing to tell you the guy's name, if you explained that it was really important, and might save somebody's life."

"I haven't seen Tory since June, when he stopped by to see Judge Gianfortoni," Laura said, "but I'm going up there this weekend for a reunion of her clerks, since she just retired after twenty years on the court. I could call and make a date with him, since he doesn't know I'm engaged, although that probably wouldn't bother him. Tory still wants to get in my pants, since leopards don't change their spots, and a few beers might loosen him up. Plus, he's basically a decent guy, and might tell me who confessed to killing a girl, if I told him there's an innocent guy on death row for killing a girl from William & Mary."

"That would be great, Laura," Andy said. "You think maybe he'd be willing to sign an affidavit that names Early Junior, if it was him? I mean, it's probably hearsay, and might not be admissible at a habeas hearing, but it's worth a shot, don't you think?"

"Worth a shot," Laura agreed. "Maybe even worth taking off my pants." Andy's eyebrows shot up. "Just kidding, and don't you dare tell Dave I said that. Promise?"

"Stick a needle in my eye," Andy promised. "You know," she added, "if it *was* Early Junior, Tory must have known he was talking about Laurel, and never told anybody. If he's a decent guy, maybe his conscience is bothering him, and he'd be willing to get it off his chest. So, give it a shot. If it doesn't work out, we still have a really strong case against Junior."

"Okay," Laura said, as they got up and headed back to the clerks' office. "I'll let you know on Monday."

Andy spent the rest of the afternoon working on her opinion. At five-thirty, Dave and Laura invited Andy to join them for dinner at the apartment they now shared, having moved from their one-bedrooms into a more spacious place on the east side of Capitol Hill. Laura made a big pot of chicken cacciatore, Andy contributed two bottles of Italian red, and the evening ended with Dave's hilarious—and spot-on—impersonations of all nine justices, down to their quirky gestures and verbal inflections. Andy walked back to her place with a warm feeling to counter the first-taste-of-winter chill.

31

The weather people were right. December began in Washington with snow, earlier than usual. Just two inches overnight, not a traffic-halting and office-closing snowfall, but enough to slow down commuting and fill the streets with slush. Bundled again in her parka and scarf, Andy arrived at Novak's chambers just as Angie hung up the phone on her desk.

"Good morning, Andy," Angie said. "That was Alex, saying he won't be in until after lunch. He's taking his dad back to GW hospital for another test, an MRI on his bladder. He said the doctor should have the results right away, and he'd let us know when he gets here. But he didn't sound very positive, which is unlike Alex." Angie shook her head and sighed. "I know his dad is over ninety, Andy, and something like this, which Alex told me is cancer, well . . ." She trailed off, reaching for the box of tissues on her desk.

Andy tried to sound positive. "Angie, I've gotten to know Anton, and he's a survivor, if you know what I mean. So let's just wait until Alex gets here, and hope for the best." She didn't tell Angie what Anton had survived, but she'd never met anyone, even people decades younger, with his stamina and resolve. But even so, cancer at his age would be hard to endure for someone used to two-mile daily walks and visits to museums and galleries. And what would this do to Gloria, she worried, whose wheelchair Anton had pushed for hundreds of miles and who helped her with tasks she couldn't perform herself.

Angie opened her desk drawer and pulled out a black-beaded rosary. "Andy, I know you're Jewish," she said, "but let's both say a little prayer for Anton, since we both pray to the same God." This caring gesture moved Andy to tears, which she blotted with one of Angie's tissues.

The sight of the two tearful women stopped Dave and Laura, who'd just come into the office, laughing at something, in their tracks. "What's wrong," Laura asked, "did something happen to Alex?"

"No, no," Angie replied. "But Alex just called, with some bad news about his dad." She briefly explained what Novak had said about Anton, which was the first Dave and Laura had heard about his condition. That news cast a pall over the office, and the clerks spent their morning working quietly at their computers, Andy on her opinion in the bill of attainder case. Returning from a short lunch break in the cafeteria, she spotted Novak coming down the hallway, dressed again in his pea jacket and watch cap.

"Alex, what did the doctor say about Anton?" she asked, guessing from his expression that the news was not good.

"Let's talk in my office, Andy," he replied. "I'm just going to tell Angie and Dave and Laura that they're going to treat Anton with some medication, and that his prognosis is hopeful. I don't want to upset them, and Doctor Huang says things might actually go better than he expects. But you should know what he realistically expects, after the pathology report and the MRI this morning."

"They're still out for lunch," Andy said, "but Angie told Dave and Laura about your call, and they're all very concerned about Anton. And about you, Alex. And I'm concerned about Gloria, too."

Hanging his jacket and cap on the coat tree in his office, Novak motioned Andy to a chair around his low table, sat beside her, and took both her hands in his. "Andy, your kindness is amazing," he said. "And both Anton and Gloria have told me that, too." Releasing her hands, Novak took a sheet of paper from his shirt pocket. "I made some notes on what Doctor Huang told us this morning, but I'll just summarize it for you, okay?"

"Sure," Andy said. "But first, Alex, tell me how Anton is doing now."

"He's home with Gloria, and says that your visit to the Phillips Collection tomorrow is still on. In other words, he's just like always, looking ahead to the things he enjoys doing. Including his walk tomorrow morning." Novak shook his head. "My dad is a real inspiration to me, Andy. Anyway, here's what Doctor Huang said, from the pathology report and MRI." He glanced at the sheet. "Anton has what they call a Stage One tumor in his bladder, meaning it hasn't gone into the muscle layer of the bladder wall. They're going to treat it with something called BCG, which is a live bacillus that's inserted into the bladder. They do that every week for six weeks, then there's several follow-up treatments. Doctor Huang says it's effective in wiping out the tumors in about seventy percent of cases, although Anton's age cuts those odds. But he's hoping it works."

"I hope so, too," Andy said. "But if it doesn't?"

"That's the problem," Novak said, with a grim look. "If it progresses to Stage Two, where the tumor spreads into the muscle wall, and maybe into the surrounding tissue and lymph nodes, the only effective treatment is what they call a radical cystectomy. That means surgery to remove the bladder, and replacing it with part of the intestine, to allow urination. And they usually also remove the prostate."

"Is Anton prepared for that, Alex, if the first treatment doesn't work?"

Novak shook his head again. "Here's what he told Doctor Huang, Andy. 'You're not going to cut me open. I'm too old for that. So if the first treatment doesn't work, Doctor, I'll let my body decide when it wants to return to the earth from which we all came.' And I can't say I wouldn't make that choice myself, if it came to that."

"Well, what could they do for Anton, if he won't allow any surgery?"

"Just what they call palliative care, Andy, which is mostly pain medication. And Doctor Huang, who's very straight-forward, told us that if it progresses to Stage Two, Anton would just have six months left, maybe a year at most, if he decided against surgery."

"Oh, Alex, that would be so sad," Andy said, reaching again for Novak's hand.

He nodded agreement, then smiled. "Here's the last thing he said, Andy, before we left Doctor Huang's office. 'At my age, every day is a mitzvah. So let us enjoy the blessings of today, and let tomorrow decide if it will come.'"

Novak took a deep breath, squeezed Andy's hand, then smiled again. "So, Andy, my dad knew I'd see you this afternoon, and asked me to invite you to come with us tonight for Friday services at Temple Shalom. He said he'd get a better seat if he came with a pretty girl."

Andy couldn't hold back her smile. "Well, tell him I'll try to find one for him. But seriously, I'm terribly flattered and I'd be glad to go with you. Was this something he'd discussed with you before your visit with Doctor Huang?"

"No, I was actually surprised, Andy. But Anton said he wants to be a good Jew for the rest of his life. So, the service starts at six-thirty. Why don't we pick you up at six, at your place? Gloria's friend Marjory will stay with her."

"That's fine with me, Alex. And I assume you still have your yarmulke, and I'll bring some bobby pins to make sure it stays on your head."

The sound of voices from the outer office signaled the return of Andy's fellow clerks, along with Angie. As they stood up, Novak leaned close to Andy and whispered, "And I want to be a good Jew, as best I can, Andy, now that I know more about who I am. Can you help me do that?"

"I'm not the best person to ask," she whispered back. "But I'm sure that Anton can help both of us do that."

Andy worked on her opinion until five, then went home and changed into the black dress she'd worn to Sam Terman's service at Temple Shalom. Alex, wearing his black suit, rang her bell at six, and she went out to his car with him, stopping to secure his white yarmulke with bobby pins. "Andy, it's so good to see you," Anton said as she settled into the seat behind him, "and to have you with us for Erev Shabbat. And, of course, the Phillips tomorrow, with Gloria."

"Thank you for inviting me, Anton," Andy said. "It's been quite a while since I've been to Friday services, to be honest, although I'd go with Bella and my parents to High Holy Day services back home in Yonkers before I started law school."

"Dad," Novak said as he pulled into traffic, "you probably haven't been to synagogue since you left Warsaw, and that was seventy-five years ago. Do you still remember any of the service? Like what to say, or when to kneel?"

Anton laughed. "Alex, Jews don't kneel. That's for Catholics, although I did kneel, back in Chicago, when your mother would insist that I go with her to Mass at St. Agnes, once or twice a year, before she passed away." He paused for a long moment. "Alex, I have something to tell you, and I apologize for not telling you earlier." He paused for a short moment. "Before I married your mother and settled in Chicago, I would go to synagogue on my travels, if the town had one. And while we lived there, I belonged to a Friday-night poker group that met at the Polonia Club. Once in a while, I would skip the game and go to services at Temple Zion. Your mother never knew." He chuckled. "So, Alex, I have been a fairly observant Jew most of my life, although I have not been to synagogue since you and I moved to Washington. But, to answer your question, Alex, I do remember most of the prayers." He chuckled again. "Sometimes, during Mass at St. Agnes, while the Catholics were praying in Latin, I would recite the Shema prayers to myself in Hebrew. They may have been the same prayers, and I am sure that God does not care which language his people speak."

Pulling his car into the Temple's parking lot, Novak chuckled. "I do remember, Dad, that you would come home some nights from your poker game and tell Mom, 'Well, I won some hands and lost some, and broke even for the night." As they walked from the car to the Temple entrance, Anton reached into his jacket pocket and pulled out a blue yarmulke. "Andy," he asked, "if you have any of those pins, can you fasten it for me?" As he bent his head while she pinned it to his shock of white hair, Anton noticed the surprised expression on Novak's face. "Alex, I have kept this yarmulke in my dresser for years. Now I am glad to wear it again." He lifted his head and smiled. "Thank you, Andy. Now we are all properly attired for services."

In the vestibule, Anton picked up three prayer books from the table by the door, handing copies to Novak and Andy. Opening his, he said, "I see that this siddur has both Hebrew and English on facing pages, so you can follow along, Alex. And Andy, you can choose which language is best for you."

She smiled, as they found seats near the front of the sanctuary. "Anton, I'm very rusty, but I do remember most of the prayers in Hebrew," Andy said. Sitting between the two men, sharing the new-found bond that linked them to millennia of tradition, struggle, and survival, Andy realized that neither would be here tonight had Bella not spotted a photograph of a young man with a distinctive scar, and had Andy not recognized the old man with the same scar. And now the lives of the father and son, however long they lasted, had been irrevocably changed by these chance events. And hers as well, Andy thought as the congregation stood for the Aleinu, the benediction prayer of praise to the Creator of the universe.

As they turned to leave, Rabbi Margolis appeared, smiling broadly. "Alex," she exclaimed, "I shouldn't be surprised to see you here, although I am, since this is just our regular Erev Shabbat service. But I'm so glad to see you again. Have you finished the books I gave you when you came to chat with me?"

"Actually, I have," he replied. "The Buber was a little hard going, but very thought-provoking. And I apologize for not returning them sooner." He turned to Anton and Andy. "Rabbi Margolis, I'd like you to meet my father, Anton, and one of my clerks, Andy Roboff."

They shook hands, and she gave them appraising looks. "It's nice to meet you both, and welcome to our Temple. Alex has told me about both of you, and that you have both helped him to discover more about his heritage. It's quite a story, and I hope you don't mind that Alex shared it with me."

"Not at all, Rabbi," Anton replied in his courtly voice. "But it was Andy and her grandmother, Bella, who made that possible."

"Call me Lisa, please," she replied, "now that I'm off duty, so to speak. Andy, I recognize you from Sam Terman's service, sitting with his family. Barbara told me that you are related to Sam, back in the shtetl. And Anton, Alex has told me of your escape from the Warsaw ghetto, and your courageous fight against the Nazis. So you are both very special, and I hope to see you again at our Temple. Maybe not every shabbas, but whenever you can."

"Thank you for that invitation, Lisa," Andy said. "This was a very inspiring service, and I appreciated your words about the duty we, as Jews, owe to those in our society who are treated as outsiders and outcasts, as we have been for so long."

"I agree, Lisa," Novak added. "It's been a while since I heard a sermon that made me think about the people who don't share the comforts and advantages people like us, or at least people like me, take for granted."

The rabbi smiled. "You know, Alex, a big part of my job is to comfort the afflicted and afflict the comfortable. I forget who first said that, but most of us here are pretty comfortable, and a lot of people out there are afflicted with all kinds of problems we can help them with."

"Come to think of it, Lisa, that's what Sam used to say," Novak said. "And I guess that's a big part of our job at the Court, too." He smiled. "Although some people seem to think I haven't done such a good job of that. But I'm starting to explore the world outside the boxes I grew up in, thanks to Anton and Andy. And you, too, Lisa."

Rabbi Margolis smiled back. "Thank you for that, Alex. I'd be glad to point out some paths you might want to explore. You know, the whole world is right here in Washington, if you know where to look." She glanced at her watch. "I've got to meet with someone about a bar mitzvah, but I hope I'll see you all soon."

Novak dropped Andy back at her place. "I'd invite you over for a nightcap," he said, "but it's getting close to Gloria's bedtime, and it takes both of us to get her settled. And thanks again for coming with us, Andy. Why don't I pick you up at noon tomorrow for your visit to the Phillips."

"That's fine," she said. "And thanks for inviting me. I hope we'll all go back." As she prepared for a hot bath in her stretch-out tub, Andy reflected on this unexpected experience, and her unexpected role in bringing it about. Who could have predicted any of the long chain of events that culminated—at least for tonight—in this visit to a place she would not have visited on her own? And what next event would extend that chain? Hot water put these thoughts to bed, followed shortly by Andy.

The visit to the Phillips Collection on Saturday was enjoyable. After being dropped off by Novak at the museum, a block from Dupont Circle, Andy and Anton took turns pushing Gloria's wheelchair through the exhibits, stopping first to admire Renoir's "Luncheon of the Boating Party," with Anton pointing out the exact table in the painting at which he had sat, on a long-ago trip to France, for lunch at the Maison Fournaise on the Seine. Andy was amazed at his knowledge of art, sounding like an experienced docent as they viewed the works of Gaugin and Degas. He said nothing, and Andy did not ask, about the diagnosis that might end his life within a year. When Novak picked them up at four, Andy gave Anton a kiss on his cheek. "I learned more from you today," she said, "than I did in my class on French art in college. So, I will call you Professeur Novak when we visit more art."

"Merci, Andy," he replied. "I am flattered, but I have much to learn from you as well. Especially about the Italians. And more visits, of course."

After spending a rainy Sunday working on her bill of attainder opinion, Andy walked past the Court on Monday morning to the Hart Senate Building, for the confirmation hearing on Kathryn Ikeda's nomination as Chief Justice. Ever since President Chambers had surprised everyone outside the Court by naming her to replace Sam Terman, pundits on both the right and left had speculated about his motives. The consensus was that Chambers, having tried and failed, with Judge Early's abrupt withdrawal, to place a conservative in the center seat, had listened to his political advisors, well aware of the president's substantial gender gap in the polls and the very small number of minorities among his nominations to federal courts. Choosing Ikeda made political sense, the pundits agreed, despite its likely effect in maintaining liberal control of the Court. Conservatives grumbled, but none proposed mounting a major campaign or filibuster to block her confirmation.

The Judiciary Committee hearing room was again packed, and buzzing with chatter, but Andy found an empty seat three rows behind the table at which Ikeda sat, flanked by Washington's two senators, both Democrats and both women. As the committee members rustled papers and chatted with each other, Ikeda turned to scan the audience, spotting Andy and giving her a broad smile and a wink. She seemed perfectly composed and confident, turning back as Charter Weeks rapped his gavel and hushed the chatter. Without a mention of the debacle in that room, just three weeks earlier, Weeks welcomed Ikeda with a quip. "This is the first time in our history," he began, "that this committee has considered the nomination of the Chief Justice of one court to become the Chief Justice of our nation's highest court. So, it's sort of a lateral promotion, so to speak." The chuckles were sparse. "Before we begin with statements from Justice Ikeda's home-state senators," he continued, "I want to commend President Chambers for recognizing the equal role of our state courts in our federal judicial system. And for increasing the diversity of the Supreme Court. I might note that six of the justices on Justice Ikeda's court are women. The day might come when the fair sex has a majority on the Supreme Court, but three out of nine is a sign of progress." A few more chuckles, but more groans at this politically incorrect gaffe.

After the laudatory introductions by the Washington senators, Weeks turned to Senator Ted Tillman, the committee's ranking Republican. He surprised no one by asking a predictable question: "Justice Ikeda, can you assure this committee, and the senators who will vote on your confirmation, that you will follow the original intent of the Constitution's framers, and the text of that hallowed document, in your interpretations of its provisions?"

Ikeda's answer surprised everyone who expected the usual platitudinous agreement with this unspoken slap at "legislating from the bench," which no nominee—liberal or conservative—had ever endorsed, but that many—both liberal and conservative—had promptly done after securing their lifetime positions. "That's a fair question, Senator Tillman," she replied, "but my answer depends on which intentions, and what provisions, to which you refer." She smiled at Tillman, then glanced at a sheet before her. "Keep in mind, Senator," she continued, "that when the Constitution was ratified in 1788, there were only four million residents of the thirteen states along the east coast. There are now more than three hundred million in fifty states, spread across a vast continent and stretching halfway across the Pacific Ocean. In 1788, more than twenty percent of the entire population were slaves, with a majority of slaves in several southern states. It was the intent of the Constitution's framers, over the strenuous objections of some, to protect that infamous institution in three of its provisions. As you know, Senator, it took a bloody civil war to erase those provisions from the Constitution. On the eve of that war, Senator, almost half of your state's residents were slaves. If protecting slavery was the framers' intent to which you refer, I'm sure you and I agree, Senator Tillman, that it should not have taken a civil war to repair their disregard of our common humanity."

Sitting behind Ikeda, Andy could see the shocked expression on Tillman's florid face. Before he could even sputter, Ikeda continued. "It was also the framers' intent, Senator, to restrict the ballot to the minority of white males, with some states requiring property ownership to vote. Consequently, only one out of four adults could cast ballots for their elected officials. That was the framers' intent, Senator, and it took constitutional amendments to give voting rights to African Americans and women. We can mark those amendments as progress, Senator Tillman, or look back and see how the prejudices of the framers have yielded, grudgingly and belatedly in my opinion, to the justified grievances and demands of those excluded groups."

My God, Andy thought, she's breaking the mold, and giving the senators a lesson in plain-spoken honesty. But Ikeda was not done with Tillman. "Senator," she said, "since you asked about my approach to constitutional interpretation, may I refer you to a passage in a Supreme Court opinion that I take as my touchstone?" She looked directly at Tillman, then at the sheet before her. "It says, and I'm quoting, that our Constitution was 'intended to endure for ages to come, and, consequently, to be adapted to the various crises of human affairs. To have prescribed the means by which government should, in all future time, execute its power, would have been to change, entirely, the character of the instrument, and give it the properties of a legal code. It would have been an unwise attempt to provide, by immutable rules, for exigencies which, if foreseen at all, must have been seen dimly, and which can be best provided for as they occur.'"

Ikeda looked up, smiling at Tillman. "I've been reading, Senator, from an opinion by perhaps the greatest Chief Justice who ever headed the Supreme Court, John Marshall, and whose words, written in 1819, seem to me still relevant to the 'various crises' our society has encountered since that time, and to which the Supreme Court must respond in its decisions." She smiled again. "I can't help but wonder, Senator Tillman, if John Marshall were sitting here today, instead of me, facing your committee, whether you would consider his answer to your question satisfactory. That's for you to decide, of course, but it satisfies me." She paused for a moment. "Senator Tillman, I apologize for my lengthy response to your question, but I'd be glad to answer any more you have. And I won't quote John Marshall again. I'll speak in my own words." Laughter, both from the spectators and on the bench, swept through the hearing room.

Even Tillman joined, conceding Ikeda's besting of an experienced politician. "Justice Ikeda," he said, "I think you have already answered any more questions I might have posed. Or John Marshall answered them. And I thank you for that history lesson. I hope there won't be an exam at the end of this hearing." The next round of laughter sent a message to the other Republican senators: Ikeda's confirmation was now assured. Tillman's junior colleagues were unlikely to abandon the ranking member and rebuke the president who nominated her. Tillman turned to Weeks. "Mr. Chairman," he said, "I yield the remainder of my time. And the next round of questions, too."

Andy stayed for the rest of the morning session, bored by a succession of softball questions from both Democrats and Republicans. Ikeda handled them with aplomb, some with humor and others with serious discourse. Only one senator broke ranks with his colleagues. Roland

Crespo of Montana, a Tea Party favorite, had squeaked into the Senate after the Democratic incumbent was caught in the wrong bed, two weeks before the election. A sheep rancher and the committee's only non-lawyer, Crespo won the nickname of "Roly-Poly Rollie" for his girth, and he seemed immune to mirth.

"Justice Ikeda," he began, "I noticed from your biography that you are a Buddhist. Would that prevent you from supporting any use of force, including military force at the president's direction and with the authorization of Congress, should a case raising this issue come before the Court?"

Before Ikeda could answer, Charter Weeks swiveled toward Crespo. "Hold on, Senator," he said firmly. "I'm going to rule that question out of order. It's inappropriate and, you may not know, also unconstitutional." Weeks picked up a pocket-size Constitution from the bench and flipped through it. "Article Six of the Constitution you have sworn to uphold, Senator, provides, and I quote, 'no religious test shall ever be required as a qualification to any office of public trust under the United States.'" He turned to Ikeda. "I apologize for the committee, Justice Ikeda, for a question that has no place in this hearing."

"If you don't object, Mister Chairman, I'd be glad to answer Senator Crespo's question," she replied. "You noted that he had sworn an oath to protect and defend the Constitution. I have also sworn that oath in my current position, and hope to swear it again. And, in reply to the question, I never have, and never will, allow my personal religious beliefs to affect my decisions as a judge. I'm sure that's true of your votes on legislation as a Senator." Ikeda changed her tone. "By the way, Senator Crespo, I learned a while ago that Buddhists are the largest religious group in Montana, after Christians. There are a dozen temples in your state, and they'd be glad to welcome you to their services. Or, if it's more convenient, I'd be glad to accompany you to a Buddhist service in the DC area. I'll help you with the lotus position, although that's optional at our services." The laughter that ensued turned Crespo's face a bright red, and rendered him speechless.

Weeks ended Crespo's embarrassment. "May I take it, Senator, that you yield the remainder of your time?" He got a nod in response. More softball questions completed the morning session, gaveled to a close by Weeks. "The committee will reconvene after a one-hour recess. Thank you, Justice Ikeda."

Walking back to the Court, Andy took a slight detour at the entrance into its Great Hall, pausing—as many tourists did—to touch the outstretched hand of John Marshall, whose larger-than-life statue was seated in the Court he led for thirty-four years and shaped into an institution that dealt with many crises in America's later history. Its future history might well be changed by a new Chief Justice who took Marshall for her touchstone. Heading for Novak's chambers, Andy reflected on her small role in this chain of events. But it was the small roles of many people from whom she drew inspiration—Mother Jones, Linda Brown, Rosa Parks, Fred Korematsu—that had changed the arc of history. Andy gave Marshall a smile and wink as she left the Great Hall.

32

"*Got it!*"

Laura jumped up from her desk as Andy returned from the Great Hall to the clerks' office, waving a sheaf of papers and grinning broadly. "An affidavit from Tory Tucker, signed, sealed, and notarized." She handed it to Andy, who quickly scanned the three pages, then gave Laura a high-five.

Dave wasn't at his desk, so Andy gave Laura a Just Between Us Girls look. "This is fantastic, Laura," she exclaimed. "I hope you didn't have to take your pants off to get it."

Laura laughed. "No, although Tory did cop a feel on my butt when I gave him a hug. Twice, actually. But that's a small price to pay for nailing Junior's confession to killing a girl when they played the 'Worst Thing I Ever Did' game. It had to be Laurel, although Tory said Junior didn't mention her name. None of the other guys knew he'd been involved with Laurel, and they all thought he was joking, just trying to get a few free beers. But Tory said that after the game, he walked back to campus with Junior, before they split up to go to their apartments, and asked him if he'd been serious, or just joking around. 'Dead serious' is what Junior said, 'but any word about this, Tory, and you're dead, too, just like that nigger-loving slut, who deserved what she got. I couldn't ever screw her after that. You wouldn't, would you? Listen, bud, I shouldn't have opened my fucking mouth, and you better not open yours.' That's all in the affidavit."

Laura shook her head. "Tory said he knew Junior had a violent temper, he'd once seen him sucker-punch a guy at a party who spilled a little beer on him, and he was genuinely afraid of Junior."

"So, how'd you get Tory to open up?"

"Well, I called him before I went up to Philly," Laura answered, "asked if he'd like to go out for drinks after Judge Gianfortoni's retirement party, and said I had something important to ask him. So, we had a couple beers, a bit of catch-up chat, and then I handed him Josh's memo on the DNA tests. 'Does that ring any bells, Tory?' I asked him. He read it, then burst into tears. Surprised the hell out of me. And then I explained why it was so important, that he could help get OD Beasley off death row and out of prison, and would he sign an affidavit of what he told me. So we went over to his office, he wrote it out on his computer, and had his office manager notarize it. I asked him if he was still afraid of Junior, and he said that if he ever saw him again, he'd sucker-punch him for what he did to Laurel and OD. And he asked me to apologize to OD for him. Oh, he also said he'd be glad to testify at a habeas hearing or trial, if we needed him."

"My God," Andy exclaimed. "Imagine carrying that around for fifteen years." She chuckled. "I'd let him cop all the feels he wanted to get that."

"What's this about copping feels, ladies?" Dave had just walked into the office.

"Oh, nothing, Dave," Laura replied. "Just reminiscing about high-school days, and boys who thought girls enjoyed getting pawed at parties and movies. But I'm sure you never did that, dear."

Dave laughed. "Thought about it a lot, but never got up the nerve." He noticed the papers Andy was holding. "Did you get a cert petition in a sexual harassment case, where the guy copped too many feels and claims he was a victim of old male cultural habits and new feminist political correctness?"

"No," Andy replied, handing the affidavit to Dave. "But Laura brought this back from Philly, and I'm giving it to Josh for the original habeas petition he's drafting for Alex to sign."

Dave read it carefully, then smiled at Laura. "I won't ask how you got this, dear, but if it involved letting this guy cop some feels, you are forgiven. Since I get a lot more than that now, and I'm not the jealous type."

"Okay, okay, you two," Andy chided. "Enough of the suggestive banter, before Angie comes in and reminds us we're not in a locker room, but the chambers of a Supreme Court justice. She's got very good hearing, you know."

"Yes, she does," came an amused voice from the outer office. "But I'm not too old to remember high school. And I guess boys haven't changed much since then."

The clerks all laughed, then went to work on tasks more appropriate for the chambers of a Supreme Court justice.

Andy took the Metro over to Josh's place at seven, bringing Tory's affidavit and a bag of Indian take-out. Josh was working on his laptop at the dining-room table, and cleared the folders spread around him to make space for the cartons of rice and chicken curry. He read the affidavit while Andy brought back bowls and a bottle of Carlo's pinot grigio from the kitchen.

"Holy shit," Josh exclaimed as Andy filled the bowls and glasses. "You told me Laura would try to get an affidavit from this guy, but I didn't expect more than Junior saying he'd killed a girl, without any clue about who it might have been. And being drunk when he said it. That probably wouldn't impress a judge who already denied one habeas petition for OD." Josh tapped on a page of the affidavit. "But this part about the nigger-loving slut who got what she deserved. That's a pretty clear reference to Laurel. Not exactly a confession, but close enough that Judge Jacobs couldn't just dismiss it. This is great, Andy."

"So, you'll attach it to the original habeas petition for Alex to sign, right?"

Josh thought for a moment, while he ate some curry and sipped some wine. "You know, I'm not sure about that, Andy," he said. "I'll ask Jim Carruthers, but I'm thinking we already have enough evidence to convince Jacobs to order a new trial for OD, without naming the 'other dude who did it.' Maybe we should keep Tory's affidavit in reserve, in case Jacobs seems reluctant to order a new trial. 'Cause if we do name Early Junior as the guilty dude, he just might retaliate against Tory, or even OD. He's obviously got a violent streak, and gave Tory a death threat if he ratted him out. I'd rather not take that risk. And there'd certainly be a media shit-storm if the affidavit became a public record. I'd rather have Jim make that decision, to be honest."

"Okay," Andy agreed. "So, how are you doing with the cert and habeas petitions?"

"Getting there," Josh replied. "I should have them both ready to file by Friday, which is, what? December eighth, right?"

"Right," Andy said. She pulled out her phone and punched up a calendar. "Let's see, that would make the state's reply to the cert petition due on January eighth, and then a pool memo by whichever justice it gets assigned to, and probably a vote at the Court's conference on the nineteenth, or maybe the twenty-sixth. Which leaves plenty of time for briefs and argument this term."

"But what if the cert petition gets assigned to one of the conservative justices?" Josh asked. "I mean, they're assigned randomly, and no guarantee it would go to Alex or one of the liberals. So, a conservative could drag his feet on the pool memo, keeping it off this term's docket."

Andy nodded. "Good point, Josh. Let's just see what happens, and deal with that after we know who gets it. More indeterminacy, though."

"Always," he said with a grin. "And, since Carlo's on an overnight shift at the hospital, how can we determine what will happen after we finish the curry and wine, and maybe a bowl of Lemon Haze?"

Andy laughed. "Finishing the curry and wine is fine, to make a rhyme, but then it's time for me to, um, decline." Josh gave her a faux frown. "Actually," she said, "I'm having my monthly, to use an archaic term, but you can cop a feel or two before I go home to recline."

Josh laughed even harder. "Okay, I won't whine, but next time is mine, which would be fine." An hour later, Andy replaced her bra, buttoned her shirt, kissed Josh goodnight, and headed for the Metro. On her way home, she realized that she hadn't told Josh about her interlude with Alex Novak, which she'd intended to do. Oh, well, that might not happen again, she thought, so maybe it's not something she needed to get off her chest. Although she enjoyed the enjoyment Novak and Josh both got from her chest. Angie was right, she concluded. Boys haven't changed much since her high school days, but girls haven't either. There weren't as many "good girls" as there used to be, and probably never were, at least since Queen Victoria died, and cars became mobile bedrooms.

Andy busied herself during the rest of the week—the last before the Court's month-long winter break—with the final touches on her opinion for Novak in the bill of attainder case, and bench memos for the argument sessions that would begin on January 8. Down the street from the Court, the Senate Judiciary Committee, after two days of hearings on Kathryn Ikeda's nomination as Chief Justice, recommended her confirmation to the full Senate by a vote of fourteen to one, with "Roly-Poly Rollie" Crespo the only dissenter. On December 8, the last day before the Senate's winter recess, the full body approved her confirmation by a vote of ninety to eight, with only the hardest of the hard-line Tea Party stalwarts in dissent. But they limited their opposition to brief written statements, warning against "judicial activism" and "legislating from the bench," submitted for the Congressional Record that hardly anyone read. Like all their colleagues, the Tea Partiers were more eager to leave the Beltway for their home states than to make futile speeches to an empty chamber.

Josh filed both the "Petition for Writ of Certiorari Before Judgment" and an "Application for Original Writ of Habeas Corpus" in the Supreme Court Clerk's office on Friday, with Jim Carruthers listed as counsel of record on both. He and Andy had spent two evenings that week polishing them, although both were what Josh called "just enough to get the job done," since Novak had assured Andy that getting at least four votes to grant the cert petition was "in the bag," as he put it. Josh had done some research and found studies, which he cited in the petition, estimating that between two and three hundred of the three thousand inmates currently on death rows across the country would qualify for new sentencing hearings under the *Hall v. Florida* standard for intellectual disability.

The habeas petition incorporated the evidence in the stay of execution application that Andy had signed for Novak in OD's case. Jim Carruthers had agreed with Josh to request that Judge Jacobs keep Tory Tucker's affidavit under seal and out of the public record, to avoid any media attention and—more importantly—any possible retaliation by Early Junior. Along with the petition, Josh had drafted a brief order that Novak signed, directing Judge Jacobs "to commence a hearing on this writ within 90 days of its issuance," setting a deadline of March 8.

To celebrate the culmination of all this work on OD's case, Andy organized a dinner party that night for the "OD Team" of the three clerks and Josh, at the historic and iconic Old Ebbitt Grill, a fixture in DC since 1856 at various locations, now across the street from the Treasury Department and a block from the White House. Josh had not yet met Dave and Laura, and their Getting To Know You stories and banter lasted through the Maryland crab cakes, New York strip, and Atlantic salmon they all shared, along with Beringer chardonnay and Kendall-Jackson cabernet. Before they left, Andy raised her glass of Beringer and said, with a serious tone, "Let me propose a toast. To a person who could not be here tonight, but who will hopefully be home with his momma before too long, since it's been far too long already. To OD Beasley."

A tear slid down Andy's cheek as the four young lawyers clinked glasses. They had all broken rules to get here tonight, she thought, as they sipped wine and remained silent for a long moment. But without breaking rules, an innocent man would likely be dead by now, his body poisoned by a system whose rules were made by men long since dead themselves, and administered now by men—some in black robes, others in state-issued uniforms—for whom unquestioned rules shaped and guided their separate roles in that system.

Andy's private reverie ended with Dave's voice. "Hey, guys, it's time for Final Jeopardy! The category is Big Game Hunters, and the clue is, 'This occupant of a nearby house shot the animals whose heads are mounted over the bar in the Old Ebbitt Grill.' You have thirty seconds to make your answers, contestants." Dave hummed the Final Jeopardy! theme music, while Andy glanced over at the bar, above which were the heads of a ten-point buck and a prong-horned antelope. But she didn't have a clue. She looked at Laura, who shook her head. Josh, however, could barely contain himself. "Andy? Laura?" Dave asked, getting Beats Me looks from both. "Okay, Josh thinks he knows."

"'Nearby house' gave it away, Dave," Josh said with a grin. "Too easy. Teddy Roosevelt."

"We have a new champion," Dave said in a perfect Alex Trebek imitation, "whose cash winnings total . . ." Dave picked up the check on the table and grinned. ". . . one hundred seventy-two dollars."

Josh took the check from Dave's hand and pulled an AmEx card from his wallet. "What better to spend it on," he said, "than dinner with friends, old and new."

On that note, the serious work that prompted this dinner ended with a release of the tension the four young lawyers had shared as they plotted ways around the rules of a rule-bound system. The banter and levity they also shared, Andy reflected as they parted, sharing hugs, was a necessary antidote to that tension. Her week ended with a hot bath and the words in her mind of the refrain to an old prison song she'd once heard at a folk festival, by a black group from Mississippi: "Ain't no chains can drag my spirit down, ain't no bars can hold my soul inside."

Everything and everyone in Washington slows down in December. With Congress and the Court in recess, Capitol Hill has none of its usual bustle. Lobbyists and lawyers have no lawmakers to button-hole or cases to argue, leaving the corridors and chambers of power almost deserted. Those who staff these offices tend to arrive late and leave early, and many use their vacation days to visit Caribbean beaches or Colorado ski resorts. Andy spent a "Hanukkamas" week with her parents and Bella in Yonkers, with excursions to Broadway shows and museums in Manhattan. Josh spent a week with his parents in Idaho, zipping along forest trails with his dad on snowmobiles. Dave and Laura spent a week with his parents in Los Angeles, during which Dave's mom gave Laura her secret kimchi recipe as an engagement present. With the filing of the cert and habeas petitions in OD Beasley's case, the OD team could only wait until Virginia's attorney general filed his reply to the cert petition and Judge Jacobs set a date for a habeas hearing.

The Court held its first session of the New Year on Monday, January 8. For the first time in three months, the center seat was occupied, and for the first time in the Court's history, by a woman. Chief Justice Kathryn Ikeda smiled broadly as she took her seat and called the first case for argument. Andy, seated in the clerks' section, had made a Loser Buys Lunch bet with Dave that the lead-off lawyer would begin with "Madam Chief Justice, and may it please the Court." She won the bet, as chuckles filled the chamber at Ikeda's reply, delivered with a smile: "Counsel, a word that conjures up bordellos isn't necessary. 'Chief Justice' will please the Court just fine."

Although the case being argued was hardly earth-shaking, involving a circuit split over standards for Social Security disability benefits, Andy was impressed by Ikeda's even-handed and incisive questioning of both lawyers. At one point, after the respondent's lawyer gave a long-winded and evasive answer to one of Ikeda's questions, she smiled down at him. "Help me out, counsel," she said. "Should I take that as a 'Yes' or a 'No'? Or would you like me to rephrase my question and give you those options?" Andy was sure that lawyers with cases later on the Court's docket would get Ikeda's message: Don't waste your thirty minutes with equivocation. The lawyer who suffered this gentle rebuke got the message. "I'm sorry, Chief Justice," he replied. "My answer should have been 'Yes.'" Her response eased his discomfort and produced another round of chuckles: "See, that wasn't so hard, was it, counsel?" Ikeda was off to a good start in the center seat, Andy thought, with a no-nonsense approach behind her warm smile.

Stopping by the Clerk's office after the second argument, during which both lawyers took pains to give direct answers to all the questions, Andy checked to see if Virginia's attorney general had filed his reply to the cert petition, which was due that day. It had just come in, the young man who handled documents told her, and a little mild flirting allowed Andy to learn that OD's case would go to Justice Alice Schroeder for one of her clerks to prepare a pool memo. That was good news, since Dave knew all the clerks and would make sure the case would get Express Lane treatment. A little more eyelash-batting got her one of the forty copies that would later be distributed to all the justices.

Heading to Novak's chambers, Andy glanced at the reply and was shocked to read the caption: "Brief in Opposition to Petition for Certiorari and Motion for Recusal." Oh shit, she thought. Bill Samuels of the Virginia AG's office had ignored Novak's warning not to divulge his ex parte visit with OD at the Sussex prison. Even worse, once the reply was docketed, the recusal motion would become a public record. Most Supreme Court reporters, including Bob Barnes of the *Post*, regularly checked the docket—posted on the Court's website—looking for newly-filed cases that might warrant some coverage. And Barnes already knew about OD's case from Andy. He would hardly pass up this story. Even if he did, some other reporter would certainly jump on it.

Angie was away from her desk, and Novak's office was empty when Andy entered the clerks' office. Dave and Laura both swiveled around from their desks when she loudly exclaimed, "*Shit!*"

"What's wrong, Andy?" Dave asked. "Don't tell me Chief Justice Ikeda collapsed on the bench." Her expression quickly told Dave that whatever was wrong was no laughing matter.

"Here, take a look," Andy replied, handing Dave the reply, as Laura scooted her chair over to share a look. They both glanced at the cover, then Dave flipped the pages to the end. He and Laura both knew of Novak's visit to the prison, and of the warning he gave Samuels to pass on to his boss.

"The recusal motion requests that Alex take no participation in OD's case," Dave said, after skimming the last few pages, "and attaches an affidavit by Samuels that recounts Alex's visit with OD. Fortunately, it doesn't include Alex's warning to Samuels that the AG should drop his opposition to OD's petition."

"Is there any way we can head this off?" Laura asked. "Like, I don't know, keeping it off the docket somehow?"

"Too late for that," Andy replied. "It's already been given a docket number, and by tomorrow morning, anybody can read it on the Court's website. The Court's new digital technology just bit us on the ass." She shook her head. "Any ideas, guys? I don't know where Alex is, but I'll bet he gets a call from Bob Barnes, first thing in the morning."

"Actually, I do have an idea," Dave said. "Alex has every right to ignore the recusal motion. It's entirely voluntary for Supreme Court justices, and nobody can force them to recuse themselves, even a majority of their colleagues. So, my advice to Alex would be to say 'No comment' and just hunker down." Dave chuckled. "Of course, Alex isn't exactly the 'hunker down' type."

Just then, Novak stuck his head in the clerks' office, scanned their faces, and said, "I just heard that I'm not the 'hunker down' type, guys. Hunker down from what, if I may ask?"

"From this, Alex," Dave replied, handing him the reply to OD's cert petition. "This just came in, and the Virginia AG has moved that you recuse yourself because of your ex parte visit with OD at the prison. It's got an affidavit by that Samuels jerk about running into you there, and your admitting that you'd talked with OD. And Bob Barnes or some other reporter is bound to see it, and discover your incognito deal with the warden. Andy told us about that."

"So you think, I presume, that I should hunker down and ignore this," Novak said. "But, as you said, Dave, I'm not the 'hunker down' type." He noticed the concerned looks from the clerks. "Tell you what, guys. Let's go in my office and figure out whether hunkering down is the best response, or whether I should go down to Richmond and deck the jerk, which I should have done when he started bad-mouthing the death-row inmates for complaining about the conditions in solitary confinement."

The clerks still looked concerned. "Come on, guys, don't worry about me," Novak said. "Remember, I've got lifetime tenure, as long as I keep up my 'good behavior.' That's all the Constitution requires, as you know. And who's to say what's 'good' and what's not? I don't think listening to OD Beasley was 'bad behavior,' but I'll let others make their own judgments."

On the way into Novak's office, he stopped at Angie's desk, to which she'd returned from lunch. "Angie, could you call the Chief's office and see if she could come down here for a brief confab?" He handed her the state's reply, flipping to the recusal motion and Samuels' affidavit. "And can you make five copies of these pages?"

With the clerks seated around Novak's table, he explained his call to Ikeda. "The last thing I want for Kathryn's first week as Chief, guys, is for her to get blind-sided by this when she picks up Wednesday's Post. So I'll level with her about the reason for my visit with OD Beasley. And if she decides I'm guilty of 'bad behavior' for doing that, I'll recuse myself in his case." Then he smiled. "Of course, unless I'm mistaken, we'll still have at least four votes to grant cert, and I can visit the Zoo during the arguments. I haven't seen the baby pandas yet."

Angie came in with the copies, handing them around. The clerks read them over again, shaking their heads at the recusal motion's final sentence: "The ex parte visit by Justice Novak to petitioner in this case showed a blatant disregard of judicial rules and ethical standards, requiring not only his disqualification from all further proceedings in this case, but formal censure by the Court."

Two minutes later, Kathryn Ikeda entered Novak's office. "Sorry to keep you folks waiting," she said, "but I was just wrapping up an interview with Bob Barnes of the Post, who's doing a story on my transition from one Supreme Court to another, and my first day on the bench." She took the final seat around the table, and smiled broadly. "I told him the biggest difference was that my new chair is too low, and makes me look like a midget." Novak and the clerks all laughed. "So, it's great to see you again, Andy, and congratulations to you, Dave and Laura. Alex told me of your engagement, and I offered to officiate at your wedding, if you haven't already made other plans." She chuckled. "I've already married a pair of my clerks, Ann and Judy, at the top of the Space Needle, although I have a fear of heights, so I wouldn't suggest the top of the Washington Monument for yours."

"That would be great, Kathryn," Laura replied. "Dave and I were going to ask you, but I'm not big on heights, either, so we'll find a more earth-bound site."

"Maybe around the statue of John Marshall in the Great Hall," Dave suggested. "He really sealed the deal on your confirmation, the pundits all agreed."

Another round of chuckles, then Ikeda turned serious. "So, Alex, I'm guessing you had something more on your mind than wedding plans. You all looked a bit serious when I walked in. Anything I can help you with, my first day on the job?"

Novak handed her a copy of the recusal motion and affidavit by Samuels. "I'm not sure how serious this is, Kathryn, but I thought you should have a heads-up before Bob Barnes gets ahold of it. And maybe I should give you some background, okay?" For the next twenty minutes, Novak laid out the basic facts of OD Beasley's case, his clerks' involvement in it, the stay order—leaving out Andy's signing his name to it—that blocked OD's execution, his prison visit with OD, his conviction that OD was innocent, and his encouragement of Josh Barfield to file the cert and habeas petitions.

"So, Kathryn, that's it," he concluded. "I got involved in this case to save the life of a man who I'm absolutely certain is innocent, and would have been executed if I hadn't broken a bunch of rules to stop it. And I'm more than willing to recuse myself, to spare you and the Court any embarrassment. And to answer any questions you have."

Ikeda had sat through Novak's presentation without interrupting, just nodding her head as he made each point. She nodded again as he concluded. "Thank you for that, Alex," she said, then smiled. "I almost said, 'Thank you, counsel, the case is submitted,' because that was a very persuasive argument." She paused for a moment. "But I hope you don't mind a few questions."

Novak smiled back. "After the arguments this morning, Kathryn, I'll try to give you 'Yes' or 'No' answers. I don't want to waste my thirty minutes."

"From what I've heard, Alex," she replied, "Sam Terman let the lawyers and your colleagues go on until they ran out of breath. Nothing wrong with that, of course, but that's not my style. Different strokes, as they say. Anyway, here's one question." She opened her copy of the recusal motion and tapped a page. "This motion, as I understand, relates to the petition for cert before judgment. Am I right?"

"Yes, Your Honor," Novak answered, then smiled. "How was that?"

"Excellent," Ikeda said. "Now, if I understand correctly, from what you said about your visit with Mister Beasley, your talk with him was limited to the question of his innocence of the murder for which he was convicted, which is the issue raised in the original habeas petition that you issued. Your talk didn't deal with the issue in the cert petition, the retroactivity of the Hall versus Florida case. Am I correct?"

"Yes, again, Your Honor." The clerks were all smiling at this exchange.

"Thank you, counsel," Ikeda said, obviously enjoying herself. "One last question, if I may. I looked over the recusal motion while you were speaking, although I paid attention to what you said. That motion cites as authority a section of the United States Code, Title 28, Section 455. Do you see that on your copy, counsel?" Novak nodded agreement. "The pertinent part of that section reads, and I'm quoting, that 'Any Justice of the United States shall disqualify himself in any proceeding in which he has personal knowledge of disputed evidentiary facts concerning the proceeding." She looked up at Novak. "Here's my question, counsel. Did, or did not, your talk with Mister Beasley give you personal knowledge of any disputed facts relating to the issue raised in the cert petition, concerning the retroactivity of Hall versus Florida?"

Novak and the clerks immediately got the point of Ikeda's question. "It did not, Your Honor," he replied.

"Well," Ikeda said, "that answers my question, counsel. The case is submitted." She gave a smile of satisfaction. "In my opinion, Alex, there's no need to recuse yourself in this case." She paused a moment. "I'm not sure I would have done what you did, Alex, but I learned in my tenure on the Washington supreme court not to question the actions of my colleagues, or their motivations. Some of them, I know, occasionally went outside the record of a case and did some research of their own."

Ikeda glanced at her watch. "Well, this has been fun, but I've got a lunch date with a couple of my former clerks, who are now practicing here in DC. Oh, and I'll check to see if it's okay to hold a wedding in the Great Hall." She chuckled as she rose to leave. "Of course, I now get to set the rules about this building, like adding sushi to the cafeteria menu. That's the best thing about being Chief Justice, having unquestioned power over minor matters that nobody can overrule. So, Dave and Laura, you can start planning your ceremony."

With that, Ikeda left Novak's office. "Well, guys," he said, "as much as I loved Sam, and miss him, I must admit that Kathryn is a breath of fresh air. Although I think I'll pass on the sushi. Okay, no recusal, and back to work. I'm sure you've all got pool memos piled up, since my inbox is empty."

Back in the clerks' office, Andy turned to Dave and Laura. "Wow!" she exclaimed. "Can you imagine what the Court would be like if Early Senior was sitting in the center seat? And you guys helped avoid that disaster."

"Andy," Dave said, "it was really you and Josh. We just pitched in. Seriously, you two changed history."

Andy laughed. "I'll think about that while I'm having sushi for lunch." With that, the clerks got to work on pool memos.

33

Tuesday morning at nine, Andy peered into Novak's office, where he was sitting behind his desk, reading what she recognized as a bench memo for the oral arguments that would begin at ten. "Excuse me, Alex," she said. "Can I interrupt for just a minute? I'm almost done with the opinion in the bill of attainder case, but I've got a quick question before I print it out."

"Of course, Andy, have a seat," he replied, waving her in. "I'm not due in the robing room for another half hour, and then I have to sit for two hours of arguments in a couple of really boring cases. I've got this bench memo from Laura in the first case, but I doubt I'll ask any questions, except maybe, 'Counsel, why are you wasting our time on a case you and your opponent should have settled, except you both want to keep your billing clocks running?'" He tossed the memo on his desk. "Just kidding, Andy, but I'd say more than half the cases we hear are just so the lawyers can tell future clients they've argued before the Supreme Court, and then jack up their fees. Sounds cynical of me, but it's pretty much true."

He came around his desk and sat next to Andy around his low table. "So, question away, although my answer will probably be to ask Dave or Laura, since they both know a whole lot more than me about whatever you want to know." Before she could ask her question, Novak's desk phone rang. "Excuse me, Andy, it's Angie," he said, reaching back to pick up the phone. "Sure, put him through," he replied, giving Andy a wink. "Good morning, Bob," he said. "I know why you're calling, in fact I was expecting it, and I'm tempted to say, 'No comment.' But I do have a comment, which you're free to quote. You ready?"

He paused for a moment. "I can hear you tapping on your keyboard, Bob, so I'll talk slowly. Anyway, yes, I'm aware of the recusal motion and the affidavit the Virginia AG attached to his reply to the cert before judgment petition in the Beasley case. And yes, I did visit Mister Beasley at the Sussex prison. I can't tell you what we discussed, but I can tell you it had nothing to do with the issue raised in that petition. Therefore, our conversation was not prohibited by any Court rule or statute, and I have no reason to recuse myself Did you get all that, Bob?"

A short pause. "Good, although I doubt that's front-page news, or even back in the classifieds. But I will tell you one more thing, Bob, strictly off-the-record, okay?" Another short pause. "Why don't you call the AG, Clark Shotwell, his number's on the reply, and ask if he had any ex parte communications with any of the Fourth Circuit judges about holding up Mister Beasley's appeal from his habeas denial by Judge Jacobs. I have it on good authority he did that, which is why Mister Beasley's lawyers filed the cert before judgment petition." Short pause. "No, I can't tell you that, Bob, but it's someone in a position to know. And if Shotwell denies it, which I'm sure he will, you might get one of your lawyers to file a Freedom of Information request for all records of Shotwell's communications with Fourth Circuit judges about the Beasley case. Under Virginia law, those are public records." Novak paused, then chuckled. "Bob, let's just call this tit-for-tat. Sauce for the goose. It's up to you, but off-the-record. Hey, I've got to run, Bob. Nice talking with you."

Novak hung up, then grinned at Andy. "In case you're wondering, Andy, my 'good authority' is actually me. But I'll bet Shotwell did that, and that former Judge Early called in chips to have him file the recusal motion. And getting a call from Bob Barnes might give Shotwell second thoughts about pushing the case. Bob probably won't call him, but he probably also won't write a story about this, since the Post's lawyers wouldn't file a public records request, and Shotwell would drag it out for months even if they did. So, Kathryn won't have to read about the recusal motion."

Novak glanced at his watch. "Sorry, Andy, but I really do have to run to the robing room, with a quick stop in the men's room on the way. I don't think Kathryn would hold up argument for a tardy justice." He picked up Laura's bench memo, looked out the door, then kissed Andy on the cheek. "You didn't get to ask your question, Andy," he said, "but here's mine. Maybe a little night music, sometime soon?"

"Um, sure, Alex," she replied, a bit surprised by his request. "You pick the night, I'll pick the music. Maybe Vivaldi, Le Quattro Stagioni."

"The Four Seasons, right? That's the only one I know. But it sounds perfect, maybe with a nice Italian white. Chilled, of course." Novak smiled, then left for the robing room and the boring arguments.

Back in the clerks' office, Andy thought about what she'd just done. Inviting Novak to "chill out" at her place was the real reason she'd gone in with a question she didn't actually have, but had decided it would sound too much like seduction. Maybe he sensed her intention, or maybe he'd been waiting for a chance to invite himself. Either way, they both were breaking rules. The fact that millions of other people, probably some in the Marble Temple, had also broken rules was a pretty lame rationalization, she reflected. Pushing those Bad Andy thoughts aside, she pulled up her opinion and pushed the Print button.

Coming into the clerks' office after a coffee break in the cafeteria, Andy was greeted by Dave, who handed her a sheaf of papers. "Hot off the printer," he said with a grin. "The pool memo on OD's cert petition, recommending a grant, of course. Not a bad job, if I say so myself. Of course, I'm biased, as the author."

Andy took the memo with a puzzled expression. "What do you mean, Dave, that you're the author? I thought the case went to Justice Schroeder's clerks. And they couldn't have finished a pool memo so quick."

"Networking, my dear," Dave replied. "Actually, I made a deal with Krista Kiger, the clerk who got the case. I already had the pool memo pretty well drafted over the weekend, and I offered Krista two bench memos from me and Laura in return. Pretty good deal, and she snapped it up. So, we'll send this off to the other chambers, and it'll definitely be on the discuss list for the conference on the nineteenth."

"Dave, you're amazing," Andy said. "I never would have thought of that."

"Aw shucks," he replied. "As they say, it's not *what* you know, it's *who* you know. And a little knowledge of horse-trading helps. Not that I've ever traded a horse, or even been on one. But don't look a gift horse in the mouth, as I told Krista. Anyway, I'll give this to Angie and it'll go out today."

"That's great, Dave," Andy said, giving him a high-five.

Settled at her desk, she pulled up a calendar on her computer and made a list of the dates on which subsequent events in OD's case would most likely occur: January 19 for the conference at which the justices would vote on the cert grant; January 22 for the grant to be posted on the Court's website; February 21 for filing of the merits brief by OD's lawyers; March 8 as the deadline for Judge Jacobs to begin a hearing on OD's habeas petition; March 23 for Virginia's attorney general to file his reply brief to the cert petition; April 16 as the most likely date for oral arguments on the cert petition; April 20 for the conference to vote on the case; and June 25 as the most likely date—probably the Court's final session of the term—on which the decision would be announced.

Andy knew that some—maybe all—of these dates could be changed, but lawyers rarely filed briefs before their deadlines, and Judge Jacobs, having denied OD's first habeas petition with unconcealed hostility, was unlikely to schedule a second hearing before the 90 days allowed by Novak's order would expire. Andy couldn't predict, of course, how long the habeas hearing would last, or how long after that Jacobs would issue an opinion and any orders, either granting or denying OD's request for a new trial. That might stretch out for months, so Andy just put question marks after those events. Also, she realized, even if the Court ruled that *Hall v. Florida* would be applied retroactively, it would take another hearing before a ruling on whether OD's intellectual disability qualified him for resentencing.

Printing out this calendar, Andy taped it above her desk as a reminder. Lots of indeterminacy, she thought, but with a feeling of optimism that—barring some unexpected setback—OD would spend his next birthday in December with his momma in Williamsburg. But she also worried that she might have given OD and Mamie the impression that his return to freedom would come much sooner. Andy wished she could somehow speed up the wheels of justice, but they were designed to turn slowly, giving lawyers and judges—comfortably ensconced in their offices and courtrooms—more time than they really needed to argue and decide cases. Meanwhile, OD spent twenty-three hours of every day in solitary confinement, out of their sight and hearing. But he was innocent, Andy reminded herself, and shouldn't have spent even one day in his six-by-nine cell on death row.

These thoughts tempered Andy's optimism with a tinge of melancholy, prompting a big sigh, which was interrupted by Angie's cheerful voice. "Mail call!" she announced, entering the clerks' office and handing Andy a package. She'd never received mail at the Court—and most of what came to her apartment was utility bills and pitches for unwanted credit cards—so she took the package from Angie with a puzzled look. Checking the address label, her puzzlement instantly turned to excitement. It was from Hank Lorenz at Harvard Law School. Almost ripping the package open, Andy pulled out two copies of a book: *Dismantling the Machinery of Death*. She'd hardly thought of the book since she submitted her paper on "Traumatic Brain Injury As A Bar To Capital Punishment" to Lorenz, eight months ago. The book jacket showed a photo of a gurney, taken through the viewing window of an execution chamber, with a sign taped to the window that read: "Out Of Business." Opening the cover, she found an inscription: "For Andy, whose compassion is matched only by her competence, with admiration and affection, Hank."

Flipping open the cover, Andy found her chapter. At the foot of the first page was this identification: "Andrea Roboff is a graduate of Harvard Law School, where she served as Senior Articles Editor of the *Harvard Law Review*. She is currently a law clerk to a United States Supreme Court Justice." Going back to the table of contents, Andy found an Introduction and Conclusion by Lorenz, and chapters on such topics as the effects on capital punishment of unscrupulous prosecutors, incompetent defense lawyers, racial bias in jury selection, flawed forensics, DNA exonerations, stories of inmates who were executed despite compelling evidence of their innocence, and a half-dozen other critiques of capital punishment. The authors were a roster of eminent law professors, academic researchers, and experienced death-penalty lawyers.

Andy couldn't restrain her excitement. "Wow!" she blurted, causing Dave and Laura to swivel their chairs around. "Hey, guys," she said, holding up a copy of the book, "you are now privileged to be in the presence of a published author."

Scooting over, Dave and Laura shared a copy, thumbing to Andy's chapter and then the table of contents. "Wow!" Laura echoed. "I recognize almost all of these people. They're the best critics of the death penalty in the country." She chuckled. "And our modest Andy is in their ranks, and never told us about this."

"To be honest," Andy said, "after I handed this paper to Hank Lorenz last April, I sort of forgot about it. You know, lots of work here, things came up, and I had no idea when the book would come out. But it looks pretty good, huh? And the book jacket is really eye-catching. That should get people to at least pick it up in bookstores."

Andy had picked up the other copy, which had a yellow sticky note on the cover: 'Please give this to Alex. Thought I'd save a little postage.' "I'd give this copy to you guys," she said, "but it's for Alex. But I'll loan my copy to you, as long as you don't drip kimchi on it. Or pasta sauce." Dave and Laura grinned, then said they'd decided to work at home for the rest of the day. Uh huh, Andy thought, their computers were just a few steps from their bed. "Have fun, guys," she said as they left the office.

Novak wouldn't return from boring arguments until noon, so Andy went back to work on her pool memo. She planned to give him the book, and then invite him to "chill out" with Vivaldi and vino that evening, if he wasn't needed at home. He'd told her that Anton was still able to care for Gloria, and that his treatment for bladder cancer hadn't slowed him down. Quite frankly, Andy admitted to herself, Novak seemed eager for another session of what she now thought of as "sensual massage," and she was also eager. If he couldn't make it tonight, Andy was sure he'd find time very soon. Her sudden morph from Modest Andy to Lascivious Andy caused a momentary pang of guilt, but she quickly morphed again into Diligent Andy, intently focused on her pool memo.

Ten minutes later, her desk phone rang. Oh, no, not Bob Barnes, she thought, hoping to weasel something from her about the story behind the recusal motion. Readying herself to give him a polite brush-off, Andy picked up the phone. But she was wrong.

"Andy, this is Hank Lorenz," her caller said. "Did I catch you in the middle of a pool memo?"

She laughed. "What perfect timing, Hank," she replied. "Actually, you did, but I was planning to call after lunch and thank you for the books, which arrived twenty minutes ago. I'm really flattered and impressed, and the jacket cover is fantastic."

"Well, your chapter is fantastic, too," he said. "So, how do you like clerking for Alex? I hope you don't regret my sending you into the lion's den."

"More like a pussycat," Andy said. "Actually, working for Alex has been much more exciting than I could have anticipated. He's a wonderful boss, and person, although a lot of people still think he's a right-wing ogre. But they're wrong." Andy decided not to share with Lorenz the events that had caused Novak to explore the world outside the "boxes" in which he'd been raised, educated, and worked.

"You're probably wondering why I called, Andy," Lorenz said, "and it's not to check on the Postal Service." He paused, while she waited to learn his reason for calling. She could hear him take and expel a deep breath. "Actually, I have a favor to ask, a pretty big favor."

"Well, I owe you more than one, Hank," she replied, "so what can I do for you?"

"Okay, let me explain, briefly," he said. "Do you remember that case from a few years ago, where the city and state officials in Flint, Michigan, switched their water supply from Detroit to the Flint River, and the river water contained corrosive chemicals that leached out lead from the water pipes?"

Andy was puzzled, but did recall reading about the high levels of lead that put Flint residents, especially children, at risk of permanent damage to their brains and other organs. "Um, yes, I do remember that, Hank," she replied, "but I don't know what's happened since then."

"Well, some families filed a class-action suit for damages in federal court," he continued. "They claimed the lead exposure caused things like hypertension, depression, skin lesions, auto-immune disorders, and seizure-like convulsions. They also asked the judge to order the state to provide lifetime medical monitoring of all Flint children."

"Uh, huh," Andy said, wondering where Lorenz was going.

Sensing her impatience, he spoke a bit faster. "Anyway, the district judge dismissed the suit, saying it didn't raise a federal question, and suggested the plaintiffs bring suit in state court for negligence. They appealed to the Sixth Circuit, claiming the state had violated the federal Safe Drinking Water Act, but the Sixth Circuit held they hadn't pleaded that properly in their complaint. So they filed a cert petition in your Court, Andy."

"Uh, huh," she said again.

"So, I've got some clients over in Worcester who've also been exposed to high levels of lead in the water supply," Lorenz said. "Very similar to Flint. But I don't want to file a suit in federal court unless your Court grants cert in the Flint case. If it does, it's a pretty good bet a majority will reverse the Sixth Circuit and send the case back to district court for trial."

Andy was still puzzled. "I haven't heard about this lawsuit, Hank, but if the Flint people filed for cert this term, you'd probably find out pretty soon, maybe later this month. Is there some reason you can't wait?"

"Actually, there is," he replied. "If I don't file a suit in state court by this Friday, there's a statute of limitations for negligence cases that expires on that date, and my clients would be up a creek without a paddle, so to speak. Or a river full of lead."

Andy suddenly realized the reason for Lorenz's call. "And if this Court grants cert in the Flint case, you can file in federal court with a good chance of getting a trial there. Am I right, Hank?"

"Right," he replied. "And I'm pretty sure the cert petition will be on the docket for the conference this Friday," Lorenz said. Andy heard him take and expel another deep breath. "Here's the favor you can do for me, Andy. The pool memos for that conference should have been circulated by now, and Alex should have a copy in his office." He paused for a moment. "If you can look at that memo and tell me if it recommends a grant, I'd be immensely grateful, Andy, and I promise not to tell a soul. And that could give a lot of people in Worcester, and their children, a better chance of a trial in federal court, where the judges aren't influenced by local and state politicians."

Andy was torn by this Save the Children appeal. "Hank," she said, "you're asking me to reveal confidential information. You know I can't do that."

"Andy," he replied, "all I'm asking for is something everyone will probably know by next Monday. That's not too much to ask, is it?"

"Hank," she replied, a touch of sarcasm in her tone, "that's asking a lot. But as I said, I owe you a favor. After all, you've given me several favors. Green-lighting me for admission to Harvard, giving my mom a painting worth twenty thousand bucks, putting my paper in your book, getting me the clerkship with Alex. And now you want one in return, right?"

Lorenz sounded plaintive. "Andy, that's not fair. I didn't expect anything in return from what I did. You deserved all of that, and you earned it. But if you can't do this, I apologize for asking."

Listening to Lorenz, Andy thought back to Bob Barnes's praise of her deal-making skill. "Hank, I'll tell you what," she said. "Let's make a deal, okay? If I tell you what the pool memo recommends, will you agree to argue a case that's going to get a cert grant, and will probably be argued in April. If you agree, I'll get you everything you need, but all I can tell you now is that the issue is whether Hall versus Florida should be applied retroactively. You remember that case, Hank?"

"Of course," he replied. "And I read the Eleventh Circuit opinion holding they wouldn't apply it retroactively, which I thought was terrible. But why ask *me* to argue the case? Doesn't the counsel of record want to argue it himself, or herself?"

Josh had told Andy that Jim Carruthers had never argued in the Supreme Court, and was afraid he'd freeze up or stumble. Finding an experienced and confident lawyer to argue for OD wouldn't step on his toes. "Actually, Hank, he'd be glad to let you argue the case," Andy said, sure that Carruthers would agree. She paused for a moment. "Do we have a deal, Hank?"

She heard a sigh of relief. "Deal, Andy. But I'd have agreed even if you declined the favor I'm asking. There's no good argument to deny retroactivity in Hall."

"Okay," Andy said. "As I said, I'll get you everything you need for that argument. You won't have to write the brief, but you can certainly suggest revisions. And I'll text you in the next ten minutes about the pool memo in the Flint case. I know where Alex puts the memos, and he's on the bench until noon. But I think we're even in favors, Hank, so please don't ask for any more."

"I promise, Andy," he said. "To be honest, I wasn't sure you would agree. And I feel guilty for asking you."

"I'm just doing this for the kids in Worcester," Andy said. "You pushed the right button, so don't feel too guilty, Hank. I'll just text you a 'Yes' or 'No' in a few minutes. And thanks for the books. I'll give Alex his copy." She hung up, went into Novak's empty office, thumbed through the pile of pool memos on his desk, found the Flint case, flipped to the last page, and texted a 'Yes' to Lorenz. Having broken another rule, Andy needed to chill out, and hoped Novak would break one with her.

An hour later, after grumping about the morning's boring arguments, he smiled broadly and agreed to an evening of Vivaldi and vino. Andy gave him the copy of the book with her chapter, which he said he'd read during the next round of boring arguments. Justice Bill Douglas, he told Andy, used to actually *write* books while he sat on the bench, occasionally looking up to skewer a lawyer with a pointed question.

Before leaving the Court at five, Andy called Josh—whose phone said he'd be in court all afternoon—and left a message about Lorenz's agreement to argue OD's case, leaving out the deal she'd made to get that agreement. Back at her apartment, she pulled out the Four Seasons CD, made her bed with clean sheets, took a hot bath, put on jeans and a thin white tee-shirt, and dropped her bra into the laundry hamper.

34

January 15 marked the midpoint of Andy's clerkship. She didn't usually pay much attention to such demarcations, but Josh—who did—reminded her of the date's significance when he called to invite her to dinner that evening at Fiola Mare, a fancy Italian seafood restaurant on the Georgetown riverfront, to celebrate the award he'd been given by the director of the Federal Public Defenders as the "outstanding" assistant defender in the Fourth Circuit. "It came with a bonus check," Josh said, "five hundred bucks, which will just about cover dinner tonight, and a modest tip."

Josh wasn't kidding, ordering an $85 bottle of blanc de blancs champagne from the low end of the wine list. "Congratulations, Josh," Andy said as they clinked crystal flutes. "I'll bet you got the award for using the 'necessity defense' to get an acquittal for the gravestone pisser at Arlington Cemetery."

"I remember that," he said with a grin. "Back at the Hark, after Hank offered you the clerkship with Alex. Best legal advice I've gotten." He gave Andy a serious look. "So, now that you're halfway through your term, any regrets? I mean, I really coerced you into coming here, for very selfish reasons. And dragged you into a case that has become the poster child for breaking rules. I know that's bothered me, and I'm pretty sure it's bothered you."

"Truthfully, Josh," Andy replied, "it doesn't bother me, because breaking those rules was the only way to save OD's life. Remember when you assured me that the end can justify the means, provided they're both reasonable, or necessary? Well, that's what allows me to sleep at night. Most nights, anyway."

"Hmm," Josh mused. "I'm sleeping most nights, too." He gave Andy a wink. "At least when I'm not thinking about you, and your you-know-whats."

"Josh," she interrupted. "Let's be serious, okay? You might actually get to see what you're thinking of, if you stop by my place for a wee while after dinner. But seriously, I don't regret coming here." She paused a moment. "But now that I'm at the halfway point, there is one thing I'd like for the second half."

"A wee while sounds fine," Josh said, "but what is it you'd like? Something different, I assume."

"Well, something less, um, stressful, I guess," Andy said. "I don't mean the work we've done for OD, but all the fallout from that. The whole thing with Senator Weeks and President Chambers, basically blackmailing them into letting Alex pick the new Chief Justice. And before that, catching Amanda Cushing and Todd Armistead at their insider-trading scheme, and forcing them to resign. Those were both *very* stressful."

Josh nodded agreement, then smiled. "But, you know, Andy, after we filed the cert and habeas petitions, most of what's left in OD's case is just lawyer stuff. Filing briefs, and the oral argument that Hank Lorenz is going to do. And the habeas hearing, unless Judge Jacobs wants to risk getting bench-slapped by the Supreme Court, probably will get OD a new trial and home to his momma. So, the last half of your clerkship should be pretty routine, which might be pretty boring, after the last six months. Pool memos, bench memos, probably another opinion or two. You know, what all the other clerks do. How does that sound?"

Andy laughed. "Pretty boring, actually. But I could use boring for a while. Except for tonight, of course." With the arrival of the first course of their *frutti di mare* repast, they shifted gears to eat and chat about sports, the weather, and—along with all the highly-paid and free-spending K Street lobbyists and lawyers around them—politics, relishing President Chambers' bashing from the far right for naming a radical feminist, and godless Buddhist to boot, as Chief Justice. If only they knew, Andy thought, why and how Kathryn Ikeda got picked for the center seat, the bashing Chambers was getting would turn into aggravated assault by Rush Limbaugh and his airwave flock.

A bottle of Toscana sauvignon, from the middle of the wine list at $145, washed down their meal and left Josh's bonus with enough for a generous tip. Not wishing to get stopped for being tipsy in public, they asked the doorman—another generous tip—to hail a cab for them. On the ride to her place, Andy decided, once again, to put off telling Josh about her "sensual massage" sessions with Novak. She found a reasonably persuasive rationalization for her decision. After all, she thought, Josh has both Carlo and me. And I have both him and Alex. Two for each of us. That's fair, and she doubted Josh would fault her for that. And besides, she didn't *really* have sex with Novak, if you defined the term to mean crossing home plate, which seemed a defensible definition. After all, a former president had used it to claim he didn't *really* have sex with "that woman" in his Oval Office bath-room, and remained highly popular. Getting out of the cab, Andy smiled at Josh. It's already been determined, she thought, that he'll slide across home plate tonight. Unless a plane crashed into her building, which was possible, but unlikely.

As Andy had planned, the "wee while" turned out to last all night, since Carlo was still on overnight duty. It also turned out to be one of the most pleasurable nights Andy had ever spent, although she didn't get much sleep. But neither did Josh. They both found new places to explore, and new ways to explore them. Boring can start tomorrow, Andy thought, sharing a bowl of Lemon Haze with Josh during the seventh-inning stretch of this high-scoring game, which went into extra innings, finally decided by a bases-clearing, walk-off grand slam, sparking a spectacular fireworks display.

Josh's prediction proved wrong. The second half of Andy's clerkship remained boring for just an hour. Plugging away on a pool memo, she was torn between recommending a grant or denial. Dave and Laura had gone to the library, so she tapped on Novak's office door to seek his advice. He waved her in with a broad smile, tossing a bench memo onto his desk.

"Sorry to disturb you, Alex," she said, "but I've got one of those Solomon cases here. Both sides have really good arguments, but we can't just cut this baby in half. Can you take a look at what I've drafted and give me your advice?"

Novak chuckled. "I'm guessing Dave and Laura are both elsewhere, otherwise they could give you better advice than me, which is probably to flip a coin. But I'll take a look, sure. Have a seat and let me see what you've got."

Handing Novak her draft, Andy turned at the sound of a loud, peremptory voice in the outer office, which she recognized as Justice Karl Sorenson's. "I'm sorry, Angie, but this really can't wait, and Alex can finish with his clerk later."

Novak got up from his desk and went to the door. "Karl," he said, obviously annoyed. "What brings you here, without any notice? And don't bark at Angie, or I'll send you packing."

"My apologies, Angie," Sorenson said. "I didn't mean to bark, and I hope you won't bite." She smiled, briefly showing her teeth. Sorenson turned to Novak. "Alex, I apologize for barging in like this, but I need to talk with you right now." He turned to Andy. "And I'm sorry, Miss Roboff, but I need to speak with Justice Novak privately. Can you excuse us for a few minutes, please?"

"Just hold on, Karl," Novak shot back. "These are *my* chambers, and I'll decide who can stay, and whether I should excuse *you* until Miss Roboff and I have finished our discussion, which just started." He checked his watch. "Maybe we can talk in the robing room before this morning's arguments, say in half an hour. Can your urgent matter wait that long, Karl?"

"I'm afraid not, Alex," he replied. "All I can tell you, in front of Miss Roboff, is that Bob Barnes has a deadline in thirty minutes, and wants a comment from me, which I'm tempted to give him." He shook his head. "I hate it when reporters play the 'thirty-minute-deadline' game, but Bob's a good guy, and says he can't hold the story any longer."

"Karl, I know what Bob wants you to comment on," Novak said, "and I'd advise you to say 'No comment.' But that's up to you. However, if you want to talk about it with me, before you comment, Miss Roboff will stay here. She knows more about what prompted Bob's call than I do, and certainly more than you." He gave Sorenson a Make Up Your Mind look. "That's the deal, Karl. Miss Roboff stays, or you leave."

Andy had been watching this Who's The Bigger Dog exchange with a mixture of amusement and apprehension. Sorenson, spare and sour looking, reminded her of the Midwest farmer in Grant Woods' iconic "American Gothic" painting, standing beside his wife, pitchfork in hand. He tucked his tail first. "Very well, Alex," he replied. "But I assume nothing we say here will be repeated outside your chambers."

Novak stiffened. "If you assume Miss Roboff would repeat anything to anyone, Karl, remember when you called one of the liberal judges on the Ninth Circuit 'a disgrace to the bench,' and one of your clerks got a bit drunk at a party and told people what you'd said, and it got back to the judge. So don't lecture me, Karl, or Miss Roboff."

Sorenson capitulated. "Very well, Alex." He held up a sheaf of papers in his hand. "Yesterday afternoon, Bob called and asked me to comment on the recusal motion that was attached to the state's reply in the Beasley case. I got the pool memo, but I hadn't seen the petition or the reply. So I had one of my clerks dig them up, and I must admit, Alex, that I was concerned about your ex parte visit with Beasley."

Novak held up a hand. "Hold on, Karl, and sit down, will you?" Sorenson took a seat, across the low table from Andy. "I did have that visit, Karl," Novak continued, still standing. "But, as I told Bob, my conversation with Mister Beasley had nothing to do with the issue in the cert petition. I even consulted with Kathryn about this, and she agreed I had no obligation to recuse myself. My visit with Mister Beasley was unusual, I admit, but I had a very compelling reason to talk with him. And it didn't violate any rule of this Court." He looked down at Sorenson. "If you think otherwise, feel free to tell Bob that." Novak chuckled. "That's your First Amendment right, Karl. Although you might think twice about suggesting I should recuse myself." He grinned at Sorenson. "Remember the case, a couple years ago, in which your daughter was on the brief as co-counsel, but under her married name? Nobody noticed that, except me, I guess, not even opposing counsel. And you voted for her side." He gave Sorenson a Gotcha! look. "I didn't say anything, Karl, since I knew how you'd vote, regardless of who was on the brief." He checked his watch. "Bob's still got fifteen minutes to deadline, and he might find that worth putting in his story, along with your comment."

Andy barely succeeded in suppressing her laughter, as Sorenson's jaw dropped. Novak twisted the knife. "Tell you what, Karl. You might want to call Bob back and tell him you don't think there's a story here, and that all your colleagues agree I have no reason to recuse myself in this case." He pointed to his desk phone. "And since time's short before his deadline, and both of us are due in the robing room, feel free to use my phone. His number's on my Rolodex."

Without a word, Sorenson got up and left the office. Andy waited a second, then lifted a hand for a high-five, which Novak gave with a palm-tingling smack. "Holy shit, Alex," she said, "that was awesome. I had no idea you could throw a punch like that."

Novak laughed. "Actually, I wouldn't have cared if Karl told Bob Barnes that I should recuse myself. I think Bob was just fishing, looking for somebody to criticize me. Otherwise, he won't have a story, since there wouldn't be any conflict, and that's what sells papers. But, frankly, Karl's always rubbed me the wrong way, with his smug, holier-than-thou attitude. And he lectures us in the conference room, like we're all a bunch of first-year law students. Felix Frankfurter used to do that, pontificating like the Harvard professor he used to be, but that pissed off his colleagues, and probably cost him votes." He checked his watch. "Gotta run, Andy, but get back to me about the Solomon case, if Dave or Laura can't help you burp that baby."

Back in the clerks' office, Andy wished she could tell Dave and Laura about the smack-down she'd just witnessed, but decided not to be a tattle-tale. Well, not right now. Maybe later, since it was a great story. After a second look at the Solomon case, Andy decided to recommend a cert grant, sparing the baby from dismemberment. The rest of her day was pretty routine, but not really boring. Andy wasn't easily bored, heeding her grandma Bella's sage advice: "Keep your fingers busy, bubeleh, and your mind will pay attention. Otherwise, you might lose a few." With this thought, she kept her fingers busy on her keyboard.

The next day's *Post* had no story by Bob Barnes, whose fishing expedition hadn't gotten a nibble from Sorenson or any other justice. So that's over, Andy thought, thanks to Novak's threat to turn the tables on his sanctimonious colleague. Skimming the paper over coffee in the Court's cafeteria, she wondered if Novak kept a mental list of other deviations from the "good behavior" the Constitution required of those who shared the bench with him. Black robes could hide many spots and stains, and the path to the Marble Temple wound through tempting byways of avarice, lust, and other appeals to human frailty. Finishing her coffee, and this rumination, Andy resolved not to judge others harshly for whatever "bad behavior" they might have committed, thinking back to her own deviations from rules that had been designed to keep such temptations at bay.

Back in the clerks' office, Andy joined Dave and Laura in the routine tasks for which they were being paid, and that—she presumed—the clerks in other chambers performed without breaking rules for which they could justly be fired. Tackling her pile of pool and bench memos, Andy got some measure of relief from her fleeting pangs of conscience to see that Dave and Laura seemed quite content—even cheerful—as they tackled their own piles. Perhaps, she briefly reflected, her conscience deserved a rest. Glancing at the "OD calendar" above her desk, Andy saw nothing that might disturb her sleep for the next few months.

The next few months, in fact, passed with very little that disturbed Andy's sleep. She settled into a routine that kept her fingers busy, clearing her desk by most Fridays of the pool and bench memos that kept Novak and his colleagues busy, choosing which cases to hear and preparing for oral arguments in those that made the cut. She also settled into a routine outside the Court. Every couple of weeks, Andy invited Novak to her place for an evening of music—mostly classical—and wine, to accompany the "sensual massage" they now played with well-practiced fingers. Most alternate weeks, she and Josh sampled the cuisine at one of Washington's many ethnic restaurants, with music—mostly Dave Matthews—and weed as dessert at her place, to accompany their well-practiced duets in her bed. This routine never bored Andy or the guests at her intimate soirees. Knowing that Gloria and Carlo had both blessed her liaisons with their spouses eased Andy's conscience over not telling them about each other's visits to her bed. If either one asked, she told herself, she'd be honest. But she hoped they wouldn't. That would put her conscience to a serious test.

The dates on Andy's "OD calendar" arrived on schedule. Novak returned to his chambers on January 19 from the Court's weekly conference and stuck his head into the clerks' office. "Good news, guys. Bill Brennan used to say that with five votes, you could do anything around here," he said with a grin. "Well, OD got six votes to grant his cert petition, so we can probably skip the oral arguments and start writing the opinion." He chuckled. "Just kidding, of course, but it looks like a bunch of other death-row inmates will also get new sentencing hearings under the Hall precedent. There's no good reason it shouldn't be applied retroactively. Keeping some poor guys on death row while others get off, just because of when they were convicted, doesn't make any sense. Especially when they're mentally disabled, and probably didn't really understand what they were doing."

"That's great, Alex," Andy said. "I'll let Josh know he can start working on the merits brief with Hank Lorenz, and I'll start writing the opinion." She smiled at Novak. "That is, assuming you get the assignment, and give it to me."

"Maybe I'll let you guys draw straws for it," Novak said. "That's fair, right?"

Dave shook his head. "Sorry, Alex. Laura and I will be too busy planning our wedding, so we'll pass. Right, dear?"

Laura gave him a light shoulder punch. "Only if you stop insisting on serving kimchi at the reception, Dave. I tried your mom's secret recipe, and almost passed out from the smell." They all laughed, as Novak gave them a thumbs-up and left the office.

During the month after the cert grant, Josh worked on the merits brief, sharing drafts with Andy, who spurred him on with praise and a few suggestions for tightening the argument. Josh also made a couple of trips to Cambridge, meeting with Hank Lorenz to polish the brief and prepare for the oral argument. Reporting back to Andy, Josh confessed a few qualms about Lorenz. "He's really smart, of course, and very experienced before the Court," he told her over dinner at Mi Havana, a Cuban restaurant that served heaping plates of ropa vieja, Spanish for "old clothes" but actually a tasty and spicy dish of stewed beef and vegetables. "But Hank seems to think this case is a slam dunk, and turned down my offer to set up a moot court at Georgetown Law before the argument, for him to practice before some really sharp professors. Said he was really busy with a lead exposure case, but that he'd be prepared. Hank's a bit full of himself, in my opinion."

"Well, from what Alex says, it *is* a slam dunk," Andy said. "Hank could probably win the case by reading from War and Peace."

Josh laughed. "Or maybe from Molly Bloom's soliloquy in Ulysses."

"Ah, the man with just one thing on his mind," Andy said, "so let's take home some flan and have it with the Cuban rum I bought this afternoon."

"That sounds almost as yummy as you," Josh said with a faux leer. "But I hope you're right about OD's case being a slam dunk. There's always some . . ."

"I know," Andy interrupted. "And a plane could crash into the Court during the argument. So, let's get back to my place and take it to the hoop, since baseball's not in season."

Another part of Andy's new routine was going with Novak and Anton most Friday nights to Erev Shabbat services at Temple Shalom. Anton showed no signs of discomfort, although he walked more slowly and welcomed Andy's helping hand on his arm, getting from Novak's car to their seats in the sanctuary. The treatment for his bladder cancer had seemed to work, Novak told her, although Doctor Huang would monitor Anton's condition over the next few months, and perform new tests if necessary.

Rabbi Margolis made a point of greeting them after each service, gently teasing Novak one night. "I can hear you, Alex, stumbling through the Hebrew in the siddur, with your booming voice," she said. "If Anton had brought you up as a proper Jewish boy, you wouldn't have trouble saying 'Shema Yisrael adonai eloheinu, adonai ehad.' You make it sound like 'sheema,' and 'eehad,' Alex. But at least you're trying."

"Very trying," he replied with a grin. "By the way, Lisa, I've decided to join the Temple, if that's possible. Would I have to do a bar mitzvah, at my age, or just write you a big check?"

She laughed. "Neither, Alex. Lucky for you, Anton is Jewish, even though your mother wasn't. Most Reform congregations now accept Jewish descent through fathers, so you can join our Temple, and I'll give you a pass on the bar mitzvah. Of course, contributions to the Temple are always welcome, but that's up to you."

"Tell you what, Lisa," Andy said. "I'll give Alex some lessons on Hebrew pronunciations, and tell him to lower his voice during the prayers. He's used to bellowing at lawyers in our Marble Temple, where the acoustics aren't very good."

"I do *not* bellow," Novak retorted. "Well, only when lawyers try to avoid answering my questions. But point taken, Lisa. And we'd love to have you over for dinner, sometime soon, Andy too, and have you meet Gloria. She told me to tell you she's very glad that Anton and I are coming to services here, and wants to know more about Judaism. Gloria was raised Episcopalian, but she's really an agnostic now. She says she can't understand why a loving God would inflict so much pain and suffering on innocent people. Especially the Holocaust, now that she knows Anton survived it, but his family and millions of other Jews perished at the hands of evil people, who claimed that God was on their side."

Lisa nodded her agreement. "That's a question we all struggle with, Alex, and probably Jews more than people in other religions, although I know many who do. But I'd love to meet Gloria, so just let me know what night is good for you."

The following Tuesday, Andy arrived at Novak's front gate just as Lisa pulled to the curb in a bright red Mini Cooper, with the convertible top down, despite the chill. Noticing Andy's expression as she got out, she said, "What, Andy, you were expecting a rabbi in a black Cadillac? I love zipping around in this little car, with the wind in my hair, and it reflects my true personality. You know, it's a lot easier to be serious if you also have fun."

"I know what you mean, Lisa," she replied. "And you can have fun even when you're doing something serious, if that makes sense."

"Oh, I have fun even when I'm in my robe, Andy. Because my job is lifting people's spirits, and that's fun, when I see their faces light up with words and songs of hope and joy." Seeing Novak coming toward the gate, she smiled. "Well, enough rabbi talk for now. Let's go in and have fun."

Dinner *was* fun. Novak had made what he called "Bella salmon," explaining to Lisa that Andy's grandma had showed him how to broil the steaks and prepare the sauce. After finishing dinner and moving to the living room, the conversation turned to the essential teachings of Judaism, with Gloria asking penetrating questions about the persistence of evil and suffering. Lisa answered that Jews—however much they and other people had endured—found solace in the renewal of life from the ashes of death. "The light of life," she said, "however dim it may seem, can never be extinguished. That's why, Gloria, we have the lamp we call the 'ner tamid' hanging over the ark in our sanctuary. It is always burning, a reminder that the forces of darkness can never snuff out the light of hope and joy." She paused. "I don't know if that answers your questions, Gloria, but that's what I believe, and that's what makes my life meaningful."

"Lisa, that was beautiful," Gloria answered. "You know, I can see that light in Alex's eyes when he comes back from services at your Temple. They just seem to shine a little brighter."

Novak chuckled. "That's because I light up when I see you waiting for me, dear." He turned to Rabbi Margolis. "But seriously, Lisa, I'm convinced now, especially after my dad's story about the horrors he witnessed in the Warsaw ghetto, that no life should be extinguished before its natural end. Whether it's by a German soldier shooting a little Jewish girl in the Warsaw ghetto, for bringing food to starving people, or someone we think deserves to die for ending another person's life. As they say, who are we to judge others?" He swirled the glass of wine in his hand. "Except that my job requires me to judge others. That makes it hard, sometimes, to come home from the Court with the light in my eyes that Gloria sees—or says she does—when I come back from Temple."

"Alex," Lisa said, "there *are* situations in which we must judge others, and punish them for harming others. But the ultimate punishment, ending someone else's life, I agree with you is not a judgment our tradition allows us to make." She paused, swirling her own wine glass. "May I ask you a question, Alex?" He nodded agreement. "I know you can't talk about any cases before your Court, but if one did raise the question of whether capital punishment violated the Constitution, have you thought about how you'd vote on it?"

Novak took a sip of wine while he pondered for a moment. "Lisa, I have, but there's a problem. On the Court, we can only consider the issues and questions raised by the lawyers on each side. We haven't had a case, since I've been on the Court, that raised the basic question you posed. And I'm still thinking about how I'd vote if one did, to be honest. After all, not to put on my black robe here, but the Constitution *does* allow capital punishment, as long as the defendant is given due process. And virtually all the death penalty cases we get raise due process questions, not the basic constitutionality of capital punishment. So, I'd have to wait for a case that raises this issue, listen to both sides, and then decide how to vote." He shook his head. "Not a good answer, Lisa, but a very good question."

She nodded, appreciatively. "Thank you for that, Alex." She smiled. "Well, that's enough rabbi talk, as I told Andy on our way into your home. So, let's have fun by clearing the table and washing the dishes." She held up a hand. "Don't object, Alex. That's what my Jewish grandma raised me to do, as a guest at a wonderful dinner. I have a feeling my grandma and Andy's must have gone to the same grandma school."

Novak laughed. "Okay, since I've been known to drop a few dishes."

Gloria smiled. "And on your way to the kitchen, Alex, can you fix your dad a vodka and tonic? Anton, you just stay here and be comfortable." She turned to Andy. "Can you wheel me into my room, dear? There's something I'd like to show you."

"Of course," Andy said. "I'd love to see some of Alex's baby pictures, if that's what you want to show me."

Once in her room, Gloria quietly asked Andy to close the door. "Can you sit down next to me, dear?" Andy took a seat on a brocaded chair, feeling a bit apprehensive. Gloria reached out a trembling hand and took one of Andy's in it. "Andy, dear, I want to tell you two things. One is to thank you for making Alex very happy. When he comes back from evenings with you, and he always tells me where he's going, he is full of cheer. So, however you are loving him, it gives him something he needs and that makes him happy. And for that I am very grateful."

Andy took a breath of relief. "Thank you, Gloria. I very much enjoy my time with Alex, and I'm glad he enjoys it too. And I'm glad you can see that."

"Well, dear, it's not hard to see." Gloria gave Andy's hand a squeeze, then released it. "There *was* something I wanted to show you, Andy. But I need your help. Can you open the bottom drawer of my dresser?" Andy went over and opened the drawer. "You'll see in the back is a notch that lifts the floor up. Can you do that?" Andy did, finding a lower floor, on which a large manila envelope rested. "Can you close the drawer and give me the envelope, dear?" Andy did, resuming her seat next to Gloria, who slowly opened the envelope and pulled out a photograph. She handed it to Andy. It showed a young man, perhaps twenty, dressed in a military uniform and standing before a brick wall. Andy recognized the uniform and recoiled in shock.

"Yes, dear," Gloria said, "that is my father, in a German uniform. He joined the army in 1943 and served until the surrender. For some of that time, I don't know how long, he served in Poland. But I never had a chance to ask him about that. He died in 1962, when I was just two, in an automobile accident, and I was raised by my mother and stepfather, who was a wonderful parent. I rarely talked to Alex about my father after I met him, and I left out his army service when I did." Gloria held out the photo and looked at it for a long minute, then slowly returned it to the envelope. "Can you put this back in the drawer, Andy, and replace that floor?"

Andy did that, then resumed her seat.

"That is my secret space, Andy," Gloria said. "I feel bad keeping it from Alex, but what it contains might very much upset him. And I know this is almost certainly not true, but it is possible, even if that possibility is close to zero, that my father might have harmed, or even killed, Jews or other people who weren't enemy soldiers." She looked into Andy's eyes. "I asked you to bring me in here, Andy, to ask a question which I could not ask Lisa." She paused. "Andy, do you think I should tell Alex about this? Anton opened his secrets when Bella was here, which was very brave. I don't feel brave, but I feel as if I don't tell him, he'll be able to see that I'm hiding something from him. He's very good at that, and I can't hide it." She gave Andy a Please Help Me look.

"Gloria, Anton never told Alex about his past in Poland," Andy answered, after thinking for a minute. "I doubt he would have, if Bella hadn't seen his photograph in the Holocaust Museum. But, when he did tell Alex, I don't think it hurt him that Anton had been hiding secrets. In fact, Gloria, I know that knowing them has changed Alex's whole outlook on life, for the better. To be honest, I doubt that knowing the secret about your father would upset him. Surprise him, yes. But make him think badly of you for waiting so long, no." Andy took a long breath of relief, having been as honest as she could.

"Thank you, dear Andy," Gloria said, reaching for her hand again. "I will. Maybe not now, but soon. I'll work on my bravery, first."

Just then, a light tap on the door. "Come in, dear," Gloria said, a bit louder. "I know it's you."

Novak came in. "I'm sorry to interrupt you beautiful ladies, but Lisa has to leave, and wanted to say goodbye. Would you like to come out, or have her come in here?"

"Oh, we'll come out," Gloria said. "I've just been showing Andy your baby pictures."

"Not the naked-baby pictures," Novak said in mock horror. "But I know you don't have any."

At the door, Lisa offered Andy a ride home in her sporty little car. Considering the time, she agreed, saying goodbye to Anton before she left. They spent the ride to Andy's place chatting about their respective jobs. After thanking Lisa for the ride, Andy poured a glass of chardonnay, sat on her couch, and thought about her talk with Gloria. What would I do, she wondered, if I faced that dilemma? Another glass later, she had come up with no answer. A hot bath and a warm bed put her troubling thoughts to sleep.

The next morning, Andy was finishing up a pool memo when Novak stuck his head into the clerks' office. "Andy, can you drag yourself away from your exciting work for a few minutes, and join me in my office?"

"Sure, Alex," she replied, "as soon as I type 'Recommend denial' on this total waste of some poor client's money. I can't believe how this ridiculous case even got here. The circuit opinion below didn't leave a single issue for appeal. And the respondent didn't even bother to file a Brief in Opposition, which saved that client some money."

Ten seconds later, Andy followed Novak into his office, with no idea of what he wanted to discuss. He closed the door, and motioned Andy to a seat at the low table, sitting next to her. He smiled at her Is This Good News Or Bad News? look. "Andy, I want to thank you," he began. "Gloria told me this morning about the talk you had last night, while you weren't laughing at my nonexistent baby pictures." He smiled again at her This Must Be Good News look of relief. "Do you know, Andy," he continued, "what a burden you took off Gloria's mind? You know, ever since our dinner with Bella and the story Anton told us, I've had a feeling that something was bothering Gloria, but I figured it was something I shouldn't ask her about, and just wait until she wanted to tell me. After thirty years of marriage, I've learned to let Gloria decide when she wants to bring up anything that troubles her."

Novak picked up a folder from the table and pulled out the photograph of Gloria's father, in his German army uniform. "Remember when Bella handed Anton the picture of him in his Ghetto Police uniform? And how that ended all those years of keeping that secret from me?" Andy nodded, as Novak went on. "And what knowing the truth about who Anton really is, and who I really am, has done to bring us even closer together?" Novak tapped on the photo. "So, the secret Gloria told me this morning, and Anton too, has brought us closer than we've ever been, ending a distance that I felt in the last few months." He reached out and took Andy's hand in his. "And that's really due to you, Andy. Not just finding Anton's picture at the Holocaust Museum, but giving Gloria the bravery to show me hers. That's what she told us this morning, that you gave her that last night. And decided not to wait any longer, knowing I could sense there was something she'd been holding back."

"Alex, that really wasn't due to me," Andy replied, squeezing his hand. "I just told Gloria that I was sure you wouldn't think badly of her if she told you about her father, and neither would Anton. Her bravery came from knowing that, and I just assured her that your love for her was stronger than any secret she might have been keeping from you."

Novak squeezed back, then released Andy's hand. "I still think that's due to you, at least mostly, and it deserves a reward." He reached into a jacket pocket and pulled out a small box. Oh, no, Andy thought, not a pair of diamond earrings. Novak handed her the box, which she held in her hand, afraid to open it. "Andy, nothing's going to jump out and scare you," he said. "No Jack-in-the-Box. So just open the box, or I'll take it back. Just kidding."

"Sorry, Alex," she said. "I'm just a bit surprised. And I don't need a reward for telling Gloria not to worry about how you'd react to her secret. But thank you anyway." She opened the box, took out a wad of tissue paper, unfolded it, and gasped. "Oh, my God, Alex!" In her hand was a gold Star of David, attached to a thin gold chain. She looked at the Hebrew letters embossed on the pendant. "L'Chaim," she read. "To life."

"I know you've already got one," Novak said, "the one you wear to Temple services. But this one is very special, and it's actually a present from Anton." He noticed Andy's puzzled look. "This belonged to Anton's mother," he explained, "and it's the only thing he took with him when he left his parents behind and escaped from the ghetto. He never showed it to me before this morning, but he said he wants you to have it, to remind you of what you've given him, and me, and Gloria."

Tears streamed down Andy's face as she held her gift, swinging on its chain in her shaky hand. Novak reached out, took it from her, and said, "Bend your head down, Andy, and let me put this around your neck."

She did, then took the tissue Novak pulled from his pocket and dabbed her tears. "Alex, I'm so touched by Anton's gesture," she said, her voice trembling. "I'm going to wear this every day, now. And tell Anton his life has given me inspiration for mine."

"And mine, too," Novak said.

A gentle tap on the door, and Angie stuck her head into the office. "Sorry to interrupt you, Alex, but you're due in the robing room in ten minutes."

"Thanks, Angie," he said. "Duty calls, and I must answer." He turned to Andy. "L'Chaim," he said. "And a lesson in Hebrew pronunciation, whenever you have time."

Andy smiled. "I have time tonight, if you do." He smiled his agreement. "We'll start with 'ani ohevet otcha,' and 'ani ohev otach,'" she said. "They sound different, but they mean the same thing. I'll tell you what they mean tonight, and you can practice your pronunciation."

Back in the clerks' office, Andy sat for a moment. Well, I *do* love you, Alex, she thought. And I know you love me. And if we don't say it in English, Hebrew is just as good. Although it's odd there are different forms for men and women. Then she answered the call of duty, picking up another pool memo.

35

Josh picked up Andy—dressed in her go-to-court outfit—at her apartment at seven on the morning of March 8. They were headed to Richmond for the habeas hearing that Judge Marvin Jacobs had scheduled for ten this morning, having taken all 90 days that Alex Novak had given him. Josh had borrowed another Ford Fiesta from the Justice Department motor pool, and Andy leaned over and kissed him lightly as she slid in beside him. "So, are you nervous, Josh? I mean, this is OD's only chance to get a new trial, and Judge Jacobs already denied his first petition."

"I'd be more nervous if I had to stand up and argue the case," he replied, pulling into traffic. "But Jim Carruthers is going to do that, and he seems pretty confident Jacobs won't have much choice, considering our DNA evidence that Early Junior had Laurel's blood on his glove, which puts him at the scene of her murder. Plus, we have Tory Tucker's affidavit that Junior admitted killing a 'nigger-loving slut,' which gives him a motive for bashing in her skull after OD ran out of her house. Put those together, and that's enough to create reasonable doubt that OD killed her."

"Well, you've convinced me," Andy said, "but remember the Paul House case that we cited as precedent for OD's 'actual innocence' claim? His lawyers had really strong evidence, including a confession, that the victim's husband killed her. But after the district judge heard all this evidence, he denied the habeas petition. It took the Supreme Court to get him another hearing, and an order for a new trial."

"That's true," Josh replied, "and that might happen again. Jim says that several lawyers have told him Jacobs is really pissed the Supreme Court might reverse his denial of the first habeas petition. But we're stuck with him, so cross your fingers and wish us luck." He turned and grinned at Andy. "Just kidding, as you know. Although, of course, you never know."

Andy was surprised as they walked a block from a parking lot to the federal courthouse on East Broad Street in downtown Richmond. Unlike the pile of masonry she expected, this building—fronted by a curving glass exterior—looked more like the headquarters of one of Virginia's corporate giants. Inside, a hundred-foot-high atrium swept Andy's gaze up to the glass ceiling that filled the center with sunlight.

After they passed through security, Andy heard a deep voice. "Morning, Josh, and I see you brought Portia Bradwell with you." She turned to see a tall, fortyish man, holding a large briefcase, who stuck out his free hand to shake hers. "I'm Jim Carruthers," he said, "and I wouldn't be here today if you hadn't pulled off the greatest heist since Butch Cassidy and the Sundance Kid."

"But I got busted," Andy said, "and they got away and were never caught."

Another voice, this one a woman's. "Mister Jim, I'm so glad to see you. Thank you for telling me about this hearing. And these nice young people got to be Mister Josh and Miss Andy." The short, plump black woman held a red-covered book in her hand. "I'm Mamie Beasley, and I came up on the bus from Williamsburg to be here for my son. You going to get him home, I pray on my Bible." She opened it to a marked page. "It says here," she read, "'Keep far from a false charge, and do not kill the innocent or the righteous, for I will not acquit the guilty.'" She nodded, emphatically. "That's the word of the Lord, and I pray this judge is a God-fearing man."

Andy reached out and hugged Mamie. "Mrs. Beasley," she said, "thank you for that. You know, that verse tells you why we're here. To tell the judge that OD was put in prison on a false charge, and is an innocent man." She tapped on Mamie's Bible. "It also says in here to honor your mother, and OD has a lot to honor you for."

Carruthers checked his watch. "Folks, we'd better get up to the courtroom. Pickles fines lawyers who show up late." He noticed Andy's puzzled look. "That's what lawyers here call Judge Jacobs, because he always looks like he just bit into a big, sour Vlasic. Not within his hearing, of course." He led them over to a bank of elevators, pushing a button for the fifth floor, then led them down a marble-floored hallway to a door marked 'Courtroom Five.' "Before we go in," he said, looking at Mamie, "remember that we can't guarantee OD will get a new trial. But Judge Jacobs also knows the Supreme Court is peering over his shoulder."

Mamie nodded. "And God also be looking down at him," she said. "But don't you worry, Mister Jim. I know you going to do your best, and I'm praying for you."

Entering the courtroom, Andy was struck by how small it was, with just four rows of benches outside the bar. "This is just for hearings," Carruthers explained. "No jury box. Trials are conducted in bigger rooms." He motioned to the first row on the right. "This is right behind the defense table." He reached into his briefcase and pulled out a notepad and pen. "Andy, if you have any thoughts during the hearing, jot them down and pass them to Josh, okay?"

Andy and Mamie took seats, while Josh and Carruthers pushed through the swinging bar gate and pulled out chairs at the defense table. Voices behind her turned Andy's head, to see two briefcase-toting men coming in, pushing through the gate and plopping their cases on the prosecution table. One was in his sixties, stocky and with a full head of wavy silver hair. He exuded an air of authority. The other was in his thirties, as average as they make lawyers. Every Biglaw lawyer who argued before the Supreme Court, Andy thought, seemed to have one at his table, furiously scribbling notes.

The senior lawyer stepped over to the defense table and shook Carruthers' hand. "Jim," Andy heard him say, "we might be out of here in ten minutes, if you're reasonable today." He flashed a power smile and took his seat.

Just then, a side door opened. Andy was surprised to see OD Beasley, dressed in a blue shirt and pants, escorted by two khaki-clad officers, both black, one male and one female, each loosely holding an arm. She hadn't anticipated that OD would attend the hearing, but suddenly realized that 'habeas corpus' was Latin for 'bring the body before us.'

OD, handcuffed but not shackled, wrenched an arm free when he saw Mamie. "Momma," he blurted, "Jesus tole me you be here to take me home." Mamie started to rise, but the officers put OD into a seat at the defense table, next to Josh. The female officer leaned over and whispered something into his ear. He nodded agreement. She reached over and removed his handcuffs, then took an arm and led him to the bar.

Mamie, overcome, reached across and hugged her son. "Thank you, Jesus," she said, her voice trembling. "And thank you, officer." She held the hug for a long moment, until the officer gently led OD back to his seat. Mamie sat down, pulled a tissue from a pocket, and dabbed her tears. "Miss Andy," she said, "this the first time I been able to hold my son since he be taken away, fifteen years ago. That was very nice of the officer. She didn't have to do that, you know." Andy was touched by this expression of gratitude. A mitzvah, she thought. And maybe Judge Jacobs would grant OD a mitzvah.

A door behind the bench opened. A stocky black man and a young white woman entered the courtroom, coming down two steps and standing behind small tables on either side of the bench. The woman pushed a button on her desk to record the proceedings. "All rise," the bailiff commanded. "The United States District Court for the Eastern District of Virginia is in session, the Honorable Marvin Jacobs presiding." The judge, short with thin grey hair in a comb-over, came through the door, scanned the room, then said, "Please be seated." He took his high-backed seat. "Miss Clark, please call the case."

"In the matter of Odell Beasley," she read from a sheet. "Docket number CR-213-MJ. Hearing on an Original Writ of Habeas Corpus, issued by the Supreme Court of the United States."

"Good morning," Jacobs said. "The record will show that Mister Beasley is present. Will counsel please state their appearances?" He nodded at Carruthers, who stood.

"Good morning, Your Honor. James Carruthers, Office of the Federal Public Defender, for Mister Beasley."

Josh stood. "Joshua Barfield, Your Honor, for Mister Beasley."

Jacobs nodded, then turned to the other table, smiling broadly. The silver-haired lawyer stood, smiling back. "Good morning, Your Honor. Clark Shotwell, Attorney General of Virginia, for the Commonwealth. It's always a pleasure to appear before you, Judge Jacobs."

"It's always a pleasure to have you here, General," Jacobs replied. "And I have read with great interest the brief you filed." Oh, my God, Andy thought. No pleasure at having OD's lawyers here, and he already telegraphed his decision.

Shotwell's minion stood. "Good morning, Your Honor. Paul Purvis, for the Commonwealth."

"Be seated, gentlemen," Jacobs said. He picked up a sheet from the bench. "I have been instructed by a Justice of the United States Supreme Court to convene this hearing on the petition for a writ of habeas corpus filed on behalf of Mister Beasley." He looked down at Carruthers. "Mister Carruthers, I have here the brief you filed. I also have the report of Doctor Vito Petrocelli, director of the Forensic Sciences Department of George Washington University. I have a stipulation from General Shotwell that, for the purposes of this hearing, he waives his right to have Doctor Petrocelli appear in person and testify as to his report. And I have an affidavit from Miss Martha Radford of Williamsburg, although I don't, quite frankly, see its relevance to this proceeding."

Jacobs picked up a document from his bench, and looked at it with an expression that justified his nickname. "I also have an affidavit from Mister Tory Tucker, an attorney in Philadelphia, Pennsylvania." He gave Carruthers a stern look. "I have put this affidavit under seal, Mister Carruthers. It names a person who has not been charged with any offense related to this proceeding, and whose reputation might well be harmed if this affidavit were made a public record. That is not to say that it might be unsealed in any further proceeding in this or another court, at some point." He dropped the affidavit with an expression of distaste. "Mister Carruthers, I expect you to abide by my order to seal this document, and not disclose its contents to any person. Sanctions will be prompt and severe if you violate this order." Jacobs raised his voice a notch. "Have I made myself perfectly clear, Mister Carruthers?"

Carruthers stood. "You have, Your Honor." He sat down.

Oh shit, Andy thought. Early Senior and Junior have a friend on the bench, and this doesn't look good for OD. She turned to Mamie, who clutched her Bible tightly against her chest, her eyes closed and lips moving in what Andy knew was prayer. Then she shot a glance at Shotwell, a shit-eating grin on his face. And the Top Lawyer has a friend on the bench. The Old Boy network takes care of its friends, and srews its enemies.

Jacobs went on. "Gentlemen," he said, "I have convened this hearing as I was instructed by the Supreme Court. And I have received the documents you submitted." He looked at both Carruthers and Shotwell. "Unless either of you wish to prolong this hearing with argument, I will take this matter under consideration and issue an appropriate order in due course."

Shotwell stood up, as Jacobs raised his eyebrows in surprise. "If I may beg the Court's indulgence," Shotwell said, "the Commonwealth would like to propose a resolution of this matter that might obviate the need for any further proceedings in this Court." He paused, as Jacobs nodded agreement. "After careful consideration, Your Honor, the Commonwealth is prepared to offer Mister Beasley the opportunity to make an Alford plea in state court, and to facilitate his immediate release from confinement in return for that plea, which could be entered today."

At these words, Mamie bolted upright. *"Praise the Lord!"* she blurted. "My prayer is answered! My son is coming home!"

All heads in the courtroom swiveled at this outburst. Jacobs picked up his gavel, holding it as a warning. "There will be no further disruption of this hearing," he said firmly, "or the bailiff will remove that person." Mamie looked abashed. Andy reached and took her hand, which was trembling. She had no idea what an Alford plea might be, but immediately suspected a ploy on Shotwell's part.

Jacobs put his gavel down. "General, you may proceed," he said.

"Thank you, Your Honor," Shotwell said. "I know you are familiar with the Alford plea, and I assume Mister Carruthers is as well, but let me briefly explain the Commonwealth's proposal for the record of this hearing, if I may." Jacobs nodded agreement. "An Alford plea is based on a United States Supreme Court decision in 1970," Shotwell continued. "It allows a criminal defendant to enter a plea of guilty, but to assert his innocence of the charge against him. In this case, we are prepared to allow Mister Beasley to plead guilty to second-degree murder in state court, and to maintain his innocence. We are also prepared to recommend to the presiding judge that he be sentenced to time served, and to be released from confinement. I have confidence, Your Honor, that our recommendation would be accepted by the judge, who has made time for an appearance this afternoon.."

Shotwell looked over at Carruthers. "Should Mister Beasley accept this offer, Mister Carruthers, we have arranged with Warden Zook at the Sussex prison to complete the processing and release him by five o'clock this afternoon, to the custody of his mother, without bond." He looked back at Jacobs. "Your Honor, the Commonwealth remains convinced of Mister Beasley's guilt in the murder of Laurel Davis, and that we can prove his guilt to a jury, beyond a reasonable doubt. Nonetheless, taking into account the time Mister Beasley has spent in confinement, we believe that justice in this matter should be tempered with mercy." With a look of satisfaction, Shotwell resumed his seat.

Jacobs paused for a moment. "Mister Carruthers," he said, "considering the Commonwealth's offer, about which I will express no opinion at this time, I think you should have an opportunity to consult with your client before you make any response. There is an attorney consultation room behind the holding cells. Do you wish to consult with him there?"

Carruthers stood, shooting a glare at Shotwell. "With all due respect, Your Honor, I wish to state for the record that making such an offer with no advance notice to me, or to you, I presume, is both unfair and unprofessional. However, I have an obligation to consult with Mister Beasley before I respond. May I suggest a brief recess to do that?"

"Would thirty minutes be adequate?" Jacobs asked. Carruthers nodded agreement. "The Court will be in recess for thirty minutes." With that, he rose and left the bench. Followed by Carruthers and Josh, the officers escorted OD through the side door. He looked back at his mother, confusion on his face.

Holy shit, Andy thought. Shotwell *knows* that OD is innocent, and that Junior murdered Laurel Davis. But this deal would avoid a new trial, the embarrassment of an acquittal, and—Shotwell's obvious purpose— allow Junior to get away with murder, scot free. The price would be OD's pleading guilty to a crime he didn't commit. What a fucking hypocrite! She turned to Mamie, who looked both puzzled and torn. "Mrs. Beasley," she said, "would you like to step outside with me? I think we could both use some fresh air in the courtyard off the lobby. And some tea from the snack bar." Mamie smiled, her eyes shining with tears, and followed Andy.

Twenty-five minutes later, Andy and Mamie returned to the courtroom and took their seats. Shotwell and his minion were seated at their table, chatting with looks of unconcern. Two minutes later, the officers escorted OD back to his seat, followed by Carruthers and Josh. Three minutes later, Judge Jacobs entered through his door and took his seat. "This hearing will resume," he said, nodding at the clerk to push the recording button. "Mister Carruthers, did you have adequate time to consult with your client?"

Before he could respond, OD stood up, brushing off a restraining hand from an officer. "Mister judge," he exclaimed, "*I did not kill that girl!* I swear to Jesus I did not kill that girl! I rather you kill *me* than say I did!" He turned to Mamie as the officers took his arms and pushed him onto his seat.

Jacobs raised his gavel, then put it down. His tone was calm as he spoke. "Mister Beasley, your attorney will speak for you in this court. But I understand what you said." He paused. "Mister Carruthers, do you wish to respond to General Shotwell's offer for the record?"

"Your Honor, I think Mister Beasley has responded." He turned to Shotwell. "We will let Judge Jacobs make his decision on the habeas petition, General. But Mister Beasley has made it clear to me that he would welcome a new trial, should the Court order one."

Jacobs looked down at Shotwell. "General, do you have any response to Mister Carruthers?" Shotwell shook his head. "Very well," Jacobs continued. "This Court will issue a conditional grant of the habeas writ. That grant is conditioned on the Commonwealth's commencing a new trial of Mister Beasley within a reasonable time. He will remain in custody during that time, but will be moved from death row at the Sussex prison to less-restrictive quarters. General, can you give the Court a time by which you can commence a trial in the state court?"

Shotwell sat for a long minute, then stood up. "Your Honor, the Commonwealth is disappointed that Mister Beasley has rejected an offer that would release him from custody today. However, as I stated before the recess, we have full confidence that we can secure his conviction, and convince a jury to find him guilty of this brutal murder, beyond a reasonable doubt."

Jacobs broke in, obviously annoyed. "My question, General, was how much time you would need to prepare for trial. Can you answer that for me?"

Shotwell leaned over and whispered to Purvis, who opened a calendar, scanned it, then whispered back to his boss. "I'm sorry, Your Honor, but Mister Purvis has the trial calendar for my staff. We have two trials scheduled in Williamsburg that are complicated and will take considerable time to complete. One is a drug conspiracy, the other a bank embezzlement case." He paused. "May I suggest a trial date in late June, Your Honor? Frankly, an earlier date might strain my staffing resources."

Carruthers jumped up. "Your Honor," he said, anger in his tone, "General Shotwell is stalling for time. Every day Mister Beasley remains in custody is a violation of his right to a speedy trial. And fifteen years is far too long to vindicate his innocence."

"Mister Carruthers," Jacobs replied, "I understand your frustration, but General Shotwell cannot rush his other cases." He flipped through the pages of a calendar on his bench. "Gentlemen," he said, "my order will require the Commonwealth to commence a trial no later than June twenty-fifth. I will entertain no requests for extension. And further, all filings in this matter will remain under seal, subject to further order." He gave both lawyers a searching look. "Anything further, gentlemen?" Carruthers and Shotwell both shook their heads. Jacobs nodded. "In that case, this hearing is concluded." He rose and left the bench.

The officers allowed OD another hug with Mamie before leading him out. She turned to Andy. "Don't you worry, Miss Andy. OD did the right thing, and Jesus going to take care of him."

Josh came through the bar, over to Andy and Mamie. "Mrs. Beasley," he said, "we got OD a new trial. That's what we wanted. I'm sorry he'll have to spend more time in prison before that trial, but at least he'll be off death row, and able to move around. That was something Judge Jacobs didn't have to do, but I think he realizes that OD is really innocent."

"Thank you, Mister Josh," Mamie said. "You and Miss Andy the ones who did this for OD, and God going to reward you for that. Give you a special place in his kingdom."

"Mrs. Beasley," Josh replied, "being able to help OD is all the reward I need, but thank you for that." He looked at Andy. "I've got an idea. Since Mrs. Beasley came up here from Williamsburg on the bus, how about we give her a ride back?"

"That's a great idea, Josh," Andy said. "Can you come with us, Mrs. Beasley?"

Mamie smiled. "Bless you both. And I got some fried chicken and greens, if you can stay for a bit. I made that for OD, case he come home today, but he'd want you to have it. And he *will* come home. I know that for sure."

They said goodbye to Jim Carruthers, drove to Williamsburg, and enjoyed every bite of fried chicken and greens.

"Do you think Shotwell was bluffing, Josh?" While he navigated the traffic back to DC, Andy nibbled on the chocolate-chip cookies Mamie Beasley had baked for OD's homecoming, but put in a box for them after the last exchange of hugs outside her modest home. "I mean, if he actually intends to try OD again, all the evidence that points to Early Junior as the killer will come out. How could he possibly get a conviction with that shit all over his case?"

Josh looked over, taking a cookie from Andy. "Mmm," he said, "better than Mrs. Fields. But seriously, Shotwell's not stupid. He knows we found the 'other dude who did it.' And don't forget, Andy, he's also a politician, up for reelection this fall. Letting a black guy out of prison for murdering a white girl wouldn't sit well with the white voters who put him in office. But getting a guilty plea from OD probably wouldn't hurt him."

Josh took another cookie, then reflected while he nibbled and drove. "On the other hand, even smart lawyers can miscalculate," he said. "Maybe he really expected OD to take the deal he offered with the Alford plea. After all, OD could be home today, eating fried chicken and cookies." He looked over at Andy. "I was sitting there, next to OD, wondering if I would have taken that deal. And I just couldn't decide. How about you, Andy? Home today after fifteen years on death row, or back to prison for who knows how long?"

"Josh, that's a decision I'm glad I didn't have to make," she replied. "But you have to remember that OD really believes God will make sure he doesn't die for a crime he didn't commit." Andy sighed. "Sometimes I wish for that kind of belief, but I just don't have it."

"Neither do I," Josh said. "But I'd never tell someone who does that there's no way to prove their belief is true." He chuckled. "And who knows? Maybe they're right. Maybe I made the wrong bet on Pascal's wager. You know, his argument that if God actually does exist, but you don't believe that, the consequences could be eternal torment. But if he doesn't, even if you believe he does, no harm done. "

Josh reached for another cookie, but Andy pulled the box away. "Don't tell me I missed a philosophy class, Professor Barfield." She relented. "Okay, have a cookie, but leave room for more dessert at my place. Something even more tasty you can nibble on." She put a hand on his thigh. "Unless, of course, you'd rather curl up with a volume of Pascal."

He laughed. "Care to make a wager on that?"

Back in the clerks' office the next morning, Andy added June 25 to the "OD calendar" above her desk. Probably a coincidence, she thought, but the deadline for OD's new trial was also the most likely date for the Court to announce its decision on the petition Hank Lorenz was scheduled to argue for OD on April 16. She worried a bit that his assurance to Josh of a "slam dunk" outcome might reflect the hubris of a Harvard law professor. But Alex Novak's assurance of six votes to hold that Hall v. Florida should be applied retroactively, and to reverse Jacobs' ruling on OD's 'intellectual disability' claim, eased her worries. Meanwhile, Andy resumed the tasks for which she was being paid, and her routine outside the Court, mixing work with pleasure and enjoying both.

One date was not on her calendar. But it was on Josh's, who called on the Monday after the hearing in Richmond. "Hey, Andy, just wondering if you had any plans for tomorrow night."

"Sure," she replied, not sure why he asked. "I'll be working on a bench memo until my eyes glaze over, then soaking in a hot bath and crawling into bed. Why, do you another plan in mind?"

"Obviously, Miss Perceptive," he replied, "otherwise I wouldn't have inquired. Don't you know what tomorrow is?"

Andy suddenly realized why Josh had called. "Oh, right, tomorrow is my birthday. Thanks for reminding me of my advancing age. But do you want me to change my plans for tomorrow night?"

"Just a bit," he said. "Maybe you could squeeze in dinner with me and Carlo. We found a new place you would like. Nothing fancy, but not jeans. Just a light repast with friends, and bring you back in time for that hot bath. Date?"

Andy laughed. "Well, I haven't seen Carlo for a while, so it's a date. But no surprises, okay? No loud rendition of 'Happy Birthday.' Just a light repast with friends."

"Deal," he agreed. "Pick you up at six?" Andy agreed, touched that Josh had remembered, and would bring Carlo.

They picked her up in Carlo's car, dented from his "terribile" driving but still running. Andy had dressed in black slacks and blazer, with a green silk blouse, safely between fancy and casual. She kissed them both, then said. "So, where's the hole-in-the-wall you're taking me to?"

"Oh, not far," Josh said. "But it's in sort of a dangerous neighborhood, so you stick with us." Andy figured he was kidding, but you never knew with Josh.

Ten minutes later, Carlo pulled up at the entrance to the Hay-Adams Hotel, perhaps the most elegant hostelry in the Capital, right across Lafayette Square from the White House. "Oh my God," Andy exclaimed, "this is some hole-in-the-wall! And I was going to order a grilled cheese sandwich."

"We could probably arrange that with Chef Michel," Josh said, "but you should listen to the specials first." Carlo turned his car over to a valet, then Josh led them into the lobby. "We're here for dinner at the Lafayette," he told a clerk, who directed them to a restaurant far more elegant than Andy had ever seen. Stopping at the reception desk, Josh said "We're here for a private dinner. It's in my name, Mister Barfield." With a smile, the greeter led them through the main dining room, then opened the door to a small room.

"Oh my God!" Andy exclaimed. Sitting around the impeccably set table were Alex Novak, Gloria, and Anton. "I can't believe this." She turned to Josh, with a faux frown. "I said no surprises, and here you've gone and surprised the hell out of me." She kissed all three Novaks. "I'm so touched that you all have come. But I sense some kind of conspiracy here."

"Actually, Josh called me just before I was going to call him," Novak said, "so we're both guilty." He chuckled. "I just picked the restaurant, since it's a short ride for all of us."

Josh introduced Carlo to the Novaks, whom he charmed with his Italian accent and animation, and even—to everyone's surprise— exchanged a few words with Anton in Polish. Their dinner—Andy had the grilled rockfish—was delicious, the wines from the best vineyards. Their conversation was light and full of amusing anecdotes, mostly about exotic places they'd visited and exotic people they'd met. Andy mostly sat back and enjoyed the stories.

With the table cleared, Andy sipped on a silky cabernet while she chatted with Gloria and Carlo, on either side of her. Across the table, Josh and Novak whispered to each other, then stood up. "Excuse us, everyone," Novak said, "but it's time for birthday presents." Each held a small box in his hand, wrapped in gold paper. Oh no, Andy thought, not matching pairs of diamond earrings. Novak handed his box to Andy. "This is from all the Novaks," he said. "Happy birthday, Andy."

Aware of the eyes on her, she slowly unwrapped and opened the box. "Oh my God!" she gasped. Inside *was* a pair of teardrop diamond earrings, set in a lacework of gold filigree and obviously antique.

"Andy, dear," Gloria said. "Those were my grandmother's, and I wanted you to have them, for bringing your love into our lives." Overcome, Andy leaned over and kissed her check.

Josh then handed Andy his box. Opening it, she gasped again. Inside was a cameo brooch, obviously antique, with a carving of a woman's head. "This wasn't my grandmother's," he said, "but it was somebody's grandmother's. Carlo brought it back from Rome. That's Venus, if you didn't know. And, as Gloria said, this is for bringing your love into our lives."

Still overcome, she kissed both men, then gave way to tears of happiness. "I don't know what to say," she said, through sniffles, "except to thank you all for bringing your love into my life."

After rounds of hugs, they all went down and waited for their cars. When Carlo reached Andy's building, he smiled. "Buon compleanno, Andy," he said. "As a final present, I'm giving you Josh for tonight." Josh seemed surprised, but kissed Carlo and followed Andy into her apartment.

Before they moved from her couch into her bed, having shared a bowl of Lemon Haze, Josh surprised Andy once more. "By the way," he said, almost offhandedly, "Alex and I know about each other. We both already *did* know, the way guys know these things, but we wanted you to know that we both know, if that doesn't sound too stoned." He gently stroked Andy's bare breasts, which enjoyed the attention. "So Alex gets an extra visit, since I hadn't planned this one."

An hour later, Andy snuggled against Josh and thought briefly about the end of her clerkship in July. What might follow that, she reflected, could not be determined. But for now, she thought no further than a night filled with surprises. This was a birthday she would never forget, come what may.

36

On April 15, the night before Hank Lorenz was scheduled to argue OD's case before the Court, he met for dinner at Buon Appetito with Andy, Josh, and Jim Carruthers. He seemed confident and calm. "Jim, I want to thank you for giving up your first chance to get one of the goose-quill pens they give the lawyers who argue," Lorenz said, over a final glass of wine. "But I've already got a dozen, so I'll give you mine." He chuckled. "And filch a couple for Andy and Josh. Either one of you guys could probably do a better job than me."

"Thanks for that, Hank," Carruthers said. "You know, I've argued in a lot of courts, state and federal, but for some reason, the prospect of facing the Supreme Court made me nervous. But you don't seem nervous at all. What's your secret?"

Lorenz laughed. "Appearances can be deceiving, Jim. Of course I get nervous, every time. But I look over at the lawyer on the other side, and realize that he or she, no matter how many times they've been there, is just as nervous. If you're not, then you're probably over-confident. And you'll probably get a question you hadn't anticipated, and start bumbling. Or even worse, try to wiggle around it. In fact, in my experience, the more eminent and experienced the lawyer, the more likely they are to assume the justices will ask only easy questions." He took a sip of wine. "So, my secret is to pretend this is my very first Supreme Court argument, and that I'll get hit by a pitch before my first swing."

"Hank," Josh said, "can I throw you a hard, high fastball, just to see if you can hit one?"

Lorenz laughed. "Try one, Nolan Ryan."

"Okay, here it comes," Josh said, leaning across the table as if it were the Supreme Court bench. "Can you explain, Mister Lorenz, how your client, if he is supposedly 'mentally disabled,' has the obvious intelligence to retain an esteemed Harvard law professor to represent him?"

They all laughed. "That's an excellent question, Your Honor," Lorenz replied. "Once your Court decides this case, we'll see how intelligent his decision was." They all laughed again. He checked his watch. "My other secret is to get a good night's sleep before the argument. And hope that opposing counsel has insomnia. So, dinner has been great, and I'll see you all when our new Chief Justice says 'Play ball.'"

The next morning, shortly before ten, Andy took a seat in the guest section of the Court's chamber, along with Dave and Laura. Hank Lorenz was seated at the counsel table, thumbing through a loose-leaf notebook. Beside him were Jim Carruthers and Josh, who turned and gave Andy a Look Where I Am smile and a thumbs-up. She blew him back a kiss.

After the justices took their seats on the bench, and the traditional recitals, Kathryn Ikeda looked down and smiled. "We will now hear argument in Number 1347, Odell Beasley versus David Zook, Warden. Before you begin, Mister Lorenz, the Court will admit Mister Joshua Barfield this morning as pro hac vice, which, for those who flunked Latin, means 'for this matter.'" Chuckles greeted this light touch.

"Chief Justice, and may it please the Court," Lorenz began, "this case raises the question of whether this Court's ruling in 2012, in Hall versus Florida, should be applied retroactively. And, if so, whether the district court erred in ruling that Mister Beasley possessed sufficient 'adaptive capability' to make him eligible for the death penalty to which he was sentenced."

A sharp, nasal voice interrupted Lorenz. "Mister Lorenz," Justice Karl Sorenson said, "it is not necessary to recite the Questions Presented from your brief." He pursed his lips with displeasure. "But let me ask you a question before you proceed. Let us assume, for purposes of argument, that this Court holds that Hall should be applied retroactively. That remains to be seen, of course. And let us assume, as a study cited in your brief states, that such a ruling would entitle some two or three hundred inmates now under sentence of death to hearings on whether their asserted 'intellectual disability' requires commutation of those sentences to life in prison without parole."

Lorenz nodded as Sorenson spoke, having anticipated the question that would follow. "Mister Lorenz, here's my question. Would not such a ruling produce a flood of litigation, and impose a considerable burden on hundreds of judges to hold these hearings? And most likely, additional suits by inmates who take any chance to prolong their cases? That seems to me the inevitable consequence of such a ruling."

"No, Justice Sorenson, it would not have that consequence." Lorenz had no need to thank his inquisitor for his question, knowing Sorenson would vote against him. "But let me turn your question around, if I may. Assume this Court holds that Hall should *not* be applied retroactively. The inevitable consequence would be that hundreds of inmates now on death row, including Mister Beasley, with evidence of their intellectual disability, would remain on death row, subject to execution at any time, while Freddie Hall and defendants sentenced to death from today on, with similar evidence, would never be executed." Lorenz paused, then spoke firmly. "Is that a consequence, Justice Sorenson, that you would consider fair? The date of your conviction determines whether you live or die? Is that fair?"

Andy turned her head to the bench. Sorenson did not answer the question, sitting impassively. She knew that questioning the justices, particularly in the assertive tone Lorenz used, was rarely welcomed, even by sympathetic justices. But Lorenz had knocked that hard, high fastball out of the park. Andy saw Josh hold one hand up and give her a covert thumbs-up behind it.

Lorenz faced only one more critical question, from Justice Cormac McCarthy. "Turning to the second issue in this case, Mister Lorenz, and the district judge's finding that your client had sufficient 'adaptive ability' to function in society, don't you agree that he must have had sufficient intelligence to understand what he did, in murdering that young woman?"

Lorenz did not change his tone. "Justice McCarthy, there is no question that Mister Beasley's IQ scores fall within the parameters this Court set out in Hall as being 'intellectually disabled.' That undisputed fact requires a new sentencing hearing. Your question, however, assumes that only those defendants who lack the 'adaptive ability' to even tie their shoes or brush their teeth, or who violate prison rules, will be exempt from execution. Such a holding, in my view, would be unfair. Mister Beasley is being punished, in effect, for being a model inmate. And that punishment, should this Court rule against him, will be his death." He paused. "Let me ask, Justice McCarthy, as I did of Justice Sorenson, would you consider that fair?" Like Sorenson, his conservative colleague declined to take the bait, and remained silent.

Lorenz spent the remainder of his thirty minutes fielding technical questions about judicial standards for deciding what kinds of cases qualified for retroactive application. Andy, sitting only twenty feet away, heard Josh quietly give him a "Good job, Hank," as he sat down.

Attorney General Shotwell, probably wary of facing Lorenz himself, had dispatched Virginia's newly-appointed Solicitor General, Ralph Stuart, thin and thirtyish, for that unenviable task. Andy noticed a slight tremor in his hands as he approached the lectern, gripping it tightly to stop the shaking. Stuart quickly faced a question from Justice Dwight Stokes, an affable Tennessean. "General Stuart, let us assume, hypothetically, that a physician in Virginia lost his medical license for assisting a terminally ill patient to end her life, with drugs the physician supplied her. That would be grounds for revoking his license in your state, as well as a criminal offense, would it not?"

"Yes, it would, Your Honor," Stuart admitted, having no choice.

"Good," Stokes continued. "And let us assume, hypothetically again, that this Court subsequently ruled that your state's law against assisted suicide, and those of other states with similar laws, violated the Due Process clause of the Constitution. You with me, General Stuart?" He nodded agreement, looking puzzled. "Under those assumptions, would that physician be entitled to have his license restored, and his conviction vacated?"

Stuart made a rookie mistake, turning to the two lawyers at his table, hoping for a 'Yes' or 'No' nod to answer this loaded question. Stokes noticed this. "Have I asked a question, General," he pressed, "that has no answer?" A quick frown by Chief Justice Ikeda shushed the wave of chuckles.

"Well, Justice Stokes, I presume he would," Stuart finally replied.

"Thank you, General," Stokes said. "So I presume that you would support giving decisions of this Court retroactive application to doctors, but not Mister Beasley and other inmates on your state's death row?" He gave Stuart a Welcome To The Big Leagues smile.

"Well, Justice Stokes, I think we have different fact patterns here," Stuart replied.

"Of course we do, General," Stokes replied. "That's the purpose of a hypothetical. But if there's a different principle here, would you kindly elucidate it for me?"

Chief Justice Ikeda rescued the hapless lawyer. "Justice Stokes, I think you should let General Stuart discuss whether Hall established a new constitutional rule, similar to your hypothetical, or simply a procedural rule that doesn't require retroactivity, as his brief argues. That might answer your question."

Stuart quickly grasped her lifeline. "Thank you, Chief Justice," he said, launching into a technical discussion that allowed him to cite several cases as precedent, and avoid answering Stokes. He faced only a few more questions before Ikeda said, "Thank you, General Stuart, and thank you, Mister Lorenz. The case is submitted." As the justices rose to leave the bench, Alex Novak—who hadn't questioned either lawyer—looked over and gave Andy a conspiratorial wink.

In a post-mortem at the Emerald Isle, Josh hoisted his pint of Guinness. "Hank," he said, "congratulations. You won hands down." He took a foamy draft. "But it was like the Redskins thumping the Little Sisters of the Poor. I thought that poor guy was going to pee his pants." They all laughed.

Lorenz took a swallow of his Harp lager. "Don't forget," he cautioned, "even if we win, Odell Beasley still remains in prison, even if he's now off death row. You know, I wish I could have argued the death penalty itself is unconstitutional, but we're chipping away."

"Maybe you'll get that chance, Hank," Andy said. "The Court has done enough chipping away that it's going to collapse, one of these days."

"I hope you're right, Andy," he said. "But since we're in an Irish bar, I'll remind you what Mister Dooley said, a century ago. 'The Supreme Court follows the election returns.' And the death penalty still has a majority of voters who support it. So I doubt the Court would risk the backlash if it did what we all think it should."

"Not now, Hank, you're right," Andy said. "But we'd still have segregated schools and abortion would still be illegal if the Court hadn't been willing to risk a backlash in those cases, a lot of it violent and even murderous."

"Good point, Andy," he conceded. "But we'll have to wait and see. Meanwhile, another round?" That vote was unanimous.

The justices usually met in their private conference room on Fridays to discuss and decide the cases argued that week, but moved this session to Thursday, since Chief Justice Ikeda would be speaking on Friday to a bar association meeting in New Orleans. Andy was sure—even taking indeterminacy into account—they would vote at the conference to hold the Hall case retroactive, giving OD a new hearing on his 'intellectual disability' claim. Fingers flying on her computer to finish the last pool memo on her week's pile, which would free up her weekend, she was startled by Dave's excited voice as he trotted into the clerks' office.

"Wow!" he exclaimed, as Andy and Laura both swiveled to hear what prompted his Wow! "Did you guys hear the commotion down the hall? I thought you'd come running out to see if the cops were coming."

"No, dear," Laura said, "we were so focused on our jobs while you went to the men's room that we couldn't have heard a bomb go off. Why, did a bomb explode while you were peeing?"

"Actually, it did," Dave replied, catching his breath. "Not the kind that brings the bomb squad, but some kind of explosion inside the justices' conference room." He suddenly noticed his fly was unzipped, and discreetly turned around to fix it. "Anyway," he continued, "I was finishing my business when I heard some loud shouting down the hall. So I dashed out—hence my wardrobe malfunction—and heard it coming from the conference room. Being the curious guy I am, I went over, about ten feet from the door, and noticed a guard down the hall, turning his head. So I bent down and pretended to tie my shoelaces, while the shouting went on."

"What was it about, Dave?" Andy asked. "Did you hear what anyone was saying?"

"No, and I wasn't going to put my ear to the door, in case someone opened it and caught me eavesdropping. Or if the guard came down to check it out, which he didn't. But I did recognize some of the voices that were shouting." Dave checked to see if Angie was at her desk, which she wasn't. "I recognized five," he continued. "One was our not-always-soft-spoken boss. Another was Karl Sorenson, shouting through his nose. I

436

did hear Dwight Stokes yelling at someone to sit down. Alice Schroeder said 'Will you all calm down and listen to each other.' And, much to my surprise, Kathryn raised her voice, although not to shouting level."

"My goodness," Laura said. "Any idea what might have caused them to lose their cools? Maybe they were squabbling over what to order for lunch, and the roast beef sandwich people lost to the tuna salad people."

"No idea," Dave said. "But we can discreetly ask Alex when he gets back, like 'So, how'd the conference go, Alex? Any surprises?'"

Just then, Novak stuck his head into the clerks' office. His expression was somber. "You won't believe this," he said, "but we voted on OD's case and . . ." He paused for dramatic effect.

Andy looked stricken. "He didn't lose, Alex, did he?"

He chuckled. "Sorry, guys. Just kidding. So, you can start writing the opinion, Andy."

"I've already got it outlined," she said, looking relieved. "But were there any surprises on other cases? Maybe some, oh, disagreement from your disagreeable colleagues? You know who I mean, Alex."

Novak gave Andy a searching look, then nodded. "Actually, there was some heated discussion about a case that was argued on Tuesday. The negligence and malpractice case against the VA, by the family of a Vietnam vet who was on a waiting list for six months, then died of pancreatic cancer. And the jury gave the family six million bucks." He paused, looking a bit uncomfortable. "Anyway, six of us voted to affirm, but a couple of my quote, 'disagreeable' colleagues disagreed pretty strongly." He chuckled. "But they'd vote to reverse if the Court ruled in favor of motherhood and apple pie." He checked his watch. "Well, I've got a meeting downtown, so I'll see you all tomorrow. Andy should have OD's opinion ready by then, right?"

"I'll pull an all-nighter, Alex," she said, "and have it on your desk by eight." After he left, Andy turned to Dave and Laura. "Did you guys notice that Alex looked a bit, um, frazzled? You think maybe he really lost his temper in there, and got a 'sit down, Alex' from Alice and Kathryn? And have you noticed that he's been a bit touchy lately?"

"Yeah, I have," Dave replied. "But you know what it might be?" Andy and Laura waited. "I heard him say to Angie yesterday that his dad is having problems getting around. I know that would be hard on Alex, since Gloria's in a wheelchair, and relies on his dad to help her. That might explain why he's looking frazzled."

"Alex told me that, too," Andy said. "And I'm guessing his meeting downtown is actually with his dad's doctor at GW hospital. That's probably what's bothering him."

"Well, let's all hope for the best," Laura said. She turned to Andy. "Say, how about dinner tonight at our place? I'm giving osso buco a try, and you and Dave can tell me if I should stick to pasta."

Andy grinned. "One of my favorites in Italy. Even though I feel sorry for the little calves that don't get to be cows. I'll bring the vino, at eight, okay? It takes a couple hours for that dish."

Friday morning, Andy was heading back to the clerks' office from a coffee break when she saw Novak coming down the hallway to his chambers. He walked slowly, his head bent down. She waited until he reached her. "Alex, are you okay? Is something wrong?"

He looked up, startled. "Oh, good morning, Andy," he replied, a wan smile on his face. "No, I'm okay, but can you come into my office?" She followed him, hoping her sudden premonition was wrong. He closed the office door, turned, and took a deep breath. His voice quavered when he spoke. "Andy," he said, "Anton is going to die." He spread his arms wide and she stepped into a tight embrace, feeling his body quiver.

"Oh, Alex, I'm so sorry," she said quietly. "I love Anton. He is such a brave and wonderful person." They released each other and sat at the low table. "You met with Doctor Huang yesterday," Andy said, reaching to hold Novak's hand. "And he told you that Anton's treatment didn't work. And what else did he say?"

"You're right, Andy," he replied. "Anton and I did meet with Doctor Huang. He said the prognosis from the initial treatment was hopeful, but the tests he ordered last week showed that Anton's cancer had spread outside his bladder." Novak shook his head. "It's now invaded the muscle wall and the lymph nodes, and would probably spread into the pelvic bone. The only possible treatment would be to remove the bladder and attach a section of intestine for urination."

"And Anton refused, I'm sure," Andy said. "You told me earlier that he would."

"You're right, again," Novak said. "Doctor Huang and I both knew better than to argue with him. So, according to Doctor Huang, Anton's got somewhere between three and six months left. His heart and lungs are in good shape, at least now, but his muscles are getting weak, and he'll need a walker or even a wheelchair to get around. That's mostly a natural consequence of his age, not the cancer. And he'll probably be bedridden in a month or two."

"You know, Alex, it's hard to imagine Anton giving up his two-mile walks," Andy said. "But if he can't get around, or has to stay in bed, what will happen with Gloria? She really depends on him when you're not home."

"Well, two things," Novak replied. "I'm going to spend more time at home, except when I come in for arguments and conferences. I can work there, with my computer and phone. That's why I came in this morning, to pick up things I need for that. And I'm arranging for a home-care service to help with cooking and shopping and caring for both Anton and Gloria. That should start next week."

"Don't forget about me," Andy said. "I'd love to help out any way I can, and spend time with all of you."

"Andy, you are beyond wonderful," Novak said. "Anton and Gloria both told me they hope you can come over whenever you can. You mean so much to them. And to me, of course." He smiled. "What is it you taught me to say properly in Hebrew? 'Ani ohev otach.' I love you."

"Very good, Alex. And I say 'ani ohevet otcha.' I love you, too." Andy looked down at the Star of David around her neck, and held the pendant in her hand. "L'chaim," she said. "To life. And to a life that has made us both more caring of those whose lives touch ours."

Novak chuckled. "You know, Andy, if Lisa Margolis ever needs someone to fill in for her, you'd make a perfect rabbi." He stood and picked up a stack of papers from his desk. "Come over tonight, and bring your caring with you. And I'll call Loeb's New York Deli and have them deliver a nice Jewish dinner. You like brisket?"

"Love it," Andy said. "Bella makes the best brisket ever, but we'll see if Loeb's can match it." She kissed Novak. "You're a real mensch now, Alex. Just like your dad. Mazel tov."

Over the next two months, Andy settled into a new routine. The circled date of June 25 on her "OD calendar" gave her plenty of time before the Court's final session and the deadline for OD's new trial. Both dates could change, of course, but she took them as goal-posts for the drive to secure his freedom.

Andy spent most days at the Court, working on pool memos for cases on the docket for the next term, but with arguments for this term concluded, there were no bench memos to write. She also devoted many hours—often at home on evenings—to her opinion in OD's case. She took her time, determined to make it air-tight and water-proof, impervious to criticism from the three "disagreeable" dissenters, whose arguments Andy tried to anticipate and counter in advance. She figured any dissenting opinion would echo—and perhaps crib from—the state's brief in the case, although it might raise new objections to the majority's holding. Normally, drafts of opinions on both sides of divided votes were circulated between the chambers, allowing their authors to respond and perhaps revise opinions before they were announced. Andy also knew that dissenters were not obligated to follow this procedure, so she didn't worry as weeks passed with no delivery of any dissent.

Andy also kept to her routine outside the Court of the spouse-endorsed weekly musicales at her place with Josh and Novak, each now aware—and approving—of the other's visits to her couch and bed. The two men complemented each other in their contributions to Andy's erotic life: passionate and often sweaty with Josh, playful and languorous with Novak. Between them, she experienced pleasure that more than satisfied her needs for physical and emotional intimacy. Sometimes, alone in her bed, Andy reflected that sex—like wine—was best enjoyed with different varieties and vintages. Now a connoisseur, she sampled and savored both the tangy and smooth flavors her two lovers offered for her tasting.

The biggest change in Andy's routine was spending two or three evenings each week at Novak's house with Anton and Gloria. She discovered that both enjoyed board games, and spent hours with them at the dining-room table, playing Monopoly, Clue, Scrabble, and Sorry! Andy and Gloria both played for fun, laughing over miscues, but Anton turned into a ferocious competitor, although a gracious winner. Increasingly, he moved more slowly, accepting Andy's helping hand, but never complaining about the pain—expressed in occasional grimaces—he clearly felt. Novak told her that Anton took only the lowest doses of pain medications that would ease his discomfort. "I'd be gobbling pills like candy if I were him," Novak said one night, "but Anton says too many and he misses some great Scrabble words and Monopoly purchases."

The newest member of the Novak household was a home-care helper, who usually left before Andy arrived, but sometimes over-lapped with her. Their first meeting, at Novak's front gate, gave Andy a pleasant surprise. "Hello, I'm Andy Roboff, and I'm here to spend the evening with Anton and Gloria," she introduced herself.

"Young lady, I know who you are, and I been hoping to meet you here," replied a tall, wiry, black woman in her fifties. "I'm Marvella Owens, and Clarence tells me you always make his day a bit more cheerful, with your smile and kind words."

"Oh, my," Andy said. "Clarence is my favorite person at the Court, and he always makes me smile, too. So, you're the woman he says keeps him out of trouble."

Marvella laughed. "Well, you're even prettier than Clarence says, so I better make sure he don't get in trouble, 'cause he likes pretty women." She opened the gate for Andy. "You know, Anton and Gloria are just about the nicest people I ever helped," she said. "Some older people, they complain if you don't fold napkins just the way they want, things like that. Or make you call them Mister or Missus, and don't call you by your name. But the first thing Gloria says to me was 'Marvella, you going to be part of our family now, so you do things just like you want.'" She smiled. "The good Lord don't make everybody that nice, so I feel blessed."

"Me, too," Andy said. "And tell Clarence he's already got a pretty woman, right at home." Marvella laughed again as she headed for the bus on Connecticut Avenue.

Andy paid more attention to the calendar, and the time remaining in her clerkship, when June arrived, along with warm and sunny days in Washington. She had finished her draft of the opinion in OD's case, which was circulated to the other chambers, but hadn't received drafts of any dissents. "Alex," she asked him one morning, "any idea when I might get a dissent from your 'disagreeable' colleagues?"

He paused before answering. "You know, Andy, it's possible you won't get any. Dissenters don't *have* to write opinions, and from what I recall about the oral argument, back in April, Hank Lorenz pretty much shamed Karl and Cormac into silence. His line about 'whether you live or die shouldn't depend on the date of your conviction' really shut them up. And there wasn't any debate at our conference, just a vote on the case. So, if you don't get a draft in the next week or so, I'd assume there won't be any. That happens in several cases every term, dissents without opinion."

"Hank really *did* shame them," Andy agreed, "and you'll get praised for a brilliant opinion."

Novak chuckled. "I'd put your name on it if I could, Andy, but that would blow the worst-kept secret in Washington. Most people already know, or suspect, that clerks write opinions that we just skim, maybe adding a word or two. But we get all the credit, or blame, while you toil in obscurity."

The next morning, Dave came into the clerks' office, shaking his head. "By the way, Andy," he said, "I checked with my colleagues in the dark chambers, just out of curiosity, and they all said there's no dissenting opinion in the works in OD's case. So, your soaring prose and heart-tugging stories will stand as the last and only word on this issue."

"Thank you for those kind words, Dave," she said, "but Oliver Wendell Holmes I'm not. He was pithy, and I'm not. Of course, he was the son of a famous essayist, so he inherited his writing gene. I'm still looking for mine."

Andy also called Josh for any news about preparations for OD's new trial, scheduled for June 25. "Hey, Andy," he said, "Jim thinks they're going ahead with the trial. Shotwell named his top trial lawyer to replace the Commonwealth's Attorney in Williamsburg, who stepped aside because he had some conflict of interest, although Jim didn't know what. Anyway, they filed their list of witnesses, which means we can interview those who agree to talk with us."

"Any surprises on the list?"

"No, not really," he replied. "Most of them are cops who worked on the case, or experts and technicians on fingerprints, DNA, the autopsy, stuff like that. Some of them testified at the original trial, and others will testify about reports by people who have died since then or moved away. Needless to say, Junior's not on their witness list."

"Well, that's a surprise," Andy said. "Just kidding. When is your list due?"

"Next Monday. So far, we have Vito Petrocelli, Martha Radford, Tory Tucker, and Mose Townley. Mose, by the way, has agreed to testify that he screwed up by not asking for testing on the brown glove and not asking Martha for more details on the red car." Josh paused for a second. "Oh, and we put you on our witness list, Andy."

"*What!* Me? You're kidding, right."

"Actually, not," Josh replied. "Vito can testify that he got the glove from Mose, and the blood and hair from the bathroom sink from the state. But the state's lawyer will ask, 'Where did you get the saliva from the glass and cigar in your report? How did you know they're from Mister Early? Did you get them yourself?' And he'll have to say they came from you. And that, Miss Portia Bradwell, puts *you* on the witness stand."

"Holy shit, Josh." Andy said. "I'd have to admit I stole the glass and cigar under false pretences."

"That you did," he replied. "But not to worry. Stealing the actual glass and cigar could get you a fifty-buck fine for petty larceny, but how you got them is perfectly legal. Undercover cops do it all the time, like in sting operations for drugs or bribes. And fibbing about your name isn't a crime. Junior could have checked you out, or asked for ID, but that was his mistake. But Jim *does* need you, to get the glass and cigar from Junior to Vito. Capice?"

"Um, I guess," Andy replied. "I'll bring fifty bucks with me just in case. But not Junior on your witness list?"

"No," Josh said. "First, we got him with the glove, and the red Corvette, and his confession to Tory, which creates enough reasonable doubt to get OD acquitted. And second, even if we did call him, he'd take the Fifth, which he's entitled to do." Andy heard a voice behind Josh. "Sorry, Andy, gotta go, but I'll let you know if anything comes up. Otherwise, we're on schedule, and we have to assume there will be a trial. We can't just walk in like, 'Oh, can you give us some time to prepare, Your Honor? We thought the state was bluffing.'"

"Okay," Andy said. "I understand. Talk soon. Love you, Josh."

"Love you too."

37

June 25 began for Andy at six. She left plenty of time to get ready for the Court's final session of the term, beginning at ten, at which Alex Novak would read from her opinion in OD's case. Also at ten, OD's retrial was scheduled to begin in Williamsburg, starting with jury selection. Josh had told her Jim Carruthers would handle that, freeing him to join Andy at the Court. She had actually slept well that night, reasonably sure that OD would soon win his release from prison after fifteen years on death row. But, she reminded herself, you never know for sure what might happen to your confident predictions.

Andy's phone rang, startling her, but she recognized the ring-tone. "It's just past six, Mister Night Owl," she said, cheerfully, "and I'm surprised you're up this early. Actually, I just stepped out of the shower, and I'm bare-ass naked. How about you, still in your jammies?"

"Normally, Venus, I'd offer to dash over and help you dry off," he replied, not sounding cheerful. "But this isn't normally, unfortunately. Can you quick dry off, and sit down while I tell you what happened last night?"

"Not Carlo, I hope," she said. "I know he's doing a cardiac surgery rotation, and had an open heart yesterday. Was it his patient?"

"No, that went fine," Josh said. "Are you sitting yet?"

"Yes, in my robe, with a cup of coffee. But what happened last night? You sound upset."

"I am," he replied. "Very upset. But let me tell you what happened last night, okay?"

"Go ahead," Andy said. "Just calm down, and I'll listen."

"Okay," Josh said. "Jim Carruthers called me last night, around ten. He'd just gotten off the phone with Warden Zook at the Sussex prison. OD was scheduled to be driven up to Williamsburg this morning for his trial. But he's in the Williamsburg hospital."

"In the hospital?" Andy said. "Did he get sick, or try to kill himself, God forbid?"

"No," Josh said. "Here's what happened, according to Jim. After OD left death row, they moved him to a block where the cell doors are open until lights out. Anyway, he was in the shower room, by himself, when two inmates came in and stabbed him several times with the sharpened end of a toothbrush. They also whacked him in the head with a metal chair leg, and kicked him when he went down. They broke three ribs, and his left arm, and he's got a bunch of contusions and cuts on his head and body."

"Oh shit," Andy said. "Is it really bad, Josh? Is he going to be okay?"

"Yeah, thanks to another inmate who came into the shower room and scared these guys away. And a bunch of guards showed up right away." Josh paused. "Hang on, Andy, while I get my coffee from the Keurig." Another short pause. "I'm back. So, there's no video in the shower room, and these two guys had pulled their tee-shirts over their heads. But their torsos were exposed, and video caught them running down the hall. Zook told Jim they ID'd them right away, from distinctive tattoos on their arms and backs. They keep a photo file of all inmates with tattoos."

"Any idea why these guys would try to kill OD?" Andy asked. "I doubt he had any enemies there."

"Well, Zook pulled these guys in as soon as they were ID'd. Needless to say, they both denied attacking OD. But Zook said he had them on video, so cut the shit, and tell him who put them up to this, since he knew OD didn't have any enemies, as you said. They both clammed up, but Zook said he could have them tried for attempted murder. That didn't seem to faze them, since they're both already doing long time. So, Zook upped the ante. Cough up names, or he'd have them transferred to a Supermax in Colorado, and stick them in solitary forever."

"Did that work?" Andy had taken her phone into the kitchen for another cup of coffee, and was back at the table.

"Yep, although it took a while," Josh said. "So, they both said they'd been offered five thousand bucks, to be paid to their 'old ladies' on the outside. Zook pressed more, threatening to arrest their old ladies, and they gave him a name."

"Was it Junior?"

"No, a guy named Artie D'Amico. Zook knew him, he'd done time at Sussex with these guys, and was now out on parole. He did a quick check, and found that Artie was now working as a groundskeeper at a country club in Richmond."

"Let me guess," Andy said. "Junior belongs to this club, right?"

"Hang on, Special Agent Roboff," Josh replied. "You're getting ahead of me. I'll get there, okay?"

"I'll bet I got there first, Barney Fife," she said. "But take your time, and I'll let you catch up."

"Thank you," Josh said. "Anyway, Zook called the Richmond cops, gave them Artie's address from the parole records, filled them in, and they found him at home, smoking weed. Said they'd come to arrest him for conspiracy to commit murder. Needless to say, Artie denied everything, until the cops found ten thousand bills in his fridge. They offered him a deal, Zook didn't tell Jim what it was, if he'd give up who paid him to hire the hit guys."

"And now you're caught up with me," Andy said. "Junior knows Artie through the golf club."

"Great deduction," Josh said. "Anyway, to wrap up, the cops went to Junior's house, rousted his wife out of bed, and she told them Junior left the day before, said he was going to Boston to wrap up a real estate deal, but she didn't know his hotel. So, that's where we are. The Boston cops are looking for Junior as we speak. Jim will let me know when they find him, assuming he's not on a plane to Rio."

"Holy shit," Andy said. "So, what happens to OD's trial? Obviously, he's in the hospital and can't be there."

"Right," Josh said. "So, Jim will inform the judge as soon as the courthouse opens, tell him that Junior's plot and disappearance leaves no doubt that he killed Laurel Davis, and ask the judge to dismiss OD's murder charge and order his immediate release. Jim will let me know what happens right away."

Andy had a quick thought. "Should we tell Alex about this? I mean, if the judge dismisses the charge and orders OD's release, it could make his petition moot, and Alex wouldn't need to announce the decision this morning."

Josh chuckled. "And your brilliant opinion would be lost to posterity. Actually, let's wait on that until this gets wrapped up. Besides, the opinion would affect a lot of death row inmates, and pulling it might cost them a chance for new sentencing hearings."

"Good point," Andy said. "Hey, while you're waiting to hear from Jim, how about coming over here before we go to the Court. I'll make scrambled eggs, bacon, and English muffins. But no fooling around, okay? That can also wait."

"Deal," Josh said. "I'll shower, dress, and cab over. Say, an hour?"

"Deal," she agreed. "And I'm going to call Mamie Beasley and tell her what happened, that OD's going to be okay, and that she can make another batch of fried chicken and greens for when he comes home. And chocolate-chip cookies,"

"That's very thoughtful, Andy," Josh said "And tell her we'll come down for the homecoming." He paused. "Can you believe all this happened? Just goes to show, well, you know what."

"I *do* know," Andy said. "So don't say it. Just get over here, and mind your manners. 'You know what' can wait until tonight."

Dressed in her go-to-court outfit, Andy walked to the Court with Josh, holding hands on a warm, sunny morning. "You know, Josh," she said, "this will be the last time I'll sit in the chamber before my clerkship ends. It's sort of sad, but not really, if that makes any sense."

"Yeah, it does," he replied. "We all have to move on when the time comes. But look at it this way, Andy. Your last time in the chamber will end with a really important opinion that you wrote, that will save a lot of inmates from execution, and that wouldn't have happened without you."

"And you, too, Josh," she said, squeezing his hand. "Don't forget that, partner. This opinion is as much yours as mine."

Andy stopped and gave Clarence Owens a hug before she and Josh went through security. "In case you didn't know, Clarence," she said, "you're a very lucky man. Marvella is just marvelous, and Justice Novak's wife and dad love having her make them comfortable."

"Oh, I knew she was marvelous, first time I met her," he replied, with a smile. "I said, 'it's time to settle down, Clarence, and that's the woman you're going to marry.' And she really loves helping those wonderful people. That's a blessing from the Lord."

At quarter of ten, Andy led Josh into the guest section of the Court's chamber, finding Dave and Laura already there. "Showtime, guys," Dave greeted them. "But you don't come on stage until Act Three, Andy. Two opinions first, the Clerk told me. Then Alex gets to end the erm with a bang." He chuckled. "I passed Bob Barnes and a couple other reporters on the way in, and I heard him say this has been the most boring term in several years, and he's only here today out of duty."

"Oh, he's just pissed that he didn't get a story out of the recusal flap," Andy said. She turned at the sound of familiar voices, to see a Court attendant wheeling Gloria into the guest section, followed by Anton, slowly pushing a walker. "Oh, my goodness," she said to Gloria, "I wasn't expecting you and Anton to be here this morning. Did Alex tell you to come, for his opinion in OD Beasley's case?"

"Yes, dear," Gloria replied, making way for Anton to sit next to Andy. "But he said we shouldn't miss *your* opinion. He said it's really going to make news, and that Anton and I should be here to witness that."

"That's nice of Alex," Andy said, "but I doubt it will be headline news." She leaned over and kissed Anton's cheek. "Tell you what," she added. "We still haven't finished our last Monopoly game, and I'll come over soon and try to buy Park Place from you. Unless I get a bad roll and wind up in Jail."

The "All Rise" command from the Marshal hushed the chamber. Gloria and Anton remained seated while he intoned the traditional opening, as the justices entered through the velvet drapes and took their seats behind the bench. "Please be seated," Kathryn Ikeda said as she took the center seat. She looked out and smiled. "This is, as you know, the last session of our current term. And we have saved the best for last." When the chuckles subsided, she went on, her tone serious. "It has been my privilege, these past few months, to serve with my distinguished colleagues. We do not always agree on the cases we decide, but we all take our responsibilities very seriously. I hope you will keep that in mind as we announce the decisions in our three remaining cases."

With that, the Chief Justice turned to her right. "Justice Hanlon will announce the decision in our first case." For five minutes, his voice barely audible, Parker Hanlon summarized a unanimous opinion in a case that pitted several states against federal regulators, over protection of coastal wetlands, with the states winning. No surprise there, Andy thought, having read the draft opinion on which Novak had scribbled "Join."

Hanlon was followed by Juan Pablo Romero, who spent ten minutes reading excerpts from a six-to-three opinion, holding that Boston's public schools could not allow white teachers to opt out of assignments to majority black and Hispanic schools, based solely on seniority. Cormac McCarthy spent just three minutes summarizing the dissenting opinion. Again, no surprise, Andy thought. Bob Barnes, who had predicted the outcome of both cases in a *Post* article, and certainly knew how OD's case would be decided, could have skipped the session without missing anything.

After McCarthy sat back from his microphone, Kathryn Ikeda leaned forward into hers. "Justice Novak will announce the Court's decision in our final case, Odell Beasley versus David Zook, Warden." She paused, then her voice took on emphasis. "Let me underscore what I will say next. The opinion of the majority has been signed by six justices as joint authors. Each of us felt a need to express our support for the holding in a case that raises the most profound issue in our legal system, and our society as well."

Andy raised a mental eyebrow at these words, but Novak, she thought, might have persuaded his colleagues to sign his opinion to deflect possible criticism of his refusal to recuse himself in this case. Her thought was interrupted by Ikeda's voice. "Justice Novak, would you please announce the opinion of the Court." He picked up a sheaf of paper from the bench, looked over with a smile at the guest section, and began speaking, his voice firm and measured.

"This case," he began, "as the Chief Justice has stated, raises the ultimate question to which the Constitution and its framers provided conflicting answers. And that is the question of deciding who shall live and who shall die for the ultimate crime, taking the life of another person." He paused. "This Court has dealt, over more than a century, with hundreds of cases that challenged various aspects of capital punishment. Despite the different issues these cases raised, they all rested, fundamentally, on the underlying issue of the death penalty's constitutionality. In its often-divided rulings in these hundreds of cases, the Court has declined to decide, unequivocally, whether the death penalty violates the Constitution. We believe that this case offers the opportunity to decide that basic question."

Unless Novak was ad-libbing, Andy suddenly thought, this was *not* the question raised or addressed in her opinion. She gave Josh a What The Hell? look, getting a Beats Me! in return.

"Let me make one point," Novak continued, "before I turn to our opinion." He looked out at a sea of quizzical expressions. "This Court has the power, infrequently exercised but nonetheless available, to decide questions not presented by the parties to a case, but implicated in them, as it is in the case before us. This is the power to decide these questions sua sponte." He looked up, with a smile. "For those who flunked Latin, it means 'on our own volition,' or something like that." Only a smattering of chuckles greeted this reprise of Ikeda's witticism, most spectators frowning with puzzlement. "Only the gravest of constitutional issues," Novak continued, "merit a sua sponte disposition, and we agree on the gravity of this issue. Those who might question our use of this power, we think, might well recognize that the time is long overdue to face this issue, and that it would inevitably come before us in any event. In our view, that time is *now*." The chamber was perfectly still as the significance of Novak's words sank in. Andy turned and gave Josh an I'll Be Damned! look, getting a Me Too! in return.

Nokav looked out again, and smiled. "Now that I have your attention," he said, "I will read the most significant portions of the opinion that my colleagues in the majority have jointly authored. The full text, with citations to cases and other material, can be found in the printed copies that are available in the press room, and will be posted on the Court's website, for those who actually *read* our opinions." A final round of chuckles, followed by silence and rapt attention as Novak—for the next twenty minutes—read from an opinion that Andy had not written, but which she would have, given the opportunity.

"Forty years ago," Novak began, "this Court upheld the death penalty under statutes that, in the Court's view, contained safeguards sufficient to ensure that the penalty would be applied reliably and not arbitrarily. The circumstances and the evidence of the death penalty's application have changed radically since then. In 1976, the Court thought that the constitutional infirmities in the death penalty could be healed; the Court in effect delegated significant responsibility to the States to develop procedures that would protect against those constitutional problems.

"Forty years of studies and experience strongly indicate, however, that this effort has failed. Today's administration of the death penalty involves three fundamental constitutional defects: first, serious unreliability; second, arbitrariness in application; and third, unconscionably long delays that undermine the death penalty's penological purpose. Perhaps as a result, most places within the United States have abandoned its use, either in imposing death sentences or carrying them out over the past decade.

"I shall describe each of these considerations, emphasizing changes that have occurred during the past four decades. It is these changes that lead us to address the question of whether the death penalty, in and of itself, now constitutes a legally prohibited 'cruel and unusual punishment.'" Novak waited for the buzzing—and an audible "Oh, my God!"—to subside before he continued.

"It hardly needs stating that the execution of an innocent person would violate the Constitution, and even one such execution argues against the constitutionality of the death penalty. Let me point out here that researchers have found convincing evidence that, in the past three decades, at least two innocent people have been executed. They are Carlos DeLuna and Cameron Todd Willingham, both executed in Texas.

"In DeLuna's case, no forensic evidence tied him to the murder for which he was executed; the prosecution relied solely on the testimony of an eyewitness who identified him on the basis of a few seconds of passing the killer as he exited the convenience store in which the victim was stabbed and later died. After DeLuna's execution, a thorough investigation identified the actual killer, Carlos Hernandez, who confessed—too late to save DeLuna—to the murder. In other words, Texas executed the wrong Carlos.

"Also in Texas, Cameron Willingham was accused of setting fire to his house and killing his three young children, although no motive was ever suggested. Subsequent investigation, after his execution, showed that the deadly fire could not have been deliberate arson, and that the state's arson investigators relied on totally discredited procedures. The evidence of DeLuna and Willingham's innocence of the crimes for which they were executed is overwhelming, and can be found in the citations in this opinion. There were undoubtedly more executions of innocent defendants than these two men, but those examples will suffice for this opinion. The burden of refuting the evidence of these men's innocence falls squarely on those, including today's dissenters, who continue to claim that no innocent person has been executed since this Court revived the death penalty in 1976." Novak shot a glance at Karl Sorenson, who looked away, his lips pursed.

"Furthermore," Novak continued, "the growing number of exonerations of inmates sentenced to death, but who were later found to be innocent of the crimes of which they were convicted, adds another argument for the unconstitutionality of the death penalty. Since 1973, there have been 156 exonerations of death-sentenced inmates, many of whom served thirty or more years on death row before their exoneration. Many of these exonerations resulted from evidence, including DNA evidence, that had not been available, or had been withheld by prosecutors, at the time of conviction. Had this new evidence not been available, many— perhaps a majority—of those 156 inmates would now be dead, beyond the reach of corrective action."

Novak paused for a long moment. "Speaking for myself," he said, "today's decision, in many respects, is both a mea culpa and an apology. I once stated in an opinion that 'We cannot have a system of criminal punishment without accepting the possibility that someone will be punished mistakenly.' That may well be true, and unavoidable, but if that punishment is death, a posthumous exoneration will not correct that mistake. I also once stated that 'This Court has never held that the Constitution forbids the execution of a convicted defendant who has had a full and fair trial but is later able to convince a habeas court that he is 'actually' innocent. Quite to the contrary, we have repeatedly left that question unresolved, while expressing considerable doubt that any claim based on alleged 'actual innocence' is constitutionally cognizable.'"

Novak took a deep breath, then continued. "I now regret those words. Fortunately, I have the chance, in this opinion, to resolve that question, and remove that doubt. Speaking again for my colleagues, what we mean by 'actual innocence' was best stated by this Court in 1992: it 'is the case where the State has convicted the wrong person of the crime.' Such a case *must* be constitutionally cognizable, or the Constitution protects no person from wrongful conviction and punishment that may be irrevocable.

"Let me raise, and answer, another question. As I noted, there have been some 156 exonerations of death-row inmates since 1973. That is certainly a substantial number, one that should give pause to those, like me, who expressed doubt that any innocent person has been sentenced to death, or executed. But they indisputably have, which raises the question: Why is that so? To some degree, in capital cases, there is a greater likelihood on an initial wrongful conviction. And how can that happen? In large part, because the crimes at issue are typically horrendous murders, and thus accompanied by intense community pressure on police, prosecutors, and jurors to secure a conviction. This pressure creates a greater likelihood of convicting the wrong person.

"If we expand our definition of exoneration to also categorize as constitutionally erroneous those instances in which courts failed to follow legally required procedures, the numbers soar. Between 1973 and 1995, courts identified prejudicial errors in 68 percent of the capital cases before them. State courts on direct and post-conviction review overturned 47 percent of the death sentences they reviewed. Federal courts, reviewing capital cases in habeas corpus proceedings, found reversible error in 40 percent of those cases. Unlike 40 years ago, we now have substantial evidence that courts sentence to death individuals who may well be actually innocent or whose convictions do not warrant the death penalty.

"If the death penalty suffers from serious unreliability, which it does, it is also arbitrary in its imposition. When the death penalty was reinstated in 1976, this Court acknowledged that it would be unconstitutional if 'inflicted in an arbitrary and capricious manner.' The Court has consequently sought to make the application of the death penalty less arbitrary by restricting its use to those whom one justice called 'the worst of the worst.' But this goal has failed. Leaving aside the fact that those who commit horrific, gruesome murders cannot be executed in almost half the states, there are numerous examples of its arbitrary imposition.

"I will give only three to make this point. In North Carolina, a defendant who committed a single-victim murder, John Badgett, was sentenced to death, while another defendant, Andre Edwards, was not, despite having kidnapped, raped, and murdered a young mother while leaving her infant baby to die at the scene of the crime. In Pennsylvania,

Richard Boxley, a defendant who committed a single-victim murder, was sentenced to die, while another, Matthew Eshbech, was not, despite having committed a triple murder by killing a young man and his pregnant wife. In Connecticut, before the state legislature voted to abolish the death penalty, a single-victim defendant, Eduardo Santiago, was sentenced to die, while Scott Pickles was not, despite having stabbed his wife 60 times and killing his six-year-old daughter and three-year-old son while they slept. In each example, the sentences were imposed in the same State at about the same time. Those different outcomes meet the very definition of arbitrariness." Novak looked up briefly, turned a sheet, and kept reading.

"There are other factors that show the arbitrary nature of the death penalty. Numerous studies, for example, have found that black defendants accused of murdering white victims, as opposed to black or other minority victims, are more likely to receive the death penalty. Geography also plays an important role in determining who is sentenced to death. This is not simply because some States permit the death penalty while others do not. Rather, within a death penalty State, its imposition heavily depends on the county in which the defendant is tried. In 2012, for example, just 59 counties, fewer than two percent of all the counties in the country, accounted for *all* death sentences imposed nationwide. What accounts for this county-by-county disparity? Some studies indicate that the disparity reflects the decision-making authority, the legal discretion, and ultimately the power of the local prosecutor.

"Within a single State, Texas being a good example, prosecutors in one county are much more likely than those in another to seek, and obtain, death sentences. One person in these counties, quite literally, holds the power of life or death over those accused of capital murder. And that power is often exercised in an arbitrary manner, unreviewable by the courts. One Louisiana district attorney, speaking in 2015, frankly voiced his belief that the state needs to 'kill more people.' Four decades ago, this Court believed it possible to interpret the Eighth Amendment in ways that would significantly limit the arbitrary application of the death sentence. But that limitation no longer seems likely."

Novak paused, as if pondering what to say next. Andy could see the indecision in his expression. Then he nodded, to himself, and continued.

"It may seem unfair and inappropriate," he said, "to chastise a former member of this Court, now deceased, for making statements that have since been proven wrong. But one example of this wrongness, in my opinion, warrants chastisement. Writing in an unrelated case, this justice referred to 'the case of an eleven-year-old girl raped by four men and then killed by stuffing her panties down her throat.' One defendant in that case, a mentally deficient black man named Henry McCollum, was sentenced to death for his participation in this horrific crime. Our former colleague wrote, referring to McCollum: 'How enviable a quiet death by lethal injection compared to that!' But the death of Henry McCollum, eagerly awaited by our former colleague, did not happen. After thirty years on death row, and years of struggle by his attorneys against recalcitrant prosecutors and compliant judges, DNA evidence conclusively proved that Henry McCollum was innocent, and he was released from death row in 2014."

Novak took another deep breath before continuing. "Given his oft-stated and enthusiastic support for capital punishment, our former colleague might well have volunteered to insert the intravenous needles into McCollum's arms, and pull the levers that released the lethal drugs into his veins. In doing so, he would have executed an innocent man, despite his confident claim, in one of his opinions, that he could not find 'a single case—not one—in which it is clear that a person was executed for a crime he did not commit.'"

A buzz of whispers swept the chamber, as spectators traded guesses— most of them correct—as to which former justice had written these callous words. Novak waited a moment for silence to return. "As this opinion documents," he continued, "there have been persons executed for crimes they did not commit. Even one such case not only violates the Constitution, it makes a mockery of the values most Americans share, the values of fairness and the equal protection of the laws for every person, regardless of a community's pressure for vengeance against those—most often poor and non-white—accused of horrific crimes.

"The problems of reliability and unfairness lead to a third constitutional problem: excessively long periods that individuals typically spend on death row, alive but under sentence of death. In large part, lengthy delays between conviction and execution result from the Constitution's own demand that 'every safeguard' be observed when a defendant's life is at stake. In the past few years, executions occurred, on average, nearly 18 years after a court imposed the death penalty. Nearly half of the 3,000 inmates now on death row have been there for more than 15 years, many for 30 or 40 years. At present execution rates, it would take 75 years to carry out those 3,000 death sentences.

"These lengthy delays create two special constitutional difficulties. First, a lengthy delay in and of itself is especially cruel because it subjects death row inmates to decades of severe, dehumanizing conditions of confinement. Nearly all death penalty States keep death row inmates in solitary confinement for 22 or more hours a day. These conditions produce many cases of insanity and suicide. Some may say that such results of delay are the just deserts for those who have ended another person's life, but their cruelty cannot be denied.

"The second constitutional difficulty resulting from lengthy delays is that they undermine the death penalty's penological rationale, perhaps irreparably so. The rationale for capital punishment, as for any punishment, classically rests upon society's need to secure rehabilitation, incapacitation, deterrence, or retribution. Capital punishment, by definition, does not rehabilitate. It does, of course, incapacitate the offender. But the major alternative to capital punishment—namely, life in prison without possibility of parole—also incapacitates. This is an alternative that every state allows, including those that have abandoned the death penalty.

"Studies of the deterrent effects of capital punishment generally have concluded that such effects are minimal at best, while others have found none. In fact, a study of homicide rates between 1980 and 2000 found that rates in death-penalty States were 48 to 101 percent higher than in non-death penalty States. Another study showed that of the 8,466 inmates under a death sentence at some point between 1973 and 2013, 16 percent were executed, 42 percent had their convictions or sentences overturned or commuted, and six percent died of other causes, usually natural, while the remaining 35 percent were still on death row. Thus, an offender sentenced to death is three times more likely to have his sentence overturned or commuted, or to die of natural causes, than he is to be executed. Taken together, these factors make any deterrent effect of capital punishment remote and attenuated."

Another short pause. Andy realized that much of what Novak had said, and the facts he cited, came from chapters in *Dismantling the Machinery of Death*, which she had seen on his desk, slips of paper stuck between pages. She smiled as he continued.

"But what about retribution, one may ask. Retribution is a valid penological goal. I recognize that surviving relatives of victims of a horrendous crime, or the community itself, may find vindication in an execution. But the relevant question is whether retributive vindication comes, if at all, only several decades after the crime was committed. The victims' families have grown far older. Feelings of outrage may have subsided. The community itself is a different group of people. In any event, whatever interest in retribution might be served by the death penalty is equally served by a sentence of life in prison without parole, an option now supported by a majority of Americans. We recognize that many people believe that retribution, even decades after the crime, satisfies their desire that offenders die at the hands of the state. But such attitudes, in my view, take little or no account of the constitutional flaws that are discussed and documented in this opinion.

"Some have argued that capital punishment itself is dying out in this country, and have advised this Court to allow its natural death and not to hasten its inevitable demise. In some respects, this prognosis is correct. As of today, nineteen states have abolished the death penalty, along with the District of Columbia. Both the numbers of those sentenced to death and those executed have dropped dramatically since a peak in the 1990s. In 1999, 279 persons were sentenced to death, and 98 were executed. By 2015, those numbers had declined to 52 death sentences and 28 executions. In that year, just three states—Texas, Missouri, and Georgia—accounted for all but four of those executions. The vast majority of Americans now live in states in which executions are performed rarely or not at all, making the penalty increasingly 'unusual.'

"It is also worth noting that few other nations still carry out executions. No countries in all of Europe, Central Asia, and South America, still retain capital punishment. In 2015, only eight countries executed more than ten persons: China, Iran, Iraq, Saudi Arabia, Somalia, Sudan, Yemen, and the United States. Those other countries are certainly not places any American would wish ours to emulate in how they deal with accused or convicted criminals."

Novak scanned the chamber, then turned another sheet. "Finally," he read, "we recognize a strong counterargument that favors constitutionality, and is made by the dissenters to this opinion. We are a court, not a legislature whose members are elected by, and answerable to, their constituents. Why should we not leave the matter up to the people acting democratically through their legislators? The answer to this question is that the factors I have discussed, such as lack of reliability, the arbitrary application of an irrevocable punishment, individual suffering caused by long delays, and lack of penological purpose are quintessentially judicial matters. They concern the infliction—indeed the cruel and unusual infliction—of a punishment that cannot be undone, should evidence of innocence later emerge."

He turned a final sheet. "We recognize that in 1972 this Court turned to Congress and the states in its search for standards that would increase the fairness and reliability of imposing a death penalty. The legislatures responded. But, over more than four decades, considerable evidence has shown that those responses have not worked. Thus we are left with a judicial responsibility. The Eighth Amendment sets forth the relevant law, and we must interpret that law, no matter how many people question our competence or authority to do so."

Novak paused one last time, taking a deep breath before he spoke, in a voice that quavered with emotion. "For the reasons set forth in this opinion, the Court concludes that the death penalty, in all circumstances, constitutes 'cruel and unusual punishment' and violates the Eighth Amendment."

The chamber remained totally silent as Novak turned to Kathryn Ikeda. "Chief Justice, I appreciate the opportunity and honor to deliver the Court's opinion in this case. My thanks to you and the colleagues who have joined us in this final dismantling of the machinery of death."

As he sat back in his chair, Novak turned to the guest section, both relief and satisfaction on his face. Andy turned to Josh, blinking back tears. "Oh, my God," she whispered, "I can't believe what Alex has done."

"What *you* have done, Andy," he whispered back. "Don't you know how you have changed his life? He's not the same Alex he was, before you first walked into his chambers." Not just me, she thought. Bella, Anton, Gloria, Lisa, Dave, Laura, and, of course, Josh--all had roles in changing Novak's life. And now, three thousand men and women on death rows across the country owed their lives to him. Andy struggled to keep inside the tears of joy that she would soon allow to escape.

A gentle rap of Ikeda's gavel—her first since taking the center seat—stilled the whispers in the chamber. "Thank you, Justice Novak," she said.

Ikeda then turned to her right. "Justice Sorenson, you may present your dissent."

Sorenson turned to Novak, an accusation of betrayal on his face. Without a word, he rose and left the bench, followed by Parker Hanlon and Cormac McCarthy. A startled attendant parted the velvet drapes as they departed. Ikeda watched them leave, then turned to the chamber. "The Court is now adjourned for the term," she said, rising to lead her remaining colleagues through the still-parted drapes.

Andy looked across the chamber to the press section, rapidly emptied as Bob Barnes and his fellow reporters hustled to file stories that would make headlines around the world. She felt Gloria's trembling hand reach hers. "Andy, dear, now I know why Alex made sure Anton and I would be here this morning." Gloria smiled. "Before he left to come here, Alex said, 'I don't want you and Anton to miss the opinion that Andy would have written.' I thought he was making a joke, but he was giving me a message that I didn't grasp until now." She squeezed Andy's hand. "And I feel sure that *was* the opinion you would have written, had Alex told you what he planned, obviously in great secrecy."

"I wouldn't have changed a word," Andy said. "And I have a guess about why he wrote that opinion in secrecy. Although he's entitled to keep it secret."

Two Court attendants appeared, one to wheel Gloria out of the almost-empty chamber, another to help Anton with his walker. Before they left, Andy kissed both on the cheek. With a last look around the majestic room in which history had just been made, and which she would not enter again as a clerk, Andy led Josh, Dave, and Laura to Novak's chambers. Her mission had been accomplished, she reflected, through a series of events she couldn't possibly have foreseen, nor could anyone else. Whoever said "You never know" *did* know that lives could change with a chance encounter, like hers with Josh. Andy looked at him, and noticed a solitary tear on his cheek. She reached over, very gently, and brushed it off.

38

Andy entered Novak's chambers, trailed by Josh, Dave, and Laura. They found Angie in his office, the TV tuned to CNN. Under a "Breaking News" banner, Novak's face and name filled the screen. "Oh, my goodness!" Angie exclaimed. "Can you believe this? I had no idea Alex was going to make the news today. But he told me, before he left for this morning's session, to turn the set on and listen for the top story at eleven. And there he is!" The clerks and Josh took seats around the low table to watch, and wait for Novak to return from the robing room.

The familiar faces and voices of Wolf Blitzer and Jeff Toobin replaced Novak on the screen. "Jeff, it's an understatement to say the Court's decision today was a shock to everyone," Blitzer said. "Until Justice Novak read his opinion this morning, nobody anticipated that six justices would strike down the death penalty, especially in a case that didn't challenge its constitutionality. Can they really do that, Jeff?"

"You're right, Wolf," he replied, "that nobody, including me, thought there was even the remotest chance the Court would do that, certainly not now. Maybe in ten or twenty years, but the majority of people still support the death penalty. Now, asking whether the Court could do that in today's opinion, the answer is probably yes. It's very rare, as Justice Novak said this morning, for the Court to use this 'sua sponte' procedure, but it's been done before, with no repercussions."

"So is there any way for death penalty supporters to undo that decision?" Blitzer asked.

"Well, not by asking the Court to overrule itself in this case," Toobin replied, "and that's hardly likely, unless new conservative justices replace the sitting liberal ones. However, Wolf, there *are* two possible ways to reverse the decision. One is through a constitutional amendment that would allow states to restore the death penalty. But that's a cumbersome process, and I doubt it would succeed. It would take just thirteen states to block one, and there are twenty that have abolished the death penalty, and probably wouldn't vote to reinstate it."

Blitzer nodded. "And what's the other way, Jeff?"

"The only other way, Wolf, is through impeachment," Toobin answered. "But that would be even less likely to succeed than a constitutional amendment. As we learned this morning, six justices signed that opinion, and they'd all have to be impeached. Some death penalty supporters might agitate for impeachment, but it won't happen. So the decision to strike down the death penalty will hold, unless there's a big turnover on the Court, which I don't see happening."

A familiar voice interrupted the pundits. "Did he say impeachment?" Novak came into his office, smiling broadly. "Hah! Bring it on. Nothing I'd like more than a trial in the Senate, telling those Republicans what hypocrites they are." Behind him was Kathryn Ikeda, also smiling broadly. "Kathryn, take a seat," Novak said. "I've got to pop into Angie's cabinet and fetch something." He popped out, returning with Angie. Novak carried two bottles, wrapped in wet towels, Angie a box of plastic cups.

Novak and Josh each popped the cork of a bottle that fizzed out the top, then poured champagne into seven cups on the table. Each person took a cup and raised it. "This is a celebration," Novak said, "that would not have happened without every one of you, working hard and caring for people that very few of our fellow citizens even think about. So, cheers!" They all touched cups—no clinking of crystal flutes—and sipped the bubbly.

Dave turned off Blitzer and Toobin. "Alex, I've got a question," he said. "Did you and your colleagues have a yelling match when you voted on OD's case?"

Novak laughed. "How did you know, Dave? But yes, there were some raised voices. Not mine, of course."

"Hah! I just happened to be passing the conference room door, and heard your dulcet tones, above the din. And you weren't arguing about the VA case, like you claimed."

"I plead no contest," Novak said. "We justices never reveal any-thing that happens in that room." He paused, with a grin. "However, after another cup of this Moet & Chandon, I might be sufficiently inebriated to unintentionally reveal a confidence."

"Oh, hell, Alex," Kathryn Ikeda retorted. "Considering who's in this room, I'll do that for you. Because you're too modest to take the credit you're due." She took a sip of her cup. "Here's why none of you knew what happened at the conference, or saw any of the opinions before this morning." She took a longer sip. "When we got to the Beasley case, Alex said, 'Any discussion before we vote?' And guess who piped up?"

"Karl Sorenson?" Dave ventured. "I heard his voice, loud and clear."

"Nope," Ikeda replied. "It was Alice Schroeder, who's our expert on obscure rules. So she said, 'Alex, if you had your druthers, would you strike down the death penalty?' And Alex said, 'Sure, but we can't, not in this case.' And Alice said, 'How about we do that sua sponte?'"

Novak broke in. "And I said, 'What, Alice? Speak English.' Then she explained what sua sponte was, and a couple cases the Court had used it before. And I looked around the table, and saw Dwight, Maggie, J.P, and Kathryn all nodding, like 'Yeah. Why not?'" He chuckled. "That's when you heard all the ruckus, Dave."

Laura piped up. "But how come we never saw any opinions, Alex?"

"I can answer that," Ikeda said. "After we voted, and Alex volunteered for the opinion, I looked at Karl, Parker, and Cormac, who were about to explode. 'Listen carefully,' I said. 'None of the opinions, including any dissent, will be shown to anyone outside this room. Especially your clerks. If you write one, you'll do it yourself.'" She chuckled. "Karl never writes a word of his opinions, and he said, 'I couldn't do that without my clerks.' And I said, 'Too bad, Karl. But if I hear that anybody sees any opinion, I'll tell you what will happen.'" Ikeda paused, for dramatic effect. Her audience rapt, she continued. "I said, 'Starting next term, if any of you votes with the majority in any case, I'll make the assignments. And all you'll get is the dogs. But you can write dissents, to your heart's content.'" Everyone laughed.

Just then, Josh's cell rang, and he pulled it from his pocket. "Hey, Jim," he said, "did you hear what Alex did this morning?" He paused. "Yeah, we're celebrating now in his office. So, any word on Junior, and what's happening with the judge?" Josh stepped to the other side of the office, and listened intently for several minutes, all eyes on him. "Wow!" he finally said. "That's unbelievable. Can I tell everyone here what you just said?"

He got an answer, then said goodbye and hung up. Everyone gave him a Please Tell Us look. "Well," Josh said, "if somebody will pour me another cup, I'll give you the news." Andy handed him a cup, and Josh took a long sip. "Okay, they found Junior. He wasn't in Boston, as his wife said. He was in Manhattan, on a sidewalk outside the Waldorf Astoria."

"Did the cops take him in?" Dave asked.

"In a manner of speaking," Josh replied. "What was left of him, anyway. Turns out he got to the sidewalk from a window on the thirtieth floor, no elevator."

"Oh, my God!" Andy exclaimed. "You mean he jumped?"

"Without a parachute," Josh replied. "That was at three this morning, but it took them a while to identify him, since he was only wearing a pair of boxers and nobody saw him come down. Took the cops and hotel staff a while to find a room with a broken window, since they don't open. Turns out Junior smashed it with a chair. And on his phone they found a text message from his wife: 'The police know, and are looking for you. Please turn yourself in.' And they found an empty fifth of Jim Beam."

"Any note?" Dave asked.

"No, but jumping actually *was* his note."

"And what did Jim say about OD's trial?" Andy asked.

"The charges are dismissed, and OD is a free man," Josh said. "He's still in the hospital, but he'll go home in two or three days. Jim says when he went to the hospital to tell OD, he said, 'I always say I did not kill that girl, but nobody believe me. Until you, and Mister Josh, and Miss Andy. Now I go home to my momma.'"

"Oh, Josh, that's wonderful," Andy said. She lifted her cup. "Can we have a toast? To a man who never gave up hope. And who gave us hope to get him home to his momma." They all raised their cups and drank to that.

Kathryn Ikeda put down her cup and glanced at her watch. "I got the gist of that, Josh, and you can fill me in with the rest of the story later. But I've got to run. And hopefully not into any of the reporters and cameras that are still lurking outside. Thanks, everyone. And Alex, you need to thank Alice for coming up with sua sponte. Otherwise, we might be drinking warm beer." She left the office to a round of laughter, while the remaining champagne was consumed.

Shortly, Dave and Laura returned to the clerks' office, Angie to her desk. Andy walked Josh down to the Court's entrance, heading back to his office in Alexandria. She gave him a long hug. "You know, Josh," she said, stepping back and looking him in the eyes, "my clerkship is almost over. A couple of weeks clearing the decks for the next group of clerks, then off to Texas. Hank called to tell me the job with the Defenders is still open. But they won't have any death penalty cases, after today, although I assume they have other clients who didn't get fair trials and have pending cases." She paused. "But, Josh, I don't want to leave you here in Washington, or Carlo, either. And I don't want to leave Alex, and Gloria, and Anton."

"I don't want you to leave, either," he said, moving them both out of the flow of traffic at the door. He put a finger on her lips. "Andy, have you thought of getting a job here, and staying in DC? Maybe with the ACLU, or a public interest law firm? I'll bet any group would be thrilled to get you. I could help you with that." He gave her a beseeching look that Andy couldn't resist.

"Tell you what, Josh," she replied. "I'll check the help-wanted ads, and give it a try. Besides, my parents and Bella still think Texas is full of drug dealers and trigger-happy cops. But if I do stay here, can we keep things the way they are? You know what I mean."

"I know just what you mean," he said, "and that's fine with me. In fact, it's more than fine, if you know what I mean."

"Okay," Andy said. "That's a deal. I'll start looking right now." She put a finger on his lips. "I love you, Josh."

"Love you, too."

Andy turned back, to see Clarence Owens with a grin on his face. "I couldn't help but hear what you and your boyfriend were saying," he said. "Tell the truth, Miss Andy, I don't want you to leave, either. You cheer me up every day. So if you do stay, promise you'll come by whenever you can."

Andy went over and gave him a hug. "That's a promise, Clarence."

Back in Novak's chambers, just a bit tipsy from the champagne, Andy decided to unwind from the day's unexpected events at her apartment, with the Dave Matthews Band and a glass of Beringer for company. She told Dave and Laura that she was playing hooky, and they assured her, jokingly, that she wouldn't be missed.

Andy was on her way out, when Novak walked into his chambers. "Are you still here, Andy? I thought you'd be taking the afternoon off. That's what I'm planning, too. Gloria and Anton want to know what happened, leading up to this morning, so I'm heading home to fill them in. I'd invite you, but something tells me you need some time to unwind at your place. And Gloria's friend, Marjory, is coming over for dinner. So, I'll invite myself to your place later this week for a musicale." He chuckled. "That is, if I'm still welcome after I didn't read your brilliant opinion this morning."

"I'll forgive you for that," Andy said. "But, do you have to leave right now, Alex? Can you spare a minute to give me some advice?"

"Of course," he said, then paused for a moment. "Actually, I wanted to ask for your advice, also. I have a decision to make, and it involves you."

Andy was a bit taken aback. "*Me*, Alex? And what kind of decision? What kind of wine to bring when you come over, maybe?"

Novak chuckled. "No, I've already picked that out. But it's a pretty serious decision, and I can't make it without asking you a question. Let's sit in my office, okay?"

They sat, Andy sensing that Novak did, indeed, have something serious on his mind. He surprised her with his question. "Andy, are you still planning to take the job with the Texas Defenders? Hank told me they were keeping it open for you."

Andy took a moment to think. "Actually, Alex," she replied, "until ten minutes ago, I *was* planning to take the job. But I just now changed my mind, and decided to stay here and look for a job with a public interest law group. Can I ask why you asked me that?"

"Because I know of a job with a public interest group," he replied. "One that you'd be perfect for. But I was going to wait until I knew about your plans, before I made my own." Novak smiled. "And I just made my decision."

"Alex, I'm totally confused," Andy said. "Why would my decision affect yours?"

He reached over and took her hand. "Okay," he said. "You know I kept the opinion this morning a secret from you. From everybody, in fact. And there was a good reason for that. But I've been holding another secret, and now that I know you're not going to Texas, I'll tell you." Novak took a deep breath, then slowly let it out. "Andy, I'm going to resign from the Court, and take a new job."

"Oh, my God," she said. "Why resign, and what job? And how does that involve me?"

"That's three questions, counsel," Novak said with a smile. "But all related, so I'll answer them in turn. First, what's happened this term with OD's case, and the rules I broke to help him, made me think I'm not really suited for the job of impartial judging. I became, in effect, one of OD's lawyers, and that's *way* outside the rules. Plus, I don't think I can still work with Karl Sorenson and his two henchmen, after our fights over the decision we announced this morning. I'm just lucky it didn't turn physical, thanks to Kathryn. By the way, she's the only person here who knows that I'm planning to resign."

"Don't you think things will cool down, after a summer off? Would they still hold a grudge?"

"I doubt they'd cool off," Novak replied. "Karl and I have been feuding for the last couple years, and I think he heard something about how Kathryn got here, although I'm not sure. Anyway, it's been pretty uncomfortable in the conference room, and I can hardly stand being there with him and Parker and Cormac. So, resigning would spare us all a lot of, what's that Yiddish word, Andy?"

"Tsuris? Unpleasantness, if that's what you mean."

"Exactly. Too much tsuris." Novak held up a finger. "That's your first question." He held up another. "Second question, what job? Actually, it's just a few blocks from here. I've been offered an endowed chair at the Georgetown Law Center."

"Wow!" Andy said. "Hank's got one, as you know, and he gets a lot of perks with it. And you'd be a great teacher, Alex."

"Thank you," he said. "Although teaching at Georgetown would only be half-time. The other half is directing a new center to do educational work for criminal justice reform. The guy who endowed the chair, Larry Bernstein, is a Georgetown graduate who's now a hedge-fund manager with a social conscience, if that's not an oxymoron. He put up five million bucks to start the center."

Andy whistled. "That sounds great, Alex. But how would that affect me?"

"Because I'd need a co-director to do the real work," he replied. "The job's yours, Andy, if you want it." He grinned. "Of course, I can only offer a salary of a hundred-twenty thousand, and that's hardly enough to live on in DC, these days. Just kidding. But does it sound tempting? If you say yes, I'll call the Georgetown dean this afternoon and tell him it's a deal."

Andy pretended to ponder, then stuck out a hand and shook his. "Deal," she said. "Although I'd have to scrimp on that salary." She smiled. "Just kidding. In fact, I don't know what I'd do with all that money. That's a forty-thousand buck raise from what I'm getting here."

He smiled back. "Buy more classical CDs, and stock up on good wine."

"Good idea," Andy said. "I could use more of each, to share with my guests. Well, one guest in particular." She paused. "Can I tell Josh, and my parents and Bella? Unless it's still a secret."

"Not any more," he replied. "And when I get home, I'll tell Gloria and Anton, who will be delighted to know you'll be staying here and working with me." He paused for a moment. "And I have more news, Andy. It's been a hectic day, to say the least, and I forgot to tell you that Anton changed his mind about the surgery. He just told me this morning. Doctor Huang thinks he can get the cancer out, if he does the surgery soon, and that Anton has a good chance of living a relatively normal life for a few more years. He's otherwise in good health, even with the walker. But no guarantees." He smiled. "Anton told me he wants to give you more chances to beat him at Scrabble and Monopoly."

"Oh, Alex, I'm so glad to hear that," Andy said. "And tell Anton I'll spend even more time with him and Gloria."

"We'd all like that, Andy," Novak said. "Tell you what. I'll go home and call the dean, and you go home and call Josh and your family. And I'll set up a meeting with the dean later this week to start planning for the center."

They both got up to leave. Andy put her hands on Novak's shoulders, and looked him in the eyes. "Can I tell you one last thing, Alex, before we both go home?" He nodded. "Well, two things. One is that I love you, but you already know that. The other is that this has been the most exciting, and rewarding, day of my life. And year of my life. So, thank you for that."

Novak smiled. "Same here, on both things."

Epilogue

On Thursday, June 28, Novak drove to Williamsburg with Andy, Josh, Dave, and Laura. They joined OD—with a cast on his left arm, and bandages over stitches on his chest and head—and Mamie Beasley, for a homecoming party. Platters of fried chicken, greens, and chocolate-chip cookies disappeared quickly, followed by two hours of happy conversation on Mamie's front porch. The guests departed with a round of hugs, tears, and a final "Bless you wonderful people for bringing my son home, and thanks to Jesus" from Mamie. Andy and Josh each held one of OD's hands as they walked slowly to Novak's car. "Nobody believe me," he said, "until you bring me home to my momma. But Jesus tole me you be coming."

On Monday, July 2, Alex Novak announced his resignation from the Supreme Court, releasing a brief letter to President Chris Chambers, in which he wrote: "It is my hope and expectation that my successor will bring both stability and moderation to an institution I leave with fond memories." Two weeks later, Chambers nominated Marcellus Passmore to replace Novak. A judge on the Sixth Circuit Court of Appeals, Passmore was African American and a former Republican mayor of Cincinnati, known as a judicial moderate. He was confirmed unanimously by the Senate on September 14 and took his seat on the Supreme Court bench at its first session of the new term on October 1.

On Saturday, July 14, Alex Novak hosted a barbeque in his backyard, grilling rib-eye steaks and shrimp kebabs, with coolers of Sam Adams and sodas. Anton and Gloria, both in wheelchairs but in good spirits, were surrounded on the patio by Andy, Josh, Carlo, Dave, Laura, Dick and Jane Wadleigh—holding their two-month-old daughter, Molly—Clarence and Marvella Owens, Angie Conforti, Lisa Margolis, Kathryn Ikeda, and Bella

Warshofsky, down for a weekend with Andy. At the party's end, Lisa asked everyone to join hands in a circle. One by one, they all said "L'Chaim, to life."

On Sunday, July 15, Andy, Josh, Carlo, and Dave and Laura—married the week before by Kathryn Ikeda in the Great Hall of the Supreme Court, around the seated statue of John Marshall—left from Dulles Airport for two weeks in Italy. They spent time with Carlo's parents in Rome, at the Uffizi Gallery in Florence—with Andy and Laura as tour guides—and with Laura's aunts, uncles, and cousins in her father's hometown of Siena.

On Monday, August 6, Alex Novak and Andy Roboff began their new jobs at the Georgetown Law Center. Novak had a spacious office as the Lawrence Bernstein Professor of Constitutional Law, with a reception area for Angie, who had come with him from the Court. Down the hall, Andy had a three-office suite, staffed by an Executive Assistant and Georgetown students who volunteered for internships with the Georgetown Center for Criminal Justice Reform. Above Andy's desk, she hung her poster of Mother Jones, with her rallying cry to striking workers: "Pray for the dead, and fight like hell for the living!"

A Note to Readers

This book is a work of fiction. Like many novels, however, it includes a number of real places and people, all used, of course, for fictional purposes. In setting the book in the Supreme Court, I have striven for verisimilitude (one of my favorite words), but have changed or made up some aspects of the Court's layout and procedures. Readers should not assume that the Court works just the way I describe, although most of it is pretty accurate.

It might help to identify some of the places and people in the book that are real, although used solely for fictional purposes. Some of the restaurants in which my characters converse over meals are real: Grendel's Den in Cambridge; Chowning's Tavern in Williamsburg; the Bull & Bear Club in Richmond (it closed in 2015, after I set a scene there, but kept it in); and the Capital Grille, the Capitol Hill Club, the Old Ebbitt Grill, Fiola Mare, and the Lafayette in the Hay-Adams Hotel in DC. Many readers will recognize Wolf Blitzer and Jeff Toobin of CNN, and Bob Barnes of the Washington *Post*, but the words I put in their mouths are entirely made up. The Sussex and Greensville prisons in Virginia are real, as are David Zook and Eddie Pearson, their respective wardens at this writing; again, their words are fictional.

Some of the cases in the book are also real: *Roper* v. *Simmons*, *Hall* v. *Florida*, and *House* v. *Bell* are real death penalty cases; I won't give formal citations here, but interested readers can easily find them (including full opinions) on the Internet. In chapter 1, the studies of traumatic brain injury in death-row inmates by Drs. Dorothy Lewis and Jonathan Pincus are real, as is the Texas Defender Services and its trial director, Lee Kovarsky. In chapter 2, David Dow and his book, *Executed On a Technicality*, are real. In chapter 11, the excerpts from the "firing squad" opinion (believe it or not) are real, from a 2014 dissent by Judge Alex Kozinski of the Ninth Circuit in *Wood* v. *Ryan*.

In chapters 16 and 17, Irena Sendler was a real person, as is her daughter, Janka, whose Polish surname, Zgrzembska, is so unpronounceable I've left it out, and the account of Irena's work in rescuing Jewish children from the Warsaw ghetto is real. So is the play, "Life in a Jar," although it hasn't been, to my knowledge, performed at the Jewish Community Center in DC. The Holocaust Museum exhibit, "Some Were Neighbors," is also real, although it does not contain the photo I describe of Anton Novitsky/Novak, who is fictional, but does contain a similar photo of the Jewish Ghetto Police, which was real.

In chapter 37, the opinion from which Justice Novak reads is largely based upon, and quotes liberally from, Justice Stephen Breyer's dissenting opinion (joined by Justice Ruth Bader Ginsburg) in a lethal injection case in 2015, *Glossip* v. *Gross*, in which he laid out the case against capital punishment, urging the Court to address this issue directly. I have, of course, changed its conclusion, and added and updated some material. And the quotations I have attributed to Novak and an unnamed justice are from former Justice Antonin Scalia. Novak's posthumous chastisement of Scalia, however, is not from Justice Breyer but from me.

A few words about me: No, I was not a Supreme Court clerk. I am, however, a Harvard Law School graduate, and a member of the Supreme Court bar. Although I haven't (so far) argued before the Court, I represented a client in a First Amendment case, challenging a giant Latin cross in a San Diego park, in which the Court denied cert from the city's appeal, making my client the winner, missing my chance to get a goose-quill pen as a souvenir. I've also written and signed amicus briefs in several civil rights and liberties cases, and have attended many arguments in the Court's chamber.

My own career has combined teaching, writing, and pro bono legal work. After brief stints at Boston College Law School and the University of Massachusetts-Amherst, I taught constitutional law from 1982 until my retirement in 2004 in the political science department at the University of California, San Diego. During and since that time, I've written ten non-fiction books on the Supreme Court and constitutional litigation, which I've listed below. Now I've turned to fiction, freeing me from pesky footnotes and factual accuracy, and allowing me to make stuff up and create my own characters. More seriously, writing this book gave me an opportunity to explore—through my characters and the events in my story—a basic question in law: does the pursuit of justice allow, or even require, breaking rules or laws to rectify injustice? People I greatly admire—Homer Plessy, Rosa Parks, Lillian Gobitas, and my former clients, Fred Korematsu and Gordon Hirabayashi, among them—violated laws that punished them for protesting racial segregation, religious intolerance, and wartime hysteria. But did their stands of principle and conscience undermine respect for law and social order? There's no easy answer to this question, posed in this story through the efforts of Andy Roboff, Josh Barfield, and Alex Novak to free an innocent man from death row. Readers can decide for themselves whether their rule-breaking is justified, and hopefully think seriously about what they would do in confronting these difficult questions and choices. But even serious people have fun, with banter, music, dinners with good friends, mood-altering substances like wine or pot, and mutually enjoyable sex, and I've given my characters time and opportunity to have tension-relieving fun. Why not? Life isn't all about facing hard choices and making tough decisions. And I had fun writing the scenes in which my characters have fun. My two daughters, Maya at 21, Haley at 25, helped with making my 25-year-olds more contemporary, since I passed that mark in the Sixties, a far different culture than now.

This novel also expresses the relevance of Josh's favorite word: indeterminacy. Every turn of events—Andy meeting Josh at the first-week mixer, Hank Lorenz's offer to Andy of a clerkship with Alex Novak, Andy reading about the "Life In a Jar" play, her grandma Bella's chance discovery of a photo in the Holocaust Museum, Andy and Josh finding the brown glove and the red Corvette, and others—could not be foreseen. My own life, and those of everyone I know, has taken unexpected turns with chance meetings, difficult choices, even accidents and illnesses. Hardly any of the events in this book that culminate in its unexpected ending could have been clearly foreseen. That's also true of most cases that wind up at the Supreme Court. It's that aspect of law that makes its development so unpredictable. The death of one justice—my fictional Sam Terman and the actual Antonin Scalia—can shift the Court's balance and the outcome of contentious cases. That's a very relevant fact at the time I'm writing this, and the identity of Scalia's replacement is, to coin a phrase, indeterminate. By the time readers open this book, the next justice may be known, but not now, and that indeterminacy is also essential to my story. But enough pontificating. This is a novel, not a sermon.

Finally, let me acknowledge, with thanks, the support and advice (not always taken, but much appreciated) of friends who helped along the way to this book's completion. Andy Siegel of Seattle University, Kermit "Kim" Roosevelt of the University of Pennsylvania, and Jay Wexler of Boston University are law professors and former Supreme Court clerks who shared their knowlege of the Court and the clerking experience. Kim and Jay have also written novels set in the Court, *Allegiance* and *Tuttle in the Balance*, very different in style but equally entertaining. Bella Suchet and Philip "Fishl" Kutner are native Yiddish speakers who graciously translated for me the dialogue between Bella Warshofsky and Anton Novak about their daring escapes from the Warsaw ghetto and the Holocaust. And my oldest and dearest friend, Priscilla Long, a brilliant writer and punctilious editor, gave the manuscript a reading that made it more readable.

My Other Books

The New Deal Lawyers

Justice at War: The Story of the Japanese American Internment Cases

The Courage of Their Convictions: Sixteen Americans Who Fought Their Way to the Supreme Court

Justice Delayed: The Record of the Japanese American Internment Cases (edited, with an introductory essay)

Brennan Vs. Rehnquist: The Battle For the Constitution

A People's History of the Supreme Court

Jim Crow's Children: The Broken Promise of the Brown Decision

War Powers: How the Imperial Presidency Hijacked the Constitution

God on Trial: Dispatches From America's Religious Battlefields

The Steps to the Supreme Court: A Guided Tour of the American Legal System

P 31 Late term abortions ... is there ... "cut off
limbs & crushing heads" ?
- "so he sued them..." who?? his
   Neighbors who stopped talking to him ?

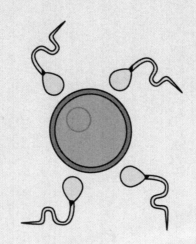

El óvulo femenino es la célula más grande del cuerpo humano. Es unas 175.000 veces más pesado que la célula más pequeña, el espermatozoide masculino.